Yukon Quest

TRACIE PETERSON

Yukon Quest

BETHANYHOUSE
Minneapolis, Minnesota

Yukon Quest
Copyright © 2001, 2002
Tracie Peterson
Previously published in three separate volumes:
   Treasures of the North © 2001 by Tracie Peterson
   Ashes and Ice © 2001 by Tracie Peterson
   Rivers of Gold © 2002 by Tracie Peterson

Cover design by Eric Walljasper
Cover photo by Randall Hop

Scripture quotations are from the King James Version of the Bible.

Published by Bethany House Publishers
11400 Hampshire Avenue South
Bloomington, Minnesota 55438

Bethany House Publishers is a division of
Baker Publishing Group, Grand Rapids, Michigan.

Printed in the United States of America

Library of Congress Cataloging-in-Publication Data has been applied for

ISBN 0-7642-0214-6

TRACIE PETERSON is the bestselling, award-winning author of more than seventy historical and contemporary novels. Her books make regular appearances on CBA bestseller lists. For more information on Tracie, visit her Web site at *www.traciepeterson.com*. She and her family live in Belgrade, Montana.

BOOKS *by* TRACIE PETERSON

www.traciepeterson.com

The Long-Awaited Child • *Silent Star*
A Slender Thread • *Tidings of Peace*
What She Left for Me

BELLS OF LOWELL*
Daughter of the Loom • *A Fragile Design*
These Tangled Threads

LIGHTS OF LOWELL*
A Tapestry of Hope • *A Love Woven True*
The Pattern of Her Heart

DESERT ROSES
Shadows of the Canyon • *Across the Years*
Beneath a Harvest Sky

HEIRS OF MONTANA
Land of My Heart • *The Coming Storm*
To Dream Anew • *The Hope Within*

WESTWARD CHRONICLES
A Shelter of Hope • *Hidden in a Whisper*
A Veiled Reflection

RIBBONS OF STEEL†
Distant Dreams • *A Promise for Tomorrow*

RIBBONS WEST†
Westward the Dream • *Ties That Bind*

SHANNON SAGA‡
City of Angels • *Angels Flight*
Angel of Mercy

YUKON QUEST
Treasures of the North • *Ashes and Ice*
Rivers of Gold

*with Judith Miller   †with Judith Pella   ‡with James Scott Bell

TRACIE PETERSON

Treasures of the North

Part One

JUNE–AUGUST 1897

In thee, O Lord, do I put my trust: let me never be put to
confusion. Deliver me in thy righteousness, and cause me
to escape: incline thine ear unto me, and save me.

PSALM 71:1–2

⊣ CHAPTER ONE ⊢

A GOSSAMER WRAP of glittering ivory danced across Grace Hawkins' shoulders and enveloped her in its folds like the kiss of a summer breeze. Huge brown eyes stared out from a china doll face, serving only to accentuate the delicacy of its owner. Her expression might have suggested serenity, but the mood in her heart suggested quite the opposite.

"My dear, you look radiant."

"Thank you, Mother," Grace replied, trying hard to smile. She had no heart for this evening or for the charade she was about to play. This should have been the happiest night of her life; instead, Grace dreaded it as she would have a dose of the cook's tonic. Neither she nor her governess, Karen Pierce, could abide the smelly concoction and usually found an unlikely place to dispose of it before being found out. Pity Grace couldn't dispose of her unwanted fiancé as easily.

Grace sighed. There were a great many things she and Karen had managed to avoid in life; however, engagement to Martin Paxton didn't appear to be one of them. Karen's quick thinking and understanding of the world would do little to free Grace from her father's demands.

And unlike Karen, who held animosity for any man's demands, Grace had worked hard for a genteel balance. She could be her father's obedient daughter, gentle in spirit and silent unless spoken to, but she could also be a reflection of her teacher. Unfortunately, as Grace grew older and began to see life for herself, the two natures warred against each other, causing her no end of frustration and confusion. Underlying Grace's seemingly serene personality a storm was brewing, and she couldn't help but wonder if this particularly unpleasant situation would be the missing element to unleash that storm.

"Your fiancé will be very impressed, I've no doubt," her mother chattered on. "A woman of quality and beauty is not easily found. You will make him proud."

But what will he make me? Grace wondered. She'd already met the formidable man, and while he was handsome enough, despite a thin jagged scar that marred his jawline on the right side of his face, his personality suggested an aloofness, a kind of cold shoulder that left Grace wondering if there could be any hope for love to grow.

Looking up, Grace caught sight of her own reflection in the mirror. *My, but I'm all grown-up.*

The gown, of ivory and rose, seemed to shimmer at her every move. Tiny summer roses fresh from the garden had been sewn into the neckline, sending a delectable fragrance—sweet and airy—wafting through the air. Their deep pink color appeared shaded and muted through the veil-like covering of Grace's wrap. The teasing effect hinted of something more—something pure and special. Grace thought it a symbolic statement of her own purity, veiled and delicately concealed, yet evident for the world and one man's picking.

Her mother had commissioned the gown in honor of her engagement, and Grace could tell by the pleased expression on her mother's face that the dress was exactly what she had hoped for. Status and appearance were of great importance to her mother. The society pages would be positively ringing with praises for the couple on the morrow, giving fuel to her mother's energies to plan the wedding of the century.

"Karen, put another pin in her hair," Mrs. Hawkins commanded. "Right here where the curl seems wont to slip away."

Karen, ever patient with her employer's demands, did as she was instructed, then stood back. Mrs. Hawkins nodded and lifted her chin as she drew a deep breath. "There will not be another young woman half so beautiful. I will go and attend to our guests. Karen will bring you to your father when the time is right." She looked back at Grace and nodded again. "Oh, I do hope the photographer has arrived!"

She opened the door, then paused again, her nervous excitement irritating Grace. "Whatever you do, Grace, don't sit down! We mustn't have you wrinkled. Karen, you remind her," she said, as if Grace were only five years old instead of twenty.

Both Grace and Karen nodded in agreement. Myrtle Hawkins seemed satisfied and turned to go.

Watching her mother leave, Grace felt her hopes and dreams dissipate. "How can they do this to me?" she whispered loud enough for only Karen to hear.

"I can't abide it," Karen agreed. "It's tantamount to slavery."

Grace lifted her sorrowful face to her governess, the term revealing little of the depth of affection the two women shared. "That's exactly what it is. They are selling me to the highest bidder. Oh, Karen, what am I to do?"

Shaking her head, Karen moved to close the door between Grace's bedroom and her sitting room. "You could always run away. We've discussed this before."

"I know," Grace said, moving to sit, then remembering the warning. Her mother would never forgive her for showing up wrinkled to her own engagement party. She sighed. "They're all going to know the truth of it. All of society—all of Chicago." Her mournful words hung heavy on the air. "Everyone who is anyone knows I've not been courted by Mr. Paxton. He's nothing more than my father's business associate."

"Well, he certainly thinks of himself as something more," Karen replied. "I've never seen a man hold such influence over your father. Why, the man practically ordered your father into giving this party tonight. I heard him myself. So did the rest of the house staff."

"I know," Grace replied. "I don't understand the situation any more than you do. I want to be a good daughter and do what is expected of me, but frankly, Mr. Paxton frightens me."

"Did you tell your mother?" Karen questioned.

"I tried. She said it was a simple matter of virginal nerves," Grace stated, her cheeks warming. "She said all young girls fear the expectations of their husbands and that I should simply pray on the matter and trust God for the best."

"I agree we should pray, but I know better than to believe this is simply a case of pre-wedding jitters. You do not love the man and he clearly does not love you. In fact, he almost seems to resent you and everyone else in this house."

"I know," Grace moaned, "but what can I do? I've tried to talk to Father, but he'll not see reason." She paced nervously, the glimmering gown swirling around her heels. "I'm a mere woman of twenty. Father still sees me as a child, and children, in his estimation, should be seen and not heard."

"I believe that to be his estimation for women in general," Karen replied with a hint of resentment in her tone.

"Father treats Mother with respect," Grace countered. "He used to listen to her counsel all the time. It was only in this decision to marry me to his associate that he rejected any influence from her."

"Probably because he knew what she'd say. I believe your mother wants to see you happy, even while pleasing her social circle. I also believe she had planned for you to marry one of the Willmington boys."

Grace nodded. "Poor Mother. Father actually yelled at her."

"Well, don't take it on your shoulders," Karen encouraged. "Your mother has known well enough how to make a go at marriage. She's shared a silver wedding anniversary with him. That must account for something."

"Perhaps if my brother, Amon, had lived. Mother said that Father was so happy having his firstborn to be a son. When Amon died, Father was inconsolable. I must have been a poor substitute."

"One child is never a substitute for another," Karen chided. "Now listen. You cannot go downstairs looking all glum. Whatever choice you make in the future, whether to go through with this and get married or run away, you must at least give your mother and father a pretense of contentment. It would greatly shame your parents in the eyes of their peers should word get out that you do not desire this union."

Grace contemplated her governess's words. She was so grateful for the companionship she shared with Karen. They were more like sisters than anything. Karen had been her teacher and friend for over ten years, and Grace loved her more dearly than anyone else. Karen's wisdom had always been a gentle guide, directing Grace to acknowledge her position and duties.

A quick glance at her watch and Karen motioned to the door. It was time for Grace to make her appearance at the party. "Well, we cannot delay this another moment. Chin up."

Grace took a deep breath and lifted her face. With the slightest hint of a nod, she followed Karen. They passed from the bedroom into the sitting room and out into the long hall of the west wing. Grace tried not to feel unduly worried—in fact, she tried not to feel anything at all. Her fear for this evening was beyond anything she had ever known. She remembered her mother suggesting that with any luck they would persuade Mr. Paxton to have a long engagement, maybe as much as three or four years. Grace agreed that perhaps in sufficient time she could come to fear him less and care about him more. But while her mother had hopes for such delays, her father implied that quick action was of the utmost importance. His attitude and insistence were puzzling.

Myrtle Hawkins had told her husband that in no uncertain terms could the wedding take place before a period of one year had passed. She would not have society believing her daughter in need of marriage. The scandal would be hard-lived, and even if the couple were slow in producing heirs, Myrtle knew how tongues would wag if the proprieties were overlooked. But despite her mother's protests, her father was unwavering in his decision. Grace had been heartbroken over her father's firm resolve to see her quickly joined with Mr. Paxton.

"I wish you could stay with me," Grace said, breaking free from the memories. "Mother has always been generous about allowing you to accompany me."

"But this is an occasion for grown-ups, not innocent maids with their nannies," Karen countered. "You are already such a delicate and petite thing, most people assume you to be years younger. My appearance would only enhance this."

"I cannot bear it," Grace said, fighting to hold back her tears. "I cannot have that man handling me."

"He won't be allowed to touch you," Karen replied. "Not in this ever-so-proper social gathering."

"But remember what he did last night after dinner?" Grace said, shuddering. "He thought nothing of touching me." She could still feel his warm hand upon her arm. He had stroked the smooth skin of her forearm in a most intimate manner before bringing her hand to his lips.

Karen reached out to dab the corners of Grace's eyes with her handkerchief. "Put those thoughts aside. The man was out of place, but no doubt he was simply overcome by his admiration for your beauty." She smiled. "Now, be brave and strong. The Lord will go before you."

Grace nodded. She could only pray it was true.

Karen's plans were for a quiet evening in Grace's private sitting room. Reading a fashionable ladies' magazine would help to wile away the hours and hopefully keep her from worrying too much about Grace. It was true that in the last couple of years—years in which Grace had not really needed a governess—the two women had grown very close. Karen enjoyed their relationship, perhaps partly because she had been raised in a big family with plenty of siblings. She had always known what it was to have company and someone to whisper silly secrets to. Grace was an only child who had often seemed lonely.

Karen had first come into the Hawkins home when Grace had been but ten years old. The child already commanded proof of impeccable manners and rigid social graces, but she bore evidence of something else as well. Grace seemed lost—almost shunned. Her mother, a wealthy socialite, and her father, a successful entrepreneur, seldom had time to share with their child. They appeared to love Grace, to hold genuine affection for her, but their busy lives seemed far more important. Grace had been left at the mercy of nurses and the house staff, despite the fact that she adored both her mother and father.

Private schooling had been considered prior to Karen's appearance in their lives. Myrtle Hawkins had heard of the social benefits of boarding schools abroad, but Grace had pleaded with her mother not to send her away. Myrtle Hawkins seemed to understand her daughter's fear of separation and finally gave up the idea. After that, Karen had been hired and a new kind of family was born.

Stretching, Karen glanced at the clock. The party had scarcely begun. And it would be the first of many to come. Over the next few weeks there would no doubt be a parade of events to honor the couple.

The thought of Grace marrying brought another realization into Karen's life. At thirty years old, she was hardly good for anything but serving as a governess or a maid. No man would want to marry her at such a late stage of life, and few women would want an attractive woman in their house, even to perform the duties of governess.

Karen tried to play down her appearance. She felt blessed to have been given thick hair the color of strawberries and honey, but given her position, she bound it tightly in a bun and covered it with a net. No sense in giving anyone a chance to accuse her of prideful behavior by wearing her hair lavishly pinned, as she might style Grace's hair.

Her figure, while less curvaceous than desired in society, was long and statuesque. She stood at least half a foot taller than her charge, but she was not unreasonable in her height. By wearing her corset fairly loose, Karen had been able to avoid displaying any accentuated womanly curves, and taking the advice of her aunt Doris, herself a spinster teacher, Karen chose to dress in dark, matronly fashions.

"Do not give yourself airs, child. The more simplified your appearance, the less threatening you will be," Aunt Doris had declared.

Thinking of her aunt caused Karen to automatically think of other concerns— of her father. Wilmont Pierce, Doris's brother, had gone north to the Alaskan Territory some five years earlier. He and Karen's mother had felt a calling to minister to the Tlingit Indians who lived in and around the southeast panhandle. Things had gone well at first. After trying several locations, the Pierces finally settled near the area of Skagway and Dyea. Other missionaries were already set up in the area, but the husband-and-wife team was well received by their brothers and sisters in Christ. Those already stationed in the wilds of this new land felt gratitude at seeing yet another American couple. Homesickness abounded and everyone desired news of home.

Karen's mother had written of great happiness in her new home. But as time went on, Alice Pierce found herself weakened by the elements. Months of sickness led to Alice's becoming bedfast, and weeks later she had succumbed to pneumonia. The news of her mother's death had devastated Karen.

Staring into the fireplace, Karen contemplated her position. She could now go north and help her father. In the absence of her mother, her father could probably use someone to assist him in his work. She was, after all, college educated and trained to teach. She could certainly make more of a difference there than she would in Chicago.

"Perhaps once we find out what the terms of Grace's engagement will be," Karen whispered, "then I will know what to do."

The idea of leaving Grace sorrowed Karen. Grace had been much like a little sister. Karen had been put in charge of Grace's education, teaching her all manner of basic learning in addition to foreign languages and etiquette. While Karen's family was hardly equal to the social standing of the Hawkins family, her own background had afforded her a complete and well-rounded education, including extended time spent at a rather refined women's college back East.

Karen could have married on at least four different occasions. The men had been well-heeled and respected in the community. Their growing importance in the city could have seen Karen as mistress of a considerable fortune by now.

She smiled, however, and shook her head as the flames in the hearth danced hypnotically. "But you would not release me to marry them," she murmured prayerfully. And indeed, that was exactly why she had remained single. God had called her to singleness, at least for a time. He had made it clear to her that her focus at this point in her life was to be Grace Hawkins.

"But that's changing now," she said aloud. Then a thought dawned on her. Perhaps Grace would want to keep Karen on as her personal attendant. Assuming the new responsibilities that would be expected of Grace, in addition to possibly moving to another city, would surely warrant the desire to have someone familiar at hand. Perhaps that was where God would lead her next. From there, maybe she would be allowed to stay on and help rear Grace's children. This thought, however, gave no real comfort.

Her father's lack of communication over the past few months was a growing concern. He should have written by now. *Unless something has also happened to him*, Karen rationalized. *He should have informed me that things were well or at least have noted his future plans.* The absence of a letter was giving Karen much reason to fear for her father's well-being. She even sensed that Aunt Doris was rather worried, although she would never admit it.

Bowing her head, Karen began to pray in earnest. "Show me the way, Lord. Show me what I am to do, because I fear I have two paths before me and neither one suggests itself over the other."

—{ C H A P T E R   T W O }—

GRACE FELT A CHILL run up the length of her spine when her father presented her to Martin Paxton. It wasn't the first time they'd been introduced, by any means, but it was the most important.

"Mr. Paxton, may I present your future wife, my daughter, Grace."

Grace looked to her father, wondering momentarily if he could read the displeasure in her eyes. Quickly, she lowered her gaze to the ground and extended her gloved hand to Mr. Paxton.

"Miss Hawkins, may I say you are looking particularly lovely. Our engagement must certainly agree with you." Paxton's tone was edged with sarcasm.

The scoundrel! Grace thought, trying her best to refrain from giving any outward appearance of contempt.

"Mr. Paxton," she murmured, waiting while he kissed the top of her hand.

Involuntarily, she began to tremble. There was something about this man that exuded distrust and . . . evil. He smelled of it—if that were possible.

Grace attempted to pull her hand away, but he held it fast. The action caused her to meet his gaze, and she discovered an inkling of evidence for the power he held over her father. As he narrowed his emerald eyes, Grace couldn't help but feel drawn into his spell. He was handsome in a rather ruthless fashion, and his confidence made clear that his affections were seldom rejected.

Grace wanted to run away from this man as quickly as her gown would allow, but of course, she could not. To put up any kind of protest would signal to the guests, just now assembling in the drawing room to their right, that all was not as it seemed.

As if reading her apprehension, Paxton smiled. He knew how he was making her feel, yet he continued to do everything in his power to keep her feeling as she was. He was, she believed, reveling in her discomfort.

Grace looked to her father for help, then realized he was a poor source. Her father was already wiping great beads of sweat from his brow. The poor man looked terrified of Martin Paxton.

"I believe we should attend to our guests, Father," Grace said in as calm a tone as she could muster.

"Yes. Ah . . . yes. Of course . . . ah . . . you are right," her father fairly stammered, looking to Paxton as if for permission to move.

"Yes, we wouldn't want to delay in announcing our engagement, now, would we?" he questioned, leaning close to reach Grace's ears alone.

He spoke in such a way that his very words seemed almost threatening. Grace was beginning to weary of his manhandling of her father and of herself. Pulling away with great dignity, Grace tilted her chin enough to give the sensation of looking down her nose at Paxton.

"I believe, Mr. Paxton, it would be unseemly for you to escort me prior to the announcement of our engagement. In my father's house, he alone would have the right to escort his unmarried daughter."

Paxton straightened and gave her a rather cruel smile. "But of course, we wouldn't want to displace the rules of society."

Grace gave him a curt nod and turned to her father. His face had reddened considerably at her suggestion, but seeing that Paxton was unwilling for a scene, Hawkins quickly took hold of his daughter's arm.

"Shall we join our guests?" he asked.

Grace gave his arm a gentle pat. She wanted to reassure him that she could make peace with his decision, but in truth, she wasn't at all sure that it was possible. She knew the Bible commanded her to honor her father, but this wish—this command to marry Martin Paxton—was almost more than she could consider.

"Yes, let us join Mother and the others," she finally replied, entwining her arm around his.

They entered her mother's favorite drawing room, with Paxton close behind them. Grace allowed her father to circulate her through their many guests, while Paxton remained near the door. She prayed he might think better of the evening and escape before making her the object of his intentions.

"Why, Grace, you are positively glowing. Love will do that for a woman," a jovial Mrs. Bryant announced. Mrs. Bryant had been her mother's best and worst friend for some thirty years. Best—because the two had known each other since childhood and had endured many of life's trials and joys together. Worst—because the two women seemed to constantly be in battle to rival the other.

"Mrs. Bryant, it is good of you to come," Grace replied formally.

She completed the remaining introductions with the same patience one might need to endure a physical examination. It was a necessary yet troublesome event. One to be tolerated but certainly not enjoyed.

Grace remained at her mother's side after the introductions while her father stood nervously twisting his pocket watch chain. He was working up his nerve to announce the engagement, and had Grace not been angry with him for his lack of consideration, she might have felt sorry for him. But one glance across the room at Martin Paxton, and Grace felt anything but sorry. How could her father do this? How could he simply give her over to a stranger she did not love?

"My dear ladies and gentleman," Frederick Hawkins began, "we have—that is, Mrs. Hawkins and I—have invited you here this evening to share in a very important occasion."

He held the attention of every person in the room. Every person, with exception to Martin Paxton and Grace. Paxton had fixed his gaze on Grace and his piercing green eyes bore into her own. She felt undressed by his cool appraisal and reached up to tightly clench the wrap to her neck. He gave her a tight-lipped smile from beneath his pencil-thin mustache. He appeared amused and quite pleased with the knowledge that he'd unnerved her.

"And so we happily announce," her father continued, "the engagement of our daughter, Grace Hawkins, to Mr. Martin Paxton of Erie, Pennsylvania."

The looks of the assemblage passed from Frederick Hawkins to Martin Paxton, almost completely excluding Grace. She felt rather insignificant for the moment, though she hadn't long to suffer in that state.

Paxton gave a stiff, formal bow to the guests before crossing the room to join Grace. "I am quite honored to make the acquaintance of this dear family's friends. I have long sought the hand of my bride and will know great pleasure in your attendance at our wedding."

"When is that day to be?" Mrs. Bryant questioned, her exuberance extending beyond the proprieties.

On an occasion such as this, Grace knew it was an acceptable faux pas. She could have predicted such a question. What she could not possibly have anticipated, however, was Martin Paxton's response.

"Because there has long existed an informal agreement between families, I am certain we will marry without delay."

It took every ounce of willpower to keep Grace from pushing Paxton away. She held her tongue, controlled her expression, and refrained from balling her hand into a fist and putting it aside Paxton's Romanesque nose.

"Surely you do not mean to marry before the end of the summer?" Mrs. Bryant questioned, rather aghast.

Grace's mother laughed nervously. "Of course not."

Paxton threw her a glance that might have completely wilted a woman of more delicate constitution. Myrtle Hawkins, however, stood her ground.

"We've not arranged for dates and places," she said, smiling. "We want to enjoy the moment of this intimate announcement among friends. Come, enjoy some refreshments and perhaps we can convince Grace to perform for us."

"Oh yes, do," several women said in unison.

Grace felt Paxton tighten his hold on her arm. He probably knew nothing of her singing or playing of the piano and harp. He probably had no idea of her education or fluency in French and German. Looking up at the man who was to be her husband, Grace realized with great apprehension that this man knew nothing at all about her.

Grace sat down to the piano and began a rather melancholy sonata. Always one of her favorites, Beethoven's "Moonlight Sonata" stirred her in a way that she could scarce put into words. The progression of the chords, the melodic appeal of the haunting tune . . . it was something that reached deep into her soul.

Looking up only once, Grace found Paxton watching her with an unveiled expression. She could only equate the look to one of hatred, and yet he had no reason to hate her. She had not forced herself upon him.

As the last notes died down and the audience applauded her efforts, Grace got to her feet and gave a brief curtsy. Paxton was immediately at her side, offering his arm, along with a look that suggested she make no move to refuse him. Smiling in a rather fixed manner, Grace placed her gloved hand atop his and allowed him to lead her from the piano. Mrs. Bryant's youngest daughter, Hazel, quickly took her place at the bench and soon a rapid-paced Mozart tune sprang from the keys.

"I would have a private word with you," Paxton told Grace in a commanding way.

"It would hardly be fitting for us to be seen leaving the party," Grace replied, unwilling to look at him.

"I really care very little for the rules of society."

"So I had gathered from your comment of hurrying our wedding."

"I take it you disapprove," he said in a low, sarcastic tone.

"How astute of you to notice."

He pulled her arm against his side. "I pride myself in keeping track of the details, Miss Hawkins." He pushed her toward the open French doors and out into the garden. Swinging her around rather abruptly, he pulled Grace into a strong-armed embrace, then assaulted her mouth with his lips.

Pushing against the man, Grace struggled to end his liberties. Paxton would have no part of it, however. He was much stronger than she had anticipated and much more determined to explore her feminine charms than even Grace would have believed. When he dared to trail his fingers down her bare neck to the swell of her breasts, Grace brought her tiny heeled slipper down on his foot. The action surprised Paxton enough that he momentarily loosened his hold. This allowed Grace enough room to maneuver. With all the strength she could muster, Grace slapped Paxton's face.

"How dare you!"

Within a heartbeat, he slapped her back. Open and bare-handed, he struck her with enough force to knock her back against the garden gate, the blow causing her to see stars.

Scarcely able to draw a breath, Grace struggled, unaided, to right herself. Protecting her throbbing cheek with her gloved hand, she looked up hesitantly as Paxton advanced. The look of hatred had returned to clearly mark his otherwise handsome features. Grace couldn't imagine why he should be so brutal with her. She had gone along—or at least pretended to go along—with the engagement. She hadn't caused him any embarrassment or reason to so abuse her.

Dragging Grace even farther into the garden, Paxton twisted her arm painfully and finally deposited her on an iron bench.

"Do not ever presume to put your hand to me," he said, his tone edged in a quiet rage. "No wife of mine will ever put me in line."

She looked up at him, still stunned by the sudden turn of events. In all her twenty years, Grace had known nothing but protection and security. Suddenly it was clear that this was all behind her now.

"You have no right . . ." she began.

His eyes narrowed, and in the moonlight Grace could see his leering expression as he sat down beside her and pulled her back into his arms.

"I have all the right I need. I will take what I want, when I want it," he said, his mouth beside her neck. He placed kisses down her shoulder, pushing aside the gossamer wrap. While holding her in place with one hand, he allowed the other to freely explore.

Grace knew she had only to scream. The open doors of the house were not but ten yards away. Someone would hear her and come to her rescue. She drew a deep breath.

He stopped kissing her momentarily and looked hard into her eyes. "Don't even think about it."

Her heart raced wildly. "What are you talking about? Unhand me!"

"Don't think to escape me or call someone to your side. Your father will lose everything if you refuse me."

Grace studied him carefully. "What are you saying?"

He reached up to draw his finger along her still-throbbing cheek. "I'm saying I can cause you far greater pain than a mere slap." He grabbed her chin and held it firm. "I'm saying that unless you cooperate with me and do exactly as you are told, I will ruin you and your entire family."

Fear as she had never known descended over Grace. She looked into the harsh face of her captor and couldn't so much as pray. The man clearly had plans for her family and those plans included their marriage. But for what purpose?

"Why are you doing this?" she finally found the courage to ask. "I've done nothing to you. I'm a proper lady, pure and innocent, yet you treat me as a harlot. Why should you take offense that I would defend my honor? Engagement or none, there are still proper behaviors to be expected."

He brushed his thumb against her lips. "I will brook no nonsense from any woman. You will do as you are told and never will I allow you to question me. You are property and nothing more."

"Nothing more?"

"Nothing more. This is obviously no love match. This is business—long over-due business. You may have no understanding of such matters, but your father's very existence teeters precariously on the edge of your actions."

"My actions?"

"Of course," Martin Paxton replied. "No decent clergy will marry us unless you are willing, and no doubt your mother already has the church picked out. You will cooperate and willingly consent to this marriage or I will see your father destroyed."

"But why?" Grace questioned, her own fear now replaced with concern for her father and mother. "How has he so offended you?"

This question actually caused Paxton to release her. Standing up, he eyed her with a look of pure contempt. "It is a matter between men." He turned away from her as if contemplating further consideration.

Grace felt too shaken to stand, but her instincts told her that if she was to escape without further harm, she would have to make her way now. Without a sound, she got to her feet and hurried for one of the closer entrances into the house used by the house staff when collecting flowers for dinner arrangements and such.

She barely reached the door when Paxton seemed to realized her escape. She heard the heavy footsteps upon the garden path just as she closed the door behind her and slid the lock into place.

Paxton began pounding on the wood, threatening to shake the very foun-dations of the house into rubble. "Let me in, you fool!" he declared in a voice hardly louder than a whisper.

"Go back to the party," Grace called. "Go back and give my regrets. Tell them I've grown ill and my governess has seen me to bed."

"Open this door now!"

"No," Grace said, knowing there would be a heavy price to pay for her defiance.

⟤ C H A P T E R ⟤ 3 ⟤ T H R E E ⟥

"I CAN'T BELIEVE he did this," Karen said angrily as she pressed ice against Grace's swollen cheek. A reddish purple discoloration was already starting to mar the pale white skin.

"I can't believe it either. I honestly have no idea what is to be done."

"Well, it's obvious," Karen replied. "You must break off this engagement and tell your father why it is impossible to go forward with marriage to such a monster. I'm certain that if he knew how you were treated, he'd never consent to see you wed to Mr. Paxton."

Grace shook her head. "Mr. Paxton said he could ruin Father. Something has apparently happened between them, and Mr. Paxton has great power over Father."

"Perhaps your mother would know what it's all about."

"I don't know if she would or not. All I know is that I cannot marry this man, and yet there seems to be no other way to help Father in his need."

"But, Grace, you don't even know what that need is. Perhaps Paxton is doing nothing more than bullying you. He probably knows of your apprehension and maybe has even heard rumors of your disinterest in marrying him. He probably hoped to frighten you into the union."

"Well, he did a good job."

Just then Grace's mother came into the room in a rush. "I heard that Grace was ill. Whatever is wrong?" She looked to Grace and then Karen. "Why has she an ice bag?"

Grace slowly removed the bag and could tell by her mother's reaction that the cheek was no better.

"Who did this?" Myrtle Hawkins demanded.

"Mr. Paxton." Grace's words were flat and unemotional. She had no way of knowing what her mother's reaction to the news might be. She hoped she might be sympathetic, but her parents were both acting very strange as of late.

Her mother came forward and studied the damage more closely. "What happened to provoke this?"

"I slapped him for taking indecent liberties with me," Grace replied. "He slapped me in return and told me that I was never to strike him again or question his actions."

"The cad!" Her mother's reaction was clearly one of disgust. "I shall speak to your father on this matter."

Grace reached out and touched her mother's hand. "Please, Mother, sit with me for a moment. I need to ask you something."

The older woman seemed to understand the importance and nodded. "We have a house full of guests, you know. I can't possibly stay long."

"I understand," Grace replied. "I wouldn't ask you if it weren't of the utmost concern."

"I'll go," Karen suggested.

"No!" Grace declared. "I want you to stay. You know all about this, and we might very well need your thoughts on the matter."

"Whatever are you talking about?" Myrtle questioned.

"Mother, something is wrong. I can't even pretend to know what it is, but Mr. Paxton apparently has some sort of control—some power over Father. I wondered if you knew what it might be."

"Power over your father? Why, that's nonsense. Frederick would never allow anyone to dictate his choices."

"Mr. Paxton told me that should I be less than cooperative in giving myself to him, apparently with the benefits of marriage or without, that he would ruin our family and Father would suffer greatly."

Myrtle stiffened. "He has no power to ruin the Hawkins family. How dare he imply such a thing merely to obtain liberties with you!"

"So there is nothing he can do to hurt Father?" Grace looked at her mother to ascertain her confidence in the matter. Unfortunately, the older woman looked away, but not before Grace detected uncertainty in her mother's eyes.

Grace took hold of her mother's hand. "What is it?"

Karen watched in silence, but Myrtle seemed more than aware of her presence. She looked to Karen and then back to Grace, as if hoping someone might instruct her as to what to say.

"Your father hasn't been himself in weeks. I haven't any idea what is wrong. He used to be quite willing to talk freely to me, but lately he refuses. He came home one day and announced that you were to marry Martin Paxton, and when I chided him for inappropriately suggesting such a thing without a period of courtship, he told me to keep such thoughts to myself. He told me you would marry Paxton and that was his final word."

Grace shook her head. "Mr. Paxton must have some influence over Father that we are unaware of. But, Mother ..." She paused and looked to Karen for reassurance. "Despite my love for you and Father, I cannot marry Mr. Paxton. He is much too cruel, and I will not suffer a husband who beats me."

"Neither would I ask you to," Myrtle said, her expression softening as she reached up to touch her daughter's cheek. Tears came to her eyes. "No one has ever laid a hand to you before this. No one ever had to. You were always such a sweet child, good as gold and never a problem. That he should strike you so offends and wounds me that I must say something to him before the night is out."

"Don't," Grace replied. "He might very well do the same to you."

"Nonsense. He wouldn't dare," Myrtle said, raising her chin defiantly. She thrust her shoulders back and appeared to take on a new resolve. "I will speak to him and to your father as well."

"Please, Mother, do not speak to Mr. Paxton on any of this. Talk to Father if you like, but leave it at that. Perhaps Father will finally relent and tell you what has happened. We should know the truth of that prior to making any other decisions."

———

With the last of the party guests on their way home, Martin Paxton bid Mr. and Mrs. Hawkins good-night with the best of wishes on the speedy recovery of his fiancée's health.

"I hope Miss Hawkins will feel better in the morning," he said rather smugly.

"I'm certain she will," Frederick replied, then turning to the butler, he checked to make sure Mr. Paxton's carriage had been brought around.

Myrtle Hawkins could barely contain her emotions as she bid the man farewell. "Good night, Mr. Paxton."

"If you'll both excuse me," Frederick interrupted, "my man tells me there is something that requires my immediate attention."

"Of course," Paxton said with a slight nod.

Myrtle waited for Paxton to leave, but instead he seemed to study her for a moment before speaking his mind. "Your husband knows very well what I expect, and now I believe your daughter knows as well."

"How dare you?" she barely breathed the words. Gone was any hope of containing her anger. "That child has never been struck in her life until now."

"She'd do well to learn quickly or she'll find herself receiving worse," Paxton said, eyes narrowing. "I tell you this and something more." He paused to make certain he held her attention. "You would do well to heed your husband's wishes and leave Grace to me."

"You, sir, are out of line," Myrtle replied. "I will not see my child married to a man such as yourself: I will not see her cruelly treated, beaten, and tormented."

Martin's expression suggested he held the upper hand. "Better beaten than on the street—or worse."

Myrtle had no idea what the man meant by his words, but one thing she knew for certain. Her husband had some explaining to do. Slamming the door behind Paxton only to hear him laugh from the other side, Myrtle went in search of Frederick.

Finding him just on his way up the stairs, she called out, "I would have a word with you, Mr. Hawkins."

"It's late. Must we talk now?" he questioned.

"It is imperative," she insisted.

"Very well." He led the way to his upstairs study and opened the door with his key. "Now, tell me what this is all about."

Myrtle began without hesitation. "That brute has struck our child."

"What? What brute?" Frederick asked in confusion.

"Mr. Paxton."

Her husband paled and took a seat behind his desk. "I'm sure you are mistaken."

"I am not!" she declared. "Grace has the bruise on her face to prove it. He tried to force himself upon her, and when Grace defended her honor, he struck her."

"Well, there you have it—just a lover's quarrel. I'm sure it will right itself within a day or two."

Myrtle could scarcely believe her husband's tone. "I tell you this man took liberties with our daughter, struck her for defending herself, and you believe it will right itself in a day or two? How can you be so heartless and cruel? Surely you cannot want to move forward with Grace's marriage to such a brutal man?"

Frederick Hawkins looked at her rather guiltily before turning his attention to the papers on his desk. He gave a pretense of shuffling the papers into order, but Myrtle knew he was simply doing this to avoid answering her question.

"Well?" Myrtle pressed.

He looked up. "The arrangements have been made. I've given my word."

"Then take it back."

"I cannot."

She shook her head. "Why? Why can't you dissolve the engagement?"

"Well . . . it is . . . it's just that . . ." He stammered and stuttered, seeming desperate to find an answer that might explain his insistence. "I cannot."

Myrtle folded her arms against her breast. "Frederick Hawkins, do you mean to sit there and lie to me? I am your wife. You have always discussed things of importance with me, yet two weeks ago you came home to announce that you were pledging our daughter in marriage to a complete stranger. Now that stranger turns out to be a monster, and you suggest it will right itself and that we should simply overlook the matter. I want to know what is going on! Why have you suddenly taken to cowering to Martin Paxton?"

Her husband's expression turned angry. "I cower to no one, dear woman. I simply believe this to be more of a lover's misunderstanding."

"One which resulted in our sweet child hideously bruised," Myrtle retorted. "Come see for yourself if you doubt my word."

"I do not doubt your word, but apparently you doubt mine."

Myrtle Hawkins sat down on the chair in front of her husband's ornately carved desk. The desk had been a gift from her own father upon the celebration of their marriage. A matching, more feminine counterpart stood in her own private sitting room. It was there that she wrote her correspondence and instructions for the servants. She had addressed the invitations to Grace's engagement party from that same desk. The party had seemed the right thing to do, in spite of her misgivings. Now she wished fervently that she might have fought harder to impose her own thoughts on her husband's rash actions.

"I do not doubt that you feel you must cooperate with this man's wishes, but what I do not understand is why. Grace suggested that Mr. Paxton was threatening in regard to our well-being. The man himself spoke threateningly to me only moments ago."

Frederick's face reddened. "The scoundrel! How dare he talk of our business to my womenfolk?"

Myrtle realized her husband's anger was motivated by some unnamed fear. "What has he to do with you, Frederick? What has happened? Please tell me."

He looked at her with such a pained expression that for a moment Myrtle nearly took back her request. Perhaps there were some things a wife shouldn't know in regard to her husband's business arrangements.

"I owe Paxton money," he finally said with great resignation. "A great deal of money."

Myrtle considered the words for a moment. "How? Why?"

He shrugged. "Bad business dealings. Paxton came along and bailed me out, but the price was Grace, along with repayment of the debt at an exorbitant interest rate."

"But why Grace? Why should the man impose himself on a young woman he doesn't even know?"

"I don't know!" Frederick answered, running a hand through his hair in frustration. "I just know that I cannot back out of the arrangement for Grace to marry Paxton." He drew a deep breath. "This union will allow for us to continue in the fashion and society for which we've become accustomed."

"But at the price of our daughter's happiness?"

"Since when has that figured into our decisions?" Frederick asked his wife quite seriously. "You've had your heart set on being the social matron of Chicago. You've worked hard to position this family among the very cream of the crop."

"With the intentions that our daughter might marry well, yes," Myrtle said, beginning to feel a strange sensation of misgiving and guilt course through her heart.

"Our daughter will marry very well. Paxton is worth a fortune. He may treat her with a heavy hand, but he has the money to give her whatever she desires. That is what counts, after all. I know it has always meant a great deal to you, and perhaps Grace will now understand why all those sacrifices have been made. Perhaps now is the time she make a few sacrifices of her own."

Myrtle felt rather sickened by his suggestion. She didn't like the woman he portrayed her to be. A money-hungry, social-climbing, coldhearted fish who put her position above her child. The realization overwhelmed her.

"I see by your silence that you agree."

"I do not!" Myrtle said, shaking her head. "What I agree with is that I have been mistaken. I have been cruel in my own fashion. I have worried over issues of society instead of working to draw our family closer. I have been a poor mother, indeed."

"Nonsense. You have done your duty as I have done mine. There is no backing out now."

"This is absurd. Of course you can back out." She reached up to unfasten the multiple strands of pearls around her neck. The symbols of their wealth weighed heavy on her throat, almost as if a noose were tightening. "Start with these. We shall sell whatever we need to in order to pay back the debt, but Grace need not be a part of the bargain."

"You pride yourself on your social standing in Chicago," Frederick began. He sounded quite weary, as if the words themselves were exacting a great toll upon him. "Word would get around quickly. Our name would be ruined."

"I don't care," Myrtle replied. For all her previous concerns about such things, she quickly realized that Grace's safety and well-being were all that mattered. "Possessions are wonderful, charming creatures, but certainly no more so than the love of a child. Our daughter needs our protection."

"I cannot give it," Hawkins replied sadly. He hung his head. "We cannot go back on our word in this matter. You must understand."

"I do *not* understand!" Myrtle said, getting to her feet. "Your child is in danger for her very life."

"Now, Mrs. Hawkins, you know very well that many men are given to slapping their wives. Granted, I do not approve the practice, but perhaps in time—"

"I cannot believe you would even suggest such a thing. I will not stand here and listen to another word. If you will not protect our child and speak to that brute, then I will."

Frederick jumped up from his desk and crossed the room rather quickly. His portly frame did nothing to keep him from beating Myrtle to the door. "I forbid it! Do not put yourself in the position of going against my wishes. You cannot speak to Paxton on this matter. Do you understand me? If you care one whit for our own vows, you must agree to obey me in this one thing."

Myrtle felt floored by his appeal. Nodding her agreement seemed her only recourse. She reached out to touch her husband's face.

"I know you are keeping something from me. I don't know why. We used to be able to face anything together. You cared about my opinion at one time. I fail to understand why now you withhold your heart and instead interject your demands."

Frederick's expression softened. "I do not seek to wound you, my dearest wife. But this is a matter that I must see through for myself. Our welfare is at stake, just as you suggested, but it would be even more so should you go to this man and try to arrange your own terms."

Myrtle nodded. "Very well, then. I won't speak of it to Paxton. But what do you wish for me to tell Grace? I will have to tell her that I appealed to you for help in the matter. Short of leaving her to believe you without feeling or concern, what am I to say?"

Frederick shook his head. "Tell her nothing. Say only that her father knows best."

The finality of her husband's words whispered over and over in her head, but still Myrtle knew no peace with his decision. She thought to go back on her own promise and telephone immediately for Paxton to return to the house. But instead she wearily made her way down the long hall, past the staircase, and down the wing where her daughter's suite could be found.

She paused at the door when she heard voices coming from the sitting room.

"I know it's just a matter of time before you marry some man," the governess was saying. "I really must consider what I am to do with my life now."

"But I want you to stay with me. Couldn't you be my personal maid? Oh, not as a maid, but as a companion?" Grace questioned. "You are my best and dearest friend. I cannot stand the thought of losing you to the northern wilderness."

"I would not be lost," Karen replied with a laugh. "At least I hope I would not be lost. I would, hopefully, be allowed to live with my father and help with the missions work. My aunt Doris would probably want to go as well. She's retired from teaching school now, and I know she worries about my father. If I leave Chicago, there would be no further reason for her to remain here."

"But you're talking of such a great distance. Thousands and thousands of miles. I could never just come for a visit and spend time with you."

"Then why not come with me now?" Karen suggested. "I would never want to be one to encourage you to go against your parents' wishes, but if what Paxton said in regard to ruining your father is true, then perhaps your father's decisions will be less than soundly based. Perhaps we should take matters in our own hands—after all, you will not turn twenty-one until December. If we can but delay any true decision until that time, you will have more legal right to refuse such a marriage."

"I believe your idea to have merit," Myrtle Hawkins said, coming into the room.

Karen and Grace both revealed stunned expressions. They had no idea anyone was overhearing their discussion.

"I apologize if my words seem out of line," Karen said, meeting Myrtle's fixed gaze. "I didn't mean to overly influence Grace's thinking, but rather seek to protect her."

"I realize that, my dear. You are not to receive an upbraiding by me." Myrtle looked to her daughter. "Would you like to consider accompanying Karen north?"

Grace seemed even more shocked by this question. She was speechless for a moment, so Myrtle continued. "If your aunt would act as chaperone," she told Karen, "I would be willing to consider the matter. We, of course, cannot say anything to Mr. Hawkins. He has his reasons for being fixed in his opinions, but I will agree with you—his thinking is less than rational in regard to whatever debt he owes Mr. Paxton."

"I would like to go with Karen," Grace finally replied. "I would do anything to keep from marrying Martin Paxton . . . even risk Father's disassociation."

Myrtle nodded. "We may both have exactly that by the time this ordeal is completed."

⊣ CHAPTER FOUR ⊢

AFTER A WEEK of feigning ill in order to allow the bruising on her cheek to heal, Grace was surprised when her mother suggested they go en masse and visit with Karen's aunt Doris.

"I'm certain the woman can help us to figure out what should be done," Myrtle said rather conspiratorially.

"But, Mother," Grace said as she adjusted her walking-out bonnet, "what would Father say if he knew you were doing this? I don't wish to come between you two. If Karen and I arrange this on our own, you can honestly say that you had no knowledge of the circumstances."

Myrtle looked at her daughter with such sorrow that Grace nearly broke into tears. It wasn't like her mother to have fears and regrets. Until now her mother's only concerns had been their social status, and this sudden change in her left Grace confused.

"I've been dealing with my heart, Grace. I know how consumed I've been by things that are unimportant." She reached out and lovingly touched her grown daughter's face. "I suppose seeing the way Mr. Paxton hurt you opened my eyes— rather like having the scales fall off. I think I was like the blind man in the Bible. Remember when the pastor spoke about the man whom Jesus touched? At first he only saw people as trees. Oh, God forgive me, but I think that is how I have been these long years."

"No, Mother, you only did what you thought right. You wanted us to have good things."

Her mother nodded. "Yes, but I sacrificed a good relationship with you. We could have been great friends. Instead, Karen knows you better than I do." She glanced to the governess and smiled. "How grateful I am that God sent you into our lives, Karen. I know He realized exactly what Grace needed. A big sister and mother all rolled into one. I'm glad she loves you so."

Grace reached out and embraced her mother. The tears were no longer held back. "But I love you as well."

Her mother held her tightly for several moments. "I know," she whispered. "I love you too. I love you enough to take you away from this situation until I can find out what is causing your father such a lapse in good judgment."

———

Hours later Grace found herself seated between Karen and her mother, while Doris Pierce, a rather severe-looking spinster, considered their plight.

"I do agree it's well past time to do something about Wilmont. I cannot abide that he should be among the tribes of the frozen north and not know whether he lives or has gone on to glory."

"I suggest that we might go north to Skagway, Aunt Doris," Karen began. "The situation is most urgent, and I fear that my father might very well need me."

"He may need us both, child. There is much to be done among primitive peoples." She smiled, suddenly breaking the look of sternness, "And much to be done with the Indians as well." She laughed at this, but it puzzled Grace as to what she was talking about.

"I've heard tell that more and more folks are headed up that way. Fur trapping, outlaw dealings, gold . . . You know, it's enough to cause a man to kill." She sobered. "I suppose that would be my biggest concern. How can I possibly agree to take two young women into the unknown with nothing more than myself and my trusty Winchester for protection?"

"I'm hardly one to be worried over, Aunt," Karen replied. "And we'll be careful with Grace—we'll dress her in unattractive clothes, bind her hair, and keep her head covered. As you have always told me, there is much a woman can do to refrain from bringing herself undo attention."

"Oh goodness, yes," Doris Pierce replied. "Why, we could even dress in breeches if the notion took us." She laughed again and to Grace she seemed such a mixture of contrasting personalities. One minute she was stern and severe, relating nothing but the worst of agendas. The next, she was laughing and making humorous statements—downplaying the dangers.

"The situation is most grievous to me," Myrtle suddenly offered. "I worry that should Grace remain anywhere in close proximity, Mr. Paxton and her father would simply find her and bring her back to face a fate worse than death."

"Well," Doris answered, "death is very much a reality up north. Alaska killed my sister-in-law. It could well do the same to your child."

Myrtle nodded and seemed to contemplate the words. Grace felt as if she weren't even in the room. They didn't need her in order to continue the conversation.

"Perhaps better to die at the hands of God's creation than at the hands of a cruel man," Myrtle finally replied. She reached out and squeezed Grace's hand. "I feel confident that despite the defiance of my husband's wishes, this is exactly the right thing to do. I cannot hope for you to understand, but I feel very much as if I am saving Grace's life."

Grace felt her pulse quicken. She'd never heard her mother speak in such a fashion. Did her mother know something more than what she'd revealed? True, Paxton had cruelly hit her, but Grace hardly saw that as a suggestion of deadly intent. Still, she knew a growing worry that Paxton would hurt her in many ways beyond just the physical. She didn't want to be wife to him, neither did she want to see her father ruined.

"What about Father?" she questioned.

All three women turned to look at her rather intently. Grace felt the need to explain. "What will Mr. Paxton do to him?"

"Your father owes Mr. Paxton money," Myrtle Hawkins replied. "I feel there is surely more to it than that, but if there is, he will not tell me. Part of my penance for this situation will be that I sell whatever is necessary for him to meet his debt to Paxton."

"No!" Grace exclaimed. "I won't allow you to suffer on my behalf."

"Grace, should I allow you to marry Mr. Paxton, I will suffer dearly on your behalf."

"Well, it sounds as if we have no choice," Doris interjected. "We can make our way within a fortnight. We'll take the train to Seattle, where Karen's oldest sister lives with her husband and family. From there, we will secure passage on a steamer and go north to Skagway."

"You will need money," Myrtle declared. "I will provide enough to help with the journey for all three of you. I know it is the only way to keep Grace safe. Once Mr. Paxton and Frederick realize she has gone, I'm certain my husband will do whatever it takes to locate her. It could very well be possible that Mr. Paxton will initiate his own search."

"If he is as determined as you suggest, what is to keep him from hiring someone to follow you and Grace even now?" Doris questioned.

Myrtle looked to Grace and then to Karen. "After encountering Mr. Paxton's threats, it is very possible. I hadn't even considered it. We should take every precaution."

"Well, for all purposes, Mrs. Hawkins, this looks to be nothing more than a social visit. We have gone together to visit your friends on many occasions. This will look like nothing more than that," Karen suggested.

Grace nodded, seeing how pale her mother had become. "Yes, I agree. We need to concern ourselves more with how to escape when the time comes to leave for good."

"Perhaps we can work on ways to throw this Mr. Paxton off the trail," Doris said, strumming her fingers lightly on the armrest of her chair. "I do believe there are some rather capable theater students who live just two blocks down. They were once students of mine when I taught secondary classes. I just might enlist their help. Perhaps we could have them pose as Karen and Grace and send them in one direction, while the girls join me to head in the other."

"Do you think we stand a chance of making it work?" Myrtle asked quite seriously.

Doris smiled. "I have a reputation for making the impossible work. With God, all things are possible."

Karen laughed aloud at this. "And with Aunt Doris, God has extra help to see matters to completion."

"Then can we count on you to aid us in our hour of need?" Myrtle asked hopefully.

"Oh, absolutely. I've not had a great adventure since five years ago when I accompanied several maiden teachers to tour the falls of Niagara."

Karen smiled reassuringly at Grace. "She didn't lose anybody then. I'm certain she'll not lose anyone this time."

———

Myrtle sat quietly in Grace's sitting room. Grace sat near her on the sofa and together they whispered and plotted while Karen made notes.

"My heart is so heavy," Myrtle said, leaning back as if physically taxed. "I have wasted many good years on the insignificant."

"But, Mother, you were brought up to care about such things. Grandmother placed great importance on social standings. You mustn't blame yourself for what has happened."

"Oh, but I do," Myrtle replied. "When your brother died as a little one, I thought my heart might break within me. Then I had you and I feared letting the bonds be too close. I didn't want to endure that pain again. I put you from me and chose instead to care about things."

She looked into her daughter's face. Only the slightest hint of the bruise remained on Grace's cheek. The handprint had been a strong reminder to Myrtle that her priorities had suffered greatly over the last twenty years. The past week had been a time of deep prayer and regret. Regret that she could have been so blind. Regret that she could not take back the choices—that she could not turn back the hands of time.

"I shall miss you so dearly," Myrtle said in a whisper. Her voice broke despite her efforts to keep her emotions at bay. "I feel as though I'm just seeing you for the first time, only to send you away."

"No more trees?" Grace asked softly.

Myrtle shook her head and reached out to take hold of Grace's hand. "No more trees. No more wealth above people. No more concern over social matters at the detriment of my loved ones. Grace, you must listen to me. I have no idea what kind of power Martin Paxton has over our financial well-being, but I do not want you to concern yourself with it. If we should lose it all, then so be it. I cannot stand by and be the woman I once was." She bowed her head. "I'm so ashamed that it should take something like this to open my eyes. How blind I have been."

"Mother, I don't understand," Grace said, putting her free hand atop her mother's chilled fingers. "This matter is grave, no doubt. But the seriousness in which you see it alarms me. I don't understand."

Myrtle met her child's gaze. "I can't say that I totally understand it myself. I have never been given to questioning your father's authority, but something in me rises up to rebel. I fear for you. I do not like Martin Paxton, and that he should exercise such demands on your father only proves that he is ruthless and unfeeling. I simply fear the outcome might be far worse than any of us could even now suspect."

"Then I will go, and I will endeavor not to fret over you and Father. You must promise to write me, however. You must write or I will go mad with worry."

"I will write," Myrtle promised. "When it seems safe to do so, I will write."

⊣ CHAPTER FIVE ⊢

DEVIL'S CREEK, COLORADO

BILL BARRINGER paced the small cabin in a determined manner. For all intents he looked to be a man with a purpose, but nothing could be further from the truth. If he did have a purpose, it was only to keep the fear he felt inside from finding an outward expression. He tried very hard, for the sake of his two children, not to look worried.

"Will Mama have the baby soon?" twelve-year-old Leah asked softly.

"I'm sure she will," Bill replied. He ruffled the dark curls of his youngest. "Pretty soon you won't be the baby of the family anymore."

"But I'll still be your princess, right, Papa?"

Bill smiled. Leah looked so much like her mother. Soft dark curls, big blue eyes. Why, even at this tender age she bore the clear markings of a beautiful young woman. Before he knew it she would be courting and then married, and forgotten would be the days when she was her papa's princess.

"You'll always be my princess," he promised. "No matter if this baby is a boy or a girl, you'll have that special place."

Leah smiled and went back to her sewing.

"Why can't Leah cook the supper?" Jacob grumbled from the hearth. At fourteen, he was absolutely convinced that cooking was woman's work.

"Leah's doing the mendin'," Bill answered. "Besides, you're perilously close to being a grown man. You need to know how to fend for yourself. Cookin' a meal ain't nothing to be ashamed of."

Jacob lifted the ladle to sample the stew. "I think it's just about done."

Bill nodded. "Better check on the biscuits."

With his son momentarily occupied, Bill cast a quick glance at the bedroom door. His wife, Patience, as good as her name, hadn't uttered a sound since taking to her bed. A midwife from nearby had come to tend to the delivery, but other than an occasional instruction murmured in a low, hushed voice, even the midwife was silent.

I should never have left Denver, Bill reasoned as he resumed his pacing. At least in Denver they had lived in a decent house and he had held a regular job that brought in steady pay. But Denver had represented failure to Bill. A dozen years earlier he had been on top of the world. Rich from a bonanza of silver, Bill had taken the world for a ride—a wild, exciting ride that had merited him a house of some means and a happy family. Patience had lived the life of privilege he had always promised, and Bill had actually felt proud of his accomplishments.

They weren't rich by Vanderbilt or Astor standards, by any means. But they were happy and comfortable and well set. At least they had been until silver was devalued in 1893 and depression set in across the country. Bill had gone from a life of happiness to one of fear and worry practically overnight. But that fear and worry were nothing compared to what he felt now.

Patience had delivered Jacob with relative ease, but Leah had come in a more difficult fashion and the doctor had suggested that additional children would be a risk. Patience, a god-fearing woman, had told the doctor flatly that she would have as many children as God gave her to bear. Bill, on the other hand, had been far more practical about the situation. He had suggested they do their best to refrain from additional pregnancies, pleading with Patience to stay strong and remain at his side. And with some disappointment, she had agreed.

Bill had figured them pretty much out of the woods when no other children followed Leah's birth. After nearly twelve years, he figured Patience was strong enough to endure whatever God sent their way. Now he wasn't so convinced.

Her labor had started at dawn, and after fixing breakfast for the family, she had taken herself to bed and asked Bill to fetch the midwife. There was an air of excitement among the family. This new baby, although unexpected, was a blessing they were all anticipating with great joy. Patience had told them all that God had smiled down upon them for a reason and that this baby would be a great happiness to them. Bill could only hope that to be the case.

Life was hard in the mining camps of Colorado, and Devil's Creek camp was certainly no different. If anything, it was only worse. Bill had tried to find other accommodations closer to town, but this run-down cabin was the only thing he could afford. Patience had assured him it would be sufficient, but Bill wasn't convinced.

Supper passed in a tense silence. Usually Patience would ask the children about their friends and what they had spent the day doing. Then Bill would ask them about their chores and make certain the tasks of the household were complete. This time Bill had no interest in conversation, and he could see that the children felt likewise.

By the time the clock on the mantel struck nine, Bill was nearly beside himself. There was no sense in pretending ease and assurance. The children knew he was afraid.

"Mama says when you feel bad, you should pray," Leah offered.

"Yes. Your mama would say that." Bill smiled. "That's why we're going to do just that. Jacob, leave off with those dishes and come on over here." Bill knelt down beside his chair. Leah smoothed out the skirt of her dress and did likewise.

Jacob lumbered over and yawned as he got on his knees. They were usually retiring by this time, yet Bill didn't have the heart to send them to bed before the baby was born.

Joining hands, Bill drew a deep breath, hoping it might put a tone of confidence in his voice. "Lord, we thank you for our blessings," he began. "We thank you for watching over us, and we ask that you would go now to be with our dear Patience. Help her to have a safe delivery. Give health to the baby and to Patience. In Jesus' name, amen."

Leah and Jacob both looked to their father as if to question what they should do next. Bill knew they were tired. They'd all been up since four-thirty that morning. "You can go to bed if you want," he finally said, "or sit here with me."

"I want to wait," Leah replied. "I want to see Mama and the new baby."

Bill nodded. "How about you, son?"

Jacob shrugged. "Guess I'll wait too."

Just as they were getting up from the floor, the midwife came out from the bedroom. "I need a word with you, Bill."

Bill felt his chest tighten. "Leah, help your brother finish up the dishes."

"Yes, Papa." She watched him with wide eyes that betrayed her fear. "Is Mama all right?"

"I'm sure she is. You just let me talk to Mrs. Reinhart and then I can tell you more."

He followed the midwife outside. The ink-black night was illuminated by thousands of pinprick stars, and Bill knew there was no other place he'd ever been where God seemed so close.

"I'm sorry, Bill," Mrs. Reinhart began, "but Patience isn't doing well. I'm afraid we may lose her and the baby."

Bill felt as if she'd delivered a blow to his midsection. For a moment he found it impossible to breathe. *Lose her? Lose the baby?* Although he had known it a risk to beat another child, he couldn't believe that God would wait twelve years to rob Bill of both the baby and his wife.

"I don't understand."

"Baby's caught," the woman said. "Patience is just too small. The baby is caught up inside and there's no way to get him down. I've tried, Bill, but without a doctor to take the baby through surgery, I'm afraid we won't be able to save them."

"Where is the doctor?"

"I couldn't say. He was on the other side of the pass. I doubt we could bring him here in time, but if you want to give it a try, that will be our only hope."

"No, don't say that," Bill said, shaking his head. "She can't die."

Mrs. Reinhart gently touched Bill's shoulder. "You could send your boy for the doctor, but I don't think you'd want to leave her now. She's askin' for all of you. I think she knows she's not going to make it."

He heard the words, but they made no sense to him. How could this be happening? Why would God do this to him? He'd tried to live a good life. He hadn't complained, even when the silver had dropped in price and they'd lost everything. Patience had helped him to see that God was in the details and that even in losing all their worldly wealth, they still had one another. How could he go on if he didn't have Patience to encourage him?

"I'll send for the doctor," he said, struggling to find some point of hope. "There has to be a chance."

"You do what you think is best," she replied. "But right now I think you'd better go talk to her."

Bill nodded. "All right. But I don't know what I'll say. What can I say?"

They went back into the cabin only to find that the children were nowhere in sight. The bedroom door was open, and from the dimly lit room, Bill could hear Patience's weak voice.

"Sometimes things don't work out the way we want them to," she was saying.

Bill moved to the door and could see that she had gathered her children to her side, much like a mother hen would gather her chicks.

"Please don't go, Mama," Leah said, her tearful voice cutting Bill to the heart. They already knew. Patience was already preparing them.

Patience opened her arms to her darlings, and Leah snuggled down beside her, putting her teary face to her mother's breast. Bill knew she was probably comforted by the steady beat of her mother's heart. Even Jacob, who considered himself too old for hugs and kisses, had knelt beside his mother and had now leaned across the bed to put his head in the crook of her arm.

"Remember what Jesus said," Patience whispered. She looked directly at Bill, even as she stroked the heads of her children. "He said he had to go to prepare a place for us. Remember?"

The children nodded, but neither spoke. Bill could see they were trying hard not to cry. He was trying hard too, but his vision was already blurred.

"I'm going to go to the place Jesus prepared," Patience said, her loving gaze never leaving Bill's face. "I want you to remember that, just like Jesus wanted us to remember it. I want to see you again in heaven, and there's only one way to get there. You must give your heart to Jesus and continue to live by what the Bible tells you. Will you do that for me?"

Leah lifted her head. "I will, Mama. But why do you have to go now? I don't want you to go." Her voice broke into a sob as she buried her face against her mother's neck.

"Oh, sweet baby, I don't want to go away, but God knows best."

"I think God's bein' mean if He thinks it's best to take you away," Jacob said, wrapping his arm tightly across his mother's still-swollen abdomen.

"No, Jacob, God is not mean," Patience said, trying her best to soothe his anger. "You mustn't be mad at God. He loves you so. Please promise me, Jacob, that you'll love Him and keep His word."

Jacob raised up to meet his mother's eyes. His lower lip quivered as he opened his mouth to speak. No words came. He bolted from the bed and flew across the room, knocking Bill backward as he fled the room.

Bill could no longer stand the pain of the moment. "I'm going to send Jacob for the doctor," he said, struggling to keep his voice steady.

"No," Patience said, shaking her head. "It wouldn't help. God is calling me and the baby home. You must let us go."

Bill crossed the room and knelt down on the floor beside Leah. "Don't leave me, Patience. Don't leave us."

She reached out her hand and Bill took hold of her. "I would stay if I could," she whispered, her voice sounding even weaker. "You must all surely know that I would love to stay here with you."

"Please, Mama," Leah cried, wrapping her arms around her mother's neck. "Please."

His daughter's pleading only mimicked the cry of Bill's own soul. *Please stay with me, Patience. If you die, I die as well.* The words went unspoken, but they were forever chiseled on his heart.

"Oh, my precious ones," Patience murmured, "Jesus is here—He won't . . . leave . . . you." Her blue eyes met Bill's gaze for only a moment. Even in death, they were filled with the hope she'd known in her Savior. Without a word, she closed her eyes and said nothing more.

Bill saw the life go out from her. Still clinging to her hand, he knew the very instant she left his side for her heavenly home. Leah, still holding tightly to her mother, didn't seem to notice for a moment. Then, raising her head, her expression became the very image of brokenness.

"No!" she cried. "No!"

Leah's mournful wailing brought Mrs. Reinhart into the room. The older woman reached down to comfort the girl. "Oh, darlin', your mama wouldn't want you to fret so." She led the crying child back into the front room.

Only Bill remained.

Looking down at the angelic face of his wife, Bill let go of her hand and reached up to touch her face. The woman he had loved so dearly for over fifteen years had gone to her reward without him. Somehow he had always figured they'd die together. He knew it was silly, but it was born out of the reasoning that he surely couldn't remain alive if she were not at his side.

"I love you, my darlin'," he said, smoothing back the dark curls that framed her face. Leaning down, he placed one last kiss upon her lips. She had deserted him, taking with her their unborn child . . . and his heart.

⊣ CHAPTER SIX ⊢

THERE HAD BEEN no money for a stone marker, but because the Barringer family was so well thought of, the mining association put together a collection. Someone voluntarily carved a headstone, chiseling the words *PATIENCE BARRINGER, 1865–1897*, while someone else agreed to make the casket. The local ladies' sewing circle came and dressed the body for burial, and the little congregation of the Baptist church brought contributions of food to help the family during their time of loss.

Leah and Jacob Barringer were rather relieved to see the townsfolk rally around them. Their father had spent that first week after their mother's death in near total silence. He cried a lot at night, and it frightened Leah, who herself felt rather lost without benefit of father or mother. Jacob did his best to remain strong and supportive. He hadn't teased her at all that week, but instead had surprised her with his kindness. Perhaps the most startling example came when Leah had been fighting to brush her long dark ringlets. Finding her hair hopelessly tangled, she burst into tears, wishing fervently for her mother. Without a word, Jacob had come to her, taken the brush from her hand, and had carefully, lovingly, worked through the tangles until her hair was completely brushed and in order. She had thrown herself into his arms, crying softly against the cotton shirt she had mended only the day before. They'd always been close, but now their bond had strengthened.

"Pa says we're leaving in just a few more minutes," Jacob called from the side of the little church.

Leah stood beside her mother's grave. The dirt was still mounded up, and the rocky terrain surrounding the little cemetery looked rather bleak. Leah hated to leave her mother and baby brother there. She had decided for herself that the baby was a boy. Her mother had thought to have another son and call him Benjamin. Leah had figured her mother to know best.

Kneeling in the soft dirt, Leah put a fresh bunch of wild flowers atop the grave. "We're leaving now, Mama. Papa says gold has been found up north. He believes we'll make our fortune there. When we do, I'm coming back to see that you have a beautiful new stone—one that has brother's name on it as well."

She arranged the flowers carefully and ignored the droplets of rain that began to fall. It rained almost religiously every afternoon about this time. Leah had learned to take it in stride along with everything else related to their life in Devil's Creek.

"I don't know when I'm coming back, Mama. I don't know if you can see me in heaven or not, but you told me when I was afraid, I could come to you and tell you. And, Mama, I'm afraid. I don't know where we're going. I don't like our new life without you." She tried hard to keep from crying. "I know you said that God is always with us and that when we're afraid, the psalms said we could trust in Him. I know that bein' a good Christian girl is what you want for me, but I'm still scared."

Leah glanced up at the sky and let the steadily building rain mingle with her tears. "I just know you can see me, Mama. Please ask God to help me 'cause Papa just isn't the same. He's talking about glory and gold again, but his heart is so sad. Sometimes he just sits there staring at the fireplace, and I don't know how to make him feel better, 'cause my heart hurts too."

"Leah! Come on!" Jacob called.

Leah got to her feet and bowed her head for a little prayer. "Dear God, please keep my mama and little Benjamin safe. Don't let nothin' hurt them no more. And, God, if it ain't too much trouble, could you please help us on our way? My pa doesn't always think clear. Mama said he's a dreamer, and I know you understand what that means. So now we're headin' off for another one of Papa's dreams, and I'm afraid."

"Leah, Pa says come right now or he's heading out without you!"

Leah smiled. She knew better, but the threat meant business nevertheless.

"Amen," she whispered, then with one last glance at her mother's resting-place, she hurried down the slippery path to where Jacob stood.

"I had to pray," she explained.

"I know," he replied. "We're going to need a lot of prayers before this adventure is through."

Leah nodded solemnly, and she could tell by the look in Jacob's eyes that he meant every word.

———————

"We'll stay in Denver long enough to put some money together," Bill explained to the children that night. "I've got a couple of folks who still owe me money, and who knows, maybe they've struck it rich while I've been away. Anyway, I know Granny Richards will put us up until we can get on our feet."

Granny Richards wasn't really their granny, but the kids knew her to be a kind old woman who had given them treats when they were young. Bill knew the old woman would be delighted to see them again. He could only hope that she was still alive.

There hadn't been much in the way of possessions to either bring with them or leave behind. Bill felt profound sorrow that in the end, his wife had no more than two dresses to her name and a wooden crate with a few odds and ends of memorabilia. Pots and pans, along with other kitchen goods, and the meager furnishings that had made the cabin a home were hardly a legacy to leave to her children. But, knowing Patience, she'd probably never considered it a problem. She'd left them the important things. She'd given them love and acceptance, hope and a basic understanding of God. Those were the legacies Patience Barringer would want to be known for.

The mining company had owned the property, and because of that, Bill couldn't even raise a traveling purse by selling off the cabin. Instead, he sold off his furniture and what household supplies he didn't deem as necessary to take with them north to the Yukon.

Yukon. Even the sound of it promised something exciting and different. With Patience gone, it left only Jacob and Leah to reason with him and keep him from making rash decisions, and neither one of them were in any mood to argue his choice. Not that it would have mattered. Bill knew he couldn't have remained in the same town where he'd buried Patience and their baby. The very thought would have driven him mad. No, by leaving he could almost pretend that she was still alive—that circumstances had sent her elsewhere. Elsewhere, but not into the grave.

When the trio finally managed to arrive in Denver, no one was prepared for the madhouse of activities. Denver had grown up considerably over the last few years and was now a rather impressive town. Sitting like a sentinel at the base of the Rockies, the town seemed to almost shimmer in the golden summer sun.

Bill wiped sweat from his brow and headed the horse in the direction of the poorer district. Granny Richards, if she still lived, would not have moved. Of that, Bill was certain. She always joked that they would have to take her out feet first, and Bill had no doubt of the old woman's stubborn determination to make that true.

"When will we get there, Pa?" Jacob asked. "I'm so empty my ribs are touching my backbone."

"We ought to be there in a short while. Traffic is pretty bad here. This city is a lot bigger than it used to be. More people and more activities."

"More money, too?" Leah asked hopefully.

Bill smiled. "You bet, princess. More people always means more money. People go where the money's to be had. You'll see. We'll be on our way before you know it."

They all sighed in relief when they finally found their way to Granny Richards'. The little run-down house wasn't much to look at, but it beckoned them nevertheless. Bill spotted Granny first thing. She was working the rocky soil at the side of the house. She seemed to work in a rhythm. Hoe a patch, pick out the rocks. Hoe a patch, pick out the rocks.

"Granny!" Bill called, jumping off the rickety buckboard.

The old woman looked up and put her hand to her head to shield her eyes from the sun. Lacking the funds and not caring one whit about convention, Granny saved her only straw bonnet for Sundays and church. Because of this, her skin was leathery and brown from the harsh Colorado sun.

"Bill? Bill Barringer?" she questioned, limping forward in an awkward manner. No doubt her rheumatism was taking its toll, Bill surmised.

"It's me," he called and went forward to greet her.

The old woman hugged him with an impressive grip. "So you've come back down out of the clouds."

"I have, Granny, but only for the moment." He grinned. "I was wonderin' if you could put me and the kids up for a few days?"

Granny looked past him to the wagon. "Where's Patience?"

Bill looked to the ground. "Uh, Granny, she passed on."

The old woman looked up and nodded. "The mountains are hard on folks, and your little Patience wasn't much more than a mite. How'd it happen?"

"She was trying to deliver a baby. Midwife said she was too small."

Again Granny nodded. "Just a mite. Just a mite. Well, God rest her soul."

Bill fumbled for the words. "I'm . . . well . . . I mean, the children and me—"

"No nevermind about explaining. You just bring down your things and come inside. Old Granny will fix you up with something to eat, and then we can discuss your plans."

Two hours and a full belly later, Bill found Jacob and Leah stretched out asleep on Granny's bed. He closed the door so as not to disturb them, then went to join Granny for another cup of coffee.

"Heard about gold in the Yukon," he said, as if Granny had asked him where he was headed. "Nuggets as big as a man's head. Just lyin' around for the takin'."

"It always is, isn't it?" Granny asked in a knowing tone. She looked at him with steely blue eyes that seemed to bore right through him. "Have you heard tell yet of a gold rush where the nuggets weren't as big as your head? What would the attraction be otherwise?"

Bill shrugged. "I saw the newspaper. They had a picture and everything. Two boats, one in Seattle and one in San Francisco, and both of them loaded down with gold."

"Until you see it firsthand," Granny suggested, "it's still just a rumor."

"No, Granny, these aren't just rumors. The papers wouldn't have run the story otherwise."

She laughed. "Put a lot of stock in papers, do you, boy?"

"Not near as much as in pictures," Bill admitted. "I saw the pictures. I'm tellin' you, Granny, there's gold in the Yukon."

"Bah! Who needs it? Better to do a decent day's job and be paid a decent wage."

"Well, that's why I'm here," he said, finishing off the coffee. "I plan to get me enough for the trip north, anyhow."

"What about them young'uns?"

"They're coming with me. They'll enjoy the adventure."

"What about schoolin'? Their ma, as I recall, held a high opinion of schoolin'."

Bill nodded. "Yes, she did. I'm certain there are schools up north. We're not the only civilized folks in the world, after all."

Granny went to the cupboard and took out a big yellow bowl. She went to the counter and put a smaller, red bowl heaping with green beans inside the first bowl. Bringing both to the table, she sat down and began to snap beans. "So what kind of work you thinkin' to find here?"

"Whatever makes me fast money. I can still deal a pretty fair game of cards," Bill said with a smile. "You know how it goes, Granny."

"Indeed I do," she answered. "I remember you gettin' into a fair heap of trouble with them cards, too."

Bill shrugged. "I was just a boy then. Patience . . . well, she changed my mind about games of chance. Guess her death has changed my mind again. At least it's a way to lay my hands on some cash."

"Don't reckon I can talk you out of it. Hate to see you spending your nights in places better left unvisited. Laws have changed, don't you know. Some of them activities are more likely to see you in jail rather than the bank."

"I don't plan to put myself in too much danger," he told her. He thought of Patience and how she would have given him the devil for even considering what he was about to do. He had to have money, however, and he had to have it fast. Anyone who understood gold rushes knew that you had to act without hesitation. If not, the land got snapped up before you even had a chance to show your face in the territory.

"Well, the young'uns can stay here with me. The garden needs weedin' and waterin'. There's always something they can help with."

"Jacob's big enough to get a job of his own," Bill said rather thoughtfully. He'd not thought of putting his son to work until just that moment. "Maybe he could deliver groceries or shine shoes. He's good with horses. Maybe he could work at one of the liveries."

"Could be. Sounds a heap better than what you have in mind."

Bill yawned and rubbed his bearded chin. "A man has to do what a man has to do, Granny."

"Especially when he's got no woman to fuss over him and keep him on the straight and narrow path."

Bill felt his throat constrict, guilt washing over him. Patience had always talked about the straight and narrow path. She believed that God's way was far more narrow a path than most folks wanted to believe. Bill considered himself a rather religious man, but he knew God understood when he ventured off the path to one side or the other. In fact, he believed God looked the other way in some of those particularly messy points of life.

"I saw you had a stack of wood in the back," he said, suddenly unable to deal with his own discomfort. "I'll just mosey on back there and split some of it for you. I want to earn my keep, after all."

"You'd earn it a sight better doing that than gambling it away or dealing in some other underhanded fashion," Granny said, never looking up from her beans. "Suit yourself."

———

Jacob woke up in a pool of sweat. The heat of the Denver afternoon had joined together with a hideous nightmare of being thrown into the pits of hell. Trembling, Jacob eased off the bed so as not to disturb Leah. He wiped his forehead with the back of his hand and tried to steady his rapid breathing.

From the time he'd been little, Jacob had known that his mother's fondest wish was for him to accept Jesus as his Savior. In all the days that had followed from that first introduction to the Gospel message, Jacob had known that someday he would be left with a choice between deciding for God—or against Him. But someday always seemed far away. At least it had back then.

Years ago, he had figured his folks to live forever. The reality of death made little impact on his world. He'd known of folks who'd passed on. Had even heard stories of his grandparents and how they had died, but death didn't seem anything so immediate that he needed to actually make a commitment to God. After all, his mother said, it would be the most important decision in his life.

"Don't promise God anything, Jacob, unless you intend to keep that promise," she had said. *"Even the Word says it's better to make no vow at all than to make one and then not keep it."*

So Jacob had made no vow. Much to his mother's disappointment.

Now in the dark, musty room, Jacob felt overwhelmed with grief. His knowing God was the one thing his mother had longed for, and he hadn't even been able to give it to her on her deathbed. He shivered in spite of the heat. He could still see her eyes fixed on his face.

"God knows your heart, Jacob Daniel," she had whispered. *"He knows your mind. Whatever it is that's troubling you about saying yes to Him—He already knows."*

Jacob had supposed she had told him this to make him feel better, but instead it only bothered him more. If God knew—truly knew his heart and mind—then He knew that Jacob was a coward.

Leaning against the wall for support, Jacob bit his lower lip to keep from crying. He'd failed his mother and he'd failed God. What hope could there be now?

┤CHAPTER SEVEN├

CHICAGO, ILLINOIS

"BUT, FREDERICK," Myrtle Hawkins tried to reason with her husband, "it's impossible to give our daughter the wedding she deserves on such short notice. Why, July twenty-fourth is scarcely but days away."

"It's just under a week. Good grief, woman, God only needed a week to create the entire world. Do you mean to tell me a wedding takes more than that?"

Myrtle tried to soften her tone. "My dear, I am hardly divine. I can't possibly be called upon to perform miracles. A proper wedding takes months to plan, organize, and prepare."

"Well, you have five days. I suggest you get on with the arrangements."

Myrtle folded her hands and tried hard not to lose her temper. She had already told Grace that this would be her final effort to get Frederick to see reason. If he refused, then Grace would accompany Doris and Karen north to Alaska.

"Freddy," she said, using her old nickname for him, "our daughter has pleaded to be heard on this matter. Won't you reconsider?"

Frederick Hawkins looked up from his paper. "I should certainly reconsider the matter if it were in her best interest, but it is not. I've tried to explain this to you. . . ." His words trailed off as he looked suspiciously at the table maid. "Leave us!" he commanded, and the young woman scurried from the room as if her skirts were afire.

Leaning toward Myrtle's side of the table, Frederick lowered his voice. "This wedding is imperative. I can say no more. Our family will see ruin if we refuse Mr. Paxton."

"But surely what the man has in mind—this blackmail—" Myrtle protested, "it can't be legal. Can't we go to the police or the courts? We have good lawyers on retainer; can we not present the case to them and allow them to earn their money?"

"No!" Frederick said, pounding his fist down on the table. "Confound it, woman, if you do not hear anything else I say, then hear this. Our Grace will marry Martin Paxton on July twenty-fourth. You will plan out the wedding and provide what comforts you can. There will be no other discussion on the matter."

Myrtle realized in that moment that her husband had just set her plans into motion. *Forgive me, God, if this is wrong, but I can't help but feel that I'm saving Grace from complete destruction,* she silently prayed.

Getting to her feet, Myrtle swept the train of her gown aside. "Very well, Frederick. I will go forward with my plans." At least she wasn't lying.

"You'll see in the long run that it's all for the best," he assured.

"I hope you'll try to remember those words," Myrtle replied. "I hope when Grace is far from us and you are lying awake at night wondering if you made the right decision . . . I hope your words still ring true."

He said nothing, but the expression on his face spoke volumes. Myrtle wanted nothing more than to burst into tears, but she was no young maid to be given to moments of emotional waterworks. As a matron of society she had often had to stand her ground in stoic fashion. She would lend an illusion of wedding preparation to their home, but all the while she would be plotting with Grace for her escape.

———

"Aunt Doris said the actresses will come tomorrow at exactly seven o'clock," Karen confided to Myrtle and Grace. "They will be dressed as maids and appear for all purposes to have come from one of the local agencies in order to help with the wedding."

"Wonderful!" Myrtle declared. "I will ring up and have other girls sent over as well. That way they may all mingle together. No one will be the wiser."

"I thought you might see the benefit in such a ruse," Karen replied.

Grace noticed the worry lines around her mother's eyes. She looked so tired and so worn from the events of the last few days. "Mother, are you certain that when all is said and done, you and Father will be able to patch this up?"

Myrtle patted her daughter's hand. "I know my husband very well. I know him so well, in fact, that I know this Mr. Paxton has done more than cause him to build an indebtedness in monetary means. No, there is more to this than meets the eye, and once you are safely away, I intend to know what it is all about.

Frederick will calm down and see the sense of it. Whatever the price, it will be worth knowing that you are protected."

"But I don't feel that way. I don't wish to be protected at all cost," Grace protested. "If it means that either you or Father are left to suffer, then I want no part of that."

"We won't suffer, my dear. Just remember that. I have the jewels and other trinkets that can be sold. And there is property and such that can also be arranged for. Do not worry about us."

Grace nodded, but her heart felt even more heavy. Her mother had already given them a great deal of money. Money that Grace wasn't entirely sure couldn't be better spent elsewhere. Perhaps even in buying off Mr. Paxton.

The next twenty-four hours passed in a flurry of activities for Grace. Her father presumed her to be resolved to the wedding, and at one point over breakfast he had even made a rather pleasant speech about how this choice would have a way of benefiting them all in the long run. He was certain Grace could come to care for Paxton, while Grace knew in her heart that she had no intention of ever caring for the man.

After lunch in the afternoon, Grace and Karen pretended to be busy fitting Myrtle's wedding dress to Grace's more slender frame. No one anticipated seeing the women for the rest of the afternoon, and when dinner came and Grace pleaded a headache, no one thought it amiss that she should take her meal upstairs in the privacy of her room.

By seven o'clock, the temporary maids arrived and with them two actresses who were rather eager for their parts. Slipping the two women upstairs, Myrtle Hawkins met with Karen and Grace to listen to the final plans.

"This is Mavis and Celia," Karen explained. "Mavis will pretend to be Grace and Celia will be me. They will leave in the morning for a day of shopping. Should anyone be watching them, they will see the ladies in the carriage, making arrangements for Grace's trousseau.

"Meanwhile, dressed in their clothes," Karen continued, "Grace and I will accompany several of the maids on various tasks that you have outlined."

Myrtle nodded. "I have a list already prepared."

"Good," Karen replied. "Have it designed so that at the appropriate time, Grace and I can slip away unnoticed. Perhaps at the market."

Myrtle smiled. "That would work perfectly. I can assign each of those who accompany you to different tasks. One can go to the baker and one to the florist."

"Exactly. If anyone is watching, which hopefully they won't be if they believe us to be nothing more than servants, they'll suspect nothing," Karen replied.

"I do so appreciate what all of you are doing to help my daughter," Myrtle said, looking first to Karen and then to the other women. "I know that in time this will right itself and Grace will be returned to us. But in the meanwhile, I also know she will be safely kept from the ugliness of this situation."

Grace frowned. That her mother expected this to develop into something ugly and distasteful worried her greatly. Certainly she expected Paxton to be angry, even threatening, but he was a businessman and as such, surely even he would recognize there to be more power in keeping her father on his feet than in defeating him. He might never recoup the full extent of his losses otherwise.

Sleep came fitfully to Grace that night. The biggest worry they had was how to arrange clothing and traveling needs for the two women. Karen had finally hit upon having a couple of the carriage servants deliver two crates marked *Oranges* to her aunt. Inside would be trunks of neatly folded clothes, shoes, and other personal articles. When Karen and Grace finally made it to Doris, they would simply change clothes and slip away to the railway station, hopefully unnoticed.

Hopefully. It wasn't a word that held the greatest reassurance for Grace. Sitting up, unable to sleep, Grace drew her knees to her chest and tried to pray. Oh, how hard it was to pray when her world seemed amiss and words refused to come. She rocked back and forth, laboring to voice her petition to God, but her mind refused the order she so longed for. Rational thought was not possible.

I hope God understands. Surely He does, she reasoned. *He is, after all, God. He knows all—sees all.*

Outside a summer storm raged over the city, flashing brilliant streaks of lightning. In those moments when her room was illuminated ever so briefly, Grace caught glimpses of her many beloved possessions—her vanity chest lined with all kinds of perfumes and accessories, her books and cherished trinkets from childhood. How could she leave them all?

They are so much a part of me, she thought. Her doll collection was extensive and had been started when she was born. There were eighteen very special dolls, one given each year of her life. After that, her father had chided her when she'd questioned why the dolls had stopped. Instead, very prim and proper gifts were received. A carriage of her own with matching bays. New bedroom furnishings. Those were the type of gifts a grown woman of means might receive. The dolls, like her childhood and innocence, were to be packed away and given to another.

"Oh, Father," she murmured, "why did this ever happen? What did you do to cause such grief to fall upon your shoulders—and my own?"

She loved her father and mother despite their distance during her younger years. She had watched them from afar. Though not as the stick figures her mother had mentioned in her own confessions, but rather as beings of importance. People to be revered and in awe of, but not to be close to or loved by.

Grace supposed she understood that her parents, in their own way, did love her, but their love was far more calculated than Grace desired it to be. She had seen her friends and other families from the church or social settings. She had watched mothers and daughters share amiable moments of what could only be described as true camaraderie. And she had longed for that type of friendship with her own mother.

"Now it seems I might have it, but for my escape," she thought aloud. "Mother is so changed. She feels so responsible for this, and yet I know she doesn't approve of Mr. Paxton any more than I do."

His very name caused her to shudder. Suddenly feeling chilled, in spite of summer's warmth, Grace slipped beneath her covers just as another flash of lightning illuminated the room. Pulling the sheet high, like she did as a child, Grace murmured a prayer for protection.

"See me here, O God," she whispered. "See me and guard me. Protect me from harm and deliver me from the hands of my enemy."

Morning came too soon, as far as Grace was concerned. She dressed as she'd been instructed, shared breakfast with her mother and father, then upon her mother's comment to see to assigning duties to the staff, Grace asked to be excused.

"My dear, if I might have a word with you first," Frederick Hawkins requested.

Myrtle and Grace looked at each other as if to question which woman it was he spoke to.

"I only wish to speak with Grace for a moment."

Myrtle nodded and went about her business, while Grace tarried behind her chair. Clinging to the high wooden back for support, Grace waited to hear what her father might have to say.

Looking genuinely sorry, he met her eyes. "I would not have caused you pain for all the world. I know you fear this arrangement, but believe me when I say, in the long run, it is for the best."

"I know you want the best for me, Father," Grace replied, barely able to keep her voice even. "I have prayed about this and will do what I must."

He nodded. "Good. So long as you understand. A father must do what seems best—even when all around him suggest it to be otherwise. I am only doing what I feel will benefit you. Becoming a wife is a wonderful event in a young woman's life. I feel confident that you will want for nothing. Paxton is quite wealthy and has assured me that you will live in grand style at his home in Erie."

Grace nodded. She wanted so badly to explain herself—to tell him everything and hope he might understand her decision to defy him. Doing the only thing she could, Grace left the security of the chair and went to embrace her father.

Kneeling beside him, she threw her arms around him in an uncharacteristic display of affection.

"I love you, Father. I know you have only tried to do your best for me. I'm sorry I haven't been the obedient daughter you deserve."

"Nonsense," he said, his body rigid and unresponsive.

Grace straightened, looked into his eyes, and realized he had put a wall up between them. He appeared to be fighting with every ounce of his strength to reveal nothing more than manly resolve.

Standing, Grace bit her tongue to keep from confessing her plan. *Better to leave now,* she told herself. *Leave quickly and quietly, remembering that you did what you could and that you aren't going out of a spirit of willfulness, but rather desperation.*

She fled the room, narrowly missing the butler as he came in to make the announcement that the minister had arrived to discuss the wedding arrangements. The words caused Grace to flinch as if struck. She hated lying to her father, but how would she feel knowing she had lied to a man of God as well?

Their plans went through as anticipated, and it wasn't until after she and Karen exchanged places with the actresses and were dressed in servants' uniforms that Grace realized the finality of the moment. For reasons that were beyond her understanding, she suddenly feared that she might never again step foot in her childhood home. Looking beyond the kitchen entryway, Grace found herself wanting to memorize every detail she could set her sights on.

Myrtle came to bid her daughter farewell, and in spite of their resolve to be brave, both women broke into tears.

"Please know how much I love you," Grace whispered against her mother's ear.

"I do know," Myrtle replied. "I love you with all my life." She pressed something into Grace's hand.

Looking down, Grace found a velvet bag. "What is this?"

"Consider it additional insurance," Myrtle replied. "I sold more jewelry. This is the money I received, as well as a few other pieces that you could sell later. Nothing sentimental, I promise. I want you to take it and be safe. Sew the money into the lining of your dress or jacket. Hide it away so that scoundrels and ruthless men will not seek to harm you in order to take it from you. The world is not a kind place, Grace darling. You must look to God for protection and wisdom."

Grace nodded and kissed her mother's cheek. "Don't forget to write to me when it is safe to come home."

Myrtle nodded. "I will. You know I will."

Grace tucked the bag inside her uniform apron and turned to Karen. "I suppose I am ready," she told her companion.

"Then let us be on our way. The world awaits," Karen said with a smile before adding, "or at least the nine-fifteen train does."

Grace refused to look back. She boarded the carriage along with the other maids and didn't so much as wave. Her mother had told her to act no more attached to the place than would a servant and to give it no further thought than one who was about her chores, soon to return.

But I'm not returning, Grace realized. *At least not for a very long time.* Somehow she knew this would be the case. With each turn of the carriage wheel, Grace felt her serenity and security slip away. Defeat weighed heavy on her shoulders. Mr. Paxton had taken her home away from her, after all.

Martin Paxton paced the confines of his hotel room and studied the papers he'd been given. The businesses he'd acquired while on his trip to Chicago were a critical start to helping him in his shipping endeavors across the Great Lakes. A start, but certainly not a completion.

"Boss?" a scruffy-voiced man asked in the doorway of the suite.

"What is it?"

"Came to report in. Davis is on the job now."

"Very well," Martin said, lowering the papers and waving him forward.

"The two young ladies, your fiancée and that Miss Pierce, they left the house this morning. Davis and I followed them."

"And?" Paxton questioned, irritated by the man's slowness.

"And they went to the dressmaker. They looked to be settin' up for a long spell, and so I told Davis to sit tight while I came back here to report in."

"Good. Now get back out there and keep an eye on them," Paxton replied. "I won't have Hawkins backing out of our transaction. Not after all he's done to cause me grief. It would be just like him to let his womenfolk talk him into other arrangements."

The man nodded. "Yes, sir. I'll get right back like you said."

Paxton flipped the man a coin and went back to considering the figures on the papers. Soon his plan would be well underway. He had Hawkins right where he wanted him, and in time he would exact his revenge. The very thought caused Paxton to feel energized and alive. Casting the papers aside, he decided an early celebration was in order. He would find himself a willing companion and a case of good liquor. Then he'd spend the evening in company of both—until one or both were completely used up.

—{ C H A P T E R   E I G H T }—

MARTIN PAXTON read the final paragraphs of the morning paper before casting it aside with a smile. The proclamation from nearly every page had to do with the new discovery of gold in the northern territories of Canada. Not that gold hadn't been a disputed commodity from that area of the world for years, but it appeared that this time things were different. There were stories declaring the authenticity of the find and warnings from the Canadian government regarding the laws and conditions of coming into their fair country, as well as a bevy of advertisements that spoke to the heart of the matter.

GET YOUR GOLD RUSH BOOTS HERE!
DON'T FREEZE WHILE GETTING RICH—
BUY BREMEN'S LONG UNDERWEAR.
Guaranteed to keep you warm or your money back!
MOTHER MADISON'S TONIC!
Guaranteed to ward off the cold and
keep your bones strong
as you journey north to fortune and fame.

Paxton would have laughed if it hadn't been so completely pathetic. So what if two ships had docked on the West Coast bearing more gold than people had seen in their lifetimes? Was the average man really so dense that he believed himself to be the one exception to the rule? Did those people not realize what slim chances were to be had in amassing a fortune in such an unconventional way?

They heard the stories of riches and glory and were blinded to the truth. Never mind that alongside the story of one miner's newly gained wealth, another told of the hardships endured by those who had been less fortunate. Was it truly so easy to look beyond the several-thousand-mile journey to the hope that gold awaited them?

But in truth, Paxton couldn't have cared less. The Yukon gold rush was rapidly making him a wealthy man. Or at least in time it would. Already in the last week he'd bought up six small businesses and one rather large freight company, all because their owners were set ablaze by gold fever.

"Ridiculous fools!" Paxton declared to no one but himself. They were exactly the kind of men he'd spent his life preying on. Men easily turned by the glitter of gold or the flash of a woman's smile. Men who would sell their souls, and had, in order to have their dream.

Paxton found the entire matter to be one of clear profit. The country had long been in a depressed state since the silver panic of 1893. Parts of the country suffered more than others, with the western coastal states perhaps hardest hit. The timber industry slowed to a crawl and with it, jobs were lost in great numbers. Canneries, vineyards, and farms were also to share in the struggles. The gold rush came at the perfect moment—offering the perfect hope.

Taking up his freshly brushed suit coat, Paxton finished dressing for the day. He would call on Frederick Hawkins and see what news could be had of his upcoming wedding. The twenty-fourth was but two days away, and as of yet, the details coming from the Hawkins house regarding the arrangements were few.

He smiled to himself. His plans were so close to being realized. After a lifetime of plotting and planning his own brand of revenge against Frederick Hawkins, Martin Paxton was soon to know the satisfaction of breaking his adversary. The thought was exhilarating—it fueled him—fed him in the darkest hours of his life.

"You'll know what it is to lose the things you love most, Mr. Hawkins," Paxton murmured.

He checked his appearance in the mirror and thought of Grace Hawkins. Such a delicate and petite flower. It would be easy to crush her—to break her of anything even remotely related to a spirit or free will. It hadn't been his original plan to insist on marriage to the girl, but seeing how beautiful she was and knowing that it couldn't help but add injury to insult once the truth was learned, Paxton knew he had to have her. Knowing she was her mother and father's pride and joy made it only that much more satisfying.

The real dilemma was Grace herself. He hadn't figured it would be a challenge to win her over. Women usually came quite willingly when he beckoned, but Grace had been different. Her naïveté in dealing with suitors made her fearful and cautious. Those qualities did not suit Paxton's plan very well. He had figured on seduction, fooling the daughter right along with the father. But no matter what he had done to try to entice Grace, she steered clear of him, hardly giving him more than a second notice. It was enough to wreak havoc with his rather over-sized ego.

"She'll pay soon enough," he said, grabbing a brush to adjust the ebony wave of his hair. Grace Hawkins would hardly be so high and mighty when he dumped her in a hovel in his hometown of Erie and left her to fend for herself. Oh, he'd visit just often enough to threaten her and see to it that she stayed put. He'd alternate his visits so that he never arrived at the same time of day. That would keep her guard up constantly and wear her down more rapidly. She'd always be watching and waiting, never knowing for sure when he might return. He'd use her and abuse her as he willed, and when he was completely finished with ruining Frederick Hawkins, he'd return her to her father—a broken woman, a mere shell of the beauty she'd once been.

Delighted by his own deviousness, Paxton went downstairs to breakfast. The day was young and promised great reward.

Cooling his heels in Frederick Hawkins' study, Martin Paxton was not happy when word came that Grace was ill and would not be receiving visitors.

"I find your daughter's lack of cooperation disturbing," Paxton told a rather ashen-faced Hawkins. "She's refused to attend parties with me, denied me the pleasure of her company for dinner or other outings, and now, not but two days until we are to be married, she is too ill with a headache to see me."

"I cannot force her to get up out of bed for a social call. You want her well for the wedding, don't you?" Frederick replied rather angrily.

Paxton raised a brow. "Be careful how you address me, good sir. I might find myself forced to divulge information that you would rather see forever silenced."

The effect of his words was clearly noticeable as Hawkins took the seat behind his desk. "You're getting what you want, but still I have no guarantee that you won't deceive me and tell your tales anyway."

Paxton smiled in great satisfaction. "No. You don't have any guarantee. You are completely at my mercy, and the sooner you accept it, the better off you'll be." He got to his feet and narrowed his gaze. "I will be here tomorrow at precisely four o'clock. Tell Grace to be ready for a carriage ride in the park. Tell her I will not brook any nonsense."

Hawkins nodded, and without another word Martin Paxton turned and left the house. A slow, burning anger stirred memories that he would just as soon have left in the darker recesses of his mind. Clenching his fists as he reached his carriage, Paxton vowed that nothing would keep him from bringing this fine family to the ground. He would leave them completely demoralized and penniless. They would have nothing but the clothes on their backs and the shoes on their feet, and even that, in Martin Paxton's opinion, would be too much kindness.

Back at the hotel, Martin let the strain of the day leave him. He studied a bundle of letters that had arrived with the afternoon post. One in particular caught his eye. Opening it, he read,

> *Dear Martin,*
>
> *It was our pleasure to hear from you once again. I cannot say the times have been kind on this most westerly coast of America. Here in San Francisco, shipping has seen both increase and decrease, and with the rapid growth of the rail lines, I worry that it will somehow fade altogether and Colton Shipping will be no more. Many of our dear friends have suffered grave financial setbacks, and some have even fled California for more lucrative promises back East.*
>
> *The family is well; thank you for asking. I think often of you and your dear mother. I was truly sorry to hear of her passing. Please know you are welcome anytime in our home and please let me know if there is anything that we might do to help you.*
>
> *Your servant,*
> *Ephraim Colton*

Martin refolded the paper and smiled. Ephraim Colton had been the only truly selfless person he had ever known. The man had shown great kindness to his mother and her family. In fact, at one time the two families had been the best of friends. Long before Martin had been born, the Coltons and Paxtons had shared a common interest in shipping on the Great Lakes. When Ephraim had moved his wife west in order to take over a San Francisco shipping firm, Martin had genuinely mourned the loss.

With barely a dozen years between them, Martin had looked to Ephraim as a father figure and older brother. Martin's own father had died when Martin was just a few months old. His mother blamed it on typhoid, but it was rumored and later confirmed by Ephraim that there had been trouble of a different kind. Martin Paxton, Sr., had been given to great bouts of drinking. It was far more likely that alcohol had killed his father rather than typhoid.

Over the years, Martin had done his best to keep in touch with Ephraim. But in this recent correspondence, he didn't like the tone and worried that perhaps his friend was suffering his own financial setback. Ephraim would never be one to ask for help, but Martin knew his mother would expect no less from her son.

He contemplated the situation for a moment. Never one to give handouts, Martin knew the situation with the Colton family was unique for him. He didn't really care if the Coltons succeeded or failed in business, but if he helped them, he just might help himself as well.

Thoughts of the gold rush once again came to his mind. *There shouldn't be a ship on the West Coast that isn't benefiting from this rush,* Martin thought. *Railroads can hardly take people north to the Alaskan shorelines. They need ships.*

He quickly penned some thoughts related to Colton Shipping and arranged for a runner to deliver a message to the telegraph operator. He would do what he had to in order to see the Coltons back on their feet. If it benefited him in the process, so much the better. After all, he was a businessman.

Martin glanced at his watch as soon as the message was on its way. He had agreed to meet with a Mr. Jones in regard to selling him a warehouse near the docks. When a knock sounded on the suite door, Martin nodded, glad to see that the man was punctual.

"Come in," he called in a loud, booming voice.

The man, a few years Paxton's senior, bounded into the room. "Have you heard it, Mr. Paxton?" he questioned enthusiastically. "Gold! Imagine gold nuggets as big as dogs."

"Are we talking poodles or wolfhounds, Mr. Jones?"

Jones stopped for a moment as if considering the question, then laughed. "Who cares, so long as it's real and worth a fortune!"

"So you've caught the fever, eh?" Martin leaned back in his chair, already knowing the answer.

The man nodded. "I'm selling everything and going north. I plan to make my fortune and live out life as a wealthy man."

"Do you know anything about gold mining in the Yukon?"

Mr. Jones could not contain his excitement. "It's really rather simple. The stuff is spread atop the ground for the taking. I've already heard tell that you just walk about picking up the gold until you've collected your fill. It's in the creek beds and the rivers, it's on the mountainsides and in the streets. Why, one man said the natives use the stuff to make fences and to line their wells."

Paxton would have burst out laughing had the man not been so pathetic. "So you've come to sell me your warehouse?"

"That's right. I want to have traveling money. I plan to go in grand style."

"And just what style would that be in this situation?"

"I'll take a ship all the way around Alaska. A man can pay a pretty penny for it, but there are steamers to be had out of St. Michael that will take you east along the Yukon River and eventually land you in Dawson City. None of that strenuous hiking for me. I'm no billy goat to be climbing over mountains." He laughed in a grating manner that set Martin's nerves on edge. "No, sir, I'll stay aboard the ship until I reach the land of milk and honey."

"I thought it was all made of gold," Martin chided.

"And so it is," Mr. Jones replied. "And I intend to see my name assigned to a good portion of it."

"Very well," Martin replied. "Then let us get down to business. I'd hate to delay you further."

"Well, ladies," Aunt Doris began, "it appears we have arrived."

"Do you suppose anyone will be here to meet us?" Karen questioned, stretching across Grace to look out to the depot platform. "I suppose what with this craziness to go north, we'll never get out of here."

"What did the paper say about the gold rush?" Doris questioned. "Is it happening near Skagway?"

"No, the gold is much farther north. However, Skagway is the stopping-off point for northbound ships. The paper said the two towns are hardly more than tent cities, but that they are sure to grow with the popularity of the routes they offer. I remember mother's letters saying there was little more than a trading post and a Tlingit Indian village in Dyea and nothing of value in Skagway."

"Your sister stated that the ship they've booked us on will dock in Skagway. Do you suppose there is transportation to Dyea?" Doris questioned.

"I'm sure there must be. Both towns afford a passageway over the mountains and north to the Yukon, but apparently the trail is shorter or better out of Dyea. The papers don't give much information on it, but my deduction from personal accounts would seem to suggest that one route is superior to the other," Karen replied.

"My, my," Doris said, shaking her head. "Such a fuss. Greed. That's all it is, pure and simple."

Karen knew it to be true, but her heart was heavy nevertheless. With so many people vying for positions on the northbound ships, there would be no hope of privacy. On the other hand, with such a crowd they would not be easily remembered. What bothered her most, however, was how they would find her father with thousands of people pouring into the territory on a weekly basis.

"It looks rather frightening," Grace said, turning her pale face to Karen.

Karen smiled and clutched her friend's gloved hand. "Think of it as an adventure," she said. "An adventure that is certainly better than the one planned out for you back in Chicago."

Grace nodded. "I didn't mean to sound ungrateful."

"You didn't," Karen reassured. "Just remember what awaits you back there, and the future can't seem half so frightening. In this case, the evil we know is far worse than any supposed trouble we might conjure to mind."

At least she hoped that was the case, because given her own vivid imagination, Karen could conjure quite a few unwelcome thoughts.

—⟨ C H A P T E R N I N E ⟩—

SAN FRANCISCO, CALIFORNIA

ABOARD HIS SHIP, *Merry Maid*, Peter Colton pulled off his bandana and wiped it over his sweat-soaked hair. The day had been nothing but trouble. First he'd had to deal with torn cargo nets and a broken hoist. Then there was a mix-up of invoices and lack of cargo to load once the nets were replaced. Nothing was going right. In fact, not much had gone right in months.

Retying the scarf around his neck, Peter snugged a blue cap over his damp hair and wondered what he was going to do about getting the hoist repaired. He gave the bill of his cap a quick solid yank to shield the sun from his eyes and squared his broad shoulders. He'd have to reason it through later. Surely an answer would come to him.

"Captain, this message came for you," a scrawny-looking teenager announced. He thrust a piece of paper into Peter's hands before heading back to his original task.

"'Come home at once,'" Peter read aloud. The script was clearly his father's handwriting. Fearful that something worse than a broken net had befallen his family, Peter barked out orders to his men, then hurried in the direction of home.

At nearly twenty-seven years of age, some thought it rather strange that he should still live at home with his father, mother, and younger sister, Miranda. But in truth, with the shipping business he was so often away that he thought it completely unreasonable to consider marriage and a home of his own. Not that he didn't long for a wife at times. There were always quiet moments when Peter silently wished for a companion with whom to share his ambitions and dreams.

There were even moments of longing for the passionate touch of someone he could love. But he always put such notions aside. The shipping business was failing. His father's lack of direction and interest had cost them dearly. Bringing a woman into his life at this point would only complicate matters.

Besides, women were of a queer state of mind these days. They were more outspoken and demanding—so unlike his demure little mother who lived to serve her husband and children. So unlike his sister who, at four years his junior, worshiped the ground he walked on and sought him without fail for advice. In fact, his entire family looked to him for advice and wisdom. Even his father recognized that Peter had a certain gift for working a matter through to a more positive benefit and often yielded his own authority to Peter. That kind of adoration was hard to find in anyone, much less a wife.

Hiking up the dock to the embarcadero, Peter hailed a ride with a passing freighter and jumped off several minutes later. He was still a good six blocks from his family's three-story home, but he crossed the distance in brisk strides. He tried not to worry. The note did not necessarily denote a problem. Knowing his family's high regard for his opinion, they might just as well need him to make the final choice in some purchase. He breathed a little easier, sure it was nothing worth fretting over.

His home came into view. Sandwiched between and connected side by side with other town houses, the Colton home was not anything to brag about. It was clean and well kept by the women who loved it, but Peter knew there were repairs that desperately needed to be made. A broken step, a cracked window, and a desperate need for paint and a new roof were all listed in a ledger Peter kept. These, along with a dozen other minor problems, were enough to keep Peter on the ship as much as possible. There was no money to see to the upkeep of their home, and he hated that his family should have to live in such disrepair. But like the problems of his ship, Peter buried his concern in order to focus on the matter at hand.

Bounding up the front steps two at a time, Peter pulled open the screen door and called out, "Father! I'm here!"

Ephraim Colton, a wiry and weathered fellow in his fifties, appeared at the end of the hall. "We've gathered in the music room, Peter. Miranda was keeping us entertained while we waited to share the news."

"Good news or bad?" Peter questioned, tossing his cap aside.

"Good. Come and hear for yourself," he said, beckoning Peter to come quickly.

Peter nodded. His father's spirits seemed considerably lifted since their earlier talk at breakfast. In fact, he looked as if he could break into a jig at any moment.

Glancing at his sister, Peter took up a straight-backed chair and sat. Miranda, ever prim and properly attired, grinned and nodded at Peter as if to suggest he was in for a treat. Easing against the chair, he looked back to his father. "So tell me everything."

"Oh, Peter, it is the very best of news," his mother, Amelia, stated before her husband could take the letter from her hands. "Indeed it has made us all very happy."

"So tell me and let me share in your happiness."

"The letter is from our good friend Martin Paxton. He's been spending time in Chicago these past two months," Ephraim told his son. "While there, he's benefited from the news of the gold rush and wishes to help us benefit as well."

Now Peter's interest was captured. "In what way?"

"He wants to hire us to take freight to Skagway. With folks making their way north, Martin sees the profit of selling goods. He wants to give it a trial run and if the money is good, he will continue to invest with us. He's wired money to the bank here in San Francisco and told me to use it as I wish to get the ships up and running."

"Isn't Mr. Paxton generous to offer us such a commission?" his mother said with obvious adoration.

"What sort of interest is he charging us?" Peter asked quickly, as if to cast suspicion on the generosity of Mr. Paxton.

His father looked confused. "No interest. This isn't really a loan in full. The money is there for our use, true enough. But we will be purchasing supplies for Mr. Paxton's store and moving them north. We can take a reasonable shipping fee and take on passengers as well—if we choose."

"Sounds most agreeable," Peter replied, thinking of what it could mean for the family.

"Son, what are your views on this push to the north? Apparently there are more willing souls to head north than there are ships to crate them. Shall we join in this rush?"

"In truth, Father, I've considered this very thing," Peter admitted. "Seems like good money for minimal work, especially if we haul passengers without extending a lot of fancy services. Charge a fair price, but offer nothing more than two meals a day and shared quarters. Out of Seattle and with good weather, it would take no more than five days to reach Skagway."

"But I thought the most coveted route would go north around Nome and up the Yukon River," his father said.

Peter was surprised his father had become interested enough to remember these details. Even the excitement of easy gold had never been enough to turn his father's head.

"It's true," Peter began. "Many of the lines are offering service to the Yukon via an all-water route. But there are just as many who are dumping loads of passengers and goods off at the towns of Skagway and Dyea. I was talking to the captain of the *Florence Marie,* and he told me about the passageway and the harbors there. Neither town has much in the way of a dock, but that will soon change. They generally anchor offshore and use barges to take the goods and people to awaiting wagons. He assures me plans are already in the making for proper docks."

"And you think it would be better to bring folks into this Skagway rather than take the Yukon River route and deliver them to their destination of Dawson City?"

Peter nodded. "Much shorter time and less trouble; thus, we could charge customers less. I could make several trips a month and see immediate results. The Yukon route would take months, and frankly, without extensive repairs I doubt either *Merry Maid* or your *Summer Song* could withstand the harsh conditions."

"Aye, *Summer Song* would need work, that's to be sure. But what of the trip to Skagway. She'll need work for that as well."

Peter considered the situation for a moment. "My suggestion is to take Mr. Paxton up on his offer, but to advise him that certain repairs and alterations will have to be made up front before we can proceed."

"But that might well result in him canceling his plans," Ephraim said. The worried look on his face spoke more than his words.

"If Mr. Paxton is the friend you claim him to be, he would not want you or me to risk our lives. In addition, he'd want to know his cargo was safe."

"Aye. I'll get a telegram off to him straightaway. But what of the alterations and repairs?"

"Yes, Peter, is there anything we can do to help?" Miranda asked.

Peter looked to the eager expressions of his sister and mother. "I can get Jim Goodson down to look over the accommodations on the *Merry Maid.* He can work miracles, and if there are funds to pay for them, Jim is the one I'd trust to do the work."

"Do you suppose he would have time to get right to it? Time is of the utmost importance," Ephraim replied.

"I'll clean up and go to see Jim. Meanwhile, Father, you must arrange for the goods Mr. Paxton wants shipped. I'm supposing he sent you a list?"

"Aye," Ephraim replied. "I can get to it after sending the post. We should make certain he wants us to continue despite the need for repair work."

"Very well. If his reply is positive, we will need to act fast. There is always the possibility that in the midst of this gold madness supplies will be unavailable. I would hate to disappoint such a generous man." Peter looked to his mother and sister. "As for you two, if you wish to be of the utmost help, assist me in planning for the sleeping arrangements. We'll need blankets and sheets, pillows and such."

"Of course," Amelia Colton replied, nodding. "We can see to all of that."

For the first time in months, Peter felt truly encouraged. "Good. Then let's get to work!"

Hours later after arranging with Jim Goodson for several alterations to the *Merry Maid*, Peter headed home. He'd decided it was in their best interest to get Jim right on the job. If Paxton wouldn't advance them the money, Jim was a good enough friend to wait until Peter could return. *One run*, Peter thought, *one run is all I need to make enough to pay off Jim*. Then he could see to their debts and get both ships properly fitted.

He hated that *Summer Song* and *Merry Maid* had suffered such wear over the years. It reflected poorly on him. He wanted nothing more than to show his father that he was fully capable of seeing to the needs of their family, and yet they were hopelessly in debt and perilously close to bankruptcy. Paxton's offer couldn't have come at a better time, and yet Peter had to fight back feelings of inadequacy.

"I should have figured a way out," he muttered to himself. He kicked an empty can out of the way and watched as the wind picked up the game and sent the object clattering down the road.

"If only Father would have—" He stopped himself in midsentence. He wouldn't bad-mouth his father. Ephraim Colton was simply not the best of businessmen. He'd made an adequate living for his family. Peter could not fault him for holding steady rather than pushing for great wealth. Neither could he fault his father for the depression that had robbed the shipping industry and everyone else of their well-being.

Merry Maid and *Summer Song* had been fairly new when his father had taken them on. They were small, classy new steamers with sail capabilities that made them both economical and efficient. The elder Colton had invested heavily, mortgaging everything he had and throwing in all his savings, which at that time had been considerable due to a family inheritance. But twenty years and a depression later, Peter could hardly find a way to keep their heads above the debt.

It was quite late by the time he reached the house, and Peter knew his family would already be asleep. Slipping quietly up the steps, he paused at the top and without thinking much about what he was doing, he sat down to contemplate their new situation.

The past months had weighed heavily on Peter, and he had worried over what they would do and how they would manage to keep in business. The gold rush news had brought a fury of activity to the Bay Area, but Peter had felt too cautious to simply jump in with both feet. It wasn't a lack of desire that had kept him homebound, but rather a measure of respect for his less-adventurous father. Ephraim Colton took things at a much slower speed these days. His father had suffered the past ten years, fretting and worrying about poor decisions. It had taken the spirit out of him. For as long as Peter could remember, he had known the business to be in trouble. Living in the West had seemed like Ephraim's dream come true, but the life here had been harder than he had anticipated, and his worries over his wife and children had caused him to change his thinking. He had once told Peter that nothing grieved him more than the thought of leaving a penniless widow behind to raise two children on her own. When a modest inheritance had come to Ephraim, he saw it as his ability to ensure his family's needs. His choices, however, hadn't been the wisest. The ships he'd purchased were costly and the resulting business transactions were not to the family's advantage.

With a sigh, Peter looked out past the streets and down over the hilly landscape to the Bay. He could just barely make out the water—inky black but glistening in the moonlight. Yet he could see the ships' masts rising up like apparitions from a life forgotten. Sailing was not as popular as steam these days, and while *Merry Maid* and *Summer Song* were fitted for both, Peter still held a passion for a ship dressed in full sail.

He reflected once again on the day's events and realized that at just the moment they had needed it most, fate had intervened to give them an answer. Some might have said it was a divine intervention, but Peter found religious nonsense to be wearisome. There was no doubt a God in heaven, but Peter believed God must expect more of man than blind faith in a Savior. There had to be many people who walked the earth and did more than their share to aid and comfort the people around them. No doubt there were more ways to please God than merely accept faith in a solitary man who had walked the earth so many hundreds of years ago. Why would a God of infinite resources rely upon only one Savior for His world?

Smiling to himself, Peter felt a revival in his spirit. His family believed him to be fully capable of leading them into the next century. He wouldn't let them down now that he himself could see a way out.

Paxton's money was just the thing they needed. There had been no hope of taking out further loans against the ships or the house. Peter saw the mounting debt and lack of business and fretted that he'd never see Colton Shipping on solid ground. He worried that his family would see him as less than capable in ascertaining the proper business plan. The last thing Peter wanted to do was to disappoint his family.

The gold rush will be our deliverance, he now told himself. *There is more than one way to make a fortune from this adventure.*

Hearing the door open behind him, Peter turned. Miranda stood peering out. "I thought I saw you coming up the walk," she said softly.

Peter got to his feet. "I was just enjoying the evening air."

"May I join you for a moment? I have something to discuss."

"Wouldn't you be more comfortable inside?"

Miranda slipped out the door and pulled her shawl tight around her long, flowing nightgown. "No, I think the evening perfectly lovely, and since it is rather late, no one will see me here."

The breeze blew her long brown hair away from her face, and in the moonlight Peter could see the questioning look in her expression. "So you have something of great importance to discuss? Come sit with me."

Miranda joined him and together they sat down on the top step. "I wanted your opinion on a suitor. Well, a gentleman who would like very much to be my suitor."

"Who is this man?"

"Mr. Plimpton."

Peter thought for a moment. "The man who owns the grocery two blocks down?"

Miranda nodded. "Yes. He attends our church, and last week he asked me if I would consider walking out with him."

"And what did you tell him?"

Miranda smiled and reached for her brother's arm. Squeezing him gently, she replied, "I told him that my father and brother would have to be consulted."

"And how did he take this news?"

She frowned. "Well, not as I would have liked. He suggested that in this modern age it was hardly necessary for a woman to consult her family before giving her heart."

Peter bristled. "And your reply to that?"

"I was quite taken aback. I had heard other women talk thusly, but never a man."

"He doesn't sound like much of a man to me," Peter replied. "Not if he's suggesting an innocent young woman need not consult with her elders—her male elders—for proper direction."

"I felt certain you would see it that way," Miranda said, sounding a little disappointed.

Peter did not miss the tone in her voice. "Do you really wish to spend time with a man who would have so little regard and concern for your safety? A man who obviously would not find it necessary to take charge of your needs in a traditional manner, but rather would leave you to fend for yourself?"

She quickly shook her head and again squeezed his forearm. "Oh, Peter, it's not that. It's just that I'm nearly twenty-three. And I've already been engaged once and that turned out so poorly that I do not even wish to remember it."

"That is because you failed to bring it to me prior to agreeing to marry that cad. It's to your benefit that we found him out before you were legally bound. A divorced man would never be an acceptable mate. Much less a man twice divorced." Peter had offered to pay the man in order to send him packing and leave the naïve eighteen-year-old Miranda behind. It took less than half of what Peter had been willing to spend, and the scoundrel had disappeared without so much as a letter of explanation.

"I know," Miranda said wistfully, "but I long to marry and have a family of my own. I know there are good men out there—somewhere." She gazed off across the valley and out to the harbor. "I used to pretend when I was little that one day a man would come to me from the sea. He would have to be a sailor, of course, because Papa was a sailor. I used to sit and imagine that he would be a great ship's captain and that he would be tall and handsome like Papa." She paused and shook her head. "Such silly dreams."

Peter felt sorry for her, recognizing the longing in her voice that was so evident. He hoped a suitable match could be made soon; otherwise she might very well sink into a mire of sadness and regret.

"Not silly at all," Peter said encouragingly. "I promise that when this gold rush nonsense is settled, I shall pursue the matter of finding a suitor for you. There are indeed good men out there, both on the sea and off. I will prove it to you when time permits."

Miranda nodded. "I trust you to do right by me. You are so wise, Peter. You always see a thing for exactly what it is."

"I try to keep informed so that my family might not be caught unaware. You mean the world to me, little sister. You and Mother and Father. I will not see harm come to any of you."

"We are fortunate to have you, Peter. I know there are perils in making the wrong choices. I have friends who are so miserably matched that their hearts will forever be broken. I do not wish to be one of their number."

He smiled, feeling completely assured that he was doing the right thing. "You have put your trust in the right place," he told her. "I will never let you down."

⊣{ C H A P T E R T E N }⊢

AFTER THREE WEEKS in the cramped quarters of her sister's home, Karen was more than ready to negotiate with anyone who had a boat in order to get out of Seattle. The town itself was an absolute madhouse, but sharing space with five rowdy nieces and nephews, as well as a disgruntled sister and brother-in-law, made for an even more unsettling scene.

Willamina, nearly ten years Karen's senior, was not at all pleased to learn of her baby sister's desire to go north. Especially in light of the current run for gold.

"Father would never want to see you subjected to such people as you will find on your trip to Skagway. Such hoodlums and scalawags are not to be equaled. Why, just trying to go to the general store down the street here is like being thrust into a war zone," Willamina had declared. She had droned on for hours, suggesting that the sensible thing to do was for Karen and Aunt Doris to take Grace and go back to their home.

But Karen couldn't go back. Even if Grace relented to her father's wishes and Aunt Doris grew too weary, Karen couldn't go back. With each passing day she longed for her father's company—longed, too, for a place she'd never before set eyes on. She had reread the letters that had been sent to her prior to her mother's death. How she missed her mother! Each letter was like a precious gem, rich with a wealth of information and tender affirmations.

Now, as Karen waited with Grace and Doris in the outer suite of some sea captain's room, she longed only for a quiet fire and solitude in which to read her letters once again. Instead, she found herself fashionably dressed in her navy walking suit with a straw and cloth bonnet she had never cared for, waiting on a man who seemed to have no idea of the time. Reaching up her hand, she wondered if she looked as misplaced as she felt.

The door to the adjoining room opened to reveal a girl with dark hair and eyes. Her dress was of a well-worn red gingham that came about four inches higher than fashion dictated. No doubt the child had grown some in height, but given their look of poverty, they probably couldn't afford to remedy the situation.

Behind her stood a boy probably somewhere in his middle teen years. With a wild tousle of golden brown hair, he stared at Karen with eyes that seemed hollow and lost. His dirty white cambric shirt was tucked into equally dirty jeans, and his boots sported a hole from leather so dried and marred that Karen wondered that he could even walk in them.

The girl stumbled as she reached the door, and Karen watched as the boy gently took hold of her to keep her from falling. The girl looked up at him with a gaze of adoration and appreciation. He patted her shoulder as if to set her back on her way but said nothing. They didn't look much alike, but the obvious protective nature of the boy for the girl led Karen to believe them to be siblings.

Turning back, Karen watched as two men shook hands. The bearded, dark-headed man, dressed little better than the boy, quickly joined his children.

"Let's go. We'll have to hurry to get everything we need for the trip," he told them.

Karen only realized she was staring when the man turned to her and nodded in a brief, almost matter-of-fact manner. She returned the nod, then dismissing any further contact, quickly turned her attention to the other man. He stood at least six feet in height, with broad shoulders and a lean waist. He had attired himself rather casually for a man of business. Truth be told, he was nearly underdressed for any occasion, yet where the other man and his children had been shoddy, he could be better described as careless in his fashion. His simple white shirt, sporting the newly popular turned-down collar, was unbuttoned at the neck to reveal just a hint of tawny gold chest hair. It was positively scandalous. His navy slacks were tucked into black knee boots and an unbuttoned vest of matching navy serge hung open as if to suggest the man had been disrupted in his morning toiletries.

"I'm Captain Peter Colton," the man boomed out the words authoritatively. "And you are?" He spoke particularly to Doris, much to Karen's relief. She had no desire to focus any more attention on this man than absolutely necessary.

"I'm Miss Pierce. My nephew by marriage arranged passage for us several weeks ago. I believe he told you we'd be coming by."

Colton nodded. "Come and join me." He looked past Doris to Karen and then to Grace. His attention lingered on Grace. "Are these your daughters?"

"Mercy, no," the woman replied. "I told you I am *Miss* Pierce. I am unmarried. This is my niece Miss Karen Pierce and her friend Miss Hawkins."

The captain frowned. "Where are your menfolk? Why are they not here? I thought you were to be accompanied by the gentleman who arranged this passage."

"No, my nephew merely booked passage for us in our absence. We had heard it was nearly impossible to arrange transportation to Skagway and wired ahead that he might secure us a position."

The captain sighed. "I'm not used to dealing with women and would prefer to talk to someone in authority over you."

Karen found his attitude unacceptable. "My father is already in Skagway, Captain, but at my age I'm quite used to fending for myself. My suggestion is that we find some middle ground on which we can deal respectably with one another. We are neither addlepated nor incapable of caring for our own affairs. My aunt and I have attended and graduated from one of the finest women's colleges in the country, and I feel confident we can fully understand and comprehend any contractual arrangements you wish to discuss."

Colton studied Karen for a moment, causing her to blush when his gaze traveled the full length of her and returned to settle on her face. "I can see you'll be nothing but trouble."

"How dare you!" Karen declared. "You are most insufferable."

"As are you," he countered under his breath.

Karen's eyes widened at this, but it was Doris who sought to intercede and smooth things over. "Captain, we are all a bit testy and tired. We have been traveling now for some time and at present do not have calming accommodations."

He smiled. "I seriously doubt there are calming accommodations in Seattle." Just as quickly as the smile had appeared, it disappeared and he continued. "I know there are many women joining the throngs headed north, but I'm not sure I'm comfortable with having you aboard my ship. You are unescorted and a danger."

Karen opened her mouth to protest, but Doris again moved to settle the situation. "I assure you, Captain, we are quite capable as God has made us so in the absence of reliable men. We will not be a bother or trouble you overmuch. We only ask for a room and meals, and we're willing to pay handsomely."

Karen watched as the sea captain rubbed a hand across his clean-shaven chin and cast another quick glance at the silent figure of Grace. "And what of you, miss? Have you a comment to make on your behalf?"

Grace smiled. "I am certain you are a reasonable man, Captain Colton. We are reasonable women. There must surely be a meeting of our minds somewhere within the confines of this predicament."

He smiled as if amused by her gentle spirit. Karen wanted to slap the smug expression off his face and demand that he give them passage. She was tired and grumpy, just as Aunt Doris had proposed, but the last thing she wanted to do was watch some seafaring oaf with a mean temper make moon eyes at her young friend. Feeling rather protective, Karen moved to position herself between Colton and Grace. She heard the captain's man arguing in the hallway with hopeful passengers. Realizing that she would have to soften her approach, Karen drew a deep breath and prayed for strength.

"So might we be allowed to continue our journey, Captain?" she forced herself to question in a calm and collected manner.

"I don't like the idea of taking unescorted women north, unless of course they are women who thrive on the arrangement of being unaccompanied for the purpose of their manner of employment. You aren't one of them, are you?" he questioned, giving Karen a look that provoked her spirit to anger.

Holding her temper, Karen replied, "You know very well we are not of that working class. We are only asking to take our place using the passage we have booked and paid for. We are not asking for you to be responsible for us."

"I am responsible for anything and anyone who boards and travels upon my ship," Colton replied. "And I do not like to take on unescorted women." He held up his hand as Karen opened her mouth to comment. "However," Colton continued, "since you are making your way to your father and will have the benefit of male protection once you have reached Skagway, I am more inclined to allow you to accompany us."

How very gracious of you, Karen thought sarcastically. She hated this man's condescending tone. Here it was, nearly the twentieth century, and he was acting as though they hadn't a brain or lick of sense among the three of them. She nearly smiled at the thought. Maybe they did lack sense. After all, here they were on the run from a powerful man who would no doubt strike out in some form of pursuit. Karen wasn't foolish enough to believe for a single moment that Martin Paxton would just leave off with his demands after finding out that Grace was gone. No, he'd follow them or at least break himself trying.

Then, too, there was the entire issue of having no idea whether or not her father was still alive. And if Wilmont Pierce was still alive—where could he be found?

"I'll take you. I have a single cabin left," Captain Colton said, motioning the women to his table in the inner room.

All three followed, rather stunned by his announcement. Karen watched him closely. He was a very strange man indeed.

"You will have to share this cabin and do the best you can. There are two bunks with four beds available. Should I acquire another female passenger, I will be obliged to give her passage and the remaining bed. Take it or leave it." He looked at them hard as if to gauge their acceptance of this arrangement.

"We'll take it, of course, Captain Colton," Doris announced. "And should there be a need to share our cabin, we will do so quite willingly. I assure you, we'll be no trouble at all."

Peter Colton looked at all three women, then fixed his gaze on Karen. "I would not deem to call you a liar, miss, but in this case I will reserve judgment on the matter until time has proved the truth one way or the other."

Karen lifted her chin defiantly and narrowed her eyes. A thousand retorts ran through her mind, but she remained stiff and silent. There was no way this rogue was going to get the better of her.

———

Concluding his dealings with the three women, Peter announced that he would take no further appointments until after lunch. He closed the door of his suite and stretched out in utter exhaustion. What a day it had been!

He thought back to the trio of women and chuckled in spite of himself. There before him had been his complete summary of women. The younger dark-headed woman with her mild spirit and gentle manner. The older spinster with her no-nonsense approach and logical reasoning. No doubt she could take care of herself as well as any man could. Then there was the other woman. Miss Karen Pierce. Her spirit defied definition. Peter frowned. She was everything he had come to despise in women of the age. Self-assured, combative, and temperamental, Miss Pierce was the epitome of the modern women's movement. No doubt she had never married, and without explanation Peter was certain she had contentedly made that choice based on her own self-sufficiency and determination to prove herself. Not that he was generally so judgmental, but frankly, the woman screamed such declarations in her very mannerisms.

But he had to admit she was beautiful. What little he could see of her light reddish-gold hair struck him as appealing. Her eyes, blue as the sea on a clear day, blazed with a passion for life that promised some excitement for those who beheld them. They were so very different from the large brown eyes of Miss Hawkins. Those eyes reminded him of a frightened doe—so big with wonder and curiosity. She comported herself as a proper woman should. Her silent reverence and gentle manner were an attraction to Peter. He couldn't help but wonder at her age and her people. Why was she here? The Pierce women were heading north to family, but not so Miss Hawkins.

He pondered the matter for several minutes, then smiled. Perhaps he would have a moment to find out on their journey north. Perhaps he could get to know Miss Hawkins better and see whether her actions were genuine.

Peter picked up the log where he'd just registered his newest passengers. Pointing his finger to the place where Miss Hawkins had signed, he found all the information he was looking for. Her name was Grace. A perfectly suitable name for such a lovely woman. And she was twenty years old. A perfectly suitable age for a twenty-six-year-old sea captain.

The thought rather startled Peter. He'd given no serious thought to women in some time. After all, the business had been in trouble and he had had nothing of his own to offer a wife. Grace's lovely image suddenly caused him to rethink his circumstances, and that was most frightening. Shaking off the thoughts, Peter was determined to think on the woman no more. At least that was his intention.

─{ C H A P T E R   E L E V E N }─

MARTIN PAXTON cooled his heels in the Hawkinses' small front parlor. His patience at an end, Paxton tried to reason what his next step would be. If he pushed too hard, Frederick Hawkins would break and be of little use to him. However, if he didn't push hard enough, the man would simply string him along. The entire matter was quite irritating, but certainly no more so than the appearance of the parlor.

Fashioned to bear a flavor of the Orient, the walls had been papered in dark red with gold trim. Added to this, an artist had created a mural of silhouetted figures standing upon a curved bridge. The setting suggested a garden scene; the figures appeared to be lovers.

To accent the decorated walls, expensive oriental rugs were placed upon the dark wood floors. The wood trim along the doors and windows had been painted black and several large decorative chests had been placed amid dark walnut furniture to further set the mood. It all appeared quite fashionable—the smart sort of room a socially conscious family might promote. The kind of room Martin Paxton had no patience or appreciation for.

"We're sorry for having kept you waiting," Myrtle Hawkins announced as she slid back the double doors and entered the room. She refused to make eye contact and Frederick Hawkins cowered behind his wife, appearing ill at ease. Martin immediately sensed there to be trouble.

"Where is Miss Hawkins?" he asked, looking beyond the couple to the open hallway.

"I'm afraid Grace still has not returned," Myrtle explained.

Martin was livid. For over three weeks they had given him one excuse after another. First, Grace was to have been taken ill and quarantined as the doctor attempted to figure out what the problem might be. Next it was suggested that Grace needed to recuperate in the mountains where the drier climate might see her more rapidly healed.

"I've had all I'm going to stand for," Martin announced. "I warned you, Hawkins, what would happen if you failed to come through on this. You owe me a great deal of money, and I'm not a patient man."

Frederick Hawkins took out a large handkerchief and wiped his sweat-drenched forehead. "She has a mind of her own. I tried to tell you that when you insisted on Grace being a part of the arrangement."

"Grace is really rather young," Myrtle began.

"She's twenty years old. Most women are married by this age," Paxton retorted. He tried to keep his anger under control.

"Can't we all talk reasonably about this?" Myrtle suggested. "I'm sure we can come up with an acceptable alternative."

Martin wanted to slap the foolish woman. "And I am equally certain we cannot. I won't stand for being double-crossed."

At this, Myrtle crossed the room to a black lacquered cabinet. Opening the intricately designed doors, she reached inside and returned with a large black velvet case. "I assure you, Mr. Paxton, no one is trying to double-cross you. We apologize for our daughter's actions, but we can't very well force her to marry you when she's not even here." She placed the case on the table beside Paxton and opened it.

Gleaming up from a bed of velvet, Paxton found an elaborate diamond and emerald necklace, complete with bracelet and earrings to match.

"What do you think you're doing, Mrs. Hawkins?" Frederick asked his wife. "I've already told you Paxton isn't interested in your baubles."

Paxton studied the flawless gems for several moments before reaching over to snap the case shut. "Your husband is right. I'm not interested in your baubles."

"I assure you, Mr. Paxton, they are worth a great deal of money. I have more and you could easily sell them to meet whatever debt my husband owes."

"You're trying to back out of our arrangement. You are trying to dupe me," Paxton said sternly. His tone suggested he was reprimanding children. "I do not take kindly to being dealt with in this manner."

He casually reached inside his coat pocket and took out a cigar. Mindless of etiquette, he snipped the end and let the tip fall to the expensive carpet. Fishing a match from his pocket, Martin reached over to strike it on one of the artfully designed cases. Myrtle gasped as he lit his cigar. Taking several long draws of air to ensure the tip was lit, Paxton finally blew out the match and tossed it aside. Mrs. Hawkins' gaze followed the match all the way to the floor. "I warned you, Hawkins."

The older man began to pale. The reaction was not lost on Paxton. He leaned back casually against the doorway and eyed his adversary carefully. "You know what this means."

"I assure you that Grace simply needs time. Isn't that right, Mrs. Hawkins?" Frederick said, turning a pleading expression on his wife. "She needs time and consideration. She's led a very sheltered life."

"Regardless, she's still under your authority, not yet twenty-one. I fail to see why controlling her is such a difficult task. Then again, given the man I'm dealing with, perhaps it's not so difficult to understand."

Myrtle looked first to her husband and then to Paxton. "I fail to see why the jewels won't settle this between you." The expression of confusion lingered, even as she voiced her concern.

"The matter will not be settled because your husband fails to yield to my demands."

"Unreasonable demands," Myrtle Hawkins replied, squaring her shoulders.

Martin resented the woman's interference in the matter but knew Frederick Hawkins was perilously close to breaking. He had seen the man cower in fear as Martin's plan was laid out before him. He had watched the man slowly succumb to fear and anguish with every suggestion or requirement Martin had placed upon him. He was weak, and Paxton hated him for it.

"My dear madam, I fail to understand why you are even a part of this conversation. I have conducted business with your husband and do not mean to begin a new term with you."

He drew leisurely on the cigar and blew out a great puff of smoke before flicking ashes onto the carpet. The look of horror in the eyes of his hostess only served to urge him on. Without warning, he tossed the cigar to the floor and ground it out beneath his boot. It was exactly as he wished to ground out the very memory of Frederick Hawkins—a complete eradication.

"Neither of you seem to understand the severity of this situation, so let me enlighten you. I mean to see our businesses joined through my marriage to your daughter. I mean to see your assets as my own. Your status in Chicago will be negated by my own higher, more influential position." He picked up the jewel case and flung it across the room, causing both Frederick and Myrtle to take a step back in fear. "I will not settle merely for baubles and trinkets. Grace is the price. I expect for you to have her delivered to me within the week."

He paused and eyed them both with a stare that drew upon all his hatred. "If you should either one believe me incapable of rendering your estate and circumstances to complete ruin, then by all means fail to meet this requirement."

Myrtle seemed to get her wind back. "I will never allow my daughter to marry you. You haven't the common decency of a true gentleman to respect a lady's lack of interest. Grace wants no part of you and I'm glad I helped her to escape!"

"Myrtle! Please be silent!" Frederick declared.

"Let her speak," Paxton said rather smugly. "This isn't anything I haven't already figured out. What I fail to understand is how you pulled the entire matter off right under my nose and the noses of my surveillance crew."

Frederick appeared stunned. "You had my daughter watched?"

"I have had you all watched," Paxton replied. "I will continue to have you watched. I will arrange for your mail to be gone through and I will study your every move, if necessary. I will find Grace, and you had better pray that when I do, I'm still of a mind to marry her."

"Never!" Myrtle cried. "I'll never agree to you marrying my child."

"Madam, marriage is the better alternative, believe me. I could do many things to discredit and disgrace this family. Just remember that and remember that I will find your daughter. You may count on it."

He walked to the front door where the butler stood stoically as if he'd not overheard the entire argument. "My hat!" Paxton demanded.

The man nodded and retrieved the black felt from the receiving table. Paxton turned only long enough to reiterate his demand. "One week. If she's not here in that time and standing with me to take her vows, I will bring you to the ground!"

Myrtle Hawkins felt the racing of her heart and actually feared she might collapse at any given moment. She could scarcely draw a breath after encountering Martin Paxton's rage. She looked to her ashen-faced husband and watched him as he clutched his chest.

"Frederick? Are you all right?"

"Leave me. I am well enough to know that if you do not rectify this situation immediately and bring Grace home, you will live to regret it. I, on the other hand, most likely will not."

"Please, Frederick," she pleaded. "Please tell me what this is all about. Tell me why you would rather give your daughter over to this man than face the loss of everything else."

He looked at her with such an expression of hopelessness that Myrtle worried he might indeed drop dead where he stood. "I cannot explain."

"Then I cannot contact Grace," Myrtle said sadly. "We may both be dead tomorrow, but I will not bring that child back to a life of brutal bondage with a man who so clearly holds no love for her. Had Martin Paxton voiced even a moderate amount of kindness and respect, I might well have gone along with you on this, but as it stands, I see him for the cruel monster he really is."

"Do not toy with him," Frederick pleaded. "He holds the ability to rob us of every happiness."

Myrtle shook her head. "He has already done that. He has driven our Grace away from us. We might never see her again, and we will have no one to blame but Martin Paxton and our own foolishness."

————————

Paxton shook with fury as he threw his hat and coat across the room. Cursing, he poured himself a drink and tossed it back as if it could quench the fire that raged inside him.

How dare Frederick Hawkins stand up to him—knowing that Martin could and would crush him for his inability to meet the demands placed upon him? Pouring another drink, Martin paced the confines of his suite and tried to figure out what he would do next. Hawkins would suffer for this. So would his wife. They would feel the pinch as Martin began the systematic collection of all they held dear. By the time Chicago figured out what had happened, the Hawkins name would lay smoldering in ashes, just like part of the town had so many years ago after the great fire.

Then, when he finally had defeated them collectively as a family, he would destroy that bond between members by giving Myrtle the full knowledge of why he had come and why he held the power he did over her husband. With that, he would forever separate their close family, sending Myrtle one direction and Grace in another. Frederick would be left to perish in the mire of his own making. The thought left Martin with a smugly satisfying feeling.

"I will destroy your family as you did mine," he promised to the empty air.

Part Two

AUGUST–NOVEMBER 1897

But where shall wisdom be found?
and where is the place of understanding?
Man knoweth not the price thereof;
neither is it found
in the land of the living.
The depth saith, It is not in me:
and the sea saith, It is not with me.
It cannot be gotten for gold,
neither shall silver be weighed
for the price thereof.

JOB 28:12–15

—{ C H A P T E R   T W E L V E }—

"WE WILL BE UNDERWAY within the hour," Peter Colton explained to the three women. "I will lay out the rules for you so that there will be no question of them in the days to come. The first and most important rule is that I am in command of this vessel and you must heed my every demand."

Karen eyed the captain in irritation but said nothing. Grace was glad that her friend had taken the route of silence. It was frustrating enough to see that these two people clearly angered each other, but Grace's head was already hurting and she had no desire to listen to an argument.

"Number two," Colton continued, "you will remain inside your cabin with the door locked. The only exception to this is for the purpose of allowing your meals to be brought inside."

"And what are we to do about personal needs, Captain?" Karen questioned sarcastically. "Surely we will be allowed access to a bathing room."

"There are pots under the beds for the obvious," he replied, "but there are no baths on this ship. The trip lasts but five days in good weather and the need for such luxury is quite unnecessary."

"I should have guessed. You smell as if you haven't had benefit of such a feature in some time."

Doris reached out and pulled Karen back a pace. "We understand, Captain, that these are your instructions. But might you humor us and explain why these regulations are necessary?"

Peter scowled and fixed his gaze on Karen. "This ship is loaded past maximum safety with men bound for the Klondike gold fields. They are bored and excited all at the same time. They are confined to a smaller space than even you have been privileged to manage. They will roam this ship at will and, short of causing trouble with my crew, will be allowed that free range for the duration of the trip. For your safety, these rules are put into place. I have no other choice."

"And what of the other women on board? Are you locking them up as well?" Karen asked snidely. "Are we all to be prisoners merely because we wear petticoats?"

Grace could see the captain had reached the end of his patience. "Perhaps we will feel better after some rest," she said, putting her hand on Karen's other arm. With Doris on one side and Grace on the other, it rather looked as if they were holding Karen back. Perhaps they were, for Grace could clearly sense her friend's desire for a verbal boxing match.

"I believe Miss Hawkins is right," Doris said, nodding enthusiastically. "A nap would be a proper thing for all of us."

Grace exchanged a look with Peter and gave him the tiniest smile. He seemed like a nice enough man. Pity that he and Karen had to be so constantly at odds.

To her surprise, the captain's expression softened, and he bowed before her and then nodded to Karen and Doris. "As I said, we will shortly be underway." He took his leave without so much as another word or look. Grace was almost relieved when he closed the door to their very plain cabin.

Releasing her hold on Karen, she wasn't at all surprised when Karen flew to the door and opened it as if to call out some further retort. Pausing, however, she seemed to realize how brazen she'd become. Slamming the door, Karen slid the lock in place.

"Have you ever known such an ill-mannered oaf? I cannot abide that man's company, even in moderation."

"So we've noticed," Doris said, smiling patiently. "He does seem to have an easy time of setting you off."

"It's his entire manner. He believes us to be subservient and incapable of tending to our own welfare. He thinks us scandalous for our unescorted travel—and he called us 'trouble'!"

"No, dear, I believe he called you, in particular, 'trouble,'" Doris replied.

"Exactly. He's hateful and mean-spirited." Karen pulled out her hat pin and jabbed it at the air. "That's what I'd like to give you, Captain Colton."

Grace couldn't help but smile. Her friend's rage at the man was a most uncommon reaction. Generally Karen held her tongue and her temper. She knew what was expected of a lady, and she had been schooled in genteel manners and acceptable decorum. Grace had never seen her overstep those bounds—until now.

"I believe the captain is merely trying to attend to our safety," Grace said, smoothing down the windblown collar of her brown- and cream-colored afternoon dress.

"And we did not exactly endear ourselves to him with our additional luggage and goods," Doris reminded her.

"Everyone is shipping an exaggerated amount of goods. It's required of them," Karen replied. "Ours should be no different. Besides, I heard it said that one of those women of ill repute was even bringing a sewing machine. How necessary is that?"

"Well, perhaps she's in the process of changing occupations," Doris suggested with a pondering look that made Grace giggle. "Either way, it's not of any further concern. Dear me, five days from now you will never have to lay eyes on the man again."

"Thank the Lord for that," Karen stated, giving her hat a toss to the tiny wooden table.

"We should thank God for a great deal more," Grace interjected. "Did you see the thousands lining the docks, just pleading to be allowed passage? Why, I heard the captain say that some men even jumped off the docks and tried to swim out after the ship and sneak aboard."

"Gold fever will make a man do ridiculous things," Doris agreed. "And yes, we should thank God for our passage and our safety. I believe Captain Colton will work hard to ensure our welfare. He seems a most conscientious young man."

"Well, he gets no such kind word from me," Karen replied. "He's given us a cabin hardly bigger than a wash closet and insisted that it be our cell for the next five days. There is no privacy whatsoever here. A person cannot even tend to their needs without an audience."

"We'll make do," Doris replied. "Mercy, if we can't figure out how to afford ourselves that much consideration, we are not half the women I believe us to be."

"What do you suggest?" Karen questioned. "I mean, just look at this place."

Grace followed the sweep of Karen's arm with her own scrutinizing gaze. It was indeed a small cabin, probably only eight by eight. Two bunks had been built against the wall. One butted up against the other to make an *L* shape. Other than this, the only furnishing was a small crudely fashioned table and two chairs over which a lantern hung to provide their only light. The entire cabin, including the beds, table, and chairs had been whitewashed. Grace supposed it also helped to make the windowless room seem brighter.

At least it appears clean, Grace thought. *We could be stuck in a dirty steerage area where everyone lives atop everyone else.* Here the room might seem understated, but it was their own hiding place.

"There aren't even enough chairs for us to all sit around the table together."

"I suppose that will do away with any plans for a game of cards," Doris teased.

The things they had deemed necessary for the trip had been packed together into two steamer trunks and positioned against the wall. The sight of them gave Grace an idea. "We could use one of the trunks for a third seat. It's very nearly the same height as the chairs and that way we could all eat together."

"I suppose for five days we can endure most anything," Karen muttered. "And as long as we keep the door bolted, we won't have to endure Captain Colton's attention."

"He is a dashing young man," Doris said with a smile.

Grace felt her cheeks flush, for she'd already thought the same thing. Turning toward the trunk, she hid her face for fear of being questioned.

"Too bad he doesn't have a decent personality to go along with those dashing looks," Karen remarked. "Perhaps God thought giving him both would rob a more deserving man of at least a positive personality."

Grace said nothing, but even hours later when the walls of the cabin began to close in on her, she was still considering Karen's words.

I think him to have a rather nice personality. He's stern, true enough, but there is something about him that appeals to me. Mr. Paxton is stern and demanding as well, but there is a cruelty in his actions that is lacking in Captain Colton's demeanor.

Thinking of Martin Paxton, Grace couldn't help but worry after her parents. Were they safe? Had he hurt them? She tried not to let the thoughts give way to fears, but inevitably images of Paxton had a way of tearing apart her confidence.

Tossing back and forth in the rock-hard berth, Grace finally gave up trying to sleep. Pushing back the covers, she slipped over the side of the berth and climbed down from the upper bunk. Fully clothed for fear of the ship springing a leak and requiring them to make some midnight escape, Grace tiptoed to the door. She had to have some fresh air. Even if she only opened the door for a moment.

Catching her toe against one of the chairs, Grace covered her mouth with her hand to keep from crying out. Pain shot up her leg for a moment, but she ignored it as best she could. She glanced over her shoulders to make certain she hadn't awakened Karen or Doris, but in the darkness, it was impossible to see.

Such blackness, she thought. It was rather like a tomb. The feeling caused the hairs on the back of her neck to prickle. The stale salt air, combined with the moaning and shifting of the ship, left Grace in an alarming state of discomfort.

Just a little fresh air. That can't possibly hurt anyone. She slid back the lock and opened the door ever so slowly. Dim light flooded the room to her surprise. Outside in the narrow passage a wall fixture had been lit, much to Grace's delight. To her disappointment, however, the air inside the enclosed passageway was just as heavy as that of the cabin. Dare she go up to the deck?

She considered Captain Colton's words of warning—his orders were to be followed under penalty of expulsion. Surely he would understand. Beneath his gruff exterior, he seemed like a reasonable man.

Quietly, she pulled the cabin door closed behind her and decided to risk it. The feeling of being sealed in her own grave was much too great. It didn't help to have the snarling face of Martin Paxton haunting her sleep. The nightmares that concerned him were of no matter to anyone else, but Grace instinctively knew that this man would not give up without a fight. She felt certain inside her heart that he would seek to cause her family great harm.

Just thinking of the man caused Grace's pulse to race. What if he had already exacted his revenge? What if he had ruined her family and they were even now penniless and destitute? Her breathing quickened as she picked up her pace. As if Paxton himself were chasing her, Grace hurried up the steps and flung open the passageway door.

Cold damp air rushed over her face and body. It had a sort of calming effect that caused Grace to lean back against the frame, panting. Closing her eyes, Grace tried to settle her spirit. Prayer seemed difficult.

"Lord, I want to trust you. I want to believe I'm doing the right thing," she whispered.

"What are you doing out here?" Captain Colton's voice growled out, demanding an answer.

Opening her eyes slowly, Grace swallowed the lump of fear in her throat. She could see the displeasure in his face. His jaw was set firm and his eyes narrowed in a menacing way.

"I couldn't breathe," she said softly. "The air was so heavy and the room began to close in on me. I didn't seek to be disobedient. Please don't be angry."

He stepped forward and Grace cowered back, flinching as if he might hit her. Her action stopped him in midstep.

"I won't hurt you, if that's what you think." His expression softened. "I would never strike a woman. Let me escort you out on the deck." He extended his hand and Grace hesitated. "What is it?" he asked softly.

"I don't wish to cause you any trouble. You were so reluctant to take us on board, I won't have it said that I caused your disapproval," Grace replied. "I'll just go back to our cabin."

"Nonsense," he said, reaching for her. His grip was firm but gentle. "I promise not to say a single word about this to anyone. You will not bear any punishment from this on my part."

"I have your word?"

His lips curved into a smile and his eyes fairly sparkled. "You, Miss Hawkins, may have my word."

Grace allowed him to lead her to the deck rail. An invigorating breeze blew across her face and Grace breathed deeply and felt instantly refreshed.

"You are a puzzle to me, Miss Hawkins. I am usually a decent judge of character, but you have me completely stumped. You are nothing like your friend, Miss Pierce."

Grace smiled. "Karen has spent the last ten years as my governess. It's a wonder that I am not more like her. I always admired her spirit and tried to imitate her."

Peter shook his head. "Do not continue with that line of study. It would do you a grave injustice."

"You like her so little?"

"I find her annoying and troublesome."

Grace smiled, for her father had once said the same thing—or nearly so. "She is spirited and driven. Men seem to find that annoying in a woman."

Peter's brow raised. "So have you given yourself to the league of women who believe themselves to be poorly used by men?"

Grace could only think of Martin Paxton and the smile left her face. "Perhaps only by some men."

"Perhaps this is only true for some women," Peter countered.

Grace looked out at the black water, unable to discern much of anything. "I have myself been the victim of cruelty, Captain Colton. I did nothing to premeditate the action, but because I am a woman, I had no say in the matter."

"So you are running away?" he asked, then added, "I don't believe I would have thought you capable of such an action. No doubt your companions have influenced your choice."

"My companions have saved my life."

He turned and the collar of his shirt fluttered in the breeze, widening the opening at the neck. Grace watched in fascination as the wind toyed with his shirt and hair. In spite of the travelers who walked about the ship's deck, she suddenly felt very alone with this man.

"I should go," she said.

"No, stay a bit longer. I must know what you are running from."

Grace wondered if it could hurt to tell him the truth. Surely now that they were on their way to Alaska she could honestly explain her circumstance and not expect him to put her off at the next port. Her heart told her she could trust this man, and there rose up a longing inside of her to talk about her escape.

"I'm afraid you would simply find it unacceptable," she began. "A dishonoring of my father's wishes is where it all begins."

"Oh," he said, leaning casually against the rail. "How so?"

"My father arranged a marriage for me to one of his many business partners. The man was considerably older and I had never met him. When we did meet, I was still troubled by the arrangement but was willing to give it my best."

"I suppose he was ugly and fat?"

"Not at all," Grace replied, shuddering as she remembered the severely handsome face of Martin Paxton.

"Then what caused you to flee?"

A steel band seemed to tighten around Grace's chest, making breathing difficult. She hated even thinking about Paxton and his angry words to her the night of their engagement.

"He was unkind," she said softly, not wishing to go into the details of that event.

"Unkind?" Peter questioned.

He studied her for a moment, then reached out to touch her cheek. She flinched and moved away. He frowned, then a look of understanding came into his eyes. Grace flushed at his expression. He knew.

"He struck you." He said the words matter-of-factly, not expecting any admission on her part. "The brute. What was his supposed justification for hitting you?"

Grace licked her lips, tasting the salty air. She looked once again to the water. "He attempted liberties with me and I struck him first. This angered him and he hit me quite hard. It knocked me down and left a horrid bruise. Afterward, he gripped me tightly and shook me, promising worse if I refused him in any way or ever laid a hand to him again." Her voice broke. "I wanted to do what my father asked of me, but I could not. I could not marry that man."

"But why run away? Surely no one expected you to marry him after he revealed such a violent nature."

"My father apparently owed him. Perhaps in more ways than one. I don't pretend to understand or know why he made the arrangement in the first place, but once he knew how I was treated, I expected him to release me from further obligation."

"But he didn't."

Grace shook her head and reached up to wipe away a tear. She'd tried so hard to be brave about the entire matter. She loved her mother and father and missed them terribly. She could still see her mother's tearstained face as Grace climbed into the carriage with Karen. She could still feel the panic that rose up inside her as the carriage passed through the back gate and took her away from the home she loved.

"So I have become a part of your little scheme," Peter said, almost good-naturedly.

Grace suddenly realized he could make life difficult for her. "Please, I beg of you. Please do not tell anyone of my passage north."

"I wouldn't," he assured. "I'm quite sorry for what you endured, Miss Hawkins. I would be the last one in the world to see you back in such a predicament.

I have a younger sister, and should a man treat her in a similar fashion, I would probably break his neck."

Grace looked up at the captain, feeling he had become an immediate champion to her cause. "Thank you for your understanding. I do apologize again for breaking your rule about remaining in the cabin. It's just that it's so dark there, and with no light and little fresh air, I found myself quite overcome. I'll do my best to see that it doesn't happen again."

"I'm the one who is sorry. I'll do what I can to arrange better quarters for you on the morrow."

"Oh, please don't feel that you must go to any trouble," Grace replied. "I wouldn't wish to see anyone inconvenienced."

He reached out toward her again, this time more slowly. Hesitating before touching her arm, he seemed to ask permission with his eyes. When Grace didn't draw back, he placed his hand atop her forearm.

"I'll escort you back to your cabin. Tomorrow morning I would like to have all three of you as my special guests for breakfast. Do you suppose your companions would agree to this?"

Grace smiled, feeling almost giddy from the closeness of him. "I'm certain I can convince them. After all, it will get us out of that cabin."

He laughed softly. "Good. Then I will send someone to show you the way."

They walked back to the cabin and paused in the dim light of the hallway. Grace thought the captain even more appealing than she had before. His chin was covered with a light stubble and his wind-blown hair seemed hopelessly tousled. His lips were moving as he spoke of some matter, but Grace found herself unable to concentrate. Suddenly her mouth felt dry, and she had no idea what she should say or do.

"Until tomorrow," he said. "Sleep well."

Grace nodded and went quietly into the cabin. Sleep? How could she sleep after such a wonderful moment? Her heart felt lighter than it had in weeks.

"Where have you been?" Karen called out in a hushed voice as Grace climbed back into her bunk.

"Arranging breakfast with the captain," she replied rather coyly.

"What?"

Grace giggled and settled into her berth. "Go to sleep and I shall tell you all about it in the morning."

—[C H A P T E R   T H I R T E E N]—

GRACE SLEPT THROUGH the night with nothing but pleasant dreams of her time with Peter Colton to mark the hours. She had surprised herself by realizing the awakening of her heart. Could this be what it was to fall in love? Smiling to herself, she stretched as best she could in the narrow berth and yawned.

"Are you going to tell me what happened last night?" Karen's voice questioned out of the silence.

Grace leaned up on an elbow as Karen managed to light the overhead lantern. With her golden red curls hanging limp to her waist, Karen looked years younger than her matronly thirty.

"I found the cabin closing in on me," Grace said, forcing herself to get up. She climbed down from her bunk and stretched. Aunt Doris moaned and rolled to her side from the bottom of the opposite berth.

"Oh, my dear girls, this is without a doubt the most uncomfortable bed in all of North America."

"I'm sure you are mistaken," Karen replied, "for I am certain my berth holds that honor." She grinned at her aunt's appearance, then laughed aloud. "We look as though we'd experienced a tornado last night. Sleeping in our clothes, wrestling comfort from beds that refused us comfort." She turned to Grace. "Only Grace appears to have faired well through it all."

"That is because she is younger," Doris declared. "Youth has its advantages."

"I'm not that old," Karen replied.

A knock sounded on the cabin door, and Karen quickly pulled back her hair and tied it with a ribbon. "One moment," she called.

Aunt Doris got up out of the bed, holding a hand to the small of her back. "Oh my, there is no way to make ourselves presentable. Someone's at the door, and here we are looking a fright."

Karen unlocked the door and opened it only a fraction of an inch. "Yes?"

"Captain Colton says I'm to escort you three ladies to breakfast in his quarters."

Karen looked back at Grace before replying. "We'll need a few moments to freshen up."

"Aye. I've fresh water for you," the young man replied.

Karen opened the door a bit wider. Grace could see that the boy couldn't have been more than sixteen. "Here, I'll take it," she said, reaching out for the gray enamel pitcher and galvanized wash bowl. "Give us ten minutes, and we'll be able to join you." The boy nodded and Karen quickly closed the door.

"Well, what a pleasant surprise," Aunt Doris declared. "See there, Karen, our sea captain isn't quite so harsh as you would make him."

Karen placed the pitcher and bowl on the table and eyed Grace carefully. Grace felt her cheeks grow hot under the scrutiny. "What have you to say about this, Grace?"

Shrugging, Grace went to the pitcher and poured water into the bowl. "I say we have less than nine minutes left. You promised the boy we'd be ready."

Dipping her hands into the icy water, Grace splashed it against her face. It was only then that she realized she had no towel. "Oh, bother," she said, then without ceremony, she lifted the hem of her skirt to dab the water around her eyes.

"What are you doing?" Karen questioned. "One night on this ship and you've taken on the manners of a sailor?"

"I can't say that I've ever seen a sailor dry his face with his skirt," Grace said, laughing. "I'm merely doing what you've always taught me. I'm making do with the provisions at hand. I have a feeling we'll be doing a lot of that in the days to come."

Karen eyed her suspiciously. "You've taken on a new attitude. When we left, you were afraid—terrified, in fact. The world and everything around you was a threat to your well-being. What has changed?"

Grace hadn't realized her feelings were so transparent. She shrugged. "I guess the salt air agrees with me."

Aunt Doris took a comb from her bag. "A new attitude could suit us all. We've taken on a big challenge, and we'll need the heart of a lioness to fearlessly march into the days ahead." She combed out her long brown hair, then began braiding it. "I, for one, intend to be prepared for the change."

"As do I," Grace said, smiling. "Now, as for breakfast, I told you I had word from the captain last night that he would like to have us as his guests this morning."

"You spoke to the captain last night?" Doris questioned.

"Yes, she did," Karen answered for Grace. "I heard a noise and awoke to find Grace sneaking back into our room in the middle of the night."

Grace nodded when Doris looked at her in sheer horror. "I did leave the room, but I was not unescorted. I felt the walls closing in on me and the air was so heavy I could scarcely draw a breath. I went up the stairs at the end of the passage, planning only to get some fresh air, but Captain Colton found me there and offered to see me safely to the deck. We spoke on the matter of this cabin and he even said he would try to arrange better accommodations. Then he told me we were to be his guests this morning. Which, I suppose we must hurry to do or risk making him angry." She pulled down her own handbag and took out the key to her trunk.

"Well, I'm not convinced of his goodwill," Karen replied. "Suppose he just wants to have us to his cabin in order to announce that he's putting us off at the next port? You did break the rules, after all."

Grace unlocked her steamer and retrieved her brush. "I apologized for that."

"And he accepted?" Karen questioned. "That doesn't seem to fit the personality of the man who barked out commands to us just yesterday."

Grace thought Karen a very harsh judge. "I believe him to be concerned with our general well-being. Rather like you when you worry over a collection of children, wondering whether or not they are being schooled properly. You can't really control their destiny, but if you have anything to say about it—"

"Which I usually don't," Karen interjected.

"But if you did, you would voice your opinion and seek to aid them as you could. Captain Colton holds the responsibility for the crew and passengers on this ship. I'm certain he was only seeing after everyone's best interest." She finished combing out her hair, then twisted it into a lazy knot at the nape of her neck. "Now, will you help me pin my hair in place so that we aren't late?"

Karen said nothing more until they were marched to the captain's quarters and seated at his table. Grace felt suddenly shy and rather dowdy as Peter Colton joined them. He looked simply marvelous in his navy-colored coat and trousers. His white shirt was buttoned to the top, while the opened coat revealed a smartly cut waistcoat, complete with a gold watch fob, which he pulled from his pocket. Checking the time, he smiled.

"I hope I haven't kept you waiting too long." He snapped the watch case closed and returned the watch to his pocket.

"Not at all," Aunt Doris said, acting as spokeswoman for the group. "We were rather surprised at your invitation and prayed that we had not tarried too long in our morning routines for your sake."

Peter shook his head, and Grace noticed his clean-shaven chin. It was such a lovely chin, not too pointed or too square. There was just a hint of a cleft in the middle, and Grace found it rather attractively placed. Somehow, it added true character to the captain's face.

Peter motioned for them to take their seats but actually came to assist Doris as she pulled her chair out from the table. Grace could not fault him for his deference to the older woman's status. Among the three women, Doris was certainly the one who should receive the most consideration.

The women couldn't contain their surprise when breakfast arrived. Brought to them by two of Peter's men, Grace found the service quite commendable and the menu most appealing. Scrambled eggs, fresh biscuits and gravy, and thick slices of bacon were the order for the day. This, accompanied by strong black coffee, left Grace no doubt how Peter managed to maintain his muscular frame.

"This looks fit for royalty," Doris announced.

"It does look good," Karen muttered.

Grace couldn't be sure, but she thought she heard her friend whisper something about being poisoned. She smiled to herself.

Peter started to dig into his food, but the three ladies remained motionless. He looked at them oddly for a moment.

"Might we ask a blessing?" Grace suggested.

Peter put down his fork and nodded. "If that is to your liking."

She felt a minor strain of disappointment that asking God's blessing was obviously not to his liking—or at least not to his routine. Bowing her head, Grace quickly asked God's guidance and safety for the trip and thanked Him for the food and Peter's generosity.

With the unison of amens from the women, Grace looked up to find Peter having already returned his attention to the food.

"Miss Hawkins mentioned the discomfort of the cabin," he said after several bites. "I have arranged new quarters for you. Even now your things are being moved. I hope you'll find the new cabin to be more to your liking."

Grace was deeply touched by Peter's generosity, but before she could comment, Karen jumped in. "You must have known it would be like a tomb," she said sarcastically. "Why your sudden change of heart?"

Captain Colton smiled rather stiffly as he addressed Karen. "I found your friend's manner and genteel expression to appeal to my sense of duty. She treated me with consideration, and in turn I find it quite natural to extend the same to her—to you all."

"I hope you will not be so unreasonable as to toy with her affections," Karen stated without warning. "As her guardian on this journey, I must say I would brook no nonsense in affairs of the heart, either real or imagined."

Grace felt her face flush with embarrassment. She wanted to melt into the rough wooden floor beneath her and never be seen again. She threw Karen a look that suggested it was uncalled for, but Karen would not be silenced.

"I suppose you are a worldly man, Captain, but my dear friend and charge has led a sheltered life. As a good Christian woman she believes the best of everyone around her, thinking that all people are honest with their intentions."

"Perhaps you would benefit by learning from her example," Peter suggested.

"Captain, you are an ill-mannered man!" Karen declared, pushing back her plate.

"And you are a self-centered woman who, seeing another, less sour-dispositioned woman receiving kindness, questions the motives of the giver without any real knowledge of the person or his desires."

"I know full well about the desires of men such as yourself," Karen answered angrily.

"That, Miss Pierce, truly surprises me, for I cannot imagine any man taking the time to express his feelings to you for any extended length of time."

Grace saw her friend's face redden and knew her temper to be clearly pricked by Peter's upbraiding. Looking to Doris for help, Grace prayed that the matter might be put behind them.

"Captain, I wonder if you might tell us of a reliable hotel in Skagway," Doris said as if nothing were at all amiss.

"No, ma'am, I am not at all familiar with anything being reliable in that town. Deviousness runs rampant and decent people are not without risk to their well-being."

"Sounds like life aboard your ship," Karen said, lifting a cup of coffee to her lips.

Grace could not understand why Karen had so completely taken a disliking to the captain. Certainly he had spoken his mind on the matter of women traveling unescorted, but that was his prerogative. She knew Karen to be outspoken on her views and to have a view on nearly every matter, but her response to Captain Colton was so intense and so evident that Grace couldn't help but wonder if her reactions were born of something else.

A sinking feeling came over Grace. Surely Karen couldn't find the man attractive and therefore be miffed to find her interest not returned. Or perhaps it was returned. Perhaps this was how people in love reacted to each other. There was a sarcastic playfulness to it. Neither one seemed completely disturbed by the other's actions, and the captain had positioned Karen at his left, while Grace had been appointed to sit directly opposite him at the small table.

The idea of her governess, who was so obviously closer to the captain's own age, falling in love with this fascinating man left Grace feeling rather under the weather. She pushed her food around the plate as if she were participating in the feast. But she never managed to eat more than a few morsels.

"Are you ill, Miss Hawkins?" the captain asked as one of his men returned to pour more coffee.

Grace looked up to find all eyes fixed on her. "I suppose I'm still trying to get used to sea travel. It is my first time."

He nodded sympathetically. "It sometimes takes a bit of an adjustment."

Grace nodded, then bowed her head and ignored Karen's look of concern. *Please don't love him,* her heart silently begged of her friend. *Don't be in love with Captain Colton, for I fear my heart has already taken up that occupation.*

———

Peter Colton knew his time would be better spent elsewhere, but nevertheless, he chose himself to deliver the trio of ladies to their new quarters. He was un-explainably drawn to Grace Hawkins, and even now had no desire to return to his duties. He wondered if she had slept well after her time with him on the deck. He wondered if she was still haunted by the painful memories of the fiancé she'd left behind. There was, of course, no opportunity to ask such personal questions, but that didn't stop Peter's mind from pondering the answers.

He stopped abruptly outside the door to the cabin and smiled. "Here we are," he announced. He hesitated, his gaze meeting that of Miss Hawkins. She smiled. Grateful for the excuse to further his stay, Peter spied the Barringers coming up behind the women and decided introductions were in order.

"Mr. Barringer, this is Miss Pierce, her niece Miss Pierce, and their friend Miss Hawkins. Ladies, this is Mr. William Barringer and his two children, Leah and Jacob. They have the cabin next to yours."

Doris extended her hand. "Glad to meet a family man, Mr. Barringer. Is your wife traveling with you as well?"

Mr. Barringer looked to the deck. "My wife passed on some weeks back."

"Oh, I am sorry," Doris replied. "Life is such a precarious act. One minute we walk the wire with the greatest of ease and the next moment we find ourselves falling to the net below."

"And sometimes there's no net to catch us when we fall," Barringer countered with a sad sort of smile.

Peter thought the circus analogy rather amusing. The older woman was quite a character. Her trim little frame seemed more imposing than most. She could hardly have stood more than five foot two, certainly no taller than Grace Hawkins.

She had been a schoolteacher, he'd been told, and given her prim and proper appearance he could well envision her in that position. No doubt she would have tolerated little nonsense from her charges. Still, he knew the woman to have a sense of humor. She'd entertained them with several stories over breakfast, and in spite of her independent nature, Peter found her to be enjoyable company.

Not so her niece, who seemed to take great delight in tormenting him. Her gold-red hair suggested trouble from the start, but even with his own superstitious tendencies, Peter had tried to give the younger Miss Pierce the benefit of a doubt. She had quickly proven his concerns on target, however.

Watching the women exchange pleasantries with the Barringer family, Peter found himself studying Grace. He had thought himself thorough in his assessment of her, but with each new opportunity to observe her, Peter found something new to consider. She wore her hair rather simply. Parted in the middle and pulled back into a casual loop at the base of her neck, the rich cocoa color beckoned his touch. The style seemed to suit her, but Peter couldn't help but wonder what her hair would look like, feel like, once Grace released it from the confines of the bun. Last night she'd been a bit disheveled, but nevertheless her hair remained in fair order and all the while he had envisioned it blowing in the wind.

As if realizing his consideration of her, Grace looked up and smiled. Peter felt his heart skip a beat. Her smile warmed him from head to toe. Chiding himself for feeling like a schoolboy, Peter couldn't help but enjoy the gift of her open friendship. He was glad she had defied her father and cruel fiancé to run away. If she'd remained in whatever place she called home, he might never have met her. And that, Peter decided, would have been a grave injustice to them both.

"So, Mr. Barringer, are you headed to the Yukon for gold?" Doris questioned.

"We are. We'll work a bit in Dyea or Skagway. I didn't have enough for supplies and passage north," Bill Barringer admitted, "but we'll manage it just fine. My children are hard workers and together we'll soon earn enough to send us north."

"Your children should be preparing for the school term," Doris said in a stern manner. "I spent my life teaching school, and I would not see a gold rush push aside the importance of education."

Barringer shrugged. "Folks have to do what they have to do. Jacob here is fourteen. He's had enough schooling to get him by. He can read and write better than I can. Leah is twelve, and I don't rightly figure a man is going to much care whether she has an education or not. She's as pretty as her ma was, and when she grows up she'll have suitors enough to keep her from having to worry about such things."

"Mr. Barringer, that is hardly a proper attitude to take," the younger Miss Pierce joined in. "We stand on the threshold of the twentieth century. Education is of the utmost importance for our children."

"I didn't realize you had any children," Peter couldn't help but comment.

Karen glared at him, her blue eyes narrowing. "I do not have children of my own, Captain, but like my aunt, I have dedicated myself to educating other people's children."

"Then perhaps you can start up a school in Dawson City or Skagway or help an existing one," Peter replied. "Either way, this man has the say over his family."

"I am fully aware Mr. Barringer is in charge of his family," Karen retorted.

"I wonder," Grace interjected, looking a bit tired, "if we might be allowed to go to our new quarters. I fear I'm feeling a bit overcome."

Peter wasted no time. "Mr. Barringer, please remember to keep your family contained to this end of the deck." Bill Barringer nodded as Peter turned. "Come, ladies, your cabin is just here on the other side of Mr. Barringer's."

He was grateful for Grace's interference, but at the same time he felt it necessary to put Karen Pierce in her rightful place. He had a low tolerance for arrogant women. Perhaps it was because they grated on his sense of propriety, but it was even possible they simply threatened Peter's own sense of power. He didn't like to think of it in that way—didn't like to imagine his own arrogance going toe to toe with someone else's, yet he knew very well that he could be a most prideful man.

She isn't going to usurp my authority on this ship, pride or no pride. I am in charge here. This is my domain, Peter thought quite seriously. He looked past Grace to Karen Pierce and decided then and there that he would do whatever it took to make her realize she had clearly met her match. He would stand his ground with her, and she would not get the better of him in any manner.

—{ C H A P T E R   F O U R T E E N }—

THE STEAMER *Merry Maid* sliced through the gray-green waters of Lynn Canal and slowly but persistently transported its passengers ever northward toward Skagway, Alaska. Skagway had become the start of the path to the Yukon, with its sister town of Dyea being the fork in the path. Both towns had their benefit for the gold stampeder, but neither were perfect.

Skagway had a better harbor, but Dyea was working on the possibility of extended wharfs. Dyea had the shorter Chilkoot Pass, but Skagway offered White Pass, a route that allowed for animals to pack supplies for a good portion of the distance. At least that was the theory. No matter the path, those who found themselves drawn north by the call of gold also found themselves face-to-face with a rugged, austere beauty that defied them at every turn. Some gave up to go home empty-handed and heavyhearted. Others pursued the dream and lost their lives, while a few fortunate souls managed to actually strike it rich.

Karen thought the stampeders rather amusing and sad at the same time. They were searching for something they'd never had, something they only dreamed of finding. They had risked life and limb to endure the difficult climate and conditions, and all for the remote possibility that they just might find gold.

Grown men—men who should, for all intents and purposes, be in their right minds—honestly believed the exaggerated stories of their predecessors. They talked of fortunes to be had for the taking—of a land where the biggest effort required of you was to bend over in order to pick the gold up from the ground.

Of course, Karen reasoned, they would probably think her decision for coming north to be just as crazed. But hers was a journey of purpose and need every bit as much as theirs. She, too, felt called to the desolate lands of Alaska, but the gold she sought came in human form.

She thought of her father momentarily. Wilmont Pierce was a hero of sorts to his youngest child. Karen knew him to be a wise and fair man, with both feet firmly planted on the ground. When he'd suggested the journey north, Karen had been surprised. It wasn't like him to go off on a whim. But somewhere along the way, he had read of missions being set up in the north. Missions that with the government's blessing were starting schools and changing the face of culture and purpose in the Alaskan wilderness. Her father had been appalled to hear that the natives were being stripped of their own ways and imposed with the manners, practices, and speech of the white American. He believed there had to be a way to blend both and still accomplish a positive result. And it was with that dream in mind that he took his wife and independently traveled north.

She admired her father for his decision. He was an opinionated man, but he was not unwilling to yield his philosophies if someone could make an argument for a better way. Unlike Captain Colton, Karen thought, who seemed only to find value in his own thoughts.

Still, he had managed to give them a lovely room with a window. Arranged at the bow of the ship, Peter had also quartered off a section of the deck that was to allow for private moments of refreshment for the little family and the trio of proper ladies.

Karen had figured the captain to be completely indifferent to their needs, but apparently he was not completely indifferent to Grace. The idea that he might well entice Grace with his charms, only to crush her spirits in the end, troubled Karen and made her quite anxious. Men like Colton and Paxton, men of power and knowledge, often believed the world and its people to be their playthings. How different they were from her beloved father.

Distancing herself from Grace and Doris, Karen spent a quiet morning moment to stand at the rail and study the landscape before her. The canal was not all that wide, but it was glorious. The day before, thick patchy fog had negated any possibility of studying the scenery around them. The captain had briefly shared of glacier ice and its pale blue beauty and dangers, but there was no hope of sight-seeing until the fog lifted. The weather had also slowed *Merry Maid* considerably, and at one point they barely crawled through the canal, the chugging rhythm of the engines bouncing off the fog to echo back at the passengers. It had been eerie, almost worrisome.

But that had been yesterday. Today the sun had already burned off the heavy cloud cover and the blue skies overhead promised a pleasing morning. The brisk breeze blew across Karen's face and body, chilling her thoroughly, but she didn't mind. It made her feel closer to her parents and the land they came to love.

It is a cold country, her mother had written. *Almost as if it played the part of the inhospitable neighbor.*

Karen had mused at her mother's poetic description. She called to mind other descriptions, however, that suggested the neighbor had softened enough to embrace and welcome her parents. They had made their home here, and her father had remained even after his beloved wife's death. That action spoke more than any words he could have written.

Calling upon her education and love of all things botanical, Karen studied the dark green carpeting of spruce and hemlock. Interspersed nearer the edge of various inlets, Karen made out black cottonwoods with their rough-ridged bark and droplet-shaped leaves. White-trunked aspen set amid lacy-leafed ferns seemed recklessly thrown out among the coastal setting, as if for variety.

With snow-capped mountains that jutted straight up out of the waters, the canal needed no man-made touch to maintain its course. Peter had told Grace that the waters were deep and cold—that a man overboard ran a bigger risk of freezing to death most times of the year than of drowning. No doubt freezing in this far north region was always a great concern.

There is a coldness to the interior lands beyond the pass that gives a person cause to wonder if ice would not better suit the tormenting regions of hell rather than fire, her mother had penned. *It chills the bones and leaves a body without hope of ever feeling warm again.*

The thought stimulated Karen's senses, however. She had known cold winters in Chicago. Days when the wind blew in off Lake Michigan and iced the air for weeks at a time. She had also known blazing hot summers that contrasted the winter in extreme opposition. She was ready for a change—ready to see this land her parents had so loved, to know the people her mother had given her life for.

What have you brought me to, Lord? Karen silently prayed as the glory of God's handiwork displayed its majesty before her. *What would you have of me? How can I best serve?*

Her thoughts went to Grace and her predicament. Karen didn't trust Martin Paxton and worried that, weakened by his threats, Grace's parents might well give in to his demands and tell him where their daughter had gone. If that happened, how could Karen hope to keep her young friend safe? She would not yet reach her majority for another four months, and besides that, Karen reasoned, as a woman her options were so limited. Grace was hardly trained to do anything but play hostess to a wealthy man. She could speak French and German fluently, sew beautiful pieces of fancywork, and sing and play the piano and harp as well as those talented souls they had often heard at the opera house.

But how could those skills possibly keep her alive and independent? Karen fretted, knowing that viable skills were absolutely necessary for survival in the icy north. Her mother had made that quite clear. She had written of chopping her own wood and piecing together fur-lined moccasins for herself and Karen's father. She had included entire stories in her letters that dealt with the harsh realities of life among such a hard and unyielding land. Alice Pierce had learned to hunt and fish as well as her husband, and in turn had spent a good deal of time smoking the meat to see them through the long winter months—months that could very well extend from September to May.

"What have I done?" Karen whispered to herself. *I should have required Grace to stay on with Willamina. At least in Seattle she might have been safe.* But even as Karen allowed the thought, she knew Grace would probably have become discouraged before long. And that in turn would have seen her heading home to Chicago and Martin Paxton's vicious cruelties.

Grace had developed into a much different woman than Karen had imagined. When she'd first taken the job as Grace's governess, Karen had seen the opportunity to mold and make Grace into an image of herself. Independent, intelligent, and completely self-sufficient. And while Grace was intelligent, she was far from independent and self-sufficient. *Perhaps my own strength overshadowed her development,* Karen thought.

Shaking her head, Karen tried not to allow her spirits to be overtaken by such thoughts. Surely God had a plan. He had seen them through this far, and with great success. He had given them a safe journey from Chicago to Seattle, and he had allowed for her brother-in-law to book them passage in such a way that they were not long delayed in heading north. Some folks who had booked passage after their arrival would not head north for months.

We've been blessed, she decided. *But where do we take ourselves from this point?* Her own plan was to find her father. No matter how long it took or how arduous the search, Karen would find him. His absence and lack of communication ate at her like a cancer. She felt with some certainty that he was still alive, but whether or not he was in peril or ill, she had no way of discerning.

What did worry Karen was that she had no idea how she might go about finding her father once they arrived. Surely with the influx of gold rush hopefuls, the towns of Skagway and Dyea would be flooded with people. It would be rather like trying to find a needle in a haystack. Not only that, but even if she were able to locate locals who knew her father, they would probably only tell her that he'd gone over the mountains into the interior. Could she follow him? Would that be an option? She'd heard from her brother-in-law that already the Canadian government was tightening the reins on the rush into their Yukon. There were certain requirements to be met. *No doubt,* Karen thought, *women are discouraged altogether from the trek.*

"If Captain Colton had his way, there would be no women in the far north," Karen muttered, turning away from the railing. An image of Grace came to mind.

There was one woman he would no doubt allow. Especially if she stayed within his reach. Somehow, Karen reassured herself, somehow there would be a way to keep Colton from hurting Grace. He would hopefully depart Skagway after depositing his passengers and their goods. She had heard him say that even though he was mostly working out of Seattle, his home was in San Francisco. Maybe he would return there and never pester Grace again. Maybe, but not likely.

Karen felt her irritation with the captain begin to mount. Surely he could see that Grace was special. That he needed to treat her with great care. At least he didn't stomp and snort at her like he did with his crew and Karen.

The entire matter made Karen feel very uncomfortable. Why did she feel so protective—so possessive of Grace? Was her anger at Peter Colton truly nothing more than a rivalry for Grace's affections?

"But she's like my own daughter in so many ways," Karen murmured, shaking her head. Had she grown as overbearing as Grace's own parents? The thought brought about a resurgence of pride.

But I am like a parent to her—like a mother. I've been her companion since she was ten. I've been the one to calm her fears, to hear her prayers. I've been there when she's needed a friend, and I'm the one who taught her about the world and the kind of people who inhabit it.

And now he comes along thinking to . . . to what? Karen realized she had allowed her imagination to run wild. She had already determined that Peter Colton was up to no good. Had she falsely judged him? Had she assigned him a motive where there had been none?

The arrogance of her own heart weighed heavily on her mind. She had become a prideful woman, especially where Grace was concerned. Until that moment, Karen had never seen herself as anything more than the voice of reason and love for her young charge.

"But she's not so young anymore, and truly, she is not my charge. She ran away, and my own influence took her from those who were her authority. Oh, God, forgive me if I have erred," she prayed. "Help me to let go of this bond—to see Grace as the grown woman she is." She sighed and leaned back against the rail, adding, "And please help me to find my father, Lord. Finding him might well settle everything else, for if I can find contentment under his direction, perhaps the future will not seem so worrisome to me."

Upon their arrival in Skagway, Karen very nearly forgot her prayer, along with the hope and promise she felt for the future. Hundreds, maybe even thousands of people were in residence along the shores of Skagway. Not much to look at, the town seemed mostly to consist of tents and a very few clapboard buildings. All of these meager dwellings were outlined in muddy walkways and roads, if one could call a path still dotted with tree stumps a road.

"We've come to the end of the world," she muttered.

"That's certainly one way of putting it," Aunt Doris agreed. "My, but I thought for sure we'd find more civilization than this."

Even as the words were spoken, two parties of nearby stampeders broke into an argument that brought about the hurling of insults and more than a few threats. One man lifted a rifle and fired it into the air, but no one paid him any attention, except to push him backward into the shallow shore waters of Skagway Bay. This event seemed to signal a free-for-all that sent all parties into a full-blown war.

"I don't think civilization has yet arrived in Alaska," Karen replied with a sigh. "In fact, I seriously doubt they have even heard the word."

Peter found Skagway a little different with each new trip north. As more lumber was cut for buildings, the tent city was rapidly taking on a new shape. Docks were already being considered so that ships like *Merry Maid* might not have to put down their anchors in the harbor far from land while passengers and freight were ferried into the town. The current arrangement was most annoying to Peter, who had been spoiled by intricately designed harbor piers in his hometown of San Francisco.

Of course, Dyea had it worse still. The inlet was even more shallow as it approached that tiny town. Tidal flats stretched out far, making it risky and difficult to deliver passengers and their goods. In both places, the use of barges and scows took the people and products from the ships to the drier patches of tidal land where wagons would meet them. Then, for outrageous sums, these entrepreneurs offered to carry the crates to dry land. Early on, many people had protested the extortion and had decided to carry their own goods to shore piece by piece. They were to realize, however, that moving a ton of goods could be a lengthy process. This, coupled with the fact that tides came in with such ferocity and quickness, sometimes bringing thirty feet of water within eighteen to twenty minutes of time, left many a person minus their much-needed equipment. It didn't take long for word to get around and for most people to pay the money due the freighters.

All of these arrangements created a strange sense of community, to be sure. The gold rushers needed the shipping companies, the ferriers needed the passengers and goods, who in turn needed the freighters. It was like a society of mad dogs feeding off one another. And now Peter had joined their ranks.

It didn't bother him so much as annoy him. There was a good deal of money to be made in Skagway and Dyea. Perhaps in truth, the real gold could be found here rather than across the mountains and north. Passengers often waited months to recover lost supplies, meet up with loved ones, or make enough to equip themselves for the journey north. People like Bill Barringer who had come north with barely enough money for passage and who planned to work at whatever he could turn his hand to.

Peter thought them all fools. His steady income, although increasing from inflated rates, was a sure thing. After the rush died down, he would simply return to his home and continue the shipping business. So many of these people, however, would have nothing to return to—if they returned.

Mucking through the rain-soaked street, Peter made his way to a tent marked *Hardware and Stoves.* Seeing Martin Paxton profit from the loads brought north by his father, Peter had taken some of his own passenger profit and purchased a variety of items that he thought might suit the northern traveler. He'd tucked the goods amid the passenger supplies, telling no one of his plan. First he wanted to see if a profit could actually be made. Then he'd worry about where to go from there.

He'd made provision for the load of camp stoves, cots, and canvas tents to be brought ashore by one of the freighting companies. The goods came compliments of an arrangement he'd struck with Sears, Roebuck & Company, the entire package having cost him an investment of some twenty-two hundred dollars. He added in the inflated cost of the freighter, and still he could reap a handsome profit. If not, at least he could break even, and that would be the end of his private scheming.

"Welcome, friend," a man called from behind a makeshift counter as Peter made his way inside the tent store.

Peter eyed the man cautiously. The clerk wore an eye patch over his left eye and had a thick gray scar that started somewhere beneath the patch and ran down the side of his face to blend into his ragged-looking beard. When he smiled, he revealed that at least a half dozen teeth were missing.

"What can I do fer ya?" the man asked in a lazy drawl.

"I'm the captain of the ship *Merry Maid.* We've just put in this morning. I have a load of camp stoves, cots, and other equipment that would no doubt interest those heading north."

"Cheechakos!" the man declared and spit on the dirt floor.

Peter had never heard the word. "I beg your pardon?"

The man laughed. "Them wet-behind-the-ears stampeders. Cheechakos is what we old sourdoughs call 'em."

Peter nodded. "Sourdoughs, eh?" He smiled. No doubt those veteran souls of the north had plenty of other names to call each other as well as their newcomers. Peter decided against making a lengthy conversation. "So are you interested in my freight?"

"You betcha," the man replied. "I'll take it all. How much?"

Peter related the number of stoves and cots and proceeded to explain the size and style of canvas tents. "I have well-made tents, poles and pins included. All of the finest duck cloth—"

"You don't have ta sell me on 'em, Cap'n, just name your price," the man interjected.

Peter thought of his investment. "Four thousand dollars for the entire lot." He fixed his jaw, waiting for the man to protest.

"No problem. Wait here."

Peter nodded and quickly realized he should have been more careful in naming his price. The man hadn't even so much as raised a brow at his suggestion.

Glancing around as he waited for the man to retrieve his pay, Peter spied the price of a nearby cot made from duck cloth similar to those he'd brought with him. Five dollars! He'd paid only a dollar apiece for the ones he'd brought with him from San Francisco. With that kind of profit to be had, Peter could easily see the Colton Shipping firm on solid financial ground. They'd not be obliging in any way to Martin Paxton.

Thinking of Paxton caused Peter to think of his father. He'd have to help his father set prices for any freight not associated with the store Martin Paxton intended to build. Paxton would pay for shipping, but Peter knew his father would be a fool to let *Summer Song* be completely given over to Paxton's needs. Why, with this kind of money to be made, Colton Shipping could build their own store. The idea held great appeal to Peter. Diversifying their holdings could possibly prevent another run of bad luck. Perhaps building a store here while the rush was going strong, then selling it and reinvesting that money in yet another scheme later on, would see a continual flow of funds into the Colton coffers. Peter smiled. Financial independence suddenly seemed very possible.

"Here ya are," the man replied, bringing with him a canvas bag, along with a stack of paper bills. "There's coins and a few nuggets in the bag. Ya can have the nuggets double-checked at the assayers, but my scales are just as good."

Peter took up the bag. It was heavier than he'd expected. *What a strange way of doing business,* he thought.

Opening the bag, he had to see what was inside. He had to know what all the fuss was about. His eyes widened. Reaching inside, Peter drew out a nugget and held it up to the light. So this was what all the fuss was about.

His expression must have amused the store owner. Laughing, the older man muttered under his breath and slapped his knee. One word was all he said, but for Peter it said it all.

"Cheechako!"

⊣[C H A P T E R   F I F T E E N]⊢

KAREN WASN'T SURE what she'd expected of Skagway, but what she got wasn't exactly what she'd hoped for. Rough-looking buildings in various stages of construction were few and far between. Tents were the mainstay and were erected in a marginal semblance of order, some with signs declaring them to be hotels, restaurants, or shops. The streets themselves were in no better shape. It looked as if the people upon arriving in Skagway had literally had to hack their way through the forest. In many places, tree stumps were still standing in the middle of what appeared to be the planned roadway, and there was absolutely no consideration of a boardwalk for the pedestrians who crowded the streets.

The place was even more primitive than Karen had imagined. Somehow she had believed the place would have been settled by their arrival. She knew from her mother's letters that there was very little in the way of an established town, but given the stampede north and the modern innovations for settlement, Karen had honestly expected something more established.

Staring at the activity down the main street of Skagway, Karen felt like crying. Disappointment had washed over her from the moment the ferryman helped her to transfer to an awaiting path of tidal mud, and it was certainly no better now that the freighters had delivered their trunks and crates of supplies.

"Where do you want this stuff, ma'am?" a bearded man called down from his wagon.

"Goodness," Doris answered before Karen could think to reply, "where should we have it taken?"

The man shrugged. "Ain't a hotel room open in town, and I don't see a tent here amongst your goods. What'd you ladies think you were comin' to? A tea party?"

Karen resented the man's flippant attitude almost as much as her own disappointment. "We have come to be with my father, if you must know." She stood with her hands on her hips, hoping the stance looked intimidating.

"Well, he don't appear to be here. Probably already hiked over the pass," the man suggested.

"He's a missions worker with the Tlingit Indians," Karen informed him. "He was here long before the fuss over gold, and he'll be here long after the others have gone. Yourself included."

"Feisty thing, ain't she?" the man said, looking to Doris. "Feisty is good up here, but it still don't tell me where you need these things taken."

Doris nodded. "I'm sorry, young man. I'm not at all familiar with where my brother is staying. I believe he's often in Dyea, but the ship wasn't headed to that harbor."

"Iffen you're headed Dyea way, you'd do best to have me take this to the flatboats on the river side of town. It's just down that road over yonder," the man said and pointed at a muddy path barely wide enough for the passage of a single wagon. "The best way to get this load to Dyea would be by having it floated over. You can ride as well." He tucked his thumbs into his suspenders and added, "And I've got a friend who runs some boats. He'll give you a fair price."

"That would be a first," Karen replied.

The man laughed, seeming unconcerned with her comment. "Take it or leave it, but iffen you want Dyea, that's my advice."

"Well, I trust you to know what's best," Doris said. "Should we walk or ride with you?"

"Ain't room but for one or two of you," he said. "'Course, that feisty redhead could probably put us all to shame. She's probably got more energy than these old nags."

Karen felt her cheeks redden. "I'd rather walk than ride with such an ill-mannered man."

"I'll walk with Karen," Grace suggested. "Why don't you go ahead and ride, Aunt Doris? You can arrange everything ahead of time, and when we arrive you can tell us all about it."

Doris nodded. "I believe that would be most advisable."

The teamster reached down to hoist the older woman up. Seeing this, Karen hurried to her aunt's aid and helped her from below. Together, they soon had Doris settled on the wood seat beside the driver.

"You gals just stick to the road. It goes straight away to where ya need to be. Just follow us."

Karen nodded, uncertain as to what they were getting themselves into. For all she knew the man could be leading them off to their demise. Bill Barringer and his children, Jacob and Leah, came upon Karen and Grace just as the wagon pulled off. Each of the trio was heavily laden with backpacks and cases.

"You're the ladies from the boat," Leah said, smiling at Karen. "I remember you 'cause I liked your pretty hair."

Karen's anger eased a bit, but her fears mounted ever higher as the wagon moved off down the road. *Please help us, Lord,* she prayed before turning her smile on Leah Barringer.

"I remember you too. I wish I had time to chat, but we have to follow that wagon. We've a boat to catch that will take us to Dyea."

"That's where we're headed too," Bill replied. "Might we walk with you?"

Karen looked to Grace and nodded. "I think that would be very nice. In fact, I would call it answered prayer. I'm not sure either Miss Hawkins or myself expected to be quite so liberated upon our arrival to Alaska."

Mr. Barringer smiled from behind his beard and mustache. Karen thought him a sad sort of figure given his recent loss, but he always seemed to have a smile and warm word for his children. She had heard him one night when they had been gathered at the rail of the ship. He had promised them that God would make a way for their steps. That God knew what was best for their lives and that He honored a man who was willing to put his plans into action, counting on God for direction. Karen had thought it wise enough counsel, even while questioning the sanity of a man who would bring his children into such a chaotic environment.

"Mr. Barringer, isn't it?" she asked, not wanting to appear too forward.

"Yes," he replied. "But call me Bill. *Mister* hardly seems well-suited to this place."

"Perhaps that's all the more reason we should stand on formality," Karen replied.

"No, I like the idea of going by our first names," Grace interjected, surprising Karen. She smiled at Bill. "I'm Grace Hawkins, Bill. You feel free to call me by my given name."

"Grace is a pretty name," Leah remarked. Jacob, however, remained sullen and silent.

"Very well," Karen said, giving in. "My name is Karen."

"I like that name too," Leah said.

Karen couldn't help but be taken with the girl. She appeared so friendly and outward in her manner. She seemed needy for attention from other women. And why not? Karen thought. Her mother had just died and she was at a most precarious age.

"I think we'd better put our best foot forward," Karen said, watching the wagon disappear around the bend. "I wouldn't want my aunt to have to be alone for very long." Bill nodded and the group proceeded after the wagon.

Karen found the mud impossible to navigate. Her boots were hopelessly ruined and she only had two other pairs of shoes to use after these were spent. Perhaps her first purchase would have to be a sturdier pair of hiking boots.

We've been quite silly, she thought as they walked in silence. They'd purchased a variety of things—blankets, heavier clothing, gloves and such, prior to leaving Seattle, but there were so many things coming to mind that they were without. Good quantities of soap, for instance, and of course decent boots and heavy woolen hose.

"We used to live in Colorado," Leah said rather suddenly. "It kind of looked like this, only maybe not as much water."

"Definitely not as much water," Bill replied.

"We lived in Chicago," Karen told the little girl. "And we had plenty of water, but no trees like these and no mountains. My, but I really have enjoyed the sight of these mountains."

"Mama used to say mountains gave her hope for life's problems."

Karen smiled. "Why is that, Leah?"

" 'Cause they have an uphill climb on one side and a downward slide on the other. No matter what kind of problem you have, Mama used to say you could always count on there being a downhill side eventually."

Karen saw Jacob's jaw clench tight at the mention of his mother. He looked away and acted disinterested, but Karen could tell he was hanging on his sister's every word. Bill Barringer, on the other hand, seemed to drift into a world of his own thought. From the way his eyes glazed over at the mere mention of his dead wife, Karen figured him to be pushing the thoughts of her aside. It was funny how everyone dealt with grief in their own way.

"So, Leah," Karen said, realizing that sharing conversation was much preferable to the silence, "tell me about Colorado."

"Oh, we were mining there. Pa used to have a lot of money in silver, but then it went bust."

Karen nodded. "I remember there were many problems with silver and a great many people lost their fortunes."

"Yup, our pa was one of them. So we stayed in Colorado and moved from our nice house and went to live in Devil's Creek. But there wasn't much there," she said rather sadly. "Our mama's buried there now, but someday we're going back to put a nice headstone on her grave. Pa said we could after we strike it rich."

Karen smiled, but inside she felt a deep sense of sorrow for the child. To live on such hopes and dreams seemed almost cruel. But living with no hope would be even more cruel, and so she said nothing.

"What did you do in Chicago?" Leah asked. "Why'd you come to look for gold?"

Karen wondered how much they should share of their lives. After all, the fewer who knew of Grace's predicament, the better.

"I didn't come to look for gold," Karen replied. "I came to look for my father."

"Your father?"

"Yes. He's a missionary up here—somewhere. He works with the Indians."

"I didn't know there were Indians up here," Leah said, her eyes growing wide. "Are they the killing kind?"

Karen shook her head. "I don't think they'll mean us any harm. My father and mother lived here quite comfortably and never knew harm by the Tlingit."

"Klink-it?" Leah questioned, trying the word. "Is that what the tribe is called?"

"Very good," Karen answered with a smile. "I'll bet you were a top student in school."

"Used to be. I liked learning, but it's been a while since I got a chance to study."

Karen realized that the girl's father probably held little interest in his children's education. Conversations from the ship came back to remind her that he figured Leah to marry well and never need an education.

"I was Grace's teacher, so maybe when you're around in Dyea, you could come and study with me sometime."

Leah's entire face lit up. "I'd like that a whole lot. Do you think I could do that, Pa?" she asked, hurrying to keep step with her father. "Could I go and learn from Miss Karen?"

Bill and Jacob had remained silent as they plodded the trail in front of the women. At his daughter's question, however, Bill Barringer slowed a bit and looked down.

"Don't know where we'll be or what we'll be doing, princess. If we're around Dyea for a spell, you could sure enough go see Miss Karen from time to time."

"Oh, thank you, Pa!" Leah squealed in delight. She threw a look back at Karen that suggested she'd just been given a very precious gift.

They concluded their walk at the edge of a small boat dock. The teamster and Aunt Doris were already haggling prices for transportation, and Karen knew without a doubt her worldly wise aunt would never let anyone get the best of her if she had any say in the matter. Aunt Doris finally extended her arm and shook hands with a man they'd never before laid eyes on. Apparently he was the one who would take them to Dyea.

"Well, I arranged passage and transportation for our goods. The bad part is, it's going to take several hours before our turn comes up," Doris announced as she rejoined the group.

"I'd best go see what I can do about getting us passage," Bill mumbled before heading off in the direction Doris had just come from. Leah and Jacob seemed indifferent to the matter. Leah was already captivated by some strange tracks she'd found in the mud, and Jacob was staring off toward the mountains, as if to size up the challenge.

"I suppose if we must wait," Karen said, looking around her, "we should at least find some comfortable place in which to do so."

"Doesn't appear to be much available," Doris replied.

Grace surprised them all. "Why don't we just have them unload our things by the dock, and we can set up a little resting area."

Karen looked at the younger woman with a smile. "You're turning out to be more innovative than I would have given you credit for."

Grace laughed, appearing freer than Karen had ever known her to be. "I had a good teacher."

The change in Grace was startling. Karen couldn't help but wonder what had brought it about. There was that irritating matter of Peter Colton and his obvious interest, but it seemed that something more profound should account for this new side of Grace.

As the women went to work to arrange their trunks and crates in such a manner as to have a place to sit comfortably and rest, Karen couldn't help but tease Grace.

"You are different. I surmise that the mountain air has brought about a change in your personality."

Grace took off her jacket and tossed it aside. "No, I think it's the liberty this place suggests. What freedom! Have you ever seen the likes?"

Karen was enthralled. "What are you talking about?"

"This!" Grace exclaimed, waving her arms. "All of this. Look at the people here. Why, they come and go, dress in such a variety of fashion that no one pretends to know what is acceptable and what is not. You have men speaking to women and all go by a first-name basis. It seems that someone threw away the rules to proper society, and I'm surprised to say I like it." Her face took on an expression that suggested a pranksterish schoolgirl had replaced the prim and proper Chicago socialite.

"I would have never expected this," Karen replied. "Your mother would be horrified." She laughed, but there was a certain amount of uneasiness that came with it. Had she unwittingly awakened a behavior in Grace that would have been better left at rest?

"Stop worrying," Grace said, sitting down atop her trunk. "I haven't lost my mind. I won't go off embarrassing you by frequenting the wrong places."

Karen sat down beside her while Doris busied herself with accounting for her latest crocheting project. "I'm not worried about having you embarrass me," Karen said, studying Grace very closely. "I just don't know what to think. When we left Chicago you were a frightened girl who was running away to put a nightmarish arrangement behind you. In Seattle, I found you ever the peacemaker, intervening when things were uncomfortable and certain to become unpleasant. On the ship . . . well, on the ship I saw you practically blossom overnight under Captain Colton's appreciative eye, and now here we are in Skagway and you are bold and radiant with joy, and I really don't know what to make of it."

Grace laughed and patted Karen's hand. "I was afraid. For a very long time I've been afraid. I don't even know that I can tell you why, but I felt that the only safe place for me was in the confines of four walls. Four very familiar walls. But spending time away from home, seeing new people, experiencing new lands . . . why, it's all enough to fuel my bravery and give me hope."

"And were you so very hopeless before?"

Grace sobered and nodded. "You know I was. I was so dependent upon you for hope and faith. I trusted God, but not enough. I prayed and pleaded my case, then cowered in the corner as if He'd never heard my words."

"I suppose I was also at fault in that," Karen replied, knowing that she had never pushed Grace to be too independent for fear she might not need her governess-friend anymore.

"Not at all. You taught me all manner of things in which to find strength," Grace replied. "And God was at the very top of the list. I feel as if this trip has been my coming of age. I've opened my eyes to see the life around me and to realize for the first time that there is so much more than my own little world. I want to experience it all. I want to learn how to work with my hands and to cook and clean. I want to sew and see something take shape, something more important than a cloth for the table." Her words were spoken softly but with such great excitement that Karen couldn't help but get caught up.

"Good thing I came along, then," she told Grace with a grin.

"Why do you say that?" Grace asked, then quickly added, "Of course I'm glad you are here and know that none of this would have been possible had you not taken the first step in our escape."

"I say it because I've taught you many useless things throughout your childhood. Things your mother thought befitting a socialite's daughter. But now perhaps you would like to learn more beneficial skills. Between Aunt Doris and I we can surely teach you how to cook and sew. And maybe, once we find my father, you can learn a great deal more."

"I'd like that very much," Grace replied. Then holding up her feet she wrinkled her nose. "I'd like it even more if we could find some of those thick-soled boots like the men are wearing."

Karen laughed. "Me too. Who would have ever thought that the most enviable possession would be a pair of ugly old leather boots?"

"Hello, ladies."

Grace quickly put her feet down, and Karen knew without looking that Captain Colton had joined them.

"Why, Captain, how is it that you are here and your ship is out there?" Karen questioned, pointing toward the general area of the harbor. "We presumed you'd be gone by now."

"I had some things to arrange," he replied without the slightest hint of irritation at her manner. "What of you, ladies? Why do I find you here?"

"We were discussing boots and waiting for our turn to be taken to Dyea," Grace offered.

"Boots?"

Grace laughed and Karen watched as Colton's face lit up at the sight. "Yes, boots. Thick leather boots that do not fall apart in the mud," Grace proclaimed. "We were rather remiss in our preparations for Skagway." She lifted one foot and revealed her mud-soaked shoe.

"That will never do," Peter replied. "You must all give me your sizes and let me see what is to be done."

"Why would you spend your time in such a manner?" Karen questioned. She knew the answer but also knew Colton would never admit to it.

"Wet feet are a danger to survival. Being a schoolteacher, I would have presumed you to know such things," Peter said rather sarcastically. "But with Skagway given over to such rowdy dealings, I would much rather you allow me to go in search of proper footwear while you are safely awaiting your passage to Dyea."

"Hello, Captain," Doris said as she joined the party. Her crocheting was neatly tucked in the crook of her arm. "Are you bound for Dyea?"

Peter smiled and gave Doris a little bow. "No, Miss Pierce, I came for another purpose. But when I found your party here, I couldn't help but stop. I worried that perhaps something was wrong."

"Only in the sense of there being no hotels and that passage to our destination should take so long."

"No hotels?" Peter questioned. "But I thought you were joining up with the younger Miss Pierce's father."

"We will join up when we can find him," Doris replied. "He's a missionary in this area, but there's no telling exactly where he is. At times he lived beyond the mountains and north toward where everyone is fussing to be. Other times he lived near Dyea."

Peter frowned and Karen could see he was not at all pleased. "So you are to be three women alone?"

"It would appear that way," Doris replied. "But fret not, Captain. We will find some nook or cranny in which to stay."

"Have you a tent?"

"No, but perhaps we can buy one," Doris said, looking to Grace and Karen as if to ascertain their thoughts on the matter.

Before either could reply, Peter interjected, "I have a tent for you. I also have a proposition that until this moment seemed not at all reasonable. Now, however, I wonder if you might not find it to your liking."

"Tell us," Grace said enthusiastically.

Karen was more hesitant. "Remember, Grace, not all suggestions are necessarily beneficial ones." She watched Colton carefully, hoping he might betray some sign of his secret thoughts. Thoughts he might be unwilling to reveal. But to her amazement, he quite openly shared them.

"I believe this idea would benefit us both. I wonder if you ladies would have an interest in keeping a shop."

"A shop? What kind of shop?" Doris questioned.

"A dry goods—a supply store for miners and stampeders."

"And who would set up this shop?" Karen asked.

"I would. I see the immense profitability in transporting goods as well as people to this region. With you ladies running the store, I would never fear being cheated."

"It wouldn't work," Karen replied without waiting for anyone else. "We have to find my father, and that will take time and effort."

"But a store, Miss Pierce, would allow you to meet many people without the need to frequent places maybe better left untraveled."

"But we will be in Dyea, not Skagway where the harbor is better."

"They are working on the harbor in Dyea, and while it isn't ideal, it's quite possible to put in and transfer the goods to barges. A store would give you an opportunity to make friendships and get to know the sourdoughs from the area."

"Sourdoughs?" Karen questioned.

Peter nodded. "Those more grizzled veterans who've been here more than a few months."

Grace reached out to touch Karen's arm. "I, for one, would like to consider this idea."

Karen felt a strange sense of being overruled. Especially when Doris nodded her enthusiasm. "Why, of course," she replied. "It would present a perfect solution. But wherever would you find a building for such an operation?"

"The tent," Peter replied. "I have a tent among my goods that's big enough to house a circus, or nearly so." He grinned and Karen turned away, feeling he was somehow mocking her.

"You could live in part of the tent," he continued, "and sell out of the other part. I could see to it that you have provisions for such a thing when I return on my next trip. I should be back here in a fortnight. In the meanwhile, you'd have no goods to sell. We could merely arrange for the tent to be put up on an accept-able site, and you could live there and even seek out Miss Pierce's father while awaiting my return."

"I think it sounds wonderful," Grace replied, getting to her feet. "Then if Karen and Doris wish to join up with Mr. Pierce, I might even choose to stay on and run the store on my own."

Karen turned around and looked hard at Grace. She was definitely not the same young woman. "Perhaps we're being hasty here."

"Well, you'll have a good two weeks to consider it," Peter replied. "For now, I'll arrange to have the tent put up and secured for your living. I can even supply you with a camp kit and three cots."

"Wonderful!" Doris exclaimed. "Ask and it shall be given."

"But you didn't ask me for a thing," Peter said, laughing.

"No, but I did ask God," Doris replied.

Grace laughed. "As did I."

Karen was the only one who said nothing. Somehow she just couldn't look at Peter Colton as a blessing. He seemed much more to be a thorn in the side. A handsome thorn, but a thorn nevertheless.

BILL BARRINGER checked his pockets one last time for any loose change he might have overlooked. Nothing! He had less than two bits to his name and no hope of getting north before the heavy snows unless he left soon.

The problem, as he saw it, was twofold. First, he didn't have the supplies necessary to go into the Yukon. The Canadians were rigid in their requirements to enter their country. They'd set up duty stations at the border and patrolled them with red-coated Mounties who would collect tax duties and enforce their demands. And those demands were even more impressive than they'd been rumored down in the lower states.

A ton of goods per person is what one person called it, but the real aim was to see that each traveler had the means of supporting himself for a year in the wilderness. Bill thought it all nonsense. There were surely game to kill and goods to purchase. It might be isolated on the other side of the mountain pass, but he'd heard of many a small town already being developed to accommodate the stampeders. And if that were the case, why should any man have to lug around four hundred pounds of flour or one hundred pounds of sugar? Not only this, but many of the requirements came in the form of tools, and why in the world couldn't a man just borrow what he needed from his neighbor?

The second obstacle and liability was the fact that he had children. Bill was quickly coming to understand that Leah and Jacob could never hope to pack their own provisions, and hiring packers from the local Indian tribes was clearly out of the question. Bill hadn't even figured out how to buy the provisions, much less pack them. The entire matter was enough to leave him completely discouraged. And while he'd never express himself in such a way as to let his children know the truth, Bill was beginning to think God held him a grudge.

After two weeks of working odd jobs, Bill's suspicions toward God were more firmly rooted. He could clearly see he was going to have to go this alone, if he was going to go at all. He had never for once imagined leaving the children behind, and even now as the solution became increasingly evident, he argued the point with himself.

Patience would never approve of leaving Leah and Jacob behind, he argued with himself. Standing over a stack of logs, Bill split the pieces into firewood and continued his internal conversation.

I could leave them with Karen Pierce and her aunt, he reasoned. *Leah adores them and is looking forward to getting some education from Karen. Those women would see to it that the kids were safe and sound. Jacob wouldn't like it, but he'd have no choice. He'd have to obey me.*

Bill brought the axe head down on the log. The dry wood split easily. *I could talk to the Pierce woman and see if she would allow me to leave Leah and Jacob. I could promise to send for them or return myself. I could promise her some of the gold I collect.* The entire matter seemed quite reasonable. Surely she would see the importance of keeping the children safe in Dyea while he went on into the Yukon.

Nagging doubts began to form in his mind, however. How would the children perceive this action? Coming so soon after the loss of their mother, they would certainly feel he was deserting them as well. Bill didn't want to give them that impression, but he also knew finding gold was their only chance to get back what they'd lost so many years earlier.

I'll just explain it that way, he reasoned. *They'll understand. They're good children.* He felt the sweat trickle down his back as he continued to chop the wood. He would still have to convince Karen Pierce, even if he could persuade Jacob and Leah. Then a thought came to him. Karen was looking for her father. As far as Bill knew, she hadn't found him, nor heard any word of him. *Perhaps I could offer to look for him.* The idea began to take root. *If I offered to look for him, the children could just naturally stay with her until my return.* The idea had great merit. Never mind that he'd be looking for Wilmont Pierce on the Chilkoot Trail north to the Yukon.

He finished his work and collected his pay before heading over to the Colton tent store. He tried to plot out how he might approach the subject without seeming desperate. Already the autumn had set in and time was getting away from them. Most folks told him he was a fool to even consider going on—that the police would close down the borders when the blizzards set in. But Bill didn't care. Even if he only made it as far as Sheep's Camp, some twelve miles away, he would be that much closer once the Mounties actually allowed folks to head north again. Besides, the bad storms might not even come and things would remain open and the travelers could just keep moving north. Either way, he didn't want to lose out on the chance of a lifetime.

Dusting wood chips off his jeans, Bill entered the store to find it stocked with goods. For the past two weeks there had been nothing but plank board stacked neatly in a pile at the side. Karen had informed him that these would be set atop barrels once Captain Colton arrived with the said barrels, the goods stored within them.

"Hello, ladies," Bill called out as he pushed through the already gathered crowd. "Looks like you're getting things set up for a day of selling."

"That we are, Mr. Barringer," Doris announced. "Have you come to purchase something, or were you looking for Leah?"

"Actually, I came to talk to Miss Karen, if she has a spare moment."

"Well," Karen said, looking at the growing crowd, "right now doesn't appear to be a good time for a talk."

"I understand," Bill replied. "Maybe later?"

Karen hurried to tuck the straw packing back inside the crate. Straw was just as valuable as most anything else. *She could probably sell it for a fortune,* Bill surmised.

"Look, Papa," Leah called from behind a stack of duck cloth tents, "I'm helping with the store."

Karen blushed slightly. "I hope you don't mind," she said, holding out a lantern for a potential customer to inspect. "We put her to work. We'll pay her, of course."

"I don't mind at all," Bill replied. "I was hoping both Leah and Jacob could find something decent to put their hands to." He wondered silently what Patience would have thought. Would she have been proud to have her able-bodied children working, or would she have been disappointed that he had taken them away from the safety they knew in Devil's Creek?

We were happy in Colorado, Bill thought. *We might have gone on being happy, even if we were poor, had Patience lived.* Even if she'd lost the baby they would have grieved, but together they would have made it through. Bill sighed and couldn't help but think of how it might have been.

Karen returned her attention to the customer. Within a moment she made the sale and stuffed the bills in her apron pocket. "I could meet you in a couple of hours," she suggested, seeing that Bill was still standing idle.

Bill hadn't realized how quickly he'd allowed his mind to wander. It took very little to find himself drifting back to Colorado and happier days. "Two hours would be just fine. How about we meet out back behind the tent?"

"Sounds good."

For the next two hours Bill attempted to think of various things he might say.

He wanted to appeal to Karen's friendship with Leah. The two had formed a steady bond since Karen first offered to school Leah. They were often together, especially when Bill and Jacob headed off in the early morning hours to help with road improvements to Skagway. Leah liked Karen a great deal, and Bill couldn't help but wonder if she'd been seeking to fill the void left by Patience.

But while Leah was close to Karen, Jacob was close to no one. Not even to Bill. He rarely talked and was always moody. He wanted nothing more than to be left to himself. The boy was hurting, but certainly no more than Bill. It was impossible to help someone with their speck when the log in your own eye was blinding you to their need. Jacob had said very little since his mother's death. He'd been faithful to see to Leah's safety, but other than that, he was clearly not the same vibrant boy who'd pleasured their household some months earlier with tall tales of adolescent feats.

But then, Bill wasn't the same happy-go-lucky father, either. Patience's death had taken a big toll on all of them. The children mourned their loss of a mother, and Bill mourned the loss of his heart and soul. Patience had been his anchoring stone. She had kept him from being too headstrong or self-serving. Patience would never have approved the trip north, but then, if Patience had lived, they probably would never have thought to join in such chaos.

No, that wasn't true. Bill would have thought of it. The moment word came about two tons of gold shipping into Seattle's harbor, he would have been digging up maps and information to see what the easiest and quickest route north might be. He would have plotted and planned it out, and then he would have taken it to Patience, extolling for his wife all the virtues of such an adventure. Then after he had settled down, Patience would have explained the pitfalls. She would have no doubt talked to him about the children's needs and how such a plan would require far more investment than they could ever manage. She would have explained how supplies for just one person would have cost at least five hundred dollars and that they were lucky to have five dollars to their name on payday.

Bill smiled and he fixed her image in his mind. Soft, dark curls like Leah's and a face that must have been lent her by an angel. He could almost smell her sweet lavender soap. Almost touch her and . . .

"Pa? Are you all right?"

He hadn't realized that tears were streaming down his cheeks until he heard the voice of his daughter. Looking up, Bill wiped his face with a dusty handkerchief. "I'm fine, princess. Just fine." He looked at Leah and shook his head. She looked too old to be only twelve. What kind of trouble would that prove to be? Hadn't he already seen men eyeing her in a way that suggested they were considering how she might figure into their lives?

Studying her for a moment, Bill patted the crate beside him and motioned her to sit. She was the very image of her mother. How could he possibly leave her behind? How could he leave Jacob, whose spirit was still so wounded?

"Are you all right, Pa?" Leah asked again. She reached out her hand to take hold of his.

Bill closed his fingers over hers. "I'm fine. I was just thinkin' about your ma. I think she would have liked it up here. Don't you?"

Leah smiled. "I think she would have thought us plumb crazy."

Bill smiled and nodded. "I believe you're right." He gave her hand a little squeeze. "Fact is, I was just thinkin' that as well."

Leah shifted her weight and leaned against Bill. Her presence comforted him. How could he dare to venture north without them?

"Pa, are we always going to live in a tent?"

Bill put his arm around Leah's shoulders. "Of course not. Someday we're gonna have a fine house."

"Like when we lived in Denver?"

"You can't remember back that far," he said, reaching up to tousle her curls.

"I remember the way Mama talked about it, though," Leah replied. "She said it was so pretty. She had dainty cups and saucers to serve the church ladies tea."

Bill frowned. He was happy that Leah couldn't see his reaction. He remembered Patience boxing her collection of fine china and selling it to the secondhand store. It brought them just enough money to pay off one of their more pressing debts. He'd hated himself for letting her sell the collection, but hate soon turned to pity and misery. He could hardly even bear to look Patience in the eyes for weeks. She had told him it was all right, that they were only dishes. But he knew otherwise. He knew how much she'd loved her china.

"I promise you, Leah, one day you'll have a set of china just as pretty as your ma's," Bill declared. "As soon as we strike it rich up north, that'll be one of the first things we send off for."

Leah snuggled against him contentedly. Bill felt sheer gratitude that she didn't question him. She believed in him. Somehow that almost allowed him to believe in himself.

"I'm sorry it took so long, Bill," Karen said as she stepped around to the back of the tent. "Now, what can I do for you?"

Bill finished stacking some of the shipping crates and wiped the sweat from his neck and forehead. "I was just wondering if you'd had any word on your father."

Karen shook her head. She'd talked to so many people in the last couple weeks, and while some knew her father, none knew where he could be found. "I still have no idea where he is, if that's what you're wondering."

"I'm sorry. I was hoping maybe you'd found him and that I just hadn't heard."

"It's very kind of you to care," Karen replied, surprised by his concern.

"I wonder if you would mind," he began, "if I asked around and gave a bit of a look for him myself?"

Karen looked at the bearded man with surprise. "You? But why would you want to spend your time that way?"

"Because I know what it is to lose someone," he replied softly. "I can't go finding what I've lost, but you can."

Karen felt an overwhelming sensation of emotion. That this near stranger should care so much for her happiness and father's well-being was a pleasant surprise in this land of greed.

"I'm very touched that you would give of yourself in that way. My father is very precious to me," Karen said. She looked beyond Bill to the mountains. "I know he's out there somewhere. I feel it—down deep." She turned to Bill. "Do you know what I mean?"

He nodded and his expression suggested that he, too, had known what it was to be so closely bound to someone that he could tell whether they lived or died, even if they were far away.

"I have a photograph," she said. "I could give it to you and you could use it to ask questions. I've shown it around a few places, but of course there are places I cannot go—or maybe better said, I *should* not go." She grinned. "But I would go into the pits of hell itself if it meant finding him."

Bill nodded. "I understand."

His soft-spoken nature put her at ease. Looking at the man, Karen firmly believed he knew and understood her grief. Then it dawned on her that with Jacob and Leah, Bill would be rather tied down.

"Since you offer to do this for me, might I suggest something in return?"

"What?" Bill asked.

"Leah is a great help in the store. We've already sold most of the supplies Captain Colton brought this morning. However, we still have a few things and she could continue to help and I would also be happy to school her. Jacob too."

"Jacob has a full-time job. He just got it today. He's going to be helping to put in some of the dock piers. I'm not sure when they'll get started, but he shouldn't need you to fuss over him. It would be good to know that Leah is taken care of, however. I wouldn't want any of the menfolk getting the wrong idea about her."

"Absolutely not," Karen said, knowing full well the kind of ideas the gold-rushing fanatics might get. She'd already turned down eight proposals in fourteen days, most from men who were old enough to be her father, much less know him.

"If you would be willing to keep her here with you," Bill suggested, "I could put the tent up right here in back of the store. She and Jacob could sleep out here in case I was gone late into the night."

"Oh, Bill, you mustn't spend all your time searching for me," Karen chided. "You have to earn a living and see to those children. I wouldn't feel right if you sacrificed your own family for mine."

"I wouldn't be doin' that," he said. "I just figured your pa might well have taken himself up the trail a bit. It's only twelve miles or so up to Sheep Camp. I hear tell from the Tlingits here in Dyea that there are a lot of the Indian folk living in and around there, what with that being a good place to hire packers."

"Packers?"

"The Indians are packing goods over the Chilkoot Pass for the stampeders. Many of the Tlingits that were living down here have gone up the trail to earn money from the white stampeders. Since your pa is involved with teaching the Indians about God, I thought maybe he'd followed them to that place."

Karen felt a twinge of excitement. "You're sure it's the Tlingits? I mean, my father might have involved himself with other tribes, but those were the main people he felt called to minister to."

Bill nodded. "It's the Tlingits, all right. They used to have all the rights to the pass. I heard one old sourdough tellin' that they used to charge their own fees for crossing over the land. In fact, they wouldn't even allow traders in or out. They would buy the goods themselves and go over the pass and north to trade with the Yukon First Nations people."

"You've certainly learned quite a bit in your short time up here," Karen said, greatly impressed.

Bill nodded. "Pays to keep an open ear. Anyway, this fella told me that there were a great many Tlingits—men, women, and children—getting paid handsomely to pack the miners' goods up to the Scale and then up and over the summit."

"Is it a bad climb?" Karen questioned. "I've heard so many talking of the difficulties. I presume that this is the same pass."

"It is. It's the shortest route north and that's why so many folks are using it."

Karen realized that this might well be the answer to her long and arduous prayers. She would have a difficult time leaving Grace and Doris to go scouting about. Especially miles down unfamiliar trails, with little to protect herself and no one to help her.

"Well, is it a deal, then?" she asked. "I'll see to Leah and Jacob. You can bring the tent here around back, but the children are welcome to stay inside our tent on nights when it looks like you might not return until late. I couldn't sleep knowing they were out there by themselves. I'll give them chores and they can earn their keep." She smiled and extended her hand. "Deal?"

Bill smiled and nodded. "Deal."

—| CHAPTER SEVENTEEN |—

KAREN STOOD OVER a pot of hot water playing referee to a washboard and her best Sunday blouse. It came as an amazing fact that she was so clumsy with such a simple task. She had once been responsible for washing all of her things, but after a time in the Hawkins household, she had been relieved of such duties. She had been happy when such menial tasks were passed to servants, but now she wished she were more competent with such handwork.

The afternoon was quite lovely, however, and if a person had to be battling the laundry, Dyea was a very scenic place to do it. There weren't very many businesses, and in spite of the multitudes of people passing through, the area wasn't nearly as lawless as Skagway.

People passing through seemed to be her biggest problem, however. No one stuck around long enough to suggest whether they'd met up with her father or not. They were hurriedly passing from Skagway to the Chilkoot Trail with Dyea as nothing more than a resting-place. Or they were returning dejected and broke from the trail, with no time for the nonsense of talking with Karen about her missing father. She found herself lost in thoughts of what they'd do if she couldn't find him. She worried even more that he might not even be alive. If he was dead, what would she do? There certainly wasn't enough money to return to Seattle. Besides, did she really want to return to Seattle? *I don't know how we'll get through the winter,* she thought. *If we can't live in a proper house, with the necessary articles to protect ourselves and keep warm, we might all die.*

Casting a glance toward the mountains, Karen couldn't help but feel the hypnotic lure of their beauty. It was a kind of madness, someone had said. A kind of sickness that got into a man or woman's blood and refused to be purged. It was as she stood pondering this very issue that Bill Barringer chose to again appear in her life.

"Karen! Karen!" Bill called out as he trudged down the muddy alleyway with two other men.

Karen felt an electrifying tingle go up her spine. Bill was back! That had to be good. He'd been gone for weeks, and the days were getting colder, the threat of snow gradually giving everyone concern for their future. He ambled down the road, however, as if the weather and timing were of no concern.

Karen noted that none of the men seemed in too much of a hurry. The smaller of the two was clearly a native. His shoulder-length black hair stuck out from an exaggerated white felt bowler, while the rest of his costume was a mix of heavy canvas pants, woolen jacket, and handmade knee-high boots. Their companion, a big, broad-shouldered man with dark hair and a thick mustache, appeared similarly dressed, with a rifle and pack slung over his back.

"Bill, have you found my father?" Karen asked, unconcerned with awaiting introductions.

"I haven't found him," Bill admitted, "but both of these men know him and said that up until three weeks ago when they saw him last, he was doing just fine."

Karen drew a deep breath to steady herself. "You actually saw him?" she said, looking to the men collectively.

"Sure did. Brother Pierce was headin' inland last we saw him," the bigger man announced. "Makin' his rounds."

"And he was healthy?" she asked the man.

His dark eyes were fixed on her face as he smiled. "Fit as any man can ever be."

She nodded and allowed herself to relax a bit. "Do you know how I can reach him?"

The smaller man joined in the conversation. "He be back before first snow. He stay here in winter."

"When can we expect first snow?" she asked anxiously.

"Signs don't seem to show it coming for at least a week or two," the big man replied. "Then again, with snow, you can never be sure. A snow could come up tomorrow and seal the pass for a time or just leave a dusting. You can bet he'll pack his way back here unless a blizzard comes. He won't stay in the interior all winter."

"Why not?" Karen asked.

"Brother Pierce has always done business this way," the man replied. "Don't see why he'd change now."

"So you think it might be a week, maybe more, before he heads back here to Dyea?"

"Looks like it. I'd just hold tight."

"Thank you, Mr. . . ."

"Ivankov," he replied. "Adrik Ivankov."

"Adrik is a guide in these parts," Bill explained. "And this is Dyea Joe. I'm afraid we weren't very proper with our introductions."

"That's all right," Karen said, reaching once again for the laundry board. "I'm learning very quickly that time spent in formalities down in the continental states is much better spent elsewhere up here."

Adrik grinned. "Yes, ma'am, now you're learning the Alaskan way."

Karen smiled. "Is that what you call it?" Her mind was still reeling from the news that her father was safe and would return to them in a few short weeks, maybe even days. This thought gave birth to another. "Oh, by the way, has my father a house here in Dyea? I've tried to ask around, but the place is in such a state of confusion. Those who know of my father weren't well enough acquainted to give me much detail."

"He stay with my people," Joe announced. "He no build house."

"Oh," Karen answered, knowing the disappointment she felt was clear in her tone.

"Tent life unbecoming to you?" Adrik asked.

"I just can't imagine living in a tent all winter," Karen replied. "I was kind of hoping to have something more substantial come winter."

"A tent will keep you fine, even at forty below, Miss Pierce. The secret is getting it set up properly. There are a great many ways of keepin' warm up here." He winked.

Karen felt her cheeks grow hot. "I think I'd prefer a house, just the same."

"Looks to me things are being slapped together every day. Why not build yourself a place?" Adrik suggested, as though she had somehow overlooked the possibility.

"We have discussed it," she admitted. Prior to Peter Colton's return from Seattle, they'd been quite low on funds, but Peter had been most generous with his cut to them for their hard work and now they were actually flush again. "I'm afraid," she continued, "I don't know who could do the job. Most of the good contractors are tied up with Skagway and Dyea hotel plans. If not that, then they're busy planning main street shops and such."

"Wouldn't take much to put a place together," Adrik said. "The three of us could do it. And if you womenfolk joined in helping, we could probably have something put up in a day, maybe two."

"You're joking, right?" she said, looking deep into the man's rugged face. She figured him to be somewhere near her own age or older, but the elements had taken their toll on his skin, as had some obvious encounters with danger. From the looks of several small scars on his face and neck, Adrik Ivankov had obviously had his share of run-ins with the wildlife.

"I'm not joking at all," he replied. "If we can lay our hands on the lumber, it won't take any time at all. If we have to fell and prepare logs, then it will take the better part of a week."

Karen's mind began doing mental calculations of what they could accomplish prior to her father's return. Perhaps if she had a house already established for him, he'd feel free to stay with her and the others. That way they could spend all winter discussing plans for spring. On the other hand, if she waited until her father came back, he might have suggestions of his own. She would hate to leave him out of the decision-making process.

"Let me talk to the others," she said, again abandoning the scrub board. "Why don't you all stay for supper and we can discuss this some more?"

Bill looked to the men, then returned his gaze to Karen. "I'll stay. That way you can fill me in on things that happened while I was gone."

"And you can be with the children," she reminded him.

"I'm afraid Joe and I can't stay. We have business elsewhere. We'll stop by tomorrow morning and see what you've decided," Adrik said.

Karen nodded. "Until tomorrow, then." The big man tipped his battered Stetson while Dyea Joe took his hat off completely and gave her a little bow.

After they'd gone, Karen turned to Bill with a smile. "I can't thank you enough for helping me. I was beginning to worry about you, however. I thought maybe we were going to have to send a search party out for you instead of Father."

Bill looked away as if he'd been caught doing something he shouldn't. "I know it wasn't very thoughtful of me. But by the time I got up Sheep Camp way, there were far too many folks to allow for easy questioning. There were a lot of Tlingit up there, and most of them, even the women and children, were helping to pack the gold rushers up to the summit."

"Sounds like horribly hard work."

"It is," Bill agreed, then looked at her rather sheepishly. "I needed some money myself, so I gave it a try."

"Was it bad? I've heard so many rumors, stories of men who've given up and come back to sell out and go home. Why, we bought up the supplies of at least a half dozen men who were too discouraged to continue."

"There are a lot of them out there. Only the strongest and bravest are going to make it north. That's for sure."

"I read up on this gold rush. The area of Dawson City is still hundreds of miles away. These people are going to be months, maybe even years on the trail.

Do they even realize that? Did you, when you began to head north to search for gold?"

Bill shook his head. "I figured it would be hard, but I didn't know just how hard. Sure enough isn't a place for children."

Karen could see the worried look in his eyes. No doubt his concern for Leah and Jacob weighed heavy on his heart. "No, I don't imagine it is a place for them. You could certainly stay here and earn enough to take you home again."

"We haven't got a home anymore," he said, his voice laced with sorrow. "I was hoping we'd find a home up here."

"But this country is hardly suitable for bringing up a family. You have to consider their needs as well," Karen answered. "What happens when the gold plays out and the crowds leave for the States? Will you just uproot them and follow the masses?"

"I don't know," he replied, looking up to meet her eyes.

Karen had never seen such a lack of hope in a man's face as she had come to see in those lost souls who had given up on their dreams of gold and were headed back to wives and families in homes so far away. But even knowing that look— that despair—she was almost stunned by the depths of desperation and sadness in Bill Barringer's eyes. It was as if a curtain had been lifted on an empty stage. A dark, bleak, desolate stage.

"Bill, I know it isn't my place to speak on such matters, but I feel I must say this," she began. She watched him for any signs of anger or emotion, but there were none. "I'm sorry for the loss you suffered. Your wife was obviously very precious to you—to your whole family. I see the pain in Jacob's eyes, and I've heard Leah speak of things about her mother and then burst into tears. I look at you and I know that you must have loved her a great deal." His eyes sparked with a glint of interest. Karen took the opportunity to drive her point home.

"I cannot imagine that your wife would want you to grieve so deeply for her. She no doubt loved you and your children and she would want you to go forward with life, living each day to the fullest and experiencing great joy, even in her absence. Forgive me for being so bold, but a woman as you have described her to be would never rest knowing you are spending your life—dying. Mourning yourself to death. Leaving your children to fend for themselves in their sorrow."

Bill looked to the ground. "I know, but I have nothing to give them." He looked up, and Karen could see that the emptiness had returned. "I'll think on what you've said, but I need to earn a living and the best place I can do that is packing goods up the trail. I can get the children jobs as well, and then maybe they won't be so lost in thoughts of their ma."

"No!" Karen declared. "They are children and they deserve to be educated and cared for. I will not permit you to drag them off to pack for the miners."

Bill looked at her with some surprise. "You won't permit me?"

Karen drew a deep breath and fought to control her anger. "Bill, just leave them here. They aren't going to do you that much good. You'll earn very little for their work and then just have to turn around and feed and clothe them. Winter is coming up and they'll never make it. Oh, Jacob might be able to withstand the cold, but Leah would probably die of pneumonia. Do you want that on your conscience?"

Bill's expression changed as suddenly as if she'd slapped him across the face. He seemed genuinely overcome by her words and turned away. "They can stay with you, but I have to go. If I can't earn a livin' one way or another, it's not going to much matter whether they have a father or not."

"Bill, that's not true. They love you—love you deeply. I can see that. I've heard Leah talk about it almost daily. She fairly worships the ground you walk on."

"Even so, I'm not doin' right by her or Jacob." He stood with his back to Karen for several minutes before finally looking over his shoulder. "I'll get money to you as I can, but the camps are a good piece up the trail."

"Don't worry about it. Jacob and Leah can do less-strenuous jobs around here and earn their keep that way," Karen replied. "I can also work with them on their schooling. I think both would benefit from it, and that would give them something to do over the cold winter months."

Bill nodded. "I'm obliged. I just wish I could do more."

"Find your will to live," Karen replied softly. "That would be the very best thing you could do for them both."

He shook his head. "I don't know that I can do that. Patience was my life."

"Give it over to God, Bill. He knows your hurt and sorrow. Leah tells me her mother was a strong Christian. That she believed in the power of God to heal and direct. She also said that you used to believe the same. Have you given up on that?"

He shrugged. "I don't know. I guess I've come to realize, as the weeks and days go by, that much of my faith was wrapped up in Patience's faith."

"That can easily happen," Karen said, praying that she wasn't driving her point home too hard. "Sometimes it takes something like this to truly bring a person to God."

"Seems kind of cruel of God to be that way, don't you think?" he asked, and for the first time Karen denoted some anger in his tone. "Why should it be that one person should have to die in order for another person to get cozy with the Almighty?"

"I've asked myself the same thing," Karen replied. "Every time Easter rolls around, I ask myself that question. Why should Jesus have had to bear my stripes on his back? Why should he have borne my punishment and sorrows?" She softened her voice. "Bill, I don't think God took Patience in some sort of trade-off. Jesus already died for your sins and for your reconciliation to God. Patience had no need to offer that sacrifice a second time. But because we are fragile human beings, we die. She died, not because you were bad or good, but because it was time for her to go home."

Bill dropped his gaze again and nodded. "I know she's in a better place. I'll think on what you've said." He walked away, not even waiting for her to comment.

Karen felt sorry for the man, her heart going out to him in his suffering. He stood on the edge of a towering cliff. One strong breeze could push him over. One simple step back into the arms of the One who loved him could ensure his safety.

"Karen!" Leah called her name, gasping for breath as she ran around from the opposite side of the tent. "Karen, come quick!"

"What is it?" Karen asked. She saw the fear in the child's eyes. "What's wrong?"

"It's . . . it's Jacob!" she panted. "He's been in a fight."

Karen turned back around to see if Bill was still in sight, but he'd disappeared between the rows of tents.

"Please hurry," Leah said, beginning to cry. "He's bleeding."

Karen went quickly with the child, hoping to reach Jacob before anything worse befell him. They found him slumped over between a couple of the newer buildings. His left eye was already swelling shut and blood trickled from his nose and lip.

"What happened?" she asked, kneeling in the mud beside him.

He looked at her with seeming indifference. "None of your business."

"When there's blood to clean up and you're in my care, it becomes my business. Now tell me what happened."

He shrugged and tried to move away from her. "It's not important. I just got into a fight with some other guys."

"What was the fight about?"

"Nothin'," he answered, struggling to get to his feet.

Karen got to her feet as well, while Leah clung to her brother's arm. "Please let Karen help you. Please!"

Her pleading seemed to affect him, and he leaned back against the wall of one building and eyed Karen as best he could.

"They said my pa was no account. They said he'd deserted us and that he wanted the gold more than he cared about us."

Karen nodded. "That must have hurt you very much, but it's not true. Your father is back, even as we speak. He'll be at supper." At least she hoped he'd still be taking his meal with them.

"He's back?" Jacob said, wiping at the blood on his face. "When'd he get back?"

"He just now stopped by to bring a couple of men who knew about my father," Karen replied. She reached up with a handkerchief and tried to help Jacob tidy himself. "I know he's anxious to be with both of you."

Jacob nodded. "Come on, Leah. Let's go find Pa."

Before Karen could say another word, he had taken hold of his sister's arm and was pushing her in the direction of the main road. Karen frowned. How would Jacob ever be able to deal with his father's decision to go packing up the Chilkoot Pass? She hadn't the heart to try and explain it to the boy. Hopefully Bill would help him to understand and reinforce that he wasn't leaving them indefinitely.

Karen paused to reconsider the house plans. Perhaps they could all live together. Having Bill around would allow her father to have another male presence, and for those times when her father wanted to minister to the Tlingits, Bill could be the male protection they needed as Dyea grew in size. It was definitely worth considering, but something she would have to take up with Doris and Grace first.

Heading back to the tent, Karen began to pray for guidance. *Show us what we're to do, Lord. Bring my father home safely and help us to know how best to help him. Deal gently with Bill and his children. They are hurting so much, Lord.* She rounded the corner to see Bill embracing his children. Her heart was uplifted by the sight. Surely this was a sign that all would be well for the little family. But in spite of this thought, the sight left her own heart aching.

Please bring Father home soon, she added with a quick glance upward to the mountains. *I miss him so much. Please bring him back to me.*

-{ C H A P T E R E I G H T E E N }-

BY OCTOBER, neither word from Myrtle Hawkins nor the appearance of Wilmont Pierce had arrived in Dyea. Grace felt sorry for her friend and tried to offer
what comfort she could, but often her mind was otherwise engaged. Peter Colton
kept her thoughts dancing on air most of the time. With each of his trips and
comments of pride for her hard work, Grace felt invigorated against the growing
cold of the Alaskan autumn.

Now, even as she watched Peter pay the freighters for their final delivery, she
felt gooseflesh on her arms. He looked up to catch her watching him and gave
her a grin. The action made her knees turn to jelly. In all her twenty years, no one
had ever made her feel so lightheaded and excited.

He tipped his cap to the men, and then before Grace knew it, he was striding
in his self-assured manner right toward her. She drew a deep breath, hoping it
might boost her courage. Why was it whenever she saw Peter, a part of her felt
like running away, while the other part felt like running into his arms?

"You grow more lovely with each passing day," he said, stopping to formally
lift her hand to his lips.

Grace blushed and looked to the ground. "I see you have brought us an abundance of goods."

"I'd like to think so, but at the rate you sell them, I doubt they'll be abundant
for long."

"The stampeders do seem to enjoy the selection," she admitted.

Peter roared with laughter. "They enjoy being waited on by womenfolk. Lovely womenfolk. They come to my store instead of buying in Skagway because you ladies have made a name for yourselves."

"Oh," Grace said, knowing the surprise showed in her voice. "I never really considered it. I just thought that your products were superior."

Peter shook his head. "My father is bringing some of the same goods on behalf of a friend of his who's settled a store in Skagway. You are his biggest competition, and I'm sure if he ever makes his way up here for a personal inspection, he will be green with envy."

"How is it that a man has a store in Skagway but isn't there to run it himself?" Grace questioned.

"How is it that I have a store in Dyea and leave it in your capable hands? People are not always wont to move to a place such as this and set up shop. However, if they have enough money, they can always find a willing soul to help."

Grace smiled and tucked her hands into her deep coat pockets. "I suppose I can understand that. Especially since I'm one of those willing souls."

"So can you slip away for a short walk? I can't stay. I must have my ship ready to leave in a few hours. But I want very much to hear from your own lips as to how things are going."

Grace hid her disappointment at his announcement of a rapid departure. He never stayed long, and she found herself intensely longing for his company when he was away. Was he driven just as mad by the separation as she was? Did these feelings happen to the same degree for both of them? She knew Peter cared, knew he sought her out before he saw anyone else in their party, but he never said anything to indicate or imply more than friendship.

"I can spend a short time away, but just like you, I must return quickly to my work. After all, we've a new delivery to deal with." She smiled rather shyly. "Lead the way."

Peter glanced around. "Things are certainly changing. There are more tents."

"Yes, but not too many buildings. Karen has suggested we build a house before winter, but a friend of Mr. Barringer tells us that tenting through the cold weather is not that difficult. He has offered to help us with whatever we decide."

"A house would be good, but it would leave the store unprotected."

"We've thought of that," Grace replied. "That and many other things." She smiled. "I'm sure God will direct us."

Peter looked away uncomfortably. "You'll find I've brought you all some personal items and some special gifts of appreciation."

Grace looked up to find him watching her. Could he hear her heart pounding? Could he see the way she felt about him in her eyes?

She pushed the thoughts aside. "Gifts?"

He laughed. "Yes. I asked my mother and sister about the things they would most miss if they were taken away from all civilization. They made a list and I went to work selecting a good many of their suggestions."

"Such as?"

"Well, you can see for yourself once I'm gone, but I've brought some teas and woolen cloth, as well as some books for fireside reading."

"Karen will be delighted to hear that. She's been working to help Bill's children to improve their reading. Since they are staying with us, it seems a good way to pass the time after chores."

"The children are staying with you and the Pierce women? What of Miss Pierce's father and Mr. Barringer? Have they deserted you?"

His voice denoted alarm, and Grace quickly worked to sooth his worries. "Not at all. Mr. Barringer, in fact, is the one who found people who knew Karen's father. He is expected back at any moment. Mr. Barringer then took a job with those who are packing supplies over the summit on the Chilkoot Trail. He's trying to earn enough money to get the things he and his children will need so that they can head north as well."

"It was foolish for him to bring those kids up north. They'll never survive."

"Oh, don't say that, Captain Colton. I'm sure God has them here for a reason."

"They are here because their father is a foolish man. I would never so poorly advise my sister or mother on such a matter. Men need to keep their family members in mind before making such harsh decisions. We are to guide and direct, not strike out at whatever appeals to our fancy."

"I'm certain you would no doubt make wiser choices," Grace replied, trying hard to think of another topic of discussion. "So is your sister very young?"

"She is older than you by three years. She's a very beautiful young woman and very proper in her attitudes."

"Is she married?"

Peter shook his head. "No, I've not yet found someone suitable for her."

Grace stopped in her tracks. "You've not found someone? What of her desires? Has she found someone?"

Peter studied Grace closely for a moment. "I forgot that such matters were a delicate topic to you. Forgive me."

"There is nothing to forgive, Captain. I was not offended by your choice of words, but rather the attitude behind them." She could see that he was thoughtfully considering how to reply. Instead of waiting for him, however, Grace continued. "I do not suppose that every woman with an arranged marriage should meet the same fate as mine. However, I do have a strong regard for the American way of finding true love."

"I have nothing against true love, but I only ask Miranda to exercise prudence and not allow her choices to be dictated by emotional heartstrings. She seeks me out on everything, trusting that I can make a better choice for her than she can herself."

"How very sad," Grace said, suddenly seeing Peter in a new light.

"Why do you say that?" he asked. His tone suggested annoyance as well as anger.

"It's just that I believe God has made both male and female to be very intelligent and capable. It would be a tragedy if your sister never felt confident enough to stand up for herself and make a few of her own decisions."

"Why tragic? Women are the weaker vessel. They are to be protected and cared for. Why should that be a tragedy?" He kept his voice very even and calm. Grace couldn't help but wonder if he was worried that she was too weak to hear the full force of his argument.

"I'm only suggesting that your sister would be better served if she were taught how to handle some things for herself. After all, it is nearly 1900 and women are pressing ever closer to having the vote. Times are changing."

"You sound like your mentor," he chided. "I only do what's best for Miranda. My entire family seeks my guidance on a regular basis. They trust me to know the truth of most things, and they need me to give them counsel."

"How very powerful that must make you feel," Grace replied, finding herself growing rather annoyed with Peter's arrogance.

He frowned and narrowed his eyes. "You're suggesting I do good by my family for my own sake?"

"I'm suggesting that God would not have you replace Him in their lives."

Peter stared openly for a moment and looked as if he might reply, but instead he gave Grace a bow and apologized for needing to get back to his ship.

"I'm sorry if I have offended you, Captain."

"Do not trouble yourself with such thoughts. I assure you I am quite capable of hearing your concerns and arguments without buckling under."

He took his leave after escorting Grace back to the tent store. She watched him go with some disappointment. She had offended him with her sudden outspokenness, but she couldn't stand back and allow for his attitude to be viewed as truth and what was right. That attitude, if coupled with a cruel nature, could easily turn Peter Colton into another Martin Paxton. And that would surely break her heart.

"Where's the captain?" Karen questioned as she came out of the tent.

"He's on his way back to his ship. See," Grace pointed, "there he is now."

"I have a list for him," Karen said, holding up her hand. "I suppose I must chase him down to deliver it."

"I suppose so. Just be cautious. He seems to be in a rather troubled mood."

Karen smiled. "And just what could possibly have troubled the dear captain?"

Grace shrugged. "I suppose it was me."

———————

Peter Colton was in no mood for any woman, much less Karen Pierce. Her incessant calling of his name, however, left him little choice but to turn and await her.

"What is it, Miss Pierce?"

"I have a list for you. The supplies and things we need most. The ones we sell the most," she added.

Her blue eyes seemed to twinkle in delight at delaying him, and her long golden red hair caught ever so casually with a ribbon at the nape of her neck blew across her face as the breeze picked up. She easily controlled the hair with one hand, however, as she handed him the list with the other.

Peter stared at her for a moment, almost mesmerized by her hair. Why did a woman her age allow her hair to be down in such a fashion? Didn't she realize the inappropriateness of it? Peter watched, fascinated as the curls wrapped around her fingers.

"Are you quite all right, Captain?"

He snatched the paper from her hand and looked at it momentarily. "I'm very well, thank you." His words were gruffly delivered, but he didn't care. Miss Pierce had been an improper influence in Grace Hawkins' life. It was her fault that Grace would question his actions with his family. Before he knew it, she'd have Grace running about with her hair down as well.

"Do you have questions about any of the items?" Karen questioned.

"No," he replied angrily. "I'm quite capable of reading a list and understanding its meaning."

"Would that men were as easy to understand as lists," Karen replied snidely. "Grace said you were a bit out of sorts, but I couldn't imagine it should make any difference. When aren't you out of sorts?"

"If I am in such a state as you suggest," Peter replied, "it is because of women like yourself."

"Me?" she questioned, raising a hand to point at her throat. "Me? Whatever do I have to do with this?"

"Plenty. You have poisoned the mind of that beautiful young woman with your claptrap about women's rights and personal capabilities. I know she has run away from the authority of her father, and you no doubt had a hand in it."

"I did," Karen replied proudly. "The man her father would have seen her married to beat her. His demeanor was something similar to yours. Women were nothing more than property to him. They were to be silent when told to be silent and useful when told to be useful. You would have liked him, no doubt."

Peter felt his face redden as his hands balled into fists. The list was crumpled in his anger and forgotten as he considered how best to put Karen Pierce in her place.

"Either way," Karen continued, "I know you've hurt my dear friend's feelings. If that is what you consider proper, then I will continue to encourage Grace against your brand of male civilization."

"It was not my intention to hurt Miss Hawkins, but she made some rather strong statements regarding the way I do business with my own family members."

"Good for her!"

Peter felt his control slip away. Raising his voice, he challenged the woman before him. "I understood you both to be god-fearing women. It was even suggested that you put much of your faith into the teachings of the Bible."

"That's true," Karen replied. "What of it?"

"Is it not a matter of your spiritual teaching that the man is to be the leader of the house?"

"In a manner of speaking, you are correct. The spiritual leadership of the house is indeed the position of the man. He is also to be a civic leader and provider for his family. Oh, and a protector as well."

"Very good. Then I suggest both of you remind yourselves of this when looking to cast disparaging comments on the role I take with my family."

Karen Pierce was undaunted. "It also provides that women are to be the *despot* of the *oikos*. That's Greek, for your information, and a roundabout definition would be 'controlling ruler of all that encompasses her house.' Women are to be the keepers of the home. They are to work with their hands, feed and clothe their families, purchase and plant the lands, and make all other manner of individual choice and decision while their menfolk are off learning God's truth for them in spiritual training and acting as leaders for the community, as well as earning a living to provide those things the woman is incapable of growing or making on her own."

Peter looked at Karen in amazement. She always had an answer for everything. Now she was even quoting Greek to him.

"Perhaps it is you, Captain Colton, who should take another look at the Word of God."

"I have no time for such things," Peter replied. "I believe the Creator of this world to have endowed human beings with great capacities for learning and knowledge through their daily living. I believe I am quite capable of making sound judgments to guide the steps of my family. I don't need a list of rules and regulations to tell me what is sound."

"Ah," Karen said with a knowing nod. "It isn't Grace who bothers you half so much as what she represents."

"I don't know what you're talking about, Miss Pierce."

"God is what I'm talking about."

He shook his head. "Are you now telling me that Grace is God?"

Karen laughed. "Hardly. I'm saying that Grace's relationship with God is intimidating to you. You aren't half as angry with Grace or with me as you are with the idea that you might need someone bigger than yourself to get through life."

Peter had all he was going to take. Pocketing the mangled list, he tipped his hat. "Good day to you, Miss Pierce. I will endeavor to secure the items you've requested."

"I will pray for your safety and quick return," Karen replied with a smile. "And perhaps I will even pray that God might open your eyes to the possibility of His love and direction."

"Do what you think best, Miss Pierce. So long as you leave me alone and only pester God."

Karen laughed and continued to chuckle even as he turned and walked away from her. How was it that in such a short time he'd left one woman behind with a grievous expression of hurt, and another with a laughter that suggested complete joy? Things were certainly not as they should be. Chaos had crowded in on Peter's very organized life and that was a completely unacceptable condition to be in. He would have to find a way to take charge again—at least so far as his own thoughts were concerned. But while he was confident he could control his own thoughts, he wasn't at all sure about controlling his heart.

-{ C H A P T E R N I N E T E E N }-

THE HEAVY BROCADE DRAPERIES that lined the floor-to-ceiling windows of Frederick and Myrtle Hawkins' bedroom were pulled shut against the daylight. Myrtle sat silently beside her husband's sickbed. He seldom said more than a few words at a time, but she wanted to be there should he awaken and attempt to explain the dealings they'd endured over the last few months.

Martin Paxton had been as good as his word. He had seized control of the family businesses and stripped them of every hope of earning a living. Myrtle had immediately weaned the house of its staff, retaining only their butler and her personal maid. Together, the three of them worked to prepare meals and see to the household chores, but it was a poor attempt by people who were better suited to their known, traditional ways.

Myrtle failed to understand why her life had so suddenly taken a turn for the worse. Her daughter was now thousands of miles away, and she couldn't even write to Grace and tell her that Frederick had suffered a heart attack. Ever since Paxton had threatened to search their mail, Myrtle had realized the man to be far more powerful than she'd given him credit for. Maybe the suggestion was a bluff—something to spur her into action. But maybe it was the truth. Maybe Paxton had the ability to control every aspect of their lives.

She shook her head and calmed her own raging heart. No, God alone had control. She'd not give Paxton that power. The pastor had said they were under God's grace—that like Job in the Old Testament, the way might not make sense or seem reasonable. But who were they to question God? God had His reasons, and it was Myrtle's job to trust.

But trust came hard as she watched her ailing husband struggle for breath. He was so weary and so very sick. His color was a pasty yellow and he made gurgling sounds when he drew in air. He was dying. The doctor said that couldn't be helped now. The heart had suffered too much damage to sustain life for long. If Frederick remained completely bedfast, he might live as long as another six months, but even at that, the doctor had given her little hope.

"Oh, my darling," she whispered, drawing Frederick's hand to her lips. "We had a good life and now you are being taken away from me. I don't know that I can bear the pain of losing you." She thought of Grace and how hard it would be for her to learn of her father's illness. She would blame herself—just as Myrtle did.

"No," she whispered, "I blame Mr. Paxton more. If I am to blame, it is for somehow failing to obtain the truth of the matter from your own lips, my dearest."

"Mrs. Hawkins," Selma, her maid, called from the doorway. "Mr. Paxton has come again." Myrtle felt her resolve toward Christian charity fade at the announcement. "I told him you were indisposed, but he said he'd heard about Mr. Hawkins and wished to discuss the matter with you."

Myrtle had worked hard to see to it that no news of her husband's illness reached Paxton's ears, but apparently she hadn't worked hard enough. Suddenly she wanted to see him. To tell him what she thought of him.

"Put him in the Oriental parlor and I'll be there shortly," she commanded.

Selma left without another word, and Myrtle kissed her husband's hand once again and gently placed it at his sleeping side. Perhaps it was the effect of the sleeping medication the doctor had given him, perhaps it was a lack of will to live. Either way, Myrtle knew her husband had no concept of her presence.

She prayed on her way down the stairs. Prayed that God would give her strength to deal with Paxton and that He would also show her the truth that had so long eluded her. Something that dwelled within this evil man's heart had taken away the comfort and peace that she had come to rely on. It had also taken her daughter from her and would soon claim her husband's life. And while she could forgive Paxton for rendering them without funds, she could not forgive him for depriving her of Grace and Frederick.

"Mr. Paxton," she declared, pushing back the sliding doors. "I see you have once again come to plague me."

The man, looking far more worn than Myrtle expected, smiled rather coldly. "I feel honored that you have finally decided to share your presence with me."

"Don't," Myrtle said, holding up her hand. "I haven't come here to make you feel honored in any way. I might as well have called this meeting."

He looked rather surprised. "How so, madam?"

Myrtle took a seat and stared at him hard. "You have done your best to see my family destroyed. I think it's about time you explained yourself."

"I think you already understand perfectly well," he replied.

"No, I don't believe I do." Myrtle folded her hands. "I'm no fool, Mr. Paxton. I've realized from the start that there was more to this than mere gambling debts and a desire to marry into our family associations." She refused to look away from him. She memorized his piercing green eyes and the way his thick black brows narrowed as he considered her statement. She felt that if only there were some way to read his expressions, she might very well figure out the thoughts behind them.

"I want the truth," she stated simply.

"So do I."

"I am not going to tell you where Grace has gone. Do what you will to my husband and myself, but my daughter will not suffer your heavy hand again."

"And what will she suffer when she learns of her father's death?"

"My husband lives."

"But not for long, as I understand it."

Myrtle forced her expression to remain unchanged. He was crafty and wily, and she knew he wanted her to break. She could feel it—could feel him almost willing her to give up. *Oh, God, help me. It's like doing battle with Satan himself.*

"My husband is not the issue, Mr. Paxton. You are. I want to know why you chose our family to destroy. Why you have made it your personal desire to harm us in such a grievous fashion. I don't recall having any knowledge of you in the past. I know of no unsettled scores or business problems that should suggest such treatment."

"Of course you don't," Paxton replied, taking out a cigar.

Before he could pinch off the end, Myrtle shook her head. "I tolerated your ill-mannered behavior once before. I won't tolerate it again. If you wish to have a conversation with me, you will put that away and save it for another time."

He looked at her for a moment, and Myrtle imagined that he was trying to decide whether she'd stand her ground. He was judging her as an opponent.

Myrtle straightened and stiffened her back. She refused to back down and kept her gaze fixed squarely on his face. With a hint of a smile, Paxton tucked the cigar into the inside pocket of his jacket.

"Very well, madam, we shall play it your way for now. You have amused me with your sudden stance."

"I have no desire to amuse you or otherwise entertain you. I mean for this to be the last time you darken the door of our home. I mean for there to be an end once and for all to the destruction you have caused my family. And I mean for it to start now."

"You have no authority to create such an ending. Your husband is the only one who can see this thing through. And believe me when I say, if you knew the truth of the matter, he would no doubt face it completely alone."

"There is nothing you can say or do that will cause me to desert the man I love," Myrtle replied.

"I believe otherwise," Paxton said, this time giving in to a much more evident smile of satisfaction. "You see, this attempt to eradicate the name of Hawkins has not come about as a random act. Your husband greatly wounded my family many years ago. He destroyed those I loved and cared about most. And now, in the telling of it, I will destroy what he cares about most."

"I seriously doubt there is anything you could say or do to cause such a reaction, Mr. Paxton."

"We shall see."

Peter Colton was almost relieved to find his ship delayed in leaving Skagway's harbor. A heavy fog was moving in, making it an easy decision to remain where they were. Besides, his conscience was eating him alive and he knew that if he didn't find a way to apologize to Grace, he'd never be able to sleep through the night. It wasn't that he thought her beliefs to be right, but he hated to leave with hard feelings between them. Perhaps with a little more effort he could help her to see that he had done nothing but benefit his family. That his ability to reason through difficult decisions and issues made him an asset to those who loved and needed him.

After seeing to his ship and men, Peter made his way to the shores of Dyea once again. A cold, heavy rain began to fall before they actually made it to land, and within moments Peter was drenched to the bone. Sloshing through the muddy streets, Peter felt only moderate relief when the tent store came into sight. No doubt there would be little privacy to discuss what was on his mind, but it didn't matter. If need be, he'd wait for a time when he could speak to Grace alone, but either way, he would plead his case once again. Shivering from the cold, icy rain, Peter forced his frozen fingers to work at untying the flap of the tent. It seemed to afford a poor method of security, but within moments he found himself face-to-face with Karen Pierce and a very ominous-looking Winchester rifle.

"Oh, it's you," she said, almost sounding disappointed.

"You were expecting someone else?" he questioned.

"We weren't expecting anyone, hence the reception." She put the rifle aside and reached out to help him with his coat. "You'd better get out of those wet clothes or you'll catch pneumonia. Aunt Doris!" she called.

Doris appeared from behind the canvas partition they'd affixed between the store and living quarters. "Oh my," she said, noting Peter's appearance. "Whatever made you brave this weather, Captain?"

"My departure has been delayed by the storm, and I thought . . . well, that is to say . . . I needed to speak with Grace," he said, ignoring Karen's raised brow.

"Well, perhaps we should get you into something dry first," Doris replied. "There are some of those apronless overalls you brought up to sell to the miners, as well as a few of those chambray shirts. You should just help yourself and let us get you warmed up. Karen, go bring a blanket for the captain."

With a nod, Karen retrieved the Winchester and went into the other section of the tent. Peter, meanwhile, made a forage through the table of goods and found a pair of pants and shirt that would fit him.

"Can't do much about those boots. Boots sell out about as fast as you bring in a load. You can see for yourself the ones you brought us earlier today are already gone." The older woman seemed to size up the situation while Peter glanced at the shelves behind her. "We can set them by the stove and hope they dry out. The way this storm looks," Doris continued, "you might as well just stay the night. Won't be much of a chance for you to get back to your ship without risking great harm."

"That would hardly be fitting," Peter said, surprised to find the very proper spinster suggesting such a thing.

"Pshaw," the woman replied. "There isn't a bed available in town. You might as well take one of your own cots and bed down here. It wouldn't be the first time we had a man under our roof for the night."

"Oh?"

She smiled. "Am I scandalizing you, Captain Colton?"

Peter nodded and grinned. "I believe you are."

"Don't let it bother you. I was just referring to Mr. Barringer and his children. Someone ran off with his tent last week, and we had him here overnight before he headed out once again to help up at the Scales."

"Did he find who had taken his tent?"

"No, but I pity the man when they do. Thieves aren't well received up here. Last week I saw a group of self-appointed officials drive a man out of Dyea with nothing more than the clothes on his back, and all because he attempted to steal a man's rifle."

"Is that why Miss Pierce met me at the door with a loaded Winchester?"

Doris chuckled. "We learned early on how to fend for ourselves, Captain. We don't take chances when we hear someone breaking in to steal your goods."

"Has that happened before?" he questioned.

"Oh, once or twice, but we always get the drop on them."

Peter shook his head. He'd had no idea of what these women were up against. How could he even suggest they continue working in such an arrangement? The dangers might well be too great. On the other hand, he couldn't very well pack everything up and take it back now. The profits had done wonders for his family. He'd been able to pay back many of the debts they owed, and soon they would be back on their feet, maybe even able to completely overhaul their ships.

"Hello," Grace said, emerging from the back of the tent. She held the blanket that Karen had gone to fetch, and Peter couldn't help but wonder if Karen had thrust the duty off on Grace, or if Grace had volunteered.

"Leave the blanket and let the captain change," Doris instructed. "Afterward, you can talk by the fire. This young man is going to be in a bad way if he doesn't get warm soon." Grace nodded and placed the blanket on the back of a nearby chair. Smiling over her shoulder, she and Doris exited the room to give Peter some much-needed privacy.

Peter quickly changed his clothes and used some of the rope he'd crated in earlier in the day to assemble a clothesline to hang his wet things from. With this accomplished, he pulled the blanket around his shoulders and picked up his soggy boots.

Entering the living quarters of the tent, Peter was rather surprised at how cozy they'd made it. A large crate made a decent table, while overhead they'd managed to rig two hooks from which to hang lanterns. In the corner on cots made up with heavy wool blankets, the Barringer children were caught up reading, with Karen sitting between them to help whenever needed. Doris had built up a fire in the stove, and Grace waited with a cup of hot coffee.

"I should get soaked more often," he said, smiling.

"Sit here, Captain," Doris replied, offering a chair by the stove. Without any further comment, she went back to her sewing.

Peter did as he was instructed, positioning the boots close to the stove. Grace moved forward and took the chair beside him. She extended the cup of coffee almost timidly.

"Are you still mad at me?" she questioned.

Peter shook his head. "I wasn't mad. I was more ... well ... frustrated and maybe a bit ..." He looked around to see if the others were occupied with their own business, then lowered his voice. "I guess I was hurt."

"Because of what I said?"

"You made me out to be some sort of ogre," he said, warming his hands around the tin coffee cup.

"I didn't mean to make you sound that way," Grace replied. She kept her voice low, almost hushed, and Peter found that he had to lean close in order to hear her. "I would like you to better understand what I was trying to say."

"I felt the same way, but you go first and then maybe I can explain."

Grace glanced upward and met his eyes. "I meant no disrespect to you regarding your position with your family. I am certain you are a tremendous help to them in times both good and bad. But people will always fail. We are, after all, human. Our choices are not always the wisest, and often we misunderstand what the most appropriate response should be to any given problem."

"Granted," he said, nodding. "People do fail, but we must listen to the counsel of those who are wiser. Surely even your Bible would support this."

Grace nodded. "The Bible indeed tells us to seek wisdom, but God's wisdom—not people's. God's job is His own."

"Meaning what?"

She blushed and looked away. "Meaning that you should not attempt to take that position in the life of your family. Otherwise, what happens when you fail them?"

"I won't fail them," he replied indignantly.

"Everyone fails," Grace replied without a hint of apology. "God is the only one who never fails. You have put yourself in the position to be a god to your family. You ask them to seek you for their counsel and direction. You would preorder their steps, but God has already seen to that task. I fear your family might suffer far more than they would ever need to suffer if you continue to fight God for first place in their lives."

"This is a ridiculous conversation," he said, taking a long drink of the coffee. How could she say these things? Did she not realize how ludicrous she sounded? He pictured his sister looking up at him with great adoration. Miranda would never say such silly things. Yet there was a peaceful, purposeful manner about Grace. She wasn't ranting and raving at him like a lunatic. She was simply and calmly explaining her beliefs. Her calm only served to unnerve him all the more.

"I don't see this as a ridiculous conversation," Grace finally said. "One of these days, I fear something will happen. Your family will seek you for help—for their salvation—and you will fail them. When that happens, I can't help but wonder what will happen to their vision of God. Or for that matter, their elevated vision of you."

—|CHAPTER TWENTY|—

WITH WINTER COMING on in the northern territories, Peter was certain the demand for passage north would slow. He didn't find this to be the case, however. So despite the opportunity to service paying customers in Seattle, Peter made the decision to return to San Francisco. He needed to see his family, especially in light of everything Grace had said. For weeks her statements had lingered in his thoughts, and there was no way to exorcise the torment without spending time with those who loved and understood him.

But now, hours after enjoying a delicious meal prepared by his mother and sister, Peter was rather stunned to hear his father's comments on the past few months. Having suffered a knee injury during one of his trips, Ephraim Colton had turned *Summer Song* over to his first mate and made the decision to spend time at home recuperating.

"Why didn't you tell me about this?" Peter questioned as his father limped across the room to pour himself a glass of brandy.

He raised the bottle toward his son, but Peter only shook his head. "I can't believe you'd keep this from me. You're injured, and *Summer Song* is running without you."

"My men are good men," his father replied. "I trust them to do a proper job. They're running Mr. Paxton's goods and show true enthusiasm for their duties. Oh, we've lost a man here or there to the gold rush—I'd imagine you have as well."

Peter nodded, not wishing to remember that he'd lost an even dozen over the past few months. Replacing the men lasted only as long as it took for the next surge of excitement over gold to build and then some of the men again would go. He'd found that the best replacements were those who had already tried their hand at mining for gold and had come back discouraged and broke.

"I always believed you'd discuss such an important issue with me," Peter replied. "I've contacted you with each of my trips into Seattle and you've never mentioned the need for me to come home."

"Because there was no need," Ephraim assured him. "I'm on the mend and within a short time I'll be back on my feet and firmly planted on *Summer Song*. In fact, I've invited your mother and sister to journey north with me and see the country for themselves."

"What!"

His father threw him a surprised look, one that seemed to border on concern. "Do you perceive a problem?"

Peter shook his head. "No, not necessarily. I mean . . ." He turned away to pace the short distance in front of the fireplace. How could he explain that his father's ability to handle matters in his absence was causing him to feel rather misplaced?

"Wonderful," his father said, not giving Peter a chance to continue. "Your mother is quite excited about the prospects of seeing Alaska, as is Miranda. Both find the idea of an adventure to be something quite appealing."

Peter thought of Grace's words and tried not to feel the sting of their truth in the wake of his father's decisions. His family had once consulted him about everything, and Peter had liked it like that. Perhaps he need only stir the pot with ideas of his own in order to get back some of that control.

"I believe we should build a store for ourselves, Father," he began. Ephraim looked at him quizzically but said nothing. "I know I haven't said much to you on the issue, but I set up business in Dyea with three women to keep the store in my absence. They sell goods out of a large tent, but with winter approaching I know they're concerned about the need for something more structured. I believe we could put a store together and allow them to live in the back portion or even upstairs. They could continue to sell goods and we would net a tidy profit."

"What of Mr. Paxton? He's been most generous and I wouldn't wish to offend him. Especially now."

"I doubt Mr. Paxton would be that affected," Peter replied. "His store is in Skagway and Dyea is several miles away. Both harbors have gold rushers pouring in, and both have the potential for plenty of customers and business." Peter paused, as if suddenly hearing his father's words. "What do you mean, 'Especially now'?"

Ephraim tossed back his brandy and wiped his blond beard. "Well, that's the surprise I've been waiting to tell you about. Mr. Paxton has invested a good deal of money in Colton Shipping. We're to receive a new steamer next spring, and if business continues well we can have that paid off and perhaps even purchase another before summer is out."

"Wait a minute," Peter said, coming to where his father stood. "What are you saying? Have you signed some form of agreement with Martin Paxton?"

"I have."

Peter felt as if he'd been punched in the gut. "What kind of agreement? Why didn't you wait to consult me about this?"

His father eyed him rather intently. "Son, I appreciate the things you've done to keep this business up and running, but Martin Paxton is a longtime friend and astute businessman. I trust his word in matters such as this."

"But I wasn't even consulted." Peter knew he sounded like a whiny child, but in truth, his feelings were hurt. What was it Grace had said about his family replacing him?

"Son, this is still a family business. I didn't mean to leave you out of the discussion, but the matter needed a rapid decision. Mr. Paxton came to me—"

"He was here?"

Ephraim nodded. "He arrived by train nearly a week ago. He left just yesterday. Sudden business, something to do with a search he'd been involved with."

"May I at least read the papers you signed?"

"Of course, my boy." Ephraim moved to the secretary and opened a drawer. "You'll find a most generous offer. Mr. Paxton has done right by this family for years." He held the papers out to his son.

Peter would not find any relief in his father's words until he saw the papers for himself. Taking them up, he immediately began to search for any complications or problems. The investment was most generous, and Paxton himself was taking on the responsibility of securing the new steamer.

"What's this clause?" Peter questioned, coming to a statement regarding grounds for dissolving the agreement. "This makes it sound as if Paxton is a partner rather than a mere investor."

"Well, where the new ship is concerned, he will be a partner. He will be part owner until my debt is repaid. Surely you do not expect the man to put up his hard-earned money without any collateral to support his investment?"

Peter shook his head. "No, but neither did I expect you to take on a new partner without consulting your old partner first."

"Son, you are still in full control of *Merry Maid* and a full partner in Colton Shipping. I would have consulted you had this been an arrangement that would have threatened that partnership. Consider this a separate arrangement. Paxton and I are partnered in this new ship alone."

Peter handed back the papers, feeling completely at a loss. His father had made what appeared to be a very sound business decision without seeking Peter's help.

"You ask them to seek you for their counsel and direction. You would preorder their steps, but God has already seen to that task." Grace's words rang clear in his memory. He could see her sweet face fixed intently on him, her warm brown eyes watching his every expression as if to read his mind. Was this God's preorder for his family? Had God tired of Peter's interference?

Peter shook his head and turned to bid his father good-night. He didn't believe God worked that way. The God of the universe surely had more on his mind than to worry over whether or not Peter Colton worked overly hard to have a position of importance in the life of his family.

"I'll see you at breakfast, Father," he said, suddenly feeling very tired. "We can discuss the idea of a store in Dyea then, if you feel up to it."

"I shall look forward to it," Ephraim assured his son.

Bill knew that with the months quickly giving way to winter, he'd have no chance of getting to Dawson City before spring. Rumor held that it was far easier to get over the Chilkoot Pass on a stairway of ice and snow, but he wasn't convinced this would be true. He'd been packing supplies for weeks, and with each step up the mountain, he reminded himself that soon he'd be seeing to his own goods and his own way.

He tried not to think about the children. Jacob stared at him with accusing eyes every time he made it back to Dyea, and Leah always fretted over him. The first time he'd gone back to Dyea with his hands all blistered and torn up from the hard labor, Leah had cried and cried. Miss Pierce had dressed his wounds and left him with a new pair of work gloves and an admonition to keep the wounds clean, but even the vibrant young redhead had little comment to make. He didn't know if she understood his plan or just surmised that he was working through his grief. He felt confident that the children didn't realize his plan to leave them in Dyea. The idea both comforted and troubled him. How would they react when they learned he was gone? Hadn't Miss Pierce mentioned Jacob's involvement in a fight based on his supposed desertion of them?

Even now as he made his way back to Dyea, Bill knew he couldn't come clean with the truth. If they knew he'd been working to gain money and supplies to see himself north while they waited in Dyea, Bill wasn't sure he'd be able to leave. He could almost hear Patience's upbraiding for leaving their children in the care of strangers. She would have given him quite the lecture on his flighty behavior and dreamer mentality. She had before.

He loved and adored the woman who had been his wife, but she had never understood his aspirations, his dreams. He had wanted to give her and the children a good life. He had wanted to give them fine china and sterling silver. He had wanted his wife and daughter to know the feel of satin and silk and his son to stand among the privileged gentlemen of society.

Patience had never cared about any of that—even when he'd managed to obtain it for her for a short time. She had had lovely things and beautiful clothes, but she had been just as content when they moved to a house of less fortune and social grace.

Bill looked up to the fading twilight skies. The feel of winter was in the air—a hard bite that bore into him and urged him to be quick with his plan. The less said the better. He would make like this night was no different from any other.

When the tent store came into view, Bill straightened his shoulders and lengthened his steps. He had no idea what would await him, but he wanted to give every impression of confidence.

"Papa!" Leah shouted as Bill approached.

Dressed in a warm woolen coat and mittens and looking years older, Leah discarded the wood she'd been carrying and ran to her father's arms. "Are you back to stay? Some of the folks here said we're due a bad snow."

"Well, the work goes on whether there's snow or not," Bill replied, not willing to give her false hope. He touched her cheek lightly. *My, but you look like your mother,* he thought, and his heart ached all the more for what he planned to do.

Jacob rounded the corner of the tent, his arms loaded with wood. "Pa!" he said in a rather excited tone. "When'd you get back?"

"Just now," Bill replied. "Looks like you two could use some help."

"No, we've got it," Leah said, leaving her father's side to retrieve her own discarded pieces. "You carry things all day. We'll carry this and you come inside and rest. How are you hands?"

"Just fine, princess. I told you once they got used to totin' and fetchin' I'd be just fine."

"I'm sure glad. Karen said they would heal if you took proper care, but without anyone to help you, I wasn't sure you'd be able to do it all alone." Her voice was animated and cheerful, and Bill could have sworn she had a skip to her step.

Following his happy children into the tent, Bill tried not to think of how they would feel when they learned the truth. Somehow he would have to make them understand he was doing this for them.

Liar! his own voice echoed in his mind. He looked guiltily at the sale tables and shelves. *I'm doing this for me, not them. I'm doing this to escape the memories and the pain—leaving them to ease my own suffering!*

"Why, Mr. Barringer," Doris Pierce exclaimed, "we'd just about given you up for lost."

"It's only been three weeks," he replied. "I might not have come back this soon had I not come with word of Mr. Pierce."

"Father!" Karen came into the room just as he mentioned the man's name. "What of my father?"

"Well, he's stuck in one of the villages. Seems there's been some kind of epidemic and they're quarantining the area. Nobody in and nobody out. The Mounties are seeing to it that no one violates this order. They've caught a lot of the Indians trying to sneak out, but so far they've kept them contained."

Karen frowned and her worried expression made Bill uneasy. "Where did you hear this information?" she questioned solemnly.

"Adrik Ivankov."

"Is he here in Dyea?"

Bill shook his head. "I passed him up around Sheep Camp. He'd talked to your father prior to the epidemic hittin' the village. This is the first opportunity I've had to bring you the news."

"Was he all right?"

Bill shrugged. "Apparently so. He had plans to settle here in Dyea, in fact was moving out the next day, but the epidemic hit and Adrik figures he probably stayed to help and then got caught there with the quarantine. Now the heavy snows have come up high, and no one knows how bad this has made the trails."

"I suppose I shall have to learn better patience," Karen replied with a tone of disappointment.

"This is the place for it," Bill agreed, a hollow tone to his words.

Karen had the feeling that Bill Barringer had something on his mind. All evening he sat silently watching his children. Even after supper, when the dishes had been cleared away and the kids had offered to play rounds of checkers with him, Bill had only given it a halfhearted effort.

Perhaps he was worried. Heaven knew she was worried enough for everyone there. Her father was contained in the middle of an epidemic, and she had no way of knowing if he was safe or in danger.

She tried not to think of her father shivering in the cold of an Alaskan snowstorm. She tried not to think of his dying from measles or whooping cough or whatever the sickness that plagued the village might be. She tried, but unfortunately her imagination ran rampant. Even after the lights had been turned down and they'd settled into their beds for sleep, Karen couldn't stop thinking. Fear crept over her in a sensation of bleak hopelessness that started somewhere deep in her heart and rippled out in destructive waves throughout her body. Try as she might, Karen could not shake the feeling of desperation that consumed her.

Risking the possibility of waking everyone else, Karen slipped from her bed and put a few more pieces of wood in the stove before slipping into the outer room of the tent. Darkness engulfed her, but it was the eerie silence that frightened her. Even the town seemed strangely silent, which for Dyea was a feat all its own.

Karen moved to the tent flap, thinking perhaps she might just slip outside for a moment. She knew it would be freezing, but grabbing up a wool blanket from the shelf, she decided to risk it anyway. Unfastening only one set of flaps, Karen dodged under the remaining closure and stepped into the icy air.

The cold assaulted her nose and lungs in a way that seemed to temporarily ward off her anxiety. The sky was overcast, muting out the light of the moon. Sighing, Karen stood in silence and wondered what the rest of the world was doing. Back in Chicago, Grace's parents were probably safe and warm, sleeping in their fine feather beds under warm blankets of goose down. Winters in Chicago could be horribly cold and damp, and no doubt the servants would keep the fires going all night to make certain no member of the family received a chill.

She wondered only momentarily about Martin Paxton. She could only pray that he'd accepted his defeat and moved on to greener pastures. She hated to think of Grace married to someone so hateful and barbaric.

Peter Colton then came to mind, and she knew there was a very good possibility the man would press his interest in Grace. She wondered if he was right for Grace. He seemed to hold no interest in issues of faith and God. In fact, he seemed downright angry and defiant about anything concerning God. Grace would never allow a man to take her away from her hope in Jesus, of this Karen was certain. No, if Peter Colton wanted Grace for a wife, he'd have to come to salvation first.

Then her mind went to Bill Barringer and his children. She thought again of how odd he'd acted all evening. His expression seemed mournful, almost as if he were experiencing the loss of his wife all over again. Perhaps the children reminded him too much of his wife. Leah said she looked like her mother, that everyone had told her so on many occasions. Maybe Bill found it difficult to be around the child without growing morose. But Leah was such a joy. In spite of her mother's death, she was like a fresh spring bud just waiting to burst to life. She loved to learn, and Karen often found her devouring whatever book she could get her hands on, all for the simple love of knowledge.

Jacob was a bigger worry. He worked all day at various jobs but never seemed satisfied. The wharf business had slowed for a bevy of reasons and with it, Jacob was more often than not sent off in search of another line of employment. He had come home with word that Skagway was actually considering a railroad to the north and that he just might get himself a job laying track if they actually went through with the plans. Karen had thought to condemn the idea but had remained silent. The boy was so clearly troubled and miserable about something. She felt it had to do with his father's leaving and the resentment he felt at being left behind. He resented, too, that the other boys picked on him for it. Most of the boys his own age were laying aside money and provisions to go north, but Jacob was merely trying to survive.

"Oh, God," she whispered, looking into the murky skies, "I want to help them, but I don't know what to do. I want to find Father and help him too, but again, I'm at a loss. I want you to direct my steps, to show me where I might best be used, but am I missing your direction? Have I somehow failed to understand your purpose?"

Down the street she could see some commotion and hear voices raised in revelry. This seemed a good time to slip back inside the tent. She had barely tied the bottom inside flap, however, when she heard voices from just outside the opening.

"Yeah, it's just women in here. Women with plenty of cash and goods. We can get what we need and take what we want, if you get my meaning," the man announced. There was laughter between what sounded like two, maybe three men. The sound left Karen trembling in fear. She felt frozen in place even as she saw the canvas around the inside flap begin to move.

-| C H A P T E R   T W E N T Y - O N E |-

MYRTLE HAWKINS pulled her coat tight against the brisk November winds. She had cried enough tears to last her a lifetime, and now she was determined that placing her trust in the Lord and seeking His strength would replace her years of greed and self-concerns.

Staring dry-eyed at her husband's mausoleum, she felt her heart break again for the pain and misery he had suffered. Poor man. He had tried so hard to keep from hurting her with the truth. If only he would have shared his misery and mistakes.

I would have forgiven you, my darling, even as I forgive you now.

All that mattered was that Grace remain safe. Martin Paxton had already seized most of their wealth and possessions, at least those he knew of. Myrtle was a smart, resourceful woman, however, and as soon as her world had begun to crumble, she had had the foresight to make provision. Even now her faithful butler was off tending to her business. He would meet her one final time at her hotel, bringing with him all the money he had managed to make by selling her jewelry, silver, and other valuable odds and ends. But it wasn't much, and it certainly wouldn't last long in Chicago.

She looked again to the mausoleum. She had come to bid Frederick good-bye, even though she knew he was no longer bound by the sorrows of this earth. It seemed fitting, however, to come to his tomb for one last moment before leaving the city they had once loved.

Myrtle planned to live in Wyoming for a time with her cousin Zarah Williams.

It was here that Myrtle hoped to bring Grace when the time was right. In Wyoming, Myrtle hoped they could patch together the pieces of their shattered lives and learn to be happy again. She prayed it might be so.

Turning from her husband's grave, Myrtle made her way back to the hotel. Her knees ached terribly from the cold, but she refused to give up even the small price of a hired carriage. She would be prudent and frugal, a complete contrast to her old self.

I will make this work for Grace's sake, she told herself. *I will put aside the things of this world and the foolishness of my former self, and I will be a true daughter of God. I will put mankind before property and social settings. I will serve the needs of others instead of myself.*

She chanted this as a mantra, as she had during the days since learning the truth about her husband and Martin Paxton.

"I don't think you want to know the truth, Mrs. Hawkins," Paxton had told her quite smugly. *"Truth is not always attractive."*

"No, but it is always liberating," she had replied.

With a shrug, he seemed indifferent. *"Your husband destroyed my life. He dallied with the heart and soul of a woman who never meant more to him than a diversion. He made promises he couldn't hope to keep and used her in such a way that no decent man would have her after he'd finished. That woman was my mother, and your husband put her in her grave—just as I intend to see him in his."*

The news had come as a shock. Myrtle would never have imagined her husband as an unfaithful man. Of course, he was often absent from home, but business took him across the lake on many occasions. Weeks would pass with Frederick working away from home, and Myrtle had always endured them with patience and understanding. Her husband was making them rich. He was giving her all that she had desired and an even higher place in society. How could she fault him for that?

"I know you would probably rather dismiss this as a lie," Paxton had continued, *"but I have letters he gave her, words of love and hope, adoration and commitment. Would you care to see them?"*

Of course she hadn't wanted to see them. She wanted no visible evidence of her husband's adultery. Paxton spoke in detail of events in the life of his mother, including the miscarriage of a child—Frederick Hawkins' child. It was all so awful and complete in detail that Myrtle had no doubt of the truth. Neither did she have to wonder any longer what fueled the rage in Martin Paxton.

Narrowly avoiding an oncoming carriage, Myrtle's thoughts were instantly thrust into the present. Inside the carriage, she recognized the face of a one-time friend. The woman, however, was not wont to recognize Myrtle and quickly looked away.

That's how it had been from the first mention of the Hawkinses' downfall. No one wanted to be associated with a bankrupt man. Proper society would talk about the family in hushed whispers, but they would have no further dealings with them. Not even so much as to acknowledge them when passing on the street.

This is the life I once thought perfect, Myrtle realized. *This is what I aspired to become.* She felt deeply ashamed for her participation in such a world. What a price it had cost her. Her dear husband was dead. Her daughter was a world away. Her servants and friends were scattered like seeds in the wind, and she no longer had a place to call home.

But in her heart, Myrtle held a peace. God had not forsaken her. The trappings of the world had fallen away, but in their place she could see what was real. She could see beyond the trees—the forest she had created for herself.

"'I see men as trees, walking,'" Myrtle quoted from Mark chapter eight. She remembered the verses clearly because Jesus then touched the man again. The memorized Scripture poured from her mouth. "'After that he put his hands again upon his eyes, and made him look up: and he was restored, and saw every man clearly.'" Myrtle looked heavenward and smiled. "I am restored in you, O Lord, and in you I see every man clearly."

Martin Paxton joined the captain of *Summer Song* for dinner. Along with his good friend Ephraim Colton, Martin shared the table with Colton's wife, Amelia, and their daughter, Miranda.

The brown-haired beauty sat across from him at the small, yet elegantly set table. She smiled warmly, knowing him to be her father's dear friend, and he easily returned the smile. His attraction to her was something he had not expected; but then, he'd never seen the woman before. She reminded him something of Grace. Her sweetness and naïveté were worn openly as though something to be proud of.

She asked simple questions about a world she'd never seen, and he honored her with patient answers that he would otherwise have never wasted time sharing. *Perhaps,* he thought, *when I truly do take a wife, Miranda Colton would be a pleasing choice.* Of course, that would come much later. Later, after he'd dealt with Grace Hawkins.

Grace was now a personal issue. She had thwarted his plans, defied him to his face, and then without any difficulty whatsoever she had managed to slip from his grasp. He didn't care about Grace Hawkins in any personal way, but the fact that she was an unobtainable part of his previous plans ate at him like a disease. He would find her and he would break her.

"You haven't told us what brings you to Seattle and now here to join us on the trip north to Skagway," Amelia Colton was saying.

Martin smiled, thinking of the most recent message he'd received. "In truth, the trip was most unexpected. My fiancée was taken north with the gold rush madness. I'm hopefully going to make contact with her near Skagway."

"How delightful!" Amelia declared.

"I had no idea you were engaged to be married," Ephraim said, pouring Martin another glass of wine. "Congratulations. Although it's a pity."

"Why do you say that?" Amelia asked her husband.

"He might have considered our Miranda, otherwise," Ephraim replied with a wink. Miranda blushed and looked to her plate, while Amelia laughed at the tease.

"She would be a fair prize indeed," Martin offered gallantly. He could see she was clearly embarrassed, and he hoped to win her confidence by changing the subject. He might need Miranda Colton's allegiance at a later date, and he wanted very much for her to consider him a friend. "I am quite pleased with the profits of our business arrangements. I had meant to address the issue earlier."

Ephraim nodded. "The news just gets better with each trip north. My son is quite exuberant about his own venture in Dyea. He hopes to continue in business by building a small general store of his own. I hope you do not consider this as too much of a rivalry."

"Not at all," Martin replied. "As is my understanding of the area, there appears to be room for all."

"Very true. The harbors are poor in Dyea, but that is quickly resolved by building wharfs and docks. As it stands, a ship may drop anchor in deep water and allow barges to take the goods ashore. It's more time-consuming, but for those who prefer to begin their journey from Dyea, it truly becomes more economical."

"And what of Skagway?" Martin asked, already knowing the answer from his own hours of research.

"Skagway is good for shipping. The town is booming, as is Dyea. The passage north from Skagway allows for horses and wagons. At least this is what I'm told. There is some talk of a railroad. I wouldn't count on that, however. The talk can hardly be trusted as more than rumors and innuendoes. I can't imagine trying to cut a path through that wilderness."

"People said the same of our western frontier," Martin replied, knowing well the plans for a railroad north. He even hoped to put himself at the center of such a venture. "Look at us now. Railroads crisscross the country and everyone rides the train."

"Believe me, I know how plentiful those iron beasts have become," Ephraim said. "My business has suffered until now because of it."

"There will always be room for ships and railroads alike. I wouldn't allow it to cause you any more worry. What matters is planning. You have to think toward the future and realize what potential awaits you there. You have to decide what it is you want out of life, then take it."

Ephraim chuckled. "I wish I had more of your enthusiasm. Peter tells me I lack the type of business acumen that would see us as wealthy people, but truly I have no desire to be wealthy."

Martin couldn't imagine any man feeling like this. "What is it you desire?"

"I have all that I could hope for. A loving wife and two wonderful children. I have a home to offer them and the means to earn a living. What more could any man desire?"

Martin knew there was plenty more to be desired, but he said nothing. Smiling, he raised his glass. "To desires that are fulfilled," he toasted.

Later, in the privacy of the best cabin on board *Summer Song*, Martin leisurely enjoyed a cigar and reread a rather unexpected letter from Myrtle Hawkins. The woman had taken his news rather stoically. He had expected tears and sobs at the knowledge of her husband's betrayal, and instead she had remained calm, collected, and even-tempered. People like that unnerved him.

"My mother was your husband's lover," he had told her with great satisfaction. Here at last was the threat that had sent Frederick Hawkins to his deathbed. Here was revenge for his mother, so painfully wronged.

"She was a beauty, my mother." He had pulled a photograph of her from his pocket and offered it to Myrtle. *"Wouldn't you like to see what took your husband away from you for long weeks and months?"*

She had studied the photograph for a moment before handing it back to Martin. Her color had paled somewhat, but she remained in complete control of her emotions. *"She is a very pretty woman."*

"Was," he corrected. *"She died and your husband killed her."*

That had brought a bit of response from Mrs. Hawkins. Her eyes had grown wide and her brows had raised involuntarily.

"They had a torrid love affair. He cherished her for a time. He gave her everything she needed."

"Are you his son?" she had asked flatly, her expression recovering to one of neutrality.

Paxton had smiled. *"I could lie and say I was, but it really doesn't benefit my case. No. I am not Frederick Hawkins' son."*

Martin drew long and thoughtfully on the cigar. The cherry tip glowed in the dimly lit cabin. Hawkins had died without Martin ever having a chance to gloat over the fact that Myrtle now knew every detail of his wicked past. He would have liked to have seen the pained expression on Hawkins' face when he realized that his beloved wife knew all about his mistress. Better yet, he would have liked to have seen the woman cast the dying man aside. That would have been perfect in his estimation, for it was no less than Hawkins did for Martin's mother. But Myrtle Hawkins had remained at her husband's side—faithful and true to the end.

Perhaps that was why the woman's letter was of such particular distaste to him now. He scanned the pages and found the part that stole his delight.

> My husband never knew of your declarations to me. I saw it served no purpose but yours to give him such information, and therefore chose instead to allow the man to go to his grave in peace and comfort. He died believing that I never knew of his shame—that he had preserved his marriage and family.

Martin tensed at the statement. So smug and victorious. Mrs. Hawkins actually believed she had won some small victory. But it was Martin Paxton who had won. The entire world could see it, he told himself. He now held most of Hawkins' holdings and controlled many of his former businesses. He had forced the sale of the house and estates and now held the proceeds of those sales as well. Myrtle Hawkins had won nothing.

He looked again to the letter, frowning at the feminine script.

> I pray God deals justly with you, Mr. Paxton. I know of no man who deserves justice more surely than you. You have done what you set out to do, but I will tell you that the outcome is not what you expected. Instead of destroying my family, you have only made it stronger. You have no more power over us, and we will now go forward in a better life.
>
> The only thing in life worth living for is love—something you will probably never understand. Grace understands it, however. And I finally understand it too. You can do nothing more to harm us, Mr. Paxton. It is now your mortal soul for which I fear.

He scowled and tossed the letter to the table beside him. "You needn't fear for my soul, Mrs. Hawkins, and you needn't be so sure there is nothing more I can do to harm you."

He picked up another piece of paper and read the information aloud.

"'Grace Hawkins left Seattle for Skagway. There are no records of where she went after arriving, but her name does not appear on the Canadian records showing her to have gone north.'" Paxton smiled and stretched out his legs in front of him.

"Soon, my dear. Soon. We shall have a reckoning, and when we are through, you will be nothing more than a brief entry in my memory. A dalliance—a pleasurable moment—a recompense for my mother."

⊣ CHAPTER TWENTY-TWO ⊢

PETER ARRIVED IN SKAGWAY a day before the scheduled arrival of his father's ship. Feeling a deep sense of confusion and frustration over his father's recent decision to expand his business relationship with Martin Paxton, Peter found himself in a foul mood. He knew his father respected Paxton as a longtime friend, but the idea that another man, a complete stranger to Peter, could come in and so influence his father bothered Peter more than he liked to admit.

Snow lightly blanketed the ground, making a vast improvement on the appearance of the small boomtown, but even this didn't help to lighten Peter's heart. He felt overwhelmed with concerns he'd never before considered to be of importance. Not only was his father making choices without seeking Peter's advice, but Grace Hawkins had made him reevaluate his entire method of dealing with life and his family.

He had never seen himself ruling over his family in a godlike way, yet given his current feelings, Peter couldn't help but realize Grace had made a good point. This only served to make matters worse, however. Peter had no desire to see himself as the kind of man Grace had described, and yet he had no desire to relinquish the position of respect and authority his family had delegated to him.

I'm a grown man, he reasoned. *Things like this shouldn't be of such concern. Under other circumstances I would have married and perhaps even produced heirs by now.* The thought had crossed his mind on occasion, and now with Grace in his life, it cornered his thoughts on more than fleeting moments. Thoughts of Grace had rapidly infiltrated his daily existence.

But if he married, what would become of his family? His father had little practical sense when it came to business. Never mind that the man had managed his shipping line for longer than Peter had been alive. After all, Colton Shipping had aspired to be nothing more than a local freighting line before Peter became old enough to push for further development. Peter had helped the company expand—to reach its fullest potential. What would happen if he bowed out now?

"Martin Paxton would happen," he muttered. He didn't even know the man, and already he felt a sense of competition with him. All of his life Peter had heard Martin and Martin's mother spoken of in a way that devoted a familylike closeness. Peter's father practically considered Martin's mother to be a sister. He didn't know any real details of their past, only that the family had been friends with his own back East, but apparently Martin Paxton had grown into a man of considerable power and wealth. Perhaps that was what bothered Peter the most. Paxton was successful in Ephraim Colton's eyes, while Peter was merely the son helping to run a business, which up until recently had been failing. Did his father see him as a failure as well?

"But people will always fail. We are, after all, human," Grace had told him.

The words were still ringing in his ears even now, weeks later. Had his family perceived him to have failed? Had he not met their needs somehow? Perhaps he should broach the subject with his father and ask for the truth.

Peter thought about this long and hard as he hopped a ride on a barge up the inlet to Dyea. His anticipation of seeing Grace again was blended with a sorrow that she could not be the woman he desired her to be. Why couldn't she be more like Miranda? *Miranda adores me,* he thought. *Miranda would never question me or consider my counsel to be less than the best. Grace thinks me to be overbearing. She believes me to have placed unfair demands on my family.*

"You have put yourself in the position to be a god to your family. You ask them to seek you for their counsel and direction," Grace had said.

So what's wrong with that? Peter questioned silently. He argued the matter internally, knowing that he needed to be able to share his answer with Grace. But logic would not win out. Instead, he again heard the petite woman's comments.

"I fear your family might suffer far more than they would ever need to suffer if you continue to fight God for first place in their lives."

She's full of religious nonsense, Peter decided. *She's been brought up in such a way that she simply doesn't understand how men must be in charge to see to their family's well-being. I've not chosen to usurp God—on the contrary. God is in His heaven and I am here. It only stands to reason that God would choose certain emissaries to guide the people of this earth.* Surely Grace had not considered that. He smiled to himself. That had to be the answer. She was a very young woman. Perhaps she was simply ignorant of such matters. After all, her mentor was strong in her beliefs of women's rights, yet Grace's father arranged his daughter's marriage and future. In her simplistic manner, Grace was most likely confused by such contrasts. The thought comforted Peter and gave him new ideas for how to handle future discussions.

A fine, icy rain began to pelt Peter, stinging his face. Grateful for his heavy wool coat, he snugged down his cap and wrapped a woolen scarf around his face. A bitter wind blew from the northern snow-capped mountains. He pitied those who were probably even now trekking their way up and over the extensive passes. And all for the hope of seeing their first hint of gold. All for that elusive rock. Why was it so hard to see that the real gold was here in Dyea or Skagway? A man could get rich with nothing more than a tent and a stack of goods.

Given this scenario, Peter had foreseen great things for Colton Shipping. Had his father not committed to Martin Paxton's plans, Peter would have had them completely out of debt in another month. He'd planned to announce the news to his parents when they'd last been together in San Francisco, but that plan had been thwarted when his father delivered the news of his own venture with Paxton.

Again Peter felt the pinch of his father's decision. What if they no longer needed him? Worse yet, what if Grace was right? What if he had set himself up to be their god? Where did mere mortals go when they were cast from their lofty perches—no longer to serve as elevated deities? The thought haunted him all the way to his destination.

"Well, I must say, you're a welcomed sight for once."

The voice belonged to Karen Pierce, but it was Grace Hawkins who captured Peter's attention as he entered the tent store.

"Good day to you, ladies."

Grace smiled sweetly. "Good day to you, Captain Colton."

Karen pretended to be busy packing blankets into a crate, but Peter could tell she was hardly focused on her work. Both she and Grace wore layers of clothes, along with their coats. Apparently with the traffic that frequented the store, keeping the interior warm was most difficult.

"So I suppose I must ask," Peter said, feeling rather like an animal about to be trapped, "why is it that you welcome my appearance this day?"

Karen didn't even look up from her work. "We need to make a decision now about moving the store. If you aren't planning to do so, you may well have to run it on your own because we're moving."

Peter shook his head and looked to Grace for an explanation. It was then that he noticed Grace was also packing items into a crate. She exchanged a glance with Peter before quickly turning her attention back to her task.

"Well, it is very cold," she suggested. "We manage well enough in the back, but even so, the nights are difficult."

Peter nodded. "But I have a feeling there's something more to this than the weather. In truth, I had planned to move the store with this visit, but I haven't yet chosen a site. There is a gentleman in town who has the ability to build up a place overnight. He charges a considerable sum, but he's quite good and very much in demand."

"We know all about him," Karen replied. "We've been after him for weeks, but he's too busy making outrageous profits to worry over a trio of women who have to live in fear of their lives."

"What is she talking about?" Peter questioned Grace.

"Karen will have to explain," Grace replied. "I only saw the aftermath. She'd already shot the man by the time I came to her side."

"What!" Peter roared the word, not meaning to frighten them. He felt bad when both women jumped at least a foot in the air. His tone brought Leah and Doris running from the back. Doris held a fairly heavy pickax in her hands and looked as though she might even know how to use it.

"It's all right, Aunt Doris," Karen said, turning to comfort the older woman. "Captain Colton is just now learning of our trouble the other night. You and Leah go back where it's warm and we'll continue explaining. If he yells again, just ignore him."

"Oh my," Doris said, not at all interested in heeding her niece. "Has she told you of our peril?"

"Grace said Karen shot a man."

"She did," Leah threw in, "but she didn't kill him. He's been run clean out of town. They put him on the first ship south."

Peter's head was reeling. "Why did you shoot the man?"

Karen finally allowed her gaze to meet his. He noted the stoic manner in which she fixed her expression, but he couldn't ignore the fear in her eyes.

"I shot him because he wouldn't leave and he and his friends were threatening us with bodily harm. I'm sure I needn't go into more detail than that."

Peter felt sickened at the thought of what might have happened. Perhaps he should be grateful that these women were cut from a different cloth. Maybe Karen Pierce's strength and fortitude were a blessing in disguise. "Well, that's it," Peter replied. "You won't go long without a building. I'll see to it immediately. I shouldn't have been so eager to pay old debts. I should have insisted this tent be traded for a building."

"Don't be hard on yourself, Captain," Grace said, coming forward. "We have enough money to put together a payment for a small place, but no one has had the time. Most of the men have gold fever and little time for constructing homes or businesses. It's just as Karen said, we would have to pay double or even triple to have their consideration. We thought to have help from a local guide and a

Tlingit Indian man, but they've both disappeared and we've had no word from them in a long while."

"Not since he sent word through Mr. Barringer that my father is delayed in a quarantined village."

Peter nodded. "I'm sorry to hear that. But what of Mr. Barringer? What of his son? They both appear to be strong, healthy men. Could they not lend their hand to constructing a building?"

"Bill Barringer has taken up a job of packing people and their goods up to the summit of Chilkoot Pass. He returns to see us only on occasion," Grace told Peter. "Jacob has been working off and on in a variety of jobs, but he's hardly more than a boy."

"I was capable of running a ship at his age," Peter retorted, having no patience for weak men. "Barringer should never have left you unprotected."

"We weren't unprotected," Karen replied. "The Winchester and I had the matter under control."

"But what might have happened if you'd been asleep?"

"I had tried to go to sleep, but I couldn't," Karen replied. "Now I believe God was keeping me awake to ensure our safety."

"I don't see God providing a building for you," Peter retorted.

"Well, He did send you," Grace replied, offering him a smile.

Peter couldn't accept that answer as valid. "Think what you will." He looked around the room and shook his head. "I'll send some of my men over to help you box this stuff up. One way or another, we'll move you out. Until then, I'll post guards if need be."

———

Bill reached up to rub his tired shoulders. Stiff and sore, they served to remind him of the journey ahead, as well as the ones he'd already completed. Packing supplies up the long, difficult Dyea trail was no simple task. Day after day he'd found himself pressed to endure impossible terrain and surly-tempered clients. He'd taken to loading his packs heavier each day and now could handle one hundred pounds, same as most of the Tlingit packers on the route up the Chilkoot Pass. Nevertheless, at the end of the day, he was worn out and ready for nothing more than a hot meal and bed.

Winter had set in, and in some ways this made matters much easier to deal with. Now, instead of struggling to muck through oozing mud paths and climb over boulders and fallen trees, the ground had frozen solid and a coating of packed snow allowed for a more productive means of transporting the goods. Even better, the area between the Scales and the summit had been modified and a stairway of ice had been carved out of the mountainside. The hike was still long and arduous but much easier to master. The packers stood in line for what seemed like miles, rope guide in one hand, walking stick in the other, hunched over under the weight of their belongings.

Coming down was much simpler. Most of the packers took to the side of the carved pathway and slid down the mountain on their backsides. Sometimes they were even lucky enough to sit atop a piece of wood or a shingle for the wild ride down. It sure beat hiking down as they had before the snows were plentiful.

The cold weather actually did more to encourage the stampeders and their packers. A person needed to keep moving in the bitter winds, otherwise they could find themselves quickly freezing to death. Bill and two other men had come across a woman and child only a day earlier, half frozen and starving in a snowbank. Neither were dressed for the climate nor the ordeal of mastering the summit. After seeing them to safety, Bill couldn't help but think of his daughter. He shuddered to think of Leah lying frozen at the side of the road.

The image only increased his resolve to go north on his own. He was ready now. He'd been earning almost forty cents per pound to pack goods and had spent very little until today.

Smiling at the stack of goods he could now call his own, Bill couldn't help but feel a twinge of excitement. Several men had become discouraged with their dreams of gold and had sold out to Bill. As required by the government of Canada, Bill had enough supplies to see him through a year in the wilderness. There were some fifteen hundred pounds of assorted goods, part of which he'd already packed to the summit on behalf of his client. Now the materials awaiting him atop the pass belonged to him. He had the bill of sale and could prove his ownership.

The idea sent a surge of anticipation and excitement coursing through his body. There would still be more than a dozen trips to make up and down the ice stairway, but that was of no real concern. He could do it. He had already come this far and nothing would stop him. Everything was planned. Everything seemed in order.

Bill tried not to think about his intentions to give sole responsibility of his children's well-being to Karen Pierce. With Jacob working and Leah helping at the store, they were no doubt earning their own keep. They couldn't possibly be costing Miss Pierce that much to feed and house. He comforted himself with the reasoning that they were much better off warm and safe in Dyea, no matter who might be helping to care for them.

When I strike it rich, he thought, *then I'll send for them and we'll be a family again. They'll understand that I've done what is right and best.* At least he hoped they would.

He covered the supplies with a tarp and staked it down. His last order of business was to make one final trip down to Dyea. He had to tell Leah and Jacob good-bye, and he had to explain to Karen Pierce what he was doing and why he needed her help. It never really entered his mind until that moment that they might all protest his action and refuse to cooperate. He frowned, trying to imagine what he would do or say should they cause a fuss. Jacob would insist on going north with him, yet there were no supplies for his son. As it was, Bill had teamed up with another group of men and this was allowing for a much easier time. One man had a stove and another the tools. A third man was a walking arsenal, refusing to go north without his beloved ivory-handled pistols, two rifles, and a shotgun. Bill had an entire set of pots, pans, and camp dishes, along with some tools and something more valuable than the others combined—a working knowledge of mining.

No, he'd simply have to explain the situation to Jacob and insist he remain behind to care for Leah and await the time when Bill could send for them.

"Bill, you heading down to Dyea?" one of the trio he'd partnered with asked.

"Yeah, heading there now."

The man produced a list and a wad of bills. "See what you can get. I've already searched through Sheep Camp and wasn't able to get much of anything."

Bill nodded and pocketed the list with the bills. "My friends run a store in Dyea. I might have better luck. Keep an eye out for my goods, will you?"

The man nodded. "We'll be packing the whole time you're gone, may even get a chance to move some of your stuff up as well."

Bill hadn't considered that his team might be delayed by his brief journey to Dyea. "I could hire a couple of Tlingits to help," he offered.

The man considered the idea for a moment. "I could see to it. You can pack my goods up from Dyea, and I'll see to keeping you caught up with the rest of us."

"Deal," Bill replied, then without wasting any more time on conversation, he picked up the small sack he'd put together for his hike to Dyea. "I'd best get a move on."

The hours of daylight were lessening considerably as the sun altered its course in winter. Bill found the lack of light a minor inconvenience. Having spent most of his adult life in mines of one sort or another, the darkness had never been an impediment to him. Still, the trails were more dangerous at night and he had little desire to be lost to an encounter with wildlife, or worse yet, underhanded humans.

The road back to Dyea was easier in the snow. Hard-crusted paths had been tramped down by hundreds of feet before his, and Bill found it far less complicated than maneuvering through the knee-high mud of late summer and fall. The frozen Taiya River would also afford him an easy path. With exception to those places where fallen trees and logs made artistic combinations with the now frozen water, the river would make a straight run into Dyea and shorten the time Bill would be on the trail. *If I had ice skates, I could make the trip in half the time,* he thought, smiling.

It was nearly dark by the time Bill reached Dyea. He'd already decided he would talk to Karen first. He would just explain the situation as it was and not give her a chance to refuse him. It had to be this way, and the sooner she realized it the better. If he had to, he'd tell her some of the horrors he'd seen along the way. He'd talk about the nearly frozen woman and her child. He'd even talk about the dead—those who had succumbed to the elements or their own weak bodies.

As if by preorder, Bill arrived at the tent store just as Doris and Grace were heading out with Leah.

"Papa!" Leah exclaimed. She hugged him tight and kissed his frozen cheek. "We're just off to do some shopping at Healy and Wilson's store. Do you want to come?"

"You have a store right here," he teased. "Are you deserting the Colton Trading Post?"

Leah laughed. "No. The other store has a new load of goods. They just came in last week. They have bolts of corduroy, and Grace and I are going to make me a new skirt."

Grace smiled up at Bill. She was hardly any taller than his daughter and very nearly the same build. "It's true, Mr. Barringer. Corduroy will make for a very warm skirt, and we must hurry or it will be taken up by the other women. Besides, we want to get back before it's completely dark."

"Then, by all means, don't let me be the reason for the delay. I'll be here when you get back, princess," he said, patting his daughter's shoulder.

"Are you sure you don't want to come with us?" Leah questioned. "You could hear all the news. There's been talk that gold has been found on the river here in Dyea. You could find out all about it and maybe we'd not have to go so far north to look for gold."

"Gold, here?"

Grace nodded. "That's what's been rumored. There are probably a dozen or more claims already staked. I haven't heard much in the way of success stories and certainly no call of a bonanza strike like they have up in the Yukon. Might just be cheechakos. You know how they can be."

"You've picked up the language pretty well for bein' a cheechako yourself," Bill teased. He liked Grace very much and found her charm and sweetness reminded him of Patience when she had been the same age. The idea of gold in the area intrigued him, and for a moment he thought to abandon his plans. "So who might know more about the Dyea strike?"

Grace grew thoughtful. "I suppose you should talk to the recording office or the assayer. They'd be able to tell you what kind of color they're seeing."

Bill nodded. "I'll do that. You ladies go ahead to your shopping. I need to see Miss Pierce for a moment, and then I'll take you up on your advice and head over to the recording office."

"You won't leave before we get back, will you?" Leah asked hopefully.

"Of course not. I'll stay the night." He said the words as her expression tore at his heart. She trusted him—believed in him. How could he betray her? He watched the trio walk away. They were happy and Leah was healthy and well cared for. That was far better than anything Bill could give her on the Chilkoot Pass.

"Mr. Barringer, whatever are you doing standing out here in the cold?" Karen Pierce questioned as she stepped outside to throw out a pan of dirty water. "If you're hungry we have a pot of beans on the stove. Leah has just gone off with my aunt and Grace."

"Yes, I saw them," Bill replied. "And I'd be happy to warm up by the stove and eat. Maybe you could share a bit of conversation with me. We should probably discuss the children."

"You're right on that matter. I've had some concerns," Karen admitted. She ushered Bill into the tent and followed him back into their private living quarters. "I've been worried about Jacob."

"Jacob? Why?" Bill questioned. He looked around the room as if the boy might suddenly appear.

"He's gone off to help Captain Colton. We're to move the store into a new building tomorrow."

"A building will be a wonderful change. Where will it be located?"

"Several blocks north on Main Street. I'm sure you'll have no trouble finding us. The captain has arranged a decent-sized building with several big rooms on the back. We'll be living there and you are welcome to come and stay there as you come back and forth."

"Well, that's part of what we need to discuss," Bill began, but Karen quickly continued, giving him little chance to speak.

"Jacob has been very troubled over these passing weeks. He has few friends in this town and his heart seems quite burdened by something. He won't talk on the matter. I've tried working with him on studies, but he holds little interest and while he's good to contribute to our needs by bringing food and sometimes other necessities, he distances himself from all of us, Leah included."

"He's a young man in a house full of women," Bill replied. "I'm sure he's feeling a bit out of sorts."

"It's more than that," Karen admonished. "He's often been in fights."

"It'll do him good to fight for what he believes. That's how it is with men."

Karen shook her head. "He needs a father. As you said, he's surrounded by women. Perhaps he should join you on the trail."

Bill tensed. "I don't think that would be a good idea. The elements are killing people every day. Sometimes from workin' too hard, sometimes the weather. You know there've been floods and mud slides, snow and ice storms. It's a hard life, and I'd rather not see him exposed to it just yet. I'm sure he'll adjust to working here with you in time."

"I disagree. He needs you."

"I think, Miss Pierce, I'm better able to know what my kids need than you are."

Karen lifted her chin, striking a rather defiant pose. "I may not have children of my own, but I know children. I nannied Grace for over ten years. I know when something isn't right and your son is clearly troubled."

Bill knew he would have to explain the situation. "You have to understand that some things have changed. I've been working hard to put together supplies for the journey north, but one man working alone is hardly able to manage very well for himself. The men I'm working with would have little patience for children—that's why I've chosen to keep them here in your care."

"Your son needs you," Karen reiterated. "Who else will show him how to be a man?"

"He already knows how to be a man, Miss Pierce. He's fourteen. He'll be fifteen next month. My father was already dead by the time I'd reached that age and I grew up just fine."

"Fine enough that you give little consideration for the needs of your children. You might as well not even come back for all the good you're doing."

Bill bristled at this. "I'm not going to stand here and argue," he said, forcing his tone to remain calm. He suddenly felt almost panicked by her reaction. He couldn't very well tell her of his plans now. Not when she was being so harsh with him in regard to Jacob and Leah. Turning to leave, he stopped and added, "Jacob will be just fine. He's going to have times when he fights. It's the only way he'll learn."

"Learn what, Mr. Barringer? How to be as coldhearted and unfeeling as you?"

Bill stormed out of the tent, not willing to even answer. He wasn't coldhearted and unfeeling. If anything, his feelings were eating him alive. Karen Pierce didn't know what she was talking about.

Jacob had heard every word spoken between his father and Karen Pierce. He felt horribly guilty for what had transpired between them. After all, they were talking about him. Karen was worried about the fights he'd had—at least the ones she knew about. Trouble was, Jacob found himself so often out of sorts with folks that he was quickly gaining a reputation as being a hoodlum. He felt bad that Karen worried, but he felt worse that his father didn't. How could he just walk away and not care what those fights were about?

Jacob felt tears come to his eyes and angrily wiped them away. He wasn't a baby and he wasn't going to cry. If his own father didn't have time or concern for him, then that was just the way it would be. He wasn't going to shed tears over it, and he sure wasn't going to let anyone know how much it hurt inside.

—| CHAPTER TWENTY-THREE |—

A SENSATION OF ANXIETY and anticipation washed over Peter as he made his way up from the Skagway docks. Word had come that *Summer Song* had arrived some hours earlier, as well as news that Martin Paxton had traveled north with the Colton family.

His family was to have rooms in the upstairs quarters of Martin Paxton's mercantile. Being one of the few completed wood-framed buildings, Paxton's store would afford them the best protection from the elements, as well as allow them time to visit with Paxton and make plans for the future.

To say that news of his father's friend coming north was disturbing was an understatement Peter didn't care to explore. He should have been grateful and glad for Paxton's interest in his family, yet he felt like a jealous sibling. For reasons that were beyond his understanding, Martin Paxton's arrival was rapidly diminishing the pride Peter felt in having purchased a building for the Colton Trading Post. He had planned to sit down with his father and explain the situation and the expenditures necessary to secure the store in Dyea. He had hoped to receive his father's blessing and approval for the choices he'd made, and somehow Martin Paxton's presence robbed Peter of the limelight. Peter knew his father would be focused on the old family friend rather than Peter's accomplishments, and it made him feel most uncomfortable.

I have to stop undermining my victories and accomplishments, Peter told himself. *I've worked hard for this, and the likes of Paxton shouldn't be the cause of my defeat.*

Acquiring the building had come at no small sacrifice. He'd had to pay a great deal to purchase the building, and along with this, Peter had to pledge shipments of building supplies that he would turn over at cost to the contractor. With the purchase finalized, Peter had sent half a dozen of his best men to help with the move of the store's goods and had even hired a sign painter to mark the new business properly. He felt good about what he'd accomplished. It had cost him a pretty penny, to be sure, but Grace and her friends, along with the trade goods, would be safe. The expense was worth it. Still, the idea of having to share his news in the presence of a man he had come to feel rather negatively toward left Peter feeling foolish.

Father admires and cares deeply for this man, he reminded himself. *It's hardly fitting that I should despise the man simply for encouraging my father to take proper business risks.* After all, Paxton had the capital to offer along with his advice.

As Peter neared the store he admired an artistically painted red, white, and blue sign announcing *Paxton & Co. Mining Supplies.* An American flag was painted on either side of the name. The sign was new and Peter was notably impressed with the addition. It lent the store a certain flair of wealth and prestige, as well as patriotism. Of course, he wasn't sure that the stampeders would care about the aesthetics, but the tasteful presentation both impressed and discouraged Peter. His own store would be a shoddy example next to Paxton's. *Perhaps I can get my own painter to embellish Colton Trading Post with a bit of flair. I might even bring up several gallons of colorful paint and do the store up proper.* The thought made him feel marginally better.

Peter made his way inside, nodding at the clerk and searching the room for any sign of a familiar face. "I believe Mr. Paxton is arriving today along with my family," he announced.

"Yes, sir. They're all upstairs. You can use the stairs back there." The man pointed to an open door beside a display of sleigh runners and wagon tongues.

Peter nodded and made his way through the well-stocked store. No doubt deliveries from *Summer Song* were quick to be put into order if Mr. Paxton had anything to say about the matter.

Climbing the steep, narrow stairs, Peter wondered what his encounter with Martin Paxton might actually bring to light. The man could be someone Peter might respect and enjoy dealing with. Intelligent men with a mind for business were always of value to Peter's way of thinking.

He opened the door onto the second floor and was greeted by Miranda's laughter and his father's enthusiastic tales of boyhood.

"Peter!" Miranda declared as he stepped into the room. "Oh, do come join us. Father is telling the most delightful story of when he and Mr. Paxton's mother got lost while exploring a cave."

"I'm glad to see you all have arrived safely," Peter said, giving his mother and sister a smile. He turned his attention only briefly to his father before sizing up the middle-aged man at his father's side.

"You must be Martin Paxton," Peter said, not waiting for an introduction.

Paxton smiled and extended his hand. "And you are the man responsible for keeping Colton Shipping in the black. Your father speaks very highly of you."

Peter felt some of his confidence return. He smiled at Paxton, noting a severity in the older man's expression. While he offered a smile and friendly words, the man's eyes seemed to denote a more cautious demeanor.

"And I've heard favorable stories of the Paxtons since I was a small boy," Peter replied, shaking hands.

"We are all very much like family, eh?"

"Indeed we are," Ephraim Colton offered. "Once you have found your bride and are married, we shall endeavor to have you both spend time with us in San Francisco."

Peter was confused by the statement. "Are you looking for someone in particular or simply searching the Alaskan territory for a wife?"

Paxton laughed. "No, I have a particular woman in mind. We were engaged some time ago. She came north with friends and, well, I was to join her here. We'll marry and return to the States before winter disallows for easy passage."

"You shouldn't have any trouble. These harbors are said to remain open year-round. I've not yet experienced the situation firsthand, but have heard favorably from other captains."

"That's indeed good news," Paxton replied.

Peter couldn't shake the feeling that Paxton was considering him beyond the mere introduction of a family friend. Paxton's green eyes seemed to take in everything around him all at once, while at the same time be zeroed in on Peter as if awaiting an answer to some unspoken question.

"We told Mr. Paxton you could probably help him in finding his fiancée," Peter's mother began, "but seeing the number of people in Skagway, perhaps it won't be quite that simple."

Peter nodded. "The town is growing daily. I brought a full ship of men and women to the city just ahead of you. All were most anxious to make their fortunes. Nevertheless, Mr. Paxton, if I can be of help in your search—"

"I have hired some men to help in searching through the town," Paxton interrupted. "Although I understand there is another town a few miles away. I believe it's called Dyea."

"Yes," Peter said thoughtfully. "I have friends there who are running a small trading post for me. I would imagine they very well might know your fiancée, especially if she's to be found in Dyea. There aren't a great many women up this way, and ladies of quality seldom pass unnoticed. What's her name?"

"Grace Hawkins," Paxton replied. "She hails from Chicago and is probably traveling with a woman by the name of Pierce. A Miss Karen Pierce."

────────────

Jacob knew his father was up to no good when he announced that he would spend a second night with the family. They had just moved into the new building, and his father made the pretense of wanting to be sure that everyone was settled in before heading back up the trail. Something in the situation just didn't seem right with Jacob. He could sense his father's agitation—could feel his discomfort.

"What's wrong with Pa?" Leah asked him in a hushed whisper.

Everyone headed off to their beds with Leah, Jacob, and Bill being relegated to one room while Karen, Grace, and Doris took another. Bill announced that he'd stoke up the fire in the main living area before joining his children for the night. This gave Jacob time to ponder what his father might be up to.

"I don't know what's going on," Jacob admitted to his sister. "But he is acting strange—has been ever since coming back. Maybe he's just worried about the weather."

"Maybe," Leah replied, hurrying to bury herself under the wool blankets on her cot.

Their father entered the room rather expectantly, almost as if he anticipated their questions. When Leah and Jacob only watched him, however, Bill Barringer took the opportunity to question them.

"Have you been minding yourselves for Miss Pierce?"

Leah nodded from her bed. "Yes, Pa. I like Miss Pierce a lot. She's teachin' me the same kinds of things Mama used to show me."

He smiled benevolently on his youngest and turned to Jacob. "And what of you, son?"

Jacob tensed. He knew from having overheard his father's conversation with Karen that he would be wondering about the fights. "I'm doing my best, Pa."

Bill nodded. "Miss Pierce tells me there've been some fights."

Jacob looked to the floor as he moved to sit on the side of his cot. "Yes, sir."

"Well, she doesn't understand how it is with men. Just try to keep out of trouble. You have a sister who needs you to stay in one piece. Men up here are mighty tight strung. The gold fever is keeping them at odds with everyone, and those that can't put together the wherewithal to get north are going to be particularly surly."

Jacob looked up to meet his father's eyes. "I'm not in any trouble, Pa. The fights are usually because I let my temper get the best of me."

"You know what your ma would say about that?"

Jacob nodded. "She'd tell me to turn the other cheek. To put a guard over my mouth."

"Exactly," Bill replied. "Things will probably seem to get a whole lot worse before they get better." He sat down and began pulling off his boots. "Sometimes folks do things that others have a hard time understanding. Sometimes things don't make much sense and it leaves angry feelings between people who care deeply about one another."

Jacob knew his father was talking about something more than his daily fisti-cuffs with other local boys.

"Sometimes, without even meaning to hurt their loved ones, people do things that they have to do. Important things that will make it better for everyone in the long run."

"What kind of things, Pa?" Leah asked from her bed.

Bill scratched his beard and pulled off his remaining boot. Jacob could see that his father's hard work had worn holes in the heels and toes of his socks.

"Well, princess, it's like your mama used to say. Sometimes God sends things our way to bless us and sometimes they come to teach us. Some of those teachin' times are hard. They might even cause us pain. Sometimes they take people away from us—people we love and care about."

"Like Mama?" Leah asked.

Jacob wished they'd both just drop the subject. Thinking of his mother only caused him greater grief. Some of his fights had come about because of derogatory statements made about his mother. But more often than not, they referenced his father.

"Look," their father stated, getting to his feet. "I'm going to smoke me a bowl." He picked up his pipe and smiled at them both. "Your ma would be proud of you children. I'm proud too. Just never forget that."

He left them then, closing the door behind them. Jacob reached for the lan-tern, but before he could turn it down, Leah sat up in bed. Her eyes locked on his.

"He's leavin' us, isn't he?"

Jacob nodded. He felt a lump in his throat that refused to allow him speech. His sister had spoken the truth—an undeniable truth. Their father was leaving them here—leaving them with Miss Pierce and going north.

He blew out the light quickly, not wanting his sister to see his tears. Balling his hands into fists, he punched at the pillow as if to arrange it into proper shape for his comfort. In truth, he was beating out the anger in his soul—an anger that was threatening to eat him alive.

Karen found the coals in the stove were just barely putting off heat by the time she roused herself to prepare breakfast. Adding wood and tenderly nurturing the fire back to life, she grabbed a bucket of water and placed it atop the stove. At least the water hadn't frozen like it had all those nights in the tent. The new building would afford them a much more comfortable existence, and once her father made it back to Dyea, she'd simply convince him to stay on with them.

Finding it still dark outside, Karen lighted a lamp and went to work measuring out oats for their morning cereal. It was as she set the table with bowls and spoons that she noticed the folded piece of paper addressed to her attention.

Puzzled, Karen put down the bowls and reached for the missive. Unfolding it, she found herself completely overwhelmed by the news of Bill's departure.

It might seem unfeeling, she read halfway down the page, *that I should leave my children behind, but you don't know what the trails are like. I've seen people die—kids too. I wouldn't want that for Jacob or Leah. I'll send for them as soon as I can. Please don't be angry and take it out on the kids. I love them, and I know you've come to care for them in your own way. I'll write when I get settled, and I promise to pay you for your trouble.*

He added no personal notes for the children, and Karen couldn't help but wonder if he'd left similar letters for each of them. She glanced around but found nothing. Perhaps if he had, he would have left them in the bedroom he had been sharing with Jacob and Leah. She thought to go searching but decided against it. They would have to know the truth sooner or later. If they said nothing to indicate their father had told them of his departure, Karen would remain silent and save the news for a more private moment.

She quickly refolded the letter and put it in her pocket. A feeling of despair washed over her as the reality of the situation began to sink in. She was now mother to two motherless and fatherless children. Jacob, already angry and unreachable, would not brook this desertion easily. And poor little Leah, who adored her father and mourned her mother, would be devastated. Karen wanted to cry for them both. How could the man have been so heartless?

"I thought I heard you out here. You should have woke me," Grace said, tying an apron around her waist.

Karen smiled, but her heart wasn't in it. "You look positively domestic, Grace."

Grace smiled. "I actually like the life. I used to feel so completely useless back home. This seems much more fitting. Why should I have servants when I take such joy in doing things for myself? Mother, of course, would be horrified, but I love it all, even the cleaning." She pulled her hair back and tied it with a ribbon before adding, "Wasn't it kind of Mr. Barringer to stay another day in order to see us settled in?"

Karen nodded and turned quickly back to the oatmeal. She had no desire to broach the subject of Bill's departure with Grace. She couldn't even decide how to tell the children, much less announce to Doris and Grace that she was now fully responsible for the care of two children. "I was just setting the table."

"Then I'll finish it," Grace replied as Jacob and Leah emerged from their shared room.

"Where's Pa?" Leah asked, looking around the room.

Karen met her expression, then let her gaze travel to where Jacob stood with a look of stoic indifference on his face. *I can't tell them,* she thought. *I can't hurt them like this. Better to let them think he's simply gone back to work on the trail.*

"He left early," she finally said. At least it wasn't a lie.

Leah's face paled as she turned to Jacob. Karen could see the boy's jaw clench as if in rage. He put his arm around Leah, then met Karen's eyes. Karen trembled without knowing why. They knew. Either Bill had told them of his plans or he had left them similar letters, but either way—they understood what his absence meant.

She pulled the letter from her pocket. "Did your father give you any idea of what is in this letter?"

Leah shook her head. "He didn't say much last night." Her voice sounded frightened and uneasy.

Karen wanted to put her mind at ease but knew the contents of the letter would do nothing of the sort.

"Your father has gone and asked me to take care of you until he's settled," Karen finally stated. She looked to the letter as if to read it, then decided against it. Glancing up, she could see the anger in Jacob's eyes.

"He's gone?" Grace questioned. "Do you mean permanently?"

Karen had expected the question from Leah or Jacob, but not from Grace. She turned to her friend and nodded. "He felt the trail was too dangerous."

Grace nodded, seeming to understand that her reaction would affect the children's reaction. "Well, I suppose that must have been very hard for him," she said softly. "What a difficult choice to make."

Karen gave Grace a smile of gratitude before turning back to the children. "I want you both to know that I won't allow any harm to come to you, if I have any say about it. We can make better plans once my own father returns to Dyea, but for now, just know that you have a home wherever I have a home."

Leah burst into tears and came to wrap her arms around Karen. "What if he doesn't come back?" she cried.

"He'll come back. He promised to in his letter," Karen said, trying to sound reassuring. Her confidence faded, however, as she met Jacob's eyes. They both knew it was a lie. Bill Barringer might never again return. The leaving had been the hard part. Staying away would require little effort.

-| CHAPTER TWENTY-FOUR |-

KAREN AND GRACE poured all their energies into making bread for the days to come, while Doris and Leah minded the store. They no longer worried about their safety. Word had traveled fast about Karen's ability with a rifle, and with that reputation, a new respect for the trio of women was born. The rowdies still poured in, demanding and bellowing for their supplies, bemoaning their lack of good fortune, or complaining about some swindle that had left them penniless. But through it all, the customers maintained a kind of silent admiration for the women.

"*You ladies are known as the toughest bunch of gals in Alaska,*" one prospector had told them. "*We drank to your health last night at the Gold Nugget. Then we drank to ours, just in case you took a dislikin' to us.*"

Grace had laughed at the sentiment. She still found it hard to believe that they'd been put in such situations of peril. Her days prior to coming north had never prepared her for the life she was now living, but she couldn't help but enjoy the freedom they now experienced. She thought, in fact, she very well might like to settle permanently in this wild, rugged country.

"So what's so pleasant that I find you grinning from ear to ear?" Karen asked from across the table.

Grace was overjoyed to find she had a few moments of privacy with her dear friend. "I was just thinking about our reputation. I'm sure half the newcomers to the area are too scared to even step foot in the store."

"Yes, but the other half comes out of curiosity and maybe even the desire to consider challenging us," Karen replied. "I don't like having a reputation either way. I'd prefer we be unnoticeable, given the reason we came here in the first place."

"You aren't still worried about Martin Paxton, are you?"

"Aren't you?"

Grace was surprised by Karen's candor and considered the idea for a moment. "Not truly," Grace said as she mixed yet another batch of sourdough. Taking a pinch of the starter, which had come by way of an old Tlingit woman who traded for sugar, Grace worked in the ingredients and waited for Karen to reply. When she said nothing, Grace stopped stirring and looked up. "Are you worried?"

"Some. I guess I've known men similar to Mr. Paxton. They aren't easily swayed and not at all inclined to take defeat—especially from a woman."

"I wouldn't fret over it. We're a long way from Chicago, and Mr. Paxton must have other concerns to busy himself with. Just as we have ours. I was just thinking that I might very well like to settle here. Perhaps I'll stay on, even when Mother assures me that all is well. Maybe I can even convince Mother to bring Father and come here to join me. Although I suppose there would be little work for Father here, and Mother does love her social events."

Grace paused, noting that Karen was sitting idle, staring off as if lost in a memory. "What's wrong? I don't think you've heard a word I've said."

Karen shook her head. "I'm sorry. What were you saying?"

"Never mind what I was saying. Tell me what has you so worried."

"My mind is just preoccupied. I'm worried about Father, and I'm worried about those children."

"This doesn't sound like the same woman who told me over and over that we had to give our heartaches to God and trust that He would see us through the bad times as well as the good."

"I know God is in the midst of this, but I have a bad feeling about this matter of the Barringer kids. Leah is so heartbroken that her father would leave her behind, and Jacob is angrier than ever. His rage was already getting the best of him—what do I do with him now?"

"Have you tried talking to him?"

Karen picked up a bag of flour and measured some out into a bowl. "I've tried," she said, focusing on her work. "But he wants no part of it. He's almost grown. And with Bill's departure, he certainly isn't open to parental guidance, especially in the form of a substitute mother."

Grace began mixing the bread again and considered the matter carefully. "I would hate to be left behind like that. They must feel completely betrayed."

"And the worst of it is, I can't help them to believe that they haven't been betrayed. I can't offer support for Bill Barringer's actions because I don't believe the man made the right choice. If anything, he should have taken his savings and loaded those kids back on *Merry Maid* and headed for home."

"I agree, but we can't change the circumstances now." Grace set the dough aside to rise and turned to her friend. "And what of your father? How shall we handle this matter?"

Karen put down the mixing bowl and shook her head. "Grace, I'm afraid."

"Why?" Grace could see the anguish in Karen's eyes, but for the life of her she couldn't understand what had given birth to this fear.

"I just have a feeling that things aren't good. I keep imagining that I've come all this way only to lose him."

"He's not lost," Grace said with determination. "He's just stranded for a time. The quarantine will pass and he'll return before the heaviest part of winter sets in. You'll see."

Karen moved to check the loaf of bread already baking in the oven. "I'd like to believe that, but I just feel so . . . so . . ." She looked up as she closed the oven door. "I feel lost."

"But I don't understand why," Grace said, coming to Karen's side. She put her hand on her friend's arm. "Has something happened that I don't know about?"

Karen shook her head. "No. I've had no news, if that's what you mean."

"Come. Sit with me and talk. We've not had a really good talk in so very long."

Karen smiled and followed Grace to the table. "You seem more the mothering figure now than me."

"Then let me bear your burden and help you to release whatever fears you may be holding inside," Grace replied.

Karen folded her hands and looked at them carefully, as if studying them for answers. "I don't know what I'm called to do anymore—what my purpose is. I used to know so clearly, but now I don't."

"What's changed?"

"You have, for one. You're a grown woman," Karen said, looking up. "You don't need a nurse or teacher anymore. You've taken to menial labor like a duck to water—you're better at bread making and sewing canvas than I can ever hope to be." She sighed and continued. "See, as long as you were a child, I knew my purpose. I felt called to be your governess—to stay at your side and see you raised properly. I enjoyed our time together and felt compelled to grow close to you as a friend, as well as a teacher."

"But nothing of that has changed. You are still my dearest friend, and there is still much I have to learn. I'm learning every day."

"Yes, but much of what you are learning now doesn't require my presence. I feel a restlessness in me, Grace. A calling out, if you would. The only problem is, I don't know what I'm being called out to."

"What of the Barringer children? You are taking up with Leah where you left off with me. Then, too, there's Jacob. He needs to be softened and molded into a young man with a heart for God and for good."

Karen seemed to consider Grace's words for a moment. In the silence, Grace could feel her friend's turmoil. It seemed to permeate the air like an odor—not quite unpleasant, but not altogether welcomed.

Karen finally spoke. "I thought maybe God was calling me north to work with my father. I thought perhaps I would teach the Tlingit children."

"And why can't you?"

"I suppose I can, but I don't know that this is the proper calling either. I have spent a lifetime feeling called to specifics, and now everything seems so questionable. I knew since I was a young girl that I was being called to remain single—to receive an education. Eventually, I felt called to work for you." She looked at Grace and smiled. "Do you remember that at first your mother thought me too young and inexperienced to work as your nanny?"

Grace nodded. "I overheard her tell Father that in spite of your being an educated woman, you knew nothing of life."

"Well, she was partially right, but I knew more of life than she gave me credit for. Anyway, I had no fear of not being hired for the post. I knew God had brought me to you, and I knew it was His will for us to be together. But now I don't know what His will is. I don't know what I'm supposed to do. I can't say whether I'm to remain single or teach or to raise the Barringer children until their father chooses to show up again. I simply feel that the answers are veiled away—hidden from my sight."

"Have you prayed on the matter?"

Karen laughed. "That seems to be all I do accomplish. I pray and pray and pray again. And still I feel no peace in my heart. I feel as though I'm in a constant state of limbo. I can't move forward or backward, nor side to side."

"Perhaps, then, you aren't supposed to move at all. Maybe this is one of those times of resting and waiting. I know it is for me."

"Because of your parents and Paxton?" Karen questioned.

Grace felt overwhelmed with her own feelings and concerns. She had longed to talk to Karen and share her heart, and now her emotions welled up inside her and threatened to spill over. "I think I'm in love."

The words had an obvious effect on Karen. "Peter Colton?" she questioned.

Grace felt her face flush. "I know you disapprove and I know you two grate on each other's nerves, but I find my heart so overwhelmed when he is near. I feel like my stomach is doing flips and my head is soaring high above my body."

"Couldn't we just chalk it off to gold fever or some other type of illness?" Karen questioned. "I mean, does it have to be love? Does it have to be him?"

Grace frowned. "Why do you hate him so?"

"I don't hate him, Grace. I simply see him as the same domineering type of man you've found yourself under all of your life. Your father was like that—Paxton is like that."

"Captain Colton is nothing like Martin Paxton!" Grace declared defensively.

"But I fear he easily could be. He's only a step away from the same kind of insistent cruelty that you witnessed in your former fiancé. I just don't want you to get hurt."

"I'm already hurt," Grace replied, getting up from the table. "I can't love Peter Colton with any real hope of a future. He isn't interested in the things of God and he has no faith in Jesus Christ."

Karen nodded. "That was going to be my next point."

"Don't you think I've already considered all of this? You've told me time and time again how painfully destructive it can be for people to have split philosophies regarding religion. I know that Captain Colton has his own way of doing things and doesn't believe in a need for God, but I can't help that my heart feels as it does."

Grace's heart ached with the truth of her words. She knew deep inside she couldn't let her feelings for Peter take her away from her faith. She couldn't allow him to come between her and God. But she also knew her emotions were set aflutter every time the man walked through the door. She had never hoped to fall in love, not after her horrible encounter with Martin Paxton. She had never believed herself capable of trusting a man after her father's betrayal. But she had been wrong. Her feelings for Peter were very real, and she feared that if she couldn't find a way to control them, they'd also become very evident. After all, Karen had no problem in guessing to whom she'd given her heart.

"I won't do anything foolish if you're worrying over it," Grace said softly. "I'm old enough to know better."

"You may be old enough," Karen said, "but I'm not sure that's the issue. Knowing better is one thing—turning away from a bad situation is entirely different."

"Grace!" Leah called as she opened the door and bound in from the store. "You have a letter."

Grace felt her heart begin to race. "Is it from home? From my mother?"

Leah shrugged and handed her the envelope. "I don't know. Jacob just happened to be up at the post office and found out we had this letter waiting for us there."

Grace took the envelope and nodded. "Yes, that's my mother's script. I'm sure of it." She tore open the envelope and began to read.

Dearest Grace,

Things are quite grim, as we knew they would be, but will work themselves out in time. You must remain in Alaska for a time longer while I work to put things right again. I'll send word when it is safe to write to me, but until then, please send no correspondence. I won't be at the Chicago address anyway, and letters might only fall into the wrong hands.

Yours in love,
Mother

"I can tell by your frown that the news isn't good," Karen said, breaking the silence. "What does she say?"

"It's what she doesn't say that bothers me," Grace replied, handing Karen the letter. "She only says that things are grim. Well, we already knew they were that. She makes no mention of Martin Paxton or of Father. I can only presume the worst. Especially given the news that she won't be remaining in Chicago. Perhaps she has left Father."

Leah patted Grace's arm. "I'm sure your mama will be all right. Your pa too."

Grace smiled, encouraged by the child's words.

"Don't borrow trouble, Grace. You don't know anything of the sort. You can estimate and try to guess all you want, but it won't change matters. We must put it in God's hands and pray for the best. In the meantime, we have to have a positive outlook and believe that everything will come around right. Your mother loves you a great deal, and she would do anything to keep you from harm. It's the heart of every mother—or so I'm told." Karen gave Grace a sad little smile.

Leah surprised them by wrapping her arms around Karen in a possessive manner. "I wish you were my mother," she said without warning.

Karen hugged the child close and kissed the top of her head, all the while looking at Grace. Grace felt her heart breaking for Leah and Karen. They were both without benefit or hope of ever seeing their mothers again, until the time God would join them all together in heaven. At least Grace had her mother. She had to take comfort in that.

We might have wasted a good many years, Grace thought, *but we'll make up for the lost time when this matter is behind us. We will find a way to cross over the years of desert and make for ourselves a place of beauty and hope.*

Part Three

DECEMBER 1897–JANUARY 1898

For God shall bring every work into
judgment, with every secret thing,
whether it be good, or whether it be evil.

ECCLESIASTES 12:14

─┤ C H A P T E R   T W E N T Y - F I V E ├─

DAYS AFTER BILL BARRINGER LEFT, Jacob disappeared. Karen frantically searched for the boy, seeking out the various places she'd heard him mention and talking to those who knew him. With every denial of the boy's whereabouts, Karen feared that he'd gone north to follow his father. It seemed to be the logical thing for the troubled youth to do.

Oh, God, she prayed as she made her way to the seedier part of town, *protect and keep him. He's just a child—a lost and lonely child. He's suffered so much already, please keep him from harm. Help him to find his hope in you.*

She continued praying, finding strength in the words she shared with her heavenly Father. There was comfort for her in the prayer as well. Karen had long realized the power of prayer and the way it allowed her to feel a connection to heaven and all that God offered. She thought of her father's deep love of God, his desire to bring the lost souls to the same hope he'd found. Wilmont Pierce didn't care where that desire took him. He didn't mind the cost or the hardship. He simply loved God, and he loved the people God had created.

Karen wanted to love people in the same way, but where her father collectively embraced entire villages, Karen had always felt directed to focus on one or two people at a time. Perhaps it was just a different method of service, she thought, but perhaps it was a self-imposed limitation. She'd always felt divided and too far spread when she'd faced the situation of teaching to a group. Even when she'd worked with the children at church, Karen had found herself wondering if her time was well spent.

Maybe it's an issue of pride, she reasoned. *With one or two people I can easily see the results of my heartfelt work. With a crowd, I'm less certain. There are more possibilities for distraction.* Yes, she decided, it was pride. Pride kept her closed off from the rest of the world and limited her ability to offer herself freely to God.

Karen peered inside one tent saloon after another as she continued her search but found nothing but darkness. The morning hours brought hangovers and misery from nights spent in revelry and drinking. It seemed a shame that such beauty as was found in Dyea could be so marred by such sinful natures. She could only pray that Jacob hadn't fallen victim to such matters.

"Where can he be, Lord?" she whispered softly. She strained her eyes in the direction of the harbor. "He's just a boy."

Picking her way across the rutted frozen mud, Karen felt her efforts were rather futile. Perhaps Jacob would come back when he was good and ready. But then again, perhaps he would never come back. What was Karen to do or say if Jacob never returned? How could she explain it to his father?

Anger coursed throughout her body. Explain? To Bill Barringer? The man had deserted his children, left them to the care of a virtual stranger, and allowed gold fever to drive him away from his true responsibilities. Why, it would serve him right if she simply packed Jacob and Leah up and headed back to Seattle. Perhaps once she found her father she'd do exactly that.

But even as she considered the possibility, Karen knew she couldn't act on her anger. God had a purpose and plan for her life, and even if she was uncertain of the direction at this point, she couldn't make poor choices simply because others had taken that route.

Giving up for the time, Karen made her way back to the Colton Trading Post. She felt overcome with grief and sniffed back tears. What would become of the boy? If she couldn't find him and talk sense into him, what harm might he make for himself?

In a spirit of defeat, Karen paused at the shop door. She peered up Main Street and then down as if perhaps she'd overlooked something. The town was surprisingly peaceful. Perhaps the bitter cold had caused folks to give up the struggle for gold. Or maybe the fact that Christmas was only a few days away had given the townspeople something else to focus on.

"Kind of cold to be out here just gawking around, isn't it?"

Karen was startled by the appearance of Adrik Ivankov. She'd forgotten what a big man he was. Tall and broad at the shoulders, he looked even more massive in his heavy winter coat and fur cap.

"I was looking for someone," Karen replied, trying not to sound shaken. "Seems to be my lot in life."

"Just so long as you aren't planning on shooting anybody," he said, the twinkle in his eye revealing that he knew about her previous exploits.

"I didn't have it planned today," she replied with a smile. "Maybe I can work it in tomorrow."

He laughed with a deep, rich tone that actually seemed to give off warmth. "Given your nature, it wouldn't surprise me." He smiled and his long, ice-crusted mustache raised up at the corners.

His amusement unnerved her momentarily. "Have you had word from my father?" she questioned.

"No, but I wouldn't give it too much thought," Adrik replied. "Your pa isn't used to having to answer to anyone else. He's probably lost all track of time in helping the sick. You can't be takin' offense that he puts the Lord's work ahead of seeing you."

Karen stiffened. "I wouldn't begin to take offense at my father's work. He has a calling. He knows exactly what the Lord has asked of him—what He wants of my father's life. How could I possibly take umbrage over that?"

"How can you worry and fret about it, either?" Adrik questioned. "After all, if the good Lord called him, won't He see to him as well?"

Karen relaxed and nodded. "Of course, you're right. My nature has always taken a tendency of trying to orchestrate the details." She motioned to the store. "Would you like to come in and warm up? I'm sure there's coffee on the stove and you're more than welcome to take breakfast with us."

"Nah, I have to head up to Sheep Camp."

Karen felt a surge of hope. Perhaps Adrik could find Jacob. "Would you consider doing something for me—I mean while you are on your journey north?"

Adrik grinned. "It's hard to turn down a pretty lady. What'd you have in mind?"

Karen felt her cheeks grow hot at the compliment. "Well . . . that is to say . . ." she stammered, trying to regain her composure. "Mr. Barringer has gone north. He's heading to Dawson City, in fact. He's left his children in my charge, but the oldest has disappeared. Jacob is almost fifteen, and he's very angry that his father has left him behind. I fear he's gone off to find him."

Adrik rubbed his chin. "I'll keep my eyes open, but I only saw the boy once and that was from a distance. Bill pointed him out, and that was kind of the long and the short of it."

"He's just a couple of inches shorter than me, and his hair is kind of a tawny color and straight. He has blue eyes and," she looked upward as if to draw to mind a clearer picture, "and a sweet boyish face." She gazed back to Adrik and shrugged. "I can't really tell you much more."

"You've just described half the boys on the trail and some of the men," Adrik replied, laughing. "But don't worry. If I see anyone slinking along on their own, I'll check it out."

"Thank you, Mr. Ivankov."

"Call me Adrik."

She'd faced these informalities before, but somehow with Adrik, the notion made her feel uncomfortable. "That wouldn't be very proper. We hardly know each other."

Adrik broke into a roguish grin. "I know plenty about you, Miss Pierce. Your pa has a propensity for talk when the fire is burning down and the stars are high."

Karen felt a trembling run through her body. She looked away quickly. "If you see my father, will you please tell him I'm thinking of him? That I love him," she added, self-conscious of the words.

"Only if you call me Adrik," he replied.

She looked up to find him still grinning. As uncomfortable as he'd just made her, Karen couldn't take offense. "Very well, Adrik."

He nodded approvingly. "I'll do it, and if time permits, I'll get word back to you or make sure that your father sends some word to you."

"Thank you. I know I'll rest better just knowing you've taken the matter in hand."

"Always happy to help a lady," he replied with a wink.

————

After an absence of three days, Jacob reappeared. It was Christmas Eve and the spirits of the residents of Dyea were running high. He couldn't help but notice the various ways in which people had tried to liven up things for the holidays. Some had cut paper stars and hung them with ribbon from their windows. Some had decorated little trees with silly things like kitchen utensils and yarn. There might be a gold rush on, but the birth of Christ was still very much on the calendar.

Jacob only wished he had a heart for the celebration. After trying without luck to find his father, he'd found himself face-to-face with Adrik Ivankov. The big, burly man assured him that his father would not be easily found and that the trail was too harsh for one as unprepared as Jacob.

The comment had stung his pride, but Jacob's freezing and starving body refused to allow his emotions any leeway. Agreeing to go back to Dyea, Jacob had happily taken a meal with Adrik. Warming up in a small tentside café, Jacob had lamented his ability to only reach Finigan's Point—not but a few miles up the trail.

"You ever consider that God might not have wanted you coming up this way?" Adrik had asked him. "Maybe there was a reason for you being in Dyea."

"*I thought I could find my pa and talk him into taking me with him,*" Jacob had told the big man. He hadn't added that the pain of being left behind was more than he could bear. That he wanted to confront his father—make him answer for his actions—even fight it out. It just hurt so bad.

Coming to the little store on Main and Sixth Street, Jacob knew he'd have a lot of explaining to do. He didn't like having to answer for his deeds, but he knew Karen Pierce well enough to know that she'd brook no nonsense regarding his disappearance. With a sigh, he pushed open the door, causing bells to rings from overhead. Someone had nailed sleighbells to the top of the frame and they cheerily announced his arrival.

"Jacob!" Karen exclaimed. She rushed forward and embraced him as though he were her own. "I was so worried. Are you all right?" She held him at arm's length and gave him a cursory examination.

"Let's get you warmed up," she said, pulling him with her to the back of the store. "Are you hungry?"

He nodded but said nothing. Karen guided him to a chair at the table and proceeded to bustle around the kitchen preparing him a meal. Jacob was surprised that she asked no questions about his whereabouts or reasons for leaving. She'd likely already figured them out. Or maybe she didn't care where he'd gone or why. Jacob couldn't help but remember his mother telling him a story about the Prodigal Son in the Bible. The boy came home to a celebration. His father didn't care where he'd been or what he'd done, he only cared that the boy had come home. His mother said that God felt that way about His lost children.

"Where is everybody?" Jacob finally asked.

Karen put a bowl of stew down in front of him. "They've gone to a party, believe it or not." She smiled, but Jacob could see her concern for him in her eyes. "I'll get you some bread and something to drink."

Jacob said a quick prayer, a matter of habit that his mother had instilled in him from his very first memories. He had already started to eat when Karen returned with a huge hunk of bread and a steaming mug of coffee. He eyed the coffee for a moment, then looked up at Karen.

"You said coffee was for the grown-ups."

Karen took the chair opposite him and nodded. "I guess being almost fifteen and living through all that you've endured makes you as close to an adult as you need to be for coffee." She smiled. "With everyone else gone, I was hoping you might talk to me."

Jacob looked at her quietly. She was a pretty woman. He'd noticed that right off. She had curly red hair that she liked to braid down her back. Jacob had watched her braid it once or twice and thought it looked like nothing he'd ever seen. She was a kind woman too. Stern and rather determined to have her own way, but for a grown-up lady, Jacob figured she was decent enough.

He focused on the food for a moment, wolfing down a good portion of the stew and bread, before taking time to comment on her suggestion.

"I didn't mean to worry anybody. I just wanted to find my pa."

"I understand. I'd like to find my father as well."

He looked at her and saw a kind of sadness in her eyes. Yes, she knew what it was like. She'd come to Alaska not for gold, but to find her pa.

He tasted the coffee and frowned. It was bitter and hot and not at all pleasing. Karen laughed and pushed forward the sugar bowl.

"You might want to sweeten it a bit. I don't have any cream for it, but there's sugar."

He nodded and added a liberal amount of the sweetener before tasting it again. Finding it more palatable, he looked up and nodded again. "It's better now."

They sat in silence for several more minutes before Karen finally just opened up and put her thoughts out for him to consider.

"Jacob, I know you feel miserable. What your father did was wrong. He should never have brought you and Leah north. He should have made a home for you where it was safe and predictable. But he's a good man and he does love you. If he didn't, he wouldn't have cared what you might have had to face on the trail. I don't want you to hate him for leaving. I'd much prefer, in fact, that you try to understand that he did what he thought was for your best."

"He didn't care what I wanted. What Leah wanted." He kept his words flat and without feeling.

Karen seemed to consider the comment. "No, I suppose he didn't. I'm sure if he'd thought overmuch on anything related to feelings, he'd never have been able to go on his way."

"He ain't been the same since Ma died," Jacob said.

"I don't suppose any of you have been."

Jacob met Karen's eyes and saw the deep sympathy she held for him. He warmed to her kindness and found his hard shell of indifference falling away in bits and pieces. It was just too hard to pretend that he didn't feel anything, especially when it came to his mother.

"I miss her." The words were simple, yet heartfelt. Jacob felt his throat grow tight.

"I miss my mother too," Karen replied. "Having her die was probably the hardest thing I've ever had to deal with."

Jacob nodded. *She understands,* he thought. *She knows how much it hurts and how bad I feel.*

"I came north to find my father," Karen continued, "but I also wanted to see my mother's grave. Somehow, I figured seeing where she was buried would help me to better accept that she's really and truly gone."

"How can you accept something so awful?" The words were barely audible.

Karen leaned back rather casually and looked upward, as if the conversation were nothing of any big importance. "It's always hard to accept bad news. I take comfort in the fact that my mother loved God. She had given her heart and life to God's work, and I know I'll see her again someday—in heaven."

"My ma was a Christian too," Jacob whispered. Tears formed in his eyes, and he got up from the table rather abruptly. Karen stood too, looking as though she might try to stop him if he chose to run. Jacob could no longer stand the guilt and pain of his burden. "She put great store in the Bible and getting saved. She wanted that for all of us, but I couldn't give her the peace she wanted."

"What peace, Jacob?" Karen's voice was soft and soothing. She walked to where he stood and looked at him without any hint of condemnation.

"The peace she would have had if I'd gotten saved before she died," he said, his voice breaking.

Karen wrapped him in her arms and pulled him close. In a motherly fashion she stroked his head and let him cry. He felt miserable and stupid for breaking down. What kind of baby would she think him? He pulled away and struggled to regain control. Embarrassed, he turned away.

"Jacob, you don't have be ashamed. You can talk to me, even cry on my shoulder. We all have to shed a few tears now and then."

"Men don't cry," Jacob said, forcing control over his voice.

"Sure they do. I've seen my father weep buckets of tears over lost souls," Karen replied. She went to Jacob and gently touched his arm. "You don't have to be ashamed. I don't think less of you for your tears. Fact is, I'd think less of you if you were without feeling for the things that matter."

"I wanted to please her. I really did. But I just couldn't make a promise to God."

"Why not? Don't you believe that salvation is necessary? Don't you think you sin just like everybody else?"

"Of course I do," he replied rather indignantly. "I'm a terrible sinner."

"Then why not come clean before God?" she asked.

Jacob tensed. "It's not important." He tried to walk away, but Karen held him fast.

"It's only life and death," Karen said. "Why can't you give your heart to Jesus, Jacob?"

Her calm, loving way was his undoing. Jacob's tears returned in a torrent of emotion. "I'd do it in a minute if it would bring her back. I can't bear that I let her down."

"It's my guess that she was only concerned with seeing you again in heaven."

He nodded. "I know. She said that much. But I'm not a good person, Miss Pierce."

Karen smiled. "None of us are. And why don't you call me Karen. It seems to be the way things are done up here, and I might as well give up the nonsense of formalities, especially when much more important things are at stake." She paused and put her hands on his shoulders. "So why is it that you are so far beyond redeeming?"

"I'm just not good. I make a lot of mistakes."

"So?"

His voice rose in agitation. "I know I'll keep making them."

"So?"

Jacob frowned. "Ma said you weren't to make a pledge to God if you didn't intend to keep it. She said it was foolishness, that the Bible said it was better not to make a promise at all than to make one and not see it through."

Karen smiled and nodded. "That's true, but there's also the matter of your heart, Jacob. Would you willingly go into sin? Would you seek it out—desire it for your life?"

"No," he replied, shaking his head.

"See, God knows we're going to make a mess of things now and then," she continued. "We have a sinful nature, and we need the Holy Spirit to help guide us as we go about our way. We need God to strengthen us because we can't do anything on our own."

"But if I give my heart to God and break my promise, won't He hate me— condemn me?"

"God knows your weaknesses, Jacob. He knows exactly where you'll be tempted and where you won't. Besides, the promise is on God's part—not yours. Your part of the promise is to accept His free gift of salvation with a repentant heart. His part of the promise is Jesus."

Jacob had never heard salvation explained in such a manner. He felt a surge of hope. "And even if I mess up, God will still know that I'm trying—that I want to be good and do right?"

Karen smiled, and the look on her face reassured him more than her words. "He's already seen the future. Remember, Jesus died for you every bit as much as He died for His disciples and friends. He knew you—Jacob Barringer—would need a Savior. He knew all your sins and the things you'd do wrong. He knew the things that would come out of your mouth and the things you'd harbor in your heart. And He still went to the cross because He didn't want to lose you, Jacob. He's just waiting for you to come home—to see how much He loves you."

Jacob's eyes flooded with tears, and he couldn't even see Karen for the blur they created. His heart felt lighter than it had since his mother had first talked to him about salvation.

"*Jesus loves you. He loves you and He already knows your heart,*" Jacob's mother had said not long before her death. "*You can't keep anything from Him.*" Her words had been so tender—so gentle. They were given out of love and a desire to show her child the truth.

For some reason the memory eased the aching in Jacob's heart. "I'm just afraid of letting Him down," he finally whispered. "I'm not good at keeping promises."

Karen hugged Jacob tightly. "Maybe not, but He is."

Jacob allowed himself to rest in Karen's arms. She reminded him so much of his mother. Even the way she held him was similar. How he wished he'd allowed his mother to hug him more often. He'd always worried about what his friends might think or say. He'd told his mother he was too big for such silliness.

I'm not too big, Ma, he thought, wishing with all his heart that she might hear and know his love for her. *I'm not too big for you to love.*

He pulled away and looked at Karen quite seriously. "Do you suppose if I take Jesus as my Lord, that my ma will see and know?"

"The Bible says that all of heaven rejoices when a lost sinner gets saved," Karen replied. "I would imagine she'll be sharing that happiness right along with the rest of heaven."

"Will you tell me what to do—what to say?"

Karen nodded, and holding on to his hand, she knelt on the floor. Looking up at him, she smiled. "I've found that it's best to start from the bottom and work our way up."

PETER FELT A MOMENTARY REPRIEVE in his worries over Grace when his father announced that Martin Paxton had lost all his hirelings to the gold rush. The man was positively livid and made no secret of that fact when discussing his plans to find Grace. Ephraim had tried to console his friend, reminding him that short of catching a boat south or going north over the passes, there were only a few places Grace would most likely be found. And with winter setting in, only the hardiest souls would even consider heading into the wilderness. Paxton had been unconvinced, however.

Peter still couldn't believe that Martin Paxton was the nightmare Grace had been running from. For all his desire to dislike the man, he was practically a hero to Peter's father. And so far in their business discussions and encounters, Peter had only the highest respect for the man. It all seemed very puzzling.

Knowing that Grace was betrothed to his father's dear friend troubled Peter, leaving little room for any other thought. He'd not even been able to think of leaving Skagway for fear that Paxton would catch wind of Grace's presence in Dyea and then take it upon himself to investigate the matter. Peter felt he couldn't leave without talking with Grace and knowing the truth, and yet the idea of knowing the truth of this situation was almost more troubling.

"Peter, what's wrong with you?" Miranda asked. "It's Christmas and you haven't been yourself all day. Are you ill?"

Peter smiled at his sister. She had dressed in the merriest of holiday colors with a smart-looking green-and-red plaid skirt and a high-collared white blouse.

A wide black belt encircled her tiny waist and black patent leather boots peeked out from beneath her hem.

"I don't mean to spoil the festivities," he said as she came to sit beside him. "I suppose my mind is on other things."

She reached out and took his hand. "Such as?"

He looked at her for a moment. *I can trust her more than anyone,* he thought. *I can tell her everything and perhaps even enlist her help.* A plan began to form in the back of his mind.

"Do you remember Mr. Paxton speaking about his fiancée?"

She nodded. "Of course. He's talked about her off and on since boarding *Summer Song.* What of it?"

Peter looked around as if to make certain no one would overhear him. Knowing that Paxton and his parents had gone out to a party where they would meet with potential investors, Peter relaxed a bit. "I know who Mr. Paxton is looking for."

"What do you mean?"

"I know this woman, Grace Hawkins."

"That's wonderful!" Miranda declared. "Mr. Paxton will be so pleased."

"I don't plan to tell him," Peter said flatly. He looked to Miranda to see what her reaction might be. "At least not yet."

"But why not? He's come so far to find her."

"The trouble is," Peter replied, "she doesn't want to be found."

"I don't understand."

"I know," he said, reaching out to pat her hand. "But I want to explain it to you, and then I'd like to have your help."

"You know I'd do anything for you," she said softly.

"I believe Mr. Paxton may not be exactly as he appears. We've so long known him as our father's friend that we've never questioned what he might truly be about. We know nothing of him, except his kindness to Father."

"That's true," Miranda said, nodding.

"I met Miss Hawkins on the trip to Skagway some months ago. She was terribly distressed and told me of her father seeking to force her hand in marriage. She told me the man was a horrible monster who had been violent with her and that she had run away from her father's demands and this man's cruelty."

"Mr. Paxton?" Miranda questioned, eyes wide.

"One and the same," Peter replied. "I realize I know very little of Grace Hawkins. She could have been lying to me, but I fail to see what purpose it would have served. She had no reason to tell me such tales. I merely came upon her feeling frightened and tearful and the story poured out in a most honest manner."

"But if she's not lying, then Mr. Paxton is ..." Her words faded as she met Peter's eyes. "What are we to do?"

"I've deliberated that for days. I don't wish to anger Paxton or hurt Father by keeping this from them, but I feel I must protect Miss Hawkins. She's younger than you and very quiet and sweet-tempered."

"She sounds very special." She paused, then asked, "Could it be that you've grown an attachment for her?"

Peter smiled. "You are wise beyond your years. I suppose I can confide in you."

"You know I would never breathe a word of it or anything else. You can trust this matter to remain between you and me," Miranda assured him.

"We must seek to better understand Mr. Paxton. Perhaps I've misjudged the situation, and my feelings for Miss Hawkins have caused me to see things as less than clear."

"What can we do?"

"I propose to have you bring up the topic of Miss Hawkins. Perhaps he will discuss his feelings on her and the upcoming marriage. Seek to learn if he truly loves her or if, as Grace says, this was merely a business arrangement."

"Even if it were," Miranda replied, "I would have thought you to support such matters. You've often said that women are poor judges of such things—that our hearts often cloud our thinking and reasoning."

Peter frowned. He had said all of that. He had told her on many occasions that she was far too emotional in her thinking to make a sound, reasonable judgment in matters of matrimony and her future.

"I know what I've said in the past," Peter began, "but I would never subject anyone, man or woman, to a cruel master. Paxton should have nothing to hide in discussing the matter with you. It will appear innocent enough, and there should be no reason to conceal his heart."

"If he will discuss the situation at all," Miranda replied.

"I've no reason to believe he wouldn't. In a quiet, non-threatening setting such as this, Mr. Paxton would have little to concern himself over. He will simply see you as curious—perhaps even caring. When Mother and Father return, I shall take them aside for a private chat. Perhaps then you could have Mr. Paxton's attention." Just then they heard a commotion coming from the stairs. "They're back. Just try to think of any way in which you can get him to talk about Grace and how he truly feels about their union," Peter said, getting up rather abruptly.

Miranda nodded. "I'll do what I can."

Peter met his parents as they topped the landing, with Martin Paxton right behind them. "I wonder if I might steal my parents away from you for a moment," he said, smiling at Paxton.

Cold green eyes met his gaze as Paxton nodded. "By all means. After all, it is Christmas and we've hardly made merry together. Perhaps you had something in mind for a celebration?"

Peter shook his head. "I hadn't given it serious thought, but perhaps as we discuss other matters, we can consider that as well." He looked to Miranda and smiled. "We'll just be a minute, and then maybe we can all go out for a celebration dinner. That is, unless everyone has closed shop for the day."

Peter's parents looked at each other and then to Peter. "Would you mind accompanying me back downstairs?" he asked them.

"Of course not, but what's this about?" Ephraim questioned.

"We can discuss it in private," Peter replied, casting one quick glance over his shoulder at Miranda. "It won't take long."

Miranda studied the handsome man as he crossed the room and poured himself a generous glass of whiskey. Paxton held up the bottle, almost as an afterthought.

"Would you care for some?"

"No, thank you. I don't imbibe in spirits."

He nodded, then replaced the stopper in the bottle. "So what do you think of the frozen north? Are you ready for the warmth of your home?"

"San Francisco is a lovely place to live," she replied, trying desperately to think of how she might turn the subject to Paxton's fiancée. "Perhaps you might consider living there after you marry. My father would be pleased to have you so near."

Paxton shook his head. "I'd say there's little chance of that."

"Oh. I . . . uh . . . suppose your fiancée wouldn't care for the climate?" Miranda asked hesitantly.

"I have no idea. I do, however, have a home in Erie," Paxton replied. He took a seat opposite her and cocked his head to one side. "Why is it that a woman as lovely as yourself has not already taken a husband?"

Miranda felt her entire body grow warm. She was certain to be blushing and looked quickly at her hands. "I suppose because the proper mate has not yet come along. Peter and my father are very good to look out for me. They've not yet approved of a suitor."

"Spoken like a proper young woman of breeding," Paxton replied. "There are far too few of your kind."

"How so?"

"Women today are not at all inclined to do as they are told. Most want to marry for love—if they marry at all. This push for women's rights has become a most annoying affair. They don't seem to be able to make up their minds even among themselves. They want equal rights with men—the vote, positions in the government—including a woman president. As if that would ever be possible."

"I have never desired such things," Miranda admitted. "But I do desire love. Would you not desire love as well?" Miranda questioned, daring to raise her face to his.

He eyed her intently, almost hungrily. She felt unnerved by his sudden interest. "Desire and love," he said softly, "are often absent in a marriage. However, were you to be a part of the union, I've no doubt both would play an important role."

She felt her breath quicken. My, but he was charming. His soft, smooth voice caused her skin to prickle. "How fortunate you are," she began uneasily, "to have found those things for yourself. I'm sure your Miss Hawkins is a most honored woman."

"She is a spoiled brat," he said, tossing back the drink and breaking the spell. "Ours is an arranged marriage. Nothing more."

"You don't love her?"

He laughed and got up to pour himself another glass. "As I said, she is a spoiled child. It is hard to love someone so willful and misguided. She has no idea of how to be pleasing or properly behaved. But I'll see that taken in hand."

Miranda felt her heart racing again, but this time it was for an entirely different reason. Paxton's cruel edge seemed quite apparent as he picked up his glass and stared at her from across the room.

"Marriage is all about business, Miss Colton. I would, however, dare to say that marriage to one such as yourself might well be the exception. Business and love could no doubt be had in one union."

"Pity you are already engaged," Peter said, coming through the door.

Miranda felt a wave of relief at the sight of such support.

Paxton laughed. "Nothing lasts forever."

"Do you really believe that marriage is nothing more than business? I mean, of course, on the whole."

Paxton shrugged and reclaimed his chair. "I believe simpleminded ninnies marry on a daily basis because they cannot control their emotions or bodily urges. I believe sound-minded people consider a broader base. They look to the future and how they might benefit financially and physically by joining their lot with that of another person. It's no different than what you observe in monarchies, where brides are chosen for reasons of making treaties and pacts with other countries."

Peter look rather ashen-faced, and Miranda couldn't help but wonder if he agreed with Paxton. After all, she'd heard some of the same philosophy from her older brother on more than one occasion. In fact, Martin Paxton's views were essentially similar. Only coming from Peter they had never seemed cruel.

She looked at her brother intently, and when he turned his head to meet her gaze, Miranda felt an awakening in her soul. Perhaps a spirit of familiarity was all that separated Peter from Martin Paxton. Perhaps a kinder upbringing would have made Paxton more like her brother. The contrasts and similarities were startling.

"But it is all of little concern," Paxton replied, nursing his drink rather thoughtfully. "I cannot have a wedding without a bride. Miss Hawkins has been remiss in explaining her whereabouts, but I've hired a new group of men. Men to whom I am paying such an outrageous amount, they wouldn't dare desert me for the Yukon."

Miranda saw the flash of panic in her brother's eyes and hoped he would conceal it before turning back to face Paxton. She needn't have worried, however. Appearing as unconcerned with the matter as if Paxton had been discussing the price of fish, Peter merely shrugged.

"The lure of gold makes men do strange things."

Paxton laughed. "The lure of many things can drive a man to do what he might never have considered before. Even murder seems quite reasonable when one's own life or livelihood is threatened."

Miranda felt her blood run cold. What was he implying? Could he possibly mean to murder Miss Hawkins? Was that why he had followed her here to the Yukon? Was that why he spoke of nothing lasting forever? She shivered, feeling his gaze upon her. What if her father had chosen him for her? Might she have done the same thing that Grace Hawkins did?

—{ C H A P T E R   T W E N T Y - S E V E N }—

PETER PACED UP AND DOWN the street in front of the Colton Trading Post. The trip from Skagway to Dyea had seemed neverending. He thought only of Grace and the need to protect her, but upon arrival found her to be gone from the store. In fact, the place was locked up tight and there was no sign of the women or even the Barringer children. He rationalized that with it being Christmas evening they might have gone to a party or even to church. He shivered against the cold and wondered silently what he should do. It seemed silly that the store was his own property and yet he had no key with which to let himself in from the elements.

He heard laughter and singing coming from down the street. Perhaps he would find Grace there. He made his way in long, rhythmic strides, forcing his mind to not deliberate unnecessarily on the situation at hand. He was determined that Paxton's plans could not be allowed. Peter didn't know how he would yet stop the man, but he couldn't see such a loveless arrangement for Grace. Not when he desired to offer her so much.

He peered inside a tent marked *Coffee and Donuts* and searched the crowd for any sign of the women. It seemed the entire town was caught up in something. Laughter poured from the tent as the group broke into a hearty chorus of "Deck the Halls." A woman dressed in a flashy shade of gold and orange plopped herself down on the lap of a miner and began to play with his beard, while another woman, much younger than the first, watched Peter from several feet away. Her eyes gave a pleading, almost desperate look as she smiled and curved her shoulders forward to give herself a bit of cleavage. It was definitely not the kind of place Grace would visit.

Backing out of the tent, Peter looked frantically up and down the street. The light was fading fast and with a heavy overcast threatening snow, it would be pitch black before another half hour passed. Where could Grace be? Had Paxton's men somehow found her?

Don't let your imagination get carried away, he chided. *Grace is fine. She's no doubt with Miss Pierce and her aunt. Paxton has no way of knowing that she's here.* But even as he gave birth to this thought, another more imposing one filled his mind. Ever since Karen Pierce's shooting incident, the women had gained a bit of a reputation. Perhaps Paxton had caught wind of this. Even so, Peter reasoned, the reputations and descriptions were nothing like the real women. It was even said that their numbers were ten or more, not merely three. One rumor said they were a tribe of natives who had banded together to fight off the imposition of the gold rusher. Another bit of gossip suggested that while beautiful, they were really servants of the devil and any man who looked into their eyes would lose their soul. It might have been comical if Peter hadn't felt so weighed down with worry for Grace's safety.

He walked back to the store contemplating what he should do. He had just decided to check the windows in case any were unlocked, when he heard the unmistakable sound of Leah Barringer's animated chatter.

"I love singing songs about Jesus' birth," she was saying.

Peter watched and waited as they rounded the corner of the building before hurrying forward to greet them. "Merry Christmas!" he declared.

"Oh, Captain Colton," Doris replied, "a most merry Christmas to you."

Karen and Leah were arm in arm, with Jacob walking in close step behind them. Grace walked alongside Jacob and smiled up warmly.

"We're just returning from church. Pity you could not have come earlier, then you might have joined us," Grace said.

Peter nodded but had no desire to explain that while he was happy to make merry on the holiday, religious nonsense had never really accompanied the celebration. His family recognized the birth of Christ, knew the stories of Bethlehem and the wise men, but other than counting these as stories from long ago, they'd never given them much thought.

"You will stay for supper—perhaps even the night, won't you?" Doris questioned as Karen unlocked the front door of the store.

Peter wondered if his absence back in Skagway would be questioned. "I will stay for supper, but perhaps it would be less than appropriate for me to stay the night."

"Nonsense. As we've said before, there's plenty of room and it is your property," Doris replied. "Leah can sleep with us, and you and Jacob can share the other room. There's no room for the same proprieties up here as we clung to in Chicago. Why, we had one woman come into the store the other day telling us how she was saved from death on the trail when two complete strangers put her in a bedroll between them. Scandalous stuff for our civilized world, but not for the likes of Alaska."

Peter considered the idea for a moment, then allowed his eyes to travel the length of Grace's hourglass figure as she took off her coat. She wore a trim little gown of blue wool and black braid trim. A delicate white lace collar edged the high neck of the bodice, and blue ribbons were woven throughout her brown hair. She caught his expression and blushed. No doubt she could read his desire merely by looking into his eyes.

"Be that as it may, I'll just stay for supper," Peter said uncomfortably.

They spent a leisurely time over a most unusual Christmas dinner. Smoked salmon trimmed with a berry sauce made up the main course. Peter marveled at the flavor and complimented the women for their efforts. His favorite had been a concoction of rice and beans flavored with spices that nipped at his tongue. It wasn't at all an expected cuisine for the far north.

"I learned to make that dish in Louisiana," Doris told him as he ate a second portion. "The recipe was given to me by a Cajun woman who taught me a thing or two about cooking, while I taught her to read."

"It's marvelous," he replied. "Such a welcome change from pork and beans or dried cabbage soup."

"Even the eggs are dry up here," Leah replied. "I'd never seen dried eggs before coming up here."

Jacob nodded. "Guess we've seen a lot of things up here we've never seen elsewhere. Never had to worry with Indians in Colorado. They'd all been moved out by the time we got there."

"You don't have to worry about them at all," Karen replied. "The natives here are friendly and helpful."

"But they do look kind of mean," Leah threw in.

"You shouldn't judge people by their looks. A person can look harmless and beautiful and be deadly. Just as a person can appear unseemly and be good. Anyway, the Russians were dealing with the Tlingit for a long while before Americans started coming up here. Many of them can speak Russian and English. It's amazing, especially when you consider that most people consider the natives to be ignorant heathens. My father and mother often wrote of their generosity. A good many were even receptive to the Bible being preached. The Russians made many converts, and now the American missionaries are doing likewise."

Peter said nothing. He concentrated on the food and tried to figure out how he was going to convince Grace to come back to San Francisco with him. He'd already decided it would be to her benefit if she left the area altogether. He thought he might convince Miranda to join him and act as chaperone for Grace. He didn't want anyone getting the wrong idea, and Miranda's presence would surely put an end to any gossip.

Of course, if Martin Paxton caught wind of it, the matter might not weigh well for Peter's father. That troubled Peter only momentarily, however. Paxton would have no way of knowing of Grace's departure. *Not if they did it right. Let the man search for her and believe her to have gone farther north. Let him assume she had tired of the cold as winter came on the area and had left for warmer climates.* He didn't care what Paxton thought. He only knew a fierce desire to protect Grace at all costs.

"Captain, would you care for dessert?" Grace asked him softly. She smiled warmly and extended him a piece of cake.

"This is indeed a party," he declared, eyeing the treat with great interest. He hadn't had a decent piece of cake in a long while.

"Well, it is Jesus' birthday," Leah offered.

Again Peter said nothing. He wasn't inclined to wax theological with a child, and no one else appeared concerned with the matter. He returned his thoughts to Grace and how Paxton had talked so harshly about marriage.

Peter watched her from the corner of his eye. She was so graceful and even-mannered. Even when Jacob dropped his cake, making a big mess on the floor, Grace only laughed it off and handed him another piece.

"Why don't you and Leah take your cake over by the stove," Grace suggested as she knelt to clean up the cake. "You can play checkers while you eat and give us a little time to talk to Captain Colton about his departure."

"Talk business on Christmas Day?" Doris questioned.

Grace laughed. Her brown eyes seemed to twinkle. "No, Aunt Doris, I wouldn't consider it. I merely thought to find out when the captain intends to return to Seattle. I had hoped to send a Christmas letter to my mother. I'm hoping she'll be back home in Chicago by now. I know she told me not to write to her just yet, but I figured that if we pass the letter through Karen's sister and tell nothing of our whereabouts, then even if someone should intercept the letter, it won't give away our location."

Peter nearly choked on his cake. He coughed for a moment, gratefully accepting a glass of water from Grace.

"Are you quite all right, Captain?" she asked softly. Her hand touched his as she took back the glass.

"I'm fine," he replied. He cleared his throat. "I would like an opportunity to talk with you alone. Perhaps later." Grace nodded, and Peter turned his attention back to the other ladies. "The youngsters have certainly thrived under your care and attention. They look healthy and well-adjusted to the harsh conditions here."

Karen nodded. "We've had our moments." She lowered her voice. "It hasn't been easy, especially with their father leaving them."

"Leaving them?" Peter questioned. "You mean while he works?"

Karen sighed and shook her head. "No, he's gone north. Gold fever got the best of him and once he collected enough to put himself in good standing with the officials at the border, he took his leave."

"And deserted them?" Peter asked, looking past Karen to where Jacob laughed at his sister's antics as she set up the checkerboard.

"Mr. Barringer stated in his letter that he intends to come back for them," Grace offered, pouring Peter a cup of coffee. "But we wonder if that will truly happen. The children have been very upset."

"Yes, but I think making peace with God has helped Jacob to make peace with his father's actions," Karen said, stacking several of the dishes to make more room on the table.

Peter thought of the things Grace had said to him in the past. Such talk of God and of making peace with Him and celebrating His birth were fairly foreign to Peter. He'd gone to church long ago as a child, but for as long as he'd been able to work aboard a ship, he'd been away from religious gatherings.

Without thinking, Peter asked, "What did he do to make peace with God?"

Karen smiled. "What does anyone do to make peace with the Almighty? He accepted that he was a lost soul without Jesus and repented of his sins."

"And that made him feel better?" Peter questioned. "Seeing how bad a person he was in the eyes of God gave way to making peace in his soul?"

"But of course it did," Grace said, sitting down beside Peter. "Has no one ever shared with you the forgiveness and love of God, Captain?"

"I know God to be judge over all," Peter admitted. "I believe Him to have set things in motion, perhaps even nudged them in a particular direction, but I don't concern myself with the extremes of such things as love and joy. Emotions seldom result in reasonable decisions." Even as he said the words he thought of his own emotional heart. He thought of the way Grace made his blood run hot and his heart pound with a maddening beat. Just sitting near her made him both uneasy and elated. Then his mind went back to the conversation he'd overheard between his sister and Paxton. A sinking feeling washed over him. *I sound just like that man.*

"What of truth, Captain?"

"Please," he said, looking to each woman. "We needn't argue."

"Who's arguing?" Karen questioned. "Does talk of God and spiritual matters make you so uneasy that you instantly give it over to argument?"

Peter pushed back from the table and shook his head. "No. It's not that. I merely meant to say that it seems a very weighty subject for such a festive occasion."

"But Jesus Christ is the reason for this festive holiday," Karen countered. "I wouldn't think it a bit out of place to discuss the need and purpose of God's direction in our lives."

Peter reminded himself that his real need was to discuss Grace's circumstances and Martin Paxton's arrival in Skagway. Not feeling he could wait any longer, he said, "I really should be heading back. Supper was very good. If you ladies give up the mercantile business, you could easily open a restaurant." He stood, hoping that Grace would take the opportunity to speak with him alone.

"I'll walk you out, Captain," she said, smiling shyly.

"Don't forget your coat, Grace," Doris called.

Grace looked up at Peter and smiled. "I won't forget."

Peter lost himself in warm chocolate brown eyes. Indeed, she would need no coat if only he had the right to hold her in his arms.

They made their way outside and Peter was relieved to find the wind had died down. The cold was more bearable and the night skies overhead were clearing out to allow just a bit of moonlight. Perhaps it wouldn't snow, after all.

"What did you wish to tell me, Captain?"

Peter fought the urge to pull her into his arms. "Something's come up. I felt it was important to come see you myself."

Grace smiled. "I'm glad you did."

He sensed her approval and pleasure in his singling her out for a private moment. She showed no sign of fearing his company. She certainly bore no hint of the terror she'd felt for Paxton. He could still remember the look in her eyes as she conveyed her feelings toward the man who was to be her husband.

"Will you be leaving tomorrow?" Grace asked.

Peter nodded. "That's part of what I wanted to talk to you about." Just being this near to Grace caused him to consider running away with her. He could imagine their making their way under cover of darkness. He could see himself fighting Paxton to the death for her honor.

No longer thinking of the information he needed to relay, Peter pulled Grace into his arms. She didn't resist, and in feeling her yield to his touch, Peter tilted her head to meet his ardent kiss. He touched her lips gently at first, then more insistently. He held her tightly and although he felt her momentarily melt against him, he could also sense her tensing—pushing away.

He knew he had to let her go, but it was the last thing he desired to do. Loosening his hold, he allowed Grace to slip from his arms.

"Captain Colton! That's quite uncalled for!" She raised her hand as if to slap him, then halted in midair. Her expression softened as she lowered her arm. "The holiday spirit has made you forget yourself. I shall not be cross about it—however, you must promise to never take such liberties again!"

She left him standing in the street without any hope of explanation. Peter felt the urge to go after her but held himself in check. He had frightened her. He had treated her no better than Paxton had. Growling in disgust, Peter pulled down his cap and headed out in search of a place to spend the night. He had no desire to return to Skagway, and fear for Grace told him he'd be better off to stay close by.

"I'll tell her the truth tomorrow," he promised himself. "I'll tell her I know all about Martin Paxton and that he has come to take her back."

GRACE SCARCELY SLEPT a wink all night. Touching her lips, she kept remembering what it felt like to be kissed by Peter Colton. Her heart pounded at the memory of the experience. She had lost all reasoning in that fleeting moment—that moment when she'd known without any further doubt that she belonged to this man, heart and soul.

How was it that two men could be so different? Peter's kiss had filled her with wonder and anticipation. It was the complete opposite of the horrible treatment she'd received from Martin Paxton.

Comparing the two men made her remember the past and in the darkness of the night, she worried terribly about her mother and father. What if Paxton hadn't left them alone as they had hoped he might after Grace's departure? What if he were punishing them for Grace's actions?

She knew things couldn't be right because of her mother's last letter. The tone had been so bleak, but worse yet were the things her mother hadn't said. Reading between the lines, it was easy to see that their problems were far from over. Grace realized that as much as she loved this wild land, she wanted to go home. She wanted to see for herself that her family was safe—that Paxton hadn't hurt them in her absence. Yet she knew she'd come this far and must stay in order to see it through; otherwise everything they'd done would be for naught.

There was also another matter. Peter Colton had created a complication she'd not planned on. She hugged her arms to her body and remembered his embrace—so strong and warm. She thought of the look in his eyes, the desire and passion that she recognized when he'd touched her. She felt the same desire. Had he known?

Grace was embarrassed for how she'd reacted to his kiss. *I should never have been so harsh, especially when I wanted the kiss as much as he did.* She rolled uncomfortably to her side. The cot was a most unbearable companion and did little to afford her any real consolation.

By the time she fell asleep it was quite late. Her dreams were haunted with visions of Paxton and Peter Colton. Always she was caught between the two men and always Paxton's cruelty won over.

She awoke in a cold sweat. A dim light shown under the closed door and glancing at the empty cots, Grace realized both Doris and Karen were already up and about their business. She yawned and stretched. Her muscles ached terribly.

"Oh, I'm already old at twenty." A thought came to mind. "I'm soon to be twenty-one."

Sitting up, Grace remembered her birthday was in a few short days. She hadn't even considered this matter since coming north. On the thirty-first she would be twenty-one. Her father could no longer assert his authority in a legal manner, and therefore Paxton would no longer be a threat. The thought gave her a moment of excitement. Perhaps she could go home.

Thinking of home, however, caused her to wonder what she would find there. Had her parents been forced to sell off all of their possessions? Had they been forced to sell the house itself? She'd not considered this before. Perhaps that was why her mother had told her not to write to the Chicago address. Perhaps Paxton now owned the house and her parents were left to find a new place to live.

"Perhaps I could go to Seattle and stay with Karen's sister until I locate Mother and Father," she said softly. Even if they'd lost the house, they could start again. They were a family, after all. Perhaps she could even convince them to come north. Martin Paxton would never think to look for any of them in Alaska.

Besides, once she was twenty-one, Paxton would have no reasonable hold on her. The fact that she might have once married the man simply to keep her father in good standing was no longer a worry to her. If Paxton had carried his threats through as her mother had implied, there was probably nothing to worry about anymore. Everything he could have done to hurt them, he would have already done.

The idea gave her a new energy. Perhaps she could talk to Peter about allowing her passage to Seattle. Her cheeks heated up at the thought of Peter.

I love him, she thought. *I love him so much that I could have forgotten myself when he kissed me. Oh, God,* she prayed, *what shall I do? He's not a man who seeks after you.* She knew well enough from years of hearing Karen speak on the delicate matter of marriage that the best ones were made of like-minded people. She and

Peter were not like-minded. At least not in spiritual matters.

The idea of losing Peter before she really even had him caused a dull ache in her heart. *But I love him, Lord. I love him so and can't imagine my life without him.* The strength of her emotions was a surprise, even to Grace. *I live for his return each time he goes away. How can I leave Alaska and venture away never again to see him?*

But what if he changed? She considered the idea for a moment. Surely she could help him to see the truth. Perhaps that's why they'd been allowed to come together. Karen always said that nothing happened by chance. Everything is carefully ordered by God. *That would have to include my falling in love with Peter.* She smiled and felt a warmth of hope, whispering, "I could lead him to God. I could help him to see the truth, and then we wouldn't be unequal in our thinking."

"Oh, good, you're up," Karen announced as she opened the door and spied Grace. "I thought perhaps you were sick, then I thought I heard voices."

"I was just talking to myself," Grace said, smiling. "I'm sorry to have left the morning chores to you."

"It's of no matter. Look, Peter has come back and said it's imperative that we join him for a discussion. He says it's quite serious and that he should have told us about it last night, but he didn't have a chance."

Grace felt her heart begin to race. "I'll get properly dressed and be out in a moment."

She hurried to pull on her brown corduroy skirt and yellow blouse. The lower neckline of the blouse was better suited to summer, so Grace drew a woolen shawl around her shoulders and fastened it together with a topaz brooch her mother had given her.

The children were just sitting down to breakfast when Grace emerged from the bedroom. She finished tying a brown ribbon to the bottom of her single braid and looked up to catch Peter watching her. She could feel the heat of his stare. *Goodness,* she thought, *he doesn't even make a pretense of looking away.* She looked to Karen and forced a smile of ease, even though her hands were shaking.

"Captain Colton suggests we talk in the other room," Karen explained, heading toward the door to the store.

Peter stood just to one side of the portal and nodded. "The privacy is necessary," he assured.

Grace nodded, having no idea why he should appear so serious. He had mentioned needing to talk to them of his departure. Surely that couldn't be such a grave matter.

She followed Karen into the front area of the store, stepping out from behind the counter in order to distance herself from Peter. It was of no use, however. He simply followed to where she stood and fixed his stare on her face.

"This news will come as a surprise," he said, pausing to wait for Doris to join them. The older woman closed the door to the living quarters and positioned herself beside Karen.

"What is this about, Captain Colton?" Doris questioned.

Grace looked at Karen, who remained somber-faced. She merely shrugged as if to say she was as confused as Grace about the urgency of the situation.

The sleigh bells over the front door jingled as two broad-shouldered men entered one after the other.

"I'm sorry, but we've not yet opened for business," Karen told them.

The first man held the door while his companion moved to one side to admit yet a third man. Grace felt the blood drain from her head as she met the smug expression of Martin Paxton.

"Good morning, my dear," he said, not even having the decency to call her Miss Hawkins. "It would seem you're a bit remiss in remembering dates of importance. I've come to remind you that you missed our wedding day. It was good of Captain Colton to find you so that we might correct the matter."

Grace looked to Peter who was already shaking his head. "No, Grace," he whispered.

"You?" she could barely speak. He knew how terrified she was of this man. How could Peter have brought him to her doorstep?

"Grace, don't listen to him," Peter begged. "Listen to me. . . ."

But hearing him was impossible as the room went black and she fainted dead away.

Peter caught Grace as her knees gave way. Pulling her into his arms, he easily lifted her and held her tight.

"How could you?" Karen declared, accusing Peter.

"I didn't," he growled out. "This is what I came to tell you."

"Of course," she said snidely. "How dim-witted do you suppose us to be?"

"I suppose you all to be very dim-witted," Paxton declared, pulling off gray gloves. "Did you truly think to defy me? I've met over lunch with men more powerful than you could ever imagine, only to drive them to their knees before supper. Surely you didn't believe yourself a match for me."

He sneered at Karen as he sized her up. Doris stepped closer in an attempt to offer Karen protection. As if the women no longer concerned him, Paxton turned to Peter. "Your father will be proud of you, Captain. We were just discussing you over breakfast and I told him I could see that you were a man of action."

"Not any action that will lend itself to you marrying Miss Hawkins," Peter replied. "I came here to warn her, not to serve your purposes."

"Do say! With the interest you took in my plans for marriage, I would have thought you to feel otherwise. Well, it really doesn't matter, does it?" Paxton replied.

"I believe it does. Miss Hawkins told me of your cruelty to her. I could scarcely believe it when I learned you were the same man my father so highly esteemed. Nevertheless, as I listened to you discuss the matter of marriage with my sister, I realized that Grace had to be telling the truth about you."

"Grace, is it? I suppose you've taken quite a fancy to my bride." He raised his brow and slapped his gloves into his hat and handed it to the man on his left. "I do hope you haven't ruined her for me."

"Why you—" Peter started to charge forward, but with Grace in his arms, it would have been impossible to fight. The two men on either side of Paxton closed ranks at the perceived threat.

Karen rushed forward to take hold of Grace. "Give her to me," she told Peter. "You've done this to her. You've ruined her life by bringing this monster here."

Peter turned to Karen. "No. I didn't. I came to warn her. I came to take her away."

"That won't be necessary. I have plans for her." All eyes turned to Paxton as he added, "Long-overdue plans."

"I won't allow it," Peter replied. Grace stirred in his arms, moaning softly as she struggled to regain consciousness.

"You have no choice," Paxton stated without emotion. He pulled a folded paper from his pocket. "Grace is my ward. She is not yet twenty-one, and you'll find here that I have guardianship of her and her father's blessing for marriage."

Grace rallied about this time and looked up at Peter with a hazy expression that suggested she'd forgotten the circumstance that had put her in his arms.

"What? Why are you ..." She looked over her shoulder at Karen and then seemed to remember all at once.

"Put me down," she said, barely whispering.

Peter did as she said but held on to her arm. "Are you certain you can stand?"

She looked at him, as though uncertain whose side he was on. "Did you bring him here?"

"No. I promise you, I didn't. He's a friend of my father's and arrived in Skagway on *Summer Song*. I found out he was the man you had run away from when he told us of how he'd come to find his fiancée."

Paxton interrupted. "This is all rather boring to me. I have other things to see to."

"Then why don't you leave," Karen more demanded than questioned.

"Yes, go," Doris added.

"I have come for my bride. She is my legal charge."

"I'll be twenty-one in five days," she said, looking up to meet Paxton's eyes.

"That might be. However, you'll be my wife before the day is out," he replied.

"Never!" Grace declared with surprising strength. "I will not marry you. You have no say over me now."

"I have every say. Your father gave me the legal guardianship of you before he died."

Grace blanched and leaned heavily into Peter's side as though she might faint again. "My father . . . is dead?"

Paxton cocked his head to one side and appeared thoughtful. "Oh, that's right. You probably hadn't heard. Since you ran away and left your family, you weren't there when he grew ill."

"What of my mother? Have you killed her too?"

"Tsk, tsk," he replied, smiling. "I've killed no one—yet. Although watching the way in which Captain Colton handles you makes me wonder if there might not be a reason to consider such things."

"Your papers and pretense of law won't wash, up here, Paxton. Grace is not obligated to you in any way."

"Even if those papers are real," Karen added, "which I highly suspect they are not."

"Well, it really doesn't matter what you think, Miss Pierce. I've no doubt you've played an ample role in depriving me of my wife. But that is about to end. Mr. Roberts and Mr. Tavis here are going to watch over my little bride while I go finish up the arrangements for our marriage. The wedding is to take place at two o'clock in Skagway." He turned to first one man and then the other. "See that she is there well in advance." They nodded.

"I won't allow this mockery to take place," Peter declared. Grace was clinging to him like a drowning woman and he felt empowered by her action. No matter what she thought of him, she clearly felt safer with him than with Paxton.

"You had better reconsider your part in this, Captain. I have a new agreement with your father that extends to most all of his holdings. Holdings that I believe you have some part in. Should you insist on interfering in a matter that is clearly none of your concern, I will be forced to deal rather harshly with you."

"I know all about your new dealings," Peter countered. "I saw the contracts prior to leaving San Francisco."

Paxton smiled. "I said that I have a new agreement."

Peter tightened his grip on Grace. What had his father done now? He forced his voice to remain even. "What of your lifelong friendship with my father? What of the fact that he was the only friend your mother had when everyone else deserted her?" Paxton appeared most uncomfortable at this and it fueled Peter's anger. "That's right, Father told us many stories about her and about you."

"Then he no doubt told you of Mr. Hawkins' adulterous affair with my mother. The years of suffering and anguish he left her in once he threw her away like so much used trash."

Grace began to sob softly, and Peter wrapped his arm around her shoulder and drew her close.

"Get out of here," Karen said, moving forward. Neither Paxton nor his bodyguards moved a muscle. She raised her hand as if to strike Paxton, but he grabbed her wrist in such a lightning-quick move that even Peter was surprised.

"You might do well to ask your little Grace what happens when women slap me."

"I don't have to ask. I saw what you did to her. I dressed her wounds in the aftermath."

He chuckled as though Karen had brought to mind a pleasant memory. Releasing her, he pushed her away and refolded the paper in his hand. He tucked it carefully inside his coat pocket, then motioned to the man who held his hat. Taking his gloves, Paxton pulled them on in a methodic, slow manner as he addressed them collectively.

"You are all welcome to witness our marriage, but I will not allow for any nonsense. The law is clearly on my side." He looked up at Peter and added, "And if you don't wish to see Colton Shipping lost to your family, I would suggest you cooperate and mind your own business. After all, that is what this is all about. Business. Grace Hawkins is my business . . . mine alone."

⊣ C H A P T E R TWENTY - N I N E ⊢

THE WORLD SEEMED TO SPIN around Grace as Peter led her back to the privacy of her living quarters. Jacob and Leah had come to stand in the doorway and had apparently overheard the entire conversation.

"That man isn't going to take Grace away, is he?" Leah questioned.

"Not if I can help it," Peter replied.

"I'll help you too," Jacob stated, sounding years beyond his age.

Grace felt a heaviness in her heart as she took a seat at the table. "I can't allow any of you to get involved. I don't want you getting hurt, and I know this man well enough to know that he would do anything to have his way."

Karen joined her and patted her hand. "Don't fret, Grace. This battle isn't over. We'll find a way to defeat Paxton."

Grace shook her head. Why couldn't they understand? She sighed. "He has already ruined my family and killed my father. Oh, my poor mother. How she must grieve." Tears came unbidden. "She adored my father. They were always very close. At least until this. If what Mr. Paxton said is true, and if he shared the news of my father's indiscretion with my mother, then I'm certain her heart is broken."

"Grace, none of this is your fault. You couldn't marry that man under any circumstance. He wants only to cause pain and suffering. What do you suppose he had planned by marrying you?" Karen questioned. "You are nothing more than an extension of his revenge."

"It doesn't matter. If I'd remained in Chicago and married him last summer, my father might still be alive." She looked up to see her dear friends gathered around the table—watching her as if they were servants awaiting instruction.

"You've all been so good to help me, but the time has come for me to face facts. I have no choice."

"That's not true," Peter said. "You have many choices."

"You don't understand. He'll destroy you too," Grace replied, her once brave tone dissolving into complete resignation. "You heard what he said. He has some sort of agreement with your father. If you interfere, he'll destroy you and your family. I can't live with that on my shoulders."

"I don't care what Paxton threatens. I only care that you are safe. It won't be your responsibility—it will be mine."

Grace looked deep into Peter's eyes. How she loved this man. God help her, but she loved him more with every word that came from his mouth.

"So what are we to do?" Karen questioned.

"I have a plan," Peter replied, "but it will require all of you helping. With Paxton's bodyguards standing by to deliver Grace to Paxton for the wedding, we're going to have to act fast."

"No! I won't let you do this. You'll only be hurt!" Grace declared, getting to her feet. "I have no choice. I will marry Mr. Paxton."

"No," Peter said, coming to stand beside her. "You can't marry Paxton if you're already married to me."

"What a perfect solution," Doris said innocently before anyone could comment. "You two have been sweet on each other since our first meeting. This would solve the matter once and for all."

Grace kept her gaze fixed on Peter, her voice low and intent. "You can't do that. Paxton will destroy your family. I won't be responsible for that."

"That's exactly what I told you," Peter said, taking hold of her hand. "You won't be responsible. I can handle the likes of Paxton. You leave him to me. The real problem is going to be getting you out of here. Paxton is waiting for a bride."

Doris chuckled. "Too bad we don't have my young actress friends."

Karen smiled and then laughed. "But perhaps we have someone just as helpful."

She pulled Leah with her and positioned the girl alongside Grace. "With a heavy veil, Leah could easily pass for Grace."

"It's true," Doris replied, nodding. "They are very nearly the same height. We have that heavy lace tablecloth I brought with us from Chicago. I could fashion it into a veil for Leah to wear. No one would be the wiser."

"Unless they insist on checking her out," Peter replied. "Of course, if we delay things until the last minute, perhaps they would be less likely to worry about it. They'd see a bride and figure Grace to be cooperating."

"But that still doesn't explain how we can get you and Grace to a preacher and then safely out of Paxton's hands," Karen said, looking to Peter for an answer.

Grace felt helpless to comment. They seemed to have taken the matter entirely out of her hands. A million thoughts danced in her head. Peter was offering to marry her. He had proposed to make her his bride and to take her away from Paxton, even if it caused his own ventures to be threatened. Surely he loved her!

But what of their differing views on God? She didn't wish to go against the Bible, what she knew God intended for her. Yet what else could she do? Surely God understood her dilemma.

"We could disguise Grace," Peter finally said. "If we're disguising Leah, why not disguise Grace as well?"

"But if we make Grace over to be Leah, the men will see her and easily recognize that we've switched them around."

"True," Peter agreed. "However, if we dress Grace as Jacob, smear a bit of dirt on her face and tuck her hair up under a cap such as Jacob has taken to wearing, they just might not give it much consideration. I could make like Jacob was joining me on the ship for our departure. Once they figure out what has happened, I'll already be steaming toward Seattle."

"What a splendid idea!" Karen declared. "I believe it will work. Now what of arranging your marriage?" She paced a bit. "I just wish my father were here. He could marry you in a minute."

Doris smiled. "I'll go run for the pastor. I'll tell those ninnies outside that Grace is in need of godly counsel. We can bring Pastor Clark here, have him marry Grace and Peter, then leave with us as the wedding party heads to Skagway. With so many people to keep track of, Paxton's hoodlums are certain to be confused."

"Of course!" Karen exclaimed excitedly. "Their focus will be on our poor, veiled Leah." She turned to the child. "Do you suppose you could do this?"

Leah laughed. "I think it sounds like great fun! An adventure!"

Karen nodded. "Do you suppose you could cry or at least sound like you were crying? Nothing is more certain to irritate a man than a woman's tears. If you were wailing and crying, they might hold themselves at a distance, leaving me to tend to you."

Leah instantly began to sob and wail as though her heart were breaking.

"That's very good," Doris said, nodding enthusiastically. "You are a natural actress."

Leah halted her sobs and smiled. "I'm glad to help Grace. I'm just sorry she has to go away."

"I'll bring her back when it's safe," Peter stated. "She can visit you from time to time when I make trips to deliver goods."

Grace couldn't believe what she was hearing. They were planning out her wedding, and Peter talked like they were already well on their way to a life of normalcy and pleasure. Was this an indication of God's blessing?

"All we need is five days," Grace reminded the group. She wanted very much to know that Peter was marrying her because he loved her and not because of a misplaced sense of duty. "You really don't need to give up your life, Captain." She walked away, and Peter looked to each of them. "I appreciate what you're planning on my behalf, but I can't put your lives in danger."

"Would you all give me a moment alone with Grace?" Peter asked.

Everyone nodded and Doris even decided that she would go for the preacher, just in case the plans came together. One by one, they filed into the store while Peter closed the door behind them.

"Grace, I want you to listen to me. This is a reasonable way to take care of the matter. Your friends want to keep you safe—so do I."

Grace looked to the floor, suddenly unable to meet his gaze. "I won't be safe until Paxton is either satisfied or dead."

"Would you rather I kill the man instead of marry you?"

Her head snapped up in alarm. "I should say not! I don't desire that you suffer yourself in any manner. I cannot abide that you would sacrifice either way on my account."

He came forward and took her hands in his own. The warmth of his touch reminded her of the night before.

"Grace, marriage to you would not be a sacrifice. Surely you know how I feel."

"We hardly know each other and you've not cared at all for my opinions on your family and of God and spiritual matters."

"Grace, please listen to me. I love you."

Her heart raced and her breath caught in the back of her throat. He loved her! Oh, how she cherished the words. The nagging thought of his lack of love for God was quickly pushed aside. Surely once they were married, he would see how important God was to her and give his life over as well.

"I thought you were just doing this—"

He pulled her into his arms. "I love you and I want you to marry me, Grace."

He lowered his face to hers but didn't kiss her. The inches between them were maddening to Grace. She longed for the feel of his lips against her own. She felt her arms involuntarily embrace him, pulling him closer and closer.

"Oh, I love you, Peter." Her voice came in a breathless whisper.

"Then don't be afraid. You are always saying that we must trust God. Why not trust Him now?"

His words brought a wave of reassurance. Grace nodded. "I do trust Him."

Peter smiled. "Then trust me as well."

———————

Karen opened the door of the store to find the two burly henchmen waiting patiently outside.

"You ready to leave?" one man questioned.

"No, in fact, I was looking for my aunt. She went to bring our pastor. Grace is very close to him, and we thought perhaps he could offer her some comfort and prayer."

The man scoffed. "Praying won't help now."

Karen smiled sweetly. "I think otherwise."

Just then Doris and the preacher rounded the corner. The man had a look of sheer terror on his face. Karen felt sorry for him. He was very young and new to the ministry and no doubt this matter did not bode well with his sense of heavenly peace and order.

"Pastor Clark, we're so glad you could come," Karen said, extending her hand. "Grace will find great comfort in your presence."

The man nodded. "I will do what I can." His Adam's apple bounced up and down as he replied. Karen would have laughed at the funny, frightened man had she not had her own fears to contend with.

"You'll find Grace preparing for her wedding," Karen said, looking to the two ruffians at her side. "We're to head over to Skagway as soon as she's prepared."

"Yeah, hurry it up, preacher," the man at Karen's left said with a low, growling tone. He reminded Karen of a bulldog, complete with lower teeth that seemed to protrude just a bit up and over the top set.

Leaving the guard behind, Karen was about to follow the preacher and her aunt inside when she heard her name being called.

"Miss Pierce!"

She looked down the street to find Adrik Ivankov bounding toward her. She smiled, but the look on his face did not suggest the action well-served.

"Sorry to bother you like this," he said.

"Is something wrong?" she asked. "Have you seen my father?"

Adrik stopped long enough to take inventory of the men standing outside Colton Trading Post. "These guys giving you trouble?"

Karen smiled. "No, they're just annoyed that the store is closed for business. Why don't you step inside, Mr. Ivankov . . . I mean, Adrik."

He looked at the men for a moment. "Why don't you fellas head over to Healy and Wilson's. They're open."

"Just mind your own business, stranger."

Adrik squared his shoulders and narrowed his eyes. He was about to say something, when Karen took hold of his arm and pulled him forward. "Come, Adrik. I want to hear the news."

They stepped onto the creaky wooden floor of the store, and Karen quickly closed the door behind them. Leaning against the frame as if to keep the two men from entering, she turned to Adrik. "So what of my father? Have you news?"

Adrik looked around the empty store as if to check for anyone else. "I'm sorry, but the news isn't good."

Karen put her hand to her mouth. She didn't even realize she was holding her breath until her ribs began to ache from the tension. Adrik seemed willing to wait for her prompting, but Karen didn't know if she could ask the question that so desperately needed asking.

Letting out her breath, she looked at the floor and tried to gather her courage. "Is he . . . dead?"

"I don't know. A man brought me word that he was gravely ill. There's been a round of measles and dysentery and many in the village have died. I'm guessing that your father has fallen ill with one or the other. He may already be gone, but I felt it important to return from the Scales and let you know."

Karen didn't know what to say. It was possible that her father might still be alive, but the situation didn't look at all promising. "What should I do?" She looked to Adrik, realizing she'd vocalized the question.

Adrik's rugged features softened, his square jaw seeming to relax as he spoke. "You can't do much. You can't get to him, and most likely he'd be gone by now if he's going to die."

"But he's alone," she said, biting her lower lip to keep from crying.

"No, he's not alone. You know better than that," Adrik said, his voice low and husky. "I've never seen a man or woman who was closer to God than your pa. One thing's for certain, he ain't alone."

Karen nodded. "I know you're right. Oh, this is so hard. To have come all this way. Others came for gold and I came for him."

"Treasures come in all forms," Adrik replied.

She looked up to meet his sympathetic gaze. He seemed so concerned for her well-being. He looked at her as if he were preparing to jump into action. Almost as if he expected her to fall to pieces any minute, only to be responsible for putting her back together.

"Please don't say anything to my friends. We're in the middle of a rather delicate situation, and I wouldn't want them to fret over me."

"Does this have something to do with the men outside?"

She nodded. "But honestly, it's under control and you don't need to worry. Will you be around town until evening?"

"What'd you have in mind?"

There was no hint of teasing in his tone and for this Karen was grateful. "I'd like to discuss this further, perhaps even decide what I should do. I'd like your advice, but I can't discuss it now."

"Then I'll come back. Say, around eight?"

"That'd be fine."

Adrik nodded. "I'll return then."

Karen waited until he'd gone to make her way back to the others. She wouldn't say a word, not even to Doris. After all, if her father was dead, there wasn't anything anyone else could do.

She opened the back door and gasped in surprise as she observed Peter and a rather boyish-looking Grace embrace and kiss. Leah, dressed in Grace's cream-colored day dress, wore a heavy veil that covered her from head to foot.

"We tried to wait the ceremony for you but figured we should get first things done first," Doris told her.

"I'm glad you went ahead. Congratulations, Captain and Mrs. Colton," she said, grinning. "I guess we're well on our way to seeing this thing through to completion."

Peter nodded. "I think we'd better give some serious thought to getting on our way. Those two thugs aren't going to wait patiently for much longer."

"You're right about that," Karen replied, forcing a smile. "They were just making a fuss about all the time we're taking."

"We're ready," Leah said from behind the veil. "Jacob's even hiding."

Karen looked around the room. "Where is he?"

"He's in my steamer trunk," Doris replied. "If those men come to search out the place and see if anyone else is here, they'll only find the silence as their companion."

Karen took up her coat. "Then we'd best get a move on. Leah, you might want to start your crying. Oh, and, Aunt Doris, please bring Grace's coat for Leah. It's bitterly cold outside." Doris nodded and helped Leah into the heavy coat, while Grace shrugged into a brand-new coat they'd taken from Peter's newest shipment.

"Are we ready?" Karen questioned, looking to the conspirators.

"We're ready," Peter said, helping Grace with a pack. He took up a heavier one for himself but didn't bother to put it on.

The entourage reminded Karen of a strange, out-of-place funeral procession. Walking with a slowness that denoted sorrow and loss, the group refused to be hurried by the angry guards.

"We'll be all night at this rate," the taller of the two men grumbled.

Peter waited until Pastor Clark took his leave from the group to begin complaining about the entire matter. "Grace, I'm sorry about all this. I wish I could have helped you escape Paxton."

Karen took up the cause. "Oh, be quiet. If you weren't such a coward you would go with us and see her protected."

Leah wailed loudly and the two bodyguards exchanged a scowl of displeasure. "Does she have to carry on like that?" the bulldog man asked.

"She's hardly going into this willingly," Karen replied. "You men think you can push us around, make us do your bidding, and then you fail to understand when we dare to be less than pleased with the affair." The men muttered but said nothing more.

The party boarded an awaiting boat and set out on the short trip to Skagway. With every stroke of the oars, Karen prayed their ruse might work.

Leah continued to sob, only softer now, and from time to time Doris would lean over and gently pat the girl's arm for comfort. Other than this, the group remained silent.

Once they'd arrived, however, Peter no longer held his silence. Making a great show of his disgust, he made his move.

"I'm leaving," Peter announced. "I can't bear to watch this mockery of marriage. My condolences to the couple." He pulled the bulky pack onto his shoulders. "Jacob and I will write. And we'll come check in on you with the next load of goods."

"I'm sure you've done all the harm you can, Captain," Karen replied. "Why don't you just leave us be?"

"I'm going, Miss Pierce." He turned to Grace. "Come on, boy. Pick up your feet, no sense in us staying here any longer."

"That's right. Leave us to fend for ourselves in our darkest hour," Karen replied, trying to keep up the farce. She tried not to think about her father's health or Grace's trembling figure dressed in Jacob's clothing. She tried not to imagine the fears that were running rampant in Grace's mind because her own were so close to being unleashed it was sure to be her undoing.

Tears came to her eyes. Real tears of sorrow. She hated seeing Grace go but knew she had to let her. And she hated thinking of her father dying all alone in the frozen wilderness.

"He's not alone." Adrik's voice rang out in her memory.

He's not alone. I'm not alone, Karen thought. Glancing upward, she whispered a prayer. "Oh, God, please help us now. I know deception is a sinful thing, but this is for Grace's good." Leah alternated sobbing with a mournful, howling kind of cry. The noise was almost haunting—like something very primitive. Karen thought it would have been very easy to imitate the sound based on her own misery.

The bodyguards paid little attention as Peter and Grace hurried off toward the harbor.

"Get moving. We're already running late," the bulldog man ordered.

Leah clung to Karen's arm, crying for all she was worth as Karen gave the impression of attempting to urge her along. She had to give Peter enough time to get safely away with Grace. And somehow, she would have to keep Paxton from learning it was Leah under the veil until the last possible moment.

—{ C H A P T E R   T H I R T Y }—

MARTIN PAXTON PACED the confines of his second-floor apartment. He'd not been available when Ephraim Colton and his family had departed for San Francisco aboard *Summer Song*, but he gave it little consideration. It was better that he now had the place to himself. With his wedding about to take place, he would appreciate the privacy afforded him in their absence.

Smiling to himself, he took time out to light a cigar. The tip burned bright as he drew a long breath. The plan had taken far more time and effort than he'd originally hoped, but nevertheless, his revenge was about to be made complete. Grace would be his to do with as he pleased, and then he would discard her. Of course, there was some disappointment in the fact that Frederick Hawkins wouldn't be alive to see it. How he hated that man. Hated him so completely that the power of that emotion had killed Hawkins as sure as a bullet. Paxton rather liked the idea that his merciless drive had taken the life of his enemy.

And just as his hatred had consumed Frederick Hawkins, Paxton's lust and greed would destroy Grace. Everything precious and important to Hawkins would be destroyed and utterly wasted. This was a day of celebration, Martin decided. He sucked on the cigar as he poured himself a shot of whiskey.

Holding the glass aloft, he pulled the cigar from his mouth. "To revenge both bitter and sweet!" He tossed back the drink and turned at the sound of people on the stairs. His day was about to be made complete.

Karen Pierce was the first to pass through the doorway. She stared at Paxton with an air of haughtiness that suggested she would somehow manage to win the day after all. Her eyes narrowed as they shared a wordless exchange.

Next came the veiled figure of Grace. She sobbed softly and moved slowly. Paxton smiled and leaned over to his desk to put out his cigar. "Ah, the happy bride."

Doris Pierce came behind Grace, and the two henchmen he'd hired followed wearing a sober look of disgust.

"Mr. Tavis," Paxton began, "the preacher is cooling his heels in the storeroom below." The man needed no further instruction. He turned heel and stomped back down the stairs to fetch the preacher.

"I'm sure it's a waste of time to ask you to reconsider this," Karen stated.

"You're right. It is a waste of my time." Paxton considered the attractive red-head and smiled. His private thoughts were loosed on images of an intimate nature, but he said nothing more. First he'd deal with Grace. Then he could worry about Miss Pierce. After all, she'd helped Grace to escape to Alaska. She deserved to be punished.

The women heard the heavy steps of two men on the stairs and turned back toward the door. Paxton found the panic in their eyes a strong stimulant. He felt the blood course through his veins in anticipation. He felt empowered by their fear.

Mr. Tavis appeared first and then a pudgy man who looked to be in his late fifties. The man panted breathlessly as he bounded into the room with Bible in hand.

"I believe, Miss Hawkins, it would be appropriate for you to come to my side," Paxton stated firmly.

Karen gripped the arm of her friend and shook her head. "I cannot let this happen. To move forward with this wedding would be wrong. Grace doesn't love you. She'll never love you. Doesn't that mean anything to you?"

Paxton shook his head. "Not a thing."

"She hates you. She'll never make you happy."

"I'm unconcerned with such notions," Paxton replied coolly.

Karen turned to the preacher. "You're a man of God. You must help us here. This woman has no desire to marry this man. You must intercede on her behalf."

The man turned to Paxton, eyes widening in apparent concern.

Paxton held up his hand. "This marriage will take place. I have come thousands of miles, and I am not leaving without my bride. Whether Miss Hawkins loves me or is happy about this arrangement is of no concern to me. I have her father's legal permission to marry her. She has not yet reached her majority and therefore must heed her father's direction."

"You're a man without feeling, Mr. Paxton," Doris said, shaking her head in a disapproving manner. "Shame on you for forcing yourself upon this child."

Paxton grinned. "I'm certain she can come to enjoy our arrangement."

He crossed the room in a rather casual manner and took hold of Grace's arm. "We need to stop wasting the preacher's time," he said, pulling Grace forward.

Karen refused to let go. She followed them the few steps to the preacher and threw Paxton a murderous glance. She glanced over her shoulder as if contemplating their escape. The action made Paxton laugh.

"You'd never make it, so don't even think of causing such a scene."

The preacher quickly opened his Bible, clearly uncomfortable with the situation. "Dearly beloved," he began.

"We need no formalities here," Paxton interjected. "Just get on with it."

The preacher nodded. "Does anyone know a reason why these two can't be wed?"

"I do."

Paxton looked to Karen, not the least bit surprised that she'd made one last attempt to halt the ceremony.

"She doesn't want to marry him. That should be reason enough," she pleaded.

"We've already covered this," Paxton replied in a heavy tone of annoyance. "Let's get on with this."

"We haven't covered anything. You've dictated terms to us."

Paxton's patience had reached an end. "I am the girl's guardian. She is not yet twenty-one and therefore under my authority."

"You are correct in saying she's not yet twenty-one," Karen answered. "She's only twelve. What preacher in his right mind would marry a twelve-year-old to any man? Besides, you aren't her guardian. I am."

She's gone mad, Paxton thought. The matter has rendered her absolutely daft. Stepping away from Grace momentarily, Paxton went to Karen.

"You would do well to stop this nonsense. This wedding will take place with or without you. I'll have my men remove you, if necessary."

Karen stood her ground. "I'm quite serious," she told the pastor. "This girl is only twelve and Mr. Paxton doesn't even know her."

At this, Paxton had had enough. He yanked off the heavy veil and tossed it to the ground. "I know this woman very well," he declared. He looked to Grace, but instead of seeing his terrified fiancée, he found instead a child.

"Who are you?" he asked.

"I thought you knew her very well," Karen said smugly. The look on her face was one of pure satisfaction.

"Where is Miss Hawkins?"

"Miss Hawkins is now Mrs. Colton." Karen drew Leah close before pushing the child in the direction of Doris. With no one between them, she raised her chin defiantly. "Grace married Peter Colton a few hours ago. She is safely in his care at this time."

Paxton felt his satisfaction fade. He looked to his men. "Where is Colton?"

"He headed off for his ship," the bulldog man replied. "But he weren't in the company of no woman. He just had a young boy with him."

"Fools!" Paxton declared. "That was her!"

Karen laughed. "My, my, but you are a smart man. But not smart enough." She turned to leave. "Sorry, preacher, but there won't be a wedding today."

"You'll pay for this, Miss Pierce. I swear, you'll all pay. Colton included!"

"You don't worry me, Mr. Paxton," Karen said, putting her arm around her aunt. "With God on my side, there is nothing you can do to harm me."

"You've already seen what I'm capable of accomplishing," Paxton replied dryly. "If I were you, I'd question the loyalty of your God."

"No need," Karen said, smiling with joy. "I just witnessed it this day."

───────

It felt good to leave Paxton in stunned anger. Karen nearly jumped down the steps two at a time. She supposed it wasn't a very positive Christian attitude to display, but in light of the events, she felt it a definite win of good over evil.

"Let's hurry and get back to the store and to Jacob," she said, encouraging her aunt and Leah. "Let's hire a wagon to drive us. It's too cold to walk." She shivered and pulled her scarf around her face. The wind was no doubt responsible for her trembling. Surely it wasn't her fear that Paxton might actually cause them harm.

I won't give in to such thoughts, she reasoned. *God is more than able to deliver us from the hands of someone like Martin Paxton. Of course, Frederick Hawkins had lost everything in the battle—even his life. Poor Grace. How hard to learn of her father's death in such a brutal manner.*

This gave Karen thoughts of her own father. Had he already died? Did he lay delirious in some makeshift bed? Was there a doctor nearby to help ease his suffering? Tears came to her eyes and quickly froze against her lashes. *I can't think such despairing things. I must have hope.*

They arranged passage with a man who managed to squeeze them in between crates of dried foods and canned milk. He had a commission to haul goods up to Sheep Camp, and Dyea was one of his stops along the way.

Karen offered the man money, but he waved her off. "It's too cold to be out here walkin', ma'am," he said, barely taking time to raise his head to speak. He quickly tucked his face back into the folds of his coat.

"Perhaps you would care to come inside our store to warm up once we reach Dyea," Karen suggested.

The man nodded and gave a muffled reply. "That'd be good, ma'am."

Karen felt the barter was satisfactory and settled back against one of the crates. She tried not to think of what the hours to come might mean for either her or Grace. She wanted only to focus on the direction in which she should go. She thought of Adrik Ivankov. If he wouldn't help her, she didn't know what she'd do.

———————

After seeing that the driver had warmed up with nearly half a pot of coffee and several sandwiches, Karen bid the man farewell and checked the clock. It was nearly time for Adrik to come. She quickly made another pot of coffee and then decided to tell Doris the truth.

"Mr. Ivankov caught up with me just before we left the store earlier today," she began. "He had bad news, I'm afraid."

"Wilmont?" Doris asked. Her stern expression softened. "Is it Wilmont?"

"I'm afraid so," Karen replied. "He's not at all well. In fact, he may have already succumbed to an outbreak of measles and dysentery that has devastated the village."

"Oh dear. Oh my." She sat down hard on the nearest chair, and Karen began to fear for Doris's health as she clutched her hand to her heart. "I was afraid this might be the case. I've felt nothing but uneasiness for days."

"Perhaps God was helping you to prepare for the worst," Karen said, taking a chair opposite her aunt. She was grateful that Jacob and Leah were out collecting wood for the fire. "I suppose we have to face the fact that he might not make it. Mr. Ivankov said it was very bad."

Doris nodded and twisted her hands together. "This country has killed them both. I suppose it will kill me as well."

"No!" Karen exclaimed, reaching out to still her aunt's hands. "Don't even say such a thing. We must trust that God has a plan in all of this. No matter what, we mustn't lose hope."

"I know you're right, but my heart is heavy," Doris replied. "I think I'll take to my bed early. You don't mind, do you?"

Karen shook her head and thought how pale her aunt suddenly looked. She wasn't aging well in this harsh environment. Perhaps it was time to consider sending her back to Seattle.

"You have a rest. Mr. Ivankov should be here any minute and we shall decide what's to be done."

Doris got up from the table slowly. Squaring her shoulders, she drew a deep, ragged breath. "We can at least comfort ourselves in our deeds today. We saved Grace from a horrible fate."

Karen considered the reality of the situation for the first time. They'd married Grace off to Peter Colton without even allowing her much say in the matter.

Karen began to feel hesitant, knowing that Peter didn't know God in a personal way. All the time Grace had spent under her care, Karen had tried to stress that an unequally yoked marriage could only spell heartache.

"I hope we did a good thing," she finally replied. "It seemed like the only option at the time."

Doris nodded. "I'm certain it was."

Karen then heard the deep baritone voice of Adrik Ivankov as well as Leah's laughter. Adrik must have spotted the children as they worked over the woodpile.

"You rest now, Aunt Doris. I must see to Mr. Ivankov." She turned to head over to the door, just as an empty-armed Leah waltzed through.

"Mr. Ivankov is carrying my wood," she volunteered as Karen looked to the motley crew.

Adrik smiled and nodded down at the wood. "Where do you want it?"

"We have a woodbox beside the stove. That would work just fine," Karen answered. "Would you like some coffee? I just put a fresh pot on to boil."

"Sounds good," Adrik said, hardly seeming inhibited by the mass of logs in his arms.

He deposited the wood, and Jacob, who'd just entered the room with an abbreviated version of Adrik's pile, grunted a greeting. "It's cold out there. I fig-ured we'd better have extra."

Karen smiled at the boy. He was becoming more and more likeable. He still had his moments of rebellion, but now he seemed far freer to communicate when things were going wrong. She prayed that in time his heart would heal and the pain over his mother's death and father's desertion would subside.

"I need to speak with Mr. Ivankov in private," Karen told Jacob and Leah. "Would you mind going to your room for a time?"

Both kids grew wide-eyed. "You aren't leaving us, are you?" Leah questioned.

Karen heard the fear in the girl's voice. "Oh, Leah, I don't plan to. Something has happened, however. My father is very sick. Mr. Ivankov was given word of this by one of the Tlingit."

"I'm sorry, Karen," Leah said somberly. She came to stand by Karen and squeezed her hand.

"Come on, Leah," Jacob motioned. His eyes met Karen's for a brief moment, and in his expression Karen found a world of compassion. *He understands,* she thought. *He knows exactly how it feels to be separated from those you love.*

She waited until the children had closed the bedroom door before turning back to Adrik. Smiling rather timidly, Karen looked to the floor. "So now what do we do?"

"HOW WE DECIDE to help your father depends mainly on what you want to do," Adrik stated.

"Well, take off your coat and hat, have some coffee, and we'll go from there," Karen replied, picking up a heavy white mug. "I find that I can think best when all the other amenities are taken care of."

Adrik took off his heavy coat to reveal a well-worn flannel shirt. Red flannel underwear peeked out from the top of the outer shirt, which Adrik had carelessly left unbuttoned. He seemed to realize this, along with the haphazard way his shirt had come untucked in the front, and casually put himself in order before sitting down to the table.

Karen smiled as she poured the coffee. She liked this big man. Maybe because he was a good friend of her father's. Maybe it was just because of his open personality. He made no pretenses, yet didn't mind seeing to proprieties.

"I would very much like to see my father," Karen said, handing Adrik the coffee. "I don't know if that's possible, but I would like it nevertheless." She took the seat opposite him and folded her hands. Looking into his dark brown eyes, she questioned, "Is it possible?"

Adrik tasted the coffee, then nodded. "Anything is possible. With God, all things are possible. The question here should be, is it more beneficial than harmful. The answer to that is no."

"Why do you say that?"

Adrik scratched his dark beard and shrugged. "Because it's dangerous, even deadly. The passes are snowpacked, the storms descend on the interior without warning, and the temperature is steadily dropping well below zero. You aren't accustomed to such things—not that you couldn't get accustomed," he added quickly. "It's just not the wise thing to go trudging off just now."

"The miners are doing it. Folks are still heading north over the pass," Karen protested.

"Yes, but they're holding up when they reach the lakes. Oh, some are still working to get north. Some are trying to pack out across the frozen lakes, but many of those folks are going to die. This gold has done nothing but corrupt men's thinking. Women's too. And in the process of turning their own lives upside down, they're workin' pretty steadily to destroy everybody else's."

"I'm sure it's hard on the tribes in the area."

"You don't know the half of it. The Tlingit owned the trails up north until the white man came along. For a while they even charged those passin' over their trails. They'd charge for the trail, charge to guide them, charge to sell them goods. They made a steady income from the whites. Better still, they made a steady income from the Sticks—the Yukon First Nations people who live in the interior. The Tlingits kept the First Nations people from coming down to the coast to trade. They insisted on being their sole source of goods. Even earlier in this century, when the Russians came with all kinds of goods to trade for furs, the Tlingits ran the show."

"But not now?"

Adrik shook his head. "They're inundated with gold rush maniacs. They're sufferin', that's to be sure."

Karen felt almost intrusive for having come to Dyea. She wanted to understand the people her father so loved, but even more, she longed to know whether God would have her stay in this land and help her father with his ministry. She had never considered that he might die before God gave her a clear sign. A horrible thought crept in. What if her father's death was her sign?

Adrik seemed to understand her mood. "Look, I didn't mean to get you sidetracked. The truth is, I couldn't look your pa in the eye if I was the one who ended up riskin' your life. But I can make you a deal."

Karen couldn't imagine what he might have to suggest. "What?"

"I'll go myself. If he's dead, I'll see to it that he's properly tended to and I'll bring his things back to you."

Karen sat quietly for a moment, then realized it was probably all she could ask for. She wanted to offer Adrik some kind of compensation for his suggestion, but she didn't want to insult the man. Honesty seemed the best choice she could make. "Mr. . . . . Adrik, I don't want to insult you by making the wrong suggestion, but I would like to see you properly compensated for such a thing."

He grinned. "Well, truth be told, I would be making the trip anyway. At least I was planning on heading up near to where your pa was last situated. I don't mind making the extra leg of the journey." He sobered. "Your pa was good to me when he came up here. Good to my folks and people."

"You were already living here?"

"To be sure. Well, actually we were up and down the coast. My grandfather was Russian. He married a Tlingit woman. They met in the years after the wars between the Tlingits and Russians. They lived in Sitka and that was where my father, and later I, was born."

The man's dark hair and tanned skin revealed his heritage. Karen wondered why she hadn't thought of this possibility before now. "So you're part Tlingit," Karen said, nodding. "No wonder you care so much about their plight."

"I'm not the only one. Your father felt a calling to save their souls, but he was far less intruding than other missionaries in the area. Some came in whoopin' and hollerin', using the Bible like the natives should already know what it was all about. Others came in more conservatively but still sought to change the people. They were excited to show the Indian a new way of doin' things. Excited to show them modern conveniences, new foods, new ways of carin' for themselves. They put the Tlingit children in schools and forced them to give up their native tongue, made them dress like Americans, and cut their hair. This was just as bad. The Tlingit are very proud people."

Karen nodded, for she had dealt with some of the women from the Dyea village. She knew them to be proud, almost arrogant in their trading. Yet they were also very efficient and trustworthy.

"It must be hard on them, having the land so overrun with outsiders."

"Indeed it is," Adrik replied. "But we can't very well stop the flow. We can't even slow it down until the gold itself plays out."

Karen sighed. "Sometimes I wish that I'd never come." Her voice sounded distant—almost distracted. She felt her guard slipping away. She trembled at the thought of revealing her heart to this big bear of a man. Catching him watching her with great interest, Karen smiled. "Well, wishing it doesn't make it so, as my mother used to say."

Adrik laughed. "I can remember her saying those very words."

"You knew her?"

"Don't sound so surprised. I've known your folks since they came up this way."

Karen shook her head. "I had no idea. How wonderful! Maybe you could tell me where she's buried. I had wanted to see her grave but didn't know if anyone would know its whereabouts."

"It's right here in Dyea," Adrik said. He drank down the coffee and got to his feet. "Put on your warm things. Bundle up good. I'll take you to her grave."

Karen didn't say another word. She hurried to take up her coat and hat, then quickly checked in on the children.

"Mr. Ivankov is going to show me where my mother is buried," she told Jacob and Leah. "I'll be back soon." The kids gave her somber nods.

Adrik took up a lighted lantern and motioned toward the door. Karen drew a deep breath and followed. She tied her bonnet snugly, then fished her heavy wool mittens from the pocket of her coat. She felt silly, almost childish, at the feeling of hesitation that crept over her. Seeing the grave would make her mother's death a very visual reality. Could she handle the pain? What if she broke down and cried? Would she offend Adrik?

They didn't have far to walk. The cemetery was positioned on the northwest edge of town. Karen had known of its whereabouts, but she'd never thought to check it out. *Funny,* she thought. *It was right here all along.*

The sounds of the waterfront and gambling houses faded as they hurried in the crisp winter air. The town had probably tripled in size just since Karen's arrival, but the bitterness of the cold made everyone take to indoor activities. She suddenly felt very swallowed up by the looming mountain ranges and the passing shadows. Shivering, she tried to keep her mind on the big man at her side. He would never allow for anything bad to happen to her. She felt safe in his presence.

That's the way I'm to feel at all times with God, she thought. How silly I am to doubt God's company and care, when this man whom I hardly know has my utmost faith simply for being a friend to my father.

"Here we are," Adrik said, holding the lantern aloft.

Karen braced herself and followed the muted light to a single headstone. The simple white wooden marker bore only her mother's name and the year of her birth and death.

Kneeling down, Karen touched the marker, then looked up to Adrik. "Were you with her when she died?"

He squatted down and shook his head. "No, but I wasn't far away. Word came to me that she was sick. I was on my way to see if I could be of any help when she passed on."

"And my father?" Karen questioned. "How did he . . . manage?"

"He took it better than most men might have. He knew she was out of her suffering. The pneumonia had left her in great pain and unable to breathe without fierce spells of coughing. She was just plain worn out, he told me. We prayed together and then arranged to bury her here."

Karen nodded and fought back tears. She could allow herself a good cry later. In fact, she could mourn her mother's passing and Grace's departure all in one very long fit. The idea made her smile.

"I see that," Adrik said with amusement in his tone.

Karen got to her feet, almost embarrassed. "My mother wouldn't want me to be sad."

"No, indeed," he said, getting to his feet. "Come on. We'd better get back. Now that you know it's here, you can come see the grave in the daytime."

They walked side by side for several feet before Karen paused. She could see the stars overhead and the moonlight reflecting off the snow-covered mountainside. People were driving themselves to madness to cross those mountains. They were looking to the mountains for their salvation.

"I will lift up mine eyes unto the hills, from whence cometh my help." The psalmist seemed to have written her heart's cry in this passage. *"My help cometh from the Lord, which made heaven and earth."*

Gold wouldn't comfort her in the loss of her loved ones, but God would. She felt her spirit take rest and smiled. Looking up at Adrik, she nodded. "It is well with my soul. Should my father have joined my mother, I will yet praise God."

He smiled. "You've found a treasure that many never find. Your pa would be proud."

Grace found herself nearly as restless in Peter's cabin as she had been that first night aboard *Merry Maid* so many months ago. She was married! The very thought was only now beginning to sink in. Now, after washing up and clothing herself in her own feminine gown, now after realizing that this was to be her wedding night, Grace wondered if she'd done the right thing.

Everyone had said it was her only way out. No one seemed at all concerned that she was running away yet again. No one—not even Karen—had made mention that Peter had no interest in the same spiritual matters that were most vital to Grace.

Grace herself quickly cast those doubts aside. At least she tried to. God could work miracles. She had to trust that He would bring Peter to an understanding of the Gospel message—that His love would be revealed, drawing Peter to Him.

Grace clung to this hope. It had to be true; otherwise God would surely have given her another way out of the situation. Peter was there, convenient to her need and to the matter at hand. It had to have been orchestrated by God.

Wasn't it?

No matter her determination to see this as a positive thing, Grace couldn't help but be nagged by those haunting little doubts. Peter was unsaved. Not only that, he held an almost irreverent opinion of God. Peter was also domineering when it came to dealing with his own family. Would he be any less with Grace?

"We hardly know each other," Grace whispered. She nervously picked up her hairbrush and began working with a fury to comb through her long brown hair. "What have I done?"

Her trembling made it difficult to handle the brush. The future before her felt overwhelming. Were it just the thoughts of her wedding night and what was to be expected of her there, she might have called it "marital jitters." But this was so much more.

Martin Paxton would be livid when he learned of her deception. If Karen told him of the marriage, then Peter's own family and their business would be at risk as well. If Paxton learned of her whereabouts, he just might come searching after her—he might not even mind that she and Peter were legally married.

Her heart ached for the counsel of her dear friend, or even her mother. *Oh, Mother, I wish we would have been closer. I wish you would have understood my need for you sooner. How you must grieve without Father.*

Tears sprung unbidden to her eyes, and it was in this state that Peter came to the room. He saw her face and the tears and seemed at once to worry that he was somehow to blame.

"Did I do something wrong? Are you upset with me?"

Grace shook her head and put the hairbrush aside. "I'm sorry. I suppose I'm just a bit overcome with all of this. I couldn't help but think of my mother and father. Oh, Captain . . ." She looked down to the floor. "Peter," she corrected herself. "I can't help but worry about what Mr. Paxton is going to do when he learns of this."

"He's no doubt become completely aware. He has no power to hurt you anymore."

"That's not true," Grace replied. "And you know it."

Peter came to her and gently touched her wet cheeks. "I can take care of us, Grace. Have some faith in me. I know what I'm doing."

Her conscience was pricked again. "What if we've done the wrong thing?" She started to mention the issue of faith, but Peter interjected before she could explain.

"We love each other and this can only be the right thing. Two people who care about each other as much as we do should be together. You needn't worry about Martin Paxton. I won't let him bring harm to you."

"And if he destroys your business? What then?"

"He won't. He and father are too close. He only spoke out of anger. You'll see. By your own admission you scarcely knew the man."

"Yes, but in the short time I knew him, just look what he accomplished."

Peter shook his head and pulled Grace tenderly into his arms. "There's only room here for you and me. Mr. Paxton will have to wait."

Grace gave in to the passion of his kiss. When he lifted her in his arms and carried her to his berth, she put aside her concerns and instead lost herself in the magic of their first night as man and wife. Surely God would make everything right.

———————

Shortly before the dawn, Grace awoke to find Peter gone. Her body chilled at the absence of his warmth, she wrapped a heavy wool blanket around her flannel nightgown and snuggled against Peter's pillow. The scent of her husband warmed her more than the blanket. She was married. Truly married. The thought both delighted and terrified her.

Sometime in the night, as they'd lain together, whispering and dreaming of the future, Peter had promised her a wedding band.

"*I feel bad that you had to supply your own wedding ring,*" he'd commented. During the ceremony, Grace had slipped off a ring she'd been given for her six-teenth birthday and handed it to Peter. He'd lovingly put the ring on her left hand but later confessed to hating the fact that he'd nothing of his own to share with her.

As she'd faded into sleep, he'd told her to dream of him and the ring that he'd buy her. He promised her the most elaborate ring her heart might desire. But even now, wide awake with the memory, Grace knew her only dream was for a small gold band. A simple, understated pledge.

The idea of gold made her smile. They had traded in furs and gold at the Colton Trading Post. There had been enough gold passing back and forth across their counter that Grace could have had an unending number of rings made. *So many dreams of gold,* she thought. *So many hopes pinned on a yellow substance that could neither think nor feel.*

Oh, God, she prayed, pulling the covers ever tighter, *keep my eyes on you. Let me only desire you. Let me serve you faithfully, no matter the price. And let Peter know you.*

She thought of her husband and hugged his pillow tight. "I love him so much, Lord. The wonder of his love is more than I ever expected." She remembered his loving touch . . . the way he drew his hands through her hair . . . his lips on hers.

With these thoughts, sleep was impossible. Grace rose and quickly dressed and made her way to the deck in hopes of finding Peter. *I just need to see him,* she thought. *I just need to make certain this isn't a dream.*

The wind whipped mercilessly at her heavy wool skirts, but the glow of light just now touching the outline of the mountains drew Grace's attention. The sky suddenly seemed to glow, and gradually the heavy blue-black of night was pulsat-ing with a magenta and lavender. Grace stood transfixed at the deck rail. The sun rose in a promise of hope for the new day. The light offered a blessing in colors too wonderful for human hands to have painted.

Looking skyward, Grace thought of the psalms. "'Unto thee lift I up mine eyes, O thou that dwellest in the heavens.'"

"Have you taken to talking to yourself, Grace?"

She turned sharply to find Peter watching her curiously. "I was just inspired by the beauty of this sunrise."

He smiled and moved to stand beside her. Opening his arms to her, he wrapped her snug against his woolen coat. "I was feeling the same, only my inspiration comes from you. You're quite lovely, Mrs. Colton."

Grace would not allow him to make her the focus of the morning. "God did a wondrous thing out there. The colors and the mountains—the skies and the way the night is turning to day. I couldn't help but praise Him for what He has done. I praise God even more that I can appreciate such divine architecture."

Peter didn't seem inclined to contradict her feelings, and Grace took that as a positive sign that things would fall into place as they were meant to be. She turned in his arms and leaned back against his chest. She didn't want to miss seeing a single thing. It was as if she had been given new sight.

Slowly the ship sliced through the icy cold waters of the passage. *Merry Maid* was taking them south to freedom and a new home in a land Grace had never seen. Her heart held great hope for what could be, and God held her heart. It was enough, Grace thought and smiled in the strength of this love. It was enough.

TRACIE PETERSON

Ashes and Ice

MARCH 1898

When thou passest through the waters,
I will be with thee; and through the rivers,
they shall not overflow thee; when thou
walkest through the fire, thou shalt not
be burned; neither shall the flame
kindle upon thee.

ISAIAH 43:2

⊣ CHAPTER ONE ⊢

"FIRE!"

From somewhere in the deepest recesses of Karen Pierce's slumbering mind, she heard the word, yet she failed to make sense of it. Licking her lips, she tasted the acrid smoke in the air and felt a burning sensation in her lungs.

Something didn't seem right, but in the world in which she found herself, Karen slipped deeper and deeper into darkness. With an indescribable weight pressing her down, she was helpless.

"Fire!"

It was that word again. A word that seemed to have some sort of importance—urgency. Karen struggled against the hold of sleep. There was something she needed to do. Something . . .

Then a scream pierced the night, and Karen felt a chill rush through her body. The cry sounded like that of her young charge, Leah Barringer. Now realizing that some element of danger existed, Karen forced herself to awaken.

Groggy and barely able to comprehend the need, she teetered on the edge of her cot. Drawing a deep breath, she coughed and sputtered against the bitter smoke.

Fire!

Her heart raced. That word. That was the word she had tried to figure out— the word that made all too much sense now.

"Aunt Doris!" she called, choking on the thick air. Karen pulled on her robe and tried to feel her way through the darkness to the door. "Aunt Doris, wake up! There's a fire!"

Karen knew her elderly aunt slept not four feet away, but in the blackness, Karen could see nothing. With burning eyes and lungs that ached to draw a real breath, Karen pushed herself beyond her fear. Her hand brushed the door and finally the knob. Both were hot to the touch, but it didn't stop Karen from deciding to survey the situation beyond her room.

As soon as the door was open, an assault of more hot, smoky air bombarded her face. Flames engulfed the interior room, and panic immediately gripped her. Frozen in place momentarily, she thought she saw a figure moving through the fire. A big, broad-shouldered figure. Surely her mind played tricks on her.

"Karen! It's me—Adrik."

The voice was muffled, but nevertheless welcomed. "The children!" she called.

"I'll get them," he yelled above the crackling of the flames. "You have to get out of here. The whole store is on fire. Come on. Now!" His command alarmed her more than the sight of the fire. The urgency was clear.

"I have to get Aunt Doris."

Karen turned back to the room and saw her aunt straining to get up. "Aunt Doris, we have to hurry. The building is on fire." With the intensity of the smoke, Karen could barely make out the older woman's form.

Coughing, her aunt replied, "Hurry, child. Don't wait for me."

Karen took up the Bible by the stand at the door. It was all that she had left of her mother and father. Only a few months earlier her father had succumbed to illness himself while nursing and ministering to some of the sick Tlingit Indians. Adrik Ivankov, their trusted family friend, had set out to bring him back to her and Dyea for better care, but God had other ideas. Karen was heartbroken at the loss.

"Hurry, Aunt Doris," she begged again. "The flames are already blocking a good portion of the room. We will have to run through the fire in order to get to the door."

Doris bent over in a fit of coughing before recovering momentarily. "Wrap a blanket around you, child."

Karen nodded and struggled to breathe. She felt panic anew wash over her as she sensed her body was no longer reacting as it should. Her movements were labored, her thinking less clear. She pulled the blanket from the bed and covered her head and shoulders. It seemed like the process was taking hours instead of minutes.

"Here," she said, taking hold of her aunt's blanket. "Let me help." She secured the wrap, then kept a good hold on the blanket. "Come on. I'll lead the way."

Stepping into the interior room was akin to stepping into a furnace. The feeling of panic and desperation mounted. They had to get out now!

Flames licked at their blankets as Karen pulled Doris to safety. She stepped out into the alleyway and gasped for fresh air only to find the smoke had permeated the air there as well.

Wracked with coughing, Karen collapsed to her knees and might have fainted but for the strong arms that lifted her and carried her to safety.

She fell back against Adrik's strong chest, desperate for air . . . questioning whether she would live or die.

"Aunt . . . Doris . . ." she gasped as Adrik lowered her to the ground. "Jacob . . . Leah?"

"I got the kids out. They're over there being tended to by the preacher," Adrik replied, pushing back Karen's unruly curls.

She looked up at him and saw the fear in his expression. "You saved us," she whispered, then fell into another fit of coughing.

Adrik gently grasped her about her arms with one hand while pounding her back with the other. "You're full of smoke," he said, as if she hadn't already figured it out.

Regaining control, Karen nodded. "Help me up, please."

He did as she asked, supporting her firmly against him. Karen's knees wobbled. "Where's Aunt Doris?" she questioned, looking up at the burning building. Several men were fighting to keep the flames under control. Panic began anew. "Where is she?"

Adrik looked around. "I never saw her."

Karen tried to head back to the building. "I helped her out. She was right here with me."

Adrik shook his head. "No, you were alone."

"I had hold of her . . . I . . ." Karen came back to the spot where she'd fallen. Doris's blanket lay on the frozen ground. "I had hold of her blanket."

Adrik saw where her gaze had fallen. The light from the flames made it easy enough to read the expression of her rescuer as Adrik raised his eyes back to hers.

"She's still inside," Karen said, barely able to speak. She jerked away from Adrik as he reached out to take hold of her. "Aunt Doris!"

"You can't go back inside. The place is ready to collapse," Adrik stated firmly. He took hold of her and refused to let go.

She fought him with the last remnants of her strength, sobbing. "I have to try. I have to. She's probably just inside the door. I know she was with me as we crossed to the door."

She turned her pleading expression to him and saw him study her only a moment before letting go of her arm. "I'll go," he said.

Karen watched in stunned silence as he pushed back several men. He pulled a woolen scarf to his face and reentered the burning building. Karen felt her breathing quicken in the smoke-filled air. *Dear God, let him find her*, she pleaded in anguish.

It seemed like an eternity before Adrik returned to the alleyway door, a small, unmoving bundle in his arms.

"Thank God!" Karen cried, hurrying forward to pull Adrik to a less smoky area than he'd previously taken her. "Put her down here," she commanded. Kneeling, she waited for Adrik to do as she said.

"Karen, I . . ."

"Put her right here," Karen insisted. She patted the frozen ground and looked up to see that he understood.

Adrik lowered Doris's still frame to the ground, but instead of leaving her to Karen's care, he pulled Karen to her feet. "She's gone."

The words were given so matter-of-factly that Karen could only stare at Adrik for several moments. "What?"

"I'm sorry, Karen."

"No!" she exclaimed, pushing his six-foot-two-inch frame aside. "She's just . . . overcome."

She knelt down again and stroked Doris's hand. The heat coming off the body caused steam to rise in the icy air. Karen pushed back the old woman's tangled and singed hair and gently rubbed her cheeks. "Aunt Doris. Aunt Doris, please wake up."

The woman's silence left Karen numb inside. She couldn't be dead. She just couldn't be. Once again, Adrik pulled her away from Doris and brought her to her feet.

"She's in better hands now," Adrik whispered.

"No," Karen moaned. "No!" She looked into the bearded man's face and saw the confirmation of her worst fears. "No." She fell against him in tears. This couldn't be happening. God wouldn't take her away from them. He just wouldn't.

Adrik wrapped her in his arms and stroked her hair. His words came in soothing whispers. "She's with God, Karen. She's in a better place. No pain. No suffering."

"I want her with me. She's all I have left."

Even as she said the words, Karen knew the statement was far from true. She had siblings in the lower states and friends right here in Dyea. There were many people who cared about her, including the Barringer children. Their father had deserted them for the goldfields of the Yukon. He had left them to her care, and in doing so, the trio had learned to cling to each other through their shared difficulties. Karen mourned the loss of the father she'd come north to find, while they mourned the loss of the father they'd come north only to lose.

They needed her. And somehow, she had to stay strong for them.

Adrik's comforting touch made the horrors of the night seem less overwhelming. She wasn't alone. Karen knew that now. Remembering her father's promise that God would always be there to comfort His children, she put her head on Adrik's chest and stared off blankly at the burning building.

Everything she owned, with the exception of her father's Bible, which now lay on the ground near Doris's lifeless body, was gone. Her clothes, her books, everything. She saw the flames reach high—appearing to go upward until they touched the night skies—cinders blending with the stars to offer pinpoints of light.

She was glad her friend Grace wasn't here to see the destruction. Their home had been attached to the back of the Colton Trading Post, the store owned by Grace's husband of three months, Peter Colton. How hard it would be to share the news of this loss, Karen thought. Peter had looked to this store as a means of salvation—at least financial salvation.

Adrik released his hold. "You can plan to stay in my tent tonight, and I'll go bed down with Joe."

"Karen! Karen, are you all right?" Leah cried out as she rushed into the older woman's arms. "Oh, Karen, we could have died."

"We're safe now," Karen reassured her, holding Leah close and stroking her hair. "Are you burned or hurt?"

"No, just scared," Leah said, lifting her tear-filled eyes. "I couldn't find Jacob. I thought he was dead."

Jacob joined them. "Where's Aunt Doris?" he asked.

Karen frowned and hugged both of the children close. "She didn't make it." Tears blurred her burning eyes.

"She's dead?" Leah asked in disbelief.

Karen nodded and looked to Jacob, who stood shaking his head. "How?" Jacob asked as if he didn't believe her.

Karen felt a rush of guilt. "I had a hold of her, but she slipped away without me noticing. When I got outside, Aunt Doris wasn't with me. Adrik tried to save her, but it was too late."

Jacob turned away as Leah hugged Karen. "Will they be able to put the fire out?" she asked.

Jacob answered before Karen could speak. "It's gonna burn to the ground."

With this thought in mind, Karen gazed toward what she first thought was an illusion. But upon a second glance, she saw the man clearly and knew he was no illusion. Martin Paxton.

Paxton. The man who'd chased poor Grace all the way to Alaska in order to force her hand in marriage, their most embittered enemy, stood away from the gathered crowd. Leaning against the wall of another business, Paxton seemed to watch her with defined interest.

Karen straightened, stepping a few paces away from Adrik and the children. She barely heard his words suggesting she and the kids settle down for the night. Instead, she fixed her gaze on Paxton, knowing that he was aware that she was watching him. He tipped his hat to her as though they were attending a cotillion rather than observing a scene of devastation and death.

"He did this," she murmured.

"What?" Adrik questioned. "What are you talking about?" He reached out to touch her arm.

Karen broke away from his hold and started toward Paxton. "He set the fire. He killed my aunt!"

Adrik took hold of her arm and pulled her back. "You don't know what you're saying. You're just upset."

She looked at him, feeling a growing panic. "You don't understand. He's getting his revenge for what we did. We snuck Grace out right under his nose. He intended to marry her, but Peter Colton married her instead. He warned us. He threatened to destroy us, and now he has."

Adrik shook his head slowly. "No, he hasn't. Not yet. But if you go to him now, he will have won. Don't you see?"

Karen wanted to deny Adrik's words as meaningless, but they hit hard and the truth of them rang clear, even in her crumbling reality. "He did this," she whimpered, feeling the defeat of the moment wash over her. "He did this."

Adrik never disputed her declaration but instead pulled her back into his arms. "Now is not the time for you to face him with accusations. He would only laugh at you—deny it. Come. See to Leah and Jacob. The morning will give you other thoughts on how to deal with this."

Karen fell against him, her last remnants of strength ebbing in the flow of tears that fell. "He did this. It's all his fault."

⊣{ C H A P T E R   T W O }⊢

SAN FRANCISCO HELD a charm for Grace Colton that she never would have thought possible. She'd always disliked the confines of her childhood city, Chicago, and the thought of another big city after enjoying the wilds of the Alaskan Territory had been less than welcoming to her heart. But San Francisco had surprised her. There was something rather Old World about it. A kind of antiquated appeal that wove its spell around the young woman.

Of course, it wasn't just the city. Grace was in love with her new husband, and life seemed very good indeed. Peter Colton had a way of weaving his own charm in Grace's heart, and despite the mounting differences of opinion on religious matters and household routines, Grace was content with her new life. At least most of the time.

Tying a ribboned cameo around her neck, Grace smoothed down the layered muslin gown and sighed. Life, overall, was quite wonderful. She tried not to let her heart be worried by the increasing number of arguments she and Peter were having. Surely all couples had their quibbles. Even Peter's mother said it was true, adding also that her son was of a very stubborn cut of cloth.

"A ship's captain has to be strong and determined," Mrs. Colton had told her. "It's only natural that a certain degree of stubbornness accompany those strengths."

Grace supposed it was true, but she nevertheless found it a darkening shadow of doubt on her otherwise happy life. Had Martin Paxton not forced her hand, she probably wouldn't have married Peter—though it wouldn't have been for a lack of love, for she'd fallen in love with the man almost from the first moment they'd met. Rather, she knew the harm in marrying someone who didn't see life the same way. The issue of being unequally yoked had been something she had talked about for years with her governess, Karen Pierce. Karen was a strong Christian, knowledgeable in Scriptures and their teachings. Karen had been the one to point out to Grace that the verse warning against unequal yoking pertained to every element of life. Be it business, friendship, or love, committing yourself to someone whose convictions differed from your own would inevitably spell trouble. There lacked a common ground upon which to make decisions.

Grace could see that problem now as she dealt with her new husband. She loved him faithfully, but his negative response to her love for God made Grace quite uneasy.

"But surely God hasn't brought me this far only to leave me now," she murmured.

Her faith bolstered her spirits. God had a plan in all of this, she was certain. He had watched over her since the first moment Martin Paxton had tried to force his way into her life. God wouldn't desert her now. No, Grace's marriage was intact for a purpose. She felt confident that she would bring Peter to God. She could change the way he thought about spiritual matters. She was sure of that. After all, Peter loved her, and he would want to see her happy. In time, he'd see the truth of it all.

Sitting down to her writing table, Grace outlined her morning to be spent in letter writing. She wanted to share many things with her dear friend Karen. While Karen would forever remain her most beloved friend, Grace was pleased to discover that Peter's sister, Miranda, was a very amiable companion. The two women had grown quite close during the three months they lived together under the same roof. It helped to fill the void created by Karen's absence.

Picking up a pen, Grace dated the top of her letter. *March 26, the year of our Lord 1898*. Then she paused. Instead of writing a greeting to her friend, Grace was compelled to turn her thoughts elsewhere. She had felt for some time that she'd left unfinished business in Alaska. Martin Paxton had been the reason she fled Chicago and also the reason she fled Alaska. Now she felt it was time to settle the matter once and for all. After all, her father-in-law had been longtime friends with Paxton. She knew her arrival into the family was putting a strain on that relationship, and she had no desire to perpetuate it further. Putting her pen to paper, she wrote a greeting.

Dear Mr. Paxton,

The days of strife are behind us now. It is my hope that you have come to understand the importance of my choices and decision. It is also my hope that you would know I have chosen to forgive you the past.

Grace stared at the words momentarily, searching her heart to ensure the truth behind them. Yes, she could forgive Martin Paxton. He might have been responsible for ruining her family financially. He might even be responsible for her father's sudden onset of bad health and death. But Grace longed only for God's peace to settle upon her life, and to do that, she knew there could be no remnants of hatred or bitterness. Karen had taught her this much. She continued,

I know that by now you must realize the truth of my circumstance and marriage to Peter Colton. He is a dear man, as your friendship with his family must have made you aware. He is honorable and generous, trustworthy and truthful, and it is my prayer that our marriage will prove to be blessed by God.

That brings me to another point upon which I cannot remain silent. Mr. Paxton, you clearly harbor many painful memories of my father. Your desire for justice and even revenge on behalf of your departed mother are understandable. I am sorry for the pain my father caused you, but you must remember that people are fallible. Only God is without mistake. You will never find what you are looking for until you make right the path between you and your Maker. God is willing to hear your confession. He desires that you would give up your ways of anger and rage. He desires that you would turn to Him for comfort and peace instead of manipulating others.

"Ah, here is my lovely wife," Peter Colton called as he entered the room.

Grace looked up to find her sandy-haired husband dressed in that same casual manner in which she'd first met him. A costume of billowing white shirt with sleeves rolled up and sides barely tucked into tailored navy trousers was set off by black knee boots and a jauntily tied neck scarf.

"Good morning, darling," she said, setting the pen aside.

He pulled her to her feet and into his arms. Nuzzling his lips against her neck, he murmured approvingly. "Fortune has smiled upon me."

"I found myself counting God's blessings this morning, as well," Grace replied just before Peter's lips captured her own in a deep, passionate kiss.

Grace felt her body warm under his touch, and a tingling sensation ran down her back as she thrilled to her husband's obvious interest. She had not known that physical love could be so wonderful. She'd imagined the nervous butterflies fluttering in her stomach every time she'd set eyes upon Peter to be love's physical calling card. The sight of this man, well before they were married, could take her breath and set her heart to racing. She had presumed this was what passion and romance were all about. She was happy to be wrong.

Yielding to her husband's embrace, Grace trembled as Peter pressed his fingers into her carefully styled hair. She cared not one whit if the coiffure fell in disarray to her waist. She could remain in Peter's arms forever.

As if reading her mind, Peter pulled away to say in a low, husky voice, "I know

I have work to do, but I would much rather remain here with you."

She laughed. "Then stay. I've only a few letters to write, and those can easily be put off until later."

He kissed her one more time, then drew away. "I'll never get anything done with you in this house." His voice betrayed his pleasure. "So whom are you writing to?"

Grace's joy drained away and her thoughts turned sober as she wondered how she might avoid a confrontation. Peter hated Martin Paxton, and although Grace had spoken of forgiveness, Peter saw no need for such declarations.

"I . . . um . . ." She looked to the letter and then back to her husband, who was even now tucking his shirttails more securely into his pants. "I have several letters to write. I owe Karen one and then I wanted to send my mother another letter. I do hope she'll join us here, at least for a visit."

Peter nodded. "So whom are you writing to now? Your mother?" He stopped and looked at her as though the answer were quite important.

"Uh, no," Grace began. "It's not to Mother."

Peter noted her hesitancy and crossed to the writing table. "Then it must be to Karen." He lifted the sheet of paper before Grace could stop him. He scanned the letter quickly, then lowered it to give Grace a hard look of disapproval.

"What do you think you're doing?" he questioned. "You can't send this letter. I forbid it."

"Peter," she said softly. "Please try to understand."

His mood changed instantly. "I do not understand. You bandy about words like forgiveness and peace to a man who would have forced a life of misery upon you, had he his own way. A man who is no doubt responsible, by his own admission, for the destruction and devastation of the life you once knew—the people you loved."

"You needn't remind me," Grace said. "I am the one who dealt with him. I know him for what he is."

"Then why?" Peter asked in obvious disgust. "Why do you throw about your religious nonsense and correspond with such a man? Haven't you come to understand he cares nothing about your beliefs?"

"Neither do you," Grace said without thought. She immediately wished she could take back the words. "But I still have hope that you will come to accept the truth for what it is. I hope no less for Martin Paxton."

"Outrageous. How dare you compare me to him? I offered you rescue—salvation. He offered only pain and suffering."

Grace gently took the letter from her husband's hand. "And I offer peace between all parties. Your parents are longtime friends with this powerful man. He holds a financial interest in your shipping line. I would hate to see your company or you hurt by his vengeful nature. Peter, please understand me—I write this for you as much as I write it for me."

"Do not think to do me any favors, madam." He always reverted to formalities when angry with her. "I ask no such agreement to be made. Paxton must pay the price for his underhanded and corrupt business practices. He has caused this family grief enough already, sneaking around behind my back, loaning my father money and making contracts against the business without my approval. If you think I will overlook such matters in whimsical phrases of forgiveness, then you are mistaken."

"Peter, it will serve no purpose but that of darker forces if you continue this hateful battle." She let the letter fall to the desk and now reached out to take hold of Peter's arm. "Please listen to me. Forgiving Mr. Paxton is the only way to put the past to rest. If he sees that you wish him no further harm, perhaps your father will not suffer any adverse effects regarding their partnership. I desire only that we have a wonderful life together—you and I. I only want security for your family. Don't you see? Can't you understand?"

"What I can't understand is a wife who would undermine her husband's authority," Peter replied in a hard, cool tone. "Why not give yourself over to reading that Bible you so love and see what it says about obedience to authority."

He stalked from the room without waiting for her reply. Grace heard the front door slam shut. Despair washed over her, and she sunk to the chair and stared blankly at the piece of paper that had started the entire feud.

"How can it be, Lord, that forgiveness should wage such wars between us?"

CHAPTER THREE

"LOOK," MIRANDA WHISPERED to Grace, "Mrs. Haggarty is back."

Grace took her seat in the church pew and smiled at her sister-in-law. "I'm so glad. I know she was worried about traveling all the way to Salt Lake City to see her daughter, but she looks no worse for the wear."

"Mother says travel is for the young. She's absolutely appalled by the number of older men and women who head north for the goldfields."

Grace didn't have a chance to reply as the Sunday services began. She, too, was amazed at the sensation of gold fever in the nation. The discovery of gold had pulled the country out of a terrible slump, and everyone wanted in on the find. Never mind issues of greed and those who died for something so fleeting. People were starved for prosperity, and they were sure they'd find it in the Yukon. Grace had to smile. The Yukon had brought her a treasure in Peter. He might have his faults, but she loved him dearly. She only wished that he'd accompany her to church—to be a part of what she believed. It was her heart's only desire.

As the service continued and they joined together to sing and pray, Grace felt a loneliness that bothered her nowhere else in the world. She knew it was silly. Worshiping with God's people should be the last place to feel such longing, but she couldn't help it. Without her husband at her side, Grace felt as though she were the talk and gossip of the other married women. After all, what man of good sense and respect for his Creator would absent himself so commonly from Sunday worship? She felt separated from the others—alone and awkward.

The situation had never bothered her when she'd been single. Attending church with Karen or her mother and father had seemed a perfectly acceptable thing to do. No one anticipated that she should be accompanied by anyone else. Why, she had even attended services on her own when her mother had been ill and Karen had been visiting relatives out of town. She had never given it a second thought. She had enjoyed the services every bit as much as when in their company.

But being a married woman changed everything. She no longer fit in the circles of the young, unmarried women and men. They were still free to mingle and flirt, within proper limits, of course. But Grace no longer belonged to their world. Sadly enough, she didn't feel that she belonged to the world of those who were married, either. A woman who attended church without her husband was often seen as a rather dangerous person. After all, she had knowledge and experiences that put her on equal footing with her married church sisters, but unlike them, she had no husband to keep her in line on Sunday morning. She was free to move about and speak to whomever she chose, and that made a great many people uncomfortable.

This had been especially true in the oversized Presbyterian church she'd first attended upon her arrival in San Francisco. Women her own age seemed to scorn her, while older married women saw her as some kind of unspeakable threat. Grace found she didn't fit in with the older widows, either. They were not of a mind to have a young married woman in their midst as they talked of death, childbirth, and their grandchildren. So everyone nodded politely when Grace appeared, then turned their backs on her and hurried away.

Before long, it even seemed to Grace that the sermons were directed to her. Comments were made from the pulpit about sinful women who sought their own way in the suffrage movement, in employment, and in seeking to follow their own course rather than that of their husbands. Maybe she was just extra sensitive to the topics, but they made her uncomfortable nevertheless.

After a while, Grace simply found it easier to keep to herself, and eventually she left the stuffy and selective congregation of Presbyterians and joined a small gathering in a newly founded church within walking distance of home. Grace had learned about the church during tea with one of her neighbors. It seemed the opinion of this gathering that people had gotten too wrapped up in man-made rules and regulations. The goal of the minister was to bring his small, but growing, flock back to some of the most basic biblical truths.

That suited Grace just fine. Her hunger for spiritual truths had only been compounded since her marriage. Peter had no desire to make Bible reading and prayer a focus for his life. He'd chided Grace about things they could better spend their time doing together, and while she'd tried to take it all in stride, her heart was torn. Grace's one consolation was Peter's sister, Miranda.

Miranda's presence comforted Grace like no other. She seemed to understand Grace's loneliness and shared feelings of her own that closely matched those of her sister-in-law. Miranda had few friends and knew the same sense of isolation that Grace experienced. Miranda became more and more compelled to participate in Grace's daily schedule, and Grace, in turn, eagerly encouraged her presence. This became especially true of church attendance.

It also didn't hurt that there were several eligible bachelors in the congregation. Miranda had confided to Grace that she had begun to fear never finding an appropriate suitor, but now Grace saw her sister-in-law quite enthusiastic. After the service, a host of men descended upon the two women like flies to a picnic.

"Miss Colton," a handsome man with flaming red hair said, taking up Miranda's hand, "I wonder if I might speak to you alone."

Miranda looked to Grace as many of the other congregation members filed past them. "I'm sure that anything you have to say to me can be said in front of my sister-in-law."

The man blushed furiously, his face nearly matching the color of his hair. "It's just that . . . well . . . I wondered . . ."

"Old Corky is trying to ask you to share lunch with him," another of the men proclaimed. "But you can just tell him no, because I asked you first. Remember?"

Grace wanted to laugh out loud at the man's obvious devotion to her sister-in-law. Miranda, on the other hand, looked quite perplexed as she tried to recall the earlier invitation.

"Miss Colton has no time for either of you gentlemen," yet a third man announced. "I sent a written invitation inviting not only Miss Colton, but her sister-in-law, as well. It's what true gentlemen of society do if they desire the company of dinner guests." He hooked his fingers in his waistcoat pocket and leaned back on his heels looking quite self-satisfied.

Grace nodded. "It's true, gentlemen. Mr. Barker has indeed requested our presence by means of a formal invitation."

The other two men, though disappointed, realized they'd lost out. They gave a graceful bow and promised to send their invitations in tomorrow's post. Grace could only imagine the confusion that promised to give the Colton household.

Miranda looked up at the dark-haired Mr. Barker and smiled. "My sister-in-law has agreed to accompany us to lunch. It is with her encouragement that we accept your invitation."

"Marvelous," the man said, flashing brilliant white teeth. "I shall cherish your company."

The luncheon seemed to last forever. Perhaps, Grace thought, it was due to the monotonous self-promoting lecture given by Mr. Barker. Or perhaps it was due to the bland and unappealing food. Either way, when Grace and Miranda made their way up the steps to the Colton house, both breathed a sigh of relief. Pausing on the porch, they looked at each other and broke into fits of laughter.

"I thought that it would never end," Miranda confided. "What a conceited man."

Grace nodded, completely agreeing. "He seemed so very much in love with himself, I seriously doubt he could have shared love for anyone else."

"Not without deeply wounding his own feelings," Miranda added.

"I had so hoped you would enjoy your outing. With so many dashing young bachelors vying for your attention, it seems only fair to expect that one of them should be the right one."

Miranda's smile faded. "I know. I keep thinking that, as well. There have been others, men who Peter said were not worthy of me. He's been so good to try and look out for me."

"Peter is a good man. He cares very much for you, but you have to make choices based on what your heart tells you. Peter might well think Mr. Barker a perfect suitor. The man is a banker and holds a respected position in the community. Your brother would probably admire him greatly and think you amicably suited."

"I suppose that is true. Peter does sometimes make choices for me that I would just as soon not have made."

Grace could well understand that, her husband being a strongly opinionated man. "Well, no harm done. Mr. Barker seemed to understand quite well that you lacked interest in his need for adoration." Grace smiled and opened the front door to the house. "Perhaps we should try Corky next time, eh?"

Miranda laughed. "All that red hair. My word, but it fairly glows."

"And just think of the redheaded children you might find yourself mother to," Grace laughed, and Miranda flushed at the thought as she giggled.

Their laughter quickly faded, however. Grace stepped into the house to find Peter awaiting their return. She had thought he was on his way to Seattle and hadn't expected to find him home.

"Peter!" Grace could see the anger in his eyes and hoped to calm him. "Why, if we'd known you were still in town, you could have joined us for lunch."

"Where have you been?"

"Grace agreed to accompany me to lunch with Mr. Barker," Miranda answered.

Peter's expression darkened as his eyes narrowed. "Who is Mr. Barker?"

"Oh, surely you remember him, Peter. He came to see Father on business about a month ago."

Grace pulled the shawl from her shoulders and untied her bonnet. "He attends our church and was quite smitten with your sister."

"Why wasn't I consulted on this, Miranda?"

Grace could see the look of contrition on Miranda's face. "I'm sorry, Peter. I presumed you were quite busy with the company. You and Father have both had so much to do in transporting goods and people to Alaska. It simply never entered my mind that you would want to hear about Mr. Barker's invitation."

"Besides," Grace interjected, "she's a grown woman and fully capable of making up her own mind when it comes to the company she desires to keep. She learned easily over melon slices and strawberries that Mr. Barker is far more interested in Mr. Barker than in anyone else." Grace flashed Miranda a smile before placing her bonnet and shawl aside.

When she turned back to her husband, she found him most furious. "I will speak to you later, Miranda. For now, I will have words with Grace on the matter. Come to our room, madam, and let us resume this discussion."

Grace followed Peter, knowing that he would lash out at her in his anger. How many times would this be the course of their discussions? He always flared up like a fire feasting hungrily on old wood. Then he would become calm and apologetic, almost childlike in his desire to please. Sometimes Grace thought she'd married two different men.

They entered their bedroom, and before Peter could close the door, Grace jumped in to speak. "Please hear me out before you take offense with me."

He turned to eye her, the rage held in tight restraint as he replied, "Very well."

Grace took a seat and began to pull off her gloves. "I did not purposefully set out this morning to cause you irritation or pain. I am sorry that I have apparently managed both. As Miranda stated, we realized your busyness and thought only to take care of the situation ourselves. Your mother found it acceptable, and in your father's absence, as well as your own, we believed this to be the only necessary authority on which to act."

"Are you finished?" he asked in a low guarded tone.

"No." Grace surprised them both with her answer. She threw her gloves aside and worked to keep her own anger in check. "I'm tired of your accusing tones and angry lectures. Don't think me to be so ill-witted that I believe for one moment this is about Miranda. Oh, certainly you wish to have control over her life, but we both know that this behavior of yours is fueled by my desire to help ease the tensions between our family and Mr. Paxton. So rather than chide me for accompanying your sister on her outing, why not simply deal with the real issue at hand?"

Peter's jaw tightened, and Grace could clearly see that her words had struck a chord. He paced the room a moment before stopping directly in front of her. "You had no right to interfere. You are my wife, and as such you answer to me. My sister is unmarried and answers to our father, and in his absence she, too, answers to me. Do you understand?"

"I understand that you wish to control the lives of the people around you. I understand that you hold no respect for God or His authority over you, yet you demand that others allow you your rightful authority over them. Seems to me there are double standards in this."

Peter shook his head, his sandy brown hair falling onto his forehead. "I do not care what it seems like to you. Grace, there are certain rules of society and decorum that I expect you to honor. My father has expected no less from my mother and sister, and I expect no less from you."

"You knew before marrying me that I didn't agree with this philosophy of life," Grace replied. "You blamed it on Karen, but in truth, I was raised to believe women have the ability to reason for themselves."

"Perhaps that's why your father arranged a marriage for you with Mr. Paxton."

Grace frowned. "My father arranged that engagement based on Mr. Paxton's blackmail and nothing more. He wouldn't have forced me into such a relationship had there been another way. And you and I wouldn't be married now had I stayed behind to be the dominated little woman that you demand of me now."

"Perhaps that would have been for the best," Peter snapped.

Grace was silent a moment, the strength of his words a blow to her heart. "Yes, perhaps you're right." She bowed her head and wondered why it should be that this man she loved so dearly should hurt her so deeply.

For several moments neither one spoke, then Peter came to her and put his hand under her chin. Lifting her face, Grace knew he would see her tears and be remorseful. For just once, however, she wished he could see the pain prior to the delivery and stop before apologies were necessary.

"I didn't mean what I said."

This was always his way. His words were to be respected, honored, and obeyed—except when he qualified them in the aftermath of his anger with that simple, meaningless statement.

"I didn't mean to hurt you," he continued, his thumb gently stroking her cheek.

Grace didn't know what to say. She didn't feel like accepting his lame excuses, and yet she had no desire to continue fighting.

"Peter," she said, forcing her gaze to meet his, "words are powerful. They can maim and injure just like any weapon forged by man. They can also nurture and encourage. I can't help but believe that you know my heart—know how very much I love you. But at the same time, I find it very difficult to accept that you love me. Especially when you say the things you do."

Peter pulled her up and wrapped her in his arms. "Grace, there are just certain things I wish you'd leave well enough alone. I don't mind that you are intelligent and witty, but I do mind when your actions make me to look the fool."

Grace shook her head. "How did I do that?"

Peter dropped his hold. "I told Barker nearly a month ago that I didn't wish for him to court my sister. I knew the man was conceited and full of his own accomplishments. I knew Miranda would abhor him."

Grace felt foolish. She'd not considered that Peter might have already spoken to Barker about Miranda. "I'm sorry. I didn't realize."

"I know that, but had you simply bothered to check, I would have given you my reasons. Miranda knows that, and it grieves me that she should seek other counsel."

"But she's lonely and she desires to marry and have a family of her own," Grace replied. "You can't expect her to wait around forever."

"I don't expect that at all. I only ask that she wait until the right man comes along. I want to save her the pain of being married to someone for whom she is completely ill suited."

The words penetrated Grace's heart like no other. Tears came to her eyes and she turned away before asking, "Ill suited as we are?"

Peter turned her to face him. "Grace, we are not ill suited. We're perfect for one another. We love so many of the same things, and while you get a little spirited from time to time, I know we'll come to work through our differences."

"You mean that in time I'll come to do things your way and then you'll be happy," Grace said, reaching up to wipe tears from her eyes. "Peter, I'm not that kind of a woman. My faith is the foundation for my existence. It's not a Sunday occupation or a social matter; it is my very life. I won't give it up as you think I should. I'll go on desiring to forgive those who've wronged me."

"With exception to your husband," Peter said, letting go of her. "Forgiveness is something you offer everyone else, but not me."

"That's not true, Peter. I do forgive you. I know you don't understand my need for church or my desire for us to pray together and share God's Word. I can even admit to knowing that you don't mean many of the words you speak in anger, but Peter, those words still hurt. Even after I've forgiven you, my heart is still tender."

He frowned, as if understanding for the first time. "It wasn't my intent to hurt you, Grace. I sometimes speak without thinking."

"That is a danger we must all work to avoid. Words spoken in haste cannot be taken back. And while they may be forgiven, the memories will linger to warn the heart of future encounters."

"But I don't mean anything by it," Peter said in self-defense.

"Perhaps that is what makes it even worse," Grace replied. "If you mean nothing by those words, perhaps you mean nothing by other words. How can I believe what you say when a good portion of the time you tell me you didn't mean it?"

Peter shrugged. "I don't have an answer for you. I lose my temper and I speak out of line. I'm sorry. I'm used to dealing with people who respect me and don't question my advice."

Grace knew her next statement could either send them deeper into the argument or settle the matter more peaceably. She felt a weariness in her heart and chose the latter.

"I'm sorry, Peter. I didn't mean to make you feel that I held no respect for your advice. I will suggest to Miranda that she speak to you on all these matters. Now, if you will excuse me, I'm feeling rather tired. I think perhaps I'll rest a bit."

Peter smiled and looked as though he might suggest joining her when a light knock sounded at their door. Grace felt relieved as Peter turned to see who it was.

Miranda stood on the other side, her expression rather tentative. "Peter, Father needs to see you in the study."

He glanced back at Grace and then nodded to his sister. "Grace was just going to rest for a bit. Perhaps you and I might talk a bit on our way downstairs."

They left the room with Peter closing the door behind him. Grace sunk onto the bed and felt such utter despair that she immediately burst into tears. She loved this man so very much, yet he had the power to hurt her like no one else. Not even Martin Paxton had caused her this much pain. But then, she hadn't loved Martin Paxton.

Burying her face in the bed pillows, Grace sobbed herself to sleep, hoping and praying that God would somehow show her what she was to do in order to live in peace with this man she so dearly loved.

─┤ C H A P T E R   F O U R ├─

KAREN STOOD SHIVERING in the cold. Staring at the charred rubble that had once been a prosperous business, she wondered what she should do next.

"You were sure lucky to get out of there alive."

Karen turned to find Mrs. Neal, the proprietor of the Gold Nugget Hotel. "Hello, Roberta. Yes, I suppose we were lucky." Her words were not at all enthusiastic, but Karen felt the truth of their meaning. They had all survived, everyone but Aunt Doris. That loss was more than Karen cared to dwell on, and she tried to put on a brave front for the sake of the children.

"I came over when I saw you out here. Wanted to tell you that you and the kids could take up a room at my place. I've had a good number of fellows head off for the north. There's a nice big room on the back side of the second floor. There's only one bed, but your boy could sleep on the floor. It ain't buggy at all, so you wouldn't have to worry about that."

Karen smiled and gave the old woman a hug. She'd become acquainted with Mrs. Neal through the small community church where the old woman pounded out church hymns on a well-worn piano. Most everyone in the area knew Roberta Neal. The widow always lent her opinion and support, be it solicited or otherwise.

"Thank you, Roberta. That would be most helpful. We've stayed a few days in Mr. Ivankov's tent down by the Tlingit village, but I'm sure he'd like to have his property back. He's heading north to Sheep Camp, and I wouldn't want him to be delayed on our account."

"Well, you just move your things right on in this afternoon," Mrs. Neal replied.

Karen laughed. "Well, there really isn't much in the way of things to move. The clothes on our backs are pretty much the sum total."

Mrs. Neal nodded and headed off down the street. "There's no need to fret about that. The Ladies Church Society is collecting things for you even now. They'll be bringing items over to the hotel this afternoon. You just gather your young'uns and come."

Relief flooded her at the news, giving her the tiniest hope for the future. Karen had wondered what they would do. She'd considered trying to buy a place or have something built, but the cold weather was hardly the time to start new projects.

"We'll be there after lunch," she called out after the woman.

Turning her gaze back to the charred remainders of the Colton Trading Post, Karen wondered how best to get word to Peter. She knew he'd be back within a week or two to bring supplies. She supposed it could wait until then, since there was no guarantee the mail would reach him any sooner.

To say she was discouraged would be an understatement. Karen tried to sort through her tattered emotions and determine what was to be done. She turned away from the rubble and made her way to the small cemetery where her mother was buried. Despite the cold and the dark, heavy clouds overhead, Karen felt confident that this was the only place she would find any real peace.

A handful of other graves kept company with her mother's resting-place. Karen knelt beside the simple white marker, mindless of the frozen ground. She gently touched the letters that spelled out her mother's name and sighed.

"I came here to find you both," she murmured. "I knew I'd find you already gone, Mother, but I honestly expected to reunite with Father. How can it be that you are both gone from me now? Now, when I need you the most."

She almost laughed at how silly that seemed. She was thirty years old, almost thirty-one. Surely at this age a person no longer needed their mother and father. But Karen had no one else. Grace was gone and married, and all the time and effort she'd poured into that relationship was now a thing of the past. There were, of course, Jacob and Leah Barringer, but they belonged to Bill, and he had pledged to come back for them. Karen had no reason to believe it would be otherwise.

Then there was Doris. Her beloved aunt was now resting in the arms of Jesus, as the simplistic eulogy delivered by Pastor Clark had suggested. It had been Aunt Doris's wish to eventually settle in Seattle, so Karen had arranged for her body to be shipped there. Karen knew her sister Willamina would be happy to handle the arrangements.

"Poor Aunt Doris." Karen thought it so tragic that the once-vibrant spinster's life should end this way. She had given Karen such hope, especially on days when things had gone particularly bad. She had always reminded Karen to keep her focus on things above and not things below. But now Karen felt lost, without a purpose.

"I miss her so much," Karen again spoke aloud. "I can't remember a time in my life when she wasn't my very favorite aunt. It seems strange that she will never again advise me or speak to me of her past experiences." She turned her gaze to the thick blanket of clouds and asked, "Why, God? Why has this happened? Why have you allowed Martin Paxton to destroy my life?"

And she was convinced that the blame rested solely with Paxton. There was no doubt in her mind. The fire, according to those who had examined the remains, had begun in the front of the shop, well away from lanterns and stoves that might have sparked a flame. To Karen's way of thinking, that pretty much signaled that someone had set the fire. Martin Paxton had sworn revenge on each of them, so it seemed an easy conclusion that he had arranged the disaster— perhaps even set the blaze himself.

"I thought I might find you here," Adrik Ivankov announced.

Karen got to her feet quickly and nodded. "I just needed a few moments alone. I was about to come find you."

"It's always nice when a pretty lady seeks your company." Adrik smiled, caus- ing the edges of his mustache to turn upward. He'd shaved his beard the day after the fire, and Karen found him much more appealing without it. His smile broad- ened as if he could read her mind. "So what's your pleasure?"

Karen blushed and looked away momentarily while she collected her thoughts. "Well, I know you're anxious to get up to Sheep Camp, and I wanted to let you know that Mrs. Neal has offered us a room at the Gold Nugget. She said we could move in after lunch, so you will have your tent back."

"I'm glad that you'll be in warmer surroundings, but there was really no need to rush. I could have just as easily headed up north without those few things."

Karen met his dark eyes and felt his expression warm away the chill of the day. She found his looks most appealing. Even the scars on his neck and jaw only seemed to make him more intriguing. She'd often thought to ask him about the encounter that had left him a marked man, but just as quickly had tucked away such questions. She didn't want to presume upon an intimacy that he'd shared with her father and mother. They were acquaintances and he had saved her life, but surely there was nothing more—nothing deeper.

"You seem pretty lost in thought," Adrik said. "You want to talk about it?"

Karen shrugged and looked down at the grave. "I was just feeling a bit over- whelmed. I really miss them, Adrik. I was so sure I would come north to spend time helping Father. I mean, it seemed right and all the pieces fell into place. I thought I would learn to minister to the Tlingits at his side and that I would spend the rest of my days here. Then, too, I was confident that Aunt Doris would be alive for a long, long time. How is it that they can be so quickly taken from me? How is that fair? How does it speak of a compassionate God?"

"Your pa was fond of quoting Scripture and saying that the rain falls on the just and the unjust. Bad things happen. There's no doubt about it."

Karen shook her head, her vision blurring with tears. "I want them back. I want the past to be nothing more than a bad dream. I want to sit down to tea with my mother. I want to hear my father preach, just one more time." She looked up at Adrik, not caring that he would see her tears. "I need them and now they're gone." Her voice broke and she buried her face in her gloved hands.

She had known he would come to her, and in some ways she thought she had willed him there by her desperate need. Adrik wrapped her in the warm safety of his embrace. This was the second time in a matter of days that she'd cried in his arms.

"I know I'm a poor substitute," Adrik told her, "but I'd like to think that my friendship with your parents would spill over to a friendship with you." He paused for a moment, and Karen lifted her face to see his contemplative expression. "I miss them, too," he added softly.

"Oh, Adrik, I am sorry. I hadn't thought—"

He put his finger to her lips. "You weren't expected to. You have enough to contend with. I just wanted you to know that we can share this grief together. You needn't bear it alone."

He lowered his face to better see her. Karen grew aware of his nearness, almost as if she hadn't realized it before. With his mouth only inches away from her own, she found herself wondering what it would be like to be kissed by this broad-shouldered native her father had put so much trust in. The thought so startled her that she pushed away from him.

"I'm sorry. I didn't ... mean to ... break down." Her voice betrayed her confusion as she stepped back several paces.

"There's nothing wrong with having a good cry now and then," Adrik said, appearing for all the world as though he had been completely unaffected by their encounter. "I just want you to know that I care—that I'm here for you and the children if you need me. I'll be heading up to Sheep Camp tomorrow, but I'll be back for Easter Sunday. Maybe we can share a dinner and discuss the future."

Karen laughed. "The future. That's exactly what I can't seem to figure out. I doubt discussing it would lend any more clarity to it than I've already gathered."

"You'd be surprised. Sometimes it just takes a bit of conversation to help a person think a thing through. For instance, I know that right now you're pretty wrapped up in the bad things that have happened. I'm thinkin', however, if you were to sit down and start talking about all the blessings you still have, you'd find that a lot of things have slipped your mind."

Karen knew he was probably right. "I know I've been blessed. It's just that right now the pain is much more evident."

"Life isn't without its moments of sorrow and pain," Adrik reminded her, "but it's also not without its pleasantries and good. God has a plan in all of this. We might not know what it is, but He is sovereign and we must trust His way."

"I don't know about that," Karen said, stiffening. She was angry at God right now and far from ready to put her feelings aside. "I trusted God with everything, and now I'm like Job sitting in the ashes, with most everyone dead and everything stripped away."

"That's not true," Adrik said, refusing to leave the matter well enough alone. "You told me yourself that you have money in the bank. Money enough to start over. That's not having everything stripped away."

"All right, then. Everything that's important to me has been stripped away. Grace is gone. My mother, father, and aunt are dead. I've lost all my wordly possessions with exception to my father's Bible, and I'm left with the charge of two children who are suffering from their own losses. It doesn't seem an easy thing to me to say that God has a plan. Frankly, if this is His plan, then I'm not impressed. Innocent people are dead, while a murderer walks free to plot further revenge."

Adrik gazed at her a moment before saying, "I know you're angry."

She shook her head, the sorrow quickly being replaced by feelings of rage. "You don't know the half of it. Martin Paxton has been a thorn in my side for nearly a year. He tormented and abused Grace, and he's threatened all of us on numerous occasions. I want the man to pay for what he's done."

"You can't be sure he was responsible."

"Oh, can't I?" She shoved her gloved hands deep into her coat pockets. The cold was beginning to seep into her bones. "He was there. He the same as announced it with that smug smile of his."

"You still can't be sure. You can't go around accusing a prominent citizen of arson."

"Prominent! That's hardly the word for him."

"I've been around Skagway long enough to know that he's well respected."

"Feared, you mean."

"No, I meant respected. He's poured money into the community, and that's made folks think rather highly of him. He's involved in helping to finance the railroad out of Skagway and has invested hundreds of dollars into improving the harbor. People see that as a real boon to business. With that kind of background, I doubt seriously anyone is going to believe your accusations." He stepped toward her and took hold of her arms. "And, Karen, that's all you have. Accusations. What if you're wrong? What if you heap some form of revenge upon this man, only to learn that a passing drunk started the fire instead?"

Karen tried to pull away, but he held her fast. "Let me go. You don't know what he's like. You don't know what he's capable of."

"Maybe not, but I do know that justice and revenge rest in God's hands and not our own." His voice took on a tone of reproach. "You know full well your father would tell you to turn the other cheek. He'd tell you to suffer your enemy with patience and God's peace."

"He might very well say that, but he isn't here," Karen said rather hatefully. "And by your own words, you are a poor substitute." She saw the way her statement hurt him. She wanted to apologize, but at the same time she wanted nothing more than to get away from him.

He let her go with a nod. "That I am."

It was Adrik who walked away rather than Karen. She felt frozen to the place where she stood, her anger and bitterness now feeding off her last reserves of energy. Why did he have to say those things? Why had he argued with her in the first place? She would never have said anything so meanspirited had he not provoked her.

The argument in her heart seemed very lame considering that she could see how deeply she'd wounded him.

"But he's wrong," she whispered, putting aside her shame. "He's so very wrong. He doesn't know Martin Paxton like I do. He doesn't know what the man is capable of."

Slowly she made her way back to the Tlingit village. They were a silent and steady people, these Tlingit. They dressed for the most part like any white person, but their endurance and patience were hardly attributes Karen found in her own people. The gold fever brought new throngs of cheechakos on a daily basis, and most of them were white and incapable of the hardships of living in the wilderness. The Tlingit seemed to take the swell of population in stride. They were often misused and abused by the newcomers, but Karen saw an attitude in them that held them proud and straight. It was almost as if without words they were saying, "We were here before you came, and we will be here after you're gone."

Karen approached the tent she shared with Leah and Jacob and squared her shoulders. They would be happy to hear about the move, of that she was certain. Leah was afraid of the noises at night, and the cold left her shivering even when sandwiched between Karen and Jacob. Jacob wouldn't care either way, but he worried about Leah, and Karen knew he'd be pleased to see her comforted. She found his love for Leah almost enviable. He knew his responsibility to her—knew that they were alone in the world at this point—and yet they had each other. For all his problems and times of despair, Karen knew Jacob cared deeply for Leah's welfare.

The children were just finishing a lunch of stew and bread when she pushed back the flap and stepped inside.

"We saved you a bowl," Leah declared. She pulled back a dish towel to reveal the awaiting meal.

Karen's stomach rumbled and she only then realized how hungry she was. "Thank you. I appreciate it." She hurried out of her gloves and bonnet, then sat down on the ground between the brother and sister.

"I have good news," she said, taking up the offered bowl.

"Have you heard from Papa?" Leah questioned excitedly.

Karen felt sorry for the child and patted her head. "No, I'm sorry. It's not that kind of news. But it is good, nevertheless. Mrs. Neal has offered us a room at the Gold Nugget. She also said the ladies at the church were collecting clothes and household goods for us. It will be like Christmas to see what they manage to put together." Karen tried to make it all sound like great fun.

She ate a bit of the stew and added, "There's just one bed, so Leah and I will have to sleep together. We'll buy you a cot, Jacob, and we'll just have to honor each other's needs for privacy. I don't look for us to stay there long, so it shouldn't be too great a hardship."

"If we aren't stayin' long," Jacob began, "then where are we going?"

Karen shrugged and tore off a piece of bread that Leah offered. "I'm not sure. My first thought was to go back to the States, but I can't do that. I can't take you away when your father has promised to come back for you."

"Why don't we go north—go after him?" Jacob questioned.

"That is a thought. I suppose we have enough money put aside that we could buy supplies. We could probably even pay for packers to see us over the summit. After that, I'm not sure what awaits on the other side."

"I heard one old fellow say that the summit is the worst of it," Jacob said, his tone taking on a hint of excitement. "There's plenty of water travel after you get on the other side of the mountain. We could just float north to Dawson City and find Pa."

"Could we?" Leah asked, the hope sparkling in her eyes.

"I suppose it is something to consider," Karen replied. She ate thoughtfully for several moments, then added, "There really is nothing to keep us here now."

"I can ask around about packers," Jacob offered. "I'll bet Mr. Ivankov could tell us where we can get help."

"Mr. Ivankov might not be feeling too kindly toward me just now," Karen replied. "We had some rather heated words. We should probably stick to asking someone else."

Jacob shrugged. "That's all right. I know lots of folks I can talk to."

Karen nodded. "Good. Let's see to getting settled over to the Gold Nugget first, and then we'll discuss the matter in more detail. There's a lot of work involved. It's not just money or the supplies. There's a great deal of distance between here and Dawson and a great many people of less than sparkling character who stand between here and there. We'll have to think this through and do what's best to ensure our safety."

"And we have to pray, too," Leah chimed in.

Karen nodded, but felt no desire to encourage any further thought on the matter. She was angry at God, and talking to Him just now was the last thing she wanted to do.

⊣ CHAPTER FIVE ⊢

PETER WAS UNPREPARED for the sight that awaited him at breakfast. His father sat at the head of the table as usual, but before him was an open Bible, and he was reading to the women who sat at either side of him.

"Psalm 112 says, 'Praise ye the Lord. Blessed is the man that feareth the Lord, that delighteth greatly in his commandments. His seed shall be mighty upon earth: the generation of the upright shall be blessed. Wealth and riches shall be in his house: and his righteousness endureth forever.'"

The verse set Peter on edge. He could remember a time when he was very young that his father had read the Bible to them at bedtime, but that habit had certainly passed by the wayside for more constructive, beneficial habits. Peter cleared his throat before his father could continue. "I didn't realize we were having church this morning."

Ephraim looked up and smiled at his son. "You're often gone before the morning meal. Grace convinced us of this marvelous routine." He smiled at his daughter-in-law, and Peter watched her flush nervously. She knew he wouldn't approve, and yet she'd once again gone behind his back to manipulate his family.

Peter took his chair beside Grace and refused to look at her when he spoke. "Grace has a great many strange ideas. I wouldn't give all of them credence."

"Peter, what an ungracious thing to say. Grace is a lovely young woman with a fine mind," Amelia Colton admonished. "She has brought a certain light and joy into this house. I hardly think it fair to accuse her of having strange ideas."

"I do not recall that this family ever wasted time over meals with Bible readings," Peter said as he reached out for a platter of sausages.

"Then perhaps we should have," Miranda countered.

Peter paused, holding the platter aloft, but turned his attention to his younger sister. "I would think you, above the others, would know exactly how faulty Grace's advice can be."

"You are just being thickheaded," Miranda snapped.

"And you are being insolent, a trait I know without a doubt you have learned from my wife."

"Enough!" Ephraim declared. "I'm ashamed of your words, Peter. Did I not raise you to have respect for the women in this family? For any woman?"

Peter dropped the platter on the table. He slammed his fist down hard, causing all the contents on the table to vibrate. He got to his feet, barely able to contain his anger. Nothing had gone right since he'd brought Grace home.

"Perhaps you would find the meal less unpleasant if I simply took myself away."

"Son, we would just as soon have you stay," Ephraim began, and Peter felt some small amount of control returning. But just as he considered retaking his seat, his father added, "However, if you insist on treating your sister and wife in a poor manner, then perhaps it is just as well you go."

Peter had never been dismissed from the family table. He'd been honored and his words heeded as grains of wisdom until now. He looked at Grace, whose head was bowed, her gaze fixed on an empty plate. This was her fault. He should have known it would happen. Why had he been so foolish as to listen to his heart?

He turned and left the room without bothering to add further comment. *I will not stand around and be insulted by my own family. Let them have their Bible studies and prayers.* He turned the handle on the front door, then remembered some important papers he needed. The delay only served to anger him more.

Taking the stairs two at a time, he allowed his anger to fuel his stride. The papers were in his locked desk near the window. Leaving the door open, he fumbled in his pocket for the key and had barely managed to open the desk when Grace entered the room.

"Peter, I would like to talk to you."

He straightened and momentarily forgot the papers. He met her intense brown eyes, saw the flush to her cheeks, and thought her the most beautiful woman in the world. Why did she have to be so cantankerous and opinionated?

"I have nothing to say."

She nodded and closed the door. "Perhaps not, but I have something I want to say to you."

"I do not wish to hear it. You've caused enough harm already. I can't believe you could so quickly turn my family against me. But that, of course, has always been the power of religious nonsense. I suppose when you found you could not convert me, you went after them with the same ardor and zeal. Well, you have my congratulations, Grace. You have managed a feat I would have thought them above falling for."

"Peter, this isn't a game."

He watched her fold her hands calmly as she leaned back against the door. "I have only the highest regard for your family. They have been gracious and kind. They have willingly taken me into their fold without question and without resentment. I thought you wanted me to get along with them. On the trip here from Skagway you encouraged me to befriend your sister, and I have done that. She is a pleasant woman who has a sharp mind for detail. She knows a great deal and has much to offer. I enjoy her company, and I believe she enjoys mine, as well."

Peter gritted his teeth and turned back to the desk. He opened the drawer and took out a thick fold of papers. Relocking the desk, he looked back to Grace and cocked his head to one side. "Is that all?"

"No," she replied softly. "Peter, I love you with all my heart. I'm sorry that I have offended you by sharing my faith with your family, but I'm not sorry for having shared my faith. I did not do so with the intention of bringing you harm or causing ill will against you."

"Well, for something you never intended to do, you've done it well."

"I don't wish for you to leave in anger. We've had too many angry words of late." She moved toward him, but Peter quickly held up his hand.

"Stay your distance, madam. I will not be cajoled from my mood."

"I had no idea to offer such a plan. I merely hoped to offer my sincerest apology and tell you that my motivation has always been love. I love you and I love your family. But I also love God, and the love He has shown me gives me cause to want to share it with others."

Peter shoved the papers into his coat pocket. "I'm afraid if you are unwilling to put an end to this religious nonsense, we will constantly be at odds. I have no desire to fall into a routine of the masses. My Maker needs no such confirmation from me. God knows who He is and what He plans. He will not be swayed by my prayers or reading of the Bible.

"In turn, I need no such lessons in religious matters from my wife." He paused and eyed her hard. He knew it was a look that could wilt even the heartiest of his sailors, but he didn't care. "What I need from you is obedience and respect. Without that, we cannot have a marriage."

"I agree," Grace said. "I do respect you, Peter. I admire your abilities and your knowledge. I am sorry that I've overstepped my place at times, but I will not give up my faith because it makes you uncomfortable."

"It doesn't make me uncomfortable, madam. It makes me furious. You put a fence between us, with God sitting squarely on the top rail. You use your religion as an excuse to defy me and make me look the fool in my father's eyes, and that I find most unforgivable."

She again moved toward him, but once more he put up his arm to stop her. "I have business to attend to."

"Business that is more important than our marriage?"

"Quite frankly, I wish I had never married you at all."

He hadn't meant to say the words; they had simply poured from his mouth in his rage. So many times before he had come to regret speaking in anger, but nothing compared to the regret he felt now as he watched Grace's expression fall and tears come to her eyes.

Guilt propelled him past her and out of the room. He couldn't stand to see the anguish on her face. He couldn't bear to know that he had so neatly broken her spirit with one fatal blow. But break her he had. He was certain of it. There was a defeat in her eyes that he knew would always haunt him.

He hadn't meant the words. But he couldn't take them back.

Grace crumbled to the floor. She felt her chest tighten, her lungs desperate for air. She wanted to scream, but there were no sounds to utter. There was nothing but the hideous, abominable pain in her heart.

I only did what I thought was right, Father. She struggled to focus on prayer rather than give in to her misery. *I thought if I shared your mercy and goodness that Peter and his family would see the void in their lives and come to you. And they have . . . all except for Peter.*

Her breathing gradually returned to normal, and with it she found her voice. "Oh, Father, what am I to do? I was faithful to you. I was faithful, and now I feel as though death would be kinder than life."

––––––––––

Peter didn't return anytime during the day, and by night when Grace prepared for bed, she was certain he was gone for good. Word came to them the next morning that *Merry Maid* had set off for Seattle, giving confirmation to Grace's fear of desertion.

"I can't believe he has behaved so badly," Amelia said, putting her arm around Grace. "It isn't like him to be so cruel."

"He's not fighting against Grace, Mother," Miranda stated. "He's fighting against God."

"Not a healthy stand to take," Ephraim said as they gathered around the breakfast table. "Grace, perhaps I will have a chance to speak to him. I'm to take *Summer Song* north in the morning. I know it would be best if you could meet face-to-face to work out your differences. Once Peter calms down, he'll realize his foolishness and wish to make amends."

Grace said nothing but started when Amelia threw out the next suggestion. "Why don't we all go north? Grace hasn't seen her friends in some time, and with Easter approaching rather quickly, she could share the season with them as well."

"That would be splendid," Miranda declared. "I would love to make the trip again. I think the adventure would be perfect for all of us."

"I appreciate what you're trying to do," Grace said quietly, "but Peter has no interest in seeing me or resolving this issue. He told me he was sorry we married, and it wouldn't surprise me in the least if he sought to remedy the matter."

"He wouldn't dare!" Amelia exclaimed. "A divorce would be a disgrace. No son of mine is going to use such an underhanded method of facing difficulties. Now I'm certain we must go north. Ephraim, you need to talk some sense into that boy before he does something foolish."

"I should have taken him in hand long ago," Ephraim admitted. "I suppose it was just so much easier to give him a free hand than to oppose him."

"We can't dwell on 'should haves,'" Amelia said softly. "We can only work in the here and now. Whether or not Peter feels he needs to see Grace and work this matter out in a reasonable manner, we know the truth of it."

Grace thought of how wonderful it would be to see Karen. She longed to sit down and have a lengthy discussion with her friend. Only Karen would understand her pain and suffering. Karen's faith was so strong, and she would applaud Grace's efforts to keep God at the center of her life and to bring Him into the hearts of those around her. Karen might even give her an idea of how to help Peter.

"I would like very much to go north," she finally spoke.

"It's settled, then," Ephraim replied, taking up the Bible. "We will have our things taken down to the ship tonight and be ready to leave at dawn." He thumbed through the Psalms. "Ah, here is where we left off. Psalm 112, verse four. 'Unto the upright there ariseth light in the darkness: he is gracious, and full of compassion, and righteous.'"

Grace barely heard the words. Her heart was so full of sorrow and pain. She thought of her mother and wished silently that she could somehow materialize at the table. They had had so little time of closeness, but their letters over the last few months had given Grace such peace and happiness. If it was possible to make up the lost years, then that was truly what was happening.

"'He shall not be afraid of evil tidings,'" Ephraim read, catching Grace's attention. "'His heart is fixed, trusting in the Lord.'"

Oh, I desire that my heart be fixed on you, O Lord, Grace prayed in the silence of her heart. *You know my heart is in pieces, Father. You know the pain I suffer. Please help me in this time of need, just as you have in all the others.*

—{ C H A P T E R   S I X }—

"KAREN, *MERRY MAID* is in the harbor," Jacob announced. He came into their cramped quarters and threw his fur-lined hat onto the bed. "I saw the ship anchored there. You want me to go wait on the dock for the captain?"

Karen shook her head and put aside the mending she'd been doing for Mrs. Neal. "No, I'll go. I've just finished mending three blankets and twice as many sheets. I need some fresh air."

He frowned and reached for his cap again. "You know how crazy it gets down at the docks. Won't be very safe. I'd better go with you."

"No, I'll be fine. If you go, it will mean you missing lunch." Karen pulled on her coat and reached for her bonnet. "Leah is helping Mrs. Neal in the kitchen. They should have lunch just about ready, so why don't you get something to eat before you head back to work?"

Jacob nodded, but Karen didn't wait for him to comment further. She was out the door and headed down the steps before she finished tying her bonnet. The thought of telling Peter what had happened was something she both dreaded and looked forward to. Peter would understand her anger at Paxton, and he would know what to do. He wouldn't treat her as Adrik had, expecting more from her than she could give. The dread came in knowing Peter would be devastated at the destruction of his store. Business had been very good and the profits quite high. The fire would set him back significantly, and Karen knew that wouldn't be welcome news.

Hurrying down the oozing thaw that was the street, Karen nodded and waved to this one and that, all the time weaving in and out of the growing crowd of newcomers. Thousands of miners had poured into Dyea for the winter, and now as the weather warmed, people came out in droves. In fact, every week more and more people poured into Skagway and Dyea, and with the growing populace came all manner of evil and hardship.

In Dyea, there were now over forty saloons, most of them in tents, but nevertheless they distributed an abundance of libations. Positioned not far from the saloons and sometimes even within their confines were the brothels and "daughters of joy," as the prostitutes were often called. Karen cringed as she passed by several of these less fortunate women. These sallow-faced women generally called out their propositions to the crowd, but they held a mutual silence as Karen passed by. She could not aid their need or better their situation, and that made her useless to these women. Karen, uncertain of how to deal with the issues at hand, hurried by with her head bowed. As one who was not very well acquainted with emotional love, much less physical intimacies, the women, quite frankly, embarrassed Karen. And as one who was struggling with her beliefs, Karen couldn't even muster the interest to share her faith or suggest a better life for these lost sisters.

She wanted to be charitable and treat them with decency, for her mother had always said Jesus did the same for the prostitutes of His time. But now, with her heart so hardened, so hurt, Karen was unsure of how to respond to anyone.

Pushing through a crowd gathered around one of the many con men, Karen shook her head in amazement. How foolish they were. The eager newcomers were fresh and unspoiled by the harsh elements of the frozen north. They faced their futures with keen enthusiasm and great pride. They were going north to make a fortune in gold—their future promised nothing but prosperity.

The con man promised them prosperity, as well—the quick and easy variety. They all did. From the underhanded salesman who sold secondhand saws—so dull they couldn't slice through butter without getting caught up—to the man who played three-ball pick-any, sliding a peanut under one of three balls and letting people pay two bits a guess to find the peanut. They always lost. Always. And still they didn't learn. They lined up for their moment—their prosperity.

Some prosperity!

Karen laughed in a cynical manner and lifted her skirts as she crossed the muddy streets. The weather had been so very unpredictable, and warm winds had caused a bit of a thaw, leaving the streets almost impassable as the hard frozen ground gave way to muck and standing water. Such was the paradise she had come to.

Sandwiched between the mountains and the west branch and main stem of the Taiya River, Dyea offered as much civilization as it could. Folks had big plans for the town, and a harbor with proper docks stood at the top of the list. The docks were even now in a constant state of improvement thanks to the Dyea-Klondike Transportation Company, or the DKT. Jacob had helped work on the piers and told Karen they were rapidly becoming first rate. The town was bound for popularity and wealth.

Of course, Dyea's sister city, Skagway, already had a decent harbor and soon they would have a railroad, as well, thanks to some Englishman's ingenuity. Karen frowned, but not because of Skagway's vast improvements. Thoughts of Skagway only served to bring unpleasant contemplations of Martin Paxton. Karen had tried her best not to think of him at all, knowing that even speaking his name made her blood run cold and her temper run hot.

"Yahoo!" The cry of exuberance came from one of the gambling halls as Karen came ever closer to the harbor. Day or night you could always find someone drinking or playing any number of games. Mostly it was naïve newcomers, chee-chakos, those poor undaunted souls who had no idea what they were in for.

Having suffered an Alaskan winter, Karen was now considered a sourdough. She was well respected by the other more permanent residents of Dyea, earning her right to be among them. The thought turned bitter in her heart, however. She hadn't come here to earn rights or achieve titles. She had come to find her father—to join him—maybe even help in his ministry. Instead, she had come too late. Her father was dead, and so too her dream of working with him.

Gunfire rang out, along with laughter, screams, and the unmistakable sounds of fighting. Karen glanced ahead, cautiously watching in case a body were to be thrown out into the streets from the Lazy Dog Saloon. She passed quickly and unscathed, nevertheless glancing over her shoulder just in case something or someone came at her from behind. It was certainly no town to raise children in, and because she was caring for Jacob and Leah, her thoughts ran constantly to their welfare. She had no idea what would be best for them. Ideally, their father should have made those decisions, but Bill Barringer had selfishly headed north, deserting his family to Karen's care. And while Karen could admit that the children were probably better off with her than climbing over the golden stairs of the Chilkoot Pass, she fretted that she would somehow make a mess of their lives.

I suppose if I allow myself to stay angry all the time, she mused, *I won't be much good to them at all.* But even as she recognized the truth in her thoughts, Karen pushed it aside to acknowledge her growing desire for revenge. Paxton couldn't be allowed to go unpunished. He had long taken things into his own hands, and it was time someone stopped him. Karen knew she didn't have the ability to stop him on her own. That was why she had to enlist Peter's help. Peter would understand and help her to see that justice was done. Justice or revenge.

The shallow waters that reached the shores of Dyea were not suited for ship traffic. In the early days, boats would harbor quite a distance from shore, then small launch boats or Tlingit canoes would bring their freight to dry land. The new docks and wharves were making the task much easier, but their length required a considerable haul to bring the goods into town. It had made more than one sea captain give up the idea of docking in Dyea. And it was for this reason that Skagway seemed much more likely to succeed. Karen didn't care either way. She didn't plan to stay forever in Dyea, nor move to Skagway. In fact, her life was so topsy-turvy at this point that she really had no idea where to head.

I don't belong anywhere, she thought. *I don't belong to any place or to any person.* The loneliness of this thought was more chilling than the breezy April air.

"Watch yar step there, missy," a gruff-looking stranger said as Karen scooted past him on the docks. "Them are slippery ways."

Karen could see for herself that the docks were wet, and she slowed her steps to heed the man's warning. "Can you tell me if Captain Colton of the ship *Merry Maid* has come ashore?"

The man pulled off his wool cap and scratched his filthy head. His expression suggested his intent consideration of her question. "I kint say that I've seen him."

She nodded. "Thank you. I'll just press on."

He grunted, pulled his cap back on, and went back to his work. Karen scanned the wharves looking for any sign of Peter. She knew he would be there, for he always came ashore ahead of his freight. Even now, she could see that *Merry Maid* was being unloaded.

Soon her efforts were rewarded. She spotted Peter as he pressed through a crowd of heavily laden men. People were everywhere and so were their goods. Stacks of possessions, caches for the trip north, were guarded warily by rosy-cheeked boys who had no idea of what the days to come would bring. Some strutted around the docks as if they'd already discovered gold. Others were so eager to continue their journey that they worked at an exhausting pace. Karen felt sorry for them. Few were dressed for the north. Their lightweight coats and boots were no match for the blizzards of the Chilkoot. When she worked the store, Karen had tried to convince those poor souls coming in for goods that they'd need to buy heavier coats and snow gear. Sometimes they'd listened, but more often they'd ignored her. She'd given up trying after a time, and unless someone asked her opinion, she'd sell them only what they asked for. They'd learn soon enough that this was only the beginning of a lengthy and possibly deadly journey. No sense in wearing herself out trying to convince them of things they would blindly ignore.

"Peter Colton!" Karen called as a sea of people threatened to send her back up the wharf and onto the sandy shore. She reached out, waving her arms.

"What are you doing here?" Peter questioned. He pushed through the crowd to take hold of her arm. "It's sheer madness out here. You know it's always like this when the ships come to dock."

"I know, but I had to talk to you before you attempted to deliver goods to the store."

"Attempted?" Peter asked, raising a brow. "What's this all about?"

"There's been a fire," Karen said, seeing no reason to play out the telling of her tale.

"The store?"

She nodded. "Burned to the ground. We lost everything."

Karen could see his confusion and shock. Putting her hand on his arm she added, "The Barringer children and I managed to escape, thanks to Adrik Ivankov. But Aunt Doris didn't make it. She succumbed before reaching the door. I thought she was right behind me—in fact, I thought I had hold of her arm. I had her blanket and nothing more."

This news brought Peter from his stunned reverie. He looked at her with such tenderness that Karen knew his sorrow was sincere. "Miss Pierce is dead? I'm so sorry. I truly liked your aunt."

"It's been hard to imagine life without her—to look toward the future—but it seems the days are passing, the sun still rises and sets, and the ships still dock, bringing us boatloads of people."

Peter nodded. "There's no sign of it slowing down, either. I had to turn people away in Seattle." He glanced across the madness, then suggested they go somewhere else to talk.

"The Glacier Restaurant looks swamped with newcomers," Karen observed. "Why don't we head over to the Pacific Hotel? They're boasting chicken and dumplings for lunch. The *North Star* came in yesterday with crates of chickens and fresh eggs. They sold for incredible prices."

"I can well imagine," Peter replied. "The Pacific sounds acceptable, and quite frankly, I'm famished."

They wove their way through the excited crowd, saying nothing as if by some mutual agreement. Karen realized that once they were alone, she would have to explain her theory about Paxton. Adrik's words of warning came back to haunt her. What if Paxton were an innocent bystander? What if he were merely gloating at their misfortune? But that just couldn't be true.

The Pacific Hotel was nothing elaborate. Built nearly overnight from plank boards and sheer gumption, it could accommodate at least three hundred guests. Of course, most of those would find little other than a place to spread their blanket, but it nevertheless got them in out of the elements.

Peter found a small table and pulled out the chair for Karen. Considering her words carefully, Karen decided to ignore her pang of conscience. Without delay she leaned forward and explained what was on her mind.

"I think Martin Paxton was responsible for the fire."

Peter stared at her blankly, and for a moment Karen thought he hadn't heard her. "I said—" she began again.

"I heard what you said," he growled and slammed his cap down on the table. "What makes you think this?"

"It was after Adrik had helped us from the burning building," Karen said softly. "I was standing there crying, and I looked up and gazed across the alleyway. He was there."

"Paxton?"

Karen saw the look of disbelief on Peter's face. "Yes! It was Paxton. Not only was he there—after all, half the town had come by this time—but it was the manner in which he conducted himself. He stared at me smugly and then tipped his hat as if to say, 'How do you like my handiwork?' That was when I felt confident that he was responsible. After all, he lives in Skagway, not Dyea. Why would he even be here in the middle of the night unless it was for something underhanded?"

Peter studied the table in silence. He ignored the aproned matron who plunked down two steaming bowls of dumplings.

"What are you drinking?" she asked in a tone that suggested she had little time for dallying.

"Leave us alone!" Peter demanded. "And take this away."

"Well, if you're gonna sit in this restaurant, you're gonna have to pay."

Peter dug into his pocket and threw several coins onto the table. "There. Leave the food and take your money."

The woman smiled, displaying her lack of front teeth. "Sure now, luv. You just stake your claim here and let me know when you strike it rich." She laughed as if terribly amused with herself, then grabbed the coins, worth three times the price of the dumplings, and tucked them down her blouse.

Karen threw her an irritated glare, hoping the woman would speed up her retreat, but her action only made the woman laugh all the more.

"Where is Paxton now?" Peter asked, ignoring the woman.

"I don't know. I presume back in Skagway. Peter, I know this may sound ridiculous. After all, I have no proof. But I feel confident that he's guilty. You don't know him like I do. You know him from your father's stories of Paxton as a boy. I know him from the torment he put upon Grace."

"Grace would have me forgive him," Peter said angrily. "As if that animal deserved anything but the end of a gun."

"Grace is only trying to be a good Christian," Karen said with a shrug. "But even good Christians have their limits. Martin Paxton is evil. Plain and simple. He has caused us more problems than I can even begin to name. I have no desire to let this go unpunished."

"What about the law? Did anyone see anything?"

"Apparently not. Adrik thinks a lantern was thrown through the front window, for we found a lantern in the debris."

"But no one heard that happen? No one heard the glass shatter?"

Karen thought of the noisy nights in the small town. Gold fever combined with cabin fever made for a brand of rowdiness that could only be called chaotic, at best. Windows were often broken, in spite of the cost to replace them. Wars were waged on a nightly basis between those who felt they'd been cheated out of something they'd brought to the shores of Alaska and those who sought to relieve them of their possessions.

"I'm afraid many folks might well have heard the glass break, but they would have given it no further thought. Arson is such an unthinkable act that I'm sure no one would ever have suspected such a thing."

"But such a thing happened and it destroyed my livelihood with it. Not to mention it took the life of your aunt." Peter's face contorted in rage. "This is what Grace cannot understand. Her religious notions matter very little to men like Paxton. She believes the world to be a place of love and second chances."

"In all truth, I believe that, too," Karen murmured softly. "At least I used to."

Peter stared at her for a moment. "It doesn't take much to open your eyes if you're willing to see things for what they are. I find that religion clouds a man's judgment of what's real and what's illusion."

"And what is real?" Karen questioned, feeling a desperate need to understand. "Just when I think I have a clear understanding of that, it somehow seems to elude me."

"What's real is the ugliness and evil of some men. They will stop at nothing." His voice lowered in a menacing manner, chilling Karen with the hatred that rang clear in his next statement. "Death is the only way to keep them from causing more harm."

Karen shivered. "What are you suggesting?"

"Retribution," Peter stated flatly. "I suggest we find Paxton and exact our revenge."

"But what if he isn't guilty?"

"He's guilty. If not of the fire, then of much else."

Karen saw a blatant hatred in Peter's eyes that gave her reason to fear. He was serious. He meant every word. He had no qualms about seeing Paxton dead. There was a part of her that found his words intriguing, but there was a greater part of her that cautioned her to forget the scheme, to return to her faith and let God deal with the sordid details of her life.

"I think we should move with caution and consideration," she finally managed to say. "Paxton is revered in Skagway. People believe he's quite beneficial to their community." She remembered Adrik's words as if he'd just spoken them. "We can't just rush in with accusations and no way to prove his guilt."

"I don't plan to rush in with accusations," Peter said, meeting her gaze.

Karen saw a coldness in his eyes that reminded her of Martin Paxton. The lifelessness of it frightened her. Perhaps she had said too much—encouraged too much.

"Peter, this is very serious. You must remember Grace."

"Grace doesn't care about me. She's driven a wedge between me and my family. Taking care of Martin Paxton will return respect to me—at least in the eyes of my family."

"But it may destroy Grace's trust, her feelings for you," Karen countered.

"Those feelings are already destroyed," Peter said, refusing to look away. "Grace cares only for her God and nothing for me."

"I find that hard to believe. She's loved you from almost the very first moment you met. I can't believe she would put those feelings aside simply because you have differences of opinion where religion is concerned."

"Well, believe it." He narrowed his eyes and his tone took on an accusing nature. "I suppose you will defend her now—take her side?"

Karen realized that in order to see Paxton punished for what he'd done, she'd have to align herself with Peter. But in order to do that, she would have to put aside her friendship with Grace.

But Grace wasn't here. No one was here. Karen was left alone to fight her battles.

I will not fail thee, nor forsake thee. The verse of Scripture seemed to speak from her soul, reminding her of God's constant faithfulness.

But if you truly cared, Karen thought, *you'd never have allowed us to suffer so much.* Her anger resurfaced as she thought of the fire and of her aunt's death. She wanted revenge. She needed revenge.

"Grace is wrong," Karen finally said. She felt torn, as if she'd just put an end to something very special, but now that the words were out of her mouth, she couldn't take them back. Worse still, she didn't want to.

ADRIK IVANKOV found himself the voice of reason in a vast sea of gold-hungry travelers. The only trouble was, no one wanted a voice of reason. Gold fever made men do things they'd never otherwise consider. Adrik had seen grown men climb the trail with broken limbs and raging fevers. He'd also seen them die far from the goal that had brought them so far.

For over a week, Adrik worked alongside his Tlingit friends to pack goods from the Scales up to the summit. The Scales were so named because it was there the packers reweighed the goods they were packing and increased their fees in accordance with the steep climb to the top of the Chilkoot Trail. Adrik found the extra money he earned transporting goods a much surer guarantee than looking for gold in the ground. He had saved an impressive amount of money, even while sharing much that he had with his friends and Tlingit relatives.

Money wasn't everything. In fact, Adrik had rarely even considered the stuff over the last week. His thoughts were more easily assigned to a pretty woman living in Dyea. Karen Pierce was more than just a pretty woman to him, however. She was the daughter of a man he greatly respected—a man whose death he felt somewhat responsible for.

"We're quitting," Dyea Joe said, releasing the pack frame he used for carrying goods.

The announcement didn't surprise Adrik. For the last two days the sky had been devoid of clouds, and with the sun bearing down on them in its April splendor, a new problem had arisen. Adrik's sense of the situation was confirmed as he listened to his friends speak out.

"Snows are very dangerous," one Indian told him.

"There's gonna be slides," another muttered. "Ain't gonna stay up here. Goin' back down."

Adrik nodded. He knew as well as his friends did that the trails were threatened by avalanches. The warm temperatures were making the newer snows less stable.

"I've tried to explain the situation to our rather ignorant—perhaps short-sighted—employers," Adrik told the men, "but they don't care. The fever has them and gold is all they can think on. Safety means nothing."

"We won't pack their goods," Joe announced to his friend. "Money isn't worth a life."

"I agree," Adrik said in a tone of exasperation. "I don't blame you for sitting this out. I'm not risking my life, either. The next few days are going to prove the situation one way or another. Look, it's Saturday night. Why don't we put our lots together and feast. We'll let the cheechakos figure this one out for themselves."

Dyea Joe nodded and picked up his things. "There's gonna be big trouble if they keep climbing to the summit."

"Plenty big," another man joined in.

Adrik knew the risks. Already the weather was changing. As was typical of the area, the changes came quickly and dramatically. Heavy clouds had moved across the sky to blot out the sun. He could only nod and lend his silence to signal his agreement. Adrik greatly admired their knowledge of the land and their seeming sixth sense for danger. He had worked hard to learn from them, to take their bits of wisdom and use them to better his own existence. Now, as he tried to share such wisdom with others, he was met with disbelief and total disregard.

No one cared that the threat of an avalanche was so great that the Tlingits not only refused to move goods up to the Scales, they were heading well out of the established gathering and down to Sheep Camp. Adrik was moving as well. He knew their advice to be sound, and he cherished his life too much to risk it in pride or greed. Sheep Camp sat in the narrow valley between impressive mountains. The canyon offered no real place of escape, as was evidenced in earlier floods of Sheep Camp. But if the snowslides came from the summit, almost three thousand feet above them, they'd most likely not cause problems that far down the trail. He hoped.

Gathering his tent and a few supplies, Adrik followed the small group down the trail. The going was tough because the snow had started up again and the wind blew bitterly against their faces. Adrik didn't mind the hard climbs and descents, but he generally refused to travel when the weather was difficult. The heavy clouds stole the light from their path, and as night came upon them, Adrik was more than ready to pitch his tent and take his rest. The lantern light from the Seattle and Golden Gate restaurants perked up his spirits. He didn't plan to pay the exorbitant price for a meal there, but the light meant civilization and the end of his journey.

As if they'd prearranged the setting, the Tlingits and Adrik worked to put the camp in order beside the Taiya River. Soon a blazing fire warded off the night's worries and the chill. Sheltered among the fir, pine, and aspen, the winds and snows seemed less threatening. Adrik ate heartily, grateful for the dried reindeer meat and beans offered to him by Dyea Joe. Canned peaches were passed around the camp, and Adrik lanced a half peach with his knife and stuffed it into his mouth. The juice was icy cold and trickled down his face into the stubble of a newly growing beard, but nothing had ever tasted better.

"Say, I've got some biscuits left over from morning," Adrik suddenly remembered. Unwrapping a bundle from his coat pocket he added, "They're soaked in bacon grease and ought to warm up nice." He skewered several of the hard biscuits on a branch and held them out over the fire. The grease began to melt and popped and sizzled on the flaming logs. The aroma filled the air with an anticipated promise of filling their bellies.

"How is your mother?" Adrik asked Dyea Joe. The two were distant relatives. Joe's mother was in fact second cousin to Adrik's now deceased grandmother, and their families had always been close.

"She is well. She does not like the fuss over gold." Dyea Joe's English bore witness to his forced attendance at mission schools.

"I doubt any Tlingit or First Nations people are going to find the rush very appealing," Adrik said, shaking his head. "The cheechakos are ruining the land. They run right for the gold, never seeing how priceless the land itself is."

"You speak the truth." Dyea Joe's dark eyes seemed to glow in the light of the fire. "People often throw away the gold in their hands for the promise of the gold hidden from them."

"Amen."

Adrik pulled the browned biscuits from the fire and pushed them from the stick onto a pie tin. "Help yourself," he said, passing the tin to Joe.

The tin circulated around the fire, the biscuits being taken up quickly by the hungry Tlingit packers. Adrik took the last biscuit and leaned back on his elbow to enjoy the rest of his meal. Thoughts of tragedy and mishaps from the trail threatened to put a damper on his mood. Determined to raise his spirits, he pushed aside the threat of snowslides and instead thought of Karen Pierce.

But thinking of Karen caused Adrik to think of her losses, and again his thoughts turned bleak. First her mother had passed on long before Karen had come north. Then her father had died with only a narrow distance separating them. Her friend had married and moved away, and now Karen had lost her aunt and her livelihood, as well.

Adrik knew, however, that it was the death of her father that gave Karen the most sorrow. She had been so close to reuniting with him. She had felt called to come north—perhaps to even work at her father's side—and now she was robbed of both seeing him and working with him. And a deep loss it was. Not only for her, but for the people who had come to care so much for her father. Including Adrik.

Adrik held the highest regard for Wilmont Pierce. The man had been both a good friend and mentor. Adrik had guided Pierce on more than one occasion and had been instrumental in seeing that he was accepted among the Indian people. Wilmont had been different from other missionaries. He had come in love and kindness, seeking to meet the people where they were. He lived with them, ate with them, and studied their ways to better understand them. This gave the Tlingit respect for Pierce, and although many of the Tlingit were already baptized into Russian Orthodoxy, they embraced Wilmont's preaching. In time, Adrik had even seen a change in the hearts of many of the natives.

"Hello, camp!" came a decidedly British voice.

Adrik looked up to find a shivering man, hardly dressed warmly enough for the cold. "Come warm yourself by the fire, stranger."

"My gratitude, sir." The man hurried to the edge of the fire and held out his gloved hands. "The night came upon me unaware. I was sent back to bring hot food to our camp, but I'm afraid the restaurants are packed. There's scarcely room for even one more."

Adrik lifted the pot of coffee. "Would you like a cup?"

The man sat down on a thick log beside Adrik and nodded enthusiastically. "I would be very grateful. I'm not fond of American coffee, but at this point I'll take anything hot."

"Where you from, stranger?" Adrik asked, pouring coffee into a tin cup.

"London, England. I have family in the Canadian provinces. I was visiting there when all this news of gold came. We decided to give it a go. Make our fortunes. And you?"

Adrik thought him a very amicable sort and smiled. "I've lived in these parts all of my life." He handed the man the coffee and saw a smile of satisfaction as the stranger wrapped his fingers around the warmth of the cup.

"How marvelous." He drank for a moment, then added, "I suppose you already have a gold mine?"

Adrik laughed. "No. I'd say my people found more gold in salmon fishing and furs."

Dyea Joe passed by in silence, dropped a small package beside Adrik, and entered the tent directly behind the stranger. This drew the man's attention immediately. "Are these your packers? We hired a few, but the cost was draining our funds and there are still tariffs to pay."

"No. They're actually distant family members. And good friends." Adrik picked up the pack and unwrapped several pieces of dried salmon. Joe was offering the stranger food for himself and his companions. "This is jerked salmon. Eat some yourself and take the rest back to your friends."

The man nodded and snatched the offering quickly, as if Adrik might change his mind. Eating as though starved, the man alternated between sips of coffee and mouthfuls of jerky. When it was gone, he fidgeted nervously with his mustache, his gloved fingers pulling off pieces of ice that had become encrusted above his lip. For several moments Adrik actually wondered if he'd somehow offended the man. He seemed strangely quiet after having been so lively moments ago.

The stranger took a deep, long drink, then turned to Adrik. "So you trust these Tlingits?"

"With my life," Adrik replied.

"Our packers told us to stay away from the Scales and the summit. Said the snow is unstable. What do you make of that?"

"I make it as the truth, mister. That's the reason we're camped here. The weather has been too varied. We had a fierce snowstorm a few days back, then an icy rain. Then it dumped another few feet of snow. After that it warmed up, melting things a bit. It makes the snow on the mountains unstable. Slides are guaranteed."

As if to emphasize Adrik's words, a rumbling could be heard in the distance. It didn't last long, but Adrik knew it was a slide. "You hear that? That's the sound of snow barreling down the mountain. You don't want to hear that sound and be in the path of it. There's nothing you can do to get out of its way."

The man stood, looking rather alarmed. "My family—my friends. They're up there now."

Adrik shook his head. "I can't tell you what to do, mister, but you'd do well to get them back down in this direction. It's only the second of April. There's plenty of time to get north. I wouldn't start back up until the Tlingits do likewise. They're pretty good about figuring these things out."

Another rumble sounded, and even though Adrik knew these small slides were probably not stealing away life in the night, he also knew they were precursors of things to come.

"Thank you for your hospitality. I must go." He handed Adrik the cup and tipped his hat. "You were most kind."

Adrik saw the panic in the man's eyes. He understood his fear and could only pray that it might keep the younger man from death's clutches. Healthy fear had a way of doing that. If a person listened to that quiet little voice, a nudging of the Holy Spirit, Adrik's mother used to say, then a person could often avoid a great deal of misery. Adrik had tested that theory and knew it to be true.

With a yawn, Adrik gazed upward to the dark mountainsides before settling in for the night. The ominous sense of death surrounded him, leaving him uneasy. He began a wordless prayer, pleading with God for the protection of those who were exposed to danger. He also asked God's blessings on Karen Pierce before he crawled into the tent and fell almost instantly asleep.

Around two in the morning a commotion awoke Adrik. He soon realized that the alarm announcing an avalanche was being sounded in the small village. Uncertain where the trouble was, Adrik pulled on his boots and coat to go in search of the problem and offer whatever help he could. Taking a lantern and a shovel, he made his way up the trail in the bitter cold and wind. Along the way, he heard tales of everything from the Scales camp being destroyed to there being little or no damage. Ignoring these conflicting stories, he pressed on up the trail and finally met up with a group of men with shovels.

"We're digging out at least a dozen people," one man told Adrik. "There may be more, but we saw a couple of parties headed through this direction. One man said there were at least twelve."

Adrik shook his head and took up a shovel. "We might as well get to work," he said, eyeing the ominous mound of snow and debris.

Twenty people were eventually rescued. The workers laughed and slapped each other on the back while the injured were treated to warm beds and strong coffee. The mountain had failed to claim their lives and so the folks were generally celebratory, having defeated the slide.

Adrik, however, was more apprehensive. He studied the dark shadows of Long Hill and stared upward toward the summit. Snow swirled around him, gentle and harmless. It was hard to imagine that such a thing could be so deadly.

The next morning there was talk of how they'd escaped the perils of the mountain. How things would be easier now that the threat of avalanche had passed. Adrik reminded more than one person that the Tlingits were still not convinced of a safe passage, and since they'd been the ones to warn of the situation in the first place, perhaps they should be heeded now. But folks generally ignored his suggestion.

Then around nine-thirty the slides began again. Word came down from the Scales that they were shutting the operation down and evacuating the camp. Adrik breathed a sigh of relief. Perhaps now they would avoid real disaster.

Around ten o'clock a low rumbling came from Long Hill, signaling yet another slide. Adrik shook his head as word came back that three people had been buried in their tents. He thought of the young Englishman and wondered if he'd convinced his party to bed down in Sheep Camp for the night.

With the evacuation of the Scales came the tram workers. The tram had been set up to assist those gold rushers who had extra money to spend. The tram owners were making a bundle, much to the disappointment of the natives who had found packing for the stampeders to be small compensation for the white man stealing their trail. They didn't mind Adrik working the line, for he often gave generously to their people, but they resented the intrusion of men from the outside. So, with this thought well etched in their minds, the Tlingits had little comment when the tram workers were caught in yet a second avalanche and killed. After all, they had warned them.

Now people were staring warily up the mountain, watching and wondering. Because the wind had picked up as well as the snow, visibility was near zero. Adrik sensed the impending disaster, but knew he was helpless to stop it. Through a combination of God's grace and wisdom along with his knowledge of the land, he was standing safe and protected, while others would meet their death.

And then it happened. The roar echoed and vibrated against the mountain-sides. The very earth seemed to move as a wall of snow poured down from the mountains above. Would-be rescuers could only wonder and wait, having no idea how bad the situation might be. Had there been others on the trail? Had they met their match in this devastating play of nature?

Adrik felt certain there would be trouble. He loaded up what he could carry and grabbed his shovel. There was work to do.

Rumors ran rampant. Announcements of two hundred or more dead filtered down the trail. Gunshots were fired off to signal the need for help. The stampeders were more than generous with their offering. They came in droves, responding in a way indicative of the frozen north. You helped your brother in his need, because next time it could just as easily be you.

Adrik dug in and worked along a line where the trail had once been. Someone said that the remaining two hundred people on the Scales had been making their way down the mountain. One man claimed to have been at the end of the line holding on to a rope that simply seemed to disappear as the snows assaulted them from every side.

Bodies, some battered beyond recognition, were lined up and transported down the trail to Sheep Camp, where a makeshift morgue was set up in a donated tent. An emergency committee was appointed for the task of identifying and tagging each body for burial or shipping.

Adrik shook his head at the loss of life. They'd been warned, but greed had kept them fearlessly ensconced in the path of danger.

"Here's another one!" someone yelled.

Adrik looked up to find the Englishman from the night before. He sighed. The man was dead. Shaking his head, he went back to work only to unbury another body.

"I've got one, too," he called out.

People came to help him dig out the man who surprised them all by moving his lips and fluttering his eyes. When he opened them, he stared up at Adrik as if he were God himself.

"He—he—lp me," the man stammered. Blood streamed from his face, which was crusted from the ice and snow in his beard and mustache.

"We're doing the best we can for you, mister," Adrik told him. "Look, just lie still. You'll be taken to Sheep Camp where there's a doctor." Even saying it, however, Adrik knew the man would never make it. The left side of his face had been crushed.

The man closed his eyes, then opened them again. Adrik could see he was laboring to breathe—to live. With a power that seemed beyond the man, Adrik watched him struggle to reach his coat pocket. Realizing the man would not be settled, Adrik moved his hand aside and reached into the pocket with his own gloved hand. He pulled out the contents: a pouch of tobacco, a pipe, and a folded piece of paper.

"Letter," the man mumbled. "Children."

Adrik looked at the possessions, not understanding. "You have children at Sheep Camp?" he finally questioned.

"No," the man replied.

The workers were ready to move the man to a plank for transport down the trail. Adrik held his hand up. "Wait just a minute. He's trying to tell me something."

"He needs attention," one surly man replied.

"You think I don't know that?" Adrik snapped. Turning to the dying man, he said, "Look, friend, I don't know what you're trying to tell me."

The man looked up at Adrik with lifeless eyes. "Letter to children." With that he closed his eyes and stopped breathing.

"He's gone," the surly man announced. "Take him to the morgue."

Adrik looked at the dead man and then to the letter in his hand. Stuffing the pouch and pipe into his own pocket, Adrik opened the letter.

1898, 2nd of April.

Jacob and Leah Barringer, in care of Miss Karen Pierce, lately of Dyea.

The very breath left his lungs, and Adrik found himself almost gasping for air. Was it possible? Was the dead man Bill Barringer? "Wait!" he called. "I might know who that fellow is."

The workers paused. "Friend of yours?"

"Not exactly." He stuffed the letter into his pocket. Taking a better look at the dead man, Adrik scratched his jaw. It could be Barringer. He'd only met him twice, though, and there had been so many other men just like him.

"I'll take him down." Adrik could only pray the man wasn't Barringer.

He grabbed the end of the plank from the man who held it. "You can borrow my shovel. Name's Adrik Ivankov. Nearly everybody in Sheep Camp knows me. You can leave my shovel at the Summit Meat Market. They know me real well."

The man said nothing. He seemed surprised by Adrik's rapid instructions. Adrik motioned to the man on the other end of the plank. "Let's go." He couldn't help but think that he would once again bear bad tidings to Karen Pierce. It wasn't a job he wanted, but obviously God had given it to him for a reason.

CHAPTER EIGHT

KAREN WIPED HER HANDS on her apron and looked out the window of the Gold Nugget's kitchen. Steam fogged the windows on the inside, while ice frosted them on the outside. It was useless to try to see out.

"Fretting ain't gonna bring them here any faster," Mrs. Neal chided. The older woman dumped a huge wooden bowl filled with bread dough on the floured counter top. "Workin' will keep your mind off the rumors. I'm sure that Mr. Ivankov and Mr. Barringer are just fine."

Karen pushed her hands into the dough and began to mechanically knead the mass. "I just want to know if the slide was as bad as people are saying. That last guy said over three hundred people are dead." She fell silent, an image of Adrik Ivankov coming to mind.

"Adrik might be up there," she murmured, trying hard not to sound worried. "But I doubt Bill would be. After all, he left us before Christmas. He might have gotten held up by the weather, though."

"Now, then, the world is full of might be's," Mrs. Neal chided. "No sense frettin' until you know something for sure."

"I know you're right, but I can't help it. I've had nothing but trouble since coming north. I don't know that I can bear losing anyone else." Karen's voice broke as she pushed the dough aside. "I need a breath of air."

Wiping her hands on her apron, Karen turned and grabbed her shawl. "I'm going to check on Leah." She left the aromas of the Gold Nugget kitchen behind and stepped out into the yard behind the building where Leah Barringer was supposed to be splitting wood. Leah was nowhere in sight, however.

The wind whipped up the edges of the shawl, causing Karen to tighten her hold. Spring thaw wouldn't come for at least another month or two, and the elements were rising up just to make themselves known. Karen sighed, silently longing for warm weather. Looking down the alley to see if Leah might have gone visiting with one of the neighboring proprietors or their help, Karen found the place surprisingly deserted.

Karen felt her pulse quicken. Only the day before the fire, Leah had been the center of some much undesired attention. Drunken miners had thought her rather pretty and accosted her on her walk from church to the store. Karen and Jacob had been delayed at the church, helping to organize plans for Easter. When they came upon Leah, backed against a wall with smelly, dirty men on all sides of her, Jacob and Karen were livid. Karen could only hope they weren't repeating the scene.

Heading down the alley, Karen called to the girl. "Leah! Leah, where are you?"

She heard the girl crying before she spotted her hiding behind a stack of crates. "What's wrong?" Karen questioned, kneeling in the mud beside Leah. The cold muck seeped through her layers of skirt, petticoat, and woolen hose. "Are you hurt? Has someone bothered you?"

"No," Leah sobbed. "I'm just scared."

"What are you scared about?"

"Papa." The single word needed no further explanation.

Karen reached out and lovingly touched the girl's cold cheek. "I know you're worried about your father, but we haven't heard anything that would indicate he was in the avalanche. Besides, you know how rumors are. Things are seldom as bad as they seem."

"But I feel it here," Leah said, pointing to her heart. "I just know Papa's in trouble—that he's hurt."

"You can't know that," Karen said, trying her best to sound convincing. She wasn't about to tell the girl of her own concerns. "Don't borrow trouble. Besides, your papa should be well on his way north."

"Karen, is God mad at us?"

Taken aback, Karen cleared her throat nervously. "Why would you ask that?"

Leah looked up, her dark brown curls falling in ringlets to frame her face. Her blue eyes were huge, pleading with Karen for answers. "Mama used to say that sometimes bad things happened 'cause we didn't listen to God. 'Cause we had to have things our own way instead of His way. She said God sometimes let the bad things happen to get our attention 'cause we were ignoring Him. I'm thinking maybe God is mad and trying to get our attention."

Karen wasn't about to agree with Leah's conclusion. She wanted to keep her distance from God just now. It wasn't that she didn't want to maintain her childhood beliefs. And it wasn't that she was refuting His existence or supremacy, Karen told herself. She was just angry and nursing a grudge, and she couldn't do that and cozy up to God at the same time.

There was a part of her that already worried she'd somehow brought this disaster on them. God no doubt wanted her to see that He was still in charge—that He could further strip her of what was dear and precious. That He, as Leah put it, might be trying to get her attention.

"I know for a fact that God isn't mad at you, Leah," Karen said, feeling confident of that one thing. "Come on, let's get the wood inside, and we can go upstairs and clean up. You're no doubt soaked clear through. Mrs. Neal baked a fresh batch of cinnamon rolls, and I know she'd spare one for you."

Karen got to her feet and reached out to help pull Leah up. The last thing she wanted to do was get involved in a discussion about God.

"I'm thinking we'll both feel better when we get some official word on what's happened. In the meantime, we need to keep a positive heart."

"I know Papa loves God," Leah whispered. "I know he loves me and Jacob, too." She said it in such a way that Karen believed the girl was desperate for affirmation.

"I know he loves you, too," Karen replied, putting her arm around Leah's shoulders. "He loved you enough to protect you from the worst of the trip and wait until he could send for you in a comfortable fashion. He just wanted to keep you safe."

Leah looked up and smiled. "I'm glad you were here to stay with us. I love you, Karen. I wish I could have had a sister just like you."

Karen hugged her close. "I'm happy to be a sister to you now, Leah. I'll always be here for you and Jacob."

"Just like God," Leah said, smiling.

"Yes, just like God," Karen said, the words turning bitter in her mouth.

———

The afternoon brought more news of the Palm Sunday avalanche. Karen cringed as packers and would-be miners flooded into the Gold Nugget Restaurant with stories of the tragedy.

"We dug out bodies all day," one man said between bites of Mrs. Neal's dumplings. "Never seen nothin' like it. Don't plan to see nothin' like it again. I'm headin' back to Texas. No gold is worth this."

Karen listened to the stories as she helped Mrs. Neal serve the various customers. She finally worked up her courage and asked one particularly knowledgeable man if he knew exactly how many people had died.

The man scratched his ragged-looking beard. "I heard it said at least seventy. At first they was afeared it might be a couple hundred. The folks at the Scales were mighty slow in comin' down that mountain. There was still a few hundred up there, and we figured 'em all to be goners. Happy to be proven wrong."

Karen nodded. Seventy dead was still a high number. "How soon will they know who all was involved?"

"They been identifying bodies since the slide. Should have some of the bodies back here by the end of the day. Heard tell they was gonna make a cemetery just northwest of Dyea. There's already some folks over there lighting big bonfires to warm up the ground enough to dig."

Karen left the man to his meal and went to wait on the new group of men just coming into the dining hall.

"We've got a few places at that far table," she announced, not realizing until she came to the last man that she was staring into the face of Adrik Ivankov. "You're all right!" She surprised the entire group by throwing her arms around Adrik and breaking into tears. "I thought you might be dead."

She pulled away and found Adrik staring at her in dumbfounded silence. "Sorry," she whispered. "Guess that was rather uncalled-for. It's just with the rumors of the avalanche and all, I was starting to get overly worried."

Adrik said nothing but pulled her back toward the front door. "We've gotta talk. The news isn't good."

"But of course it's good. You weren't killed in the slide." Karen didn't want to hear anything more about the slide. She was afraid of what news Adrik might share.

"Maybe not, but others weren't as fortunate."

"I know," Karen said, nervously letting go of Adrik. "I just heard that some seventy people are dead. Is that true?"

"At least seventy. They're still not sure if they've found everyone."

"How awful. Were you in the middle of it?"

Adrik shook his head. "Not when the slides came. I'd been earning a bit of money with Dyea Joe and his family. We decided the snows weren't safe and moved back to Sheep Camp. We tried to convince other folks to move back with us, but they wouldn't hear it. Now they paid for their greed with their lives."

"I'm so glad you were sensible. We've been worried sick." She paused and looked down at the well-worn rag rug. "Look, I know I said some things—that I wasn't very hospitable . . ."

"Never mind. I knew the grief was making you say things you didn't mean." Adrik's expression softened from worry to sympathy. "Karen, there's something else you need to see."

"What?"

He reached into his pocket and pulled out a letter. "I was given this by a dying man."

Karen looked at him quizzically. "Why do I need to see this?"

"Just open it."

Karen shrank away as a strange foreboding gripped her. Fear crept up her spine and settled on her heart. Slowly she unfolded the paper and read. Glancing up to meet Adrik's eyes, Karen shook her head. "You said you took this from a dying man. Bill Barringer is dead?"

"I'm not sure," Adrik replied. "I was helping to dig out the victims of the slide and came upon a man who begged me to take this letter. He died shortly afterward. He was pretty banged up, his face crushed—probably he hit his head on rocks as the snow swept him down the mountain. I went with him to the morgue, but as you know, I only saw Bill a couple of times."

Karen felt her head begin to swim. Poor Leah. Poor Jacob. They were all alone now. Completely deserted and orphaned in the world. Adrik was speaking to her, but Karen couldn't hear the words. The only thing she heard was Leah's question, over and over in her head. *"Is God mad at us?"*

"Karen, why don't you sit down for a minute and rest?" Adrik took hold of her by the elbow and led her away from the front door and into Mrs. Neal's office.

"I can't believe this is happening. God must hate me." She let the letter fall to the floor. "I can't give them that. I can't take away their hope."

"You can't give them false hopes, either."

Karen shook her head. "You don't understand. If that man was Bill, then they're all alone."

"They still have you. You were just telling me before I left that you would stay with the kids no matter what."

"And I will," Karen replied firmly. "But it isn't the same and you know it." She looked deep into his eyes, feeling some small comfort from his closeness. "It just isn't the same."

"Yes, I know that. But I also know that having someone love and care for you, even someone who wasn't born to the task, is better than no one at all. Maybe it's even better." His words warmed her strangely. She felt drawn into his gaze as he continued to speak. "You love those kids even though you don't have to. No one would blame you if you ran in the opposite direction, but I know you won't."

Karen saw the sincerity of his words in his expression. He knelt beside her and handed her the letter. "You may be the only person left for them. You have to give them this and you have to be with them when they learn the truth."

"But we don't know for sure that it was Bill. People carry posts all the time for folks. Someone might have been coming down to one of the camps to pass the letter on."

"That could be true," Adrik said softly, "but then again, it might not be. You have to be ready for the worst."

"Seems like the worst is all I'm getting these days," Karen said, looking again at the letter. She raised her eyes to Adrik's. "This is a hateful land. Cruel and inhumane. My father must have been crazy to love it so."

Adrik shook his head and got back to his feet. "You'll learn in the by-and-by that land has no choice in the matter. It is what it is by God's design. People, however—now, people have a choice. *You* have a choice, Karen."

Karen deliberated long after Adrik left as to how she might break the news to Jacob and Leah. There was no easy way to tell them the truth. Then again, what was the truth? Had the dead man truly been Bill Barringer? Would it be cruel if she suggested he was dead, when their father might well be miles away in safety? Sitting in Mrs. Neal's tiny room, Karen longed to run as far away from Alaska as she could possibly go. Her heart urged her to pray, but in her weariness she rejected such comfort.

Nothing I do is going to change a thing. I can't bring the dead back to life, and I can't give those kids a reason to have hope any more than I can figure one out for myself.

She looked to the ceiling. "I suppose this is all my fault. Will you just keep stripping away the things I need? Will you take everyone—everything? Why not kill Martin Paxton instead of Bill Barringer?"

"Oh, here you are," Mrs. Neal announced as she entered the room. "I have a couple of folks who are looking for you."

Karen looked up and shook her head. "I don't feel like company right now. Who is it?"

"It's your friend Grace." Mrs. Neal smiled. "That ought to cheer you up."

Karen jumped to her feet. "Grace is here?"

"She sure is. Just outside by the front door. She's brought another gal with her. Pretty little thing with hair the color of brown sugar. Can't say I've ever seen her before, but I could be wrong."

"Could I talk to her here? I just got bad news about Bill Barringer."

"The kids' pa?"

Karen nodded. "Adrik thinks he died in the slide. He took a letter from a man, and it's addressed to Jacob and Leah. I need to tell the kids and give them this letter from their father, but I don't want to do it just yet."

Mrs. Neal, a softly rounded woman, put her arm around Karen's shoulder in motherly comfort. "You just stay right here and I'll get Grace. You'll need her now."

Karen knew the truth in that. She sorely missed Grace and her friendship. She wondered how Grace had found her here instead of at the burned-out remains of the store.

Mrs. Neal paused by the door. "I'll keep Leah busy, and if Jacob comes in from work, I'll see to him, as well."

"Thank you," Karen murmured, feeling a bit of peace return to her heart at the sight of her friend. It had been over three months since she'd last seen Grace. How marvelous that she should arrive at just this moment.

"Karen!" Grace called out, hurrying across the room. She wrapped her arms around Karen and hugged her tight. "Oh, I've just learned about the fire. How very awful for you. Are you all right?"

Karen pulled away. "How did you learn about it? Did Peter find you and tell you?"

Grace frowned. "I've not seen Peter since docking in Skagway. Miranda, Peter's sister, accompanied me here. Oh, goodness, Miranda!" Grace went back to the door and motioned for the woman. "Miranda, come meet my dear friend and mentor."

Karen easily recognized the resemblance between Peter and Miranda. Although Miranda's hair and eyes were darker, her chin and mouth were clearly the same. The woman smiled and extended a gloved hand. "I've heard so much about you, Miss Pierce. Grace speaks of you often."

Grace smiled. "The pleasures and joys of one's life deserve special consideration. Karen has been both to me. Karen, this is Miranda Colton."

Karen shook the woman's hand. "Miss Colton."

"Please call me Miranda."

"Only if you call me Karen."

The woman laughed. "Oh, I shall, for I feel I already know you very well through Grace."

Karen seriously doubted that either Grace or Miranda knew her at this point. She felt only rage, anger, and now complete confusion. She would soon have to tell the Barringer children about their father and then decide what was to be done in order to see to their welfare.

Grace picked up the conversation. "We went first to the store only to find it gone. Whatever happened?"

"Paxton."

Grace raised her brows. "Martin Paxton?"

"The very same. He burned down the store and killed Aunt Doris."

"What? Doris has passed on?"

Karen saw the pain in Grace's expression. She touched her friend's arm to offer comfort. "Adrik Ivankov woke us. He saved the rest of us—the Barringer children. I thought Aunt Doris was with me, but I only had hold of her blanket. The smoke had overcome her and she collapsed. Adrik went in after her, but . . ." She paused, trying to keep her voice from breaking. Taking a deep breath, Karen changed the subject. "But what of you? How is it that you're here? Aren't you worried about Martin Paxton?"

"I don't think he'll bother me now. I'm married. He knows he's lost."

"He knows nothing," Karen said, walking back to the wooden chair. Angrily she plopped down, not even caring that she had done so in a most unladylike manner. "Martin Paxton is to blame for the fire. He's promised to make all of us pay. He managed part of that threat with the fire."

"But how do you know it was Mr. Paxton?" Grace asked in grave concern.

"I saw him at the fire. He was watching us as we came out of the building. He smiled at me, Grace. Smiled that smug, ridiculous smile."

"That doesn't mean he actually set the fire," Grace protested.

"I suppose you would just forgive him even if he stood there acknowledging the deed. Peter said that would be your attitude. He said you didn't understand that men like Paxton never change."

Grace stepped back and frowned. "Peter spoke against me?"

Karen saw Miranda take hold of Grace's arm. "Surely he wouldn't," Miranda stated.

"He didn't say it to speak against you, but merely to explain to me why you wouldn't be inclined to believe anything against Paxton."

"I know Mr. Paxton to be an evil man. You forget, I was the one who had to deal with him first," Grace said, anger tingeing her tone.

"I don't forget, but apparently you do. Peter said you wanted to send the man a letter of forgiveness. Why would you ever want to do that? You owe him nothing. He's the one who should apologize."

"But the Bible calls us to forgive our enemies and do good to those who wrong us," Grace protested. "You taught me that."

"I don't care. The man is evil and deserves to pay for what he's done. The Bible is also full of examples where people were justly punished."

"That's true, and if Mr. Paxton started the fire, he should indeed pay," Grace replied. "But, Karen, what if you're wrong?"

"Do you have proof?" Miranda asked. "Proof that the authorities might recognize?"

"I know Paxton, and I know what he's capable of. It was the middle of the night, and he had no other reason to be here in Dyea. I feel no doubt whatsoever. He was responsible, and he must pay for what he's done."

"Just listen to you," Grace said, shaking her head. "You don't even sound like the Karen Pierce who taught me to trust God in matters of revenge."

Karen didn't take her upbraiding easily. She got to her feet, hands on her waist.

"I'm not the same Karen Pierce. I've lost my mother, my father, and now Aunt Doris. I nearly lost my own life. Not only that, but I just got word that the Barringer children's father has most likely died in an avalanche. Please don't expect me to be the same woman. You went off to safety with Peter. Safety and love and comfort. You had no idea of Paxton's threats, and you have no idea how badly I want that man punished."

"But, Karen," Grace tried to reason, "it isn't our job to punish him. If you have proof, take the matter to the law. Better yet, take it to God. Vengeance belongs to Him."

"If I wait for God, it might never be taken care of." Grace's mouth dropped open in surprise, but still Karen wasn't moved. "I don't have much faith in what might be done to put an end to Martin Paxton's evil deeds."

"Sounds to me like you don't have much faith, period."

Karen looked hard at Grace. "I don't want to discuss my faith or lack of it. I only want to see Paxton suffer as he's made others suffer. Peter understands me. Why can't you?"

Karen stormed from the room, knowing that she'd deeply wounded her friend. It hadn't been her intention. She had been happy to see Grace once again, but something in her gentle demeanor set Karen on edge. Something in her peaceful spirit forced Karen to think of the wall she'd put between herself and God. A wall that grew higher and deeper by the minute.

⊣ CHAPTER NINE ⊢

"JACOB, LEAH, I NEED to talk to you upstairs," Karen said as soon as supper was finished. She didn't wait for either one to respond to her, but instead got up from the table and moved toward the back stairs just off the kitchen.

For a new building, the floors certainly creak a lot, she thought. With each step, the stairs seemed to groan, evidence of their shoddy carpentry. Karen didn't mind for once. She listened to the sound and heard her own heart in those wooden moans. She felt old and tired. How could it be that she had passed thirty years and had so very little to show for it? All of her girlhood friends were married with large families of their own. She was still single and cared for a dead man's children.

"This is about Pa, isn't it?" Jacob asked.

Karen waited until they were inside their room before she spoke. "Mr. Ivankov brought back a letter."

"Then he's alive?" Leah asked with hope.

Karen met Jacob's fixed stare and knew she couldn't hold the truth from them any longer. "I don't know, quite honestly. Adrik found a man who resembled your father. He had this letter on him, but nothing else to identify him. The man had been battered by the avalanche, and Adrik had only seen your father on a couple of previous occasions."

Jacob said nothing, his face losing its color. His eyes refused to blink and he maintained his stoic gaze, while Leah cried out loud and threw herself onto the bed.

"No! He can't be dead!"

Karen handed the letter to Jacob and went to gather Leah in her arms. "I know this is hard. But, Leah, we don't know for sure that it was your father."

"I knew he was in trouble. I knew," Leah sobbed. "I told you, didn't I?"

"Yes, you did." Karen stroked the girl's hair as Leah buried her face against Karen's chest.

Karen watched Jacob as he read the letter. She knew the content, but she waited for him to say something about the message.

"Perhaps you could read the letter to Leah," Karen suggested.

Jacob looked up. "Let her read it herself." He threw the page at Karen. "Where's his body? I'll know if it's him. Even if nobody else can recognize him, I can."

Leah cried all the harder at this reminder, but Jacob refused to be moved. Karen could see the hardness in his eyes. He was walling himself in, just as she had.

"Why don't you talk to Mr. Ivankov about it?" Karen suggested. "I don't think this is the place or the time. I'll read the letter to Leah while you go find Adrik. He should be somewhere around the church. I heard him say he was helping to deliver supplies from the wharf."

Jacob, his blue eyes now damp with tears, licked his lips and pulled on his fur hat. Taking up his coat, he headed for the door.

"It won't be light for long," Karen called after him. "Don't be gone after dark. Things are getting more and more rowdy around here, and with the new load of stampeders, I wouldn't want you to get into any trouble."

"I'm not going to get into trouble," Jacob replied in a clipped tone.

He stalked from the room and slammed the door behind him. Karen felt as if her nerves had snapped with the crashing of the door. Tears came to her own eyes and without understanding why, she began to cry. It was as if all the pressures of the day began to overwhelm her all over again. Funny, she had never been given to tears prior to coming north. The long dark months of winter, the cold, the lawless greed, and the bad news that just seemed to keep coming ate away her final reserves of strength.

"Oh, Leah. I'm so sorry." Karen held the girl tight, needing comfort as much as the child did.

They cried for a time, then they just held each other as if the world had ended and they were the last ones to survive. Finally Karen spoke.

"I won't leave you," she whispered. "You don't have to be afraid of being alone. I won't let anything happen to you as long as I have breath in my body."

"But you might die, too," Leah said, straightening up to look Karen in the eye. "Everybody dies."

Karen couldn't argue that. "But while I'm here, I'll do what I can to ensure you're fed and clothed and cared for. I just want you to know that."

Leah nodded. "Will you read the letter?"

Karen edged off the bed and picked the piece of paper up from the floor. The letter looked like it had been carried around for months, even though it was dated just yesterday. Why he had felt it necessary, Karen couldn't say. Perhaps he'd seen too much death along the trail. Hadn't Adrik told her of folks freezing to death within inches of the main path? Maybe Bill had seen this, as well.

Karen cleared her throat and took a seat on the corner of the bed. Leah wiped her eyes and moved close as Karen began to read.

"1898, 2nd of April.

Jacob and Leah Barringer, in care of Miss Karen Pierce, lately of Dyea.

Jacob and Leah,

I miss you more than I have words to say. You know I've never been a man for writing letters and such, but as time weighs heavy on my heart, I felt it necessary to send a post to you. The trail is hard and cold—there's never any real warmth. I'm glad you're safe back in Dyea. I seen a woman and child die yesterday from the cold. The woman's feet had froze 'cause she had no boots. Her man must have left her behind or got separated from her, but I kept thinking of you two and how even though I missed you, I'd done the right thing in leaving you behind. You might both hate me by now. I hope not. You might not understand, even with me telling you about the bad times on the trail, but I love you more than life. I'll come back for you, I promise.

Your father,
William Barringer"

Karen folded the letter and handed it to Leah. She waited for the girl to say something, anything. Leah took the letter and reread it to herself, then tucked it inside her blouse. She looked at Karen, her broken heart so clearly reflected in her eyes.

"If Pa is dead, they won't just leave him up there, will they, Karen?"

"No, honey, Adrik said they took the body to the morgue."

"Can we take some of the money and bury him all proper like? Can we order a stone with his name so folks won't forget who he was?"

Karen thought of her own father buried somewhere out in the middle of the wilderness. How comforting it might be to have him close by, to know she could go visit the grave as she did her mother's.

"Of course. We'll use all the money, if need be."

Leah nodded and lay back on the pillows. "Thank you. I knew you'd understand."

Jacob had no words for the way he was feeling. Responsibilities had come to him at a young age, and if his father were truly dead, the burden would be even greater.

"Mr. Ivankov!" Jacob called out as he climbed the church steps two at a time. "Are you in here?"

There was no answer. Jacob looked down the aisle to the podium where he'd heard the pastor preach on many a Sunday. He looked beyond the pulpit to where a cross had been nailed to the otherwise unadorned wall.

"I don't understand this at all," he said, knowing that somehow God would understand he was speaking to Him. "I don't see the sense in it. I don't know how this can be fixed."

"Some things can't be fixed," Adrik said as he came up from behind Jacob.

The boy turned to rest his eyes on the big man's sympathetic expression. He didn't feel like being strong and brave. He didn't feel like fighting or arguing. He simply wanted to be comforted. Falling to his knees, Jacob cried bitter tears.

"He shouldn't have gone. We needed him here. He shouldn't have gone."

Adrik knelt beside him. "I know, son. I know."

"I don't know why God is doing this to us."

"Why do you suppose it to be the way God wanted it?"

Jacob shook his head and wiped his nose with the back of his hand. "God is in charge of everything."

"Well, I do believe God is in charge. I believe He has power and authority over the universe," Adrik said. "But I also know God has given us free will to make choices and decisions for ourselves. He gave it to Adam and Eve in the Garden. Told them what they could do and what they shouldn't. Then He let them decide for themselves whether or not they'd obey. They chose to listen to other voices. Your pa did the same."

"My pa was a good man!" Jacob declared, glaring in anger at Adrik. "If you say he wasn't, I'll—"

"Whoa now, son, don't go getting riled. Everybody makes poor choices from time to time, and whether you like it or not, everybody sins against God. You know that as well as anybody."

Jacob continued to glare for a moment, then looked away and nodded. "But my pa was a good man. He was a Christian man, too."

"I'm glad he was. But Jacob, being a Christian doesn't mean you aren't going to make mistakes. It doesn't mean that bad things will never happen to you, even when you're doing the right and good thing. Why, I once saw a man go after another man who'd fallen off a ship. He knew the other man couldn't swim, so he went to help him. The other man was scared and desperate, and when his would-be rescuer came, he latched on to him and drowned them both. It wasn't fair or right—after all, the first man hadn't fallen in on purpose and the second man was going to help—putting his own life in danger to help his friend."

"So what's that got to do with my pa?"

Adrik leaned back and pushed his fur hat up away from his face. "Neither man would have died if they'd done what they were told to. They didn't listen to the advice of others. The first man wasn't supposed to be playing around at the rail. He was supposed to be loading salmon into the hold of the ship. They knew he couldn't swim and had given him a job in a place where he would have been safe. The second man knew better than to jump in after his friend, but his emotions got the better of him, and reasoning and logic went out the door. He should have thrown his friend a line or a life ring. If either man would have done what he was supposed to do instead of doing what he thought best, then both would be alive today."

Jacob's eyes narrowed. "My pa was doing what he thought was right. I'm going to do what I think is right. I have to find out if that man was my pa."

"You'd be hard pressed to learn that for sure, unless you found your pa face-to-face."

"Why do you say that?"

Adrik frowned. "Most of the dead will be buried together. You're not going to find him, and even if you do, well, you can't be sure of recognizing him."

"I'd know my own pa," Jacob declared. "I have to try, Mr. Ivankov. I have to go and at least try to find him. If he's dead, then I'll take up where he left off. He had a dream of finding gold and making a better life for us. I won't let that dream die."

"It was a mighty selfish dream, if you ask me. He was a grown man with two children, and he knew you needed him here. He probably should have loaded you both up and headed back to the States, where you'd all be safe. Instead, he let himself buy into the stories of gold and put himself in danger and left you and Leah behind."

"Don't say that." Jacob's temper flared. He wasn't about to sit and listen to this man mean-mouth his father. How dare he say that his father had done the wrong thing. He got to his feet and stared down at the larger man. "I'll fight you for saying that." He balled his fists and held them up as if to prove his point.

Adrik pulled off his gloves and slapped them against his thigh as he got to his feet. "Jacob, I'm telling you this because I don't want to see you make a mistake. I know you're hurting and I know you're angry, but going north is foolish. Plain and simple. Greed is what's driving men north. Greed and wild stories about things that don't even exist."

"The gold is real," Jacob said. "My pa said it was real. Other people are coming back rich. You know it's real!" His voice was steadily rising.

"The gold might well be real, but so's the cost. Are you ready to pay that price? Folks on the trail were warned about the dangers. Avalanches were predicted for several hours ahead of when they actually started happening. The Tlingits stopped packing and went down the mountain. They told people why, but no one wanted to listen. They had to get just one more pack over the mountain. They had to press just that much closer to the goal of finding gold. Had they listened, they wouldn't be dead now. Your pa might very well be among those gone—if so, then he didn't listen, either."

Jacob felt a strange aching in his throat. He wanted to speak, but words wouldn't come. He wanted to hit Adrik Ivankov, but he knew nothing would come of it, either.

"I'm going. I have to find my pa. I was always going to leave, I was just waiting for warmer weather. But now I'm going on my own. Pa has a cache and money. If he is dead, then I'm going to see to it that his dream comes true."

"What about Leah?"

Jacob hadn't really thought of his sister. He had forced her from his thoughts because he knew he couldn't take her along. She'd be heartbroken at his departure. It would make her misery complete. After he left, she would truly have no one but Karen.

"I'll send for her. When I have enough money, I'll send some so that she can come by boat. Or if the railroad is built through by then, I'll have her come by train. Pa said the trail is too hard for someone like her. I won't have her freezing to death like that woman in his letter."

"Jacob, I wish you'd reconsider. You're going to tear that little girl completely apart if you leave her now—what with not knowing about your father."

"She'll understand," Jacob said, not at all convinced of his words. "She'll need to know the truth, same as me."

"And how do you think you're going to discover the truth? They were already lighting fires to thaw the ground for digging when I left. They aren't going to leave folks unburied so that you can get up there and figure out who's who. That man was tagged as Bill Barringer, and they won't wait on his kin to show up. Most of those fellows didn't have kin anywhere nearby. They'll bury them all quickly and probably en masse. You can't very well dig them all up to see if one of them is your father. If they can bring him back to bury in Dyea, they will. After all, I told them you and Leah were here. But chances are they'll bury him with the others. Even then we can't be sure it was really your pa."

Jacob held his ground. "I'll head north, then. I'll go to Dawson and check with the claims office and see if he has files. If he's alive, that's exactly what he'd do. If he's not alive, then there are supplies and money somewhere that belong to Leah and me."

"You don't know that, Jacob. If your father is dead, no one's going to worry about getting that stuff back to you and your sister."

"I don't care. I'm going. You'll let Leah and Karen know, won't you?" Jacob asked.

"You don't plan to go back and get your things?"

"I have some things hidden in the woodshed. Like I said, I've been planning to go all along."

Adrik nodded. "I suppose you have to do what you think is right, but just remember one thing. When you take off from here without the permission or advice of your authority figures, you are setting yourself up for trouble. When we walk away from God's authority, we are also walking away from His perfect protection. Do you really want that?"

"I'm not leaving God. I know He's got a reason for everything, and while I don't understand it, I'm not going to curse Him and die like Job's friends suggested." Jacob remembered the sermon preached on the Sunday before the avalanche. The words had impacted him. Job had lost everything and all that was left to him was to curse God and die. But still he hung on, and Jacob would, too.

"Jacob, why don't you just think about this overnight? Pray on it first and then make your decision. You don't know what awaits you out there. One trip up the summit and you'll see for yourself what a mistake this is."

"I don't care what you say," Jacob said, pushing his way past the big man. "I'm going and don't you try to stop me."

————

Leah had known about Jacob's dream to join their father from nearly the moment he'd planned it. That's why she waited for him in the darkness of the woodshed. She knew he was going to leave her, and she knew he wouldn't come to say good-bye. Clutching the satchel he'd left there in hiding, she tried to think of what she'd say to him.

When the shed door opened and Jacob entered carrying a small lantern, Leah waited until he tried to retrieve his things from their hiding place before speaking.

"You're going away without saying good-bye. Just like Pa," she murmured, stepping out of the shadows.

"Leah!" He said the word almost accusingly.

"Why are you leaving like this? How could you do this to me?" She fought back tears and shivered in the cold. She threw the satchel at him. "There. Is that what you came for?"

She heard her brother's sigh. "I don't want to hurt you, but I have to go. We have to know if that man was Pa. Mr. Ivankov can't tell me for sure that Pa was the man he saw. We have to know."

"When will you come back?"

"I don't know. I'll probably have to go all the way to Dawson before I know for sure whether the man carrying Pa's letter was him or not. You'll be safe with Karen."

"But you're all the family I have left." Leah couldn't believe he was just going off like this. She'd known of his plans but had always figured on changing his mind. After all, they were close. They'd been each other's confidants for years.

Jacob moved to close the distance and put his hands on her shoulders. "Look, I'm going to send for you. I promise. I'll get enough money so you won't have to go up the Chilkoot Trail. I'll send you enough money so you can take a steamer all the way to St. Michael and then down the river to Dawson City. You'll ride like a queen!" He tried to make it sound wonderful, but Leah wasn't convinced.

"Take me now. Take me with you."

He shook his head. "You know I can't. The way is too rough. You read Pa's letter, didn't you? The way is just too dangerous for someone like you."

"It's dangerous for you, too. Grown men died in that avalanche—one of them might have been Pa. What makes you think it'll be any better for you?"

Jacob's jaw fixed in that determined way she'd come to recognize. It was a characteristic he'd inherited from their father. "All I know is that I have to try."

Wrapping her arms around him, Leah hugged him tight. "Please don't go, Jacob. I'm scared for you. I don't want you to die."

Jacob held her for several minutes, then gently pushed her away. "I'm not going to die. You just wait and see. I'll send for you before you know it, and who knows, maybe I'll find Pa and everything will be all right again." He turned from her but not before Leah saw the tears on his cheeks. Seeing him in such pain, she decided to say nothing more.

He pulled on his pack and reached into his pocket to hand her something. "I bought this and planned to give it to you for your birthday next month."

Leah opened her hand to find a delicate gold chain. At the end of the necklace was an equally delicate gold cross. "It's beautiful. I've never had anything like it."

"I know," Jacob replied. "I wanted you to have some gold from the north. I wanted you to believe in the dream."

She looked up and saw the hope he held for his future. "I believe in *you*, Jacob—but not gold or land or anything else but God."

He kissed her on the forehead. "I love you, Leah. Stay with Karen and I'll find you again."

Then he was gone. Leah stared after him, watching the amber glow of the lantern bob and swing as he walked away. "I love you, too," she whispered. Numb from the truth of the moment, Leah made her way inside and up to the room that she now shared with Karen alone.

She opened the door cautiously. The night was still young enough that Karen might well be reading or writing letters, and Leah didn't want to make too much noise. But the room was empty.

Sitting down on the bed, Leah unfastened the clasp on the necklace. Putting the necklace on, Leah felt the cold metal against her skin. It did little to reassure her.

"Nothing has gone right today," Karen declared as she came into the room and slammed the door. Seeing Leah, she halted a moment, then went on raving. "I'm so tired of bad news. Everybody is talking about one horrible thing after another downstairs. I came up here because I just can't stand to hear another word! I'm going to go wash up for bed."

Leah nodded and slipped the necklace beneath her blouse. Giving no further thought to telling Karen about Jacob, she curled up on the bed and cried softly into the pillow. She thought for a moment of a verse her mother had once read to her about how God collected your tears in a bottle and saved them. *He's sure going to have a lot of bottles from me,* she thought as sleep overcame her.

⊣ CHAPTER TEN ├─

WHEN KAREN AWOKE the next morning, she found Leah sitting cross-legged in the corner of the room. The child, rapidly turning into a beautiful young woman, had been crying. It broke Karen's heart to see the girl so grieved. Karen saw herself in Leah, recognizing the raw misery and open wounds of her father's death. She longed to say something comforting, but words eluded her. How could she comfort Leah when Karen could find no comfort for herself?

Yawning, Karen stretched, then pushed back the covers. The room felt like ice. She was surprised that Jacob hadn't started a fire in the small stove. Pushing back long strawberry-blond waves of hair, she looked to Leah.

"Where's Jacob? Why didn't he get a fire going?"

"He's gone." Leah's flat words registered no emotion.

Karen got up and pulled on her warm robe. "It's not like him to go off to work and leave the stove cold."

"He didn't go to work. Like I said, he's gone."

Karen looked down at Leah. "Gone? You mean gone from Dyea?"

Leah looked up mournfully. "He left last night."

"Why didn't you say so? Why didn't you wake me up so I could stop him?"

Leah picked up her skirts and stood. "You couldn't have stopped him. He didn't want to be stopped. I tried."

"You should have at least told me about this last night. I could have sent for Adrik to stop him."

Leah looked almost accusingly at Karen as if she were responsible for Jacob's disappearance. "You didn't want to hear about anything else that was bad. Remember?"

Karen could hardly comprehend Leah's words. Jacob was just a boy. Where had he gone? And for what reason? She tried to remain as calm as possible. After all, the boy had probably just taken off to mourn. Maybe even find out where they'd taken his father's body.

"I'm sure he won't be gone for long. It's still winter out there and too cold for pretty much anyone, let alone an unseasoned child." Karen picked up several pieces of wood and put them into the stove atop the cold, lifeless ashes.

"He's not coming back."

Karen straightened at this and looked at Leah. "Of course he will. You're here."

Leah shook her head. "He said he'd send for me."

"Send for you from where?"

"From the goldfields. From Dawson City."

A tremor ran through Karen. It started somewhere in her heart and radiated out from there until her entire body felt like it was shaking. "He wouldn't really have gone—would he?" She darted to the window and pulled back the drapes. The frost kept her from seeing beyond the room. She turned back to Leah. "He wouldn't just go like that, leaving you here. Not when he knew what it felt like to be left behind."

Leah nodded, and her tears began to fall. "He said he had to know if that dead man was our pa. If it was Pa, then Jacob wants to take up his dream. Either way, he's gone."

Karen paced the small room for several moments. The floorboards creaked in protest as she picked up her steps. She forgot about the fire and finally plopped down on the corner of the unmade bed. Angry, she reached out and threw one of the pillows. "That's just great. Things just seem to go from bad to worse."

Leah went to where Karen sat and took hold of her hand. "I know things have been hard, Karen. I've been praying for you. For us. My ma used to say that it seemed like it didn't rain but it poured. I guess that's the way it's been with us."

Karen softened as she met the child's red-rimmed eyes. "I'm sorry. I know you're hurting." She reached out and pulled Leah into her embrace. "I'm so sorry, Leah. I know you're feeling bad and that I'm not helping it."

"You can't help it."

The truth of Leah's words seemed to hold a double meaning. There was nothing Karen could do to change the events of their lives, and she seemed powerless to even say the right thing—to point Leah back to her faith and hope in God—to bring herself along as well.

"I'm sorry," Karen murmured. "Sometimes I just feel like . . . well . . ." She wanted to say that she felt deserted by God. That He no longer cared. She wanted to say that her anger was making her forget her upbringing. Then a picture came to mind—the angry face of Peter Colton. She had stirred his anger. She had caused his rage by promoting her own hatred of Martin Paxton. She saw herself in that angry face, knowing the only difference between her and Peter was that he would actually pull the trigger and kill Paxton. Karen could only dream of his reckoning.

"I know I should have told you last night," Leah said softly. "I shouldn't have just let you go to bed without knowing about Jacob. I'm sorry."

Karen shook her head. "Don't be. I deserved it. I pushed you away, along with everyone and everything else."

"Even God?"

Leah's softly spoken question seemed to rip apart Karen's stoic facade. "Yes. I suppose I must confess that, as well." She tried to smile at Leah, hoping the action would reassure her without words. It didn't.

"It's easy to trust God when things are going well," Karen began. "There's no real effort in that. But when things go wrong and then keep going wrong until you feel like nothing good is ever going to happen again . . . well, then it gets harder."

"It has to get better." It was Leah who offered the encouragement.

Karen nodded. "I want to believe that, but right now I feel as though my life is as cold and lifeless as those ashes in the stove. Nothing makes sense anymore. Everyone has either died or gone away."

"Everyone, 'cept you and me." Leah paused and put her hand atop Karen's. "I need you, Karen."

Karen saw the fear and questioning in Leah's eyes. She reached up and touched Leah's tearstained face. "I need you, too. I know exactly what it is to lose the people you love. It makes you feel all alone—like nobody in the world even knows you're alive."

Leah nodded. "Like God's too busy."

Karen knew God was working on her spirit through the words of her young friend. She hated feeling the way she did, all bottled up and walled in, while at the same time so very resentful. "God's never too busy," she finally responded. She knew the words were true, and by speaking them she thought maybe she'd broken a little chink of the mortar in her walls.

Smiling, she took Leah's face in both hands. "Leah, I won't leave you. You needn't fear that. I made your father a promise to look after you, and I will do just that. This country is no place to be alone."

"Jacob's alone," Leah whispered.

"For now," Karen agreed. "But once we talk to Mr. Ivankov, I know Jacob won't be alone any longer. Adrik will go after him. You'll see." She tried again to smile for Leah's sake, but a weariness settled upon her. What were they going to do after they found Jacob? Should they board the next ship south? Should they return to Seattle and take up a home near Karen's sister? There were just too many questions and not enough answers.

"We should pray for Jacob," Leah said.

God still seemed so distant. So very far away. Could she possibly find her way back to His comfort? She knew He forgave sin—welcomed back prodigals. The only real question was how could she go back to God and carry with her the hatred she felt for Martin Paxton?

She looked to Leah's wide-eyed expression. The child had lost so much, but her face looked ever hopeful as she spoke of prayer. Karen nodded, knowing that she would never be able to lead such a prayer.

Leah seemed to understand Karen's reluctance. She took hold of Karen's hands. "Don't worry, Karen. I can pray for both of us."

———

"What do you mean you knew he was heading north? Why didn't you come to tell me?" Karen questioned in disbelief. "I thought you were my friend."

Adrik looked apologetic, but it wasn't an apology that came out of his mouth. "Look, I figure sometimes a man has to do what he feels he must."

"For a man that might well be expected, but we're talking about a fifteen-year-old boy."

"Fifteen is hardly a boy in these parts. There's more than a few fellows Jacob's age who are here on their own. They're out working to make their keep, to see themselves north in search of gold."

"I don't care about the gold, I care about Jacob. Adrik, it was very irresponsible of you to let him just head off like that. You should have at least convinced him to come back to the Gold Nugget and talk this through with me."

Adrik shook his head. "If you'll recall, I'm not responsible for Jacob. Bill Barringer gave that job to you, but even so, I did talk to him and I tried to encourage him to stay. He was bent on knowing the truth about his father. I remember someone else who was just as eager to know her father's whereabouts. Jacob wants to keep his father alive, and if not his father, then his father's dream. Before the fire left you so bitter, I'd heard similar things from you."

Karen hadn't expected Adrik to call attention to her bitter heart. It stung to hear the words, and she thought momentarily of some sort of defense. But there was none. She was bitter and angry, and those two qualities were slowly draining her of her strength.

Karen got up from the overturned crate Adrik had offered her as a seat. In his overwhelming presence, the tent seemed to have shrunk since she'd shared it with

Leah and Jacob. "I suppose I should just go. I thought you might understand."

"I do understand," he said softly, the tone of his voice sending a small shiver through her. "I understand better than you give me credit for."

She turned her eyes upward and studied the ruggedly handsome face. The nose was a little too large, the mustache too thick. The jaw was too square and the eyes too . . . She lost herself for a moment. There was nothing wrong with Adrik's looks. He was perfect. Her feelings startled her back into reality.

Taking a deep breath, Karen barely managed to speak. "If you understand, then why . . . why won't you help me get Jacob back?"

"Karen, the boy will most likely come back on his own. And even if he doesn't, do you really want me to go out there and haul him back, only to have him run off again? And he will. He won't stand by and let some woman who's not even kin tell him what he can and can't do regarding his father. Do you honestly want that ugliness between the two of you?"

"But I can't just stand by and do nothing," Karen protested. "There's Leah to consider. Not to mention that there's hardly any reason to stay here. Everything has changed now. Nothing's the same. I came here with one thought—one hope and dream, and that's gone now. I have no reason to stay, but without Jacob I can hardly leave."

Adrik didn't reply but moved with a quickness that took Karen's breath as he pulled her into his arms and kissed her soundly on the mouth. Too stunned to even react for a moment, Karen relished the ticklish way his mustache moved against her face. She felt a warmth spread to her cheeks as she allowed herself to realize what was really taking place.

He ended the kiss as quickly as he'd begun it, but still he held her tightly. "I can give you a reason to stay, if you want to hear it."

Karen tried not to show her surprise, but in all honesty her feelings were so confusing that she feared what she might do or say. Pushing away, she shook her head. "You had no right to do that." She broke his hold but knew that had he any intentions of forcing her to remain in his embrace, he would have little difficulty in keeping her there.

"I apologize," he said. Then grinning, he added, "Not for kissing you, but for not asking first."

The boyish amusement in his expression irritated Karen and pressed her into action. "That was uncalled-for, Mr. Ivankov. I came here to discuss Jacob, not issues between us."

"I think the issues between us need to be discussed," Adrik replied. "Seems to me you're wrestling with an awful lot these days. You worry about the future, but it's the present that's killing you."

"You're wrong," Karen said, shaking so much from the encounter that she was certain he could see her tremble. "I'm merely trying to keep things under control. I can understand that you would be less than supportive of seeing Martin Paxton pay for his deeds. After all, you don't really know him and what he's capable of. But I felt certain you would care enough about Jacob to help me keep him from further harm."

"I do care, Karen. I care about a great many things, including you."

"I don't want to hear that. I haven't any interest in hearing it. I need to think of Jacob and Leah. I need to figure out what's best for their future, as well as my own."

"What's best for your future is exactly what you're running from," Adrik said matter-of-factly.

"What's that supposed to mean?"

Adrik refused to back down. "You know what it means."

Karen fought the attraction she had for Adrik and instead put her hands on her hips and shook her head very slowly. "No . . . I don't think I do."

"Have it your way," Adrik said with a shrug. "I'm not going to play games with you. I haven't got the time for it. Look, if it makes you feel any better, I'll go look for Jacob. But I'm not going to force him to come back."

Confused by her emotions and Adrik's unwillingness to continue their conversation, Karen picked up her gloves and hat. "Don't bother. I'll go for him myself before I ask you to do me any favors."

She headed for the Gold Nugget awash in a sensation of defeat and discouragement. What was she supposed to do now? She could hardly pack up Leah and head north, yet she couldn't leave Jacob to fend for himself.

"Why are you doing this to me?" She gazed upward to the snow-covered mountains as if she might very well see God seated on a throne atop the crest. The swirling snow arched upward against a sky so blue it almost hurt her eyes to look upon it.

"Winter's not long for us now," an old man commented as he passed by her, dragging a sled full of gear. "The thaw will be here afore ya know it."

She lowered her gaze and nodded. "I'll be glad for it."

The man smiled, revealing a mouth full of decaying teeth. "The thaw will melt the ice and snow. Everyone will be glad for it."

He went on his way, and Karen watched after him. His sled made two deep indentations in the icy mud as he pulled the heavy load forward. Karen thought on his words, knowing them to be true. How many times had she heard someone praying for an early spring—an end to the relentless darkness, warming winds to melt the ice?

"I'm glad you didn't get too far."

Karen whirled around to find Adrik holding up her handbag. "You left this in my tent. I thought you might need it."

Her temper had cooled and she nodded. "Thank you. It was kind of you to bring it to me."

"Look," Adrik began hesitantly, "I didn't mean to anger you."

"I'm the one who needs to apologize. I've been so short with you—with everyone," Karen said, sighing heavily. "I just have no answers. I'm tired. And it seems that everyone wants to hurt me. Even God seems to be taking part."

Adrik smiled. "Well, I for one have no desire to hurt you. Facts being what they are, I have something much more pleasurable in mind."

Karen's cheeks grew hot, and she quickly lowered her gaze to the ground. "You shouldn't talk like that."

"Why not? It's the truth."

"Be that as it may," Karen said, trying to maintain her control, "I don't think it very appropriate. I have more than enough to concern myself with, and pleasure isn't on the agenda."

"First you complain because there's nothing but misery in your life, but when someone offers you something else, you refuse it." Karen looked up, noting his amused expression. "I think you need to decide exactly what it is you want out of life, and go after it." He smiled in his good-natured way and tipped his hat. "When you figure it all out, let me know. Especially if there's a spot for me."

─{ C H A P T E R   E L E V E N }─

GRACE SAT BESIDE the cabin window. She had returned to *Summer Song* to nurse her bruised feelings. Her heart was nearly broken by memories of Peter's rage and Karen's desire for revenge. Her dear friend had changed so much. How could she even be the same gentle woman who had so often admonished Grace to let bygones be bygones?

"I'm sure Peter will turn up soon," Amelia Colton said in motherly assurance. "He's never been one to admit to being wrong." The three Colton women had gathered in the small living space to still one another's worries.

"You don't have to take my side," Grace said softly. "You are his mother. I don't expect you to choose between us."

"But there is no us," Amelia stated. Miranda looked up from her knitting and nodded.

"The two shall be one," Peter's sister murmured.

"That's right. It's what I've often counseled Miranda about. That's why it is so difficult to be married to one who has no interest in what's most precious to you. What possible hope can you have of peace in such a household?"

Grace knew only too well of what Amelia Colton spoke. "We are, as the Bible says, unequally yoked. Like light and darkness. I have chosen to walk God's narrow path, and Peter, well, he's a good man, but being good doesn't save you for eternity."

Amelia nodded. "I blame myself, Grace. Ephraim and I . . . well . . . we got away from fellowship and worship. We got busy with life, and so often Sundays were the best days to take care of other needs. I spent many a Sunday, along with my children, on board one ship or another cleaning and scrubbing."

The expression on Amelia's face tore at Grace's heart. Her regret was so evident. "You mustn't be too hard on yourself, Mother Colton."

"Oh, but I was wrong, Grace. Miranda, I wronged you and Peter. I should have showed you a better way—a more faithful way to honor God. I never saw that it might cause you to turn away or find worship unimportant. I only desired to help Ephraim."

"I heard my name being bandied about," Ephraim Colton said, coming from the adjoining cabin.

Amelia smiled. "I assure you it was all for good. I was actually apologizing to Grace and Miranda for not having been more faithful in raising my children to fear God first and attend to duty second."

Ephraim nodded, and the same sadness that had tinged Amelia's eyes now touched his. "We've no one but ourselves to blame for taking such a lazy view of our faith and commitment to God."

"But you were and are good parents," Miranda said, putting aside her knitting. She went to her father and hugged him close. "God can restore our family and the wasted years. He's already doing quite a good job of it with us. Peter will come around."

A knock on the cabin door caught their attention.

"Peter!" Grace gasped, her hand going to her throat. She could only pray he had returned.

Ephraim went to the door, but instead of finding his son, he found his first mate accompanied by the local law officials. "Welcome aboard, gentlemen. To what do I owe this pleasure?"

"Ain't hardly pleasure," the taller of the two replied. "I have papers here from a Martin Paxton. He says he owns this ship and can take possession of it at any time. He wants you and your folks off the ship immediately."

Grace was on her feet. "*Summer Song* belongs to the Coltons. Martin Paxton has no say whatsoever."

Ephraim took the papers but continued to stare in disbelief at the lawman. "That's right. *Summer Song* is a part of Colton Shipping."

"I can't help that, mister. Read these papers, and you'll see they've been executed all legal-like back in San Francisco. We're here to uphold the law."

Grace went to Ephraim's side. "Father Colton, don't worry about this. There must be some mistake. We must go see Mr. Paxton and set things right."

It took further convincing on Grace's part, but finally Ephraim agreed. The sheriff's deputy, however, was of no mind to leave Amelia and Miranda on board while Ephraim and Grace went off to settle the affair. The two deputies ordered the party to gather their things and deboard the ship immediately.

Grace could hardly believe the order. She threw her things haphazardly into her trunks and watched helplessly as *Summer Song*'s crew went to work loading them off onto the dock. He was doing this to hurt her. Martin Paxton was doing this to punish the Coltons for helping her defy his plans. Perhaps Peter was right—perhaps Martin Paxton did not deserve forgiveness.

Mindless of the beautiful skies overhead, Grace allowed herself to be helped from the ship. The rush of activities along the harbor walk did nothing to take her mind from the moment. Peter would be furious. No doubt if Paxton thought he had rights to *Summer Song*, he would also take *Merry Maid*. *Dear Lord*, she prayed, *you must help us. Peter will kill Mr. Paxton if he hasn't already done the deed.*

They hurried along with the confusion and bustle of new arrivals and old-timers. Supplies were stacked everywhere, and the noise was enough that a deaf man might well seek solace elsewhere. Grace hardly noticed the new buildings and busy freighters. Skagway nearly doubled its size by the week, but it was so completely unimportant at this moment.

"Miranda and I will try to arrange rooms," Amelia said, putting her hand on her husband's coat sleeve. "I'm sure we'll find something nearby."

"But what if this is all a misunderstanding?" Miranda questioned. "Would we not be better waiting?"

"No, your mother is right. I can hardly have you standing here unprotected on the streets while I go find Mr. Paxton."

The deputy who had accompanied them this far spoke up. "Mr. Paxton is residing in the rooms above his store. I have to report to him, and you might as well come with me."

"I'm coming, too," Grace said firmly. "After all, he's doing this because of me."

Ephraim looked for a moment as if he might refuse her, then nodded slowly. "Get us rooms, Amelia. We can all meet for lunch at that little place on Third. Go there after you have secured us a place to stay, but be watchful and speak to no one. The town is full of ne'er-do-wells."

Amelia nodded and clung to Miranda's arm. "We'll be just fine. I'll keep two of the crew with me until you join us."

Ephraim looked past his wife to the men who had accompanied them. Laden with bags and trunks, the men's attention remained fully on their captain. "Watch over them."

The two men closest to them gave Ephraim their pledge. Grace looked to her father-in-law and saw the sorrow in his expression. Was he seeing his lifelong dream pass before his eyes? Had he come to the harsh north only to lose his fortune like so many others? She'd not stand for it! She would fight Martin Paxton with every ounce of her strength. She had to make him see that this feud was an exercise in futility. She was a married woman, and whether her husband desired her company or not, their commitment was still binding.

The deputy led them past the Pillbox Drug Company, the Yukon Outfitters, and Burkhard House. She knew well the location of Paxton's store, for it had been in place when she'd left the previous December.

Following the deputy into the store and past the curious stares of the onlookers, Grace tried to pray. She wanted to remain calm and rational. She wanted God to do her talking, rather than her own emotions. But it was hard. All she could think about was the harm Paxton had once again caused her. She thought of how Karen presumed that because Grace wanted to extend forgiveness to the man, she couldn't possibly understand the extent of his cruelty.

But I understand it only too well, Grace thought. It seemed like only yesterday that he had slapped her at their engagement party. She could almost feel his breath upon her neck, his hands upon her body. The thought made her feel physically ill.

They passed from the main floor and climbed up a dark passage of stairs. The deputy knocked at the door, and Martin Paxton himself opened it. He stared down at the man, seeing beyond him to Ephraim and then Grace. He rested his gaze upon Grace, then smiled with an expression that suggested he'd known she would come.

"Thank you, Deputy," he said and tossed the man a coin. "I can take care of the situation from here. Please make sure you have men standing guard at the dock. I don't want anyone getting the idea they can sneak back on board." The man nodded, then turned to push past Grace and Ephraim.

"Come in," Paxton said, walking away from Ephraim and Grace. "I have been expecting you both."

"Do you care to tell me what this is all about?" Ephraim questioned without waiting to so much as take a seat. "This man shows up on board my ship and demands we leave. He hands me these papers and tells me you have commanded my removal."

Paxton poured himself a glass of brandy, then took a seat behind a massive desk. He pulled a gold watch chain from his red print silk vest and popped open the cover on the piece. "I have exactly fifteen minutes. No more. If you care to sit down, I will do my best to explain. However," he paused and looked hard at Grace, "I am only doing this out of respect for my mother. I know she held you in highest regard, Ephraim. Otherwise, I'd have not let you cross the threshold."

Ephraim guided Grace to the leather upholstered chair opposite Paxton and sat down on its matching twin only after she had taken a seat. She smoothed out the soft lavender wool of her skirt and unbuttoned her jacket. She tried hard not to look at Paxton, but he seemed to pull her attention against her will.

His eyes were dark with hatred, and his hair seemed to have grayed a bit around the temples. Grace knew his severe looks were considered handsome by many women, but the coldness in his eyes only left her wanting to run from the room.

"To get right to business, you will find those papers are the ones you signed some time ago in San Francisco. Our agreement spoke of my investment and of the fact that should I feel that investment was threatened, I would have the right to withhold further support and stop any other action until I was confident that my investment was no longer threatened. It allowed me a great deal of interpretation when it came to defining 'threat to my investment.'"

"I still don't understand what that has to do with anything. We've been doing a tidy business. You've been paid back regularly," Ephraim replied. "How could you possibly see your business investment as being threatened?"

"Because there is bad blood now running between your son and me. I could only conclude that you were supportive of his decisions when you arrived here in Skagway with Miss—excuse me—*Mrs.* Grace Colton in your company." He scowled at Grace. "She was, in fact, to have married me. She broke her father's written and verbal agreement and fled to Alaska from Chicago. I took this in stride as her youth no doubt gave her over to a bad case of wedding jitters, but I had no tolerance for her deception in arranging her marriage to your son. Furthermore, Peter knew of my arrangement with Grace and chose to ignore it. Thus, I suffered great financial setback."

"I had no such arrangement with you," Grace countered before Ephraim could speak. "You are doing this only to punish me for thwarting your plans. You are throwing away a lifetime of friendship with a man who was good to you when no one else was there, all because I refused to be your wife. That hardly seems a sensible choice, Mr. Paxton."

"I've no doubt that to your simple mind, Mrs. Colton, the issues at hand seem to be less than sensible. But I assure you, they are. How much longer would it have been before your husband would have come blaming me for the destruction of his store in Dyea? Furthermore, how much longer would it have been before he and his father might have decided their arrangement with me was less than pleasant, and because many new businesses would happily purchase their goods, I might well find myself paying exorbitant prices for items of lesser quality? You do not truly believe that I would stand by and await those conclusions, do you?"

"You know very well that my father-in-law would never have done such a thing. I cannot believe you would perform such a childish deed, throwing the man and his family off his own ship, leaving us to seek refuge without warning."

Paxton swirled his brandy for a moment, then downed it quickly. He slammed the snifter to the desk, breaking its delicate stem and leaving it jagged and useless atop the now scarred wood.

He got up just as quickly from his seat and pulled on his outer coat. "Your time is nearly up. I want to add that *Merry Maid* is even now docked near Dyea. I have arranged for her to be brought here and for your son to be escorted from her as you have been escorted from *Summer Song*. I will expect your cooperation, and I will accept no further trouble in this matter."

"You . . . you . . . can't be serious," Ephraim gasped the words and clutched at his chest. "Colton Shipping is my life. It is my son's inheritance. I would never have signed it away to you. You have duped me. The business belongs to Peter."

"And Grace belonged to me," Paxton said without concern for the man's obvious distress.

Grace saw her father-in-law turn ashen. His eyes met hers, and she could see they were wild with pain. "He's sick! Can't you see that!" She reached out to touch the older man, desperate that she might keep him from further discomfort.

Paxton walked away from them and went to the door. He called out two names, and in a moment the same thugs who had tried to escort Grace to a wedding with Paxton appeared.

"Take Mr. Colton to the doctor two doors down. He appears to be suffering from some sort of heart attack."

The men moved quickly and hoisted Ephraim from his seat. The thick, stocky, bulldog-faced man was none too careful as he lead the way out of the room, knocking Ephraim clumsily against the doorjamb before heading down the steps.

Grace hurried after them, but Paxton stopped her. He closed the door and shook his head. "Sit."

"I thought you only had fifteen minutes to spare," she said with a tinge of sarcasm.

"I had only fifteen minutes for explanations to stupid men. You, however, are another matter."

"Indeed," Grace said, her anger besting her. "I am a married woman."

"I can easily remedy that. You have only to cooperate with me, Grace, and I'll see that Colton's mediocre shipping line is returned to him. Divorce Peter Colton and marry me. Do this and they will have not only their business restored, but the contract between us will be dissolved and the bill paid in full."

Grace felt her mouth go dry. "I cannot divorce. It's a sin."

"Is it not also a sin to kill a man?" Paxton asked casually. He leaned against the door and looked at her in a way that suggested less than pure thoughts.

"I've killed no one," she barely whispered.

"That man is sure to die unless he finds his company securely back in place. He's heartbroken—literally," Paxton said, laughing.

Grace hated his snide remarks at the expense of her father-in-law. She reached out to pound her fists against his chest, but he easily caught her arms and held her tight.

"You can't fight me, Grace. I have more power than you could imagine."

"God's power is greater."

Paxton laughed heartily. "Then let God get you out of this one." He released her and walked back to his desk. "You know the price and the terms, so you're free to leave. I will expect your answer before the week is out."

"You may have my answer now. I will not divorce my husband. I made a covenant before God, and whether or not such things matter to you," Grace said, her voice betraying her fear, "they matter to me."

Paxton shrugged. "It's just a matter of time, my dear. Do you really imagine that when faced with losing the family business and the livelihood he's always known, your husband will desire to remain married? Especially when I explain to him how you could have saved his father all of this grief—how you could have kept his mother and sister off the streets. No, I don't think your husband will worry half so much about keeping this covenant as the one I hold against his father."

"You're evil," Grace breathed, moving with shaky steps toward the door. "You're as evil and wicked a man as I have ever known."

Paxton leaned back against his desk and crossed his arms against his chest. His hard face tensed, and the thin scar that lined his right jaw seemed to become more prominent. His green eyes narrowed as he spoke. "Be that as it may, you have until the end of the week to reconsider this matter. Perhaps Ephraim will be dead by then—perhaps not. But no doubt your husband will be alive, and he'll want answers and he'll want his ships."

"What makes you think even if I were forced to divorce Peter that I would marry you?" Grace couldn't help but ask.

"That's simple. The deal wouldn't be concluded until my ring was upon your finger."

A coldness crept over Grace, and she feared momentarily that she might very well pass out. "Why are you doing this? You've already robbed my family of their fortune. I have nothing you could possibly want." She opened the door, feeling only slightly better for being able to see her way to freedom. She looked back to Paxton. "Why?"

"That's completely unimportant," he said, his voice low and menacing. "You have no understanding of my business, and neither will I afford you one. I want you, and that is all you need to understand. I will expect to see you again by Friday."

─{ C H A P T E R T W E L V E }─

PETER COLTON STARED back from shore at the *Merry Maid*. Not but an hour ago he had labored over the log, tallying expenses to be offset by profits. In spite of the fire and the loss of his trading post, he was doing well enough. He had sold the extra supplies to half a dozen businesses and had made a considerable profit. But then his entire world had changed in a matter of minutes. Before he realized what had even happened, a group of men, armed with guns and badges, pressed into his cabin. Papers were served, and while Peter quietly considered their content, the men began ordering his men to ready *Merry Maid* for the trip into Skagway.

Now as he stood on the docks of Skagway, *Summer Song* resting easy in the waters not far from *Merry Maid*, he felt nothing but a numb sensation of disbelief. How could it be that his ship was gone—taken from him in a heartbeat? He hadn't even known his father was in dock. He had to find him and try to figure out what had just happened.

A million thoughts rushed through Peter's mind as he made his way along the wharf. Was his father angry with him for rejecting Grace? An anger strong enough that he signed *Merry Maid* over to Martin Paxton? Surely not. The thought was incomprehensible.

He spotted one of his father's crew and motioned the man to his side. "Are you going aboard *Summer Song*? Is my father to be found there?"

The man shook his head. "Haven't ya heard? Them lawmen came and took him and the missus and your missus and sister, as well, and sent them off the ship, they did."

"What?" Now Peter was truly confused. "Grace is here—Miranda? What has happened?"

"Don't know," the man said with a shrug. "I heard the captain sold off everything to pay a debt."

"That's impossible. My father owed no man that kind of money. My papers said the *Merry Maid* had become the property of Martin Paxton. Do you know anything about that?"

"No, Captain. But I did hear that your father took an attack of the heart and is lying sick in town."

"Where is he?"

"He's been moved a couple of times. Last I knew he was at the Hotel Alaska."

"Thank you," Peter said, pushing back his billed cap. "I'll get to the bottom of this. Don't let the men lose hope. Tell them we'll fight this."

"Yes, Captain. I'll tell 'em."

Peter hurried in the direction of the Hotel Alaska. The unpainted clapboard building did nothing to raise his spirits. He bounded through the front doors like he owned the place, determined that nothing would keep him from his father and the truth.

"We're full up," a grizzled old man told him from behind the counter. The man's face was hideously disfigured, having encountered a bear or some other equally harmful beast. One eye had been lost altogether, and thick white scars intertwined grotesquely around the empty socket.

Peter thought the man should have covered his misfortune with a patch, but the man seemed not to care. "I'm not here for a room. I'm looking for my family."

"And who might they be?"

"Colton is the name." Peter knew patience had never been his strong suit, but waiting for the man to answer was severely testing his limits.

The man eyed him for a moment, then nodded. "They're up at the top of the stairs and two doors down on the right. If you're figurin' to stay with them, I'm going to have to up the rent."

"I'm not staying," Peter said. "And hopefully neither are they."

He took the stairs two at a time and pushed his way past three men who appeared to be not only drunk, but close to exhaustion as well. They were wandering back and forth as if trying to find their room or some person. Ordinarily, Peter might have attempted to help them, but with his father lying ill, he had no interest in their plight.

Pounding on the door loud and hard, Peter found himself welcomed quite happily by Miranda. "Oh, Peter, you've come. We prayed you would. We couldn't find you."

"What's happened here? How is Father?"

He looked past Miranda to where his father slept. "Is he . . . worse?"

"Oh no. No, he's much better. The doctor believes in time he will be completely healed. Mother and Grace, oh, you didn't know we brought Grace, did you?" She watched his face as if expecting some sort of response. Peter wasn't at all sure what she expected from him.

"One of father's crewmen told me she was here. What in the world is going on, Miranda? Why was my ship taken from me?"

"That question," Ephraim called weakly from the bed, "would be better answered by me."

Peter rushed past his sister, not even pausing to consider where Grace and his mother might be. "Father, are you all right? What does the doctor say?" He stared down at the ashen-faced man and shook his head. "What has happened?"

Ephraim struggled to sit up, bringing Miranda quickly to his side. "Let us help you, Father. You know the doctor said you must rest and take care not to overwork yourself."

Ephraim relaxed and let Peter and Miranda help him. Plumping pillows around her father to assist his upright position, Miranda turned to Peter. "Mother and Grace have gone to buy food. They should be back anytime now."

"Why don't you go see to finding them?" Peter suggested.

Miranda seemed to understand that Peter wanted to speak privately with their father. She took up her coat and headed for the door. "You mustn't leave Father alone. You will stay with him, won't you?"

"I promise not to leave until you return," Peter assured her.

Once she had gone, he pulled off his heavy wool coat and tossed it to one side. "Now, let us get down to business. The sheriff showed up on board *Merry Maid*. He said the ship had been confiscated as a part of an agreement with Martin Paxton."

His father nodded sadly, affirming Peter's worst fears. "The papers I signed when Paxton advanced us the money for repairs—they held a clause that said should Paxton find his investment . . . compromised or threatened . . . he would have the right to take over possession of the company until such time as he felt the property was once again on sound footing."

"But he has no grounds," Peter stated. "Even if the contract holds such a clause—and mind you, I do not remember reading such a thing when I looked the papers over—he would have to have reasonable grounds for such an action."

"He feels his actions are reasonable," Ephraim said wearily. He closed his eyes, and Peter thought for a moment that he'd never seen his father look so old and tired. The dark circles under his eyes, the sagging of his jaw—it all made him look so very fragile. It wasn't something Peter dealt with easily.

"Father, I should let you rest." Peter said the words, but at the same time, allowing his father to rest was the last thing he wanted to do.

"No," his father said, waving his hand weakly. "Don't go. We must discuss this."

Peter sat down on the edge of the bed. The mattress sagged under his weight, leaving him little doubt its support was nothing more than ropes. "Why does Paxton feel he has a right to do this?"

Ephraim slowly opened his eyes. "He feels his investment is threatened because of your marriage."

A burning sensation arose in Peter's chest. How dare Paxton take this to such lengths, and over a woman! He would strip a man of his business, leave him on his sickbed from the shock, burn down his assets, and for what? To exact revenge over a missed opportunity for marriage?

"Paxton has done this because I married Grace?"

Ephraim nodded. "Apparently because of the bad blood between them, Paxton felt you might threaten his investment by siding against him."

"But Grace has nothing to do with the business. Nothing to say. Are you certain you understood him?"

"Ask Grace. She was there with me."

"Grace went to Paxton? After I told her to never be in his company?"

"She was only trying to help. The men had come to take us from *Summer Song*. I knew I had to straighten this matter out, and Grace offered to go with me. She already felt confident that Paxton had done this as a deliberate act against her."

Peter rose from the bed and began pacing in the small room. His father once again closed his eyes, as if telling such a woeful tale had taken his last reserves of strength. And perhaps it had. Peter immediately felt guilty for not concerning himself with his father's condition.

"What are the doctors telling you?"

Without opening his eyes, Ephraim drew a deep breath. "They tell me I've suffered a heart attack. With rest they believe I will recover. They are suggesting I go home as soon as possible, where better medical facilities and doctors are available to aid me in recovery."

"Then we'll see to it that you leave immediately. I'm surprised you brought Mother and Miranda here. Whatever brought that about?" He tried to make the question sound curious rather than disapproving.

Ephraim looked at his son quite seriously. "You left in a bad way. You hurt Grace deeply."

"Yes . . . well, she hurt me, if that's any consolation."

"It's no consolation," Ephraim replied. "Such matters are never easily consoled. Peter, she is your wife. You must find a way to deal gently with her. Your temper is easily provoked these days, and I fear this news will not bode well for your marriage. You must determine to put your differences aside and let the past go."

"I would love nothing more, but apparently Grace and Mr. Paxton have other plans."

Just then Miranda opened the door. Their mother, dressed somberly in a dove gray coat, came next, and Grace entered behind her. A delivery boy stood at the door, a box of goods in his arms. With the stranger there, Peter held his tongue and said nothing. While his mother paid the boy, Peter had a chance to meet his wife's eyes.

She looked at him as though she'd not seen him in years. Her expression was one of hope. It even suggested pleasure in seeing him. Peter softened momentarily. She was beautiful. Her dark eyes drew him like a moth to a flame, and just like the moth, Peter knew he could very well be wounded to the point of death if he got too close to Grace.

Grace ignored the distance and Peter's lack of movement. She went quickly to his side. "I'm so glad you're safe. We were terribly worried about you."

Peter had no words. He wanted to jump right to the heart of the matter regarding Paxton, yet he didn't want to further upset his father by creating a scene. What he needed to do was take Grace somewhere away from his family. Once he had her alone, he could question her and learn the truth.

The delivery boy placed the contents of the crate inside the room and turned to go. Amelia stopped him and handed him a coin, then closed the door behind him as he whistled off happily down the hall. She turned and met her son with an expression that suggested veiled displeasure. Peter hadn't seen this from her since he'd been a young man. She had always hated to take him to task as a child, and her reluctance and obvious distaste for such matters kept him in line more often than the threat of punishment.

"Peter." She said nothing more, but her expression said it all.

"I've been speaking to Father," Peter began. "I'm sorry I wasn't here to help you ashore. I'm sorry you were displaced."

"We've had quite the adventure," his mother admitted and crossed the room to gently kiss her son's cheek. "But we are all well and fine. Your father is recovering his health and soon will be back on his feet."

"I think Father should go home. You all should. There are better doctors and hospitals, and who knows if he's had the proper treatment here in the wilds of the north?"

"Passage home can still be rough at this time of year," his father replied.

"Have you the money for tickets?" Peter asked, still not daring himself to speak what was really on his heart.

"Mr. Paxton has offered us free travel home," Amelia said as Miranda helped her from her coat. She pulled off her bonnet and handed it to Miranda as well. "We plan to leave soon, but not until your father has regained more of his strength."

Peter felt slightly upbraided by her response. She wasn't asking his opinion or his advice. She was simply stating how it was to be. He nodded, then looked to Grace. "I need to speak with my wife."

"I should say so," his mother replied half under her breath. She turned to tend to the groceries, then turned back abruptly. "Do so in gentleness, son. I will not brook any nonsense of ill will between the two of you. Not now—not after all we've been through."

Now Peter felt his anger stirred. His mother was treating him as if he were a young boy again, chiding him to mind his manners and play nicely with the other children.

"The matter is between Grace and me. We will speak in private." He took hold of Grace's arm and tightened his fingers around her wrist. "Come, Grace."

He led her past his mother and sister, opened the door, and fairly pushed her into the hall. "Is there somewhere we can speak privately?" he questioned in a barely audible voice.

"Not really," Grace replied. "Why don't we go for a walk? The day has turned out quite nice, and we can walk away from the town and have a moment or two to ourselves."

Peter nodded and turned back inside to grab his coat. He allowed Grace to walk ahead of him as they went down the stairs and out the door. Freighters with teams of less than cooperative horses added to throngs of people, dogs, and mules, all obstacles of living flesh for anyone brave enough, or foolish enough, to join their numbers. Peter tired of the noise and the ordeal before they'd even walked two blocks.

The buildings thinned out quickly, however, as did the crowds. The town proper was all that really held the interest of these gold rushers. That and the trails to White Pass and the Yukon.

Grace clung to Peter's arm, more for support than intimacy. The muddy streets were difficult to maneuver, and even when they were treated to a few plank boards to negotiate the muck, the walk was still quite uneven.

Peter tried not to be physically drawn to Grace's presence. She seemed so small and helpless sometimes, yet he knew she was quite capable. Her hand holding his arm was less than half the size of his, yet he knew this woman could cause him more pain than men with fists double the width.

"I'm sorry you had to find your father in such a state," Grace finally said after they'd walked a good distance from the planned tracts of Skagway.

Peter stopped and turned to her. Calmly, he asked, "What happened? Tell me everything."

Grace licked her lips and looked quickly away. "The men came to *Summer Song* and escorted us off. When your father learned that this was Mr. Paxton's doing, he decided to go see what he could do to change his mind. I accompanied him, not to defy you or your wishes, but because I didn't want him to face Mr. Paxton alone. I knew his action was most likely on account of me." She looked up as if awaiting his approval or rejection.

"Go on," he said, trying hard to keep all emotion from his voice.

Grace seemed to consider the matter a moment. "Mr. Paxton stated that there was bad blood between our families. That his friendship with your father was completely threatened by my marriage to you. He said that you had taken what was rightfully his, and in turn he would take what belonged to you."

"Why, that—"

Grace held up her hand. "Your father told him that Colton Shipping was his life—your inheritance. Mr. Paxton didn't care. He felt it was only a matter of time before you blamed him for the destruction of the store in Dyea and that soon you and your father would conspire against him."

"Is that all?"

"No," Grace said.

The wind blew loose a strand of chocolate brown hair and draped it across her face. Peter thought to reach out and push it back, but he held himself in check. If he touched her, even for a moment, he might well forget why he'd brought her here in the first place.

Grace's gloved fingers quickly tucked the hair back into place. She said nothing, but looked up at Peter as if awaiting instructions.

"What else?" he finally asked.

"When your father fell ill, Mr. Paxton called for his men to take him to the doctor. I wanted to accompany your father, but Mr. Paxton would not allow me to follow."

Peter could no longer hold back his rage. "Did he touch you? Did he?"

"He did not hurt me, except with his words," Grace replied. "He made it clear that my marrying you had caused this ordeal. I am sorry, Peter. I don't know why he insists on having me for his wife. The matter is settled, yet he acts as though it's only begun. His demands suggest he could change everything with our cooperation."

"What do you mean by that? What are his demands?"

Grace turned away. "I intend to send a telegram to my mother. I am hoping she might have some idea of what Mr. Paxton had said to my father. I am hopeful that she will have some idea of why he continues to pursue me even after he has destroyed my family and our fortune."

Peter gripped her shoulders much too tightly. He knew he was hurting her, but nevertheless, he yanked her back around to face him. "What does he want?"

Grace shook her head. "He wants me."

Peter looked at her and saw the fear in her eyes. He could feel her trembling beneath his hold and knew it was from fear of him. Ashamed, he dropped his hold and stepped back. "You're married. How can he hope to resolve that?"

"He wants me to divorce you. He's already arranged for it and wants only my cooperation. He's probably bought himself a judge and court somewhere," Grace said, her words cold but honest. "Peter, he says he'll return everything to you and your father if I leave you."

"I'll kill him!" Peter said, no longer caring. Doubling his fists, he closed his eyes. He saw hot white stars against a field of blackened emptiness. He had never wanted to kill a man before now. His earlier anger and irritation with Paxton were mere annoyance compared to the feelings coursing through his body—feelings that were quickly fueling his rage and pushing him toward action.

Opening his eyes, he saw the tears streaming down Grace's face. "I suppose you want me to forgive him, madam? Maybe pray for him? Well, there will be none of that. Any prayers said will have to originate with you. I'll kill him before I'll allow him to hurt my father any further. I'll kill him before I'll see him in charge of Colton Shipping. And I'll surely kill him before I see him lay a finger on you."

─┤ C H A P T E R   T H I R T E E N ├─

KAREN SAT DOWN on the edge of the bed and brushed out her long, damp hair. She'd hated to give up her time in the bath, but others were waiting and there was no chance of keeping the place to herself.

With each stroke of the brush, Karen couldn't help but remember Adrik's touch. She shivered, even though the room was quite toasty and warm. What had he done to her? How could she be so easily moved by this man?

She thought of her father and Adrik's loyalty to Wilmont Pierce's memory. She had at first believed Adrik's interest in her was nothing more than an expression of that loyalty. But now . . . now that he'd kissed her, she realized it was something entirely different.

Licking her rather chapped lips, she felt her cheeks flush at the memory of his touch. He sparked a fire inside her. He left her weak-kneed and full of romantic thoughts. No one else had ever done that. Was this truly what it was to fall in love? Could she give her heart to this man? Love him? Marry him? Could she develop any relationship before she'd first dealt with the past?

Karen knew she must deal with her anger toward Martin Paxton. It was affecting everything else in her life. Leah knew it. Adrik and Grace had both endured the effects of it.

Poor Grace. Karen hadn't seen her young friend since their encounter. The thought of Grace being so near yet so far away—just a few miles away in Skagway—was frustrating. Karen longed to make things right between them again. She longed to sit down and put aside talk of Paxton and even of Peter. She longed for things to go back to the way they had been before they'd come to Alaska.

How many times had Karen faced a new day only to wish—even pray—that the reality of her life was nothing more than the remnants of a bad dream? But as bad as her own nightmarish existence was, there was Leah to contend with. Leah's grief had changed the girl. She added her brother's disappearance to her list of losses, tallying them like an account she could never hope to reconcile. Karen saw the child slip further away almost daily. Gone were the vibrant smile and childlike faith. In their place had come a touch of cynicism and defeat, emotions much too adult for a girl not yet thirteen.

It could still be worse, Karen reminded herself as she began braiding her hair into a single plait. She felt her stomach churn at the mental image of women young and old working in the cribs down by the harbor. Leah would most likely be there herself if not for Karen's protection. It was only—yes, she had to admit it—the grace of God that had kept them from harm's way this far.

"I know I'm acting the fool," she said softly to the God she'd resolved to turn from. She bowed her head and tied a ribbon around her braid. "It's just so hard to be here—to endure this life. You have no idea."

But of course, she knew that was wrong. Jesus had come to earth to know every part of being human. The insults, the sorrows, the loneliness. And oh, the loneliness was so overwhelming. Karen brushed a tear away and closed her eyes. Her soul cried out for real communion with God, but even as she contemplated surrendering her will, Martin Paxton's face came to mind once again.

He had no remorse for the things he'd done. He wanted only to have his own way and to hurt those people who stood against him. Karen balled her hands into fists, fists that she'd love nothing more than to use against Paxton. Her breathing quickened, and she jumped to her feet.

"How long must I suffer like this? I'm like two different women. Just when I think I can lay this aside and make peace with God, I see that man and know that I cannot leave the matter alone and walk away."

She began to pace. "I can't allow him to ruin my life."

She heard the words echoed back to her and stopped short. "But he is ruining my life. My hatred of him is destroying everything. My friendship with Grace . . . my love of God. It's even wreaking havoc with the potential love of a good man. And for what?"

She caught her reflection in a small mirror that hung near the door. Her expression reminded her of another person. The anger and bitterness was the same. That expression had belonged to Peter Colton.

"I have become what I thought impossible to be." The sorrow of it broke her spirit and left her devoid of hope.

Grace had heard of the newly installed telegraph system and had hoped to get a message off to her mother. She had to know what it was that kept Martin Paxton so interested in her. She had to know why he refused to leave her in peace and let her life find some normalcy.

If it could find normalcy.

Grace wasn't at all convinced that anything could ever be right again, much less good. She had come to Alaska to flee one monster, only to find herself married to another. But she loved this beast. He had taken her heart as surely as she had taken his name.

Walking unescorted to the telegraph office, Grace found the strength to continue only by trusting in the knowledge that God would never leave her nor forsake her. Should everyone else desert her—leave her to die alone, she knew God would be there. Her faith had been strengthened by the adversity she'd endured. Peter's anger only served to drive her to prayer, where her heavenly Father sent comfort through His Holy Spirit.

Martin Paxton was a thorn in the flesh, to be sure, but he didn't frighten Grace half as much as Peter did, perhaps because she loved Peter and cared nothing for Paxton. Perhaps because she knew Martin Paxton could only take her life, but Peter would have her soul if he thought it possible.

Ignoring the men who eyed her and called to her, Grace quickly sent her telegram, paying the exorbitant sum of five dollars. She hurried back to the hotel, hoping that Peter hadn't returned and found her missing. He had warned her to stay off the streets of Skagway. Apparently, rumor had it that most of the passes were in perfect condition for pressing north. People were creating a new, smaller stampede from the one they'd left in the lower states. This stampede was leaving the comforts of Skagway to head into the vast unknown territories. Gold lured them forward—called to them. Gold beckoned them to forget their loved ones and face the risk of death.

But in spite of Peter's concerns, the town had emptied out onto the trails rather quickly. The stampede was gone, leaving behind those souls who had taken up residence in Skagway, along with stragglers who had lost their caches in games gone bad. Every day, however, new arrivals poured in, the fever glazing over their eyes, keeping them from seeing the truth of the disease that had come to grip them.

By night, Grace knew the rowdies would be out and about. Skagway's lawlessness rivaled nothing she had ever known, and Peter's concerns were well justified. Jefferson "Soapy" Smith and his men were notorious for the trouble they caused. They weren't alone, however. Scallywags and hoodlums of every sort were to be found in the town. Everyone wanted something from someone, and gold was almost always at the bottom of it.

In the exodus of gold seekers, Peter had managed to secure a private room next to his parents' for himself and Grace, and it was in this room that Grace sought her solace. The four bare walls offered no comfort. Gone was the beauty of the rooms she'd known growing up. Even the simplistic charm of the little room she'd once shared with Karen was preferable to these stark confines.

But as much as she desired the beauty and warmth of her childhood, she needed answers more. Answers to questions that seemed so illogical to even ask. Why did Martin Paxton desire to marry a woman who clearly held him in contempt? Why did he pursue her to the point of ruining lifelong friendships and giving old men heart attacks? Why, when she had nothing left to offer him but her body, did Martin Paxton find the price worth paying?

Then there were questions about Peter. Why did he so fervently refuse to see God's part in his life? How could he have no desire for spiritual truth? How had he lost his desire for her?

He'd not even come back to their room the night before until well into the morning hours. Grace had pretended to be asleep as he fell into the bed beside her. She had thought to herself, *If he reaches for me, I will willingly go into his arms.*

But he never reached for her.

"I love him so much, Father," she prayed. Picking up her Bible, she held it close for comfort. She didn't have the energy to read the Scriptures between the covers, but just holding it gave her a sense of peace. Settling into a chair, Grace lost track of the time. She dozed off, weary from the battle she'd been fighting, only to awaken disoriented.

She wondered at the time, then startled when a loud, insistent knock came at the door. Apparently it had been this that had brought her from her sleep in the first place.

Peter had already left by the time she'd awakened that morning and she'd not seen him since, so she hoped that it might be him. She put the Bible aside and hurried to the door. Throwing it back, she was surprised to find a boy, no more than twelve or thirteen years old, standing there holding out a telegram.

"Are you Mrs. Colton?"

"I'm Mrs. Grace Colton," she replied.

"Then this here telegram is for you." He thrust the paper toward Grace and hurried back down the hall almost before she could take hold of the missive. Apparently he wasn't concerned with getting a tip.

Opening the telegram, Grace couldn't contain her surprise. It was a response from her mother. She scanned the lines quickly and felt all hope drain away. Her mother simply advised her that she should do whatever Mr. Paxton told her. That he could still hurt them both.

Grace didn't even remember to close the door. She walked back to her chair and sat down hard. How could this be? Why would her mother direct her to do such a thing when she'd previously been so supportive of Grace remaining free of Martin Paxton?

"May I come in?" Peter questioned from the door.

Grace looked up and found him staring at her as if seeing her for the first time. "Of course you may come in. It's your room as well as mine."

Peter crossed the threshold and quietly closed the door. Grace watched him, confused by his gentle nature and uncertainty. "Is something wrong?" she questioned.

"Yes." He came to where she sat. "I've been unreasonable and owe you a great many apologies." He knelt beside her. "I never meant to let things get so muddled. I don't even know who I am anymore or why I act as I do."

Grace felt her heart nearly break. He looked so lost. She reached out and took hold of his hand and brought it to her lips. "Oh, Peter, I'm so very sorry for all that you've had to endure. Especially for those things you've endured on my behalf."

"No, it's not your fault. You have no reason to apologize. Even your faith is not an issue that should divide us. I know that now, but I cannot pretend to believe as you do. I'm sorry I've failed you as a husband. I'm a poor leader, both spiritually and physically. I'm responsible for losing my family's business, and I've nearly lost you. Please tell me I'm not too late."

Grace got to her feet, the telegram now forgotten. "You could never be too late. Oh, Peter, I love you. I'm sorry I'm not the wife you had hoped me to be. There is still so much we do not know about each other. So much that is yet to be overcome."

He held her close and buried his face in her hair. "I know I'm difficult at times. I know I've said things that hurt you." He pulled away and shook his head. "I know, too, that I can never take back those words."

He walked away from her and seemed to struggle with his thoughts. Grace stood still, afraid that she might break the fragile peace should she do anything but await his words. Turning to face her again, Peter frowned.

"I cannot make this right. I cannot hope to see Paxton pay for the harm he's caused, yet everything in me rises up to demand it. As a woman, you have no idea what it is for a man to face this humiliation. My father lies ill in the next room. My mother and sister have no hope of returning home except at the mercy of the very man who has caused their misery. The man openly covets my wife and sees nothing wrong in tempting her to divorce me and marry him."

"He has not tempted me," Grace said softly.

Peter stared at her for a moment as if trying to convince himself of her words. It was then he spied the telegram on the floor. "What's that?"

Grace looked quickly to where the paper lay. "It's nothing." She bent to retrieve the telegram and folded it to put it in her pocket. If she shared the news with Peter, he would know that she'd disobeyed him and had gone alone to the telegraph office. Furthermore, he would not be pleased by the message.

"That's a telegram. I didn't even realize they'd put a line through. Who is it from?"

"It's not important," Grace replied. "I'd rather hear what you have to say." Nervously, she warred within her mind. *If I tell him he'll be angry, and if I don't tell him he'll feel betrayed. Oh, God, what am I to do?*

"What are you hiding?" Immediately he sounded suspicious. "I demand that you allow me to see that message."

He took several steps toward her, and Grace knew she had once again managed to rile the beast. "Peter, it is to our benefit that you forget about this telegram. Please. I want only to sow peace between us." She looked up to him, hoping he could read the pleading in her eyes.

"So now you're making a habit of keeping secrets from me?" he questioned, but his tone made it clear that he'd already determined the answer.

"Peter, I do not desire to keep things from you. The telegram is unimportant. What is important is that you know you can trust me. I'm not the enemy here."

"For all I know you're in this with him."

"You don't really believe that. You can't believe that."

"Why not?" He shook his head as if he couldn't quite put the pieces together. "How am I to know what the truth is when you insist on keeping it from me? It seems quite reasonable that you could have formed some sort of alliance with Paxton."

"You aren't speaking rationally," Grace said. Fear flooded her heart, giving a trembling to her voice. "You . . . can't . . . say these things." How could this continue? She was only trying to protect him from her mother's suggestion that Grace cooperate with Paxton. He would hate her mother for saying such a thing, even as Grace suspected he now hated her for her secrecy.

"So now you think me mad? You think me incapable of seeing this situation for what it is—a betrayal of our marriage vows? Do you tell Paxton your secrets? Does he know your heart? And here I came to apologize—thinking I was the problem."

Grace drew her hand to her mouth to keep from crying aloud, but her muffled sobs were no less evident. He truly believed the worst of her. He thought her a traitor. She struggled to compose herself while Peter watched, eyes raging silent accusations at her.

"Peter," she finally managed to speak, "do you love me? Do you trust me at all?"

"Why do you ask me that now? You speak of words and their importance, yet you bandy them about as though they were halfpenny candy. I had a business and a good life before you came into my world. I should have known the worst would be upon me for disregarding my own misgivings."

Grace fought to keep her voice even. The pain was tearing her heart in two. "Then you truly wish we'd never married?"

"I wish I'd done whatever it would have taken to keep this regretful existence from happening. I wish I had a wife who trusted me enough to share her secrets and respected me enough to keep her faith to herself." He calmed considerably as he studied her. This calm was even more unnerving than his anger.

"I can't live up to your expectations, Grace. I cannot believe as you believe. I cannot provide as a husband should provide. Until I met you, I had thought my life well ordered. Now . . . well, now there's little hope that we can put this right."

Grace felt the tears stream down her cheeks but refused to wipe them away. She thought only of her mother's words to do as Martin Paxton had asked. She thought she ought to simply show Peter the telegram, but she realized the time for that had passed.

Peter went to the far end of the small room and took up his trunk. "I'll leave you to your telegrams and secrets. Perhaps you will find solace in them."

She felt ill. Would he really leave her? Divorce her? "Where are you going?"

"It doesn't matter. I know I'm not wanted here, and I don't intend to stick around and watch what I once thought of as love further crumble and die."

Grace watched him walk from the room. She crossed to the door and thought to call after him as he made his way down the stairs, but something held her back. Her hand went to the telegram in her pocket, and she knew it would have done little good to call after him.

"What are you doing out here, Grace?" Miranda questioned as she came from the room next door.

"Saying good-bye to my heart," she murmured.

Miranda came to stand directly in front of her. She took hold of Grace's arms, forcing her attention. "What are you saying?"

"Peter's left me. He's just now gone away . . . and," she looked beyond her sister-in-law to the now empty stairs, "I don't think he's ever coming back."

Part Two

MAY 1898

He discovereth deep things out of
darkness, and bringeth out to light
the shadow of death.

JOB 12:22

-[C H A P T E R   F O U R T E E N]-

KAREN CALLED IT a meeting of grave importance. She had sent a note to Adrik and now sat across the small table from both him and Leah Barringer.

"It's been weeks since Jacob left, with no word from him. The town's abuzz with newcomers and would-be miners in every shape and size. Every day," Karen continued, "more and more people pour over Chilkoot Pass on their journey north to gold and fame. I can't sit here and wait and wonder what has happened to Jacob in the midst of that onslaught."

Adrik seemed to consider her words as he thoughtfully rubbed his chin. "Well, what do you have in mind?"

Karen looked at Leah. Only that morning she'd tried to encourage Leah by suggesting they go look for Jacob. It was the first spark of life she'd seen in the child since he'd disappeared. "I think we should go after him."

"To Dawson?" Adrik questioned in disbelief.

"Yes," Karen replied. "If that's what it takes."

"And what if we did that? What if we went all that way and still didn't find him? Then what?"

Karen hadn't considered the scenario any further than the idea of going along the same path Jacob would surely have taken. "I don't honestly know. I suppose we could settle in and put out word that we were there. We could put up posters asking for information. If they have a newspaper, we might even place an advertisement."

Adrik nodded. "You've thought this all out, I take it."

Karen shook her head and looked to the table. "Actually, no. I mentioned the idea to Leah this morning, and she liked it. Other than telling Mrs. Neal that we needed a quiet place to meet this evening, I hadn't considered anything else."

"Well, there's a great deal more to do with heading to Dawson than deciding it should be so. You have no idea what the trail is like and how demanding the ordeal will be," Adrik told her. "Not only is this a wilderness with pathways barely mucked out by those who've passed before you, but there are very real dangers."

Karen felt she had to persuade Adrik. Perhaps in doing so, she might also persuade herself. "I know that, but other women and children have made the trip and lived to tell about it."

"And others have died and lay buried alongside the trail in unmarked graves. I'd hate to see that for you or Leah."

"I want to find Jacob," Leah said, speaking for the first time in days without having a direct question posed to her. "I want to know if Pa is really dead. I know it won't be easy to hike the trail. My pa told us all about it. He'd read up on it. But I still want to go. I want to try."

Adrik smiled at her, and Karen saw the sympathy and kindness in his expression as he reached out to touch Leah's shoulder. "I know you love your brother and want to know the truth about your father, and no man could ask for a better sister or daughter. But, Leah, you have no idea what you'd be up against. The nights are bitter cold, even now with the spring coming. There will be floods with the thaw and wild animals. There are miles to go between here and Dawson City, miles that you will have to walk. Are you really up to that?"

Leah lifted her chin ever so slightly. "I'll do what I have to. Ma said that was the way it was with life. You face each day as it comes. And the way I see it, every day spent on the trail would put me that much closer to Jacob and maybe even Pa."

"She's got a point, Adrik," Karen said softly. "The reason I've asked you here is to find out if you'd be our guide. I could pay you."

Adrik frowned. "I'd hoped maybe I was something more than a guide."

"You're our friend," Leah responded before Karen could speak. "You're the only one we trust."

Adrik met Karen's eyes. He seemed to demand answers from her that she wasn't yet ready to give him. Understanding this, he drew a deep breath and put both his palms down on the table. It looked as though he might push himself up and leave, but instead he blew out his breath loudly and patted the tabletop. "I suppose we need to figure out what our assets are. The supplies needed to go north are extensive, as you well know. A ton of goods per person won't be cheap. Then there are tariffs to pay to the Canadians, and we can't hope to pack this stuff all on our own. I can hire a couple of natives to help, but they probably won't want to go any farther than Lake Bennett."

Karen smiled. He was going to help them. The thought sent a wave of relief washing over her. She flashed him a look of gratitude—at least she hoped he'd see it for that. "I have the list that appeared in the paper," she said, pulling the notice from her pocket. "Does this appear to suggest all of the necessary supplies?"

Adrik took the paper and scanned it. "I have tools—we needn't have those things for each person. I also have a large tent we can share and a cookstove, so we needn't buy those things, either."

"I don't know that it would be such a good idea for us to share a tent," Karen replied. "We aren't . . . well . . . that is to say . . ." She felt her cheeks grow hot. "We aren't family."

"We could remedy that," Adrik said with a laugh. "Wouldn't hurt my feelings none." He leaned over and playfully nudged Leah. "How about you? Would you be against Karen marrying someone like me?"

Karen felt mortified. He'd never talked of marriage—not outright like this. Leah giggled. Karen hadn't heard that girlish sound in weeks. Leah had been so lost in her sorrows that laughter had been buried along with the news of her father and her brother's disappearance.

"Enough!" Karen declared. "Just buy another tent. We have the money."

Adrik turned to study her for a moment. He raised a brow as if to question her certainty on the matter, then shrugged. Karen couldn't help but see something akin to regret, maybe even hurt, in his expression.

"You talk as though money is no object," Adrik said, looking back at the list. "I think we'd better figure out how much we have for this. I have nearly eight hundred dollars from my packing experiences. I want to leave some of it for Joe and his family. Packers aren't making much money these days, what with the tramway taking their business."

"That's perfectly fine," Karen replied. "We did very well with the store, and Mr. Colton was quite generous with our profits. I have my aunt's share as well as my own. There's probably twelve hundred dollars in my account."

"Well, coming from a camp where they charged twenty-five dollars for a dozen eggs, you're going to need every cent you can put your hands on," Adrik replied. "We've also got to remember the duty taxes. I've heard it said you'll pay a pretty penny to get the Canadians to let you cross their borders."

"I'm sure the stores here will give us a good deal. I was always generous with them when they needed something from me," Karen said. "Do you think we can get everything we need here in Dyea?"

Adrik continued to look at the list and nodded. "I feel confident we can, but you'll pay dearly whether they owe you favors or not. Can you maybe get Mrs.

Neal to let you have some of her kitchenware rather than buying it all brand-new?"

"It's possible. What will we need?"

"Well, I have a coffeepot and a skillet, so we don't need to worry about that," he replied. "See if she can spare a couple of pie tins. You can use those over the fire if need be or just heat things up on the camp stove with them. You can eat out of them, wash out of them, and even dig with them if you have to. They make a very useful tool. If she doesn't have any, we'll buy rather than settle for plates."

Karen nodded. "I'm sure we can get them. What else?"

"You and Leah will each need your own tin cup and knife. I can find you a couple of good pocketknives. These are vital. You need them to stay alive. Never underestimate the usefulness of anything. Why, I once saw a man pull his boot-laces out and make a fishing line with them and a safety pin. You just never know."

"Sounds like we'll have ample chance to use our imaginations," Karen said with a grin.

He laughed and looked at her in such a way as to warm her blood. "You don't know the half of it."

They pored over the supply list for another half hour before they all felt they knew exactly what their responsibilities were to be. Leah began to yawn, and Karen finally sent her upstairs, leaving only Adrik to sit with her in the dim lamplight of Mrs. Neal's empty dining room.

"So what do we do when we find him?" Adrik asked, his voice low and appealing.

They were so very alone, Karen realized, and for a moment the idea rather excited her. She wondered if he might attempt to kiss her again. And if he did, she wondered if she would try to stop him. "Find whom?" she asked, rousing herself from such thoughts.

Adrik looked at her, rather puzzled. "Whom do you suppose? Jacob."

Karen shrugged. "I hadn't thought past the search. And I really don't have any hope of finding Bill. Even if the man you found wasn't Bill, he could be so far away by now we might never find him. He may not even have survived another leg of his journey."

"Have you ever considered settling up north? Whitehorse or Dawson?"

Such thoughts had once accompanied Karen to Alaska, but they'd died out with her father's passing. "I don't know what I want to do. Things are so very confusing right now. I had thought about teaching the native children—you know that, of course, from our previous talks. Now I just don't know."

"You don't seem quite as angry as the last time I saw you," Adrik braved.

"No, I suppose not." She brought her elbows to the table and leaned her chin against her folded hands.

"Wanna talk about it?"

She heard the desire in his voice. Not a passionate desire, but rather one of hope that she would not shut him out. "I suppose there's really very little that you aren't already aware of. I miss my father. I'm confused about God and what He wants from me. I'm angry for being angry, and torn apart for hurting the people I care about most."

"Nothing's been said or done that can't be fixed," Adrik suggested.

"I can't bring the dead back to life, and that's what I really need. I need my father to tell me it's all right—that I can stay on with him and that he'll teach me how to minister to the people he so loved. I need Aunt Doris and my mother to encourage me and love me until I'm strong enough to stand on my own again. I need Bill Barringer to come back to his children—to father them and care for them as only a parent can.

"I need things I can't even identify," she said in complete exasperation.

"Well, I can't bring the dead back to life, either," Adrik said softly, "but I can tell you that it's all right—that you can stay on with me, and that I'll teach you how to minister to the people your father loved—the people I love."

Karen closed her eyes and buried her face in her hands. Why did she have to be so moved by his words? Why did she have to feel all weak and shaken? "I don't know what's right. I don't know what God wants because I haven't bothered to ask Him."

Adrik took hold of her wrists and pulled her hands away from her face. When Karen still refused to look at him, he let go of her arms and put two fingers to her chin. "Look at me," he commanded.

She opened her eyes, but her vision blurred from her tears. She'd been so cruel to him. Why did he go on enduring her?

"God wants you to talk to Him. He wants you to put aside childish ways and trust Him. You've been fighting Him, wrestling Him for a blessing, and He's already provided."

"But He's taken away so much that I loved."

Adrik rubbed his thumb against her cheek. "But maybe He's given you new things to love."

She trembled under his touch. She wanted Adrik to hold her, to kiss her, to promise her that nothing would ever hurt her again. If only he would make that pledge, she could tell him that she loved him—would love him forever. But she wanted the same of God, and if God wouldn't give her that promise, how could this mere mortal?

Breaking the spell, Karen jumped up from the table, sending her chair flying backward to crash against the floor. For a moment she shook off the spell Adrik had woven over her, and by the time he got to his feet, Karen felt a firm resolve to send him on his way.

"I have to go," she said in a curt manner. "Leah will be wondering where I am."

She headed for the door, but Adrik caught hold of her before she could get that far. Swinging her around, he pulled her against his chest and held her fast.

"What are you afraid of?"

She swallowed hard. "Everything," she whispered.

"Don't be." He put his hand to the back of her head and buried his fingers in her coiled braid. His mouth came against hers in a kiss so sweet and passionate that Karen momentarily took leave of her senses.

She lost herself in his embrace, allowing her hands to travel up to the back of his neck. She memorized the feel of the scar that edged along the right side, leaving a deep furrow where his collar reached. She let her fingers toy with the thickness of his hair, all while being very much aware of his hands. One pressed against the small of her back keeping her snug against the warmth of his body, while he'd brought the other around to the side of her face.

He was all she wanted. Nothing else mattered. Not the trip north nor her damaged friendship. Nothing else even came to mind. She wanted nothing more than to stay forever in his arms.

Returning his kiss with a zeal she'd not known herself capable of, Karen all at once realized she was gasping for air. The smell and taste of this powerful, wonderful man had completely stolen her senses. Forcing herself to regain control, Karen brought her hand between them and pushed at Adrik's chest. She had to stop this now or she might forget herself all together.

"Adrik!" She staggered back and looked at him, embarrassment replacing the passion.

He grinned at her in an irritating manner that furthered Karen's journey back to reality. "What? Am I doing it wrong?" he asked, as if he had no idea what the problem might be.

Karen bit her lip for a moment, then shook her head. "Buy another tent. That's final."

She heard him laugh as she hurried from the room. No doubt he had no idea what he'd done to her. No doubt he had no idea how hard it had been for her to walk away.

-{ C H A P T E R   F I F T E E N }-

ADRIK GOT LITTLE SLEEP that night. And the next. Consumed with his feelings for Karen, he could only remember the way she'd felt in his arms—the way she had yielded to his kiss.

"She loves me," he said aloud as he pulled on his boots. "I'm certain of it, but how do I make her certain of it, as well?" He got up from his cot and went to the makeshift table he used for his tent. Picking up his Bible, he pored over the Scriptures between sips of steaming coffee. The book of First John spoke to him of God's love and the need to show love in return to God's children.

"I love her," he said prayerfully. "I know she loves me. I know she loves you, too. Oh, Father, she's just afraid. She's terrified that you have somehow forgotten her. She's worried that the love she's given has somehow been misplaced. Help her, Father. Help her to see that just because bad things have happened, it doesn't mean you haven't been there all along, grieving with her, sharing her sorrow."

Adrik closed the Bible and buried his face in his hands. He continued to pray in silence, losing track of the noises around him and the time.

Help me not to make a mess of things by pushing her for answers before she's ready to give them. Help me to take her and Leah north, to do it safely. And please, Lord, let us find Jacob. I probably shouldn't have let him go off like I did, but I know how it feels to mourn a father's death. I needed time to myself, and I was certain he did, too. I didn't mean to be neglectful of my duties as a Christian man. If I failed to respond in the right way, please forgive me.

He prayed for some time, and only when he felt he'd exhausted himself before

God's throne did Adrik put away his Bible and head out to tend to business.

"Where are you headed?" Dyea Joe asked. His dirty white bowler was pulled down tight over oily black hair. Added to this, his heavy pants, coat, and best boots told Adrik that Joe was ready to head back up to pack goods on the trail.

"I have to buy supplies. Are you game for a bit of a trip?"

Joe shrugged. "I was going up with the others. Why?"

"I've agreed to pack north with Karen Pierce and Leah Barringer. They're desperate to find Jacob Barringer and to know the truth about whether the man I found in the avalanche was really Bill. I'm not sure what we'll do once we're up there, but we'll go until we find the boy and then decide. I just wondered if you and your family wanted the job packing."

"Sure," Joe said, nodding. He followed Adrik to the Yukon outfitters and stopped short of going inside. "How soon you want to leave?"

Adrik realized they'd not settled on a day or time. "I'm not sure. It'll take me a day or two to put everything together. Why don't you round up some reliable men and meet me tonight at my tent? We'll discuss the time and place then."

"I'll be there."

"Good. Now I have to buy a tent," Adrik said, pulling open the door to the shop.

"Buy a tent? You have a tent," Joe declared.

Adrik turned and smiled. "I don't have a big enough tent."

Joe shrugged in confusion, tapped down his bowler as if it had come loose, then sauntered off down the street. Adrik laughed, knowing the man couldn't hope to understand the situation. Then again, Adrik wasn't exactly sure he understood it all himself.

Four hours later, Adrik shook hands on the last deal. Eight hundred pounds of flour, three hundred pounds of split peas, and three hundred pounds of sugar were to be delivered by morning. This, added to the condensed milk, coffee, dried potatoes, fruit, rice, and beans that he'd already purchased earlier in the morning would round out their supplies rather nicely. He knew they could pick up other things once they got to Sheep Camp or the Scales. Discouraged men would be turning back by that point, and there was always a supply of goods to be bought.

Stopping by the Gold Nugget for lunch, Adrik figured to satisfy his appetite and talk to Karen at the same time. He walked into the dining room and spied her working at one of the far tables. A rowdy group of men seemed to be overstepping their bounds as she worked to maneuver out of their reach. Adrik frowned. It seemed the men had escaped manners and common decency when they came north. He crossed the room just as one man put his hand out to give Karen's backside a friendly pat.

Adrik plowed his fist into the man's jaw, leaving everyone at the table to stare up in stunned silence. Except, of course, the injured man. He howled like Adrik had mortally wounded him. Even Karen turned rather abruptly, startled by her customers' expressions and the man's obvious pain. Adrik noted her face had reddened considerably.

"What'd ya do that for, mister? I didn't mean any harm." The wounded man rubbed his jaw and winced.

"I didn't mean any harm, either," Adrik replied. "Just figured if we were putting our hands where they had no business bein', then I'd get in on the fun, as well. Now, if you apologize to the lady, I might be inclined to put an end to our game."

"Sorry, miss," the man said, sounding profoundly sincere.

Karen said nothing but seemed pleased that Adrik had come to her rescue. He winked at her and asked, "Do you have a table for me?"

She looked over her shoulder and motioned with her head. "You can sit over there."

Adrik spied the small corner table. "Can you join me?"

"In about ten minutes," she replied. "Mrs. Neal has a couple of girls coming in to spell us. We've been at this pretty much since breakfast. I think this must be a new group headed north."

Adrik nodded. "I'll wait over here. Whatever you're dishing up today is just fine by me." He grinned, then leaned close enough that only Karen could hear him add, "As long as you come with the meal."

She elbowed him away. "I'll bring you fish heads and seaweed if you don't mind your manners."

He laughed all the way to the table, knowing that if Karen Pierce served them up, he'd find a way to digest them. He watched her work, admiring her stamina and grace. She conducted herself like a lady but wasn't averse to getting her hands dirty. Maybe it was because she came from a family of good hardworking folk who'd brought her up to appreciate manual labor as well as an education. And in truth, Adrik admired her mind, as well. She was smart—smarter than most women. Smart and pretty. Now, there was a combination.

Adrik continued watching her, needing to assure himself that she was safe. He caught the veiled glance of the man he'd punched and noted the fellow's nose was already turning purple. *Well, he had it coming,* Adrik thought. Then he rationalized that he probably shouldn't have hit him. He knew he could have handled it in a different manner, but up here folks seemed to better understand a physical deterrent. They weren't all coming for a summer social, after all. They were greedy and hungry for gold, and that tended to sever a man's brain from his actions.

True to her word, Karen joined him a short time later. She brought with her two steaming bowls of bean stew. One of the new serving girls followed behind with a tray of coffee and warm biscuits.

After the girl had gone, Adrik suggested they bless the food. He took hold of Karen's hand before she could protest and held it fast in his own. He prayed a simple prayer of thanks, painfully aware of Karen's presence. The softness of her hand was enough to distract the most pious of men. After he said amen, he continued to hold on.

"It's going to be difficult to eat if you insist on holding my hand," Karen finally said.

Adrik grinned wickedly. "I could feed you."

"I could toss this coffee over your head," she said, smiling sweetly. "What happened to us all keeping our hands where they belong?"

"But this *is* where my hands belong."

"Ah . . . yes . . . well, we can discuss that later. I'm hungry and would like to eat my lunch."

Adrik gave her fingers a squeeze, then let go. "I suppose you're right." He picked up one of the biscuits and downed it nearly whole. He was starved, and the sight of Karen only made him more hungry. Hopefully the food would take the edge off his appetite.

"So were you successful in getting supplies?"

"Yup. I have a vast warehouse of goods, and Dyea Joe's getting some men together to help pack. He might even consider bringing his wife, since this will be a long trip."

"Wonderful. Another woman would be very welcomed. Leah and I discussed our needs this morning, and she's going to take in some trousers for us to wear under our skirts. I figured it would be far to our benefit to wear something substantial."

"No doubt you're right. I've seen all manner of things on the trail. Some women have just taken to wearing men's clothes. Others make themselves split skirts and such. I think the long dresses are a definite danger when climbing steep grades. You might well want to shorten your skirts."

"That sounds like a good idea," Karen said, nodding. "I'll do that before we go."

"Speaking of which, when did you have in mind to leave?"

"Soon," Karen replied. "But first I have to see to something else. I wonder if you might have time to take me to Skagway."

Adrik frowned. "Why?"

"I have to find Grace. I have to apologize for the way I treated her." Karen looked down at the table. "I've let weeks pass by and I don't even know if she's still in Skagway, but I have to try to find her. I hurt her, and I can't just leave without making it right between us."

Adrik smiled, knowing she couldn't see him. God was working on softening her heart, and while he knew it was probably painful for Karen, he rejoiced to see the change. "Sure, I'll take you. We'll borrow one of Joe's canoes. When do you want to leave?"

———

Grace finished penning her note to Peter and sat back to wipe the tears from her eyes. She'd not seen him since he'd stormed out of their room. Nor did she expect to see him. She had no idea where she would go or what she would do, but she wouldn't be forced into a divorce. If Peter wanted to end their marriage, that was up to him. She would leave the decision in his hands, but she wouldn't allow Martin Paxton to dictate her future.

"Grace, are you in there?" Miranda called from the other side of the door.

"Come in."

Miranda opened the door hesitantly and stepped inside. "Have you heard any-thing?"

"No. Have you?"

Miranda shook her head. "Not a word."

She crossed the room and sat down on the edge of the bed. Her dark green skirt swirled out around her feet, revealing dainty black leather shoes. Hardly suit-able for dealing with the knee-deep mud of an Alaskan thaw.

"So what are you going to do? Mr. Paxton has arranged passage for us at the end of the week. Father is supposed to be strong enough to travel by then."

"I don't plan to stay here, but I'm not sure where I'll go. I had thought I might make my way back to my mother, but she's confusing me just now and I'm not sure that would be wise. I have some jewelry from when we first came here. I never needed to use it because the store Peter set up did so well. But I have it with me and figure to sell it. I'll give you some money so that you can see to Mother and Father Colton's needs, as well as your own. Then I'll take the rest and go wherever I feel is best."

"You can't leave us. You must come home to San Francisco," Miranda declared.

Grace shook her head. "It's not my home. It's Peter's home, and he's made it clear he doesn't want me there."

"Mother is heartbroken. Father said he would go after Peter himself if only his health would permit."

Miranda and her family's loyalty did Grace much good. It helped to know that they didn't blame her or hold her in contempt for the troubles between her and Peter.

"It's nearly suppertime," Miranda added. "I thought you might join us."

"I'm not hungry," Grace replied. "I'd just as soon—"

A knock sounded at the door and both women jumped to their feet. They shared a glance that assured Grace they were both thinking it might be Peter. Grace hurried to the door and threw it open. It was not Peter, but it was nearly as good.

"Karen!"

"Oh, Grace," she cried before entering. "I've been such a fool. Can you ever forgive me?"

Grace opened her arms to her former governess and hugged her tight. "I'm so happy to see you. I'm so sorry for upsetting you in Dyea."

"I'm the one who needs to apologize," Karen said, pulling away. "I was horrible and my anger caused me to take out all my disappointments on you. I had to come and tell you so before I left."

"Left? Where are you going?"

Miranda joined the women. "We're leaving, as well."

Karen eyed Grace. "Where are you going?"

Grace shrugged. "I don't know. I don't really have any place that calls to me."

"I'm heading north to the goldfields. Jacob Barringer has fled Dyea for Dawson. He hopes to find his father alive or at least keep his father's dream alive. He's taken off alone, and I mean to find him."

"How terrible. You must be so worried. But honestly, are you up for a trip as they describe? The journey sounds so perilous."

"Life is perilous. I can't just wait around for something to happen. I've asked Adrik Ivankov to take us. Leah and I plan to head out tomorrow."

"How exciting. I envy you," Miranda said, surprising both women.

"Why do you say that?" Grace asked.

"The adventure sounds marvelous. Besides, if I had money, I'd go north myself."

"You would?" Karen questioned. "But whatever for?"

"My family has been stripped of its fortune, so I would go north to find gold. Other women are doing it. Why, I heard one woman tell the clerk next door that she was heading up there for her second trip. She'd gone up by way of St. Michael the first time and now she was heading up over the pass."

"You could both come," Karen said, suddenly realizing the potential of such an idea. "We'd help each other. We'd be together. Grace, you said you had no other place to go, and Miranda wants to come north anyway."

Miranda frowned and shook her head. "There are no funds for such a trip.

Mr. Paxton is allowing my family passage back to San Francisco, but he has ownership of everything else. Besides, I know my mother needs me especially now."

"What is this all about?" Karen asked. "What has Mr. Paxton to do with any of this?"

"It's a very long story," Grace replied.

"And Peter?"

"An even longer story."

"Well," Karen said, taking off her gloves, "I suppose you had better start talking, then. I intend to hear it all so we can make an educated decision about what is to be done."

In the quiet of Grace's hotel room, Miranda and Amelia Colton listened to Karen's plans for the trip. Amelia nodded and asked questions from time to time, then finally grew very quiet.

"I cannot say that I don't have misgivings," she said softly. Looking to Miranda, she reached out to touch her daughter's cheek. "Your father is much stronger. I'll be able to take care of him without your help. However, I do worry about allowing you to go off without telling Ephraim exactly what you're about. I fear if I tell him the absolute truth, it could bode ill for him. I wouldn't want to risk that."

"Neither would I," Miranda replied. "Why not simply tell him that Grace needs me? That I might yet act as a negotiator between Grace and Peter."

Amelia looked at her daughter-in-law and nodded. "That would be my prayer."

Mine too, Grace thought, but said nothing.

"Oh, Mother, I just know this is right. I feel so wonderful inside—so excited." Miranda fairly beamed from the joy of her mother's approval.

"We truly are left without hope of finances. I don't know what is to be done, but God will provide. I do believe that much. Perhaps it's best this way."

"I have enough money to buy additional supplies for them," Karen assured, "and we have plenty of protection. Adrik Ivankov and some of his friends and family are going along to guide and help pack the goods. I trust him with my life."

"I, too, trust him, Mother Colton. Because I trust Karen's judgment." Grace hoped her words would further heal the relationship between her and her mentor.

Amelia smiled. "Then that will be good enough for me. Miranda may go."

FOR MIRANDA AND GRACE, their last order of business in Skagway was to bid farewell to Ephraim and Amelia Colton. Miranda and Amelia cried, as did Grace, but the Coltons were not in the leastwise worried about their daughter and daughter-in-law. Their renewed faith in God had given them hope for Miranda and Grace and for Peter's repentance and return.

Miranda left her mother with the promise that she would write often and bring home a fortune. Grace kissed her mother-in-law and pressed half the money she'd managed to secure from the sale of her jewelry into her hand.

"Tell no one," she whispered. "God has provided it, and I must share it with you. But I wouldn't want Mr. Paxton to get wind of this."

Amelia said nothing. She didn't even look at the money in her hand. She simply pressed a kiss upon her daughter-in-law's cheek and smiled.

With Amelia and Ephraim steaming off for San Francisco, Miranda and Grace took their things and, with Adrik's help, moved into Karen's hotel room at the Gold Nugget. The plans were set to leave early the following morning. Grace felt a certain amount of relief in the rapid pacing Karen encouraged. She in no way wanted Martin Paxton to catch wind of what they were about. She would much rather he assume she was hiding out or sulking somewhere than to imagine her daring to head north with the stampede to the Klondike.

Karen's pacing would also help her to conceal another situation. Grace was now certain that she was with child. Any extra time spent in Dyea or Skagway might well reveal this secret, and Grace did not wish to be left behind. She knew the trek north would be a risk to her unborn baby, but she felt confident that God had directed her this way for a reason.

She had labored long and hard with her decision of where she might go. She didn't feel right going back to San Francisco, and at the same time her mother's attitude concerned her and left Grace with little desire to join her in Wyoming. Then there was the whole idea of leaving the northern territories and Peter. She had no idea where he was or what he was doing. She longed to tell him about the baby and felt confident that it would impact his feelings toward her. But on the other hand, did she want his heart changed only because of the child she would bear?

After the Gold Nugget supper crowd had cleared out, Karen and Adrik gathered everyone for a flurry of planning for the next day's departure. Grace got a chance to better know Adrik Ivankov and thought it rather amusing to see how much he and Karen doted upon each other. Funnier still was the way they refused to give in to their feelings and made pretenses at just being friends.

"The first part of the journey isn't the hardest," Adrik told them, stretching out a handmade map. "The trail has been forged—at least better than it used to be. They've even laid corduroy roads here and there."

"Corduroy?" Miranda questioned.

Adrik smiled and explained. "The ground up here is a bit of a problem. Winter is actually the best time to pass through a great deal of it. Come thaw, the ground in a lot of places turns all boggy and wet. It makes the simplest of travel a real nightmare. So some have taken to putting down tree trunks—side by side. They cut logs or take up fallen branches, so long as they're thick enough, then strip them and cut them down to size. Some have tried to charge a toll for passing on these roads, but the gold rushers got impatient with that idea and pretty much just pushed their way on through."

"I see," Miranda replied. Then, leaning toward Grace, she added, "I sure have a great deal to learn."

"Well, Mr. Ivankov is the man to learn it from," Leah Barringer threw in. "He's taught us a whole lot, and he saved our lives."

Grace easily recognized the younger girl's glowing admiration for Adrik. If Karen wasn't careful, Leah would make herself competition for the man's affections. Although Grace doubted Adrik would consider anyone but Karen. It was nice to see that her mentor had found true love, even if she did deny it to herself and everyone around her.

"The important thing is that we pack only the essentials and outfit ourselves appropriately. None of those flimsy satin dancing slippers for this hike," he said good-naturedly. "Only sturdy boots, and pack an extra pair. This won't be easy. Spirits and soles will wear out before you know it."

Grace tried not to worry about the journey ahead, refusing to be left behind. When they were well away from any chance of sending her back to Skagway, she would tell them about the baby.

A baby! Just the thought completely consumed Grace's senses. How could this be? How, in the midst of such anger and confrontation, had a baby been conceived? God's plan for her life certainly seemed to differ from the plan Grace had thought up for herself.

She was happy about the baby, though, despite her sorrow over her current marital situation. She was glad to have some small reminder of her love for Peter. It was so hard to think of him hating her. Hating God. She mourned that thought more than his absence. If he didn't want her for a wife, she could deal with that. Her heart felt completely broken, but it was her own fault. She should never have married him—not with him so adamantly against having faith in Jesus. No, what truly pained her was that Peter should so completely alienate himself from God. God would not be mocked. Grace knew this full well, and she did not want to see Peter suffer because of his decision.

Please be merciful with him, she prayed. *Please guard Peter, Lord, and help him to see the truth about you.*

Grace scarcely heard the discussion around the table. She was lost in thoughts of Peter and the baby and had very nearly decided to go upstairs to rest when Martin Paxton came through the doors of the otherwise silent dining room.

"I've been looking for you, Mrs. Colton. I want to speak to you . . . now."

Everyone at the table looked up in unison. Grace stood, but Karen reached out to touch her arm. "You don't have to give him the time of day, Grace."

"What do you want?" she asked softly. She hoped he didn't find their little gathering too suspicious and quickly added, "We were just about to retire for the evening. Perhaps we could speak another time—say, next week."

Martin Paxton leered and folded his arms casually against his chest. "Next week won't work. I think it's time we discussed your answer."

A wave of nausea threatened Grace's resolve. "My answer?"

"Leave her alone," Karen demanded. "She wants nothing to do with you."

Adrik stood as if to challenge Paxton's claim. He said nothing, but Grace could see the protective nature of his stance. The last thing she wanted was a showdown in front of Leah and Adrik, not to mention Miranda.

"I'll talk with you," she finally said, getting to her feet. "But only if Karen is with me."

"I want to see you privately."

"I think you heard the lady's conditions on the matter," Adrik said, stepping next to Grace.

Paxton seemed to size up the situation before relenting. "Very well. Let's find a quiet corner."

Grace nodded. "Karen, where is that little office where I first met you upon my return to Dyea?"

"Right this way," Karen said, leading them across the room. "It's well within earshot of Adrik should the need arise." She looked at Paxton with great defiance—challenging him to comment on her words. He did not.

Karen and Grace went into the office first, with Paxton close on their heels. Karen protectively put her arm around Grace's shoulders for support. Grace felt blessed to have her friend so close at hand. If Paxton should have demanded she speak to him alone, she would have had little choice but to refuse him. Perhaps this way, she could resolve the past and put an end to his demands.

"Have you determined to divorce your husband and marry me?" Paxton asked without delay. He eyed Grace in the same cold, calculated manner as before.

She could very nearly feel his hot breath upon her neck—his hands upon her body. Shuddering, she shook her head. Very softly, almost inaudibly, she replied, "If my husband wishes to put an end to our marriage, he will have to do so on his own. I will not divorce him. It is against my beliefs."

"I see." Paxton reached into his pocket and produced a cigar. He toyed with it a moment, then pinched off the end and procured a match from his vest pocket. Striking the match, he lit the cigar, his gaze never leaving Grace. He puffed silently, staring at her as if deciding what to say next.

Praying silently, Grace knew she had to stand up to Paxton. She wouldn't tell him of her plans, but neither would she cower. God was on her side. There was nothing Paxton could do to further harm her.

"I don't believe you do see," Grace said, straightening her shoulders a bit. "I am a married woman. I am very much in love with my husband, and in spite of your actions to harm him and his family, I will support him and help them through."

"I saw for myself that the youngest of the Colton clan stayed behind at your side. She's a pretty woman."

"Leave Miranda out of this," Grace said firmly. "If you have some sort of vendetta against me, then hear me now. I am not afraid of you. I have a source of strength and power that you cannot even begin to understand. You are lost and alone inside the pits of evil that you've dug for yourself." Her chin raised ever so slightly, her confidence in God fueling her bravery. "You are not a threat to me, and I would thank you to give up this nonsense."

Paxton moved toward her. "Let me show you just how evil I can be." He grinned at Karen and tossed the cigar onto the paper-strewn desk. "Funny how easily things catch fire up here."

Grace saw Karen's face flush as she rushed to the desk to make certain the cigar caused no damage. Meanwhile, Paxton pressed toward Grace.

"You belong to me, Grace. Your father gave you to me, and I intend to have you."

Karen looked up and opened her mouth. Grace could only presume she meant to call for Adrik Ivankov, but Grace decided on another course of action.

"In the name of Jesus, I command you to leave me."

Paxton stopped and looked at her as if in disbelief. "I beg your pardon?"

Karen moved toward the door shaking her head. "I'll get Adrik."

Grace never faltered. She stood her ground, feeling a legion of angels as her protectors. "In the name of Jesus, I command you to leave me."

"Do you really expect that nonsense to mean anything to me?" Paxton questioned.

Karen stopped, seeming to forget about Adrik. She watched Grace with as much intensity as Paxton, but Grace could not give her attention to her friend.

"Jesus gave His children authority over the devil. And while you may not exactly be the devil himself, you are about his work. Therefore, I command you, out in the name of Jesus."

Paxton's expression changed to one Grace had never witnessed. Confusion. He looked at her and seemed to lean forward as though he might still advance, but his feet seemed nailed to the floor.

"Your faith and your God mean nothing to me," he said. He growled as if fighting some unseen assailant. His hands were raised as if to take hold of her or at least strike her, but he made no move to complete such tasks.

Grace felt awash with peace. There was no fear. It was as if all of heaven battled for her and she had only to stand and await the outcome. The faithfulness of God had been proven over and over to her, but never so dearly as in that moment.

"You're going to regret this," Paxton said. "You think you've already paid for trying to dupe me, but I've got news for you. This isn't over. It's just begun. You haven't yet tasted my wrath."

"Nor will I," Grace said, putting her hands to her hips. "I am no threat to you, Mr. Paxton. I have no interest in you and no desire for anything you might offer. I ran from you twice, taking matters into my own hands. I'm not running anymore. I'm standing here face-to-face with you. I'm here to tell you that my God is more powerful than you could ever imagine. I'm here to tell you that you have no power over me—no rights whatsoever to me. You have only accomplished what you have thus far because God has allowed it and my own hand has often even encouraged it. Well, that is done."

"None of this is done," Paxton said, his eyes narrowing. "It isn't done until I say it is done."

Grace said nothing more. There was no need. She could see that she'd shaken the man. He didn't understand this new manner of business, but Grace did. Grace remembered a sermon she'd heard not but a month ago. A sermon that talked of how God's children need not live in fear. That Satan was the one responsible for stirring fear and worry through his lies and doubts, and that God's children had power they'd never even begun to tap into. Well, she was staking her claim on that power here and now. She had to. For her sake and for Peter's, not to mention their unborn child.

Walking past Paxton without fear, Grace turned at the door. "Mr. Paxton, if you would spend half as much time in pursuing God as you have pursuing me, you would understand where my strength comes from."

She left him standing there, eyes burning and jaw fixed. His surprise was no less evident, however, than Karen's. Her friend stood with mouth agape, eyes wide and full of wonder. Grace knew Karen had been struggling with God's sovereignty and love. She could only hope that this demonstration of God's power to keep evil at bay would help to strengthen Karen's walk of faith.

Karen watched in disbelief as Martin Paxton stormed from the hotel. She followed him in silence to the open front door and watched as he joined in with the throngs of lost souls who headed to the gambling halls and saloons.

Quietly she closed the door and looked up the steps as if expecting Grace to still be standing there. She'd never witnessed anything such as what Grace had just done. The confidence and power that seemed to exude from her friend were impressive, to say the least. Where had she acquired such faith? To face evil, not but a few feet away, and refuse to back down because of the power of God—it was inspiring.

Shaking, Karen hugged her arms to her body and shook her head. It was nothing short of miraculous. Miraculous . . . and perhaps even terrifying.

⊣{ C H A P T E R   S E V E N T E E N }⊢

THROUGHOUT THE WINTER of 1897–98, Karen had understood why Skagway and the surrounding area was called what it was. Coming from a Tlingit word that meant "people of the north wind," Skagway bore the brunt of the chilled arctic air that bore down on the coast from the northern mountains. Dyea was no different. Now, however, with summer upon them, the reverse was true. Winds coursed in from the coast and rushed through the valleys and canyons toward the mountains.

This often made travel up the Chilkoot Trail very difficult. Karen tried not to think about the trials and tribulations and focused instead on Jacob and the land itself. Adrik gave her botany lessons, increasing her understanding of the land and the people who dwelt there.

Determined to carry her share, Karen had allowed Adrik to decide how much she should carry. He had fixed her with a twenty-pound pack, advising her that once she grew used to this, they could increase the weight. She adjusted well at first. She even thought him silly to have given her so little. But by the end of the first day, Karen was grateful for Adrik's wisdom. After a long day twenty pounds felt more like two hundred pounds.

Casting her load aside, Karen dropped wearily to the ground and sought the support of a nearby spruce. With its heavy branches towering above her, Karen leaned back to look toward the sky. How long had they been at this? How long would they journey until they found Jacob, Bill, or the promised land of the Yukon?

Day after day it was the same. They trudged through muck and mud, forded streams and rivers, and bedded down at night to the restless sounds of the coastal rain forest.

"When do you think we might find Jacob?" Leah asked after they'd been on the trail for nearly a week.

Karen shrugged. "With your brother's determination, that would be hard to say. He was bound and determined to get north before too much time passed. He has a two-month lead on us, and up here timing is everything."

"She's right, you know," Adrik told Leah. He threw more wood on the fire, then sat down on the ground beside them. "Jacob's probably already in White-horse, knowing him."

"Where is that?" Leah asked, her face lit up in eager anticipation. She had talked of little but Jacob since they'd begun the trip.

"Whitehorse is over the mountains and farther north. Remember the map?" Leah nodded. "It's north past Lakes Lindeman and Bennett, Taggish and Marsh," Adrik said, stretching his hands out to the fire. "You'll get your fill of it all traveling by boat, that's for sure."

Yawning, Leah stated she was on her way to her tent, where Grace and Miranda were already bedding down for the night. She first turned and looked to Adrik and Karen for hope. "You do think we'll find him, don't you?"

"You mean Jacob?" Karen asked. She couldn't really say why, but she felt that Leah had begun to give up thoughts of finding her father. Maybe it was easier for the child to think of him as gone and deal with the loss, just in case it was true. Karen smiled at Leah's hesitant nod.

"I wouldn't be here if I didn't believe we could find him," Karen replied. She sincerely hoped she wasn't giving the child false encouragement.

The chill of the evening made Karen forget that it was already the first week in June. She shivered and decided it might be just as well to turn in with the rest. Even the packers were bedding down for the night. In fact, Dyea Joe and his sturdy little wife, Merry, had long since made their way to bed.

She thought it even more sensible to leave when Adrik scooted closer and put his arm around her. Her instincts suggested she flee, but her heart bade her stay.

"The nights are unpredictable," he murmured.

She turned, her face only inches from his. More than a little aware of the intense way in which he regarded her, Karen nodded. "I'm sure they aren't the only unpredictable thing up here."

Adrik smiled in that roguish way she'd come to love. He raised his brows and leaned closer. "Being unpredictable only adds to the adventure. But, on the other hand, if you learn to watch for the signs, you'll come out just fine."

"The signs, eh?" Karen said, unable to look away. She wasn't sure at this point if she could have willed herself to look elsewhere under any circumstances.

Adrik ran his hand up her arm before giving her shoulder a squeeze. "I've lived up here all my life, you know. Maybe not right here, but close enough. You'd do well to stick close to me. I can teach you things."

"What kind of things?"

His smile broadened. "All sorts of things."

Karen lost herself momentarily in eyes dark as the coffee they'd shared at supper. She trembled, but this time it wasn't from the cold. She jumped to her feet, uncertain as to whether she'd imagined his mouth moving closer to hers.

"I think I should join Leah and the others."

He looked up at her and shrugged. "Guess you have to do what you have to do."

Karen had half expected him to try to convince her to stay a while longer. When he didn't, she couldn't help but be disappointed. "All right, then," she said, still not entirely convinced of her mission. "I'll see you in the morning."

"All right," he murmured and stretched out on his side before the fire.

She looked down at him and saw the amusement in his expression. He knew how she felt. He knew she wanted to stay, but he wasn't going to ask her. Frustrated, Karen turned sharply on her heel, causing her shortened skirt to flair.

"Nice ankles," Adrik called. "Been meanin' to tell you that all day."

Karen felt her face grow hot. If she turned around now, she knew she'd find some excuse to stay. *Stay true to the mission,* she told herself. *Go to bed with the others and sleep off this silly infatuation. Tomorrow things will seem a whole lot different.*

She reached for the tent flap just as she heard Grace pose a question to Miranda.

"Will you do that with me? We could get up before the others and pray for Peter and even Mr. Paxton. We could pray for your folks and my mother. Not to mention the trip and our safety."

"I think that would be wonderful," Miranda replied. "Of course I'll pray with you."

"I thought you would. I know Karen isn't feeling too interested in such things. We should also pray for her. She's been deeply wounded. I know exactly how she feels. Sometimes it's hard to accept that God's ways are not always our own. I haven't always liked how things turn out, believe me. Mr. Paxton has been nothing but a thorn in my side, but I am willing to trust that God's Word is true. I will pray for my enemy, and I will pray for my husband."

"I'm glad you haven't lumped them together," Miranda replied.

A deep sensation of loneliness flooded Karen. She had been replaced by Miranda in Grace's life. Grace had demonstrated such strength of character in dealing with Mr. Paxton and others around her that Karen felt almost like a student—she was no longer the teacher and mentor.

She couldn't help but remember the stand Grace had taken with Paxton back in Dyea. She wasn't afraid of the man in any way. She had simply taken a stand on her faith in God.

Have I only been playing a role? Karen wondered silently. She had been raised in a loving Christian home and had never known a day when God wasn't revered and honored. She had prayed almost before she'd learned any other form of communication. Had it all been for naught?

Grace has something I want, she thought. *She has a grasp of God that I cannot seem to take hold of. Yet I'm the one who taught her. I'm the one who brought her into an understanding of faith in Jesus. How can it be that she has grown so far beyond me?*

Miranda and Grace's words had ceased, and Karen could only suppose they'd concluded their discussion. She entered the tent, grateful for the dim lantern light. It had been very thoughtful of them to leave it turned up so that she could see.

Karen prepared for bed quickly. The choices were limited and desiring to stay as warm as possible, she wasn't about to worry about bathing or other notions. She turned down the lamp until the flame went out, then made her way to her pallet. Slipping into her sleeping bag, compliments of the latest shipment from Sears Roebuck, Karen snuggled down, relishing the feel of the sheep's wool against her cold cheeks. The contraption had cost her thirteen dollars, an outrageous sum, but Adrik had thought it a worthwhile purchase. He'd reminded her that the product would eliminate the need to bring so many separate pieces of bedding. With that in mind, she'd purchased a bag for both herself and Leah. By the time Grace and Miranda had decided to join them, however, the bags were completely sold out.

But Adrik was ever to the rescue. He had procured heavy wool blankets and promised they'd work just as well. Karen prayed it was so. The nights could still be quite cold, as tonight was.

"Karen?" Grace's whisper came through the silence of the night.

Surprised, but pleasantly so, Karen turned onto her side so that she might not disturb Leah, who slept behind her. "Yes?"

"Thank you for inviting me to come along. I don't know what I would have done without you. The months away from you were ... well ... I missed you greatly. Miranda is a dear sister to me, but you were like a mother. I needed you then, just as I need you now. I just wanted you to know how very much I love you and thank God for you."

Karen felt engulfed in her friend's love. She felt a lump in her throat constrict her words. "That means so much," she barely whispered.

Karen reached across the distance between them in the darkness. She touched Grace's shoulder and followed the contour of her arm down to her hand. There, Karen clasped their hands together.

"Grace, I want to pray with you and Miranda. I know I haven't worked through all my feelings yet, but I know that prayer is where I must begin. I need help, however. Would you and Miranda stand by me?"

"But of course," Grace whispered as if there had never been any doubt of Karen's decision.

Karen felt Grace tighten her hold. Without meaning to bring up the past, Karen said, "I see he never bought you a ring."

"No, he never did," Grace replied.

"I'm sorry, Grace. I'm sorry things have been so bad. I'm sorry Peter is so angry, and I'm sorry I helped to fuel that anger."

"Mr. Paxton has a way of bringing out the worst in all of us," Grace murmured. "It should be no different for you or Peter."

"He brought out the best in you," Karen replied. "I still have the vision of you standing up to him in defiance. It reminded me of David and Goliath."

"Me too. I kept thinking of David's declaration. 'Thou comest to me with a sword, and with a spear, and with a shield: but I come to thee in the name of the Lord of hosts. . . .' I felt the strength soar through me and imagined what David must have felt being in the presence of God's mighty protection and power."

Karen breathed a sigh and knew that God had given *her* that display of power as much as he had Mr. Paxton. He wanted her to know He was still God and He understood her pain and suffering. He wanted her to know that He had not forsaken them nor handed them over to the wicked—to Paxton.

"Good night, Grace," Karen said, giving her friend's hand another squeeze before pulling back to snuggle back down into her bag. "You are truly the image of your name, and I thank God for the honor of calling you friend."

The next morning Adrik was surprised to find Joe hunched over the campfire, talking to a long forgotten friend.

"Crispin Thibault!" Adrik called out as he bounded from the tent. "In all the world I never thought I'd find you here." He laughed heartily and waited as the man stood in greeting before wrapping him in a big bear hug.

"Adrik Ivankov, still the bear of the north, I see," Crispin said with a laugh that betrayed his absolute delight. "I saw Joe and figured you had to be close by. Then I spied your red-and-white flag and knew it had to be you." Crispin pointed to the strip of material Adrik kept tied to his tent flap. This same type of material was tied to the caches that represented the group's supplies.

Adrik had used the red-and-white material to mark his tent since he'd been a boy. His father had taught him this simple method for identification. It was almost as good as painting numbers on the doorpost of a house, and in some ways it was even better. Friends knew each others' markings, while strangers had no idea of the significance.

"What brings you back to Alaska?" Adrik questioned.

Crispin shrugged. "Gold—what else? I was residing very comfortably in the house of one of my French cousins when all this gold rush news came to entice us. I thought, why not travel north and see my old friend Adrik? I figured I'd find you in Sitka but heard tell you'd taken to living on the coast at Dyea."

Adrik nodded. "Been there a little over six years, off and on. I still travel more than I stay in one place. That's why I live in a tent instead of a house."

"You should come to stay with my French cousins," Crispin teased. "You'd not willingly go back to tenting."

"Maybe you have a point at that. So what news have you brought us? The communications are poor up here. We're lucky if we get a newspaper from Seattle now and then. What of the problems with Spain?"

"Well, let me think," Crispin said, looking rather thoughtful. "President McKinley has called for seventy-five thousand more volunteers to help out with this misunderstanding."

"It's a bit more than a misunderstanding. They blew up the *Maine*," Adrik replied. "We can't be havin' that."

"The rest of the world, including your Russia, has asked President McKinley for a peaceful end to this matter."

"It's not my Russia. I'm an American. I was born in this territory and plan to remain here," Adrik said, adding, "This land has been pretty good to the both of us, and it didn't happen by letting other folks push us around."

"Be that as it may, America may well fight this war alone."

"I'm sure we won't fight alone," Adrik replied with great confidence. "We'll fight with God on our side."

Crispin laughed. "You Americans are always believing such nonsense. I think winning your revolution went to your heads."

"You sound like an Englishman."

"Forbid that!" Crispin declared rather dramatically. "My dear departed mother would swoon if she heard it said that I remotely resembled those tyrants. She'd rather I be called an American!"

"Now, that's a thought," Adrik said, slapping Crispin on the back with a hearty laugh.

"What's all the commotion?" Karen asked as she emerged from her tent.

Miranda Colton was on her heels, tucking her long braided hair into the confines of a warm wool bonnet.

"Come meet my good friend Crispin Thibault," Adrik called. He motioned to Karen and Miranda. "I've not seen him in, what? Seven years?"

"To be sure," Crispin replied, his gaze fixed on the ladies. "My, but you travel in much prettier company than when I left you."

Adrik laughed. "There's two more just as pretty inside the tent, but these will do for starts. This is Karen Pierce and Miranda Colton."

Crispin drew his six-foot-three-inch frame to full attention, then gave a deep bow. "Ladies, I am charmed." He straightened and grinned at Adrik. "You are a man of many surprises."

"Not half as many as you, my old friend," Adrik leaned closer to Karen and added, "It is rumored that our Mr. Thibault is in line for the throne of some small European principality."

"How very interesting," Karen said, nudging Miranda. "We're in the presence of royalty."

"Nonsense!" Crispin declared rather theatrically. He waved his arm and lifted his face to the cloudy skies. "It is a very minor principality, indeed, and my place in line is a dozen or more cousins away from ever being crowned." He lowered his face and leaned toward Karen as though he would tell her a great secret. "Perhaps if I strike it rich, however, I may yet buy myself a throne."

Miranda giggled and even Karen smiled.

"So who are you traveling with?" Adrik asked, not entirely happy to find Crispin's attention so strongly focused on Karen.

"I came up with a rather disgruntled group who call themselves by the family name of Meyer. I dare say, I've little desire to go the course with these very unpleasant folk and thought I'd appeal to you, Adrik. Might I join you and your . . ." his voice fell away as Grace and Leah pushed back the flaps of the tent and joined Miranda and Karen. They looked to Adrik as if questioning him about Crispin's identity. Crispin leaned closer to Adrik and added, "Gentle women?"

Karen turned to Grace and Leah. "This is Adrik's friend Mr. Thibault. He is of some European aristocracy, and we must be very nice to him, as he plans to buy himself a throne."

"Oh!" Leah said, her mouth round in surprise. "Are you a king?"

Crispin laughed and bowed low before Leah. "Not at all, but I daresay, you are surely a princess."

Leah's expression fell and her frown surprised them all. She turned rather abruptly and ran off toward the river, leaving them all in stunned surprise.

"What was that all about?" Adrik questioned, looking to Karen for answers.

"Her father is believed dead," Karen said, looking to Crispin. "He used to call her that. I'll go talk to her."

"No, please, allow me," Crispin begged. "For I am the offending person."

"You are also a stranger," Karen replied.

Crispin smiled and pulled the woolen cap from atop his head. "I do not wish to be a stranger to either of you. I would be most stricken, however, if you refused me this. I feel quite bad for having hurt the young lady."

Karen looked to the tent and then to Adrik. Adrik nodded, knowing she was looking for his approval of the situation. "Her name is Leah Barringer and she's just turned thirteen. I do not believe she's very well acquainted with the . . . shall we say . . . charms of aristocracy." She eyed the taller man with great intensity, and Adrik might have laughed out loud had the matter not involved the child's feelings. Crispin was no threat to anyone; he knew that as well as he knew his own name. The man was one of the most sensitive and caring fellows Adrik had ever known, in fact, and should Karen deny his request, Adrik knew it would have cast a cloud of despair over his friend.

"I shall endeavor to prove myself worthy of your trust, my dear lady." He lifted her hand and placed a kiss atop her fingers.

Karen, still very serious about the entire matter, nodded as Crispin lifted his gaze. "Very well."

Crispin pulled his cap back on and headed after Leah. Adrik followed the gaze of the three women as they watched him disappear into the woods. He then observed as each woman looked to the others with grins that suggested they knew a secret he had not been privy to.

"My, my," Grace spoke first. "I don't believe I've ever met anyone quite like him."

"Me neither," Miranda replied. "Did you see his hair? All those lovely black curls."

"And his eyes," Karen added. "Such a dark blue, yet so bright and full of laughter."

"And such a regal bearing. Why, I've no doubt he must be from the lineage of kings," Miranda said, straining to catch another glimpse of the man.

Adrik rolled his eyes. Women! What a lot of nonsense. He could personally run circles around Crispin Thibault. The man possessed great endurance and courage, there was no doubt about that. And he was charming and quite the orator when necessary, but he wasn't anything that special. Scratching his chin, Adrik listened to the three women chatter on and on. At first he'd been happy to see Crispin, but maybe his initial joy would be short-lived. After all, he had no intention of fighting his friend for Karen's affection, yet she seemed just as enthralled as Miranda and Grace Colton.

"We're going to be striking camp in thirty minutes," he said after hearing his fill. "I'm not waitin' on anyone."

He doubted they'd even heard him, for not one of the women acknowledged him. Walking away, he met Joe's stoic expression and shook his head. "You've got black hair, and I never saw them get all swoony over you."

Joe pulled off the white bowler and rubbed his head. "Got no curls."

Adrik grinned. "Me neither. But I've got my sights fixed on having a bunch of redheaded children someday, so I guess me and Mr. Curlylocks better have us a talk."

⊣ CHAPTER EIGHTEEN ⊢

DAY AFTER DAY the little band of travelers pushed forward along with hundreds of other weary souls. Karen, Grace, and Miranda rose early every morning to pray, and it wasn't long before Leah was joining them, as well. Whatever Crispin had said to her had remained between her and the aristocratic traveler. But her spirits were much improved, and she shared Crispin's company very easily.

Morning prayers and Scripture reading were helping them all to keep their perspective. Even Karen, who was still confused about her feelings toward God, seemed to thrive. And she wanted very much to thrive—to put aside her anger. The labor of each day allowed little time for such grudges. Still, there was a hesitancy in her soul, the fear of one who felt betrayed. Could she trust God again? Did she have a choice?

Grace never tried to push her beyond her ability, and for that Karen knew a gratitude that went far beyond their years of friendship. It was as if Grace understood the pain and anger and was determined to love Karen right through it.

Pulling on her pack, which now weighed almost thirty-five pounds, Karen squared the load and secured the belt Adrik had fashioned to keep the pack snuggly in place. Her spirit soared on the hope of a new day. With each group of stampeders they passed, Karen searched for Jacob. Sometimes she even looked for Bill, though she felt almost certain that it must have been his body Adrik had found. Leah said nothing, but Karen was certain she was beginning to accept this as truth, as well. Perhaps the young girl rationalized that it would be easier to believe him dead and accept the loss than to have hope in his existence only to lose him again. Whatever the reason, Leah said very little about her father and only mentioned Jacob.

"You're awfully quiet," Adrik said, coming up behind Karen to double-check her load. He adjusted the straps, then nodded. "You thinking about anything you want to share?"

Karen licked her chapped lips and smiled. She felt her heart give a jump at the nearness of the broad-shouldered man. "I'm just contemplating the day ahead of us. Wondering if we'll find Jacob—or Bill."

"I wouldn't get your hopes up. This is almost the end of June. Jacob's been on the road for over two months. He didn't come up here with the tons of supplies we're packing, so he could move a lot quicker. He probably spent time here earning some money so he could buy supplies from someone who'd made it this far but was giving up. My guess is, he's found some group to hitch up with, and in trade for work, they'll help him move his supplies along with their own."

"Well, I intend to ask around when we get to Sheep Camp. You said we'd make it today, right?"

"We ought to, barring any unforeseen problems."

Karen had already begun to look forward to the little town, where Adrik promised her she could pay for a hot bath. "Your friend seems most intent on entertaining Leah and Miranda," she finally said, motioning to where Crispin carried on with sleight-of-hand tricks.

"They seem pretty intent on being entertained," Adrik replied.

"I don't think your Mr. Thibault likes me very much," Karen said, looking to Adrik. "I don't suppose you know anything about that, do you?"

Adrik's mustache twitched at the corner as he appeared to be fighting a smile. He glanced sidelong and then toward the skies overhead. "Maybe he doesn't like redheads."

Karen believed Crispin's lack of attention had far more to do with Adrik than with her honey-red hair. "Perhaps he doesn't."

Adrik leaned close and whispered in her ear. "Well, I like redheads just fine. So don't you go worryin' about gettin' lonely." He paused and dared to place a kiss upon her cheek. "I know a few tricks I can do with my hands, too."

Karen felt her face grow hot. "Mr. Ivankov!" She tried to sound indignant rather than impassioned, but her attempt sounded feeble even to her own ears. His name came out more closely resembling a term of endearment.

"It's a nice name—Ivankov. Don't you think?" His grin broadened to a full-blown smile, amusement dancing in his dark eyes.

"I think we'd better get on the trail," Karen said, grabbing her bonnet. She headed for the path only to hear Adrik chuckling behind her.

"I don't know when I'll see you again," Adrik called.

Karen turned around as she tied her bonnet snug. "What are you saying?" Surely the man wasn't going to leave her simply because she refused to play his games. She eyed him quite seriously. "You aren't leaving us, are you?"

"Nope, but you are if you keep heading in that direction," Adrik replied. "Sheep Camp is that way."

He pointed in the opposite direction, leaving Karen little choice but to retrace her steps and walk past him once again. "You're a scoundrel, Mr. Ivankov."

Adrik laughed and tipped his hat. "Yes, ma'am, I am."

"Rockslide!"

The desperate call split the afternoon air, sending a cold sensation of dread into Miranda Colton's heart. She had heard the rumbles of rock off and on all day as they tumbled down the canyon walls, and each time she had feared for her life. This time, however, she had good reason to fear.

As rock and dirt began to rain down around her, Miranda froze in place, unable to remember Adrik's instructions. Was she to try and outrun the slide? Should she back up and retrace her steps?

Without warning, Miranda felt strong hands upon her waist. Then, as if she weighed nothing more than the pack on her back, Crispin Thibault lifted her and swung her around to flee the dangerous area.

They crashed to the ground as Crispin lost his footing, but he rolled in such a way that he took the full impact of the fall. Miranda, although shaken, was cushioned against the man as rock and debris continued to rain down upon the path where they had stood.

When the noise died down to little slips of pelting gravel, Miranda seemed to regain rational thinking. She stared down into the face of the most beautiful man she'd ever seen. His dark eyes were edged with ebony lashes, so thick and long it seemed almost unreasonable that they should belong to a man. Especially the man who'd just saved her life.

"I-I-I couldn't move," she stammered.

He gave her a lopsided smile. "Just as I cannot move now."

Miranda realized all at once that she was stretched out full atop the poor man. Without giving it another thought, she rolled to the left and found herself in peril once again. She'd managed to roll right off the side of the trail and now clung precariously to Crispin's arm while her feet dangled in the air beneath her. With her free hand, Miranda fought to take hold of the rock and dirt on the edge of the ravine. All she managed to do, however, was pelt herself with a mouthful of earth.

"Be still," Crispin commanded. "I'll pull you back up, but you must stop flailing."

He held her tight and again, with surprising ease, pulled her back to safety. Together they sat, side by side, panting from the momentary exertion and panic.

"I wasn't really complaining," he said, catching his breath. "You needn't have run off like that."

Miranda swallowed dust and grit. "I'm so sorry. I just thought . . . well . . . it seemed highly inappropriate."

"So does throwing yourself off the side of a mountain," he said, grinning. He reached out with a handkerchief and wiped the dirt from her face. "Are you hurt?"

Miranda shook her head tentatively. "I don't think so."

"Crispin! Miranda! Are you two all right?" Adrik called as he climbed over the gravel and debris to reach them.

Getting to her feet, Miranda watched as Crispin surveyed the massive pile of rock and debris. He met his friend's worried expression with one of calm confidence. "We're quite all right."

Adrik looked to Miranda and back to Crispin. "You're neither one hurt?"

"Not that we have ascertained," Crispin replied. He reached down to help Miranda to her feet.

Miranda looked to Adrik and smiled. "I'm fine. I don't think anything is broken, unless it's poor Mr. Thibault. I'm afraid I used him rather abusively and allowed him to break my fall."

Crispin exchanged a glance with Adrik. " 'Twas my pleasure."

With a raised brow, Adrik began to laugh. "Yes, I'll just bet it was." He glanced back to the slide. "It's not too bad, at least. Could have been much worse. I heard them say this road was blocked for two days last week when a slide worse than this one sent boulders big as houses down the mountain."

"Now if only the gold would come in boulders that size, every man would be content."

"Every woman, too," Miranda added.

"Well, let's move out. I know the others will worry if we don't catch up to them soon." Adrik made his way up and over the debris and picked up his pack on the other side. "I'll go on ahead and let them know you're coming."

Miranda squared her shoulders and hiked up her skirt. What a nuisance, she thought. Men walked about in trousers and boots and no one thought twice about it. But let a woman wear trousers and the entire world considered her mad. Madness to Miranda's way of thinking was trying to hoist heavy lengths of corduroy and wool with one hand while steadying yourself with the other.

Crispin helped her navigate the slide, and before she knew it, Miranda was once again on the path. Contemplating the vast wilderness around her, she thought it most magnificent. Deadly, but nevertheless marvelous. Crispin Thibault was marvelous, as well. *How wonderful that he would risk his life to save mine. What more could any woman hope of a man?* Thinking such thoughts, Miranda began to see Crispin in a new light. Perhaps Peter would approve of such a man for her. That was, if they ever saw Peter again.

Her brother's disappearance had gravely worried her. Not so much for herself or even her parents, but mostly for Grace. She knew Grace was strong and full of faith in God, but the poor woman was battling her worry within herself daily and had grown quite distant. Aside from their morning ritual of praying for the men in their lives, Grace had withdrawn and kept to herself more and more.

Or perhaps I have drawn myself away to spend more time near Mr. Thibault, Miranda thought guiltily. But when Crispin turned on the trail and smiled warmly at her, Miranda lost all thoughts of guilt.

By nightfall they were settled in Sheep Camp. Grace had gone to bed very early, only minutes after a supper of rice, dried ham, and a yellow cake that Leah proudly announced as her own creation.

Adrik had walked Karen and Miranda to a place where he knew they could get hot baths for fifty cents. The Hotel Woodlawn stood just a few feet from the River Taiya, and because of this, they had set up a bathhouse behind their establishment. They'd even found a Tlingit woman who could cut hair in a decent fashion. Adrik had used her on many occasions to keep his hair from growing past his collar. Tonight, he allowed her to shave the stubble of beard from his face and trim his hair, as well. He was just splashing on tonic water when he heard Karen and Miranda approaching.

He tossed the woman four bits and jumped up from the chair to join his party. He wasn't prepared for the sight that met his eyes. Neither woman had bothered to bind up her hair, and, with the hotel's towels in hand, they were still blotting the water from their heads while carrying on an animated conversation in the cool night air.

"You'll catch your death like that," Adrik teased, but inside his heart was racing like a sled dog on the homeward stretch.

Karen looked up, and in the glow of firelight and lanterns, her eyes seemed to twinkle with amusement. Adrik figured she knew the effect she had on him. He also suspected she was rather pleased with the power she held. But when she handed him her brush, he concluded that she was meanspirited and cruel.

"Here, you brush my hair out while I brush Miranda's."

He took the brush and his hand trembled. Miranda turned obediently as

Karen took the younger woman's brush and began the process of untangling the lengths.

For a moment, all Adrik could do was stare at the wavy mass. He'd wondered—in fact, he'd wondered quite a bit of late—how she might look with her hair down and all soft around her shoulders. This wasn't quite the picture he had in mind, but it would do. He brought the brush to her hair and gently, almost fearfully, began to brush it.

He could smell the sweetness of lavender soap, something Karen had no doubt brought for herself. His hand shook as though the temperature had dropped below freezing. He reached to touch Karen's shoulder to steady himself and felt her trembling, as well.

"It's cold out here," he said abruptly. "Let's get back to camp."

Karen turned to face him, and he could see that the moment had affected her as much as it had him. "I think that would be wise," she murmured.

The next few days were devoted to moving their provisions up to the Scales. Adrik felt it unnecessary to move the women away from the safety and provision of town, so he and the other men headed out before dawn every morning and moved the tons of provisions at a steady pace that left them exhausted by nightfall. To their credit they were making remarkable time.

Karen spent her days searching through the small town, desperate to find any news of Jacob and Bill Barringer. Leah went with her faithfully, refusing to be left behind, determined to be with Karen when she learned the truth.

They finally got word on the third day. Having searched through all the hotels and stores, Karen finally broke down and began asking in the saloons. It was at the Big Tent Saloon that a burly man, who acted as both owner and bartender, remembered having given Jacob a job cleaning.

"He was here for about three weeks," the man said. Standing behind a makeshift bar that consisted of a plank board set atop two whiskey barrels, the man seemed less than inclined to offer more.

"Do you know if he continued north?"

The man wiped out a glass, spit in it, and wiped it again. "Don't guess he'd go south. He was workin' to buy provisions. Worked here cleaning every morning." The man set aside the glass and picked up another. His idea of hygiene left Karen less than eager to visit any of the area establishments.

"Do you know if he teamed up with someone? Do you know when he left Sheep Camp?"

The man shook his head. "Don't keep track of everybody that goes through. He came to me for a job and I gave him one. He worked over at the drugstore during the day—you could ask there. They might be inclined to tell you more."

Karen nodded and thanked the man before pulling Leah with her to the muddy street. "Did you hear that? He's actually seen Jacob!"

Leah nodded. "Can we go to the drugstore and ask them, too?"

Karen felt a ray of hope for the first time in weeks. "Yes. Let's hurry. Maybe they know more."

But the drugstore proved to be no help at all. The ownership had changed, and the man knew nothing of Jacob or his whereabouts. Dejected by this, the two tried to take heart that at least they'd heard something about Jacob.

"Well, we know he's alive and headed north," Karen said, trying to encourage Leah.

"Yeah, but nobody remembers Pa." She looked beyond Karen to the mountains that rose up to the north. "I don't think he's alive, Karen." She shook her head and met the older woman's eyes. "I think my pa is dead, and the sooner we accept that, the better off we'll be."

"You can't be sure," Karen said, not wanting the girl to feel too hopeless or depressed.

As if understanding, Leah pushed back her braids and pulled her bonnet into place. "I talked to God about it, Karen. I'm going to be all right, even if Pa and Jacob are both gone. God's given me a special promise."

Karen looked at the girl, who suddenly seemed years beyond thirteen. "And what promise was that, Leah?"

The girl lifted her face with an expression of peace and contentment. "God promised He was all the Father I'd ever need and that He'd see me through this."

Karen thought about Leah's words all the way back to camp. The child radiated contentment, and Karen knew that it was this very substance that she herself so desperately sought.

God, she prayed in the silence of her heart, *out of the mouths of babes come your wisdom and words. May I know the contentment she knows. May I trust the way she trusts.*

"There you are!" Adrik called out as he strode out to meet Karen and Leah. "We're packing it up and moving up to the Scales."

"Already?" Karen said, looking to where the men were already tearing down the tents. Grace and Miranda were working silently to ready their packs.

"We've made good time," Adrik said enthusiastically. "We're making good time still. We've got extra help at the Scales—more men. Our things are already being packed up the mountain."

Karen thrilled to the news and yet dreaded it. The summit seemed like the first hurdle in their path of obstacles, a monster that would stand in their way to deny them their dream.

She had heard many men say that this climb was by far the worst. In winter they climbed the ice staircase, man after man, one after the other. The row of men and women that moved up and over the pass could be seen from far below as a black, inching line that never ended. But in summer, things were done much differently. The path lost its staircase, and a treacherous mountainside of boulders and shifting rock became their adversary. There was nothing easy about climbing the Chilkoot Pass.

"We found someone in town who knew Jacob. He said Jacob moved on after working here for several weeks. Perhaps he isn't so very far ahead of us after all," Karen said, looking to Adrik for encouragement. "Maybe he even got held up at the Scales or at the summit. If he didn't have the tariff money, they surely wouldn't let him pass, would they?"

Adrik shook his head. "I don't think they would, but you need to remember, he may have teamed up with a group. It's always best that way. Someone else might well have been able to foot the expenses for tariffs and such but lacked Jacob's muscle to move their goods."

Karen nodded, feeling rather discouraged. She looked at Leah as she helped Grace pack up the kitchen equipment. "Oh, Adrik, I just want to find him. I want to be up and over the mountain and safely on our way with the worst of it behind us."

"Well, the summit is a bad climb, that's for sure, but this won't be the last of our woes by a long shot." He looked to her with such a serious expression that Karen couldn't help but grow worried.

"You don't think we'll make it, do you?"

"I wouldn't have brought you this far if I didn't believe you could make it," he replied softly. "It won't be easy, though. You have to understand that much. You have to be realistic about it."

Karen laughed almost bitterly. "Was it realistic to make this trip to begin with?"

"You've got a point. You givin' up?"

Karen looked at everyone working so willingly and quickly to break camp. They were in this together, each one with their reasons and needs.

"No, I'm not giving up," she finally murmured. "That mountain isn't going to best me." She looked up to see Adrik's expression of approval. "I'll give the mountain a run for its money, just see if I don't."

Adrik guffawed loudly, causing everyone to stop and look. Calming, he turned to go, then looked back at Karen. "I believe you will, Miss Pierce. I believe you will."

KAREN STARED in disbelief at the climb to be made. The mountain rose up at a forty-five-degree angle to a summit that was lost in the clouds. It looked as though they very well might be climbing all the way to heaven. Thankful she'd only have to climb it once, instead of the multiple times the men had endured over the past weeks, Karen steadied her nerves.

"It's only about two and half miles from this point," Adrik told them in his authoritative way. "But it's gonna feel like it's at least two hundred miles once you're climbing.

"I don't want any of the women wearing packs. We'll get your things added to our own or send them up with the packers. In the meanwhile, we're going to pair up. Joe will take Grace, Sakatook will see to Leah, Crispin to Miranda, and I'll lead Karen."

Karen knew exactly who'd been in charge of figuring out the pairing. Miranda seemed content enough and nodded enthusiastically. Only Grace and Leah remained perfectly silent. They continued to cast skeptical looks up the mountain-side.

"This isn't going to be easy," Adrik continued. "In fact, I think it's a whole lot easier in winter with the packed down snow making a pretty smooth trail. But we don't have that now. Wear your heaviest boots, as the rocks are sharp enough to cut right into them, and don't forget to take your canteens. Water is mighty important up here, and in spite of there being plenty of rivers and lakes, you'll do well to keep a canteen close at hand."

"How long will it take to climb up there?" Leah questioned.

"That depends on several things," Adrik answered. "The weather, the land, the folks around us, and each of you. We'll stop to rest from time to time—there's no sense havin' anyone collapse on the trail. If you need to stop sooner, just give a holler."

The sun warmed them generously despite growing cloud coverage to the south. After an hour on the trail, Karen paused to ease out of her jacket. The well-worn white shirtwaist that she wore underneath had seen better days. Nevertheless, it was no different than everyone else around her. She had no reason to worry or fret over her wardrobe. The Chilkoot Trail was a far cry from the ballrooms of Chicago's finer homes. Not that she'd ever spent much time upon those dance floors herself, but she'd certainly dressed Grace for enough parties.

Glancing down the mountain to where Joe carefully assisted Grace, Karen couldn't help but wonder about her friend. She spoke very little about Peter and their separation, though they prayed faithfully every morning for him, along with their party of travelers, the packers, the stampeders, and even Mr. Paxton. Karen, however, seldom allowed herself to truly pray for the latter.

Otherwise, Grace had become progressively more silent. She helped with the camp and almost immediately after every evening meal, would make her way off to where she could clean up in private, then took herself to bed.

"You coming?" Adrik asked, breaking through her worried thoughts.

Karen nodded. "Can't stop now, I guess." She wrapped her jacket around the top of the walking stick Adrik had made for her before continuing up the rocky slope.

She'd scarcely taken three steps, however, when her foot hit a shelf of loose gravel. Instantly she started to slide backward. Her balance was hopelessly lost, and for a moment, Karen envisioned herself falling all the way down the mountain. But before that could happen, Adrik's powerful grip held her fast. He looked at her as if her slip hadn't surprised him in the least.

"You've got to keep your eyes on the trail," he admonished. "Otherwise, you'll end up buried alongside it."

"Sorry," Karen muttered, embarrassed by the entire matter. She had just boasted to Adrik that very morning that she could manage no matter the route. Pride had nearly taken its toll.

An hour later, Karen was hurriedly pulling her jacket back on and wishing fervently that she'd not wrapped her coat up with her sleeping bag. The day had been so fair at the Scales, but now heavy clouds moved in, and based on her experience with her first winter, Karen felt almost certain they would see snow.

"Um . . . Adrik," she began hesitantly, "does it snow in July?"

"It can snow up here any time of the year. See those white patches up the way?" he questioned. "That's winter left over."

The wind whipped at her skirts, making Karen glad for the woolen trousers she'd fashioned to wear beneath. "Is it going to snow today?" She looked to Adrik's eyes for the truth of the matter.

He reached out a hand and pulled her up to the rock on which he stood. "It just might. But I hope we'll be to the top by then. Worried?"

Karen couldn't help but nod. "I can't lie and say I'm not. I've never known two miles to take such a long time. Then again, I've never had such obstacles to endure."

"If we keep pressing forward," Adrik said in an assuring tone, "we'll be there before suppertime."

Karen allowed him to keep hold of her hand as they maneuvered over the rocks. "What was it like here in the winter?" Her breath came in quick pants as she fought against the altitude and the angle of the mountain.

She tried to imagine the stairs cut out of ice. It was called the Golden Stairway by some of the locals. The name had spread, she'd heard from Grace, all the way to California.

"Cold," Adrik said, grinning. "They sometimes get as much as thirty feet of snow up here."

"Thirty feet? Surely you jest."

"Not at all. It's a severe land with a temperament like a feisty woman."

"My mother wrote once saying it played the part of inhospitable neighbor. Cold and difficult."

"I can imagine her saying that," Adrik answered, resting for a moment against a rock.

Karen knew he was stopping to allow her to catch her breath again. It seemed she could only take ten or twelve steps without becoming completely winded. Settling on the rock beside him, she noticed the lichen and moss that clung to the crevices of the great boulder. How could anything survive being buried under thirty feet of snow?

"It can drop to fifty below in a matter of hours," Adrik said, gazing off across the valley. "But it's really not a bad land. You simply have to respect the dangers that surround you. Just like handling feisty women." He grinned at her and winked.

Karen knew the reference was intended for her. She ignored his teasing. "Would it have been this bad in April?" She was thinking of Jacob again.

"It was bad enough," Adrik answered, reaching out to steady her as they began to climb again, this time over a rather precarious place in the trail where the rock was loose and offered no secure hold on the trail. He swung her up and over some particularly jagged rocks, bringing her back to the ground directly in front of him.

She faced him momentarily, her face lifted to his. My, but he was handsome with the wind reddening his cheeks and his dark eyes glowing. He searched her face as if seeking an answer to an unspoken question. Karen knew she might have told him most anything had he asked, for her mind and heart were so completely swept up in the moment. She thought he might have kissed her, thought she might have liked it, but Leah's laughter rang out and Karen looked away.

Crispin and Miranda walked along behind Leah and Sakatook. Crispin was regaling them with some tale or another, and Leah thought it all good fun. "Sounds like they're out for an afternoon picnic instead of the climb of their life," Karen said, smiling. It was good to hear Leah so happy. She was glad Crispin had joined them, if only because he made Leah laugh.

"Come on," Adrik said, letting go of her. "We're going to be there before you know it. Then we'll all sit and laugh and share a meal."

"And pitch tents and wash dishes and freeze in the wind," Karen said, hiking up her skirts in one hand and planting the walking stick ahead of her with the other.

"You make it all sound like such fun," Adrik said, giving her a wink. "Then again, I know I didn't have this much fun on any of my other hikes up this mountain. Must be the company."

Karen warmed under his attention. She had fallen in love with Adrik Ivankov sometime between Grace's marriage and her own departure from Dyea. Her emotions and disappointment at the sad turn of events in her life had kept her from enjoying this new discovery, but she couldn't avoid the truth forever.

———

It had started to rain as the party finally made their way to the summit. Exhausted and discouraged by the weather, the travelers wanted only a shelter from the impending storm.

They located their caches by Adrik's red-and-white flags. Two men, along with Joe's wife, had been left to guard the materials and set up camp, and Adrik knew the women were more than a little happy to see they wouldn't have to set up camp.

"You ladies go ahead and get inside the tent out of the weather. Joe and I will get dinner together and bring it to you."

Karen was too tired to argue, much to Adrik's surprise. She nodded and followed Grace inside the tent. Crispin relinquished his hold on Miranda and waited until she'd followed suit with Leah close behind before turning to Adrik.

"How can I be of assistance?" He followed Adrik and Joe into the largest of three tents.

"Help me dish up this stew. Joe's wife put it together, and she's one of the best cooks I know." Adrik directed Crispin to a stack of pie pans and spoons. Then turning to the small camp stove, he lifted the lid atop the cast-iron pot and breathed in deeply. "Oh, this is going to hit the spot."

"I heartily agree," Crispin replied.

Joe pulled out his knife and began slicing a loaf of bread. The women had made several loaves while awaiting their departure in Sheep Camp, and this was the last of them.

As the rain began to fall more steadily, Adrik hurried to dish up the stew. No sense in letting a downpour spoil the meal. Crispin transported the stew two plates at a time back to the women's tent. Miranda met him at the door and without a word took the pans inside. They exchanged food in a like manner two more times as Crispin finished by bringing them bread.

Adrik followed up with four cups of a special tea Joe's wife had brewed. The aroma made him all the more glad for having sent the woman ahead. This was going to be a nice surprise for the weary travelers. He hadn't told any of them how proud he was, but the fact was, he'd had some doubts about whether or not they could make it. He knew Karen would climb the mountain energized by sheer willpower if nothing else. But Grace Colton was such a delicate little thing, and so, too, was Leah Barringer. Miranda Colton seemed spirited enough, but he knew from what she'd said that outdoor activities had not been her focus of attention back in San Francisco.

"I have tea for you," Adrik announced as he followed Miranda into the tent. "It's pretty good and will help you regain your energy." He had wrapped his fingers through the metal rings of the cups and now tried to disengage his hand without spilling the contents.

Karen looked into the cups and then back to Adrik. "What is it? It smells wonderful."

"Joe's wife put it together. It's a concoction of rose hips and wild blackberry leaves. It's the best drink for travel and living up here. Full of good things that revive the soul."

"Sounds perfect," Karen said, pushing a cup toward Grace. "Sounds like just the thing for you."

Grace took the drink and thanked Adrik. "You've been very good to us. I can't thank you enough for agreeing to bring me along."

Adrik looked around him at the four exhausted women. "I never thought I would take a group of women on such a perilous journey, but I must say, it's a whole lot more fun traveling with you than with Joe and his sons."

Karen seemed to instantly sober at this. "They aren't really heading back tomorrow, are they?"

Adrik nodded. "But don't go frettin'. We'll pay the Canadian tax and then hire a mule team to cart our goods down to Lake Lindeman. With Crispin and me you'll be just fine. And who knows, maybe we'll pick up Jacob on the way."

Leah perked up at this. "He could be up here right now. I wanted to go look for him, but the weather got bad."

"We can look for him tomorrow. I think we should rest up a bit before pressing on anyway," Adrik said. "Now, you ladies have a nice supper. I'm going to go eat with the boys. If you get too cold, come on over to the big tent. There's still a bit of warmth in the stove, and we might even be able to build the fire back up for a short time. There's not much in the way of fuel up here, however, and you'll pay dearly for it if you have to buy it off someone else."

He paused at the tent flap and smiled. "I just want you all to know I'm proud to have been leading you. You were all real troopers, and I shouldn't wonder but that we'll make it to Dawson without any of you being any worse for the wear."

With that he left them, smiling to himself and contemplating how in the world he was going to convince Karen Pierce to marry him by the time they reached Dawson City, or maybe even Whitehorse.

After supper, Adrik decided to make his way over to the customs tent. He wanted very much to see what they might expect when they moved on in the days to come. He hadn't gone ten steps, however, when he found Karen at his side. The rain apparently was not a deterrent to her.

"What are you doing out here?" he asked.

"I want to look for Jacob."

"I thought I told you to rest. You'll have time to look for him tomorrow."

"But there's still plenty of light, in spite of the overcast."

"And there will be even more light tomorrow after the rain has passed."

Karen stopped and put her hands on her hips. "You have no way of knowing that it won't be raining tomorrow. I won't perish in the rain, you know. I just want to come along and see if anyone remembers Jacob. Surely the Canadians keep a list of people passing through."

Adrik frowned and decided to come clean with her. "They do. They also keep a list of the dead. Word is sent down from the other posts to the north. Eventually the list will make it all the way back to Skagway. I thought maybe I'd spare you from having to . . . well . . ."

"Find Jacob listed with the dead?" Karen asked softly.

Adrik nodded and wiped rain from his face. "Look, let's get out of the rain. We're going to have a hard enough time staying warm tonight, so there's no sense in being soaked to the bone."

He led the way to where the British flag hung limp and drenched. Ushering Karen inside, he introduced himself and asked first about Jacob. The Northwest Police officer appeared skeptical but nevertheless pulled a book from his desk. Adrik prayed in silence as the man thumbed through the register.

"I show a Jacob Barringer passing through on the twenty-eighth of May," the man told them, glancing up to see if they would make further comment.

"What of William Barringer?" Karen asked. "He might well have come through last winter—even as long ago as December."

The man returned his attention to the ledger but shook his head. "This register only goes back to April. We've had thousands come through," the official told them. "The other records have been passed on to our headquarters."

Adrik saw Karen's expression of hope pass to one of worry. He took hold of her hand and shook his head. "No news is good news. Bill could have passed through here months ahead of the avalanche and given that letter to someone who was headed back to Dyea. People post letters and packages like that all the time. I can't tell you how much mail I've carried down the trail."

"I wish we knew for certain one way or the other. The waiting is taking its toll on us. Leah is certain she must give him up for dead, and I can't offer her much hope to do otherwise."

Adrik understood. He felt more than a little frustration that he'd played such an inadequate role in all of this. He'd brought them the letter and word of the dead man, but he couldn't be sure it was Bill Barringer who lay in that grave and not some other poor fool.

Karen awoke quite early the next morning. The skies had cleared and the sun had come up somewhere in the middle of what would normally be night. She had trouble adjusting to the long days. The sun would stay up so long, not setting until around ten o'clock, only to rise again at four in the morning. Adrik had told her it would only get worse as they journeyed north. He had told her of a time when he'd ventured far to the north. The sun had set at midnight only to lighten the skies again two hours later. Karen didn't think she would like that very much, but it seemed to be the way of this strange new land.

Of course, winter had been even more difficult. The reverse had been true, with the sun long absent from the sky. And even when the sun made its debut, it seemed many days were overcast and gray. The darkness had nearly driven her mad. She'd had no one to talk to save Leah and Jacob, and while they were dear children, they couldn't begin to understand her feelings and needs.

True to his word, Adrik arranged for their things to be freighted down to Lake Lindeman. The Northwest Police checked through their supplies, took their money, and issued them receipts to show they had cleared the checkpoint. After this, the goods were loaded onto mule trains and transported down the rocky decline.

The weary band of travelers followed, depressed at the lack of civilization. Leah was glad to hear news of her brother, but the understanding that their journey had just begun weighed heavy on their hearts.

Adrik moved out ahead to converse with the freighters and pick up any news or information that might make their passage north a bit easier. Karen felt both a loss and a relief in his absence. Her growing feelings for Adrik were so overpowering that they terrified her at times. She found herself daydreaming constantly about what it might be like to share this man's life.

Her father had trusted Adrik, and to hear Adrik tell it, they had enjoyed a strong friendship and camaraderie. Karen had no reason to doubt the truth of his words. In fact, she worried that her attraction to Adrik had been based upon that relationship with her father. Now, however, thoughts of her father were only distant memories when she was with Adrik Ivankov.

Desperate to think on something else, Karen caught sight of Grace as she lagged behind Miranda and Leah. Crispin seemed to be once again caught up in some animated tale of his adventures. But Grace held an almost visible wall around her—a wall that seemed to keep her safe inside herself. Or maybe it just kept others out.

Karen pondered her friend for a moment. Dressed in a dark green skirt and jacket, Grace walked the trail with a refined elegance that reflected her background. She had spent a lifetime being trained for high society. Karen shook her head. Some society!

"Going down is almost harder than going up," Miranda called as she passed with Crispin and Leah.

"I was thinking the same not but a minute ago," Karen replied.

"Mr. Thibault is telling us about his adventures in Africa," Leah threw in with wide-eyed wonder. "He's actually seen an elephant!"

Karen laughed at the young girl's excitement. Here she was risking her life in the northern wilderness, her brother missing, her father possibly dead, and it was the musings of a roaming aristocrat that allowed Leah to forget it all. *Good for her!* Karen thought. And good for God, too, for having sent Mr. Thibault their way.

Grace came walking down the same trail, her walking stick clacking along the rocks as she passed by. Karen watched for Grace to lift her face and acknowledge Karen's presence, but she never did.

Preoccupied and silent, Grace had no idea that Karen even stood by watching. "I thought," Karen began, "that we might chat while we walked."

At this Grace looked up. "I'm sorry. Were you talking to me?"

Karen joined her on the trail and linked her arm with Grace's. "Yes, I was talking to you. You've been far too distant to suit me. I want you to tell me what's locked up in those thoughts of yours."

Grace looked at the ground but allowed Karen to pull her forward. They walked a few minutes in silence before Grace spoke. Her voice barely audible, she said, "I miss him so much."

The sorrow in her words was intense, and Karen was struck by the depth of her emotion. Poor Grace. Just looking at her expression caused Karen to feel like the most neglectful of friends.

"I'm sure he'll read the note you left him at the hotel and come join us. It isn't like he couldn't find us if he wanted to."

"But he may not have the funds. He might not be able to get supplies," Grace argued. "Oh, I should never have come."

"Nonsense. Peter Colton is a strong, determined man. I'm certain he probably has set aside money for just such occasions and concerns. He'll read your note and wire his bank—you did say the telegraph to Seattle was in place in Skagway now, right?"

Grace nodded. "But he may not have returned to the hotel. I only left the note on the hope that he might. I have no reason to believe he will."

"You're the biggest reason I can think of for his return." Karen squeezed Grace's arm. "He's hotheaded and worked up about all that has transpired. But give him time."

"I'm afraid of time," Grace replied, looking up to meet Karen's eyes.

"But why? Time can heal all wounds, or so they say," Karen replied, trying her best to sound lighthearted. "You'll see. Peter will think things over, and he'll go back to the hotel in search of you."

"And I won't be there, and he'll be hurt and angry with me."

Karen shook her head. "He has to make a choice, Grace. He has to put aside the past and deal with the future. There's too much at stake for him to do otherwise."

Grace nodded and returned her gaze to the ground. "Far more than anyone realizes."

Karen wondered what her friend meant by such words, but she let it go and decided against probing for more information. Grace's sorrow over her husband's absence was nothing that Karen could resolve for her friend. She would simply have to bide her time and trust that Grace would open up to her as she always had in the past.

LINDEMAN TOOK THE ENTIRE PARTY by surprise. Adrik hadn't seen the city in over three years, and he was rather dumbfounded to find it so well established and planned out. The rest of the party took absolute delight in the lakeside town. Despite being comprised mostly of tents, there were hotels, bakeries, restaurants, and stores to lure weary travelers. Promises of hot meals and soft beds were tempting, but other than stopping long enough to stock up on supplies, the plan was to move the party forward.

Adrik had planned to have them rest in Bennett, a town north of Lake Lindeman, but seeing his companions so completely worn out, he changed his mind.

"There's plenty of materials and such that we'll need for building a boat," he told the group the afternoon of their arrival. "I believe instead of building a boat in Bennett, we'll go ahead and do the deed here. Perhaps even find additional supplies and such—if they're not too expensive."

"Sounds like a capital idea to me," Crispin said, wiping his hand against his perspiring forehead.

"Where will we stay?" Karen questioned.

"Well, we can pitch our tents and make things as comfortable as possible. If the weather stays nice and the materials aren't too expensive, we won't need to be here all that long. I've built many a boat in my time, and with Crispin's help, we ought to have something decent put together in a couple of weeks. We don't want to rush and make something that will just break apart when it hits the rocks."

"It looks as if much of the good timber is gone," Karen said, looking around at the hillsides.

Adrik noted the stumps where hundreds of hemlock, spruce, and fir had grown years earlier. "It's a sorry state to see the land so stripped, but I'm sure we'll find the necessary goods. First, however, we need to make camp. I don't want you ladies worrying about anything for a few days. We can all wear dirty clothes and eat canned food. We can buy our bread at the bakery or do without if it's too expensive."

"We won't wilt, Mr. Ivankov," Grace threw out.

But Adrik wasn't convinced. The poor woman looked almost green from her travels. She'd been so tired coming through from Crater Lake that Adrik had thought it impossible for her to take one more step, much less travel for miles.

They settled the matter of their camp by following the example of others before them. Setting up with the lake a short walking distance away, Adrik was almost sorry he'd allowed Joe to head back to Dyea. He missed his companionable silence, along with that of his sons, and Adrik also felt safer having more men in their party. There were no doubt plenty of scallywags and no-goods who would be tempted to trouble the women when Crispin and Adrik were off gathering supplies. It was a grave concern, but no more so than the idea of getting the small troop north.

Two days later, with Karen looking quite rested, Adrik permitted her to accompany him while he looked for lumber. She was eager, almost restless to be doing something more than sitting in camp, while the others were still bemoaning their sore feet and weary bones.

"Are you certain you're up to this?" Adrik questioned as they hiked away from the lake and up the rising slope.

Karen kept even with his every step. "I'm doing quite well. I think this country agrees with me after all. It's difficult to get used to the long hours of light in the summer and the equally long hours of dark in the winter, but I must say, the lack of formality agrees with me." She laughed softly. "I never thought I would be saying that. I was such a stickler for keeping rules when I first arrived."

"So you think you might stay?" Adrik dared the question he'd been longing to ask. If he couldn't convince her to marry him just yet, he had to at least persuade her to stay in the north.

Karen paused and turned to look down on the lake and tent city. "I believe I could be tempted." She lifted her face to him and smiled. "It is a lovely country. I can see why my mother and father loved it. Then again, they had a purpose for being here."

Adrik sat down on a stump and eyed her quite seriously for a moment. "You could have a purpose, too."

Her expression grew quite thoughtful. Her delicate brows arched ever so slightly as her blue eyes bore holes in his heart. He felt his breath catch. He'd already teased her about marriage and about giving her a reason to remain in Alaska. What he needed to know was where her interest pointed. Could she really give up the lively civilization of the larger American cities? Could she spend her life living in the wilderness? Raise a family here?

Finally she spoke. "I have struggled—wrestled, really—with God." She looked away from him and this time cast her gaze to the mountains. "I have tried to put my anger aside. I've tried to let go of all that has caused me to question God, but I find some things are most difficult to bid farewell."

"Such as?"

She continued to look toward the peaks. "I cannot understand His ways. I try. I really do. I know that faith is required and that in faith comes the ability to trust, even when the way seems unclear."

"But?"

She looked at him now, and Adrik had never thought her more beautiful. Her hair, void of its typical bonnet, glinted gold and red in the summer sun. He longed to reach up and pull loose the ribbon that held her braid. He thought back on the night she'd asked him to brush her hair. He could almost feel himself trembling again. He was grateful she'd not asked that favor of him since, but then again, he almost wished she would.

"I suppose forgiving Mr. Paxton will have to be a daily event for me," she said in a most resigned manner. "I don't feel like forgiving him. However, neither do I desire to grant him more effort or time than is absolutely necessary."

"So wouldn't giving him to God be the wiser choice?" Adrik asked softly.

He heard her sigh, and he longed to hold her in his arms. Instead, he remained seated, hoping she would continue to open up to him.

Changing the subject, Karen returned her gaze to the lake below them. "So many people will pass through here. They'll come and go, and I can't help but wonder if many will stay."

"Will you?"

She said nothing for what seemed an eternity. Adrik could hardly bear it and stood to suggest they continue their exploration. But when he got to his feet, she turned, and he saw the tears that were running down her cheeks. What had he said to cause this? His expression must have betrayed him, for she smiled and wiped at her eyes.

"You might think me very silly," she said in a barely audible voice, "but I feel that I belong here. I feel I must stay, but I have no idea of how to do that or where to go. I can't even tell you what I would do once I figured those other things out."

He reached out to put his hands on her shoulders. "I don't think it's silly at all. I think God has a purpose in your being here. Selfishly, I want you to stay, but you know that. I think you understand a great deal more about it than you've been willing to let yourself see. You're a fine woman and a good teacher. I've seen you teach Leah, and you have a gift. Why not put that to good use up here?"

"With the stampeders' children? With the natives?" she asked.

"Why not? Either one would be a fine choice. Just look at the children here in Lindeman. There are a lot more running around than I would have ever believed. There are only going to be more in the years to come. Then with the natives . . . well, trust takes time."

"Would they ever accept me? I mean, just because they accepted my father doesn't mean they would like me, as well."

Adrik grinned and inside, his heart soared. He would find a way to convince her. "They'd like you well enough. I'd see to that."

Karen looked intently into eyes, then suddenly pulled away. "I'm heading back to camp. I need to check on Grace and Leah."

Stunned, he watched her go, not at all sure what had just taken place. Women were queer creatures, with strange ideas and ways about them. How could he ever hope for her to understand that he loved her more than life, when she wouldn't stand still long enough for him to tell her?

Working for the railroad proved to be a form of salvation for Peter Colton. With Skagway's city fathers seeing the benefit of such transportation, it wasn't long before they found the money and men to back up their dream, and Peter now played a part in it. In some ways, Peter Colton found his job with the railroad to be less taxing than his duties had been aboard *Merry Maid*. Here he was in charge of no one but himself. And in some ways not even that, for he took his orders just like the others.

He worked six days a week, helping to blast out a road from the rock and gravel. The railroad was rapidly taking shape, in spite of the difficulties. So many people were certain the plan would fail, that no one could put a railroad in the midst of such a chaotic land—but they were succeeding.

The railroad company had a bigger problem than the land, however. Keeping workers on the lines was taxing the patience of even the most saintly supervisors. The company paid the workers high wages to keep them from running off prematurely to the goldfields, and still they suffered losses. Peter had no illusions of gold, except for getting together enough to buy back his father's company—*his* company. Of course, there was still the matter of his wife to deal with. He did his best not to think of her sitting in Skagway alone and frightened.

"So you heading down to Skagway?"

Peter looked up to find Jonas Campbell studying him with an intent look on his face. "I was thinking about it."

The man nodded and pulled a pipe from his pocket. "Do you suppose you could bring me back some tobacco? I'm packing my last bowl."

Jonas had been a good friend to Peter. At least a dozen years his senior, Jonas had taken on a brotherly role when Peter had come to work for the railroad, anger and sorrow his companions. Without Peter even realizing what was happening, Jonas had managed to befriend him.

"I'll be glad to get it for you," Peter said, washing his face with cold water from a bucket. He took the scarf from around his neck and dried his face, then rinsed the scarf out, as well.

"Will you be visiting your little family?" Jonas asked, appearing not the least bit concerned about intruding on Peter's privacy.

"I suppose it's time," Peter replied rather sheepishly. "But to tell the truth, I don't even know if they'll still be there. I left without word, and it's been months. They may well have gone south, back to San Francisco."

"They might have at that, but weren't you just telling me last night that you had no notion of your wife doing that—that she'd probably stay behind?"

Peter tied the wet scarf back around his neck. "I just don't know." And that was the truth of it. Disgusted by the way he'd treated Grace and his family, he had no way of knowing how they might have responded to his actions. Surely there was a breaking point for everyone, and with the way he'd behaved, Peter feared he'd reached that point with each one of them.

"Don't give up hope," Jonas said softly.

Peter looked at the man for a moment, a question on his heart that begged to be asked. "Jonas, you've been a good friend to me these last few weeks. You've fed me when I was without food. You've talked to me when I didn't have another friend in the world. You've gotten me to talk, as well—to share things with you that I wouldn't have shared with another human soul, much less a stranger."

The older man nodded thoughtfully and dragged slowly on the pipe. Peter could read a quiet contentment in the man's brown eyes. He always seemed at peace. Jonas often spoke of longing for the company of his wife and son who'd stayed behind in Kansas. He'd not seen them in over six months, and yet he remained in good spirits.

"I envy the peace you have," Peter said, turning his gaze to the ground. "I know that I have to find a way to make things right. I have to know that peace."

"Friend, I know you're weary. I know that even though we've shared a meal and some passing conversation, you've kept yourself closed off from the rest of the world. But I know that your wife deserves to see you and to hear you ask for forgiveness."

"There's that word again," Peter said, looking up with a smile. "I used to hate that word. I thought it was nothing more than a sign of weakness."

Jonas guffawed loudly, causing several of their retiring co-workers to look their way. Jonas paid no attention to the others, however. He pulled out his pipe with one hand and slapped Peter on the back with the other. "Ain't a man alive who is strong enough to deal out forgiveness on his own. Takes a higher power than what's here on earth."

"I'm beginning to see that, but I'm not entirely sure I understand it. Grace believes in it—she believes in God and that God desires a relationship with each of us."

"And that bothers you a mite, doesn't it?"

Peter looked at Jonas and raised a brow. "It bothers me more than a mite."

Jonas nodded and said, "Well, at least you're being honest, which is more than I can say for you a month ago. Go to town. Go see your wife and have yourself a talk. Nothing says you can't come back here after it's done. If she's not there, then you take the next step."

Peter could feel all the longing and desire for Grace's company rise up in him as he asked, "Which is?"

"You go find her."

───────

Making his way into Skagway from up the rail line, Peter thought of Jonas's words and of the need to forgive. He knew Jonas was a godly man, but he was different somehow from the pious preachers and churchgoers of his home port. Jonas had never once tried to beat Peter over the head with his faith. Instead, he'd offered friendship and kindness, a listening ear, and occasional advice. And in that advice Peter heard the same truths that had come from Grace.

Just thinking about his wife tore Peter up inside. Was this what it was to be broken in spirit? And, if not this devastating void in his heart, then what? He felt as though he had irreparably damaged his wife, and even though Grace had always offered him forgiveness, how could he possibly expect such a gift now?

Still, what would she say when he suddenly appeared after so many months of separation? She might not ever want to see him again. She might have even . . . No, he wouldn't let himself think that she had sought out Martin Paxton for help.

Martin Paxton and the harm he'd caused was the reason for all of this. Peter had been so humiliated by the situation and his wife's obvious mistrust that he'd taken himself away from the town and family he loved. Now, months later, he could only hope they were still in port and that they might speak to him and listen to what he had to say.

He had enough money to take them all home to San Francisco. He knew Paxton had offered them passage, and even if his parents and Miranda had gone, surely Grace would have remained behind in hopes of his return.

But I gave her no reason to believe that I might return, Peter thought solemnly.

With determined steps, Peter walked with a single purpose. He would go back to the Hotel Alaska, and if Grace should be there, he would beg her forgiveness and offer her his plan. If his family were there, so much the better.

―――――――

But the proprietor of the hotel hadn't seen Grace or Peter's family in months. He had no idea of their whereabouts, leaving Peter quite troubled. Stepping out onto the busy street, Peter scanned the crowd for some sign of a familiar face. There was no one. He thought for a moment about telephoning Karen in Dyea. A new line had been put between the two sister towns, but Peter had no idea of where he might find Karen. What was the name of that hotel she was staying at? He wracked his memory but could recall nothing.

In complete exasperation, Peter sighed and shoved his hands deep into his coat pockets. He contemplated the people who crowded Broadway Street. There wasn't a friendly face among them. They were intent on their dreams of gold—of fame and fortune. Perhaps he should just give up and go back to camp. Perhaps this had been nothing but a hopeless cause.

For a moment he did nothing but watch the people. Fresh-faced boys mingled with grizzled old-timers, and all of them appeared to be carrying the weight of the world—or at least their homes—upon their backs. Dogs barked and strained against their owners' control, while horses laden with packs whinnied nervously when strangers drew too close. They all seemed drawn to the same purpose— gold. Picks and shovels, pans and sledges peeked out from packs along with tents and food supplies. This gathering of strangers knew what they wanted out of life. Would that Peter could say the same.

Then, against his will, Peter knew what he had to do.

Without thought, he pivoted and headed down the street to the one place he had never intended to go again. Paxton's store. If Paxton was still in town, then he would most likely know where the Coltons had gone. If not the whole family, Paxton would certainly know what had become of Grace.

Martin Paxton seemed almost to be expecting Peter when one of his thugs ushered him through the door. He smiled and casually took his seat behind a rather regal mahogany desk. It was new—something perhaps brought aboard *Merry Maid* or *Summer Song* while under Paxton's jurisdiction? Peter tried to quell such thoughts. They only served to stir his anger.

"I must say this is quite a surprise. I figured you went south with your family."

"I'm here to find out about my family," Peter replied. "Where are they? Where is Grace?"

Paxton shook his head. "What? No time for formalities? No groveling for the answers you seek from me?"

Peter's temper threatened rational thought, but still he remained calm. "Where have they gone?"

"Home, I would imagine," Paxton replied. "I gave your father and mother passage to leave and they went."

"And my sister?"

"I have no idea."

"And Grace?"

"Your wife is still here in Alaska."

"How do you know that?"

Paxton's expression grew smug, further irritating Peter. He was toying with him, playing him like a poorly tuned instrument. "How do you suppose I know? Grace did not leave with your family."

"Then she is still in Skagway?" Peter questioned. "If that is the case, I wish to see her."

"Well, she doesn't wish to see you," Paxton replied, getting to his feet. "You left your wife, Mr. Colton. You tossed her aside and I picked her back up. Ironic, given that she was always mine to begin with."

Peter took a step forward, then stopped. He gripped the back of a leather chair in order to keep from plowing his fist into Paxton's face. "Where is she?" he growled between clenched teeth.

"I am not at liberty to tell you," Paxton said, coming around from behind his desk. Peter was certain the action was to show him he felt Peter was no threat to his well-being. "She doesn't wish for you to know. She is deeply wounded. She has agreed to end this farce of a marriage."

"I don't believe you," Peter replied, torn by a wave of emotions that threatened to destroy his composure. She wanted to be rid of him. She had put aside her fear of Paxton's abusive nature and had sought him out for help. How could that be? How could it be that she saw Peter as a worse threat than Paxton?

"You must believe me," Martin Paxton said, crossing his arms. He leaned back against his desk and looked for all the world as though he'd given information no more important than his shoe size.

"You see, Mr. Colton, your wife is perhaps wiser than you give her credit for being. She listened to me, and now she is ready to settle this matter. My advice to you is that you return to San Francisco and divorce your wife. Make it easy on all parties concerned. I will pay for your transportation, and I will even accommodate you in seeking legal counsel. Once you have accomplished this and the decree is finalized, I will return Colton Shipping to you."

"What?" Peter could hardly believe the man was suggesting such things. Worse still, he could scarcely imagine that the man was serious. Colton Shipping was worth hundreds of thousands of dollars.

"You heard me correctly. I will not only return your ships, I will sign over any further interest. I will consider our transaction, my loan to your father and all the investments, to be completed. Paid in full."

Peter shook his head. "A divorce would not be possible."

"Oh, but I think you might reconsider. You see, Grace told me all about your fight. How you wished that you'd never married her—how you never intended to return to her."

"That's not true!" Peter declared. "I was angry and I said . . ." His voice trailed away. He had said things he didn't mean. He had spoken out of anger and driven away the only person who really mattered to him.

"I know what you said. She told me everything." He looked at Peter with a pitying glance. "I could have warned you that she wasn't for you. She is spoiled and willful. It was the reason her father thought best to agree to my plan. You see, in spite of my desire for revenge, Mr. Hawkins found his daughter's behavior to be a social disgrace."

"You lie, sir! You forced yourself upon that family for purposes of your own. Grace told me how you savagely attacked her."

"Much as you did, only with words. We are not so very different, Mr. Colton." His words hit like a blow to Peter's stomach. The truth of his statement was more than Peter could stand.

"Now, what of my deal? Will you return to California and do as I have asked? Better still, we could both make the journey. I could help you to find proper counsel, and you and your father could join me in arranging the transfer of the business."

Peter shook his head. "I'm not leaving Skagway until I see Grace. You'd better tell her." He forced himself to leave before he released his pent-up anger on Paxton. Opening the door, Peter dared to look up. Paxton was actually smiling. "I'll check back tomorrow. She'd better be here."

Paxton circled his desk and reseated himself as Peter Colton exited his office. "If I had the power to bring her here, she'd be here already," he muttered. He threw open his top desk drawer and pulled out two folded sheets of paper.

One was clearly addressed to Peter Colton. The other was a hastily scribbled request to send a telegram to Wyoming.

At first Paxton had found it amusing that Grace had fallen for the biggest scam in Skagway. There was no telegraph to the lower territories and states. Soapy Smith had made money hand over fist with that little gem. Too bad the man had gotten himself killed in a gunfight only days before. As irritating as Smith could be, Paxton had figured one day he would buy the man over to his side of the fence. Together they could have ruled Skagway and Dyea and controlled the commerce and people coming in and out of the north. But instead, Smith had been too threatening—too greedy. And the people had risen against him.

Paxton got up from his desk and headed over to the cast-iron stove. Poking up the fire, he took one last look at the words Grace had penned to her mother. Words that never reached the woman, but were instead answered at no small expense, with Paxton's own suggested content. He tossed the paper into the stove and smiled as the corners curled and caught fire.

Then he looked at the letter Grace had left at the Hotel Alaska for Peter. He hadn't known of the letter until just the week before. After Grace had disappeared from Dyea, Paxton had set out once again to find her. Quizzing the hotel manager at the Hotel Alaska had been difficult, for the man had taken ill and his nephew had been put in charge. Finally, however, the manager regained his health and had returned to take charge of his business. At that, Paxton's men had quizzed him about Grace. He admitted to knowing nothing of her whereabouts but added that he held a letter for her husband, Peter Colton.

Paxton had the letter in his possession before the end of the day, and with it he found all the answers he needed. She'd gone north. North to Dawson City. Once again she'd fled his hold. He'd thought to keep her in Skagway, or Dyea at least, and he'd paid a good sum of money to see that no captain would give her passage on any ship heading south. But Grace had outwitted him once again, and for that Martin burned in anger, just as the letter burned when he cast it inside the stove.

"Colton will never know the truth," Paxton said as he slammed the door shut on the stove. "But with a little incentive and a great deal of money, perhaps the man can be persuaded by a lie."

⊣ CHAPTER TWENTY-ONE ⊢

ADRIK WASN'T AT ALL SURE he should have given in to the idea of building a boat in Lindeman. He wasn't prepared for the high cost of materials and the shortage of good lumber. He also wasn't prepared to hear about the One Mile River and the rapids that connected Lake Lindeman to Lake Bennett.

Still, he had to face the truth of the situation. They needed transportation north, and they could either pay for freighting in someone else's boat or take a chance on their own. Coming from seafaring people, Adrik didn't question his ability to build a decent craft. He listened intently to the advice given him by other builders and added it to his own knowledge, designing a boat that would be ideally suited to the strenuous travel they would encounter. Still, he wished he might have considered other options.

Supplies were scarce, and the available lumber was green and spongy. Not the kind of thing you wanted for building a ship. Green wood would shrink and lead to disaster on the trip. Many people were waiting to build boats in Bennett, and while that had been Adrik's original plan, he counted it as the divine providence of God that he'd changed his mind. Bennett was quite overcome with dysentery and typhoid fever. And while one police officer told him things were looking better, Adrik didn't want to take a chance. Those were two problems he didn't care to take on. Sickness and scarcity of goods were enough to discourage and send many a man packing. But apparently it wasn't as daunting to the women in Adrik's party.

The women wanted to press on and did everything within their means to see that it happened quickly. September would soon be upon them, and their options were quickly narrowing. With God smiling favorably upon them, it would take four weeks to reach Dawson by water. Yet in that time, the Yukon could freeze up solid and be hit with ten feet of snow. Adrik didn't like thinking about the odds.

These thoughts fouled his mood, causing even Crispin to avoid him. Karen generally eyed him from afar, saying nothing—for once. He knew she had troubles of her own. She continued to fret over Jacob's whereabouts. Leah had taken a cold, causing the child to be greatly discouraged and saddened. Between her mood and his, Adrik had no doubt Karen was feeling rather overwhelmed.

"So are you still planning for us to leave tomorrow?"

He hadn't heard Karen come up behind him. He turned and smiled, determined to prove to her that all was well. "That's the plan."

She studied him for a moment. Her red-gold hair, now lightened considerably by the long hours spent in the sun, blew wisps around her face. Her eyes, so intent on understanding his mood, were exceptionally blue. He wanted to reach out—to touch her. He wanted to beg her to marry him and put an end to his loneliness. But now wasn't the time.

"I thought we were friends," she said matter-of-factly.

Adrik hadn't expected this and was taken aback for a moment. "What?"

Karen crossed her arms. "You heard me. Furthermore, you know exactly what I'm talking about. You've been nothing but a bear all week. You've grunted around here, barely talking to anyone. Your mood has sent the entire camp into a spell of depression, and I want to know why."

"I have a lot on my mind. Getting this party north is a big enough task to weigh heavily on anyone. It's already the middle of August."

"So?" She refused to back down, and her expression caused Adrik to actually smile.

"So . . . winter isn't that far off. There are signs that it just may come early. And if you'll remember, it gets kind of cold up here. And when that happens, the water freezes and the snow falls and makes living a little more uncomfortable—and transportation a great deal more difficult."

"Is that all?"

"Isn't that enough? The odds are no longer with us."

Karen shook her head. "I've never known you to be overly worried about the odds. No, this is something more."

Adrik turned away from her and picked up his hammer. He wasn't ready to tell her how he felt. How loving her was tearing him apart inside because he didn't know if she could ever love him enough to share her life with him. He began to pound a nail into the piece he'd been working on all morning, but just as he raised his hammer, Karen took hold of his hand.

She didn't say a word, and finally he had to look at her. Her expression softened as his eyes met hers. "Adrik, please don't be this way. Just tell me what's really troubling you. I promise to be understanding and to do my best to help you figure out what we should do."

"Will you, now?" he said softly. He jerked away from her and put the hammer back on the table. Then turning back around, he pulled Karen into his arms. Mindless of the crowds that worked around him and the throngs of strangers who coursed right through their camp, Adrik lowered his mouth to hers for a long and leisurely kiss. She didn't resist him. Adrik felt lost in the power of the moment. He wanted to forget that there were decisions to be made and trials to be faced. He wanted Karen, and nothing else mattered quite so much. Realizing that he had to put an end to their embrace, he abruptly ended the kiss and let her go.

"There," he said. "Figure out what's to be done about that."

She stared at him in wide-eyed surprise. Her cheeks were red and her mouth was slightly open, as if to speak. Adrik knew it would be better for both of them if he simply walked away. So that was what he did.

Miranda and Crispin had just returned from a foray into town when they came upon Adrik kissing Karen. The passion displayed in that kiss had caused Miranda no small amount of discomfort. How she had longed for someone to love her as dearly and completely as she knew Mr. Ivankov loved Karen Pierce.

"It seems we are interrupting," Crispin said good-naturedly. He leaned close to whisper, "I wonder how long it will take until they both realize they are in love?"

Miranda giggled, but Crispin's warm breath against her ear caused a shiver of delight to run up her spine. "I'm sure I don't know," she replied without thinking, "but perhaps we should invest in another tent."

Crispin laughed out loud. "What a woman. Your thoughts could well be my own."

Miranda suddenly realized how inappropriate her remark sounded. "I only . . . well . . . I meant that should they marry. . . ." She gave up when she saw that her words only served to amuse Crispin all the more.

"I knew exactly what you meant, my dear. I was thinking much the same."

They watched Adrik march off as if to war, while Karen stood looking after him in dumbfounded silence.

"Ah, true love," Crispin said, nudging Miranda. "Theirs will be a match for all eternity."

Miranda nodded, but the statement made her feel suddenly very empty. "I think I'd better take these eggs and see about supper." She held up the small basket where only moments ago she had placed the two precious eggs. Paying a dollar for the two, Miranda thought they might as well have been golden eggs.

She left Crispin and hurried to where they had set up a makeshift kitchen under a canvas awning. The awning had been stretched out between the two tents and made a nice, almost cozy living area in the evening and a wonderful kitchen in the daytime. At night Adrik would lower additional pieces of canvas from the sides and create the effect of walls. Then, by tying the canvas strips to the tents, he closed them off from the rest of the world and allowed the heat of the stove to warm both tents. At least it warmed them marginally.

Miranda actually liked the cold weather and enjoyed the crisp feel to the air. She'd heard one man say that winter was due to come early this year, and she thought that was marvelous. She wanted to see the snow stacked ten and twenty feet deep, as Crispin had spoken of. He had traveled the world and had seen all manner of things, and it thrilled Miranda to the core of her being. How wonderful to simply travel at will and see the world and all that it had to offer.

"Were you able to get any eggs?" Leah asked as Miranda approached.

"I was able to buy two, and they were quite expensive," Miranda replied. "But for one of your cakes, Leah, I know it was worth the price."

Leah didn't respond with the excitement Miranda had anticipated. "They work a whole sight better than those powdered ones we brought along."

"You're a good cook, Leah. You'll have us all forgetting the cost before the end of the meal."

Leah merely nodded and went to work. Taking the eggs from Miranda's basket, she cracked them into a bowl. Miranda's heart ached for the young girl. Leah had prayed so passionately that morning, pleading with God for the safe return of her brother. Miranda couldn't help but speak a similar prayer. They were bound in a strange way by their wayward male siblings. And until that morning, Miranda had never truly realized the connection.

"Leah," she said, knowing that she had to share this thought with the girl, "you and I are very much alike."

Leah looked up from her work and coughed lightly. "What do you mean?"

"Our brothers," Miranda replied.

Leah shook her head. "I know Jacob and Peter knew each other, but I don't see how that makes us alike."

Miranda moved closer and smiled. "We are both longing for our brothers to come back. Your brother has gone north, mine has gone away without any word of his whereabouts. You love your brother and I love mine. Both are important people in our lives, and both hold our hearts in a special way."

"I see," Leah replied, turning her attention back to the cake.

Miranda reached out to stop her for a moment. "I know how hard it is. I know you're worried and that you can scarcely think of anything else. I know you wonder about your father and long to know the truth.

"When I heard you pray this morning, I realized the words could have been from my own mouth. I long for Peter to return home, just as you need to find Jacob."

Leah's eyes filled with tears. Miranda reached up to wipe away the drops as they fell onto the girl's cheek. "My mother always said that a burden shared makes the load less heavy. I will share this burden with you if you will let me."

Leah wrapped her arms around Miranda's waist. "Thank you, Miranda. Sometimes it just scares me so much. Sometimes I'm afraid I'll never see him again."

Miranda stroked Leah's hair and sighed. "I know. I fear sometimes that I'll never see my brother again." Just then Miranda looked up and saw Grace standing not five feet away. Her expression made it clear that she'd overheard a good portion of their words.

Miranda decided to speak from her heart. "When I get very afraid, I pray that God will give me strength to endure and that He will take away my fear and help me to remember that He loves me."

She smiled at Grace and hoped that she would remember that long ago she had once spoken similar words to Miranda. The moment had been when Miranda had feared God might never send her a husband Peter would approve of. Her heart had been close to breaking at the thought of never knowing true love. Grace had comforted her with those very words.

Grace nodded, as if remembering the moment herself. She slipped off between neighboring camps and disappeared from sight while Leah raised her head and offered Miranda a weak smile. "My mama always said that I should come and tell her when I was afraid. She said that God was always with us and that when we're afraid, the Psalms said we could trust in Him."

"Your mother sounds like she was a very wise woman—and a very loving mother."

Leah drew a ragged breath and laid her head back against Miranda's shoulder. "She was a wonderful mother. My pa was a good father, too. Even though he left us, he still loved us."

"I'm sure that's true," Miranda replied, her heart filled with love for the girl. How very much she would have liked to have a little sister like Leah. Perhaps that was the reason God had allowed her to come on this journey. He knew Leah would need her. Even more, God knew Miranda would need Leah.

———

Adrik stood back with a great deal of pride and no small amount of reservation. The flat-bottomed scow he and Crispin had completed sat afloat in Lake Lindeman without the slightest hint of taking on water.

"It would appear, my friend, we have built a seaworthy craft," Crispin said joyfully.

"It would seem that way," Adrik replied, continuing to check every inch of the deck for some sign of a problem. Apparently the oakum and pitch caulking was holding well.

The flat-bottomed scow was exactly what they needed to take them north to the goldfields. Adrik knew the boat would easily accommodate their passengers and tons of goods within its forty-two-foot length. What he was less convinced of was whether or not the women would have the strength to help row and pole as they passed through the rapids.

Then, too, he'd already been warned that even with a sturdy square sail rigged to the bow mast, he'd be a fool to rely on the winds and currents alone. The doldrums, it seemed, were quite common on the still waters of the larger lakes. And when storms came up without warning, as they were wont to do, the oars would be necessary to make it to the safety of the shore. Could he and Crispin handle it alone?

"Face it, my friend," Crispin said, slapping Adrik's back, "you've built a masterpiece. Michelangelo couldn't have done better."

"Well, I don't know who he is," Adrik said, blowing out a breath of relief, "but I almost wish he were here to help us sail her."

Crispin laughed, then surprised Adrik by waving. Turning, he saw that Crispin was bidding welcome to the women, who stood watching from shore. "So what do you think?" Crispin called out.

"It looks awfully small," Karen called back. "Are you sure it's going to hold us all?"

"It's bigger than you think," Adrik answered. "Just wait until tomorrow. You'll see for yourself."

"It's nothing short of a floating palace," Crispin announced, and the ladies laughed.

Adrik gazed heavenward and shook his head. "I wouldn't exactly call it that, but it's floating and that's what counts."

"Well, it cost as much as a palace," Karen called out from the shore. "Who would have ever thought pitch would cost seven dollars a pound?"

By now a crowd had gathered to see the finished masterpiece by Adrik Ivankov. They laughed at Karen's statement and threw out comments of their own.

"No worse than paying a dollar a pound for nails!"

"If you can get them!"

"You can't even get lumber for building, and the trees to cut are five miles away."

"And it helps if you know how to build with them when you get them," another poor soul called out. At this everyone laughed, and even Adrik stopped fretting momentarily and joined the fun.

"Well, perhaps I would do better to open a boat-building school rather than to head north to the goldfields," he replied.

"No doubt the money would be better," Karen said, laughing.

"Well, be that as it may," Adrik said, putting his hands to his hips, "are you ladies ready to leave in the morning?"

"I was ready to leave a week ago," Karen answered. He watched her turn to the others. "Come on, we've got some packing to do. I know this captain of ours, and he's the pushy sort. If we aren't ready, he'll leave without us."

"That's exactly what I'll do," Adrik said, laughing, but he didn't mean a word of it.

The excitement of his accomplishment finally outweighed his worry. Looking to Crispin, he nodded. "We've got ourselves a boat, and she looks to be all that we could hope for."

Part Three

LATE AUGUST 1898

It was meet that we should make
merry, and be glad:
for this thy brother was dead, and
is alive again; and was lost,
and is found.

LUKE 15:32

—|CHAPTER TWENTY-TWO|—

TRAVERSING LAKE LINDEMAN proved to be an easy, almost carefree trip. The biggest problem was avoiding the other twenty or more boats that were attempting to launch at the same time. There was nearly a carnival-type atmosphere as the various pilots steered in one direction and then another. It soon became quite clear who had prior experience in boating. Adrik, steeped in years of childhood sailing and fishing, took to the water with great ease. Even Crispin, for all his upper-society manners, was quite adept on the boat. The boat itself proved to be a seaworthy vessel. The shrinkage of the raw lumber remained minimal, and the rocky passageways caused little damage.

Karen thought Adrik's worry was all for naught as the One Mile Rapids and Lake Bennett soon became nothing more than exciting memories. After registering their boat in Bennett, along with scores of other desperate souls, the party pushed on and made exceptional time. Even Adrik had to admit that God was smiling on them. They'd managed to keep the boat clear of most obstacles, and even when the waters had grown rough, it was almost as if an unseen hand had maneuvered them through the dangers.

The little scow proved to be much bigger than Karen had originally believed. Once they'd positioned the smaller of their two tents in the middle of the boat and set up their provisions around those canvas walls, Karen felt they were living rather well. It wasn't perfect and it wasn't anything luxurious, but it was better than most.

But perhaps most surprising of all, Karen enjoyed life upon the water. She enjoyed the passing scenery and the glorious colors of the changing seasons. There was something simply marvelous about moving to a new place every day. After living a life of rigid convention in Chicago for the ten years prior to coming north, the Yukon offered a sort of liberty that appealed to Karen. She didn't even mind the frost that touched most everything that morning.

Winter's clutches were approaching, yet Karen refused to let her spirits be defeated. She thought of her mother's letters describing Alaskan winters—bitterly cold and deep snows. Yukon winters were surely the same, and having survived the long dark season in Dyea only the year before, Karen was convinced she could manage the days to come.

That night Karen slipped away from her tent and found Adrik sitting near the small campfire they'd enjoyed earlier in the evening. She smiled at him and pulled her coat together to ward off the chill.

"I couldn't sleep," she said softly. "I'm much too excited."

"We're doing well," he admitted. "I had my concerns, but I have to say things are going along better than I could have planned."

"Hand of God," she whispered.

He glanced up. "Is that a question?"

Karen folded her arms and looked to the skies. "You needn't worry about me. I'm all right." She stated the words, knowing he would understand, but was surprised when he questioned her further.

"What do you mean, you're all right?"

Karen wondered if he needed to hear her confess she had yielded her will. Why was it that God and Adrik Ivankov always demanded she completely surrender her innermost secrets?

"Why don't you sit down here beside me," Adrik suggested, "and tell me exactly what's on your mind?"

Karen hesitated for a moment. Could she trust herself with Adrik? She knew her heart in the matter. She wanted very much to declare her love for him, but she was so uncertain of how he might respond. He obviously found her desirable, but love—now, that was a different story. Could he really love her? And if he did, what would that love require of her?

She inched closer and knelt down beside the fire. "I just wanted you to know that I've yielded my anger to God." She stared into the fire rather than risk Adrik's eyes. "You've so often borne the brunt of that anger and had to keep me from making a fool of myself—"

"On more than one occasion," Adrik interjected with a laugh.

She turned to him and saw that he intended only to lighten her mood. "Yes, well, I thank you for that. I know I can be difficult at times."

Adrik nodded. "That's what your pa always said."

"He said that?" Her tone betrayed her surprise.

"He said that you were the one pea in the pod that just refused to be alike. Your sisters were calm, quiet children who settled down to marriage and family, but not you. You thirsted for knowledge and adventure and went after both with great enthusiasm."

Karen laughed softly. "Yes, I can imagine him saying just that."

"He loved you, you know."

Karen felt tears come to her eyes. "I loved him, too. I still can't believe he's gone. I was certain he was the treasure I was coming north to find. I was certain he would give me answers and purpose for my life."

"Only God can do that, Karen."

"I know that—at least now I do. I'd always espoused that belief in words, but I guess God had to bring me through fire to help me make it something more than words."

"He's making you grow. Making your faith grow. Your pa used to say that a man's faith was like building a house. You give it a good foundation, and then you have something to build on. Even then, you have to add to that basic structure. A house has to have walls and a roof."

"A floor's nice, too," Karen said with a smile. After living with the ground beneath for her tent floor, she was ready for real wood under her feet.

Adrik chuckled, "Floors are good, too." He reached out and touched her hand. "Faith has to be added in order to make it strong. It doesn't happen overnight."

"My mother used to say that God's love for us was instantaneous, but that human beings needed time to learn to love." Karen had spoken without thinking, and now the memory burned in her heart as she looked deep into Adrik's eyes.

She knew he cared—of that she was certain. But did he love her? Did he love her enough to want the rest of his life altered by a wife—children? He'd teased her in Dyea about getting married in order to share a tent. He'd kissed her until Karen had lost all reasonable thought. But did this constitute that kind of love that meant "forever"?

Adrik was a free spirit. She'd known that from the moment she'd first met him. He'd told her tales of wandering the land, of living among his grandmother's people, of learning what the land had to offer him. He'd shared sad tales of the battles fought over the land, of whites who destroyed the Tlingit commerce and livelihood, of sickness that had destroyed entire villages. He knew this land and people and loved them both. Karen knew that in order to have Adrik Ivankov, she'd have to accept his land and people as her own. Could she do that? Could she give herself over to this frozen north—this deadly but beautiful land?

She felt his fingers stroking her hand. The sensation caused her to tremble. He was the only man in the world who could make her feel all weak in the knees.

"You'd better get to bed," Adrik said abruptly. "We've got a full day ahead of us tomorrow." He fairly jumped up from his seat on the ground.

He helped Karen to her feet but didn't wait for her response. Confused by his actions, Karen shook her head. Who was this man, and what did he want from her?

———

"What do you mean we have to walk around the rapids?" Karen declared.

Adrik stood his ground. He'd known Karen was going to be a problem. "The Northwest Mounted Police have set the regulation for Miles Canyon. The rapids are too rough there, and people have drowned while trying to make it through."

"But we made it through other rapids just fine," Karen protested.

"Maybe there's something different about this particular area," Grace suggested.

Karen shook her head. "Even if that were true, why not merely tell us of the dangers and leave the decision up to us?"

"Karen," Adrik began in a firmer tone, "I have no say over what the officials of this country dictate. They have decided the rapids are too difficult for women."

"Just women? What about men? Why don't the men have to walk?"

Adrik clamped his mouth shut and looked heavenward. The woman could be so argumentative when she decided to be. Why couldn't she just accept the ruling and deal with it in the same calm manner as her traveling companions?

"I happen to enjoy the exhilaration of the rapids," Karen continued. "I want to ride them out with you and Crispin. If Grace and Miranda and Leah wish to walk, I have no objection."

"You aren't going, and that's final!" Adrik declared louder than he'd intended.

"You're just trying to control me!"

"Well, somebody has to."

Karen gave him a look that would have frozen a weaker man in his steps, but not Adrik. He knew only too well that this was for her own good, and he wasn't about to let her run roughshod over him. "You'll walk and that's final. If I die taking the scow to Whitehorse, then I die. I built the boat and I'll stand by it. But I won't risk the rest of you, and that's my final word." He turned to Crispin and added, "They have men to help pilot the boats through the rapids, so you don't have to come with me."

"Nonsense," Crispin said with a gleam in his eyes. "I wouldn't miss it for the world."

Karen looked at Adrik as if waiting for him to change his mind. When he didn't, she stormed off to the women's tent. When suppertime came, she was still there, and Adrik knew she'd be difficult to contend with. Why couldn't she see that he was only trying to keep her safe? Personally, he was glad for the rule. He'd heard many accounts of the dangers from passing travelers. In fact, that day in the small community that had formed at the head of Miles Canyon, he'd nearly called the trip off after hearing about all the problems with broken ships and lost souls.

"It's the reason we must insist that you portage your goods and passengers," one of the officials told him firmly. "There's a tramway, and your supplies may be loaded onto flat cars. The walk is a decent one except for the mosquitos. Your women will much prefer it to the ride down the canyon."

Adrik would have laughed had the situation not seemed so grim. Most women might have preferred it, but not his women. At least not one woman in particular.

By morning Karen was still not speaking to him, and Adrik had decided enough was enough. He wasn't going to sit around and wait for her to come to her senses. He marveled that she could be so level-headed one moment and so completely obstinate the next. Resolving to concentrate on the task at hand, however, Adrik put in his request for help with the rapids and waited his turn to battle Miles Canyon.

"You're being awfully hard on him, aren't you?" Grace questioned as they washed up the breakfast dishes.

Karen shrugged. "He's just doing this to control the situation." She scrubbed hard at a pie pan, almost imagining she was scrubbing out Adrik's image. Why did the man have to so completely infuriate her one moment and leave her breathless and trembling the next? What kind of madness had overtaken her?

"The authorities have set this rule, not Mr. Ivankov. He only means to see us safe, Karen. I think you're judging him too harshly."

Karen paused and eyed her friend. Grace's color was rather pale, and Karen had worried about her ever since leaving Lindeman. Perhaps Karen's anger was only adding to Grace's exhaustion. With a sigh she set the pan aside. "Grace, I don't know what to do with my feelings. One minute I think I'm in love with him, and the next minute I'd just as soon push him into the river."

Grace offered a bittersweet smile. "I'd like to tell you it gets easier, but I can't. I'm a poor example to follow. I have no idea where my husband has gone. He could very well be dead for all I know, and it breaks my heart to think that the last words we shared were such harsh ones."

Karen nodded. "I know and I'm sorry, Grace. I shouldn't be telling my woes to you. My problems pale compared to your heartbreak."

Miranda bounded into the tent announcing, "Crispin says we're to pack up and head out within the hour. They've made the final arrangements, and we're to meet them on the other side of the rapids. We'll actually be in Whitehorse tonight!"

"I've heard it's grown into quite a city," Grace said. Then she clutched at the edge of the tent, appearing as if she might collapse.

"What is it?" Karen exclaimed, going to her friend's side. "Are you all right?"

Grace nodded and steadied herself against Karen's arm. "I just got a little dizzy for a moment. I'm sure it's just the lack of sleep and decent meals. Oh, what I wouldn't give for a large bowl of fruit." She smiled reassuringly. "How about you?"

Karen wasn't at all convinced of her friend's health. "I think you'd better see a doctor once we get to Whitehorse. You haven't been well the entire trip, and frankly, I'm worried. It isn't like you to be so pale and weak."

"I'll be fine," Grace said, walking to where she'd left bread dough to rise. "I guess we'll have to figure a way to carry this with us or throw it out. I can't see wasting it."

"Let's put it in the big kettle," Miranda suggested. "We'll cover it and pack it with the other things and let them portage it for us. Maybe it will be ready to bake by the time we get to the other side."

The two women went to work on the bread dough while Karen considered the situation. Guilt set in, making her miserable. She couldn't let things go on between her and Adrik as they were. What if something happened to him on the trip through the rapids? Other people had died. Other boats had broken apart on the rocks. A cold shiver ran down her spine. She would rather die with Adrik than live without him. For the first time in her life, Karen was certain of what it meant to be in love with a man. She couldn't let him leave without her. She just couldn't stay behind.

———————

"It's like nothin' ya've ever known," the boat pilot told Adrik as he moved them out into the water. "It's the most untamed stretch of water in the continent. We'll be through it right quick, but ya'll be wonderin' what happened to ya for weeks to come."

Adrik wanted to ask the man about his experience—his abilities—but instead he said nothing as they maneuvered away from shore. He had no idea whether the man knew what he was talking about or not, but he'd paid the exorbitant sum of twenty-five dollars to have the boat taken down the water, and Adrik would have to trust that the man knew his job. After all, his life was as much on the line as Adrik's or Crispin's. Still, he looked awfully young, and he was even shorter than Karen. He was just a kid, as far as Adrik was concerned—a kid who held their lives in his hands as he controlled the scow.

The man seemed unconcerned with what they were about to experience. He chattered incessantly as he worked the boat to the middle of the river. "Ya have to ride the midriver crest in order to survive the white water. Running the white ain't for the faint of heart. I'm glad they've taken to puttin' the ladies off the boats. Just ain't safe."

Adrik could agree with the man there, especially after conversing with one of the officials. The man seemed to positively delight in giving him the details of crafts that had crashed and broken apart on the rocks. It was as if the story were the man's own personal melodrama and Adrik was his only audience.

There was little time to worry any more about it, however. Adrik could feel their speed pick up as the current caught them and pulled them down into the canyon. The water was swift, but not unduly rough. At least not yet. Thick stretches of pines and spruce topped walls some one hundred feet high on either side. The walls seemed to narrow as the water picked up speed and roughness. As the scow lifted up and slammed down against the churning water, Adrik was glad the women had left by foot hours earlier. They'd be safe and sound once Adrik and the men got the scow safely through the canyon. If they got the scow through. Adrik had the distinct sensation they were being taken to their graves. Within a few minutes he knew he had good reason to feel that way.

"Hold on to yar hats," the pilot called, "there's rocks ahead. Ya'll want to keep yar poles ready."

The scow dipped and pitched, and Adrik steadied himself as best he could. He could have anticipated the rocks that sent the little boat into a bit of a spin. What he could not have anticipated was the crash of a human body landing at his feet.

Karen looked up from the deck with a lopsided smile. "Surprise," she said meekly as the boat pitched once again and water sprayed up around them.

———

"The man actually expects me to take this lying down," Peter told his friend. Jonas simply nodded and looked to Peter for further explanation. In the weeks since Paxton had first suggested Peter put a legal end to his marriage, Peter had received two letters from the man further outlining the procedure. "I won't divorce her. I won't give either one of them that kind of satisfaction."

"You're mighty quick to judge that she's agreeing to this matter," Jonas replied. "I would have thought if she were in such an all-fire hurry to get rid of you, she would have allowed that Paxton fellow to help *her* get the divorce rather than waitin' for you to see to it."

"Perhaps Paxton believes I would have an easier time of it," Peter said, pushing back his hair in exasperation. "But I won't do it!"

"Then don't," Jonas said, reaching across the table to help himself to his pipe and tobacco.

"I wanted to kill him," Peter said, looking to his friend for some kind of comment. "I honestly wanted to see him die on the spot."

"Can't say as I blame you. If a man were keepin' my wife from me, I'd probably feel the same way. Especially if he'd caused as much trouble as this Paxton fellow has for you."

Peter finally stopped his pacing and sat down at the table. "What am I supposed to do? Grace is gone. I've no doubt lost her forever. My anger and stupidity have put up a permanent wall between us." He buried his face in his hands. "I miss her so much. I need her."

"Then what are you doing here?" Jonas asked.

Peter raised his gaze and saw that the man was staring at him as if awaiting an answer. What could he say? Why had he left Skagway and Paxton to return to the railway camp? Why had he gone without beating the truth out of Paxton and insisting on Grace's return?

Shrugging, Peter suddenly knew the answer. "Because I'm not man enough to do anything else. I'm less than a whole man without her."

Jonas smiled. "I can well understand how ya feel. A good woman completes a man—makes him see what's been missin' in his life. God said it wasn't good for man to be alone, and it sure as well ain't."

Peter looked at Jonas, and an aching filled his heart. "Jonas, tell me about your God. Tell me why He should care about someone like me—why He should forgive me or need my adoration. Religion makes no sense to me."

"Me neither," Jonas said with a laugh. "All that mumbo jumbo and risin' up and sittin' down. I could never carry a tune, so I didn't figure it made much sense to put myself in a place that made a point of havin' singin'." He put the pipe aside and shook his head. "Knowin' God has nothin' to do with religion."

Peter shook his head. "I don't understand. Grace went to church every Sunday and read her Bible all the time. She wanted the same for me, and I couldn't give it to her. She wanted me to forgive Martin Paxton. I couldn't see the sense in that, either."

"Your little wife went to church because it pleased her to do so. She no doubt had friends there and folks who were of a like mind. That's fellowshipin', and I don't mind that one bit. But you can't box God into a buildin'. He's everywhere, Peter. He most prefers to be here." He pounded his chest for a moment. "Right here, in your heart."

"I just don't know," Peter said, getting to his feet once again. "It doesn't make sense to me. All I can think about is my family. I need to know if my father is well, if my mother is safe. I need to know where my sister is and what she's doing. And I need Grace."

"In more ways than you realize," Jonas said with a grin. "My advice to you is to skedaddle out of this place and go home. Start with your folks. And maybe on the ship ride home, you could have a word or two with the Almighty. I'm thinkin' He'd be pleased to listen to the matter if you were of a mind to tell Him about it."

CHAPTER TWENTY-THREE

THE RIDE DOWN Miles Canyon was like nothing Karen Pierce had ever experienced. Thrown first one way and then the other, she had been as surprised as Adrik to fly out of the tent and land at his feet.

"Stay put!" Adrik yelled, his face contorting in anger.

Karen had no intention of going anywhere, but as the boat lurched and crashed upon a projection of rock, she rolled across the deck. No sooner had she reached the right side of the scow when the entire platform seemed to shift directions. Without a hope of stopping herself, Karen rolled across to the left side of the boat. Only this time, there was nothing to grab on to and she felt herself slipping over the side.

"Adrik!" she screamed, her fingers slipping on the watery deck.

She couldn't see him or even know if he'd heard her. She felt the waves push them up into the air, and before she could so much as snap her fingers, the boat slammed back down in the water. For a long moment, she seemed to be suspended in the air, wondering if there would even be a deck to come back down to. But there was. Thrown against the hard wood, Karen again found herself hopelessly rolling to the right.

If ever there was a moment of reckoning, Karen Pierce found one in this moment. Catching sight of Adrik frantically working to keep the boat from the canyon walls, Karen knew he had no way to help her. The same was true of Crispin, as well as the young man who handled the sweep. There was no one to cry out to—no one but God.

"Oh, God, help me!" she cried out as the icy water poured over the side. She felt herself slipping, sliding ever closer to the edge. Why hadn't Adrik built a rail around this deck?

"Hold on!" she heard the stranger sound above the thundering rapids.

But there was nothing solid to hold on to. She couldn't quite reach the tent, and that would have offered her very little in the way of support anyway. Then Karen spied one of the benches Adrik had nailed to the deck to offer relief from the tent or standing about on deck. If she could make it to the bench, she might be able to wrap herself around it and hope for the best.

Please, God, help me. Don't let me die without telling him how much I love him, Karen thought. She continued her prayer as she fought to make her way across the deck. *Father, I know I've held a grudge, and I'm sorry. Please don't drown me here in the river just to punish my stupidity.*

Inching her way to the structure, Karen felt only a marginal amount of relief as her hands grasped the bench. "Thank you, God!" She sighed and clung to the bench as though it were the most precious gift in all the world. And for all the most important reasons, it was.

Glancing up, Karen saw that Adrik stood only a few feet away. His expression told Karen he was anything but happy to see her—either that or he was angry at the Whitehorse Rapids. *Never mind,* she thought as the boat rose up on a wave and crashed down again. Water seemed to explode around them, dousing them both. *He'll get over it. He'll see why I had to come when I explain the matter to him.*

Water poured across the deck, drenching Karen's heavy wool skirt. Earlier she'd slipped away from the other women, pretending to want to be alone, and so they'd believe her to be returning, she'd left her coat and taken only the knitted wool shawl Aunt Doris had given her last Christmas. Wrapped up in that and wearing a long-sleeved white blouse, Karen felt the icy water bite into her skin as if it had teeth.

The deck pitched back and forth while the bow forced its way through the water. As she managed to figure out the best way to secure herself, Karen realized she was having a wonderful time. The waves and water, the canyon walls—it was all rather like a carousel ride gone mad.

Laughing, she looked up to find Adrik fighting with a long thick pole. She had no idea what he was doing but surmised he was probably helping to keep the boat from crashing against the rocky cliffs.

Then, almost before the ride had begun, the waters calmed, and Karen found them heading to shore. She whispered a prayer of thanksgiving, seeing for herself that they were all still in one piece—as was the boat. The latter was a critical issue, almost on equal footing with their own safety. There was still a great distance to head via water, and they would need the scow to get them through. As they approached the land, Crispin caught sight of her and laughed.

"Where in the world did you come from? Drop down from the skies, did you?"

Karen nodded and pulled her wet body up to the top of the bench. "I felt as though I had."

"So we have a stowaway," the pilot said, taking note of Karen. "Women don't know what's good for them. They ain't gonna like it one bit that you broke the rules and rode down the rapids."

"Tell them to throw her into jail," Adrik said, turning away to help secure the scow at the makeshift dock.

Karen knew she'd have her work cut out with him. She stood and tried to wring out some of the water from her shawl. Crispin offered to help her, and while he took charge of her wrap, Karen worked on the bottom of her skirt.

She looked at Crispin rather conspiratorially and whispered, "That was the most fun I think I've ever had. Of course, I thought for a minute that I was going to go right over the side. God seemed to just pluck me right up. But as dangerous as it seemed, I'd do it again in a minute!"

He nodded toward Adrik. "Looks like there's going to be quite a price to pay."

She looked over to where Adrik stood scowling at them and said, "I suppose I should attempt to unruffle his feathers."

"I think it will take more than that," Crispin replied. "But a word of advice, my dear."

Karen leaned closer. "Yes?"

"Never underestimate your feminine charms."

Karen grinned. "Why, Crispin Thibault, what a splendid suggestion."

She forgot her shawl and sauntered rather boldly up to where Adrik stood. Her legs were a little wobbly after the ordeal, but she steadied herself and grinned. "Permission to go ashore, sir," she said in a teasing manner.

Adrik stepped from the scow and pulled her with him onto the deck. Then without warning he hoisted her unceremoniously over one shoulder and stalked off away from the river.

Karen tried to raise herself up, but Adrik's steps were bouncing her around something fierce. She caught sight of Grace and Miranda, who stood to one side with Leah. They looked at her as if to question this latest escapade, but Karen couldn't even so much as shrug.

"Adrik, put me down!" she protested as his long strides took them farther from the shore. He crossed the tramline and headed deeper into the forest, all while Karen pounded on his back to get his attention. "Adrik, I mean it. Put me down." This ride was almost as perilous as the course on the rapids.

They were well away from the crowd by now, and Karen couldn't see a single sign of civilization. All around her were spruce and pine trunks and vegetation that had begun its autumnal transformation. Then, as quickly as he had hoisted her to his shoulder, Adrik dumped her onto the ground. Her bottom smacked against the hard earth, causing the wind to go out of Karen in a great whoosh.

Gasping, she managed to sputter, "How . . . how . . . *dare* you!"

"How dare me? How dare *you*!" he countered. "You were told to stay off the boat. You were told to go with the other women. You were told a great many things, but you refused to listen."

He turned as if to go, then attacked again. "Do you realize you could have been killed?"

"Of course . . ."

"Do you give any consideration to those who travel with you?"

"Yes, you know I—"

"I can't believe," he said, stalking toward her, hands outstretched, "that you would put your life in danger." He pulled her into the air and dropped her back on her feet.

"Adrik, I can explain!" she said, demanding to be heard.

"You can explain!" He turned away and paced. "You can explain that you gave little thought to the laws of the land—to your authority? You can explain that you took matters into your own hands and disregarded everything I said to you?"

Karen could see there would be no talking to him. He wasn't at all willing to listen. Shaking the dirt and debris from the back of her skirt, she let him rant and rave. His righteous indignation, however, did much to lighten her spirits. He loved her. He would never have reacted this way if he didn't. His anger was born of fear. Fear for her. Fear that she might have died or gotten injured. Smiling, she lifted her face and waited for him to conclude.

"You could have been killed. You could have easily been swept overboard, and you very nearly were. Do you know that my heart actually stopped beating when I saw you struggling at the side and knew I could do nothing to save you without jeopardizing everyone else? The rapids have claimed many a life. The Canadian authorities wouldn't have seen fit to make laws regarding that particular passage on the river if it hadn't been for their desire to keep folks alive. But you . . ." He turned to look at her and stopped. "What are you smiling about? Do you think this is funny?"

"You're funny," she replied. "You won't let me talk or even attempt to explain. All you want to do is yell."

"You bet I want to yell. There's absolutely nothing you can say that will make one bit of difference to me." He shrugged out of his wet coat and tossed it aside. Rolling up his sleeves, Karen actually wondered for a moment what he had planned for her. His well-muscled arms strained against the drenched flannel of his shirt sleeves. It was little wonder, she thought, that he could throw her so easily over his shoulder.

Karen opened her mouth to speak, but again he silenced her.

He held up his hand. "There's nothing you can say. Nothing!"

"I beg to differ with you. I think there is something I can say. Something very important, and if you would settle down and stop being so pigheaded, I might get a chance to say it." She put her hands on her hips, not caring that she must look a sight.

Adrik waved his arm in front of him. "By all means, have your say. What in the world do you think could possibly explain what you just did?"

"I love you," Karen said matter-of-factly. She smiled and shrugged. "I love you. I think that says it all."

He looked at her as if dumbfounded. His dark eyes simply looked her up and down before he began shaking his head. "That's just great. That only makes matters worse."

"What?" Karen exclaimed. "How can you say my love makes matters worse? I know you love me, too. Tell me that you don't."

Adrik looked at her as if she'd suddenly gone daft. "Of course I love you!" he yelled. "That's what makes it so awful."

Karen laughed. "I must have hit my head on that boat ride, because you aren't making any sense to me at all."

He crossed the distance between them in two strides and took hold of her. Shaking her hard, he said, "This is nothing to laugh about. I love you so much that I would have spent the rest of my days with a broken heart had anything happened to you. Don't you understand? This is a deadly land, and you are playing at it like a child with a puppy. Instead of a puppy, you're dealing with a grizzly bear, and you don't even know the difference."

He let her go but didn't move away. Karen thought of what Crispin had said and reached up to touch the side of his cheek. The stubble of a two-day growth of beard scratched her hand as she ran her fingers along his jaw.

"I love you. You mean the world to me, as well," she said softly. She lifted her face and prayed he'd see the sincerity in her eyes. "I couldn't bear the thought of losing you. You must understand—I kept hearing all the stories of death and destruction. I couldn't bear for you to go without me."

"But if you knew the risk, why would you do that?" he asked, his voice low and guarded.

Karen wrapped her arms around his neck and laced her fingers together. "Because, my darling man, I would rather die at your side than live without you." She stretched up on her toes and placed a kiss upon his unresponsive lips. "Don't you see? I had to go with you. I couldn't bear to be left behind and know that I might never see you again."

She heard his breath catch in his throat as he grabbed her and buried his face against her neck. Sighing, Karen knew things would be all right. She clung to him as he wrapped her in a fierce embrace.

"You could have died. You will die if you aren't willing to do what you're told—if you won't learn to respect the land and the danger she hands out."

"Then I'll listen and learn," Karen promised. "Just please don't be angry with me for loving you."

He pulled back, still holding her fast. "I could never be angry at you for loving me, but I swear I'll be tempted to wallop the tar out of you if you ever pull another stupid stunt like that again."

She grinned. "You won't wallop me, Mr. Ivankov."

"Don't bet on it."

She ran her finger over his upper lip, playfully toying with his mustache. "If you wallop me, I won't marry you."

"What makes you think I want to marry you?" he asked, finally offering her a smile. The twinkle returned to his eyes.

"Hmm," she said, gazing sidelong, "maybe you should tell me. Unless, of course, you don't want to marry me. And if that's the case, then I think you should stop caressing my neck and step away."

"You are the most aggravating woman I've ever known," he said, bringing his mouth toward hers. But before he kissed her he added, "I'll have to marry you just to keep you from hurting yourself—or me."

Karen's heart soared on wings of delight as Adrik kissed her most passionately. She was in love, and though the future contained many unanswered questions, she knew the answer to the most important question. Did Adrik really love her? The answer was most assuredly yes! And that made all the other uncertainties in her life seem rather unimportant.

Adrik continued to hold her as he trailed kisses across her cheek to the lobe of her ear. "So will you?" he whispered.

Karen giggled, feeling a dozen years younger. "Will I what?" She wanted to hear him ask her properly.

"Will you marry me?" He straightened and let go of her. Stepping back, he locked his gaze with hers. "Will you?"

Karen nodded enthusiastically and threw herself back into his arms. "Yes! Yes! A million times yes!"

CHAPTER TWENTY-FOUR

JACOB BARRINGER MOANED softly as he rolled to his side. Opening his eyes in the fading light, he watched the trees swirl in circles overhead. Whoever or whatever had hit him on the head had done a real good job. Struggling to keep his eyes open, Jacob thought he heard the muffled barking of dogs. Maybe someone could help him. Maybe there was a chance they'd hear his call for help.

Pushing up on his side, Jacob cried out in pain and collapsed against the bank of the river. An icy cold washed over him, and all at once Jacob realized he was partially submerged in water.

By nothing more than sheer will, Jacob struggled to inch himself out of the water. He would freeze to death if he stayed there, and only God knew how long he'd already been there. He touched his aching head and noted that his hand was sticky with blood. Jacob's stomach gave a lurch at the sight.

The sound of the dogs seemed to fade and grow muffled. Jacob strained again to take in his surroundings. Tall spruce stood guardian around him, and jagged rocks lined the river on the opposite shore.

"Where am I?" he wondered aloud. He couldn't remember a thing. He couldn't imagine why he was here at the edge of this river. What river was it?

He heard the dogs again and called out, "Help me!" His voice sounded weak and unnatural. Straining to sit up against the trunk of a nearby tree, Jacob tried again. "Help!" He closed his eyes and thought to pray, but blackness surrounded him and there was nothing more.

When Jacob opened his eyes again, he was surprised to find himself warm and comfortable and inside a room he didn't recognize. He tried to remember what had happened, but his memory failed him. Then after a moment he remembered traveling on the river with a group of companions. He had worked to earn his keep. *Yes!* He thought for a minute, closing his eyes. *I was headed to Dawson for gold. But what happened?*

"So you're awake."

Jacob looked up to find a grizzled old man staring at him from a doorway. "Where am I?"

"Back room of the Mud Dog Saloon," the man said, then spit on the dirt floor. "Found you on the side of the river."

Jacob nodded with a brief recollection of the icy water. "I don't know how I got there."

"Well, I figure you were either coming through the rapids and got thrown overboard, or someone jumped you and left you for dead. Either way, you weren't in good shape."

Jacob reached his hand up to his forehead and felt the knot that seemed to throb with every beat of his heart. "I don't remember what happened, but I thank you for your help." He looked to the old man who seemed no bigger than his own five-foot-six-inch frame. Jacob's father might have called the man wiry. He was skinny but muscled in a way that left Jacob little doubt he could fend for himself.

"So what town is this?" Jacob asked.

"Whitehorse."

Jacob remembered the name. He had been headed to Whitehorse—that much he could remember. But why couldn't he remember what had happened?

"I know I was coming this way," he told the man, "but ... well ..." He shrugged. "Guess I'll never know."

The old man shook his head. "Don't see as it much matters. It's done happened, and you can't very well take it back."

Jacob nodded. "Did I have anything with me? My pack?"

"Nah, you barely had the clothes on your back."

Jacob eased back against the pillow. "Well, I thank you for what you did, mister. I'm beholden."

The man started to leave, then turned back around. "The name is Cec Blackabee. When you get to feeling better, we can talk about you working to pay me back."

————————

Karen put aside her happiness over Adrik in order to concentrate on Leah and Grace. Neither one looked well. "Adrik says we're stopping in Whitehorse. He wants you both to see the doctor."

"Nonsense," Grace replied. "I'm fine. A decent meal or two and I'll be back on my feet."

Leah gave her a solemn nod. "Me too. I don't want to stop now. We'll never get to Dawson before the snow if we don't keep moving. I have to find Jacob." She fell into a fit of coughing that ended with the teen gasping for breath.

"Yes, I can see that you're just fine," Karen replied. "Nevertheless, I promised Adrik I'd heed his wishes."

"Well, that's a first," Grace said, moving to sit beside Miranda.

Karen thought her pallor rather green as they floated down the river on their way to Whitehorse. "Well, now that I've agreed to marry him, he thinks I owe it to him."

Miranda smiled. "I'm so happy that you've found each other. I sometimes despair of ever finding true love."

Grace patted her hand gently. "You will. Never fear. God has a special man out there for you—somewhere."

"That's right," Leah said softly. "Who knows, maybe he'll own a big old gold mine, too."

"It couldn't hurt," Miranda said with a laugh.

"Maybe he'll be European royalty," Grace said, nudging Miranda good-naturedly. The younger woman blushed but said nothing.

Karen smiled. "Well, either way, we're tying up in Whitehorse, and I'm to see you two to the doctor."

"It'll just cost more money," Grace protested. "We've already spent so much of what we started with. The taxes, extra supplies, the boat, and the tramline—it's all taken far more than we'd ever dreamed."

"I know exactly how much it's cost us," Karen answered, "but we're stopping and that's final."

Whitehorse was already a booming town with businesses and riverboats lining her shores. Ferry service was for hire to take you all the way up to Dawson, if you were of a mind to part with your cash. Tents were staked in every conceivable nook and cranny, and saloons and gambling halls abounded.

Karen was almost disappointed to be set again in such civilization. She'd rather come to enjoy the isolated ruggedness of the life they'd been leading.

"Miranda, if you don't mind staying here with Crispin," Adrik said as he came ashore with the others, "I'll escort these ladies to the doctor. We can all go exploring later, but I'd just as soon have someone keeping an eye on the boat. We don't really know much about this territory, and I wouldn't want to see us lose everything now."

"I'd be glad to stay," Miranda replied with a glance toward Crispin. "I'll have Mr. Thibault entertain me with stories of his youth."

Crispin bowed low. "Always a pleasure, ma'am."

Karen grinned and looked at Adrik. "I don't think either one will be too put out with the arrangement."

Grace turned to Adrik, as well. "I really don't need a doctor, but I do think we should have one look at Leah."

Adrik put his arm around Grace's shoulder. "There's no sense in taking any chances. You haven't been feeling well. You might as well see if there's something wrong."

Grace shook her head and looked from Adrik to Karen. "I know what's wrong, and the doctor can't help me. At least not for several months."

Karen eyed her friend curiously. "What are you saying?"

Grace's face reddened. "I'm going to have a baby."

"What!" Karen exclaimed. "Why didn't you say so sooner? How long have you known?"

Adrik looked positively stricken, but Grace reached out to touch his forearm. "I'm sorry for not telling you, but I knew you'd leave me in Dyea, and I couldn't let that happen."

"You mean to tell me you've known about this since then?" Adrik questioned. "You climbed the Chilkoot carrying a child?"

Obviously uncomfortable with the personal nature of the conversation, she could only nod. Karen, scarcely able to comprehend this information, stepped forward to embrace her friend. The news left her completely speechless, as it did the others.

Karen looked past Grace to Adrik's accusing expression. Shaking her head, she whispered, "I swear I didn't know."

Grace pulled away. "Look, I know this is a shock, but there's only a couple of weeks left at most and then we'll be to Dawson City."

"But that's just the start of it," Adrik replied. He brushed back his dark hair and looked to the sky.

"I can't believe Peter just ran off and left you there, knowing you were going to have his child."

"He didn't know," Grace replied, tears coming to her eyes. "I barely knew the truth of it myself. I fully intended to tell him, but he never came back."

At this, Miranda rushed forward to take Grace in her arms. "Oh, poor dear. Never worry. We'll make a way. I'll be there to help you through this."

Karen felt a twinge of jealousy at the way Miranda seemed to cut in on her friendship. She had been like a mother to Grace for over ten years. If anyone would see Grace through this, Karen intended for it to be her own duty.

"We will all help you, Grace. But more importantly, we need to find Peter. He must be told about his coming child."

Leah began to cough. She'd said nothing up until that time, but the fitful spell brought all attention to her. Adrik put his hand on Karen's shoulder. "I'd suggest we get Leah to a doctor and discuss this matter with Grace upon our return."

Grace nodded. "Yes, please. Get Leah some medicine and then come back and we'll talk. I'll stay here with Miranda. You'll see, I'll be just fine."

Karen hesitated. She didn't like being dismissed from her friend's side. Nevertheless, as Leah's guardian, she had to see to her responsibilities. Looking to Adrik, she saw the deep concern in his expression.

"Come along, then." She reached out to pull Leah to her side. "We'll be back as soon as we can."

Adrik couldn't believe the turn his life had taken. He would never have seen himself playing escort to a boatload of women. Only Crispin's presence kept him from being completely befuddled. And now . . . now he had to face the responsibility of a pregnant woman being among their group. What more would he endure before the trip was finished?

God, he prayed as he wandered the street outside the doctor's tent, *I don't know what you have planned, but it sure looks like quite a confusing load. I find a woman to marry, even though I never figured to be marrying. I find myself taking on the care of not only a wife, but a young girl—and her brother—if we ever find him.*

He paused and looked back toward the river. *It wasn't what I planned on.* The turmoil settled sourly in his stomach. *And now this. Grace Colton is going to have a baby. What more can be heaped upon us?*

The real fear in his soul, however, had to do with their rapidly depleting finances. He was almost afraid to check the ledgers and see what exactly they had left. They'd all been good to pool their money and supplies, but there was only so much to go around. He'd hate to have to ask Crispin for help—or anyone else, for that matter.

"Oh, there you are!" Karen called as she came from the tent with Leah. "The doctor said her lungs sounded clear, so it isn't pneumonia." The petite girl's blue eyes were as big as saucers against her milk-white face.

"Well, that's good news," he said, forcing a smile for Leah's benefit. "I guess it's sheer orneriness that's making you cough."

Leah smiled, as he'd hoped she would. She leaned toward Adrik, rather embarrassed. "The doctor said I had to drink whiskey."

"What!" Adrik roared without thinking. "What in the world . . ." He saw Karen shaking her head as if to show her disapproval at his reaction. "What is she talking about?" he asked, calming considerably.

"He doesn't have any medicine. At least nothing that isn't laced with opium. I won't have her taking that. It's addictive," Karen answered. "The doctor suggested we give her whiskey instead. Just small amounts to help the cough dissipate."

Adrik calmed. *Of course,* he thought. That made sense. "I'll have to scout out some." He leaned toward Leah and nudged her gently. "You'll be the scandal of us all." She laughed, but this sent her into a fit of coughing once again.

Adrik straightened. "Look, I'll walk you two back to the boat and then go after a bottle."

"We could use some other things, as well."

"Make me a list, then. I'll get whatever I can find."

Adrik left the women safely in Crispin's care before heading back to the main part of town. Crispin and Miranda had already begun to set up camp not far from where the scow was docked. Adrik was glad they'd have a few days to rest and make repairs. The boat was holding up well, but there were places that had been damaged by the journey through Miles Canyon, and this would give him a chance to strengthen and improve their lot before heading back toward the Yukon.

Of course, there was still the matter of dealing with Grace's news, as well as seeing to his own change of matrimonial state. Karen wanted to marry as soon as possible, and it wouldn't surprise him at all if she suggested they wed right there in Whitehorse. Perhaps he should scout out a preacher as well as a bottle.

He tried not to have misgivings. It wasn't for a lack of loving Karen that he felt apprehensive. Facts being what they were, it was probably *because* of his love that he worried about rushing into marriage. After all, he was already facing the responsibility of one pregnant woman. What if he married Karen right away and she found herself in a similar fashion?

Listen to yourself, he chided. *You've lived in this wilderness all your life. You've gone from plenty to poverty and back again. This is a good land with a heap of opportunities. There's no reason to fear raising a family here any more than anywhere else.*

But in his heart, Adrik realized it wasn't his own inabilities, but rather Karen's that worried him. She was city born and raised. Sure, she'd endured an Alaskan winter, but there had always been a harbor and a ship that could take her back to Seattle. There wouldn't be a ship up here. At least not one that could escape the frozen north on a year-round basis. What if she found herself hopelessly unhappy? What if they married and after a time she couldn't bear living in the wilds? Adrik certainly couldn't envision living in a city down south. What would they do then?

There was no time to consider the matter further. The crooked sign of the Mud Dog Saloon caught Adrik's attention. This would be as good a place to start as any. He walked through the open door of the poorly built log cabin and waited a moment for his eyes to adjust to the dark.

"What can I do for you, stranger?"

Adrik looked in the direction of the voice and squinted at the old man. "I came for whiskey. I need a bottle."

"Well, it's not going to come cheap," the man said, reaching down behind the counter. "I only sell the best here." He slammed a small bottle up on the counter.

"It'd better be the best," Adrik said, stalking toward the bar. "I have a sick child who needs it."

The man shrugged. "Don't much matter to me one way or the other. It'll cost you ten dollars for a pint."

Adrik knew the man could probably name any price and get it. Without the promise of regular supplies, they were definitely at the mercy of whoever had the goods this far north. Still, there were other saloons in the town. Maybe he should check them out instead. He glanced at the door.

"Maybe I'll try elsewhere," Adrik said, looking back to see how his words had affected the clerk. Bartering was nothing new to the north, and Adrik was better at it than most. Problem was, he really had no desire to spend the rest of his day looking for a good deal.

The man spit again and scratched his chest. Adrik could see the ragged state of his long underwear beneath his thin flannel shirt. Apparently his profits didn't extend toward replenishing his wardrobe. Figuring the old man wouldn't budge on his price, Adrik started for the door.

The older man muttered under his breath, then said, "Well, seein's how this is for medicinal purposes and all, maybe I could give you my special rate. Eight dollars."

The negotiations were open. Adrik smiled. Perhaps they could reach a compromise. Reluctantly he pulled out the money and put it on the bar.

"Six," Adrik said firmly. "I still have food to buy."

The old man looked at the money, then back to Adrik. "Well ... I suppose . . ." He reached for the money and quickly shoved it in his pocket.

Adrik took the bottle and pocketed it in turn. He'd just tipped his hat when he heard a familiar voice ask, "Where you want these, Cec?"

Adrik turned on his heel, unable to believe his eyes. "Jacob?"

The boy's eyes positively lit up. He put the tray of glasses on the counter and ran to Adrik. "I can't believe it's you!"

The two men embraced and pounded each other's backs as though they'd been parted for years instead of months.

"You're as thin as a rail," Adrik said as Jacob stepped back.

"Oh, it's been bad. Had the typhoid in Bennett. Then I finally got started for Dawson again and met with a bad end. Cec here found me half dead."

"More like three-quarters dead," the old man said, spitting to one side.

"What happened?" Adrik asked.

"Well, as best as Cec can figure out, the men I was traveling with did me in. They took my gear and left me for dead. Either that or I fell out of the boat when we came through the rapids, but if that were the case, I would've had my watch and money in my pocket. It was all gone when Cec found me."

Adrik eyed the codger suspiciously. "I can well imagine."

"Weren't my doin', mister, so stop lookin' at me like I sunk the *Maine*."

Adrik nodded. "Well, I'm grateful you found him. His guardian is going to be mighty glad to know he's safe." He turned back to Jacob. "Get your gear—or whatever you have coming to you. We're docked on the north side."

"Whoa, now," Cec called out. "You can't just up and take the boy. He owes me."

Adrik forced his temper to remain under control. He nudged Jacob in the direction he'd just come. "Get your things." Jacob nodded and disappeared while Adrik walked back to the counter where Cec stood. "Just how much do you figure the boy owes you?"

"Well, I did save his life. And I've been feedin' him all this time. Oh, and I gave him a change of clothes."

"How much?"

He could see the old man nervously trying to figure out how much he could wheedle out of Adrik. Finally, Adrik had more than he was going to take. He reached into his pocket and pulled out several bills. "Here. I don't imagine it was more than this, and if it was, we can take it up with the law."

The old man shook his head and snatched the money. "No, this'll be just fine."

"I thought it might."

Jacob came back carrying a rolled-up knot of clothes. "I'm ready. Who'd you travel with, Adrik?"

Adrik waited until they were outside and headed back to the boat before answering. "You're going to find this hard to believe, son—after all, I find it hard to believe myself. I've come here with Karen and your sister, as well as Grace Colton and her sister-in-law. Oh, and my friend Crispin Thibault joined us along the way."

"Leah's here?" Jacob asked as if he'd not heard anything else. He stopped and turned in disbelief. Dark half-moons under his eyes were more apparent in the sunlight.

The wind picked at the boy's sandy brown hair, pushing it around just enough to reveal a rather nasty cut at the hairline. Adrik reached out and pushed Jacob's hair back. "Yes, Leah's here, and I think that old man was right. You probably were three-quarters dead with a gash this size."

Jacob pulled away and kept walking. "Don't worry about me none, Adrik. I had a headache for a few days and I bled like all get-out, but I feel fine now. Is Leah all right?"

"She's a bit under the weather, but not too bad off. I came to the saloon for some whiskey. Doc figured it would do her good, help with her cough."

"But she's going to be all right?"

Adrik could read the worry in the boy's eyes. "Why don't you ask her yourself? We're setting up camp just over there. But, Jacob, there's just one thing."

The boy looked to him and stopped in his tracks. "What?"

"I think it might be best if we leave out the part about you being three-quarters dead when we tell Karen about this. She's been worried enough about losing you, and it was all I could do to keep her from coming for you the day after you disappeared. She's here because of you, and it wouldn't do her any good to add more guilt to how she's feeling."

"She's up here because of me?" Jacob asked in disbelief.

Adrik could see it impressed the younger man. So many folks he'd cared about had left him behind, he was probably amazed to learn that someone would actually chase him down. "Yes, she's here because of you. Leah too. There didn't seem to be any reason to stay in Dyea when they were worried over how you were doing."

Jacob bit his lip and looked away. "I won't say a word about the accident."

"Believe me, things will go better for both of us if you don't." Adrik put his arm around the boy and laughed. "You know how Karen can be."

Jacob looked up, wiping a tear from his eye. "She's a real lady, Miss Karen. She's got a good heart."

"That she does, but I feel I should tell you," Adrik said, laughing, "we're going to get married. So don't be getting any ideas about her."

"Married! That's great!"

They were nearly back to the camp by now, and Adrik could see the women helping Crispin set up the second tent. Leah was nowhere in sight, and Adrik figured she was snuggly tucked inside the erected tent.

Karen was busy helping to secure the tent pegs. She worked silently with a small wooden mallet as Crispin adjusted the guy lines. Adrik marveled at her efficiency. She never complained, yet Adrik knew many a time she was spent of strength and hope. Now that she'd managed to regain her faith, Adrik saw her anger fading with each passing day. And as the bitterness left her, a new, stronger woman seemed to emerge. How could he not marry her? He couldn't imagine life without her. He'd become so attached to her these past few months that to let her get away was simply unthinkable.

"Karen," Adrik called. "I have what you've been looking for!"

Karen looked up, and for a moment her face registered nothing but a blank, rather stunned expression. Then realizing the identity of Adrik's traveling companion, she squealed with delight and came running across the short distance.

"Oh, Jacob!" She wrapped herself around the boy, who was nearly as tall as she was. "Oh, you're here. You're safe."

Adrik exchanged a smile with Jacob over Karen's shoulder. "I thought you might want me to bring him back rather than the other things you sent me for. Oh, but I did bring the whiskey."

"Oh, I'm so happy to see you!" Karen exclaimed. She stepped back and held him at arm's length. "Oh, you're so skinny. You must be starving."

"I'm doing all right, Miss Karen. How's Leah?" Jacob asked softly.

"Go see for yourself. She's in the big tent," Karen replied. "Oh, she'll be so happy to see you. This will do wonders for her—much better than any medicine or whiskey."

Jacob took off running, forgetting all about the pack of clothes he'd dropped on the ground.

"Come on," Karen said. She picked up the clothes, then pulled Adrik along. "I want to be there."

Adrik wrapped his arm around Karen's waist and together they walked past Grace, Miranda, and Crispin. Pausing at the open flap, Adrik could see Jacob kneeling beside his sister. He held Leah in his arms as she cried.

Adrik reached for Karen's hand. "Let's give them some time alone."

Karen seemed reluctant but finally picked up her steps. When they were back near the boat, she threw her arms around Adrik and hugged him tightly. "You are the most incredible man in the world," she declared. "I simply love you more and more every day."

Adrik held her tight. "There wasn't much to this one, Miss Pierce. The boy just sort of came to me. I think God had more to do with it than I did."

Karen pulled back and frowned. "Well, if He sends Mr. Colton your way, let me know. We've got one problem solved, but there's that new one to deal with. Grace's baby is due shortly after the New Year, as best we can tell."

Remembering their situation, Adrik felt the weight of his responsibilities falling heavily on his shoulders. "We ought to find a way to get her back to Dyea or Skagway. She could take a boat out and at least return to San Francisco."

"By your own admission, it's too late to turn back. She'd not make it before the snows got heavy and the rivers froze over."

"I know. It was more wishful thinking than anything."

"We'll just figure this out as we go," Karen said softly. "You keep reminding me that God has a plan."

"Yeah, but He doesn't seem exactly eager to share it with me."

⊣ CHAPTER TWENTY-FIVE ⊢

MARTIN PAXTON CRINGED at the sight of the four walls. His office and living quarters were the best money could buy in Skagway, but the walls were closing in on him. The weather had turned foul, and for three days it had rained and snowed off and on. There was little to entertain himself with, and now that he knew for sure Grace Colton had gone north to Dawson City, he was up against a major decision. Should he send someone to fetch her back? Should he go after her himself?

He thumbed through the latest packet of mail and shook his head. The game with Grace was growing rather dull. Still, he had his reasons. Money. At the bottom of everything that motivated Martin Paxton, money—and large sums of it— was generally the object that caught his attention. Grace Colton had the potential to be worth a fortune to him.

Of course, she didn't know that. No one did, short of her father's lawyer in Chicago, and that man had been paid a tidy sum to keep his mouth shut. No, Paxton was the only one who knew Grace stood to inherit a good sum of money upon the day she legally wed. Not even Mrs. Hawkins knew of the arrangement.

Martin himself had only learned the truth of this after Frederick had passed away. And nothing had ever angered him quite so much. It seemed that while Martin was systematically relieving Frederick Hawkins of his fortune, the man had connived to transfer vast sums of money to his daughter. The trust was untouchable—irrevocable. Martin could only suppose that Hawkins had figured Grace to be rid of the marriage agreement between herself and Paxton when she'd fled to the north. He probably assumed he could give his daughter the money, and once Paxton was out of their lives, Hawkins could reclaim his fortune. But he died instead. He died without telling his beloved wife yet another very important fact of his life. The thought of duping the dead man kept Martin going—pressing him to search Grace out. That and his desire to get even with the brat for making him the laughingstock of Chicago.

Even now he could remember the way people had talked about him in the finer dining establishments. More than once he'd taken a table for dinner, only to watch as those around him caught sight of him and began to whisper among themselves. He heard their snickers and knew he was the object of their scorn. Just as he had been as a boy. But no more.

Still, there he stood at a crossroads. He had the ordeal of Colton Shipping to settle, as well as other enterprises that needed his attention. Several of his investments were doing quite poorly, and without his immediate attention, they were sure to go bust. He could chase after Grace or attend to his affairs, but he couldn't do both. Not with any real assurance of success.

Getting up from his desk, Paxton walked to the window and looked down on Broadway Street. Tracks for the train had been routed through the heart of town only months earlier. And thanks to his investment along with others, the Pacific and Arctic Railway and Navigation Company would soon be the only reasonable way to make passage north.

The country had made him a very wealthy man. It should have been enough. It should have been satisfactory knowing that he had ruined the man who had destroyed his mother—that he had left that man's family destitute and miserable. He could probably go on paying Hawkins' lawyer, and Grace would never know of her good fortune. Martin would continue his revenge without Hawkins' widow and daughter ever even knowing it. But the revenge was hollow. Martin knew his mother would have been disappointed, even ashamed of the way he'd conducted himself. She would never have understood—but Hawkins did, and that was what counted. Hawkins had used his mother as a mistress, and just when she needed him most, he had discarded her, never to return again.

Martin could still see his mother day after day looking out the door or window. Watching and waiting for Hawkins' return. After a year had passed, she had begun to fade. The life went out of her in the absence of his love.

Convinced the man had met with great distress or even death, Martin had gone in search of him. It hadn't been difficult to find Hawkins. Everyone in Chicago seemed to know the man—and his family. He could still remember learning the horrible truth. He remembered seeing the grand family all together in their polished surrey. They were traveling to church, as he recalled. All prim and proper—a family.

Hawkins hadn't met with death or illness; he had simply dismissed the Paxtons without so much as a good-bye. Martin's anger started to grow on that day, roaring to life like an unquenchable inferno. Turning from the window, Martin knew the fire had somewhat abated now. There came a time when a plan merited reconsideration. He figured that time had come in the situation with Grace Colton.

He regretted having hurt Ephraim Colton. Martin wasn't, after all, completely without feeling. Still, the man had to understand that what his son had done— what he himself had condoned—did not come without a price. Perhaps the best thing to do was to let things rest for the time and see where Ephraim Colton would take them. Better still, perhaps to avoid the onset of winter, Martin would make his way to San Francisco and offer magnanimously to affect a solution or agreement.

He smiled to himself. He had earned his weight in gold and then some. He could afford to be generous with his mother's only friend. And in doing so, maybe he could even drive the wedge a bit deeper between Colton and his wayward son. If Ephraim agreed to never allow Peter to return to the business, if he cut him completely from his life, then perhaps Martin could see his way clear to returning *Summer Song*. It bore some consideration.

Peter Colton considered Jonas's words on the journey to Skagway. He had thought to force Martin Paxton to deal with him, but Jonas's steady logic kept Peter in check.

"A grizzly bear doesn't much care how you go about reasonin' with him," Jonas had said. *"He only wants one thing, and that's to kill you."*

Paxton would seemingly love nothing more than if Peter would fall over dead. But truth be told, Peter desired the same for Martin Paxton. Funny how all of his worries and problems might simply disappear with the death of one man.

It could be self-defense, Peter reasoned. Then Jonas's words of warning would come back to haunt him.

"If you go gettin' yourself in trouble with the law, you'll never see that pretty wife of yours again."

No doubt the man was right. So instead of exacting revenge, Peter would simply mail the letter he'd labored over so diligently. He had written to his parents and Miranda and begged their forgiveness. He wanted—needed—them to understand that he'd never intended to let things get so carried away. He'd hurt them. He knew that much. He could only pray they might forgive him.

Forgiveness. It was a hard word for Peter. Grace had talked about it so often that the word left a bitter taste in his mouth. But that had been before. Before his father's heart attack and Grace's disappearance. And it had been before Peter had opened his mind and heart to hear what a godly man like Jonas had to say.

Peter posted the letter, hoping it might reach his folks with great speed. He needed to hear from them—to know that all was forgiven and that they were all right. Leaving the letter behind, Peter took himself to the Second Hand Store down the street. Something had been on his mind since Jonas had first started talking to him about letting go of the past.

"Do you have any wedding rings?" he asked the clerk behind the counter.

"We've got a couple," the man said with a grin. "Find yourself a little gal to marry, did you?"

"I'm already married," Peter replied. "Just never got around to finding the ring."

The man chuckled. "Well, here's what I've got." He plopped down two rings. "Don't know what you had in mind, but I got these rings off a wealthy woman who was bartering for gear."

Peter hadn't thought of the rings belonging to someone else. He really wanted Grace to have her own brand-new ring. "Don't you have something . . . well . . . something not used?"

The man frowned. "This is a used goods store."

Peter nodded. "Do you suppose anyone else in town has rings?"

The man shrugged. "I wouldn't doubt it. There are some jewelers working down on Fourth Street. Making all sorts of doodads and such out of gold nuggets. You might get them fellows to make you a ring."

Peter thought it just might be exactly what he needed. Thanking the man, he made his way to the jeweler and posed his question.

"I just need a simple wedding band," Peter told the man.

"Do you know the lady's ring size?"

Peter's heart sank. "No."

"She a big gal or little?"

"Oh, she's small. Very small. Why, her hand is quite tiny in mine." Peter held up his hand to demonstrate.

The jeweler slipped into the back and returned with a plain gold band. The small circle seemed to gleam with a life of its own. "That's perfect," Peter declared, hoping it would be the right size.

"It should fit, if she's as small as you say. That'll be a dollar and thirty cents."

Peter put the money on the counter and pocketed the ring. "Thanks."

He drew the ring out once he was headed back to camp. Holding it up to see it in the sun, Peter thought of Grace and how he should have given her a wedding band a long time ago. Why had he put it off? Maybe his actions had caused her to think he was less than serious about their marriage, but that was far from the truth.

Peter loved his wife. He loved her more than life, and it hurt to think she no longer cared for him. After all, if she loved him, why hadn't she waited for him? Or at least left him a note to let him know where she'd be?

He wondered if Grace was really with Paxton. It didn't make sense for her to seek his help, but she *had* accompanied Peter's father to see him. *Perhaps the real problem is that I don't know her very well,* he thought. She had the loveliest brown eyes in the country, and her voice was soft and gentle—warming his heart just with the memory. But those were outward qualities. Peter needed to know her heart.

Rubbing his finger over the ring, Peter's soul cried out within him. *Oh, please let me find her.*

––––––––––

Jonas had supper on the stove when Peter got back to their tent. They had thrown their lots together, and with the snow collecting in the passes, the railroad's progress was slowing down. There were rumors that the men would all be laid off and that progress wouldn't resume until spring. Peter had no idea of what he might do in the meantime.

"So'd you get that letter posted?" Jonas asked, wiping his hands against his pants.

"I did. I also did something else I should have done a long time ago."

"What's that?" the man eyed him as if trying to guess his answer.

"I bought Grace a wedding ring. Now if I can just find her."

"The good Lord is in the business of finding the lost. You might want to ask Him," Jonas stated. Then, without waiting for further comment, he turned back to the stove. "I've got beans and corn bread if you're of a mind to eat with me."

"I'm starved," Peter replied, taking off his coat. He slipped the ring from his coat pocket to his pants pocket and grabbed a tin plate. Peter dished up beans and threw a big hunk of corn bread into the tin as well. "You suppose they'll close down the line?"

Jonas joined him at the table with his own plate of food. "They just might. It wouldn't be that strange to have them wait until warmer weather."

Peter feared Jonas was probably right. He stared at his plate for a moment, then looked at Jonas. "Are you going to pray?"

The older man grinned. "I thought maybe it was about time you did."

"You may be right at that," Peter answered, his tone quite serious. "But I think I'll require a teacher to show me how."

"Don't know as I've ever taught anything of such value before," Jonas said. "But I'm game to try."

CHAPTER TWENTY-SIX

A CROWD OF WELL-WISHERS gathered along the banks of the Yukon River in Whitehorse the next morning. Anxious for any excuse to break the routine, those who had settled permanently in the town seemed game for a party. Hearing about Adrik and Karen's impromptu wedding gave them the perfect reason to celebrate. Even those who were making their way north to the goldfields paused long enough to make certain the gathering wasn't the call to another, closer, gold strike.

The day was cold, much colder than it had been, and the threat of snow was in the air. The crowd was tense in anticipation of the winter freeze to come. Most of the sourdoughs understood the severe contrasts of this land and took the changing weather seriously. The cheechakos, however, were less concerned. They had braved the cold in their hometowns. They knew what it was to shovel a bit of snow or hunker down through a blowing blizzard. The sourdoughs laughed as they listened to the newcomers' comments; even Karen had to chuckle at their preconceived notions.

But at this moment Karen's mind was far from the comments of her neighbors. She stood in a tight-knit group of three: herself, Adrik, and a preacher who seemed happy to marry someone instead of bury them.

Nervous at the very idea of what she was undertaking, Karen twisted a handkerchief in her hands during the entire ceremony. She loved Adrik. She knew that without any doubt, but there was that nagging feeling that perhaps they should have waited. They really didn't know each other all that well, and Karen was still trying hard to figure out what her future might hold. Of course, perhaps Adrik *was* her future. It was possible that God wanted nothing more of her than to keep company with this good man and be a friend—even a teacher—to the people he loved so much. The people her parents had loved, as well.

It wasn't until the preacher asked if Adrik had a ring that Karen stopped trying to second-guess her tomorrows. And then, it was only because Adrik took hold of her hand.

"With this ring, I thee wed," Adrik said in a low but firm voice.

Karen gazed up into his dark eyes and felt her breath catch in her throat. He was clean-shaven, with exception to his mustache, which had been neatly trimmed. The ragged edges of his brown-black hair had been cut in an orderly fashion that Karen longed to reach up and touch. His rugged outdoor looks appealed to her in a way that the Martin Paxtons and Crispin Thibaults of the world never would. He was a man of action. A man who knew what he wanted and knew how to go about getting it. She supposed it had been that way with his desire to marry her. He simply had decided on her heart and refused to stop until it belonged, in whole, to him.

He lifted her hand to his lips and kissed her finger where the gleaming gold band rested. "For now and all time, Mrs. Ivankov."

Karen swallowed hard and looked at the ring. The symbol of their never-ending love—the symbol of forever.

"You may now kiss your bride," the preacher said with great gusto and enthusiasm. The crowd cheered as Karen lifted her face to Adrik's gaze.

Tenderly, Adrik wrapped her in his embrace. Karen felt the warmth of his body against her own. She was married! She, who had thought herself to be a spinster, now kissed her husband.

Adrik seemed in no hurry to end the kiss. He pulled her tighter, closer, and Karen longed for the moment to go on and on. She didn't even mind that she was the focus of so much attention. Her joy overcame any concern of what others might think.

When they finally did pull away, ruddy in the face and well aware of their crowd of well-wishers, Karen managed to catch Grace's expression. She seemed sad, almost tearful. Karen wondered if she were contemplating her own rushed wedding. Grace had married in the fear and horror of Martin Paxton's threat. Did she regret it?

Someone began playing a fiddle, and it wasn't but a moment before half a dozen other instruments joined in. Impromptu dancing broke out even while one by one people came forward—most complete strangers—to wish Karen and Adrik well on their day. Many came with a gift, usually giving the couple a few bits or as much as a dollar to start them on their way. Karen thought their generosity very touching. Some of these people were struggling and suffering to make it north before winter. Others were fighting to prepare for a winter of isolation. Reckless charity was not a luxury these people could afford.

When Karen finally had a chance to slip away and find Grace, her young friend had already retired to their tent. She could see that Grace had been crying, and for once she was rather at a loss for words. Not so Grace.

"I married Peter for all the wrong reasons," Grace said softly. "I thought I needed to help God. I didn't realize what I was doing."

Karen overturned a packing crate and sat down on it. "You did what seemed best. What we all thought best."

"But it wasn't right. There were too many crucial differences between us, and I knew that. I knew Peter hated talk of the Bible and of my faith. I knew it was a source of contention between us." She looked up, her brown eyes red-rimmed from her tears. "I dishonored God by marrying a man who had no respect for Him. Now I'm bearing the punishment of that."

"No, Grace," Karen said, reaching out to take hold of her hand. "Maybe you are enduring the consequences, but I don't believe God is punishing you. We are only human. We are fearful and weak. We make choices that aren't always God directed, but we do what we can—what we must.

"God is a loving, merciful God. I know that, even though I wanted to forget it or, better still, deny it. When Aunt Doris died, after I'd already lost Father and Mother, I felt so deserted. You were gone and I was very much alone. You had been my sole companion for over ten years. You were like a daughter and sister and friend all wrapped up in one person. But when you went away, I found an emptiness bigger than any I had ever known—even with my parents."

Grace clung to her hand. "I missed you terribly after I'd gone. I loved Peter most dearly, but he was often too busy for me. Then there was the matter of our differences." She sighed. "Oh, Karen, every time the issue of God and His love for us and our need for Him came up, Peter simply could not bear my company. I became most undesirable to my own husband."

"Apparently you weren't too undesirable," Karen said, trying hard to make Grace's mood lighter. "You are carrying his child."

"Don't remind me," Grace replied. She looked away as if ashamed. "I know that only God says when a soul lives or dies, but I don't understand why He would give this union a child. How very disappointed He must be in me."

"Nonsense," Karen answered. "Where is that strength of character I saw when you faced Martin Paxton in Dyea? I could hardly believe it. The Spirit of the Lord simply seemed to overcome you and fill that entire room. I felt almost as if I were standing on holy ground."

"I try not to battle this on my own," Grace said. "I know from everything you've taught me and from all that God has shown me in Scripture that He has a plan in all of this. That He has never turned away from me or left me to fight this alone. I know that He will give me the strength to endure whatever I must, but ..."

"But what?" Karen asked, confused by Grace's words.

Grace looked up, her eyes flooding with tears once again. "I love my husband. I love Peter more than life, and if he has no desire to be my mate, then I might as well die. This child, too."

A shudder coursed through Karen. She had never heard her friend talk in such a way. It frightened her terribly. "Don't say that," she admonished. "I would be overwhelmed with grief if you were to die."

"I'm sorry I've ruined your wedding day," Grace murmured before breaking into sobs. She buried her face in her hands and cried softly.

Karen drew Grace into her arms. "You haven't ruined anything."

Holding Grace while she cried, Karen began to pray unselfishly for God to intercede. *I know I've been far too compelled to worry about myself and my feelings,* she told God. *I know that I've been a difficult and disobedient daughter, but, Father, this child needs your touch. She needs to feel that you have not forsaken her because of her decision to marry. Please, Father, please show her that you are with her.*

Grace rested her head against Karen's shoulder for a moment, her tears abating. "I feel so foolish."

"Why?"

She lifted her head and squared her shoulders. "I feel foolish because I know better than to give in to these feelings. You taught me that God is with me through the bad and the good. I know He is faithful."

"It doesn't mean that we won't have our moments of weakness. As I said before, we're only human. Look at how I acted. I knew it was wrong to blame God for the bad in my life. I knew it was wrong to bear Him, who loved me so much, a grudge." Karen felt her chest tighten. She hadn't really thought of her relationship with God as the same as that of her earthly father. Had she acted that way with her earthly father, it would have surely broken his heart and left him in utter despair. Was that how it was for God? Did He weep when His children called Him unjust?

"Look," Karen continued, "we'll pen a letter to Peter. We'll send it on the first available post. There won't be time for him to get north before the winter freeze, so that much can't be helped. I'll see you through this, however. Adrik and I will make a home for you as long as you need it. When the baby comes, we'll help you through that, as well. Then in the spring, we'll get you home to Peter."

Grace shook her head. "But what if he doesn't want me home? And maybe worse yet, what if he does, but his heart is still bitter toward God? Maybe it's best that we remain separated."

Karen considered that thought for a moment. "Perhaps you married for the wrong reasons, Grace, but I believe God will use you and your marriage to reach Peter. I believe He already has. Let's not worry about the future. We have plenty to concern ourselves with in the here and now." She smiled and gently touched Grace's face. "You're going to be a mother. That is a precious and most wonderful thing. And it's a gift from God."

Those words suddenly shot arrows of hope through Karen's heart. Yes, a baby was a gift from God. The psalmist said as much. "Oh, Grace, I know God is with you."

Karen got up and went to where she had put her father's Bible. Turning to Psalm 127, she found the verse she was looking for. "Here, see for yourself." She handed the Bible to Grace. "Read verse three."

Grace did so. " 'Lo, children are an heritage of the Lord: and the fruit of the womb is his reward.' "

"God hasn't deserted you, Grace. He's rewarded you for your faithful love and desire to know Him better."

"But what of you?" Grace replied, looking up from the Bible. "You are a wonderful woman, and in spite of your difficult times, you have been faithful. Why did God not bless you years ago with a husband and children of your own? What of the barren woman? Does God not love her equally as much if she is seeking His heart, as well?"

"Of course God loves her, as well. Of course He loves me. It doesn't say that children are the only reward God gives. God is a god of infinite ability. His rewards are many, as are His mercies. Do not limit the Almighty God of the universe," Karen said, almost laughing. Her own heart was lighter than it had been since Doris had gone home to God. *I have limited you, Father. How like you to use my own student to reteach me a valuable lesson.*

"I know you're right," Grace replied. She reached up and dried her cheeks and eyes. "But, Karen, if Peter doesn't love God—if he still rejects the idea of accepting God into his life—I don't know what I will do. I cannot stand by and let him subject both the child and me to further tirades. I will raise this baby to love God first and foremost."

"Then we have only one choice," Karen replied with great confidence. "We must pray and ask God to bring Peter into His number." Karen got up and smoothed her blue wool skirt. "Adrik says we're to break camp and leave within the hour. I don't think they'll have much luck of it with us in here. What say I help you pack?"

"But this is your wedding day," Grace protested, getting to her feet. "You shouldn't have to work or travel. You should have a wonderful night alone with your husband."

Karen laughed. "And where would we have that? Out under the trees? We have two tents, one for the men and one for the women. There are now four women and three men since Jacob has come along."

"Then I think we should get another tent," Grace announced rather matter-of-factly.

"Well, they don't grow on trees around here. And even if they did, someone probably would have already cut down the tree to make a home or fuel a steamer."

Grace smiled and nodded. "Maybe I should ask around and see if there is anything to be done about it."

"Oh, don't bother. There's precious little time as it is. If we're not ready to go when Adrik gives the call, it won't matter that we've just wed. He'll leave me here just to teach me a lesson about heeding his directions."

Grace grew very serious. "He's a good man, Karen. I'm so pleased that God put you two together. And I know He'll give you children and great happiness."

"I know He will, too."

"I'm so glad you agreed to walk with me," Crispin told Miranda as they left the crowd and headed toward a nearby stand of spruce.

Miranda experienced both a sensation of danger and excitement as Crispin paused and looked with great longing into her eyes.

"You know that I've completely lost my heart to you, Miss Colton," Crispin said with great flair. "You are the most incredible woman."

Miranda, unfamiliar with flirtatious encounters, looked away quickly. "You shouldn't say such things. It isn't proper."

"And why not? It's true. This country throws off convention with great abandonment. Surely you won't allow yourself to be steeped in prim and proper Victorian rhetoric when my heart is overflowing with the need to tell you how I feel."

Miranda couldn't help but smile at his words. She looked up to find his dark eyes searching her own. He looked for all the world as if he might very well perish if she refused to give him the answer he desired.

"I am cautious," she replied. "Cautious because it bodes well to be so. Not because of any presupposed rules of society. Healthy fear keeps one from peril."

He grinned at her rather roguishly. "Do you fear me, Miranda?"

"I'm not certain that fear is the proper word," she answered, a charge of electricity stealing up her spine. He knew what she was feeling, of this Miranda was certain. Furthermore, he very much seemed to be enjoying her vulnerability.

When he stepped toward her, Miranda steadied her shaking knees and tried to appear as if clandestine moments in quiet woods were nothing out of the ordinary.

When he reached out and took her face in his hands, Miranda thought she might very well stop breathing. Forcing herself to maintain eye contact, she was unprepared for the kiss he pressed upon her lips. She realized all at once she was staring at his closed eyes, but soon she realized nothing at all. Nothing save the warm, delightful feel of his hands caressing her face and his mouth on hers.

"Say you love me," he whispered hoarsely. He pulled away only far enough to allow her a full view of his beautiful face.

"I scarcely know you," Miranda said, her breath ragged. Her pulse raced so wildly she thought she might actually faint.

"Then get to know me," he murmured and began planting gentle kisses upon her cheeks and forehead. "For I am in love with you, Miranda Colton. I have loved you from the first moment I laid eyes on you."

Miranda forced herself to back up, leaving the warmth of his touch. "Crispin, I'm not a fast woman. I do not play loose with any man. Perhaps I've given you the wrong idea by walking here with you today. Worse yet, by letting you kiss me."

He looked hurt, almost as if she'd slapped him. "So you are rejecting my love?"

Very slowly, Miranda shook her head. "Not at all. Merely suggesting we take it slowly. I would enjoy knowing you better, understanding your aspirations for the future. I would like to hear about your family and know what things you value most in life. I would like to know who you are. Most of the time on the trail you were busy packing goods or building the boat. I feel I know very little about you."

His expression softened, and she could see his delightful nature return. "I will spare no detail. I will keep nothing from your scrutiny. Ask me anything. Demand the moon—only promise me that you might one day love me."

Miranda smiled. "I will make no promises, but neither will I demand the moon. Let us keep company and see where our hearts lead us from there."

Adrik loaded the last of their supplies onto the scow while Jacob finished securing the tent on board. Adrik had built in special rings on the deck to which they could stretch out the base of the dwelling. This, along with the canvas ties he'd had the women sew to the tent, allowed for the structure to ride rather securely.

He worked up a sweat restacking their supplies. Jacob was a good extra hand to have on board, in spite of his thin, almost frail, appearance. Adrik knew Karen would have him fattened up in no time—at least if their food held out, she would. He had already decided they would need to start some serious fishing and hunting as they made their way to Dawson. Fish would certainly be plentiful, and Adrik was quite capable of putting together a smoker to preserve the fish for some time to come. The forests away from the rush of the gold stampede were no doubt full of wildlife. Stopping long enough to spend a day hunting might pay off in the long run. They could easily butcher the meat and use the river's steadily dropping temperature to keep it cold.

What he tried not to think about was how much he wanted to be alone with Karen. He ached to hold her—to share their wedding day isolated from the rest of the world. But it wasn't to be. They couldn't even have a decent wedding night alone together.

"We're all ready here," Jacob announced, coming up behind Adrik. "Shall I bring everyone aboard?"

Adrik glanced around to make certain everything was in its place. "Yeah, looks like we'd better get a move on. I figure we'll have at least ten good hours of light. I'd like to make it to the other side of Lake Laberge, but I'm not holding my breath. That's at least sixty miles. We'd have to have perfect winds and no obstacles to cross that distance."

Jacob looked upward. "It looks like a fair sky."

Adrik followed his gaze. "Let's just hope it stays that way."

┤ C H A P T E R   T W E N T Y - S E V E N ├

"THERE'S A LETTER for you," Jonas said, coming into the small cabin. He plopped down a cloth bundle, then reached back to close the door.

Peter had been working to build up a fire in the stove, but this news left him far too excited to worry about the growing cold. "Is it from Grace?" He picked up the bundle and began to explore the contents.

"Can't say." Jonas pulled off his fur cap and hung it on a peg. "I will tell you this much." His voice came to an abrupt halt.

Peter paused and looked up at the older man. "What?"

Jonas shrugged out of his coat and tossed it over the cap. Turning, he eyed Peter quite seriously. "There's talk that Martin Paxton is leaving town."

"Who told you this?"

"When I was over to the railway office, I heard that he was planning to head south before winter got too hard. Ain't recollectin' who exactly told it, but he sounded like a knowledgeable fellow."

"If he's leaving, perhaps Grace is leaving with him," Peter said, leaning back in complete dejection. "Maybe I should just hide out and follow him around."

"Why don't you give a look-see and read that letter first? Maybe it's from Grace," Jonas suggested.

But the letter wasn't from Grace. It was nearly as good, however. Peter's mother had penned a lengthy note full of information and good news. Peter's father was on the mend, and Amelia Colton predicted it would only be a few days before he was out of bed. Even from his bed, Ephraim Colton had hired a good family friend to see to the legal matters of Paxton's illegal action. Amelia again optimistically predicted that God would intercede on their behalf and let justice be done.

Peter didn't resent his mother's comment about God. In fact, over the passing weeks with Jonas, he'd taken on a whole new attitude toward such matters. After all, he had sunk down as far as he cared to go. Oh, he knew others had sunk further—sometimes giving themselves over to drinking and even crime. But for Peter, this lack of self-confidence and feeling that nothing was within his control was close to the lowest rung on his ladder. The last rung he reserved for the effects of Grace's absence.

"So who's it from?" Jonas questioned. He stood over the stove with the ingredients for their supper of oatmeal.

"It's from my mother. She says my father is much improved." Peter read on before speaking again. "She talks of being anxious to hear from Grace and Miranda." He looked up. "That must mean they are together. But Paxton said he knew nothing of my sister."

Jonas shrugged. "Don't 'spect you can trust that critter to tell the truth."

Peter nodded. Perhaps he had given Paxton's words too much credence. "She goes on to say that she prays I will restore my marriage. She wants me to stop being willful and prideful and seek Grace out for forgiveness. Then her heart's desire is that I would bring Grace home and settle down in San Francisco with them—to build a new future."

"Sounds like a good idea."

Peter put the letter down. "It sounds like a wonderful idea, but Grace is nowhere to be found. Even if she were, she'd have nothing to do with me. I hurt her more deeply than even Paxton did."

"Son, you keep comin' up with excuses as to why you can't fix this problem. Truth is, you can't fix it no matter the excuse or the solution. Some things are only resolved through prayer and the good Lord's divine meddling." Jonas grinned.

"But I don't know what to do," Peter admitted. He looked at the letter, then folded it up. "I don't know how to find her, when I can't even find the right road for myself. I'm lost."

Jonas stirred the pot of boiling oats and nodded. "At least you can see that much. Some folks take forever to see that. They just sort of wander in circles most all their life."

Peter knew he had nothing left to lose. The most important elements of his life were gone: his family, his business . . . Grace. He'd let pride and arrogance dictate his path, and both had served him poorly.

"What do I have to do, Jonas?"

The older man pulled the oats from the stove and plopped the pan down on the table in front of Peter. "You have to repent of doing things your way instead of God's way."

Peter met his friend's serious gaze. "Is that all?"

"Nope. You have to be willin' to accept that you're lost without Jesus. You have to accept that He died to save you."

"Save me from what?" Peter questioned.

Jonas laughed. "From sin. From the devil. From yourself."

Peter wanted to believe it was true. After all, he needed saving. If he let things go along as they had been, he might very well lose hope and give up. Then he'd never see Grace again—or his family.

"I'm as lost as a man can be," Peter finally said. His voice was low, almost a whisper. "I can believe that Jesus died, although that He would die for me is a hard stretch."

"More important, Peter, He lives for you. Jesus rose from the grave, and that's the part that makes His gift special. Ain't no simple matter of going to the death. Folks have done that for folks as far back as there have been friends. What makes Jesus' love for us different is that He not only died in our place, He rose again to show us that with Him we don't need to fear death. Death ain't the end of things."

Peter struggled against his old way of thought. To believe in the need for a savior—to believe and accept Jesus for himself—went against all the things he'd steeped his life in. He had built his world on a foundation that suggested he, Peter Colton, could accomplish anything. And now that foundation was crumbling around him.

"I want to believe, Jonas. I really do," Peter said, tears coming to his eyes. "Do you suppose God knows how hard this is for me?"

Jonas put his hand on Peter's shoulder. "He knows, son. He knows your heart, and He'll give you the strength to see this through. If your heart is willing, then all you need to do is pray and ask Him to forgive and save you."

Peter drew a deep breath and wiped his tears with the back of his hand. "I'll do it. I can't bear the mess I've made of things. His way would have to be better than my own."

Jonas smiled. "Then let's pray."

"Grace, how are you feeling?" Miranda questioned. Having seen that everyone else was busy at various tasks on the boat, she had crept into the tent to find her sister-in-law alone.

Grace sat up on the cot Adrik had fashioned for her and smiled. "I'm fine. Truly. I'm just a little spent."

Miranda pulled a crate over and sat down by Grace. "Why didn't you tell me about the baby?"

Grace smiled sadly. "I didn't want anyone to know. Not you or even Peter. I think at first I didn't even want to admit it to myself."

"But why? I know you love my brother. Don't you want children?"

Grace bowed her head and looked at her hands. "I would love nothing more than a house filled with the laughter and joy of children. But, Miranda, I can't offer this child a happy home—much less a dwelling to live in. Your brother made it clear that I wasn't welcome in his life."

"But that was before. Once he knows about the baby, he'll forget about the past and change his ways. He'll want you back."

"That's what I'm afraid of," Grace said, lifting her head.

Miranda could read the pain in her sister-in-law's eyes. "I don't understand."

Grace reached out and took hold of Miranda's hand. "I don't want Peter coming back out of obligation. I want him to come back because he loves me."

"Sometimes," Miranda began, "obligation is also important. Maybe Peter needs a dose of obligation."

"And maybe I should be less romantic in my notions," Grace replied.

"Perhaps. And that brings me to the other reason I've sought you out."

"Pray tell?"

Miranda felt her cheeks grow hot as she remembered Crispin's kiss. "I wanted to talk to you about Crispin Thibault." She lowered her voice. "He has shown, with great dramatic flair, that he's taken a liking to me. In fact, he calls it love, but I fail to see how that can possibly be the truth of it."

"Why?"

"Because we've only known each other a few short months."

"Yes," Grace agreed, "but our adversity has certainly made it seem longer."

Miranda shook her head. "He tells me he has loved me since the first moment. He kissed me," she said rather abruptly. "He kissed me, and it warmed me through and through. Still, I cannot say that I love him."

"Perhaps you should give it time," Grace replied. "I'm a poor teacher in such matters, but I know that had Peter and I more time, we might have given more consideration to our like interests. If Crispin has no interest in what you hold dear—God and the Bible—then you should definitely beware of losing your heart. After all, look what that has done to me."

"I've never heard him voice beliefs of one kind or another," Miranda said thoughtfully. "Perhaps that's where I should start. I'll ask him when the opportunity arises."

"Unless he shares your heart for God, Miranda, I fear you will never know a moment's true joy or peace."

Grace's words stuck in Miranda's heart long after their conversation. The winds had failed, and the party was forced to make for the shore of Lake Laberge before nightfall. Miranda helped to gather firewood and thought on her sister-in-law's counsel. Crispin's love of life had drawn her to him, there was no doubt of that. As had his splendid appearance and attentive nature. Still, Miranda knew very little about the man. He spoke of family and of childhood memories. He spoke of travels around the world and of the people he'd met. Miranda couldn't recall any stories related to past love affairs. If he'd shared his heart with any woman prior to Miranda, he gave no inkling of it.

When Miranda dumped a small armload of branches and kindling beside the fire, Jacob Barringer looked up at her with a smile. "I think we have enough for a while."

He was already busy preparing their food, and Miranda thought it rather odd that he should be about the chores of supper. "I can help if you like," she offered.

"That's okay. I'm pretty good at this. My pa thought it was important for me to learn, and it's served me well." He went back to preparing the fish Adrik had managed to catch. Miranda didn't recognize the type of fish, but there were two rather large ones—surely enough to feed them all. She could hear her stomach growling in anticipation.

Seeing that Leah and Karen were putting the finishing touches on the land tent, Miranda thought to offer her help. Then Crispin came into view. He carried a makeshift fishing pole and was headed down the rocky bank. Drawing a deep breath, Miranda decided to follow behind. *Perhaps I can engage him in conversation,* she thought. *I need to know more about him before I let myself get carried away.* Whispering a prayer, she slipped past Karen and Leah without a word and made her way in the direction Crispin had taken.

He walked a considerable distance from their camp, and when he seemed satisfied with the setting, he paused only long enough to bait the hook. Miranda had no idea what he was using for bait, but she took the moment as an opportunity to call to him.

"Mind if I join you?"

He looked up with an expression of pure delight. "I could never mind finding myself in the company of the most beautiful woman in the world."

Miranda shook her head. "I do not know this woman, but perhaps you will accept my company instead."

He smiled and gave her a sweeping bow. "You are most welcome here, m'lady."

"Do you mind conversation while you fish? Or are you like my brother, who prefers absolute silence?"

He finished with the hook and cast out the line. "I must say I prefer the conversation and company of a lovely woman. I have never made a good fisher-man, and I'm only here because Adrik bid me do so."

Miranda considered his comment and opened her line of inquiry. "Have there been many women in your life?"

"Oh, positively hundreds," he replied, seemingly unconcerned about such a declaration. "There are over ninety cousins in my lineage. Both my mother and father were from families of a dozen or more children, and all of them were wonderful in reproducing heirs."

"What about women who were not cousins or aunts or sisters?"

He gazed heavenward as the wind blew off the lake and ruffled his black curls. "Are you asking if there has been another lady of love in my life?"

There was a part of Miranda that didn't want to know the answer, but at the same time she knew she needed to know the truth to better understand who he was. "Yes," she finally whispered.

"There were several times when I thought I was madly in love. But they proved false." He looked back to her and smiled.

"How can you be so certain they were false?"

"Why, that, my dear, is quite easy. I recognize them as false in light of the truth. Comparing those ladies and those feelings up against what I have come to feel for you . . . why, they are only pale reminders of days gone by." He stuck the end of his pole in mud and walked to where Miranda stood.

As he drew near, Miranda felt her heart begin to race. She could feel the blood pounding in her ears. There was no denying the feelings he stirred, but Miranda knew she could not rely on feelings alone.

"I know why you're here," he said in a husky tone. "You want the same things I do, only you are young and inexperienced and do not know how to ask."

"That's not true. I'm asking you questions," Miranda countered, suddenly feel-ing very shy and nervous.

He stopped only inches from her. The heavy coat he wore made his shoulders seem much broader. The dusky twilight shadowed his face, but Miranda could still read the passion in his eyes.

As if frozen in place, she did nothing when he reached out to touch her face. His caress felt warm and soothing. He touched her neck and gently rubbed the knotted muscles that betrayed her weariness.

"You must love me," he said softly, almost hypnotically. "You simply must."

Miranda felt the worries and concerns she'd spoken of earlier with Grace dis-appear as he continued to rub her neck. When he slipped his hand behind her neck and pulled her forward to meet his lips, Miranda felt helpless to refuse.

He slanted her head ever so slightly and deepened his kiss. Miranda tried hard to remain calm and in control of her senses, while at the same time her body seemed to have a mind of its own. Crispin continued to kiss her while toying with her waist and gently massaging the small of her back. The rhythm was alluring—hypnotic. Miranda might very well have found herself swept completely under his spell, but he made the mistake of trying to pull her with him to the ground.

"Stop!" she said, pulling back in shock. She didn't know with whom she was more surprised—herself or him. Panting, she looked at him and questioned, "What are you doing?"

"I thought you were showing me how much you cared," he said without alarm. "I thought we were taking advantage of a quiet moment of privacy."

"I came to talk."

"Did you?" he questioned, his voice so smooth and low that it gave Miranda a shiver.

"Yes," she replied. "At least that's what I had thought. I cannot deny the physical attraction, Mr. Thibault, but I hardly think our behavior appropriate. I know very little of you, as I said before. I came here seeking to know more."

He shrugged and walked leisurely back to his fishing pole. "Ah, 'tis my bad fortune. The woman I love has no interest in me."

Miranda took several uncertain steps. "That's not . . . what I said." She stammered over her words, fighting the sudden urge to apologize. But for what? For defending her honor? For keeping an unseemly situation from becoming even more dangerous? Her emotions and logic were completely jumbled.

"So what would you like to know of me?" he questioned, pulling up the line. There was no fish on the end, so he cast it out again and this time bobbed the pole up and down.

"Everything," Miranda said without hesitation.

"Everything?" he asked, looking to her with a grin. "Would you leave me no secrets? No dark shady past to remain forever hidden from view?"

"No, I'd rather know everything up front."

"Starting with what?" He looked back to the lake and seemed completely at ease.

His lackadaisical spirit bolstered Miranda's courage. She studied his profile for a moment, greatly admiring the aristocratic line. Somehow his pose seemed quite regal, as if he were surveying his kingdom from some lofty perch. Thinking of him as a king reminded Miranda of why she'd come here in the first place.

"Mr. Thibault . . . Crispin . . . what are your thoughts . . . your heart toward God?"

He laughed. "Oh, that's easy enough. I have no thoughts or heart toward God. I don't believe in any god. Life is complicated enough by all manner of superstitious nonsense. I know you have your beliefs," he said, turning with a shrug. "It doesn't bother me in the least. Just as Adrik's devotion to such nonsense has never affected our friendship. Let each man be his own dictator."

Miranda was speechless. She could scarcely believe what he was saying. Here was the man she had only moments ago allowed such an intimate moment with denying the very God she served.

"I . . . don't . . . I never . . ." She halted, having no idea how to reply.

Crispin seemed to understand and turned back to the lake. "Give it no thought, my dear. It needn't come between us. I'm perfectly content to allow you to go on with your practices. It doesn't change my regard for you."

Miranda could stand it no longer. "Well, it changes mine for you," she replied and started to go.

"Wait, don't leave. I know you're confused," he called. Once again he abandoned his fishing pole and came to her. He reached out to touch her, but Miranda pulled away. "Don't let this come between us. Why should it bother you that I see no need for such matters? My educational training and life travels have proven to me over and over that there is no such thing as a divine being. And even if, on some remotely distant chance there is, I know He has no interest whatsoever in the daily lives of human beings. I mean, how very audacious of us to presume upon something like that."

"How can you say that?"

He shrugged. "How can I not? I've traveled the world over and experienced many different religions and cultures. Everyone has some notion of spiritual matters. Americans certainly haven't captured the market on it, if that's what you think. Why, I have sat in the presence of many great men who expounded on issues of faith. I believe that such matters are better left to those who need them."

"But we all need Jesus," Miranda said, unfaltering.

He smiled. "My dearest, don't you see? Everyone needs something. You won't hear me say otherwise. Please don't let it come between us that I have different ideas. Perhaps in time you will come to better understand my beliefs, but in the meanwhile you'll get no umbrage nor disdain from me in regard to what you desire to believe."

"I'm sorry," Miranda said, shaking her head. "I have to go. I don't understand you, and I don't wish to continue this conversation."

"Give it some thought, my dear," Crispin replied. "You'll see. Life is much too short and sweet to worry over such conventions."

———

It was nearly midnight before the camp grew quiet and the obvious sounds of sleep could be heard. Occasionally Leah coughed and Crispin snored, but otherwise gentle rhythmic breathing filled the air.

Karen, however, couldn't sleep. Nestled there between Grace and Leah, she longed for her husband's arms. *This is my wedding night. I should be with Adrik.*

They had already agreed to delay their consummation, given their travel situation. Had they managed to obtain a separate tent or had the nights been less cold, they might well have chosen otherwise. And Adrik had promised her they'd rent a room in Hootalinqua, but that was a whole day away.

Knowing trying to sleep was an exercise in futility, Karen slipped out of her bag and pulled on her boots. Without bothering to lace them, she pulled on her coat and unfastened the tent flap.

The crisp night air hit her face, but in the moon's brilliant light, Karen could see Adrik standing a little ways from the fire, as if waiting for her to come to him. Eager to be in his arms, she hurried to cross the distance and tripped on her laces.

Adrik caught hold of her before she fell, but it threw him off balance and sent him onto his backside with a dull *thump*. He took Karen with him, pulling her protectively across his lap. Surprised, Karen looked up and smiled.

"You do have a way of getting right to the heart of things, don't you, Mr. Ivankov?"

Adrik chuckled softly. "I wasn't the one throwing myself at folks." He pushed back her loose hair. "You don't know how many times I've dreamed of this."

"What? Having me trip over my own feet?"

"Nah, I saw plenty of that on the trail. No, holding you like this is what I dreamed of."

She sighed and nuzzled her lips against his neck. "Me too." Wrapping her arms around his neck, she added, "I couldn't begin to sleep. It just didn't seem right that I couldn't be with you."

"I know. I felt the same way."

Karen lifted her face to his and leaned forward to kiss him. She had very little experience in such matters, but prayed that she might please him. *Oh, God*, she thought, *I only want to make him a good wife.*

She needn't have worried, however, for Adrik's low moan of satisfaction told her he was quite content with her forward action. She touched his chest, feeling his heart racing—the beat clearly matching her own wild pattern. How marvelous to know this feeling. How wondrous to share this kind of love.

"I don't want to leave you," Karen whispered against his lips.

"I don't want you to go," he murmured as his kisses trailed up to her ear. "But I think you must."

She nodded even as he kissed the lobe of her ear. "I'll leave in a few minutes." Reaching up, she lightly massaged the skin at the base of his neck. His skin felt so warm and inviting. She blushed at the thoughts that ran through her mind.

In the distance a wolf cried out in lone adoration of the night. Soon other cries followed, and Karen startled. "They won't bother us, will they?"

Adrik shook his head and smiled. "You have nothing to fear. I'll never let harm come to you so long as there is breath in my body."

She forgot about the wolves' serenade and looked deep into her husband's dark eyes. "I love you so much, Adrik. I didn't know it was possible to love another human being this much."

"I know," he said nodding, "I feel the same way. I can't imagine my life without you in it."

"I want to be a good wife to you," she said, toying with the hair around his ear. "I will try very hard to be obedient." She kissed him again, slow and lingering. It was a habit she could very easily get into.

Abruptly, Adrik ended the kiss and surprised her by getting them both to their feet. "I really want you to stay," he said, his breath coming quickly, "but I need for you to go back to your tent. We'll both be better off for it in the long run."

"I know," Karen replied rather breathlessly. She turned to go, then paused and smiled. "Hootalinqua?"

He grinned. "Hootalinqua."

LAKE LABERGE ONCE AGAIN became an obstacle for the boating party. Positioning themselves among one of a dozen or more crafts, Adrik found himself confronted more than once by strangers in search of answers.

"How much farther to Hootalinqua?"

"We need fresh meat, do you have any to spare?"

"Our boat's breakin' apart, do you have any extra nails? Any rope?"

The list went on and on, but once in a while a scow would draw up close simply to exchange pleasantries. People were starved for conversation and news of the outside. But Adrik had little to offer on either account.

Concern for his own party was growing, making him less than pleasant company for his companions. Crispin had been unusually quiet, almost sullen, since the night before. Miranda and Grace were huddled in conversation, and if the expressions on their faces suggested anything, it was a sign of additional trouble. Karen concerned herself with improving Leah's health, but from time to time Adrik could see the longing in her eyes for time alone with him.

The frustration of not being allowed enough privacy to have a decent wedding night was enough to cause Adrik to consider a cold swim. Especially after last night. Oh, but the woman could make his blood run hot. He knew a good deal of his agitation was steeped in his desire to spend a good long time alone with his new wife. Still, he'd brought this on himself. He should have insisted they wait to marry until they'd reached Dawson City.

Have I been a fool, Lord? Adrik began to pray. *Tempers are running high, and patience is nearly gone.* Adrik missed his regular times of devotion and quiet moments of prayer. Perhaps that was what was eating at him. Since they'd left Lake Lindeman he'd had little time for either prayer or Scripture. He felt as if he were starving to death. Maybe he should join the women for morning devotions.

Of course Crispin wouldn't be interested, but it surely wouldn't hurt for him to listen in. Adrik thought of his friend. Crispin believed in his own power. To Crispin, the only one worth serving was himself. "Why bother with anything or anyone else?" was Crispin's declaration.

Lost in thought, Adrik wasn't even mildly concerned when the wind picked up. But soon the choppiness of the water drew his attention. Steering the boat became increasingly more difficult, and before he could make a reasonable decision, a light rain began to fall.

"Looks like we're in for it!" Crispin called, pointing behind Adrik.

Adrik turned to look to the southwest. Heavy gray-black clouds were fairly boiling on the horizon. Overhead, the brooding rain clouds were unleashing an increasing flow from their reservoirs. "We'll need to head to shore!" Adrik yelled above the winds. "Get that sail down."

But there was little time. As was often the case in the north, the storm came tearing across the sky in a matter of minutes. Roaring out across the area, it seemed to devour everything in its path.

Karen came from inside the tent and looked to Adrik. She could barely stand steady. "What's happening?"

"Storm," he said, knowing that no other explanation was necessary. "Better make sure everything's tied down tight. Get Miranda to help you, and send Grace into the tent with Leah. Jacob!" The boy turned from where he'd been working with Crispin to bring down the sail.

"We'll put her downwind and try to make our way to shore. Grab the oars! I doubt we'll have much luck in rowing, but maybe we can keep her from going broadside to the wind."

Jacob and Crispin finished securing the sail and went immediately to where the long-handled oars waited in reserve. As the wind rocked the craft, Adrik began to fear that reaching the distant shore would be more of a trial for the group than he'd originally figured. He'd have to work hard if they were going to bring the boat to land in one piece.

"Jacob, you come take the sweep. Guide her toward the shore as best you can," Adrik ordered. "I'll row." He knew his strength was greater than the boy's.

Miranda and Karen worked diligently to check the supplies. They covered the flour and sugar sacks with a canvas tarp and fought against the wind to tie it down. The storm was shaking loose everything that wasn't actually nailed to the deck, and Adrik began to worry that they'd lose their goods. Handing over the sweep handle to Jacob, Adrik went to help the women only long enough to settle the canvas in place before taking his place with the oars.

"Karen," he called over his shoulder, "keep close to Jacob, and give him any help he needs."

The skies blackened overhead, stealing the light. The storm was unlike any Adrik had ever seen. "God help us," he prayed. For surely only God could deliver them from the moment.

The boat pitched wildly, nearly sending Adrik off his feet. Water rushed over the sides and drenched his boots. He'd been a fool for his daydreaming. He knew how dangerous the Yukon could be. Why had he allowed himself to be caught unawares?

Another wave came crashing, and with it the wind seemed to change direction. The scow rode the crest and slammed hard against the lake's surface. A woman's scream pierced the air, and Adrik felt his blood run cold. Fighting for all he was worth to keep them from capsizing in the storm, he had precious little time for additional problems.

Glancing over his shoulder, he saw Karen lying in a heap on the deck. He breathed a sigh of relief. At least she was safe. He would worry about whether she was hurt after they reached dry land.

Rain pelted hard against his face as the storm intensified. The wind howled at them in protest, and the lake did its best to expel the boat from her unsettled body. Adrik's arms burned from the intensity of fighting the water and the wind. They were making precious little progress, but at least there was some.

He looked to Crispin, who fought the same battle from the port side. Adrik couldn't help but wonder what Crispin did for comfort in times like these. Adrik prayed and prayed hard. But Crispin had his own notions, and Adrik couldn't imagine how they could ever sustain a man through trying times.

Another scream rent the air, and this time Adrik knew instinctively that something horrible had happened. He turned, pulling the oar from the water lest it be ripped from his grasp.

"What's wrong?" The sound of his voice was swallowed up in the storm.

Karen and Jacob were pointing wildly at the stern. Karen shook her head and began to make her way to Adrik. At the same time, Crispin seemed to come out of his stupor and with great strides leaped over several of the crates to make his way to the back of the boat.

Karen fell against Adrik, her red hair plastered to her face, her lips blue from the cold. "Miranda!" she cried against the wind. "Miranda has fallen overboard!"

Adrik felt a sickening sensation settle in the pit of his stomach. There was no hope of finding the woman in this raging gale. But already Crispin had tied a rope around his waist, and before Adrik could stop him, he dove into the water.

"Stay here!" Adrik commanded Karen. He thrust the handle against her. "You'll have to help me! Just help Jacob keep her headed to shore."

Karen nodded, but Adrik could see the fear in her eyes. He positioned her where he'd stood, then lashed a rope around her waist. Fighting the pitching waves, he tied the other end to one of the tent rings secured in the deck.

"Don't let her go broadside to the wind, or we'll all be in the water!" he told her.

Then crossing the deck, he picked up the lifeline that connected Crispin to the scow. Pulling, Adrik fought to bring Crispin back to safety. He could barely see beyond the rope to the water. There was no sign of Crispin, but the weight at the end of the rope told Adrik the man was still fastened.

With superhuman strength, Adrik pulled on the line, all the while fighting to maintain his balance. Gradually the line yielded, and in a matter of moments, Adrik was pulling Crispin's icy frame back onto the deck.

"I couldn't find her!" Crispin called out.

Adrik shook his head. "We won't find her in this. We have to get to shore. It's our only hope to save the rest."

Reluctantly, Crispin nodded. He struggled to his feet with Adrik's help, then shielded his eyes from the rain trying to see where Miranda had gone.

"Come on," Adrik commanded. "We're nearly there."

The men finished maneuvering the scow to shore just as the worst of the storm came upon them. They secured the boat as best they could, then began unloading the supplies just in case the lines didn't hold. They could build another boat if necessary, Adrik reasoned. It would be difficult, but not impossible. But food, weapons, clothing . . . those things were much harder to come by.

The wind fairly howled around them as a deluge of icy rain tormented everything in its path. Everyone worked. Even Leah and Grace. The entire party seemed to understand Adrik's insistence at completing the task at hand. There would be time for warming up and drying off after the storm had passed. For now, the best they could hope for was to secure the supplies, then seek shelter with their things.

Grace sat huddled under the canvas tarp in a state of complete shock. She'd become so numb from the cold she could barely feel her feet or hands. The baby moved within her. The movement comforted her.

As the worst of the storm passed, leaving only a light rain falling, the men left the women and went in search of firewood. Adrik promised a large bonfire, big enough to warm them all to the bone. Grace doubted she would ever feel warm again. The worst of it was the cold that washed over her in the knowledge that Miranda was gone.

Grace hadn't even realized it until just moments after they'd pulled the tarp around them to hide from the storm. "Where's Miranda?" she had asked, only to receive the pain-filled expression of her companions.

"She just can't be gone," Grace murmured.

Karen patted her hand, and even Leah reached out to touch Grace reassuringly. "Maybe someone in one of the other boats will find her. We weren't the only ones caught unaware," Karen stated evenly.

"That's right, Grace," Leah added, "Miranda told me she was a strong swimmer. Maybe she even made it to shore."

"The storm was too bad," Grace replied. She looked to her longtime friend. "No one could swim in that weather. And the cold . . . oh, Karen . . . the temperature of the water was surely enough to . . ." She couldn't say the words.

"Adrik said they'd go down the shore tomorrow and look for any signs of Miranda. There are Indian villages in the area, and she could very easily have been swept ashore."

Grace buried her face in her hands. "Oh, what am I going to tell Mother Colton?"

The thought of having to break such news to her in-laws left Grace overwhelmed to the point of complete despair. *Oh, God,* she prayed, *please let me wake up and find this nothing more than a horrible dream. Please let Miranda come back to us now, safe and unharmed.*

"Let's wait until we know for sure that there's something we need to tell her," Karen suggested.

Grace looked up, tears blurring her vision. "It should have been me. It would have solved everything."

"No!" Karen declared, reaching out to shake Grace's shoulders. "You must not talk that way. You're just feeling the effects of the shock and the cold. You must be strong, Grace. You must be strong for your baby."

Grace felt the fluttering movement again. It seemed the child wanted to show his or her agreement with Karen's statement. She wanted to take hope in the child—wanted to have a reason to live in the midst of this awful, suffocating despair. But she felt so weak. So inadequate to deal with something so monumental. Martin Paxton's threats were nothing compared to the loss of her sister-in-law.

The men had a fire going in a short time, thanks to Adrik's knowledge of the outdoors. The rain eventually abated, leaving everything damp and cold. Grace huddled with Leah at the edge of the flames. The warmth felt good but did little to relieve her sorrow. Crispin, too, looked completely devastated. He sat opposite Grace, and from time to time their gaze met across the flames.

He must have loved her, Grace surmised. *His expression speaks it.* The pain she saw there so clearly reflected her own heart. She tried not to think of Miranda as dead, but there was nothing else to consider. The weather had been too foul, the waves too high, the water too cold. No one could have survived such an accident.

The next day, after Adrik and Jacob made repairs to the scow, they floated the remaining distance to Hootalinqua. Grace faced their arrival at the little community with mixed emotions. The Northwest Mounted Police had a station here, and she would have to go and make a report on Miranda's accident. It would be important to let the officials know what had happened in case her body washed ashore. Adrik had offered to do the deed, but Grace had insisted she be the one to take care of the matter. After all, she had stated, Miranda was family.

Adrik walked with her to the log building headquarters of the Canadian officials. "Are you sure you don't want me to take care of this?" he asked.

Grace shook her head and looked up to see his compassionate expression. He was such a kind man. So gentle and caring. "I will be fine. You need to take care of the others."

She turned away without another word and made her way inside the station. A young man in a red coat that seemed much too small for his broad-shouldered frame looked up in greeting.

"Good morning, ma'am. I'm Sergeant Cooper. What can I do for you?"

"My name is Mrs. Grace Colton. I have come north with a party of my friends." Her hands began to tremble, and for a moment she felt light-headed.

The officer seemed to understand and quickly came to her side. "You should sit," he commanded and led her to a chair.

"Thank you. I've had quite a shock." She tried to steady her nerves, but visions of Peter and Amelia and Ephraim kept coming to mind. She saw them in their sorrow and knew the pain they would feel.

"Would you care for a cup of tea?"

She looked up at the man and shook her head. "I must be about my business. My party is anxious to move on."

"Very well. Why don't you begin?"

"We were on Lake Laberge yesterday when the storm came up. It was fierce, and our boat was barely able to handle such a storm. We made for shore, but before we arrived, my sister-in-law, Miranda Colton, fell overboard. We tried in vain to rescue her."

The man took the news in a stoic fashion. "Were you able to recover her . . . well, that is to say . . . did you find her?"

Grace bit her lip to keep from crying. She forced herself to draw a deep breath. "No. We did not find her body."

"I see. Let me take this down on paper." He went to his desk and took up his pen. "The name is Colton, correct?"

Grace continued to answer his questions and waited for him to complete his task. When at last he finished writing, he put down the pen and looked up at

Grace. "We've had some trouble with the telegraph, but as soon as the lines are repaired, I'll get word of this down to Whitehorse. Should anyone find her, it would be on record for the purpose of identification."

Grace knew it made sense, but her fear was that Miranda's parents might learn the truth before she had a chance to write to them herself. "I would like to send a letter to her parents," she finally said. "It would be unfair for them to receive word of this from strangers."

"If you care to leave a letter with me, I'll see to it that it goes out with the next post."

"Thank you. I'd like that very much."

The sergeant's heart went out to the young woman. There were so many tales of loss among these stampeders. They came seeking their fortune and often lost their lives. He looked down at the report he'd just written. Such a waste. Why, the woman was no older than he, and now, by all reasonable accounts, she was probably dead.

"Sergeant Cooper," the voice of his superior called from outside the door.

Leaving his desk, Cooper made his way outside. "Sir?"

"I saw a young woman leave the office just now. What was her business?"

Cooper looked down the path to where the woman was making her way back to her party. "That was Mrs. Colton. She came to report the drowning death of her sister-in-law. Seems they were on Lake Laberge when they were caught in yesterday's storm, and the young woman, a Miss Grace Colton, fell overboard. They were unable to recover her body."

CHAPTER TWENTY-NINE

WITH A COLD OCTOBER WIND howling at his back, Peter Colton made his way to Martin Paxton's store. He had to meet with the man, though it was the last thing in the world he wanted to do. Since deciding to follow Christ as his Savior, Peter had known he would have to make this trip. Nevertheless, it was hard. He needed Paxton to tell him where Grace had gone. He needed his adversary to be gracious—merciful.

"What can I do for you?" the clerk asked from behind the counter as Peter came through the door.

Struggling to close the door against the wind, Peter barely heard the question. With the door secured, Peter turned and pulled his scarf from around his face. "I need to see Mr. Paxton. I have business of a personal nature."

The clerk recognized Peter and shook his head. "I doubt the boss wants to meet with you."

"I don't care what he wants," Peter stated, working hard to keep his anger under control, "I need to see him nevertheless."

The man stood his ground, staring hard at Peter. "And if I'm not of a mind to disturb him?"

"Then I'll start tearing this store apart until you are of a mind," Peter replied calmly.

The man weighed Peter's words for a moment, then shrugged. "I'll tell him you're here, but that don't mean he'll see you."

Peter waited until the man had moved from the front of the store to follow after him. He knew the way without an escort. He waited at the bottom of the stairs while the clerk announced him in the room above.

"Send him up," Peter heard Paxton say.

The clerk turned and saw Peter standing at the bottom of the stairs. "The boss says he'll see you."

Peter took the stairs two at a time and had reached the top before the clerk had so much as attempted to descend. Bounding into the room, he was unprepared for the sight of the once fashionable room. The furniture stood as ghostly images, covered in white sheets. Paxton's desk and chair were the only pieces not yet hidden away. To one side of the desk sat an open trunk. Paxton apparently had been packing even as Peter had come to call.

"Where are you going?" Peter asked.

"Not that it is any of your business, but I'm headed south. The winter promises to be severe, and I have little desire to find myself here when the snows grow heavy. One winter in Alaska was enough for me."

"What of Grace?"

"What of her?"

"I want to know where she is," Peter said firmly. "I don't intend to leave until you tell me the truth."

Paxton shook his head. "I have no reason to tell you anything."

Just then a big burly man stormed into the room. Peter turned, certain the man had come to take him from the premises.

"Boss, I got something you need to see. Just came in on the train about an hour ago. Mayor thought you'd want to see it right away."

Paxton slammed down the book he'd been holding. "Can't you see I'm busy?"

"Yeah, but this is important."

Paxton eyed the larger man for a moment, then held out his hand. "What is it?"

Peter watched in irritation as the man passed a folded piece of paper to Paxton. Paxton read the missive, then looked up in stunned silence. Peter thought perhaps the man might have been having some sort of spell as he moved around behind the desk and fell into his chair.

Paxton looked up at his man. "Are they certain about this?"

"Yeah, boss. Mayor said to tell you it came direct from the police headquarters in Whitehorse."

"Leave us," Paxton told the man. The man did as he was told, but not without some hesitation. He paused at the door and looked as if he might question Paxton, but he had no chance. "Go!" Paxton demanded.

Peter stood, uncertain. Would Paxton demand his exit, as well? And if he did, how would Peter ever find out about Grace?

"It would seem I was in error," Paxton began, his gaze rather glassy and distant. "I told you that I had no reason to tell you anything. It would appear that has now changed."

"I don't understand," Peter said, stepping toward the desk.

Paxton extended the paper. "Your wife, Mr. Colton."

Peter snatched the letter with great speed. Opening it, he scanned the few lines and let the paper drop to the desk. "No. Grace isn't dead."

"The Northwest Mounted Police are, I'm afraid, quite thorough and reasonably qualified at their job. If they've declared her dead, she's dead."

Peter felt the room spin. His breath refused to come, and he pulled at the scarf around his neck as though it had somehow tightened. "She can't be dead. She can't be!"

"It would seem she has eluded us both," Paxton replied.

"But you told me she was here. You said she was with you."

"I only let you believe that. I haven't seen her since she went north to Dawson with your sister and that Pierce woman."

"No!"

Peter crossed the distance between them and, without warning, reached across the desk and pulled Paxton up by his lapel. Shaking the man hard enough to rattle his teeth, Peter demanded the truth. "You're only doing this to throw me off track. You're trying to make me believe she's dead so you can have her."

Paxton shook his head. "I'm just as surprised at this news as you are and just as devastated for my own reasons. This is no game, Colton. She's dead."

"Stop saying that!" Peter declared, sending his fist into Paxton's face.

Without realizing what he was doing, Peter hit the man again and again. "She isn't dead! You're lying to me!" He felt the aching in his own hand as his knuckles made contact with the unyielding bone of Paxton's jaw.

"I don't care what you believe," Paxton said as he started to fight back. "Now leave me before I call my men." He slammed his fist into Peter's nose, causing blood to spurt out across the desk.

Peter, stunned at the blow, let go of Paxton and backed up a pace. "I'll go to the mayor. I'll go to the police. I'll learn the truth."

"You already know the truth," Paxton said, nursing his bleeding lip.

————

Hours later, after getting the same reassurance from the mayor, Peter let the realization sink in that what Paxton had said was true. It was no sham. No game to take him away from Grace. Devastated and stunned, Peter collapsed near the docks and gave himself over to his grief.

She can't be gone, he told himself. *She just can't be gone. We left on such bad terms, and there was so much that I needed to apologize for. Words I can never take back. She must have died hating me—hating me enough to go north into the wilds of the Yukon.* He thought of Jonas and of what insight or comfort the man might offer. Then just as quickly, Peter dismissed the idea. He couldn't bear to see the man and explain that his pride had caused him to be too late to reconcile with Grace. Jonas expected Peter to find his wife and head south to San Francisco and a new life in the Lord. Now that could never be.

Uncertain of how to pray for himself, Peter moaned as he buried his face against his knees. "Oh, God, what am I to do? How am I to face this alone?"

"Peter Colton?"

The voice seemed to call from somewhere out of Peter's memory. Looking up, he found a childhood friend, a rival in the shipping industry from San Francisco. "Wesley Oakes?"

"Good grief, man, what's happened to you?" the man reached out to help Peter up from the ground.

"I just got word my wife is dead," Peter said in an almost mechanical tone. "I didn't know where else to go."

The man's face contorted. "I'm sorry, Peter. I had no idea you were even married."

"We've not even been married a year," Peter replied, his brain taking on a fogginess that seemed to mute the pain momentarily.

"Where are you headed?" Oakes questioned.

"I don't know." Peter looked to the steamers in the harbor. "I should go home. There's nothing to keep me here now."

"I leave in two hours. You can have a place on my ship," Oakes offered. "Get your gear and be back before we leave."

Peter looked at the man and shook his head. "Everything of value is with me already. I signed off my job with the railroad and bid my friends good-bye this morning."

"Then come with me now. We'll find you some private quarters, and I'll send someone to tend to your nose. It looks as though it might be broken." Oakes reached out and pulled Peter to his side.

"It doesn't matter," Peter said without the will to protest the man's decision.

True to his word, Wesley Oakes had Peter put in one of the better cabins aboard the steamer *Ellsbeth Marie.* The ship's cook, who also doubled as the ship's doctor, examined Peter's nose and declared that it was not broken, then cleaned Peter up and left him in the silence of the room. Without the will to go on, Peter crawled into the berth and closed his eyes.

"Let me die, as well, Lord," he begged. "If she's dead, I can't go on." He felt hot tears on his face. "Just let me die."

Peter slept through the night and might well have slept through the entire following day, but for Wesley Oakes. The captain of the *Ellsbeth Marie* wasn't about to leave Peter to his own sorrows.

Bringing a hearty supper of dried beef stew and biscuits, Oakes acted as if nothing was out of the ordinary. "You've got to eat," he announced. "It's acceptable to miss the morning and noon meal, but I draw the line at missing your supper."

"I'm not hungry," Peter said, easing his legs over the side of the bed. He'd never known such exhaustion. His limbs felt like lead.

"I've no doubt that's true," Wesley said with a compassionate smile, "but nevertheless, you need to keep your strength up."

Peter realized the man would no doubt stay there to harass him until he yielded. "Very well. I will eat."

"That's a good man. Now I need to slip down below and check on my men. You eat up, and we'll have us a talk tomorrow."

Peter nodded and sat down at the table where Oakes had placed the tray of food. Picking up a biscuit, he put it to his mouth and bit into it. It tasted like sawdust. Peter said nothing, however, as Wesley took his leave.

Letting the biscuit drop to the plate, Peter stared at the food in disinterest. If a man could will himself to die, then Peter was eager to learn the secret.

He thought of Grace and of the letter reporting her death. It said she drowned in Lake Laberge. He couldn't help but wonder what had happened. What had been the circumstances? Why her and not Karen Pierce? Not that he would have wished either one dead, but why Grace?

Peter lost track of the time, feeling no interest in his surroundings. He had lost the love of his life. The only woman he would ever love—ever want to spend his days with.

"Why, God?" He shook his head and let out a deep sigh that went all the way to his soul. "Why?"

Boom! Suddenly the entire room rocked with the impact of the explosion. Peter looked up, uncertain of what had just happened. Another explosion followed close behind the first one, and this time Peter got to his feet and went to the door of his cabin. Flames shot up from the deck below as people screamed and ran for safety.

The black water below was illuminated by the fire on the *Ellsbeth Marie*. Peter tried to make sense of the disaster, but could not.

"Abandon ship!" the call went out. "Abandon ship!"

But to where? Peter wondered, moving stiffly toward the stairs.

It seemed that only moments passed before the entire ship was engulfed in flames. People fought each other for the few lifeboats that were on board. Peter inched down the stairs amidst the panicked passengers. He caught a glimpse of Wesley Oakes. Charred from smoke, Wesley stood as a pillar of stability in the madness.

"Peter!" he called out, "Get off, man! There's no time to lose. The *Seamist* is just behind us. She'll pick up the passengers."

Peter's senses seemed to return all at once. He knew he had to get off the ship, but a greater part of his captaining instincts told him to help the other passengers first. He made his way to the flaming deck and, dodging the fire, managed to make his way to where an older woman struggled.

"Here, let me help you," he said, taking hold of her. He maneuvered the woman to the only lifeboat nearby. Helping her gently, Peter saw her safe, then turned to help the others.

The screams and sounds of panic were terrifying. His own pain seemed insignificant compared to that of a mother who stood screaming for her baby.

"Where is he?" Peter questioned.

The woman pointed down the long deck of flames. "Our cabin—the last one on the right!"

Peter nodded, then darted through the flames and headed in the direction she pointed. He thought only of the child—praying he might not be too late. Thick black smoke bellowed up from the fire, blinding him and stinging his lungs. He coughed and pulled his handkerchief from his pocket. He had to hurry.

The door was locked tight, but Peter would not be stopped. Throwing himself against the door over and over again, he finally felt the wood give way. Gaining entrance to the smoke-filled cabin, Peter tried to see through the illuminated haze. Cautiously feeling his way about the room, he found the cradle. The baby didn't so much as cry as Peter lifted him from the bed. He tucked the baby into his coat, hoping to shield him from the heat and smoke.

Making his way back down the deck, Peter heard a man pleading for help. "I'll be right back," Peter called, seeing that the man's door was somehow jammed. The man waved his hand from the few inches of space.

"No! Don't leave me!"

Peter had no choice but to leave the man. He had to return the baby to his mother, otherwise they might both be lost. He accomplished his goal quickly, meeting the teary-eyed woman with a smile. "He seems just fine," Peter announced, then pulled the still-sleeping baby from beneath his coat.

"Oh, my baby. My sweet baby," the woman said, pouring kisses over the child's head. "Oh, thank you. Thank you so much!"

Peter didn't wait to hear more. Amidst the cacophony of certain death, he made his way back to the man in the cabin.

"I'm here!" Peter called.

"Get me out! The door won't budge. The blast sent a beam across it."

Peter pushed at the door even as the dull roar of the fire climbed the wall behind him. The heat burned the back of Peter's neck, but still he worked to free the stranger.

The door moved ever so slightly, and Peter felt encouraged. The man pressed his bruised face to the door, causing Peter to step back in shock. "You!"

Martin Paxton was unconcerned. "Get me out of here, Colton."

Peter thought of all that the man had done to harm him. Leaving him to die on the burning ship would be sweet revenge. Frozen in place, Peter contemplated what he should do. Paxton deserved to die.

"Peter, it will serve no purpose but that of darker forces if you continue this hateful battle," Grace had once told him. He could almost hear her sweet voice pleading, *"Please listen to me. Forgiving Mr. Paxton is the only way to put the past to rest."*

"Colton, I'll give you whatever you want. Just get me out of here."

"I want Grace back," Peter said, shaking his head. "But you can't give her back to me."

"Just get me out of here, and I promise to return your father's business. I never meant to hurt him anyway."

Peter recognized the pleadings of a desperate man and could only think of Grace's gentle nature and loving heart. He couldn't leave Paxton to die. It would negate everything Grace had stood for. Everything Peter now believed in.

Giving it all he had, Peter pressed his body to the wood.

"Just a little more!"

Peter felt his heart pounding against his chest as he pushed with his full weight against the door. Without warning, it gave way, and Peter fell into the room, landing soundly on his back. Looking up, he found Martin Paxton staring down at him, a smirk lining his lips.

"You fool."

Paxton kicked Peter square in the jaw, then pressed through the opening, pulling the door closed behind him. Peter barely registered what had happened. Dull-headed and struggling to see, Peter got to his feet and reached for the handle of the door just as a third explosion tore through the night and into the room.

Peter felt himself hurled through the air, the walls around him seeming to splinter into a thousand pieces as the blast carried him into the night skies. Something hit Peter hard against the head, and as he began to lose consciousness, he felt the icy waters of the canal engulf his body and pull him down.

It's only fitting, he thought as he slipped into oblivion. *Grace drowned. It's only fitting that I should drown, as well.*

—❘ C H A P T E R   T H I R T Y ❘—

PETER'S FIRST SENSATION of consciousness was the rocking of his bed. He thought for a moment he must be dreaming. Beds didn't rock. He heard voices around him, but he felt too weary to open his eyes. He heard someone call his name.

Grace! He knew it must be her.

Struggling, he tried to say her name. Nothing—not a single sound would come from his lips.

Grace, don't leave me! he silently pleaded.

The next time he awoke, Peter found himself in a hospital bed. The nurse who hovered over him was an unappealing woman whose pinched expression gave him little hope for his recovery.

"I'll tell the doctor you're awake," she said curtly before turning to leave.

Peter thought to say something, but his throat pained him. The smoke had nearly choked out his voice.

The doctor, a thin man with a compassionate look to him, came to Peter's bed. "My boy, welcome back to the living. You're at a hospital in Seattle."

Peter tried to speak, but again the words were hoarse and inaudible.

"Don't try to talk, son. The smoke has damaged your vocal cords. Just give it few days of rest and fluids, and you'll be fine."

Peter nodded. It felt as though his head were three times the normal size. Every movement hurt, and Peter couldn't help but wince.

"You took a blow to the head. You were fortunate that you weren't in the water too long. The captain saw you floating and managed to keep you that way until help arrived."

Wes had saved his life. Pity he didn't realize Peter didn't want to be saved. Peter thought of Grace and of how close he had been to joining her.

The doctor gave Peter a cursory examination, then discussed his orders with the nurse before turning to go. "We don't expect you to be here long. You're a strong young man. You'll heal fast."

The doctor's conclusion proved correct. Within a week, Peter found himself nearly as good as new and ready to leave. He'd asked the nurse to write a letter to his mother only the day before. He hoped and prayed she hadn't heard about the catastrophe on the ship. Or that if she had, she wouldn't have any reason to believe that Peter was aboard the steamer.

Now that he was out of danger, however, he wanted his parents to know where he was and to tell them about Grace. He wouldn't do that via letter, he'd decided, but he would explain his journey home and let them know he'd be back in San Francisco within the month.

"You have visitors," the pinch-faced nurse announced. Then turning to Ephraim and Amelia Colton, she announced, "You may see him for ten minutes. No more."

"Mother!" Peter said, his voice finally regaining strength and clarity.

"Oh, Peter!" Amelia opened her arms and crossed the room to embrace her bedfast son. "We were so worried. Wesley Oakes telegraphed us and had one of his ships bring us up."

Peter hugged her close, then pulled away to greet his father. "You look like a new man."

"I feel fit as a fiddle," his father announced. "But you look a little worn."

"I've had better days, that's for sure."

"Oh, we're so grateful to Wes," Amelia continued. "We had no idea you were heading home. What of Grace and Miranda? Did you see them?"

Peter didn't know what to say. He had hoped to avoid the subject of Grace until later. His mother's imploring expression, however, made it clear she had come for answers.

"Grace is the reason I was headed back to San Francisco."

"How so, son?" his father asked.

Peter eased up in bed a bit and folded his hands. Drawing a deep breath, he tried to figure out the easiest way to break the news. "Grace wasn't with me in Skagway."

"No, we realize that. She and Miranda were to travel north to Dawson City with Grace's friend Karen Pierce."

"You already knew?" Peter questioned. "Why would she do that?"

Amelia became quite grave. "She felt you had abandoned her. And after hearing what had occurred between you two, we had no reason to believe it to be other than true. Then later your letter arrived, but of course Grace and Miranda were long gone."

"Yes," Peter murmured. "Gone."

"Well, I'm certain that if you want to restore your marriage, son," his father began, "you can make your way north, as well."

"I can't restore my marriage," Peter said flatly. He knew of no other way to tell them the truth of the matter than to simply say it. "I've had word regarding Grace. It was the reason I was headed home. You see, I didn't realize she had gone north until a report came to Skagway that she had met with an accident."

"What kind of accident?" Amelia questioned, her hand going to her throat.

"Grace apparently fell overboard while their boat fought a storm on Lake Laberge. She was lost."

"No!" Amelia and Ephraim cried in unison.

"What of Miranda?" his mother quickly added.

"I don't know. Remember, I didn't even know they were together until receiving your letter. And you never said in that letter where they'd gone. The Northwest Mounted Police were merely sending down a report of United States citizens whose lives were lost in the territory. They would have no reason to speak of Miranda unless she also had been lost."

"Oh, son, we're so sorry. How very hard this must be on you," Ephraim said solemnly.

"I was coming home to tell you and decide what I should do."

"Poor little Grace. Such a sweet, sweet girl," Amelia said, shaking her head. "How very sad this news is."

"It seems unreal," Peter replied. He looked to his parents, then past them to the door. "I keep thinking that if I concentrate hard enough, she'll come walking through that door. We first met here in Seattle, you know. It would be rather seemly that she return to me here." He shook his head and sighed. "But I know she's not coming back." How very empty his life would be without Grace.

"This will not be an easy burden to bear," Ephraim declared. "But we must help one another through the pain."

"Oh, my poor sweet Miranda. She must be devastated with the death of Grace," Amelia said, looking to Ephraim. "Oh, what should we do?"

"It's too late to get north now," Peter replied. "The snow is blocking the progress of the train. The routes are often impassable from day to day and the rivers up north are freezing up. We'll have to wait until spring."

"But that's over six months away," Amelia replied. "What will Miranda do in the meanwhile?"

"She's with Karen Pierce," Peter said thoughtfully. "Karen is a good woman, and she'll be just as devastated as Miranda. They'll comfort each other. There is another matter, however, on which I wish to speak to you both."

"What is it, son?" Ephraim asked.

"I want to apologize for my behavior. My actions and opinions reflected a poor character, and I now see myself for the man I was and regret it greatly."

His mother reached out to touch his hand. "We all make mistakes."

"Yes, but mine has caused the death of someone I loved very dearly. If I hadn't acted in the manner I did, Grace would be safely beside me instead of lost in the Yukon."

"You don't know that."

His father's words did little to offer comfort. "The truth of the matter is, while in Alaska I met a man who helped me to see what Grace had tried to make me see all along. The need for God." Peter looked to his mother and squeezed her hand. "It seems too late, but I have made my peace with God."

"Oh, Peter, it could never be too late." Amelia hugged him close. "With God as your comfort, you will know joy once again. Let Him help you through this."

"I am," Peter admitted. Amelia released him and smiled. Peter thought of Martin Paxton for some reason. Perhaps it was because Paxton had become Peter's greatest challenge to his new faith.

"There's something else," Peter said. "Martin Paxton was on the *Ellsbeth Marie* when she blew up."

"Yes, we know," Ephraim replied. "He's dead."

"Dead?" Peter hadn't heard this news.

"He was killed in an explosion," his father answered.

Peter suddenly felt a chill. "I had gone to help a man who was trapped in his room. The door was blocked, and as I pushed it back, I found myself face-to-face with Martin Paxton. I wanted to leave him there." Peter looked up. "Does that shock you?"

Ephraim shook his head. "I probably would have felt the same."

"I thought of what Grace had said about forgiveness—about letting the past go so that real healing could begin. I knew if I left Paxton there, I would never be able to heal. I would never be able to face God."

"What did you do?" Amelia asked.

"I decided to help him. I pushed the door open and fell into the room as it gave way. Paxton called me a fool, kicked me in the face, and fled, pulling the door closed behind him. I was stunned for a moment and struggled to my feet. I'd barely stood when the explosion cut through the room and blasted me out into the water."

"Paxton's evil intent kept you alive," Ephraim replied. "He thought to leave you to die, but it was his own death he met. While you were protected by the walls of the room, albeit only marginally, Paxton was torn apart by the intensity of the blast."

Peter found the news disconcerting. "What he'd intended for evil, God used for good. My friend Jonas told me that's often the way it is with God."

His mother nodded and reached out to touch her son's face. "Oh, my dearest, I'm so very grateful that God spared you. I could not bear to lose you."

"I wanted to be lost," Peter admitted. "I felt no will to live without Grace."

"But we need you, son." His father's words were firm, not sympathetic or even filled with pity. They were merely stated as fact.

"But without her, my life feels useless. There's nothing to look forward to. My heart feels cold and lifeless." Peter closed his eyes and laid his head back on the pillow. "I never had a chance to tell her how sorry I was for my actions. I never had a chance to hold her again—to kiss her. She died thinking me a hateful and mean-spirited man."

"No," Amelia interjected. "That's not true. The last words she spoke to us were of her love for you. She was filled with love for you."

Peter opened his eyes. His vision blurred from the tears. "She was filled with love, period. She knew the love of God, and it permeated everything about her, including me. I wish she could know how she changed my heart."

"I'm sure she does," his mother said, her own tears falling freely. "I'm sure she does."

The taste of muddy water and grit in her mouth did little to rouse the half-conscious Miranda Colton. She had no idea where she was or what had happened. She only knew that the icy cold of the water left her numb and leaden.

Oh, God, she prayed, *I'm dying. Perhaps I'm already dead. Oh, God, help me.*

She heard voices, in a dialect she found unintelligible and senseless.

She felt herself being rolled over and then lifted from the watery grave of the lakeshore. She lay as dead weight, unable to move or even open her eyes.

Is that you, God? Have you come to take me home?

Her thoughts began to fade. Her time was drawing nigh. She smiled at the thought of heaven.

⊣ CHAPTER THIRTY-ONE ⊢

"THAT'S DAWSON!" Adrik called to his weary and sorrowed travelers.

Karen came immediately to his side and stared across the water to the buildings and tents assembled at the water's edge. Warehouses and sawmills stood near the docks, while an idle steamer and a dozen or more boats of various build floated casually in the river nearby. Chunks of ice were even now forming as a light snow began to fall.

"It's a lot bigger than I'd figured," Adrik said, embracing Karen with his right arm.

"It looks marvelous. I don't know when I've ever wanted something half as much as I've wanted to reach this town."

"Well," Adrik said, pulling her close for a kiss, "I can think of something I've wanted more than Dawson."

"Silly man," Karen replied, kissing him quickly. "You've already got me."

"Now, how did you know I was thinking of you?"

She jabbed him in the ribs, then stepped away. "You're impossible."

"Yes, ma'am."

"Is that it?" Grace asked, her voice hopeful.

Karen nodded. "Dawson City." She looked to her friend. Grace had blossomed overnight, and her rounded belly gave little doubt of her condition. "We'd better sit down. Adrik's about to dock. I don't want you to lose your footing."

They went to one of the two benches Adrik had secured and took their place.

Karen reached out to hold Grace's hand as Adrik called out orders to Crispin and Jacob.

"Just look at it!" Leah Barringer called from where she stood leaning over a crate of goods. "It's like nothing I've seen since we left Seattle."

"Well, it's not quite that settled," Karen said, laughing.

"It wasn't more than a trading post last time I was up this far north," Adrik said. "It came up out of nothing."

They docked uneventfully, and when Adrik gave the word, Karen made her way to the shore. She waited for Adrik to help Grace from the boat, wondering if her friend would ever get over the losses in her life. So much had been taken from her. Karen thought how very similar their lives had been. They both had lost people so very dear to them.

"Oh, aren't you excited, Karen?" Leah called, coming up beside her to take hold of her arm. "We're finally here." Then remembering their recent loss, Leah bowed her head and added, "I wish Miranda could be here."

"It's awful cold," Jacob said, glancing around. "Where we gonna live?"

"That's a very good question," Adrik replied. "We're going to have to check things out quickly and figure where we can best hold up through the winter."

"What about a claim? Aren't we here for gold?" Jacob questioned.

"Nothing says we can't look for it," Adrik said. "But we're also going to need some regular money coming in. We'll have to get jobs as soon as possible. That might mean working for somebody else's claim."

"No, sir!" Jacob declared. "I came here for my own claim. My pa said . . ."

Leah left Karen and reached out to Jacob. "Our pa is dead. We need to make our own dreams now."

He looked down at her with such love and compassion that Karen was nearly moved to tears. What a marvelous bond they shared. Jacob slowly nodded and gave Leah a hug. With that simple gesture, Karen knew things would be all right. Jacob had learned much about foolish choices. Perhaps it would be enough to take him into adulthood without too many additional scars.

Crispin came up from behind, his face blank of expression. He hadn't been the same since Miranda had fallen overboard. Karen felt sorry for him. Adrik had said that Crispin was an atheist—that he didn't believe in the existence of God. She wondered how he could bear the thought of a tomorrow without the certainty that God had already seen the day—had planned it through.

"Well, what now?" he asked Adrik.

"Now we start over," Adrik replied. "This is a new adventure. The old is passed away. We find a home or make one. We find a claim and work it. We settle ourselves in for the winter and do the best we can with what the good Lord has given us."

Crispin looked back to the boat. "Someone should stay here. No sense in having our things taken." He began to walk back to the boat.

"Doesn't Crispin want to see the town?" Leah asked.

Adrik shook his head. "I think he needs some time to himself. But what say we all head up that way? Might as well begin checking things out."

Leah rallied from her thoughts of Miranda and pulled on her brother's arm. "Come on. There's so much to see."

"Oh my," Grace said as it began to snow in earnest, "I forgot my bonnet." She turned to go back to the scow, but Adrik stopped her.

"I'll get it. You stay here."

"Thank you," she said, looking to Karen. "He's a good man. He'll be a wonderful husband."

Karen nodded. "I know he will. But I know something else, as well." She looped her arm through Grace's. "You make me proud to call you friend. I so admire your strength and courage. You have been put through trials of fire and still your faith has grown."

"I'm only putting into practice the things you taught me," Grace said, her brown eyes meeting Karen's gaze. "You planted the seeds within my heart, and God grew them. You should be proud of your job as a teacher, for you taught me much about life and about love."

Karen felt tears sting her eyes. "Things will be better, you'll see. God is not finished with this matter. He has a plan."

"But there's nothing left."

"Then just as the stampeders did with Dawson City, God will create something out of nothing. He can do that, you know. He thawed my icy heart after I turned away from Him. He shattered my illusions of self-sufficiency and proved to me that He alone could see me through. He'll do the same for you, Grace, because you're His and He cares for His own."

"Like He cared for Miranda?"

Karen saw the sorrow wash over Grace as she looked past Karen to the river. "He was with Miranda even when she fell. The Bible says that even the falling sparrow doesn't escape His notice. I don't know why God allows these things to happen, Grace. I don't know why bad should plague the lives of people who desire only to do good, but my faith is restored, and I know that God in His infinite wisdom will have things as He wills."

"Then there's nothing we can do?"

Karen smiled. "We can trust Him. Trust Him to know the path and the way to go. Trust Him to raise us up from our worldly, daily deaths."

Grace put her hand on her rounded abdomen. "I know He will keep us—I trust Him to deliver us."

"Here's your bonnet, Mrs. Colton," Adrik said, coming back up the walk.

Grace looked to Karen for the briefest moment and smiled. Karen knew in her heart that God would make a way for all of them, but especially for Grace, who had tried so very hard to honor Him.

"Thank you, Adrik," Grace murmured. She took the hat and started up the road toward the congestion of town.

Karen looked to her husband and saw the hope gleaming in his eyes. "Are you ready?" she asked.

He nodded. "Are you?"

"I'd follow you to the ends of the earth," she said, embracing him with great pride. "And I think I've proven that by coming here."

He chuckled. "It's not the end of the earth, but you can see it from here."

Karen smiled and leaned up on her tiptoes to kiss her husband's lips. "It's not an ending at all," she murmured. "It's a beginning."

TRACIE PETERSON

Rivers of Gold

Part One

OCTOBER 1898

It is of the Lord's mercies
that we are not consumed, because his
compassions fail not.

LAMENTATIONS 3:22

─{ C H A P T E R   O N E }─

MIRANDA COLTON floated in a sea of warmth, the sensation unlike any she had ever known. *Maybe I've died*, she thought. *Maybe I've died and this is heaven.* She attempted to open her eyes to confirm her thoughts, but her eyelids were too heavy.

Drifting in and out of a hazy sleep, Miranda knew nothing but the comfort and assurance that all was well. There was no sense of panic. No fear of the unknown. Her spirit rested in complete peace.

In her dreams, she saw herself as a young child, happily playing in fields of flowers, the mist of the ocean upon her skin, the salty taste upon her lips. She lifted her face to the sun and felt the delicious warmth engulf her. She would like to stay here forever. Safe and warm. Happily contented among the green grasses and colorful flowers. At times, a delicate aroma wafted through the air, delighting her further with the luscious scent of roses, honeysuckle, and lilacs.

Then voices called to her. Miranda didn't recognize the language, but somehow she knew the words were being spoken to her. She struggled to listen—to understand. With great difficulty she opened her eyes and stared into the brown, well-worn face of an old woman.

Miranda felt no sense of recollection at the sight of the serious countenance before her. The woman was clearly a stranger, yet she seemed so concerned, so gentle. A momentary tremble of fear seized Miranda's heart, but the woman's tender touch made her realize the old woman was no threat to her well-being.

"You wake up now," the woman said in a thick, almost guttural tongue.

Miranda opened her mouth to reply, but no words came out. Her mouth felt as if it were stuffed with cotton. Closing her eyes, she heard the woman call to her again.

"No sleep. You make too much sleep. You wake up now."

The command did little good. Miranda had no energy for the task.

She felt the woman swab her face with a cool cloth. The woman gently urged, "You wake up. You no die."

Die? Miranda wondered at the word as she listened to the woman chatter on. Wasn't she already dead? She couldn't remember what had happened to her, but she was certain that it had been a very difficult journey. It didn't startle her to think of dying or even of being dead. She merely wondered why she couldn't wake up. Weren't you supposed to see pearly gates and hosts of angels after death? Nowhere in her church upbringing could she remember anything about brown-faced women escorting a person to their reward.

The woman forced water into Miranda's mouth. The cold liquid felt marvelous as it trickled down her throat, dissolving the cotton taste. *How very pleasant,* Miranda thought.

"How is she?" a masculine voice questioned in a decidedly English accent.

Miranda started to open her eyes, certain that she was about to meet God. Funny, she had never thought of him as an Englishman. She hesitated a moment. Didn't the Bible say that you would die if you saw God's face?

Then it came to her. *If this is God, then I'm already dead and it won't matter.* She opened her eyes, prepared to meet her Maker. Instead, she met the compassionate gaze of dark brown eyes. The man had a gentleness about him as he leaned over her to touch her forehead.

"I say, seems the fever is gone. You'll soon be right as rain." His dark brown mustache twitched ever so slightly as he offered her a smile.

"What?" Miranda barely croaked the word out.

The man patted her on the head as if she were a small child. "Nellie will fix you right up. You'll see. She's quite gifted in the ways of healing."

Miranda wanted to question the man but had no energy to do so. She watched in silence as he turned to the woman. His alabaster skin was quite the contrast to the older woman's native complexion. His dark hair had a haphazard lay to it. Perhaps he had just awakened, or perhaps he wasn't given to worrying over appearances.

"I've prepared the herbs you asked for, Nellie. That should help considerably. Shall I put a pot of water on to boil?"

The old woman nodded and followed the man. Miranda wanted to call out to them and beg them not to leave her, but again her voice failed her. She tried to remember what had happened to her. *How did I get here?* But even as she worked at the foggy memories, Miranda knew only one thing for certain. This wasn't heaven—she wasn't dead.

Thomas Edward Davenport, Teddy to his friends, turned from the ancient Indian woman and went back to his worktable. He had hoped to have a better showing for a summer's worth of work, but after categorizing the plants and herbs he'd gathered, Teddy was rather disappointed. He would spend the winter recording and cataloging his finds for the botanical research book he intended to produce. This was his life's work—work that had brought him to the vast regions of the Canadian provinces. Leaving his beloved England behind had been a difficult task, but after the death of his mother, Teddy had no real reason to remain. His father had died years before, succumbing to a terrible round of influenza. And while English soil might hold the bodies of his dearly departed parents, Teddy knew their souls were safely in heaven with God.

He glanced across the cabin room and watched Nellie spooning tea into the young woman's mouth. Teddy couldn't help but wonder about the woman. Local natives had brought the half-drowned creature to his door, knowing Nellie had a gift for healing. Teddy could hardly turn the unconscious woman away, but the interruption was most unwelcome. He had no time for diversions. His work would suffer—had already suffered—because of this stranger's arrival.

Teddy toyed with a bit of dried alpine geranium. *Who is she?* he wondered. No doubt she was one of the thousands who had come north with their hearts set on gold. So many parties had been lost upon the wild and reckless waters of the Yukon. The shores along the lakes and rivers were littered with the sad reminders of the invasion from the south. Teddy wished with all his heart that the strangers would all return to wherever they had come from. In the five years he'd been at work in the Yukon, he'd known a tranquil and graceful land. That tranquility, however, was greatly diminished in the wake of the Klondike gold rush.

"She sleep again, but not so long, I think," Nellie said, coming to the table where Teddy worked only halfheartedly. "I think she much better."

Teddy nodded. "Yes, I believe you are right."

"I make you supper," Nellie said and walked back to the stove without another word.

Teddy required the old woman's presence, because without her he simply lost track of time and forgot to eat or sometimes to sleep. His work consumed him. It was a thing of great interest and passion, but it was also a challenge that he could not seem to shake. His father had always loved plant life and his desire to come to North America for the research of Canadian vegetation was a dream Teddy intended to see through to fruition. It was a sort of legacy Teddy would leave in honor of his father.

Albert Davenport had been very much a dreamer. Teddy's mother had found his love of plants annoying, for it had taken them from her beloved estate outside of London and plunged them into the heart of Cornwall. Eugenia Davenport would endure her husband's sojourns to the country for a time, but then, after no more than a month, she would announce her return to London. Declaring she would simply perish from the isolation of the country, Eugenia cut everyone's stay short, for her husband was not inclined to remain in the country without her.

Teddy had adored his mother, for she was a loving parent, but he'd also resented the pain she caused his father. Albert's dreams were unimportant to her, but not to Teddy. He had vowed to his father, even as he lay dying, that he would see to fruition his father's dream of creating a great book of botanical study on the Canadian landscape. That vow had become a driving force in Teddy's life, and he was bound and determined to see it through.

Perhaps that was why the presence of this woman bothered him so greatly. He didn't want this stranger to become a deterrent to his work, as his mother had been to his father.

Teddy glanced back across the room to where the young woman slept. She had been in his cabin for over three weeks. Off and on she would awaken and then fall back to sleep. Nellie said her lungs had been full of lake water, and at first, the old woman hadn't believed the stranger would live. Teddy had prayed for the injured woman, knowing that there were some things only God could heal. Within a fortnight, Nellie announced her belief that the woman would recover. It would take time for a full recovery, however. Time Teddy wasn't entirely sure he could offer.

It was already October and the snows had set in. Normally he would already be heading back to his hotel room in Dawson. But he could hardly pick up and leave this complication. The woman couldn't be left behind—but neither could she be moved.

Teddy pushed up his sleeves and leaned forward on the table. What was he to do? The woman needed him. She was helpless, and although Nellie felt confident of her recovery, Teddy couldn't help but wonder what he was to do with her once she regained her health.

A knock on the cabin door brought Teddy out of his thoughts. What new interruption awaited him? Nellie padded across the room, a slight limp noticeable as she walked. He had once asked her about the limp and she'd told him a horrific tale of having been caught in a trap when she'd been young. The incident had left her both scarred and crippled. Teddy offered her his condolences, and Nellie had merely shrugged, saying, "It not your trap did this."

Nellie opened the door and stood back to look at Teddy. Teddy didn't recognize the man at the door. The stranger pushed back his fur parka and brushed crusty ice from his beard.

"I wonder if I might warm up for a spell," the man questioned.

Teddy nodded. "Come in. I'm about to take supper."

"I'm much obliged," the man said. "The name's Buckley. J. D. Buckley."

"Thomas Davenport," Teddy replied. Nellie closed the door behind the man and waited to take his coat. "Feel free to warm up at the stove or the fireplace," Teddy added.

"It's not too bad out there today," Buckley stated. "I've seen worse, but I'm glad to be inside for a spell."

Teddy nodded. He didn't usually get visitors and that was the way he liked it. Though centrally located for his work, his cabin was well off the beaten path. There had been an increase in traffic since the gold rush pandemonium, but his area hadn't yielded much in the way of profitable dust. For this, he was most grateful.

"If I might ask," Teddy began, "how did you find yourself in this part of the country?"

The man rubbed his hands together. "Well, to tell you the truth, I got lost. I ain't been up in these parts long, and I guess I took a wrong turn. I was following the Yukon River, then moved inland for a ways in order to follow an easier path. I thought I'd stayed with the Yukon, but now I see I didn't."

"You most likely took the fork for the Indian River. It runs off the Yukon, and if you walk too far inland and aren't familiar with the lay of the land, it's easy enough to get waylaid. Especially as you fork off from the Indian River and follow some of the lesser creeks and streams, which surely you must have done to wind up here."

"Can you point me in the direction of Dawson?"

"That I can, but the hour is much too late to travel." Teddy knew, regrettably, that he had no choice but to offer the man lodging. It was a sort of code in the north. You dealt kindly with strangers, otherwise it could cost someone their life. Especially when the weather turned cold and unforgiving. "You're welcome to lay your blanket by the stove. I can't offer you much in the way of privacy or space, but it will be considerably warmer than a tent in the woods."

"That's mighty kind of you, Mr. Davenport."

"Think nothing of it."

Nellie dished up a thick elk stew and placed the wooden bowls on the table. "You eat now."

Teddy pushed his work aside and motioned to the man. "Please pardon my poor manners. Pull up a chair and join me. Nellie will bring us tea and biscuits as well."

"Sounds good. I'm afraid I ain't had a hot meal in some time."

Teddy frowned. "Have you been lost all that long?"

The man took out a handkerchief and blew his nose loudly. Bits of ice loosened from his mustache and beard, seeming to soften the stranger's appearance. "I ain't been lost all that time, but to tell the truth, my partners and me had a falling out. I got the sled and a few other supplies, but not much in the way of food."

"Have you dogs for the sled?"

The man laughed. "Nope, been pulling the heavy thing myself. My partners kept the dogs, knowing they'd fetch a good price in Dawson. Fact is, I really have no need for the sled. You wouldn't be of a mind to trade me for some food, now, would you?"

Teddy rubbed his chin. The stubble reminded him he'd not shaved that morning. "I just might be able to help you out. I have a guest staying with me who is quite weak. It might be a good thing to have a sled to carry her in when I make my way to Dawson."

"I'd surely be obliged."

"Then consider it a deal. We'll arrange a pack for you and load it with a variety of food. I'll be closing out the cabin and heading to Dawson myself as soon as my guest can travel, so I'll give you what I can."

The man nodded and dug into the stew without another word. Teddy cleared his throat and asked, "Do you mind if I offer up thanks?"

The man looked rather sheepish and put down his spoon. "Like I said, I ain't ate a hot meal in a while. Weren't no disrespect intended to the Almighty."

Teddy bowed his head. "For that which you have provided, oh God, we thank you. Bless us now as we share this meal. May you ever be the unseen guest at my table. Amen."

"Amen," Buckley said, barely waiting long enough to utter the word before shoveling another spoonful of stew into his mouth.

Teddy glanced across the room to where Nellie ministered to the sick woman. He had thought of giving her a name. Always calling her "the woman" seemed so impersonal and somehow unkind. But since he'd spent his life's work attaching the proper name to plants, he didn't feel right in simply attaching a random moniker to the stranger.

"So what brings you out here, mister? Gold?"

Teddy returned his gaze to the man and noticed that he looked around the room with an unguarded interest. "No, I'm afraid not. I've no interest in rivers of gold unless they hold some new botanical specimens."

"Botanical what?"

"Specimens. I am conducting research on the vegetation of the region. I'm chronicling it for a book."

"So you're an educated fellow?"

Teddy smiled. "I suppose you might call me that. I've a deep love of learning."

"Ain't had much time for such things myself. My pa didn't hold much respect for learnin' in a school. He said life was a better teacher."

Nellie brought them tea and a platter of biscuits. Without a word she placed the food on the table.

"Could you spare another bowl?" Buckley questioned, raising the empty bowl.

"Certainly. Nellie, please give the man another portion."

The old woman nodded and took the bowl. She seemed none too pleased to deal with the stranger. She hadn't cared for white men when Teddy approached her village some five years earlier. She had seen the damage done by the prospectors and others who had come north for their own greedy reasons. This was prior to the rush, and now that hundreds poured into her land on a daily basis, her feelings were only confirmed.

Teddy had won her over by first winning over her son Little Charley, so called not because of his physical size but to distinguish him from Big Charley, his father. Unable to speak their native language, Teddy had been greatly relieved to find many of the natives spoke a fair amount of English. Teddy explained his situation and offered to hire on several of the English-speaking natives to guide him and assist him in identifying the vegetation they found.

Five years of honorable relations had forged a bond between Teddy and Nellie. She now stayed with him from the breakup of the ice until the first heavy snows. She seemed to know when Teddy would return without his even telling her. The day or so before he was ready to head out, Nellie would be packed and ready to leave the cabin. Then when he returned in May, he would find her already sweeping out the musty cabin. They had a companionable relationship, and Teddy knew that part of this was due to his contentment with solitude, as well as his respect for the land.

Nellie put the refilled bowl in front of the stranger, then left the men to their meal. Teddy wondered if Nellie sensed something dangerous about the man. He eyed Buckley with a steady gaze, hoping that, should the man be more than he appeared, God would give Teddy clarity to know the truth. But Buckley had eyes only for the meal and scarcely drew a breath while devouring the stew.

Well, God always has a purpose for allowing circumstances in our lives, Teddy thought. He hadn't yet figured out the reason for the unconscious woman's appearance or the stranger's, but Teddy was content to leave the matter to God. Leaving the details of life to his heavenly Father left Teddy free to concentrate on what really mattered. Not that the woman didn't intrigue him, but he couldn't afford to let himself get carried away. His work came first. His work would honor his father and bring glory to God.

—| C H A P T E R   T W O |—

"IT JUST DOESN'T seem like Christmas should be only days away," Karen Ivankov said as she hung up a pair of her husband's trousers to dry. "I figured we'd be in a cabin by now."

Grace Colton, now swollen in the latter months of pregnancy, nodded. Her brown eyes were edged with dark circles. "I'd hoped so as well. I hate the thought of bringing a baby into this world with nothing more than a tent to offer for a home."

Karen's strawberry blond hair curled tight from the humidity of the washtub. She pushed back an errant strand, regretting that she hadn't taken the time to pin it up. The heat felt good, however, and Karen cared little for her appearance, given their setting. Living through the Yukon winter in a tent hardly allowed for niceties such as fancy hairstyles and pretty clothes. In this country everything needed to be functional and useful. Otherwise it was just extra baggage.

Her husband, Adrik, had tried hard to find them a home. He'd hoped to stake a claim and build them a house, but the pickings were slim and most of the good land was taken. Those who wanted to sell out and leave before the winter charged exorbitant prices. One man sold his claim, complete with cabin, for thirty thousand dollars before catching the last boat out of Dawson. For a family who had barely managed to hang on to the smallest amount of money, thirty thousand dollars was nothing more than a dream.

"We'll just have to make the best of it," Karen finally replied. "I know Adrik doesn't want us here any more than we want to be here."

"Of course not," Grace agreed.

"Don't worry, Grace," thirteen-year-old Leah Barringer encouraged. "We can make things real nice for you and the baby. You'll see. Jacob said he'd build you a cradle. He remembers when Pa made one."

"Your brother has his hands full, chopping enough wood to keep us warm," Grace said with a smile. "But I appreciate the thought."

"At least it's warmed up some," Leah offered. "It's not nearly as cold as it was in November."

"That's for sure. I hope I never see forty below again," Karen commented. "A person can hardly move away from the stove for fear of their blood freezing in their veins."

"Yes, it's much warmer now. I heard Adrik say this morning that it was clear up to five degrees above zero," Grace said, turning her attention back to her sewing.

"A veritable heat wave," Karen said, laughing. She wrung out the last of the laundry and hung it over the line. "We'll just pull together. I know this isn't what any of us imagined, but since Christmas is nearly upon us, we should plan for some sort of celebration."

"The Catholic church needs folks to sing in the choir for the midnight mass on Christmas Eve," Leah offered.

"We aren't Catholic."

Leah looked to Karen and shrugged. "It doesn't matter. They said they'd take anybody they could get. Apparently the other churches help them out on Christmas Eve, then the Catholics come and help out on Christmas Day with our church. I guess they just want it to sound pretty for Jesus' birthday."

To Karen, the idea didn't seem like such a bad one. It was a pleasant thought to imagine churches joining together to offer each other support in spite of their differences. "I suppose we could go sing with them on Christmas Eve. I'll speak to Adrik about it."

"Jacob won't want to go. He can't sing. He says that Ma and I were the only ones who were blessed with that talent. He and Pa couldn't carry a tune no matter how hard they tried."

Karen noted the twinge of sorrow in Leah's voice. Her mother had died prior to the family's coming north, and her father was believed to have died in an avalanche near Sheep Camp. The child had no one, save her brother, Jacob, to call family. Karen loved the girl, however. Her brother, too. Karen had become a surrogate big sister and mother all rolled into one. She had made a promise to herself and to God that she would care for these children until they were grown and able to care for themselves. It seemed a companionable arrangement, and they offered each other comfort in the wake of each tragedy.

And the entourage had known their share of sorrow. Karen had come to Alaska in hopes of finding her missionary father. He had died before they could be reunited. Grace had lost her sister-in-law, Miranda, during a storm on Lake Laberge. This had also been a huge blow to the morale of the party—especially to Adrik's friend Crispin Thibault, who fancied himself in love with Miranda. Crispin had long since parted their company—seeking his solace in a bottle of whiskey rather than God. He was one more casualty of the gold rush as far as Karen was concerned.

The frozen north was well known for exacting its toll. Families all around them had suffered loss. Babies and children died from malnutrition and exposure to the cold. Women died in childbirth, and men were often injured while working to mine their claims. Death was everywhere. It was the one thing that truly bound them all together—even more so than the gold.

"Isn't there some sort of town Christmas party planned?" Grace questioned. "I heard one of the nurses talking about it when I was over to the hospital the other day."

"Yes, there are plans for quite a shindig," Karen replied. "I suppose that will be the best we will have for a celebration. There's hardly opportunity or means to exchange gifts and certainly no room to put up a tree in here."

She looked around the room. The eighteen-by-twenty-foot tent had seemed so big when Adrik had managed to trade their smaller two tents for this one. Now, the walls seemed to have moved closer together. They had five people living in a space hardly big enough for two. Karen was most anxious to put an end to the adventure.

"So did you get a chance to talk to Father Judge?" Karen asked Grace. Grace had gone to the Roman Catholic hospital to inquire as to the expense for having her baby delivered there by a doctor.

"For all the good it did. He told me it would be one thousand dollars for my hospital and doctor's fees."

"A thousand?" Karen asked in disbelief. "That's outrageous. How in the world can he expect us to come up with that much money?"

"We can't," Grace replied sadly. "Apparently the hospitals are poorly equipped for women's needs. The nurse there suggested I talk to a midwife. So I spoke to a woman who lives just over the river. She can come to the tent and deliver the baby and will only charge me a hundred dollars."

Karen's emotions got the best of her. "Prices are so inflated a person can scarcely stand in one place without being charged for it. If we weren't squatting on this land now, we'd be paying through the nose for rent."

"Don't forget what Adrik said," Leah offered. "Nobody much cares that we're here right now. The town offers folks more interest because of gambling and drinking. But if they find gold over here or if someone decides it's worth something, then we'll be in trouble." She had quoted Adrik almost verbatim.

"Still, we need the town to survive. We can hardly head out into the Klondike with Grace due to have a baby any day. That would be totally senseless. It's bad enough that we're as far away as we are, especially with the river standing between us. Come spring, there will no doubt be problems," Karen muttered.

"We couldn't very well afford any of the sites in town. Not that much of anything decent was available," Grace offered.

Karen sighed and reached up to tie back her hair. "It's all about money—the love of it is destroying the heart and soul of the people who crave it."

"Still, we can hardly exist without it," Grace said, adding, "even if it is hard to come by."

"We'll just have to get the money," Leah said as if by saying the words the money might magically appear.

"Well, I was waiting to share this news until later, but I might as well tell you now. I heard about a job," Karen announced. "They need a cook at one of the restaurants. They're willing to pay $150 a month."

"To cook?" Grace questioned, looking up. "Are you sure about that amount?"

"Very sure. It was only to be one hundred dollars, but that was if I needed room and board. I convinced them that I didn't, but that I did need the extra cash. We settled on fifty dollars more, and I've agreed to take the position."

"What did Adrik say?" Grace asked, looking to Leah as if she might have the answer. The child in turn looked to Karen.

"He doesn't know about it—yet. I figured I'd tell him after I hear what news he comes back with this time. If he still hasn't managed to find us a cabin, then I'll tell him. We're running out of money, so someone has to do something. Besides, this is a good amount of guaranteed money. He may well change his mind and want us to stay here."

"We have plenty of food," Leah offered.

"Yes, but that won't last forever. Besides it's mostly dried goods. Our canned goods are running low and we haven't had fresh fruits or vegetables in forever," Karen replied. "And even though Adrik and Jacob managed to shoot an elk and a moose, there are so many other supplies we need. Soap, for one, and that costs a small fortune. I think the job is exactly what we need to help us fill our purses again. I can cook fairly well, and it's not like I'd be doing the job forever."

"I suppose not," Grace said, "but I can't imagine that Adrik will like the idea."

Karen thought of her bear of a husband. His large frame often caused folks to shy away, thus, they never learned of his gentle nature. Karen knew her husband wouldn't like the idea of her having to work to keep their heads above water. Especially when the jobs he'd managed to find while searching for a claim or housing offered so little pay. The real money was in the saloons and gambling houses, and Adrik refused to work for either of those. Karen wholeheartedly supported his conviction.

"He'll just have to get used to the idea. My mind is made up," Karen said firmly. "He knows I'm pigheaded. He knew it when he married me. It comes with the red hair and Irish heritage." She laughed at this, but a part of her was edgy and nervous at the thought of facing Adrik with the news.

———————

In the weeks that followed Miranda's return to consciousness, she gradually regained her physical strength. The old Indian woman she'd seen in her dreams proved to be a real person—so, too, the handsome man. Her surroundings were unimpressive. A crude log cabin with two rooms kept out most of the wind, but not the cold. A large cooking stove and small fireplace offered the main sources of heat, with a smaller stove in the solitary bedroom on the back of the house. It was in this room that the handsome man spent his nights.

Teddy was most unusual, Miranda had decided. It was evident he loved his work and God, but he seemed interested in little else. He worked until the late hours of the night before retiring and was almost always up and working again before Miranda would rise for the day.

Day. Now, that was a word Miranda thought rather a misnomer. There was no day or very little of it, for darkness surrounded them most of the time. Miranda thought she might go mad at times. The hours of hazy gray light were so few—only four or five at best. How she missed the sunshine and beauty of her San Francisco home. Even a foggy day there would be better than the muted light of the Yukon.

"How are you feeling today?" Teddy asked, barely looking up from the notes he was making as he crossed the room.

Miranda had taken her breakfast at the table and was still seated there, contemplating the dark. "I'm feeling much better, thank you."

"I'm glad to hear that. Nellie's returning to her family."

The words came out without any indication of concern. Miranda looked up, rather stunned. "Leaving? When?"

Teddy shrugged. "Today or tomorrow. She would have returned a long time ago, but . . ."

"But for me. I'm sorry to have been a burden on everyone. I'm so very grateful for all that you've done. Nellie, too." Miranda had shared her gratitude many times, but each time Nellie had only nodded and Teddy had actually seemed embarrassed—just as he did now.

Teddy turned away from her, but not before Miranda saw his cheeks flush.

"Yes, well. I must return to work. If we're going to be stranded here, I must accomplish as much as possible."

"But when will we go to Dawson? I need to find out if my friends survived the storm." Miranda couldn't really remember much of what had happened on that fateful day, but she did recall the rolling black clouds and rain. She had a vague memory of being tossed about on the deck of their scow, but little else until waking up in Teddy's cabin. Had she not been told that she'd most likely been thrown overboard on Lake Laberge, Miranda would have had no idea of what had happened. It simply didn't register in her memory.

Teddy put his journal aside and threw more wood into the stove. He dropped several pieces and awkwardly bent to pick them up. "I . . . well, that is to say . . ."

He turned and met her gaze. Gold-colored spectacles framed his dark brown eyes. Miranda had noticed he only wore them when he was busy with his writing. No doubt the dark wreaked havoc with his sight.

Teddy turned toward the window, as if surveying the weather conditions. "I suppose we'll be able to head out soon. I'll ask Nellie to send her son Little Charley over. I'll talk to him about helping us with the sleds."

"The snows are very deep, aren't they?" Miranda asked. She had peered from the doorway on more than one occasion and had been stunned to see the snow-covered landscape. Her hometown of San Francisco didn't get much snow—certainly nothing like this.

"That's why we'll go by sled," Teddy replied, turning to pull his coat from a hook near the door. "I must see to something. I'll be back."

Taking up a lantern, he hurried out before Miranda could make any comment. He was such a nervous sort. Miranda wasn't entirely sure if it was simply his nature or if she caused him this discomfort.

Getting up from the table, Miranda went to the stove and warmed her hands. She couldn't help but wonder about Grace and Karen and the others. She prayed they were safe. Prayed they'd not be worried overmuch about her. Teddy said it was nearly Christmas, and last Miranda could remember it had been September.

"They have no way of knowing I'm safe," she whispered. "They probably have given me up for dead." It sorrowed her to imagine them weeping over her when she was safe and sound. It sorrowed her even more to imagine they'd not made it through the storm. If she'd been thrown overboard, there was a good chance they had been lost, as well.

Dread washed over her in waves and continued with each new revelation. Mr. Davenport had said that Nellie was leaving. That would mean she'd be alone with a man. A man she scarcely knew. It certainly wasn't appropriate, yet there seemed to be no choice in the matter.

Thinking of Teddy Davenport only complicated things. His nervousness around her amused Miranda, while at the same time his lack of interest in sharing conversation or even a meal left her lonely and frustrated. He was unlike any man she'd ever known. He seemed to care whether she recovered, but he wanted very little to do with her otherwise.

Miranda supposed that should comfort her mind about the upcoming departure of Nellie. But it didn't. Instead, it only added to her worry. What if the man
was only acting this way because Nellie was around? True, she was an Indian and
most whites held little respect for the natives, but it was very possible it was her
presence in the house, sleeping on the pallet at the foot of Miranda's bed, that
kept Mr. Davenport silent and subdued.

Picking at the worn wool skirt she wore, Miranda could only pray for comfort.
"God, please give me hope. Please watch over me and strengthen me so I can go
to Dawson and find my family and friends. And please, God, please let them all
be safe and well." She thought again of the man who'd offered her a place in his
cabin. "Thank you, Lord, for Mr. Davenport's kindness. Please, please, let his heart
be fixed on you. Don't let him hurt me." But even as she prayed, Miranda felt the
words were almost ridiculous. Teddy Davenport had proved to be no threat to
her well-being. Perhaps she was borrowing trouble by even concerning herself
with the matter.

With little else that she could do, Miranda curled up on her bed and dozed in
the warmth of the heavy quilts. Her dreams were interrupted, however, when
Teddy came bursting through the door.

"You'll never believe what I just found!" He panted and his breath came out
in little white clouds that faded in the warmth of the room. He stomped his snowy
boots and held up a small branch of dried, dead leaves.

"It's a *Salix hookeriana.* They're supposed to be limited to the Alaskan Territory."

"I beg your pardon?" Miranda questioned and got to her feet. She'd never
seen Mr. Davenport more animated. "A *Salix* what?"

"*Hookeriana,*" he declared. "A Hooker willow. William Jackson Hooker discovered them and wrote about this species as being isolated to Alaskan plant life—
but here it is in the Yukon. He was wrong! This will certainly validate my work."

Miranda sunk back to the bed. She looked to the man and tried to gather
some excitement for his find, but her heart was still racing from the shock.

"I suppose I am very happy for you, Mr. Davenport," she finally offered.

"And well you should be. This is most sensational."

Teddy appeared mindless of the snow from his boots melting into puddles on
the floor. He crossed the room, took down a book, and without even bothering
to shed his coat, went to the stove where he kept his ink ready for use.

"I might never have found it but for your arrival and our late departure. A
rare specimen, indeed," he declared, then turned his full attention to the branch.

"Glad I could be of help," Miranda muttered and shook her head. The man
was truly a rare specimen himself.

─┤ C H A P T E R T H R E E ├─

"WELL, I'LL BE!" declared Adrik Ivankov. He slapped his right thigh and let out a loud and hearty laugh. "If it ain't Gumption Lindquist."

An old man with a full head of snowy white hair looked up from his plate of food. His thick and equally white mustache twitched in amusement. "Ja, dat be me."

"I figured you for grizzly food by now," Adrik said, pulling Karen along with him. "Gump, I want you to meet my wife. You always said I'd never get married unless I found a woman uglier than me. I just wanted to show you how wrong you were. I got the cream of the crop."

"Ja, dat you did," the Swede said, putting aside his plate. He got to his feet and without warning, pulled Karen into a welcoming embrace. "She looks like good stock. You done well for yourself, boy."

"Karen, this old reprobate is Gumption Lindquist. Gump to his friends."

Gump released Karen and nodded. "Ja, you call me Gump."

Karen smiled at the old man. He looked much like many of the other miners, well-worn and weathered, yet he had a contentment about him that others seemed to lack. "Gumption is such a unique name for someone to call their child."

Gump's smile broadened, revealing a full set of perfectly matched teeth. "My folks, they had six boys before I come along. Not a one of them was amountin' to much, so my father, he say, 'Let's call this one Gumption. I've always wanted one of the boys to have some, might as well give it to this one in a name.'"

Adrik reached out and reclaimed his wife. "Too bad they missed again with you."

Gump laughed and picked his plate back up. "Ja, they didn't think much of me leavin' the farm to come north when I was a boy."

"So were you living in America?" Karen asked.

"Ja, I was born in Sweden but grew up in Kansas. We had a farm."

"Gump came north way back when he was just seventeen," Adrik told her. "Of course, I wasn't born yet, but my father was. He and Gump were good friends. They used to fish together."

"Ja, dat's right." The old man shoveled a huge hunk of moose tongue into his mouth and smiled as if he'd died and gone to heaven.

Karen looked to her husband. "I wish Grace would have felt like coming tonight. This looks like quite the celebration."

"It's a good one, by golly," Gump replied. "I remember last year. I had Christmas dinner with some of the fellas who were working claims near to mine. We had quite the time, not near so good as this, but nearly."

Karen heard the makeshift band strike up a Christmas carol. It echoed across the main room of the log house. Donated by one of the local families, the cabin was about twenty-by-twenty and was decorated from top to bottom with whatever could be found. Greenery, guns, and even a Union Jack flag had been nailed to the wall to lend itself to the occasion.

"So, Gump, did you strike it rich?"

"Nah, I find a bit now and then. Usually enough to keep me interested," the man said in between bites of food. " 'Course, with the cold you have to wait. I light a few fires and dig up some ground. Come spring I'll go through it, all righty."

"Do you know anyone who's selling out for a cheap price? Even a fractional claim?" Adrik asked.

"Nah. Most folks are hunkered down for the vinter."

Karen liked the man's singsong cadence of speech. His intonations went up and down like a child's seesaw.

"I was afraid of that," Adrik said, frowning. "I'd heard someone mention the government was changing the rules on claims. Guess we'll have to check into it. We've not had much luck in securing a claim or a house. We're living in a tent across the river, about a mile or so from town. There's five of us, soon to be six. My wife's friend is expecting a baby soon."

"It's not a good time to be havin' a baby."

Karen tried not to let the old man's tone frighten her. She knew well enough the odds were against them. The bitter cold and lack of money did nothing to reassure her that things would be all right.

"Vait a minute," Gump said suddenly. "I know a man who says he vants to hire folks to help him. Maybe he vould hire you on and give you a place to live."

"Does he have a cabin?" Adrik questioned.

"Ja, a good big one, with two, maybe three rooms. He had him some friends vorkin' with him, but they go home before vinter. He been out there all by himself, and I know he could use the help."

"Well, I'd like to talk to him," Adrik said, looking to Karen. "We'd be happy to work for the man. Karen is a good cook and fine housekeeper."

"Not that he'd know," Karen threw in. "We haven't lived in a house since we married."

Gump laughed. "By golly, we go ask him tomorrow. He didn't come tonight or we could ask him now."

"That's all right. It'll wait until tomorrow," Adrik answered.

For the first time in a long while, Karen heard hope in her husband's voice. She knew he worried incessantly about his little band of travelers. He and Jacob had taken odd jobs from time to time—sometimes splitting wood or helping with construction. But more often than not, there was nothing to do—not that would earn them any money.

Karen thought at least a dozen times to tell Adrik about the new job she'd taken. He wouldn't be happy, however, and because of this she delayed. She didn't want to upset him. Now that he had prospects of a place to live and a real job, Karen figured she'd just wait until they knew something for sure. For the time, she'd just enjoy the holidays and the party that the people of Dawson had put together.

The celebration was a kind of combination for Christmas and Boxing Day. The party lasted well into the night and by the time they'd stuffed themselves with moose and mince pies, plum pudding, and cakes, it was nearly one o'clock in the morning.

Jacob had taken Leah back to the tent hours earlier, and now as Karen and Adrik made their way from the happy celebration, Karen couldn't help but feel a sense of desire to keep her husband to herself for just a little longer.

"I wish we didn't have to go back—just yet. I kind of like being alone with you."

Adrik looked at her and grinned. "Why, Mrs. Ivankov, behave yourself."

Overhead the northern lights danced and crackled. No matter how many times she saw it, Karen could never get used to the wonder of this cosmic show. Red and green ribbons of light danced on the cold night air. The colors changed, and white, almost as bright as sunlight for just a moment, burst through and streaked the skies. This was followed by blue and then green.

"I've never seen anything so beautiful!" Karen declared.

Adrik pulled her into his arms. "Nor have I."

She looked up and found his gazed fixed on her. "I meant the skies. The aurora."

"I didn't." His voice was low and husky. Karen hardly noticed the sub-zero temperatures around them.

"I love you, Adrik." She thought for a moment of telling him about her job but knew it would ruin the moment. "Please never forget how very much I love you."

He lowered his lips to hers for the briefest kiss, then pulled away. "We'd best get home or we just might freeze this way."

Karen giggled. "Can't you see the story in the *Klondike Nugget*? Husband and wife found frozen together."

"It wouldn't be the first time, sadly enough. When I think of all the folks who've been lost on the trail north . . . Well, it's enough to discourage a man." Adrik held her close and moved them toward home. "I'll be gone several days as I travel to speak with the man about the cabin," he said, changing the subject. "Maybe even weeks. Gump can put me up. Will you be all right?"

"I'm sure we will. We're not that far from help if we need it. Plus, we have those two other families living nearby. If I need anything I can always call on them."

"I know, but I just want reassurance. I figure to take Jacob with me. He wants to ask about his pa around the claims."

"He just isn't ready to let go of the hope that Bill is still alive." Karen felt sorry for the boy. Leah had handled her father's death better than her older brother. Jacob seemed driven to confirm his father's existence or death, while Leah was content to relegate it to the past.

"I wish we could be certain of what happened to Bill, but so many people have lost loved ones. The lists held by the Mounties go on and on. Folks get lost on the trail, freeze under an avalanche, or drown in the rapids."

"Or during a lake storm, like Miranda."

"Exactly. This territory is unforgiving—and is not in the leastwise interested in whether it hurts your feelings. It's more likely to claim a life than to spare it. My guess is that both Bill and Miranda have been sharing the Lord's table in heaven."

They were nearing the tent and Karen couldn't help but pause. "Adrik, I know God has blessed us and will show us where to go—where to settle. My biggest concern right now is for Grace. It's not going to be easy to have a baby out here—in the dead of winter."

"I thought she arranged to have the baby at the hospital in town."

"She would have, but the priest told her it would cost a thousand dollars."

"That's robbery. I thought they were doing God's work."

Karen smiled. "Well, apparently God's work costs more up on the Klondike."

"Everything costs more here. I just hope Grace can nurse that baby without any trouble. What little fresh cow's milk can be had is sixteen dollars a gallon, and canned milk is running out fast."

"I'm sure we'll get by," Karen told him, looping her arm through his. But in truth, she worried about such things as well. Perhaps if she told him about the job, he'd relax and accept that God had provided them a way to at least have money to buy the essentials they needed.

"Come on, let's get inside. The temperature's already dropped considerably. Gump says it's going way down—maybe even as low as sixty below."

Karen shivered just at the prospect of such an unreasonable temperature. "I doubt I'll ever be warm again."

Adrik laughed. "I'll keep you warm. Once we get snuggled into my sleeping bag, there won't be room for the cold to bother us."

"Won't be room for you to breathe either."

"Then I'll hold my breath. Being that close to you leaves me breathless anyway."

———

Sometimes when Miranda first woke up, she could almost believe that she was safely back at home in San Francisco. At those times, like now, she would purposefully keep her eyes closed tight and imagine that when she opened them she'd see the white fluttering curtains that graced her bedroom window at home. She could almost smell her mother's cooking. Oatmeal and sausages. Coffee and tea.

She liked to pretend what she would do that day. Thoughts of long strolls in the park or shopping for fresh fish at the wharf seemed most appealing. Funny how she had taken all that for granted.

"Oh, bother!" Teddy declared from across the room.

Miranda realized the poor man was struggling to fix his own breakfast again. Smiling, she eased out from the bed, fully dressed albeit wrinkled. She used her fingers to get the better part of the tangles out of her hair. Mr. Davenport had seemed completely oblivious to her needs. A blizzard had kept them locked inside the cabin after Nellie had gone back to her village. There had been no sign of Little Charley and the dog sleds, but in this weather, Miranda hadn't really expected them.

She quickly plaited her hair and tied it with a worn piece of rawhide. "Can I help?" she asked, coming to kitchen area.

"I would be very grateful if you would take this matter over," Teddy replied as he gestured toward a pan full of oatmeal, which was running over onto the tiny stovetop.

Miranda wanted to laugh, but the situation was such that she didn't. She merely took the task in hand. "How much oatmeal did you put into the pan?"

"I don't know. I filled it halfway and then stirred water in until it was filled."

Miranda kept her head down so that he couldn't see her smile. "That's way too much oatmeal. You only need a cup or so to make enough for both of us."

"I can see that now. At least the coffee is passable. Strong, but passable."

"Good. Now why don't you set the table, and I'll have this mess under control in just a minute."

Teddy nodded and went quietly to the task of pulling down bowls from the cupboard. It was in moments like this that Miranda liked Mr. Davenport very much. But other times she didn't know what to make of him. He seemed so closed off—so antisocial. He constantly buried his nose in his books and writings, and whenever Miranda tried to talk to him, he only grunted and murmured unintelligible answers.

This, added to the fact that he had no apparent understanding of time, left Miranda frustrated with the man. She'd asked him several times when they might find their way to Dawson. He'd only shrugged and suggested they were at the mercy of the weather and the natives. Without the sled dogs and help of his friends they were stranded, because Teddy had no way to pack his supplies and books back to Dawson.

Miranda cleared away the excess oatmeal, salvaging what she could for their meal. She turned to bring the pan to the table when she smelled the unmistakable odor of something burning.

She stopped and sniffed the air. Turning, she looked once again to the stove to make certain she'd not missed some of the oatmeal in her cleanup and was surprised to see the smoke wasn't coming from atop the stove, but rather the oven door showed the telltale sign of black wisps.

"Mr. Davenport," Miranda questioned, turning back to Teddy. "Have you something in the oven?"

"Oh, dear," he muttered, dashing across the room and sending Miranda sprawling backward onto the floor. Oatmeal flew from the pan and landed everywhere, including on Miranda's only skirt and blouse.

Teddy, meanwhile, reached into the oven, showing at least the presence of mind to use a potholder, and pulled out a pan of charred remains that Miranda supposed to be biscuits.

Thinking it all rather amusing in spite of, or perhaps because of, the oatmeal that oozed down her cheek and blouse, Miranda began to giggle—quietly at first, and then louder. Teddy caught sight of her and shook his head.

"This isn't funny. Just look at this mess. Look at yourself."

"I am." Miranda wiped away the tears that had trickled down her cheeks. "That's why I'm laughing."

Teddy cocked his head to one side and then tossed the pan into the sink. "Well, I see nothing funny about this. Our breakfast is either burned or splattered across the floor."

Miranda shook off her mirth and got to her feet, no thanks to Teddy offering any help. "My mother always said, 'When bad times come we can either laugh at them or cry.'"

"That makes no sense. Was your mother quite all right in the head?"

Miranda picked up the pan. "I assure you, my mother was quite sane. She was also very content with life because she tried never to let problems overwhelm her. I wish I could be more like her."

"I'm not entirely certain that would be to your benefit."

Miranda smiled and began wiping up the oatmeal. "Well, I know for certain that it would greatly benefit us both to stop taking things so seriously. Who knows, Mr. Davenport. You might actually have some fun."

———————

As Teddy added wood to the fireplace and prepared to retire for the night, he thought of Miranda's words and shook his head. His mother had always been one for having fun. As a young boy, Teddy had enjoyed her zest for living. Where his father would have been content to sit in his solarium cultivating a new type of rose, Eugenia Davenport was one for cultivating life.

It had been his mother who had taught Teddy to ride and hunt, his mother who had taken him to the museum and opera. She had spent hours teaching him about art and the pleasure that could be had in a single painting.

His mother had loved people with a great passion, and her enthusiasm was contagious. Teddy remembered as a boy being allowed to join his mother for luncheons and afternoon teas. The food was always an adventure of flavors served on the finest china. And it was his mother's laughter that rang out most clearly in his memory—laughter not so very much different than that of Miranda Colton.

The flames greedily consumed the dried logs, crackling and popping. Teddy's memories intertwined with the present. His mother and Miranda Colton were very much alike. They both had a flair for living that seemed to overwhelm their environment. Teddy was more like his father. He enjoyed the quietness and solitude of introspection. He preferred a good book or time spent with his plants, to conversation and revelry.

He thought of his father succumbing to an ailment the doctors were never quite sure how to diagnose. Cancer seemed the most likely culprit, but there was nothing that could have been done on any account. His father simply wasted away, day after day. His dreams of travel to North America dying with him.

"I won't disappoint you, Father," Teddy whispered, staring into the fire as if he could see the image of Albert Davenport in the flames. "I'll stay the course."

He heard Miranda sigh in her sleep and felt a foreign sensation creep up his spine. She was a lovely woman—gentle and spirited and lovely—in spite of the lack of amenities with which to care for herself.

Eugenia Davenport had also been a lovely woman—and she had broken his father's heart. Teddy squared his shoulders and firmed his resolve. He wouldn't fall victim to the same temptations as his father. He wouldn't allow a woman to put an end to his dreams.

CHAPTER FOUR

"PLEASE UNDERSTAND," Miranda began. "I don't mean to be a bother, but I'm most desperate to get to Dawson City. Is there no way we can get a message to your native friends?"

Teddy looked up, distraught to have been drawn once again from his work. "Do explain to me, Miss Colton, how we might send this message."

Miranda crossed her arms. He noted the determined look in her eye. She was a pretty young woman, probably at least five years his junior. *Her eyes are most appealing*, he thought, noticing the way she watched him with unyielding interest. He remembered his determination from the night before and shook off his thoughts of admiration.

"Please understand me, Mr. Davenport. I realize the situation is difficult, but might we simply hike out? You could leave your things here until your friends could bring the sleds. I'm completely well now, and I know you might not believe this, but I'm fully capable of hiking long distances."

"Leave my things here?" he said, hardly concerning himself with anything else she'd said. The very thought of it was absurd. The woman simply didn't have any understanding of his work or its importance—just like his mother, who couldn't understand when Teddy took up his father's torch, determined to pick up where his father left off. "I can't just leave my things here."

"And I can't just stay here all winter. I want to know what happened to my friends. I need to know whether they made it or not. Your plants will still be here in the weeks to come."

"And if your friends are in Dawson, they will still be there as well," Teddy countered. "There's no chance they could make their way out if they've not already taken their leave. At least it's highly improbable. Certainly, there are ways, as in any situation. Dog sled teams can be hired and such. Walking out is possible, but very dangerous and highly unlikely unless, of course, your friends are native to the area and quite used to the harsh elem—"

"Oh, you are impossible!" Miranda stomped her foot and moved to her corner of the cabin.

Teddy looked at her in surprise. He'd merely tried to explain the situation. There was no call for her to get so angry. He waited, thinking she might begin again. When she remained silent, he breathed a sigh of relief. Maybe she'd leave him alone now and let him work. He picked up a piece of charcoal and began to sketch the outline of a dried subalpine buttercup.

Ranunculus eschscholtzii, he wrote in small charcoal lettering. *Petals—five, colored a brilliant yellow.* He went to work sketching the petals of the flower.

"Why can't you try to understand my position?"

Bother! She is back. Teddy looked up, hoping his expression betrayed his frustration. Slowly he took off the gold-framed spectacles he used for his closeup work. "Miss Colton, I have a feeling you will endeavor to explain it, so I might as well hear you out." He put his elbows on the table and leaned his head against his hand.

Miranda took the chair opposite him and folded her hands as if he might be about to serve tea. Teddy was more frustrated at the interruptions than angry. After all, she did cook a nice meal and her mannerisms were not at all unpleasant—except for this incessant nagging. He hated to continue conjuring up the likeness of his mother, but Miranda's attitude was very much like hers. They were both very likable, but not entirely thoughtful.

"My friends most likely believe me dead. Imagine their pain and suffering. It's inhumane to sit here and let them assume the worst. What if they've written to my mother and father?

"I'm not without regard for the work you're doing here, Mr. Davenport. In fact, I highly respect it. I love books, and I well imagine that your book will be quite fascinating and accurate. I'll probably be determined to purchase a copy— not only because of having known you, but also because of the topic. Even so, you must understand my position."

Her expression bore evidence to the pain in her heart. Teddy lost himself for a moment in her huge brown eyes. Her eyes were just about the same light nutty color as the cone of the Canadian spruce. If he'd saved a specimen he could show her. He looked around the room for a moment, and then realized she'd fallen silent.

Looking back to her, Teddy offered an apologetic smile. "I say, please continue."

"Why should I? You don't care. All you can think about is your own need."

"Until recently, that was my main concentration, I must admit. However, with your arrival, I found my plans very much altered. You cannot, with any reasonable truth, suggest otherwise."

Miranda leaned forward, causing Teddy to pull back ever so slightly. The young woman made him nervous. He'd never been around many women other than his mother or servants. This woman had the ability to rattle his thoughts and leave him struggling for words.

"I wasn't suggesting that your life hadn't been altered by my arrival. I am very sorry you were delayed. But I'm even sorrier that you continue our delay." She got to her feet and put her hands on her hips. "Look, if you haven't any desire to take me to Dawson, then perhaps I'll set out on my own. I have the things Nellie left me and I'll just follow the river. It can't be that hard."

Teddy actually smiled at this. She no doubt assumed he'd find such a suggestion threatening. "You cannot be serious. The temperature is forty below, and the river is some distance from here. The creek will do you little good because it branches off in several directions—none of which lead to Dawson, which I might add is a good three days journey from here. Not to mention we are enjoying only about four hours of daylight, and most of that is spent under heavy clouds and snow."

"I don't care. My friends and family mean too much to me."

She turned to go to her bed. Teddy watched as she began pulling together the things Nellie had given her. She laced on the thick elk-skin boots Nellie had crafted while tending to Miranda. Next, she pulled on a fur-lined cloak, also crafted by the old Indian woman. Somewhat amused by her show of independence, Teddy secured his glasses on his nose and began to study the petals of the buttercup in more detail.

Maybe her persistence at gathering her meager belongings would wear Miss Colton out and leave her willing to forego her adventure. Not that he truly believed she'd step foot outside the door.

Teddy lost himself in thoughts of his drawing and the work at hand. There was no sense in worrying over his guest. She would settle herself down and realize the sensibility in waiting until help came their way. Perhaps she'd even put on a pot of tea. It wasn't until he heard the door to the cabin open and felt the cold rush of arctic air that Teddy realized he'd underestimated Miranda Colton.

Miranda slammed the door to the cabin, hoping it jarred Mr. Davenport's teeth right out of his head. The man was insufferable. He kept his nose buried in his notes and drawings from morning light until dark. Even then, he would often take up a lantern and work until the allotted supply of oil was gone.

Stepping off the small porch, Miranda felt an alarming sense of folly when her booted feet sunk into snow that came up over her knees. And this was in the area that Teddy had managed to clear away prior to the last big snow. How deep must it be in other areas?

Miranda pulled her fur hat down, trying desperately to ward off the frigid temperatures. Her eyes were crusting with ice as she blinked against the painfully cold air.

"Oh, God," she murmured as she pushed out across the once shoveled path. "I need your help. I have to get to Dawson. I have to know if Grace is safe." The frigid temperatures slowed her steps. She was so poorly prepared. Even without Teddy there to tell her so, Miranda knew she would be dead before she ever reached Dawson.

"What do I do, God?" she whispered, burying her face into the fur lining of her cloak. She was grateful Nellie had left her such a fine gift. She only wished the fur extended to cover her entire body.

A twig snapped and Miranda froze in her steps at the sound, her heart racing. Could it be wolves? She'd heard horror stories of wolves that attacked humans and fed off their bones while the person was still alive. Swallowing hard, she turned and strained to see into the darkening woods. If she were to be attacked, she would meet her assailant head on.

She let out a long breath when Teddy's bundled figure emerged from the shadows. "Why are you following me?"

"Because someone has to," he replied. "Stop this nonsense and come back to the cabin. You're lost already. At this rate you'll end up in Whitehorse before you ever see Dawson. Now come along. Much longer out here and we'll both pay the price."

Miranda knew it was hopeless to argue. Her lungs already hurt from the frigid air. "Very well, Mr. Davenport. As it appears I have no other choice, I will do as you suggest."

"This truly wasn't necessary," he said as they made their way back. "You may believe me to be heartless and completely void of understanding, but I know very well that your need is great."

"You certainly don't act like it," she said, struggling to keep up. Stubbing her toe against a buried rock or branch, Miranda cried out and would have fallen face first in the snow, if not for Teddy.

Steadying her with one hand, he reached out and took her bundled things with the other. "I say, we'll both be ready for a spot of tea when we get back inside."

Miranda felt completely humiliated. It had been purely childish and even self-ish to take this action.

Once back in the cabin, Miranda warmed her hands by the fire. Her gloves had helped to keep the cold at bay, but her fingers were numb, as were her toes.

"I fail to see what you thought that would prove."

Miranda looked up to see Teddy watching her most intently. "I thought it would prove my willingness to risk my life in order to ease the concern of my friends."

"But if you had died on the way it would have proven nothing—especially if your friends think you already dead. You see, the logical thing—"

"Oh, please don't give me your analytical review of the matter," Miranda said, closing her eyes in exasperation. "My heart has no understanding of it and it is my heart that urges me to find my friends. Can't you see that?" She opened her eyes and looked at him. His expression seemed to suggest that he could not comprehend her meaning.

"Oh, just forget about it. I don't expect you to understand." She turned back to the stove.

"I am not without concern for your emotions," Teddy countered. "But I am a man of logic, and that logic tells me that we dare not attempt the wilderness on our own. I've stayed alive up here by listening to the advice of those who know better. You'd do well to follow my example."

Miranda knew the truth in his words, but she didn't want to admit it. A tear trailed down her cheek as she realized she might well be stranded until spring. She turned away so that Teddy wouldn't see her cry. No sense in bothering him with her sorrow.

"I'm sure you know best, Mr. Davenport," she finally said. "I'll try my best to understand."

"Perhaps you should take some of your own advice and not take this situation so seriously."

Miranda realized he was using her words against her. She turned, hands on her hips. "Mr. Davenport, laughing over spilled oatmeal is one thing, but my dear sweet mother may very well be inconsolable over the loss of her only daughter. My friends may be suffering guilt and pain over their belief that they've played a part in my death. I cannot help but take this situation seriously."

Teddy gave a halfhearted smile, causing him to look youthful and vulnerable. Miranda almost felt sorry for him. His gentle spirit was no match for her temper. Calming a bit, Miranda drew a deep breath. "I know there is nothing to be done. I will try to be useful, instead of antagonistic."

After arranging her meager belongings under the bed, Miranda stretched out atop the bed and tried not to think of home. She tried her best to put aside thoughts of how sad Christmas must have been for her parents. She tried not to worry over whether or not Grace had given birth. *I might as well be stranded on the moon for all the good it does me. Never mind that we are less than one hundred miles from Dawson. Never mind that it's already January of a new year and I have no idea where any of my friends and family are.*

She thought for a moment of Crispin Thibault. Both he and Mr. Davenport bore themselves with a sort of European flair—that flavor of aristocracy that Americans always seemed so desperate to emulate. But where Mr. Davenport was driven and passionate about his work, Crispin had been a free spirit—simply living to experience life. He hardly cared where they went or when they might arrive. Crispin was the kind of man who would be just as content to get in the boat and let the river take him where it would. Mr. Davenport, on the other hand, would go no place unless it merited him to do so. They were completely opposite—and in more ways than one, for Miranda knew that Mr. Davenport was a godly man. He prayed and read Scriptures to her every day. He also talked of God on occasion, but for the most part dedicated himself to his work.

"I am taking the liberty to reheat the leftover portion of our luncheon stew," Teddy said, jarring Miranda from her thoughts.

Miranda shook her head and sat up. The man had a penchant for destroying meals. "I'll heat it," she said getting to her feet. Reluctantly, Miranda crossed the room and took the pot from Teddy's hands.

"I'm happy to help."

Miranda looked at him and forced herself to smile. He was trying to make up for his attitude and lack of interest in her situation. "I suppose you could slice the bread."

"I believe I can handle that," he said, heading to the counter.

Miranda worked in silence for several moments. Teddy Davenport was such an unusual man. She found herself wishing she knew more about him. "Tell me about your homeland, Mr. Davenport."

"It's certainly different from this place," he answered. "We would never have to endure cold like this. In fact, it rarely snowed."

"What part of England are you from?"

"Well, actually, my parents owned two estates. One was very close to London. My mother's people were from the area, and she loved the city. London, of course, is quite fascinating. There are many fine places to go—museums, shops, and such."

"But you didn't care for it as much as the other place?" Miranda questioned, feeling certain her guess was true.

Teddy smiled. "You are very astute. My favorite place was by far and away the estate of my father's people. It was in Cornwall, not far from the coast. It was quite lovely there year round. We had magnificent gardens and my father was good to train me in every area of horticulture."

"Do you still live there? I mean, when you aren't in Canada." She was amazed that he had shared so much information with her.

"I do," Teddy admitted. He took the bread to the table.

"Do you have caretakers who tend it while you're away?"

"Of course. They tend it while I'm in residence as well."

"You must be very wealthy." Miranda never heard his response, however, for without warning, the front door blasted open and Miranda reached out to take hold of Teddy's arm as if for protection. She ducked behind him when two bulky figures entered the room.

Teddy stood frozen in place, and Miranda wasn't sure if he was more concerned with his visitors or her actions. It took a great deal of willpower to let go of his arm and step back. Watching the figures shake themselves of their ice-crusted blankets, Miranda wasn't at all surprised to see that their visitors were Indian.

"Little Charley!"

Her heart skipped a beat. Could it be? Had help arrived? Were they truly going to leave this place and make their way to Dawson?

Teddy turned to her and smiled. "It would appear that, even if my knowledge of your need is less than what you desire, God has heard your prayers. Little Charley has come to take us to Dawson."

—⊣ C H A P T E R F I V E ⊢—

IT HAD BEEN MORE than two weeks since Adrik and Jacob had gone off with Gump Lindquist, and frankly, Leah Barringer was starting to worry. She knew her brother was quite capable of taking care of himself, but the separation was maddening. She couldn't seem to convince Jacob that searching for their father was a waste of time. He had no doubt died in the Palm Sunday avalanche the previous year. She could accept it. Why couldn't he?

Stirring a pot of beans, Leah heard Grace stir from her bed across the room. The tent allowed for very little privacy. Adrik had stretched a rope across the area where Grace and Leah shared a crude bed. Karen had draped a blanket over the rope to partition the room off for the sake of changing clothes and such, but it also blocked what precious heat could be had.

Leah glanced over and saw Grace struggling to sit up. Karen had long since left for her job at the Sourdough Café, leaving the two women to entertain themselves for the day. Leah knew there was washing to tend to as well as bread to make, so keeping busy wouldn't be difficult.

"I've got some prunes and oatmeal ready for breakfast," she called to Grace. "And I've already put the beans on for our supper. By the time they've cooked all day with bacon, they should taste pretty good."

"Leah," Grace barely whispered the name. "Leah, something is happening."

Leah put down the spoon and came to the bed. "What's the matter?"

Grace looked up, her eyes filled with pain and fear. "It's the baby. The baby is coming."

Leah had watched her mother die in childbirth, there was no way she wanted to be left alone with another woman who might well do the same. "I'll have to get help." She looked around the tent as if the answer might well be at hand.

Grace reached out and gripped her arm. "Remember where the midwife lives? Just down by the river. You'll have to go and bring her back."

Leah nodded. "Will you be all right while I'm gone? I mean, it's still dark, and Karen's already gone to work."

Grace released her hold. "I'll be fine." She clutched her abdomen. "Just hurry."

Leah ran for her coat and boots. "I'll be as fast as I can."

Once outside the tent, Leah quickly realized her main adversary was the weather. Heavy snow made the going difficult. She held a lantern in front of her as she stumbled again and again, wishing silently that she owned snowshoes for such occasions. Assessing the situation momentarily, Leah tried to reason out what was to be done.

"Help me, Father God," she prayed aloud. The wind bit into her face, stinging painfully as it pelted her with ice and snow. The path seemed to obliterate before her very eyes. "I don't know which way to go."

After a search that seemed to take forever, Leah stumbled down what she hoped was the path to the river. If she was on the right path, she knew she would soon be approaching the small bridge she could cross over to reach the Dawson side. The midwife lived in a small cabin behind one of the more popular saloons. Leah hated to go there alone, but there wasn't any chance of a proper companion—save God.

The snow seemed to ease up a bit, but the darkness was just as maddening. The lantern did very little to aid her. Leah slipped and felt the rock solid ice against her knee. She struggled to keep from dropping the lantern as she got back to her feet. Moving even more cautiously now, Leah continued to pray. She hated the darkness. It was frightening and so filled with death and dying. Karen had brought home a copy of the town paper that told of an entire family that had been found frozen to death in their tent. There were other deaths listed as well. Miners who hadn't been able to endure the harsh cold of winter. Babies and children who were no match for the elements. The horror of such tragedies frightened Leah more than she wanted to admit.

The north had already claimed her father's life. Would it also claim hers?

Leah finally reached the river and breathed a sigh of relief. She had only to cross the bridge and then make her way to the midwife's cabin. It shouldn't be that hard, she reasoned. The snow was lessening, and the glow of light from the windows in town could now been seen through the flurry of white. God had heard her prayers. Everything would be all right.

But it wasn't all right. After Leah had pounded on the midwife's door for over ten minutes, a woman bearing heavy makeup and a haggard look impatiently opened the door and told Leah there would be no help—the midwife had taken ill and lay on her deathbed.

"I have to have help," Leah declared. "My friend is having a baby. She's all alone."

"Women been doing that for years, sweetie," the older woman told her. "Just grab yourself a pair of scissors and a ball of string. Boil some water for cleaning up afterwards and warm some blankets by the stove. Nature will do the rest."

Leah felt her stomach lurch. "But what if there are problems?"

The woman shrugged. "Honey, I can't help you there. Get her to the hospital or get yourself another midwife." She closed the door, leaving Leah to stand alone.

Leah thought of Grace all alone and knew she couldn't leave her without someone to help. Still, she didn't know what to do. *Karen will know,* Leah thought. *Karen will know exactly what to do.*

Leah turned in the direction of the Sourdough Café. She pulled her coat tighter and hugged the lamp as close as she could. She knew it was risky to take the shortcut behind the saloon, but time was of the essence. She picked up her pace, feeling the hair on the back of her neck begin to prickle. She saw things in the shadows. Her breath came in strained pants as she pressed toward the street.

Coming out onto the main thoroughfare, Leah slowed her steps and her breathing. *I'm being such a goose,* she thought. *I'm scared of my own shadow.*

At the Sourdough, things only worsened. Karen had gone off with the owner's wife and daughter to retrieve several crates of dried fruit. The man who told her this had no idea how long she would be.

"Please tell her she's needed at home," Leah said, realizing she had to get back to the tent. Grace might very well be giving birth any moment.

"I'll tell her, but she's needed here, too," the man replied gruffly.

"Yes, but her friend is having a baby. That must be more important than cooking."

The man grunted something unintelligible and continued sweeping the wood floor. Exasperated from her lack of success, Leah bolstered her courage and headed back to the tent. She had just rounded the corner of the Klondike Gold Saloon when she tripped and fell face first to the ground.

Though she had somehow managed to keep the lantern from breaking, Leah wasn't entirely sure the same could be said for herself. She felt as though the wind had been knocked right out of her. Easing up on her hands, Leah could barely stifle a scream. The rock she had presumed she had tripped over was no rock at all, but rather the extended leg of a man—a man who appeared to be dead.

Leah picked herself up and pulled the lamp close. She gasped at the ghostly figure. "Crispin!"

She placed the lantern down beside him and reached up with her gloved hands to pat his frozen face. "Oh, Crispin, please be alive."

The man opened his eyes ever so slowly. A grin spread across his face. "I know you."

His breath reeked of whiskey. Leah frowned. He wasn't dead, but he was drunk. "Crispin, you'll die if you stay here. Come with me. I need you."

He blinked hard several times, then struggled to get to his feet. Leah helped him stand, forgetting her fall and the pain it had caused. "Crispin, Grace is having her baby, and I can't find anyone to come and help me."

"I can't help you. I have never done . . . that . . . sort of thing." His speech was slurred, and he began to weave back and forth on his feet.

Leah wasn't entirely sure she could sober him up or get him to understand the seriousness of the situation, but for the moment he was all she had. "Come on, Crispin. I can make you some strong coffee back at our tent. We're just across the river and up the path a ways."

Crispin seemed to forget her mention of the baby and put an arm around Leah's shoulder. "Are you having a party? I could use a drink."

"Yes," Leah said, pulling him toward the bridge. "I'm having a party."

How she ever managed to get back to the tent was a miracle to Leah Barringer. She struggled against the ever-increasing snow, and as the wind picked up to howl a blizzard in their path, Leah found herself half carrying the drunken man.

She almost expected to find Grace dead upon her return. She'd been able to push aside the images of her mother only by focusing on the task to retrieve the midwife. But now those images came back in a rush. She could see it all as if it were only yesterday. How very pale her mother had been just before closing her eyes in death.

Leah felt tears come to her eyes. It made a painful prickling as the wind crusted the liquid to ice. Fighting to control her emotions, Leah knew a tremendous amount of relief when she reached the tent.

"Come on, Crispin, let's get you inside."

"For the party?" he questioned.

"Yes."

Inside, Leah found Grace still very much alive. "Where's the midwife?" she asked as she realized the stranger standing next to Leah was no woman.

"She's taken sick and may not even live," Leah answered. "I found Crispin on the street and brought him back with me." She looked at the staggering man and then returned her gaze to Grace's worried expression. "I'm hoping he can be of help."

"He looks to be drunk."

"He is," Leah admitted. "But I hope to fix that with some food and strong coffee."

"We need someone to help," Grace said nervously. "I don't know how much time we have before the baby will come."

"I know. I went to the Sourdough to find Karen, but she wasn't there. She'd gone with the owner's wife to get something. I told them to send her home as soon as she got back."

Grace nodded and seemed to relax a bit. "That's good. Karen will know what to do."

"That's how I had it figured."

Leah worked over the stove to fix a pot of coffee. She noticed that Crispin hardly seemed to care that there was no real party. He had plopped down at the table and was now asleep.

When the coffee was ready, Leah brought a steaming mug to Crispin, along with a hunk of bread. "Crispin, wake up. I have something for you to eat."

He didn't rally and for a moment Leah again feared he had died.

"Crispin!"

He moaned and struggled to raise his head. "Why are you yelling at me? Why did you bring me here? There's no party."

Leah sat the cup down rather hard, sloshing some of the contents onto the table. "I brought you here to help me. You have to sober up now. Grace is going to have a baby, and Karen isn't here to help me." The wind howled loudly, shaking the tent and causing Leah to fear for the first time that Karen might well be stuck in town until the worst of the blizzard passed.

Blinking back tears, Leah tried to compose herself. She didn't vocalize her fears, but a quick glance to where Grace lay writhing in pain told her she didn't have to. Who was she fooling by trying to appear ever so strong and controlled? Grace knew very well how serious the situation was, and Crispin was too drunk to care.

With all the strength of her thirteen and a half years, Leah reached her hand into the black curls of Crispin's hair and yanked his head up and back. "You listen to me, Crispin Thibault. I need you, and I need you sober. You drink this coffee and eat what I give you, and I don't want to hear any kind of protest. Understand?"

He looked at her oddly for a moment, then smiled. "I believe I do."

"Good," she said, letting go her hold. "I'll bring you more coffee after you've finished this cup."

Grace screamed out against the pain. Leah's blood chilled her veins. A dull ache started somewhere at the base of her neck and edged its way up her head.

She thought of her mother—saw her lying pale, almost colorless against the white sheet of her bed.

Leaving her memories behind, Leah picked up the coffeepot and slammed it down in front of Crispin. "You'd better drink fast."

—{ C H A P T E R   S I X }—

MIRANDA SAW HER first glimpse of Dawson amidst a heavy snow. Buried under a mound of covers, she stayed warm enough in the lead sled, while Teddy rode in the sled behind her. The town looked surprisingly big. Miranda wasn't exactly sure what she had expected of Dawson, but after months in the wilderness, any collection of buildings and people seemed like heaven.

Sitting a little straighter, Miranda realized she had no idea what she should do. She didn't know where her friends might have gone. She had no idea if they had even made it this far. Frowning to herself, Miranda watched the rhythmic movement of the sled dogs. They seemed to pull the weight so easily. At first Miranda had felt sorry for them, but watching them work, she realized the dogs seemed to enjoy their task. Teddy had told her they were born and bred for this work, but until she'd witnessed it firsthand, Miranda had doubted the truth of that.

Little Charley brought the dogs to a halt in front of the Dawson Lucky Day Hotel. Miranda pushed back the blankets and struggled to climb out of the sled basket, but Little Charley quickly reached down and lifted her up without a word. After placing her on the boardwalk outside the hotel, he turned to unload the rest of the sled.

"Thank you," Miranda said, turning to see where Teddy might be. The falling snow seemed to lighten a bit, but the entire town was covered in a fresh blanket of white. Teddy stood a few feet away, surveying the town as if looking for something in particular.

"What is it?" she asked coming up beside him. "Is something wrong?"

Teddy looked over and smiled. "Not at all. I was merely reacquainting myself with this soiled dove."

"Why do you call Dawson that?"

"Because that's what she is. She was once pure and unspoiled, and now every man who can make his way north has come to use and abuse her. She looks good in snow, however. Almost clean again."

Miranda had no way of knowing whether this was true or not. "I suppose I can understand. Look, Mr. Davenport, I have no idea what I should do." She hoped he might have some suggestions. "I don't know how to find my friends."

"I can well understand your concerns. My suggestion would be that once we've checked into the hotel, you might make your way to the claim registrar's office. It's my understanding that everyone who seeks gold must secure their claim with the local authorities."

Miranda barely heard his words. She was still contemplating his statement about checking into the hotel. "I have no money. I can't very well check into the hotel. If I could find my friends right away, I could stay with them."

"The wind is picking up and the temperatures are dropping. It's hardly the right time for a search. Just come along with me and I'll see you receive a room. I know the management here, it won't be a problem." He smiled pleasantly, but it did nothing to ease her concern.

"But I can't pay for it," Miranda protested. "A place like this is no doubt expensive. Everything up here has been far more costly." She looked to the etched-glass doors of the hotel. "I'm sure they'll want the money up front. Besides, they might not even have room."

"It's not a problem, I assure you. I stay here every winter. I have an adjoining room where I usually set up my workroom. If the hotel is booked up, I can simply arrange my things in my room and you can stay as long as you need."

Miranda felt an overwhelming sense of gratitude. For all her anger and frustration with the seemingly indifferent Mr. Davenport, she realized he wasn't without mercy. "It would only be until I could find out what happened to my friends."

"Of course. Let's get inside." Teddy hardly seemed to concern himself with the matter. He turned away to direct Little Charley and the other man. "Bring my things into the lobby. I'll direct you from there."

Miranda followed the men inside, anxious to begin the business of locating her friends. A warm waft of air touched her cheeks as she crossed the threshold. *Oh, to be warm again,* she thought, sighing. She moved across the marble entry floor to a large, inviting fireplace. A heavy oak mantel framed a hearth trimmed in Delft tiles of blue and white. Miranda pulled off heavy fur mittens and held her hands out to the flames. She glanced behind her where she heard Teddy instructing the hotel clerk to bring them supper.

Miranda's stomach rumbled loudly. It'd been a long time since they'd shared their cold lunch of jerky and biscuits on the trail. Teddy motioned toward the stairs and Little Charley nodded and began to ascend with one of Teddy's heavy crates. The other man picked up another crate, while Teddy took up a third.

"Miss Colton, if you'll follow me, I'll show you to your room."

Miranda came alongside without a second thought. "I know it's dark, but I thought perhaps I should go check the recorder's office. What do you think?"

"I think you should eat a hearty meal and rest for the evening. Tomorrow will be soon enough to begin your search. If they're here, they aren't going anywhere tonight."

"I suppose you're right."

Miranda climbed the carpeted stairs, gently touching the polished wood banister. The hotel was more beautiful than she could have imagined. How in the world had such elegance come so far north? She marveled at the plush opulence. It was as if someone had taken the finest hotel in San Francisco and transplanted it to Dawson.

Mr. Davenport and his men seemed to take it all in stride. Apparently they'd seen the hotel many times before and the effect had worn off. Of course, she reasoned, Mr. Davenport had come from a well-to-do English family. He'd told her briefly of stately gardens where he'd learned a love of vegetation. It was really all she knew of Teddy Davenport. Funny how a person could share such close quarters with someone for months and still not know anything about them.

Reluctantly, Miranda pulled her skirt up a bit and continued her climb. Her legs felt leaden. She had lost so much of her strength by having nothing to do but sit around the cabin with Mr. Davenport. Teddy, on the other hand, hoisted the crate as though he worked days at the freight dock. His strength came as a surprise to Miranda, who had thought him a dandy at worst and a gentleman of leisure at best.

Yawning, she kept a silent vigil behind the men. In the morning she would have to get a telegram off to her parents. She worried that they had been notified of the accident. She'd been practically frantic over the thought of their suffering such news. She'd labored with images of her mother for weeks. When she closed her eyes at night, she could almost see her mother wandering around the house, crying in her grief. Miranda had to let them know she was alive and well.

"Well, here we are," Teddy grunted under the weight of his crate. He gently lowered the box as if it contained his most valuable possession. And in truth, Miranda knew that, to Teddy, those bits of dried vegetation and notes were his most valued articles.

Teddy procured a key from his coat pocket while Little Charley eyed Miranda. She felt her cheeks grow hot under his scrutiny and lowered her gaze to the floor.

"Just put those inside," Teddy instructed. He glanced to Miranda and reached out to offer her something. "This is the key to the room next door." He motioned to the right and Miranda realized he intended her to admit herself.

Without waiting for any other comment, Miranda took the key and opened the door. The room was grander than any she'd ever known. The brass bed had been done up in a heavy coverlet of brocaded burgundy and navy. Brass sconces on either side of the bed held thick white candles.

Without warning the side door opened and Mr. Davenport popped into the room. "I say, looks just as I left it."

"It's a lovely room. Much nicer than anything I expected to see in Dawson," Miranda admitted.

"Well, to be honest, it is one of the finer accommodations in the hotel. I stay here regularly, and these are my private rooms."

"I see. Are you sure you can spare the room?" she questioned. "I mean, I plan only to be here as long as it takes to find my friends or to make other arrangements."

"Nonsense," Teddy assured. "The room is no problem. I've set my things up in the sitting room and Mr. Ambrose, the manager here, will have the staff put in another bed."

"I've taken your bed? That hardly seems right. Perhaps they could move me to another room."

Teddy shook his head. "There are no other rooms available at present. Please do not concern yourself. I wouldn't have extended the offer if it were a bother. Now, do get your things settled and we'll have supper."

"I'm afraid, I have very little to settle, as you probably remember." Miranda dropped her own bundle of meager belongings on the bed.

"I'd nearly forgotten," Teddy said, frowning. "We should look into purchasing you a wardrobe."

"No!" Miranda exclaimed. "You've done enough. And don't forget, I have plenty of things, clothing especially, with my friends."

"That hardly helps you in this setting. We'll figure out what to do after supper."

"I would like to wash up," Miranda said, looking around the room.

"Of course. I'll send someone with towels and hot water. There's a bath down the hall, but in the winter it is sometimes less than congenial."

"Thank you. The water and towels will be more than enough."

"I suppose after tonight," Miranda began, "we'll see little of each other."

Teddy looked up rather surprised. He'd seemed distracted throughout the meal, but he now gave her his full attention.

"Why would you say that?"

"I'll be searching for my friends, and you have your work to see to."

"Yes, well, it may take some time for you to locate your friends. This area is more far-reaching than it seems. The claims of gold have been staked along nearly every river and creek in the area. There are hundreds of miles to cover in order to check each and every one. If your friends have failed to file a claim, or if perhaps they are working for someone else, there will be no record of them in the claims office. Short of finding someone who knows them or remembers them . . . well, it might be quite a task. I didn't want to say anything for fear of discouraging you."

Miranda hadn't considered that it would be that hard. She hadn't figured the town to be much bigger than the other stops along the way, and she certainly hadn't thought the claims to be so far-reaching.

"I suppose I didn't consider the situation in an accurate light. But then again, I had no idea I would encounter such a place."

"Of course, who's to say that God hasn't already straightened this crooked path out for you?"

Miranda nodded. Her hope was fixed on God. For the past months she had prayed and prayed for His deliverance and guidance. "I'm counting on God for just that, Mr. Davenport." And she knew in her heart it was true. For after all, what possible alternative did she have?

"The town isn't safe for you to journey too far alone," he continued. "It might be wise to check in with the officials."

"I plan to." Miranda toyed with her silverware for a moment, then cut into the thick steak on her plate. "This is quite delicious. I don't remember the last time I had a steak."

"I'm glad you're enjoying it. I wasn't sure you'd care for the flavor of moose."

"Moose?" She eyed her plate. "This is moose?"

"Indeed. It's rather an acquired taste unless it's prepared exactly right. We have a marvelous chef here at the hotel, and when he is able to get the right ingredients, he does a wonderful job."

"The entire dinner has been perfect," Miranda said, taking another bite of the meat. This time she focused on the flavor. She decided it was still quite delicious, in spite of knowing its origins.

Later that night, as she slipped beneath the thick wool blankets and heavy brocade cover, Miranda realized she'd not given any further thought to Teddy's sleeping arrangements. She thought to double check and make sure he had a bed in which to sleep, but even as she considered approaching their adjoining door, she held back.

It was hardly appropriate for her to go to him. He was a grown man and fully capable of seeing to his own needs. She thought of him, determined and focused on his work. He was probably bent over some piece of dried greenery even now.

Miranda smiled to herself and snuggled down deeper in the covers. A spirit of hope washed over her, energizing her and making sleep seem impossible. For all her exhaustion earlier, now she felt as if she could run a race.

She longed to find Grace and Karen. She longed to let them know she was alive and well. But then the reoccurring horror of knowing that they might well have died in the storm crept into her conscious mind.

What if they had all perished in the storm?

She shuddered. "Oh, God, please let them all be well and safe. Let me find them and rejoin them. Let me return to my parents and ease their worry."

But even as the words were out of her mouth, Miranda felt a strange aching in her heart. To return to her friends and family meant she would have to part company with Mr. Davenport.

"I'm being silly," she quietly whispered into the darkness. "Of course we'll part company. We are nothing to one another. We were thrown together for the sole purpose of. . . ." Her mind was incapable of completing the sentence. Why had they been thrown together? Was there some other plan for them?

Miranda thought of Teddy as a brotherly sort. He wasn't exactly like her own brother, Peter, but he was caring and kind. He didn't look at her like Crispin Thibault had. Crispin's lingering gazes had always warmed her and left her a little jittery inside. Teddy's glances did nothing but . . .

But what?

Miranda hugged her pillow. *This is so nonsensical,* she thought. *What's wrong with me anyway? Mr. Davenport is nothing more than a kindly benefactor. As soon as I find Grace, I'll be gone. I'll probably never see him again.*

The thought made the dull ache more intense. Could it be she'd come to care for Mr. Davenport? Care for him in such a manner that leaving his company could actually cause her grief?

The winds picked up outside and made a mournful whine. Miranda had heard it said that the dark northern winters could cause a madness to settle upon a person. It caused all manner of trouble. Some people went screaming into the night and were never seen again. Some retreated to the silent darkness of their cabins and weren't found again until spring.

Maybe her strange feelings in regard to Mr. Davenport were nothing more than a part of this winter madness—a sort of northern plague that would pass with the coming of the summer light. Maybe.

LEAH AND CRISPIN looked down on the wrinkled baby boy with expressions of awe. Grace smiled at her two champions. Had it not been for their devotion and determination, she and the baby might well be dead.

"He's so tiny, Grace," Leah said, shaking her head. "I didn't know he'd be so little."

"He's perfectly normal in size," Crispin stated. The haggard look on his face and dark circles around his eyes caused Grace to worry over his health. She wondered if it was the first time he'd been sober in quite some time.

"Mr. Thibault, we have quite despaired of ever knowing your fate. Have you come back to us now?"

Crispin seemed to suddenly realize not only the hour and setting, but also his state of sobriety. He reached for his coat and pulled it on without ceremony. "I have not come back. I was merely taken in hand by this lovely lady." He smiled sadly at Leah. "I'm glad I could be of help, but I must go. I have places to be and the hour is late."

"Crispin, don't leave. Karen hasn't come home, and what if I need someone?" Leah questioned.

Grace heard the concern in the child's voice, while noting at the same time the determination in Crispin's expression. "Perhaps Mr. Thibault has other obligations," Grace said softly. She pulled her son closer to keep him from chilling. The baby slept as though completely disinterested in his surroundings.

"I do indeed," Crispin said, giving the ladies a slight bow. "I bid you farewell for a time."

Leah walked to where Crispin's fur hat had been carelessly left to dry. "Here. Don't forget your hat. You might need it."

He smiled at her as he took the hat. Grace couldn't help but wonder what had transpired between Leah and Crispin prior to their arrival at her bedside. Crispin reached out and took hold of Leah's hand. Bending, he kissed her fingers.

"Parting is indeed a bittersweet sorrow."

"You don't have to go," Leah said matter-of-factly.

"Ah, but I do. You'll understand better as time goes by. Now stay here and care for our little mother and her babe. I'm sure Karen will return after the storm abates."

"But you shouldn't go out in it either," Leah protested.

"I'll be perfectly fine," he assured them and then, without further ado, was gone.

Leah's eyes filled with tears and Grace reached out her hand. "Come here," she said softly. "Come sit with me and Andy."

Leah sniffled. "Andy? You've named him already?"

"I've thought for a long time of what I would call him, if I had a son. I love the name Andrew, and if you remember your Bible stories, you'll know that Peter and Andrew were brothers who were called by Christ to become disciples. I figured with his father's name being Peter, Andrew was a most appropriate name. They just go together, don't you think?"

Leah wiped at her eyes and nodded. "He is a beautiful baby, Grace. I was so scared he wouldn't be born."

Grace squeezed her hand. "I know your mother died in childbirth. I'm sorry you had to bear this."

"I just kept thinking about Mama." The tears fell in earnest now. Suddenly it seemed that the intensity of the day had finally caught up with Leah. She sobbed into her hands and buried her face against the side of Grace's cover.

Stroking the child's head, Grace tried to think of some words of comfort. It seemed only a short time ago that she herself had been young like this—young and innocent and so very carefree. Grace thought of her home in Chicago. Of the finery and blessings they'd enjoyed. She had never known what it was to really need or want something. How very different things were now.

She let Leah cry, thinking it was probably a cleansing help to the girl. So often people buried their feelings inside and never allowed them to come out, never let their souls be cleaned and refreshed by the rain of their tears.

How very often I've tried to refrain from tears, she thought. *I've tried to feel nothing but the determined hope that God would somehow make everything right, when down deep inside I hurt so very bad.* Grace thought of Peter and looked to the baby who now slept wrapped safely in her arms. Would Peter care that he had a son? Would he forgive her the anger of the past and come to realize the importance of putting his trust in God?

Surely it was better that she remain here, separated from her husband, to raise her son in the presence of God-fearing people who cared about them both, rather than return to a loveless marriage—a union that promised all parties nothing but pain and sorrow.

Grace continued to stroke Leah's hair, even as her own tears fell. *Father, I know you have a plan in all of this. I know your love is there for me—for Andrew. But, God, it hurts so much to know that Peter is far away from us, to know that he doesn't care for your Word, or for you.* Grace cried softly while Leah's sobs still filled the room.

Andrew stirred and began to fuss. As he cried louder, Grace and Leah both looked at each other and then to the baby. Grace began to smile. A fine trio they were with their tears.

"He's probably hungry," Grace surmised. "The midwife told me he would probably want to nurse first thing."

"Is there anything I can do? Is there anything you need?" Leah asked, drying her eyes.

Grace untied the neck of her nightgown with her free hand. "No, nothing. God has seen to making this quite a self-sufficient matter." She positioned the crying baby to her breast and watched as he began rooting. She startled when he latched on and began to suck.

Leah laughed. "He must be pretty hungry. You must be hungry too. I'll fix you some food."

Grace nodded. She was feeling both hungry and weary. When Leah had gone to the stove, Grace returned her gaze to the dark-haired baby. How wondrous and awesome to hold something so tiny, so alive, and know that it came about because of the love she shared with her husband. God had given her a son—a son who would no doubt be very much like his father.

As if to concur, Andy opened his eyes and looked up at her. Grace couldn't help smiling. She saw the future in her son's eyes. She saw the hope that she and Peter could one day be united again in love.

"Oh, let it be, dear Father," she whispered.

To their surprise, not more than an hour after his departure, Crispin Thibault returned to their tent. He brought with him a none-to-pleased local doctor. The man grunted a greeting to Grace and Leah, then immediately took the baby in hand to examine him.

"I thought you might both rest better if a doctor were to declare everything well done," Crispin announced.

Leah pulled the blanket across the roping to afford Grace and the doctor some privacy. She turned to Crispin and smiled. "Will you stay?" she asked hopefully.

"No." His voice was flat and void of emotion. "I can't."

"Because of Miranda?"

Crispin looked blankly at Leah for a moment. "Yes."

"It hurts a lot to lose someone you love. I know because I've lost both my ma and pa. I was really scared to be here with Grace, and I know I couldn't have done it without you. See, my mama died trying to have a baby. I was scared Grace would die, too."

"Yes, well," Crispin stammered in obvious discomfort, "it's all behind us now."

"But it's not," Leah said, putting her hand on his arm. "You won't stay with us because of Miranda's death. You blame yourself, but it isn't your fault."

"You have no idea what you're talking about." His voice took on a gruff edge. "I need to go. The snow has abated, and no doubt Karen will return."

"Please, Crispin, don't go. I know how you feel inside, but the whiskey won't help."

"You talk as one who knows, and yet you're a child."

"My mama said whiskey was nothing more than a crutch some folks used to help them hobble down the road to hell."

Crispin actually smiled at this. "I suppose her to be correct in that statement."

"She said God was the only one who could ease our sufferings."

He frowned again. "I see God as a crutch used by mere mortals to raise them higher to some supposed glory."

"I don't mind leaning on God as a crutch," Leah declared boldly. "I'd sure enough rather lean on God than a bottle."

"That's your choice. Now leave me to mine."

Crispin turned to go, but Leah held fast to his arm. "You can't just ignore God or your need for Him. My mama always said that without God we'll never be happy. You do want to be happy again, don't you, Crispin?"

He looked down at her, his dark gaze penetrating. "I will never be happy again. Not with God. Not without Him."

He jerked away from her hold and left without even waiting to hear of Grace's condition. Leah felt a strange desire to run after Crispin. She had admired the man from their first meeting, and when she'd learned that he didn't believe in God, she felt that perhaps it was her duty to set him straight. But that chance never came, at least not until tonight. As hard as it was to see him leave, Leah thanked God for the opportunity to finally talk to him—no matter how fruitless her words seemed.

"Mrs. Colton is to have complete bed rest for two weeks," the doctor said as he came from behind the blanket. "She's clearly not a well woman. This pregnancy has weakened her considerably."

Leah nodded. "I'll see to it that she rests."

"She needs to eat plenty of meat," he stated as he pulled on his gloves. "Have you meat?"

Leah nodded again. "Adrik shot an elk. We have plenty of food. I'll see to it that she eats."

"Good. The baby is small, but time will tell."

"What do you mean?" Leah questioned.

"I mean," the doctor said, "he will need much care in order to thrive. It's nearly thirty below outside. You're going to have to keep him warm and well fed. If the mother doesn't make enough milk, you'll have to supplement his diet with canned or fresh milk—whatever you can lay your hand to. If that can't be found, fix him a little sugar water and find a bottle with which to feed him in between nursings."

Leah nodded, fearful that the baby might die. She wanted to ask the doctor of the possibility, but her mouth wouldn't form the words.

"Lastly, I would make a place for the child between you both. He'll need the warmth of your bodies to survive. This tent is no place for a newborn, but if you take precautions, he might well live."

He left in the same quick manner as Crispin had, leaving Leah to stare after him in stunned silence. She had figured now that the baby had been born, and had even cried and nursed, that he would be just fine. She hadn't even considered that he could die.

She pushed back the curtain and looked to Grace. "I suppose," she said, seeing the understanding in Grace's expression, "you heard what the doctor said?"

"I heard him," Grace replied.

Leah reached out and took hold of Grace's hand. "I'll do whatever I can to help you. We'll see to it that Andy makes good progress. You, too. You'll rest and take care of Andy, and I'll bring you meals and take care of everything else."

Grace bit her lower lip and tears came to her eyes once again. "He must live," she finally whispered.

"He will," Leah said, promising in her heart that if she could make it so, it would be.

That night, even though she worried because Karen had never returned to the tent, Leah crawled into bed beside Grace and helped her to nestle Andrew between them. The baby slept without concern for his surroundings, and Leah thought it rather a blessing that he should know so little. The dangers were something she'd just as soon not know about—for knowing only made surviving the night all that much harder.

Leah thought of Crispin and worried about him drinking the night away in one of the many saloons. She wondered, as Grace's even breathing indicated sleep, if he would get drunk and pass out in the snow as he had when she'd come upon him only that morning.

"God, please take care of Crispin," she prayed in a hushed whisper. "Let him know how much you love him. Let him come to understand that you really do exist—that you really do care."

⊣ C H A P T E R   E I G H T ⊢

KAREN DIDN'T KNOW when she'd been so tired. Even climbing the Chilkoot Pass hadn't been as exhausting as working for nearly eighteen hours without a break. First she'd gone to help unload supplies from storage, and then she'd found herself out in the blizzard bringing in wood from the stacked pile behind the café.

After that she waited tables, washed dishes, and was eventually allowed to cook—the job she'd been hired to do in the first place. They'd been so short-handed that everyone had been forced to pitch in and do a little bit of everything.

Yawning, Karen pushed back the outside tent flap and unfastened the ties of the inner flap. A lantern burned on the stove, but other than that the room was dark and quiet. Grace and Leah had no doubt gone to bed. Yawning again, Karen blew out the lantern and found her way to her own bed. Adrik had built a frame of ropes, and together they'd sewn canvas from their makeshift sail into mattress coverings. These they stuffed with pine boughs and anything else they could find to make a soft resting place.

Sinking into the bed, Karen managed only to kick her boots off before pulling the covers high. Within a moment she was fast asleep.

Strange thoughts and sounds drifted in and out of her dreams. Karen thought at one point that a baby was crying. But her eyes were much too heavy to open and investigate, and her mind was cloudy with thick fog of sleep.

It wasn't until morning, when she heard Leah moving about the tent, that Karen forced herself to wake up. She didn't have to report to work until noon and had thought to spend a few extra hours asleep, but the cry of a baby pierced the silence and caused her to bolt upright in bed.

"What's that?" she asked, throwing back the covers. "Grace, are you all right?"

Leah laughed. "Grace had her baby."

Karen looked to the wide-eyed child and shook her head. "You're just kidding me, aren't you?"

Leah took hold of her hand and pulled her to the blanket partition. "See for yourself."

Karen looked behind the covers to find Grace smiling at her from a propped up position. The nursing baby seemed completely oblivious to her intrusion.

"I don't believe it."

"Neither did we," Grace replied. "At least not at first."

"Why didn't you come get me?" Karen asked, looking to Leah for an answer.

"I did. I went first to get the midwife, but she was on her deathbed. So then I went to find you, but the man at the café said you were off helping get supplies. He promised he'd tell you to come home when you got back, but he wasn't happy about it."

"Apparently his displeasure kept him from telling me the truth," Karen stated, angry that she had been deceived.

"I found Crispin on my way back," Leah said, then frowned. "He was drunk, but I sobered him up, and he helped me deliver the baby."

"They did a perfect job and it saved me one hundred dollars," Grace said, shifting the baby.

Karen was still in a state of disbelief. "So is it a boy or a girl?"

"A boy," Grace answered. The expression on her face caused Karen's heart to ache for her friend. No doubt Grace was thinking of Peter and his long absence.

"What have you named him?"

"Andrew. But we call him Andy. Seems like a better fit," Grace replied.

"Crispin paid for a doctor to come and check on Grace and the baby," Leah said authoritatively. "The doctor said they both need rest and lots of good food."

"And no doubt a warm cabin," Karen threw in. Why couldn't they have found a home first thing? She couldn't help but wonder what plan God had for them and why it included Grace giving birth to her son in a chilly tent.

"We were worried about you," Grace stated, looking rather worried. "Are you all right?"

Karen saw the look of loving concern in her friend's eyes. "I'm fine. The blizzard seemed to drive folks in to the café rather than keep them away. We had a bevy of folks from the hotels, and those that didn't come to take a meal at the café sent someone to bring a meal back to them. We were working all day and night."

"I'll fix you some breakfast," Leah said, pushing back the blanket partition. "You just sit down and rest."

Karen smiled appreciatively and took a chair beside Grace's bed. "She's been such a help."

"That she has. She never balked at the work of helping me with Andrew's delivery. She and Crispin worked as a remarkable team."

Karen looked around the tent. "Where is Crispin?"

"He left," Grace admitted. "He left even before the doctor finished his examination. He looked awful."

Karen nodded. Adrik had told her on more than one occasion that he had seen Crispin drunk. The news positively broke Karen's heart. Crispin had cared so very much for Miranda Colton, and he just couldn't seem to let go of feeling responsible for her loss.

"I hope he's all right. Adrik should try to talk to him again."

"Leah did her best to reason with him. I figured if anyone had a chance of getting through to him, it would be her. But Crispin just bolted."

Karen watched as Grace gently lifted her son to her shoulder. Patting him firmly, she burped him, then looked questioningly at Karen. "Would you care to hold him?"

The longing in Karen's heart for a child surfaced all at once. "I would love to." She reached out and took the baby in her arms. He was so small, yet so perfect.

Andrew Colton looked up to Karen with wide blue eyes. His dark brown hair reminded Karen of Grace. "He favors you."

"He looks like Peter, too," Grace assured. "I see it in his nose and mouth." She lowered her face. "I'd give anything to have him here."

Karen cuddled the baby close and nodded. "I know you would. We'll get word to him, one way or another. We'll tell him about his son and we'll pray that he comes."

Grace lifted her face. "But I want him to come for more than the baby's sake. I want him to come because he's come to love God and he knows what's right. And I want him to come because he loves me."

Karen looked at Grace and saw the sadness in her expression. "I know he loves you."

Andrew closed his eyes while Karen gently rocked him in her arms. How wonderful he felt in her embrace. She couldn't help but feel a touch of envy. Here Grace was years her junior and she was already a mother. Karen gently handed the sleeping boy back to his mother. She smiled with an assurance she didn't feel. "I know we'll find Peter, and I know he loves you."

"I just about have the flapjacks ready," Leah called out.

A rustling at the door flap and the stomping of boots brought the attention of all three women to the front of the tent.

"You'd better throw some more of those on the stove," Adrik Ivankov's booming voice rang out.

"Adrik!" Karen exclaimed and jumped to her feet. She threw herself into her husband's ice-encrusted arms.

Adrik hugged her tight and kissed her soundly. Karen thrilled to his touch, feeling a wave of longing rush over her. They'd had so little privacy since they got married. There was rarely any opportunity for intimacy between them.

Jacob stumbled in behind Adrik. "I'm starving."

"You're always starving," Leah called out.

Karen pulled away from her husband and laughed. "Oh, it's so good to have you both back. I have wonderful news for you."

"We have some pretty good news ourselves," Adrik said, pulling off his heavy coat.

"Well, I can't imagine it can top this," Karen said, motioning to Grace. "Grace has a new son."

Adrik beamed a smile. "Congratulations, little mother."

Grace nodded. "Thank you. This is Andrew Michael Colton." She held the sleeping baby up ever so slightly.

"He's a beaut," Adrik declared.

"Leah helped deliver him," Karen told her husband. "Along with Crispin."

Adrik frowned. "Crispin?"

"I found Crispin nearly passed out in the snow," Leah said matter-of-factly. "I made him come back here with me."

"I would have paid good money to see that," Adrik said, laughing.

Jacob patted his sister on the shoulder. "She can be real pushy when she wants something."

"Well, in this case, I'm glad she was," Grace added. "She sobered him up and he helped with delivering the baby."

"Where is he now?" Adrik asked, looking around the room.

"He wouldn't stay," Leah replied. She turned her attention back to the stove. "I tried to talk to him, but he was just too sad."

"Sad?" Adrik questioned.

She nodded. "Yes. Sad about Miranda. He seems to have lost all hope and purpose."

"I wouldn't be surprised if you aren't right on that matter," Adrik said, looking to Karen. "I can well imagine how I'd feel if I lost Karen."

Karen reached out to hold his hand. "I don't even want to think of how things would be if you weren't here. I worried about you the whole time you were gone. I'd pray and pray and then worry that I needed to pray some more."

"Well, we do have good news," Jacob said, seeming to suddenly remember. "Tell 'em, Adrik."

Adrik looked at Karen. "Gump said he'd like to hire us on to work his claim. Even though there isn't as much to do this time of the year, he'd like us to come just the same. Said he'd split whatever we found fifty-fifty. We aren't going to get a better offer than that. His cabin is small, but it should be sufficient. We can add onto it when the weather warms up." Adrik puffed out his chest as though quite pleased with himself. "I told him I'd come back here and pack everybody up and be there within the week."

Karen's mouth dropped open. "What? Just like that?"

"Just like what?" Adrik seemed genuinely surprised.

"We can't just up and leave. Grace just had the baby. She can't possibly travel."

"We can arrange for her. She could stay here in town for a spell, and then we could come back and get her. Look, I borrowed Gump's dogs and sled. I can't keep him waiting longer than the week. It takes two days just to get to where his claim is on Hunker Creek."

"But I thought you went to check out another claim. Didn't Gump suggest some friend of his might need help?"

"Gump's friend didn't need the hands, but Gump did. We started talking on the trip out there, and Gump talked about how hard it is to work a claim by himself. He wants to give it one big go in the spring and then pack out by fall of next year. He figures if we help him with it, we might all come out on top. After all, most of the claims on Hunker Creek are netting good finds."

"But Adrik, we can't ... I mean ..." Karen's voice trailed off. She tried to think of how to tell him about her job. She looked to the others in the room. Leah and Grace seemed to understand, but Jacob just looked on, as if confused by the entire encounter.

Grace nodded to Karen as if to bolster her courage. Karen looked to her husband and decided it was better to just get things out in the open. "I have a job. It pays good money. One hundred and fifty dollars a month, to be exact."

"That *is* a lot of money!" Jacob exclaimed. "What do you have to do for it?"

Adrik took a step back and looked down at his wife. "Yes, what do you have to do?"

Karen felt her cheeks grow hot, but whether from embarrassment at the suggestive tone of her husband or her own anger, she couldn't tell. "Nothing that would shame either one of us. I have a job cooking. It's a good job. I figured we could use the money what with the baby and all. Grace and the baby need four walls and a roof, not a tent."

"And that's exactly what I propose to offer them," Adrik replied.

Karen looked around the room, frustrated to have an audience. That was the biggest problem with their living in a tent. There was never any place for real privacy, and outside was far too cold to take a stroll for something so menial as an argument.

"Adrik, I took the job because I thought it might ease the burden for you and Jacob. The job isn't hard, and I don't mind doing it."

"Well, I do. I don't want my wife supporting me," Adrik said sternly. "I'm the one who took it on to see to your welfare and that of everyone else in this room. I wouldn't have done it if I didn't think myself capable."

"And you are," Karen replied, hoping to soothe his irritated spirit. "I just thought this would free you up to find what you were really searching for."

"I've already found what I'm looking for," Adrik answered. "Gump has been a good friend for a long time. He needs the help and we need what he can offer. It's a good trade, and since there's still plenty of winter left, I don't intend to see you living it out here in a tent."

"But—"

"No, Karen. We're doing this my way. I'm the man of the family." He looked to Grace and nodded. "In Peter Colton's absence, I'm Grace's protector, as well. I know what's best. Grace, do you trust me to provide a place for you and your son?"

Grace looked to Karen and then back to Adrik. "I know you'll do right by us."

Adrik turned to Karen. "Will you trust me?"

Karen knew there was no reason to continue the argument. Adrik's mind was made up, and she wasn't going to change it. "All right," she said reluctantly.

Adrik took hold of her shoulders. "Karen, I've prayed this through. I know God has provided for us and at the same time, He's provided for Gump. This is all going to work out. You'll see. Gump gave me some money for extra supplies and a bit to tide us over. I'll use the money to secure Grace and the boy, then we'll get whatever else we need and head out. When the weather improves, I'll come back and get Grace and the baby."

And so it was settled. Leah stirred more flapjack batter while Jacob and Adrik went to care for Gump's dog team. Karen went to sit beside Grace, still not entirely certain this solution was for the best.

"I don't want to leave you behind," Karen said in a hushed tone.

Grace patted her hand. "Don't worry. I know that God has this completely in His care. I know Andy and I will be just fine. You go ahead and we'll join you as soon as we can. Just trust Adrik to know what's best. He's a good man."

Karen smiled. "You sound like the teacher now rather than the student."

Grace shook her head. "No, I sound like a lonely wife."

Karen took hold of her hand. "I'm so sorry, dear friend. I know you would much rather be with Peter, safe and warm in some distant home. I should never have brought you north. I should have insisted on having you return to California. I should have bought the ticket myself and put you on the ship."

"No," Grace replied. "I believe God had a purpose in allowing all of this."

"Yes, but if it hadn't been for Mr. Paxton and his unyielding desire to force you into marriage, you might never have had these problems with Peter."

"But for Mr. Paxton, I might never have met Peter. We must remember that, as well."

"I suppose you're right," Karen said, feeling overcome by a sense of defeat. "Sometimes I think this is all a dream and other times, a nightmare."

"At least we have each other," Grace whispered.

"For now. But Adrik will separate us on the morrow."

"I'm confident of our reunion. Andrew and I will join you before you know it. We'll be safe and sound and you may fuss over us as much as you like."

"I hope you're right," Karen replied, looking across the tent at all their worldly possessions. Things weren't nearly as important as the people in her life. They never had been, but now more than ever, Karen sensed the emptiness of their humble dwelling. Would things ever return to normal? *At this point*, Karen thought, *I can't even say that I know what normal is anymore.*

⊣ CHAPTER NINE ⊢

"WESLEY TELLS ME it's possible to get as far north as Lake Lindeman, even in the dead of winter," Peter Colton told his mother and father as they concluded breakfast. He'd waited for just the right moment to break the news that he'd soon be headed to Alaska.

"Does Captain Oakes tell you how to go about doing this?" Ephraim Colton asked his son.

Peter pushed back from the table and nodded. "Wes says he can take me as far as Skagway. From there I'll take the train as far north as I can and hike out from there. The biggest problem will be the cost of supplies, but I'm working on that."

"I wish you didn't have to go," Ephraim stated. He pushed around the food on his plate before focusing on Peter. "I won't rest as long as I know you're in danger."

"The danger should be minimal, Father. After all, there are far more settlements and conveniences now. The Mounties have worked hard to maintain law and order, so even the criminal problems have been reduced."

"Still, it's hard to know you'll be so far away," Ephraim murmured.

Peter knew that since his father had suffered a heart attack, he'd been far more concerned about Peter sticking close to home. It was as if the older man feared his death might yet come from the attack, leaving Amelia without someone at her side to help with the arrangements.

"I have to go," Peter finally said. "If I leave right away, I can be there when the first thaw allows travel on the lakes."

"If you leave now, when do you imagine you might find Miranda and bring her home?" Amelia questioned.

Peter looked to his mother and smiled. "I would guess late May at the earliest. If I can get to Dawson right away, say by early June, I can head home with Miranda by the end of the month. That should see us home by August at the latest."

"My poor Miranda. I fear for her having to live these long cold months alone," Peter's mother sniffed.

Peter knew the separation had been hard on his parents. It had been only compounded by the knowledge that Grace was dead. They all mourned that loss and shared their sorrows daily. Peter knew it was impossible to wish or pray his wife back to life, but he couldn't help but turn his eyes heavenward, hoping against hope that God might somehow reverse the order of the past. It seemed like only yesterday word had come from the Mountie station at Whitehorse. His wife was dead, one more victim of the Yukon gold rush. His sister was left alone, and it was his duty to bring her home safe and sound.

"We'll soon have her home, Mother. I'll see to it," Peter promised.

"I had some good news from Mr. Hamilton," Ephraim said, changing the subject.

"And what does our good lawyer tell us these days?"

Ephraim smiled. "He believes it will only be a short time before our assets are returned to us. With Martin's death and the questionable legality of the contract between us, Hamilton feels confident Colton Shipping will soon be back in family hands."

"That is good news," Peter replied. He had missed being the captain of his own ship, *Merry Maid*. "Perhaps if the details are worked out soon enough I might sail myself to Skagway. Perhaps even take a load of goods and reap a profit." But even as the thought crossed his mind, Peter couldn't help but remember Wes's prediction that the high-profit days of the Seattle-to-Skagway route were quickly coming to an end.

"It's always possible," Ephraim said thoughtfully. "You do realize the trade is slacking off."

"I was just remembering that," Peter said, smiling. "Funny that you should be on top of that, as well."

"Not funny at all, considering it's my business to know." Ephraim then turned a loving look on his son. "I know I've not always been a wise businessman. I know my choices have often been made because of ease or even the liberty involved. That is in the past, however. In coming back to an understanding of what God would have of me as a man and provider, I realize that I must also be a good steward of that with which He has blessed me."

Peter understood his father's heart entirely. Following his own will had brought him nothing but misery. Turning his thoughts to God and leaning on His ways had brought about the only peace Peter had known since losing Grace.

Peter looked to his parents. "I thought I was doing a good thing when I took control of the family business. I figured it to be an act of love, but now I see it was a deception of selfishness. I wanted to be important—indispensable."

"But, son, you already were," Ephraim said, shaking his head. "You were all we could have hoped for in a child. As you grew into manhood, you were protective and loving with your sister, and you were astute and conscientious regarding the business. The fault is on my part, if there is any to be had. I tired of the burden. I'm tired even now, which is why I plan to sign the business over to you in full, once we resolve the legal circumstances, of course."

Peter would have thrilled to hear those words only a year ago. But now they rang hollow. Grace was gone. So, too, was his chance for real happiness. He would never love another woman. Grace had made her way into his heart, and her memory refused to leave him in peace.

Peter tried hard to push aside the thoughts that Grace had died believing the worst of him. She had thought him to be a heartless cad—ruthless in his decisions and indifferent to her needs. At least, that's what Peter imagined she thought. And that hurt him more than anything else, except her actual absence. It was difficult, if not impossible, to remember that he had purposefully caused her pain.

". . . that's all I ask."

Peter realized his father had been speaking, but he'd not heard a word. "I'm sorry. What did you just say? I'm afraid my mind was a million miles away."

Ephraim reached over and gently touched his son's shoulder. "I said, it is my desire that your mother and I be allowed to live here, comfortably with your sister. Otherwise, you may do as you choose with the business and its profits."

"But of course you may live here. I would fight every court in the country to see to it that you remained in the home you love. Look, I don't wish for us to discuss any more about the shipping business," Peter said, getting to his feet. "I'm going to start putting together my plans for going north. I have a good understanding of what I need and how much money it will take. There's one benefit that the north can offer, and that is the tired souls who are giving up their dreams of gold. They will have all the supplies and tools that I'll need. And they'll be willing to sell them at a much discounted price."

Amelia dabbed her eyes and looked away. "But what if something happens to you? You could just as easily be lost on the same lake that claimed your wife."

Peter went to his mother and hugged her close. "God is with me, Mother. No matter the outcome, I am His now. I am His and He will guide me. If and when

He chooses to take me from this earth, please know that I am ready and willing to face Him."

"I might know it in my heart, but I would still miss you—need you," Amelia replied, lifting her gaze to meet Peter's.

Peter leaned down and kissed his mother's forehead. "Please don't fret, for nothing will ever truly separate us."

Just then a knock sounded at the front door. Peter exchanged a look of curiosity with his parents. "Who could that be?" He gave his mother's arm a gentle pat before heading to the door.

Peter's heavy booted steps echoed in the empty hallway. The house seemed so quiet without Miranda and Grace. Sometimes he ached to hear their girlish chatter. Sometimes the silence of the house threatened to encase him like an empty tomb.

Opening the door, Peter met the gaze of a small, simply-dressed woman. She looked to be in her fifties and there was a certain air of refinement about her. Gazing into her eyes, however, Peter saw a haunting reminder of his wife.

"I'm Myrtle Hawkins," the woman announced. "Grace's mother. Are you Peter?"

Peter felt the wind go out from him. "Yes," he managed to say.

"I recognized you from Grace's descriptions. You are a fine, handsome man," Myrtle said with a sober smile.

"I . . . ah . . . I don't know what to say," Peter replied. He had written to Myrtle months ago to tell her of Grace's death. He hadn't told of their separation or of the problems they were having. He hadn't even related the issues of Martin Paxton's continued harangue. Peter had thought to save Grace's mother from all of that, and because he had never figured to have to face her, he felt certain it was the right thing to do. Now, however, he felt like a fraud.

Myrtle reached out and took hold of his hand. "Peter, my daughter loved you very much. You needn't say anything more."

Her words only convicted him that much more. "I must say," Peter began, "I never expected to meet you. Welcome to San Francisco." He stepped back from the door and added, "Won't you please come in?" He looked past her to where a hired carriage waited at the curb. "Do you have baggage?"

"Yes, but I needn't impose on you," Myrtle replied. "I had thought perhaps you could escort me to a decent hotel."

"Nonsense. You'll stay with us. I'll get your things."

Peter quickly retrieved the bags and paid the driver. A rush of thoughts consumed his attention. Why was she here? What could she possibly want with him? What could he possibly do to ease her suffering when his own was still so raw and fresh?

"Come inside," Peter said as he climbed the steps. "I'll introduce you to my mother and father."

"Peter, before we join the others, I must tell you something. In private," she added.

Peter put her things down inside the door and waited until she'd joined him in the entryway. Dreading what she might have to tell him, Peter braced himself as Myrtle Hawkins unfastened the buttons of her traveling coat.

"I've come because I received some news from my late husband's lawyer," Myrtle said as she paused to look Peter in the eye. "News that will profoundly change your life."

┤ CHAPTER TEN ├

TEDDY ARRANGED HIS OFFICE as best he could. Working and sleeping in the same room had reduced his level of comfort, but he felt confident that he had no other choice. The hotel was full and Miranda needed his help. He couldn't just leave her to venture into the unknown.

It was strange how she'd managed to worm her way into his daily thoughts. Teddy had never been one given to daydreams, but of late, he found Miranda's sweet face ever coming to mind.

Looking over the variety of specimen bottles and crates, Teddy knew he'd have to abandon thoughts of the brown-haired beauty or fall hopelessly behind in his work. This had never been a problem in the past—when little could distract him from his botanical research.

"Lord," he prayed, "I cannot say I understand my state of mind. It seems an oddity to me at best and a fearful thing at worst. Please steady me to complete the work you've given me to do."

Teddy looked to the door that adjoined his room to Miranda's. He wondered if she was there just now. He wondered what she was doing and how she planned to go about searching for her friends. She was a delicate and lovely flower—petite and gentle, but with a fiery sting when angered. He didn't like to think of her alone on the streets, for he knew full well how some would be inclined to take advantage of her.

Crossing to the window, Teddy noted the skies were clearing. A light snow still fell, but the winds had calmed. Perhaps Miranda would choose this time to go scouting for her friends. Perhaps he should offer to help. Once again, he looked to the tables of work behind him.

"I must stop this nonsense. I have become flighty." He reached for his coat and pulled a list of needed supplies from the table. "I might as well occupy myself by attending to this first thing. Perhaps then my mind will be fixed for work."

But even as he rechecked his list, he found himself adding things for Miranda—a dress, new boots, stockings, and other such things that might be pleasing to her. She had told him not to worry about her, but Teddy didn't want her going about looking like a street urchin.

"Maybe something red," he murmured. "Something the color of the mountain ash berries."

Heading to the hardware store, Teddy tried to bring his thoughts into order. He knew it would do more harm than good to continue focusing on Miss Colton. She was a pleasant enough woman, but he had work to do. *I must stop this nonsense and turn my attention to the task at hand*, he told himself.

Squaring his shoulders, Teddy was determined to purchase the things he needed, and then return to the hotel and spend the day buried in his work. Maybe he wouldn't worry about getting Miranda a dress. After all, he didn't even know her size. And maybe she didn't like red. Tucking his face down into his coat, he put Miranda from his mind.

The ring of the bell on the door of MacCarthy's Hardware seemed to jolt Teddy's senses. He looked up, but not in time to avoid stepping headlong into the chest of a broad-shouldered man.

"Oh, please pardon me," Teddy said, stepping back.

"No problem, friend."

Teddy sized up the large man and smiled. "I'm afraid my mind was elsewhere."

The big man laughed. "Mine's somewhere to the south where the winds blow warmer and the fishing is easy. Unfortunately, that's a long way from this place."

Teddy returned his thoughts to his list just as a young man joined them. "Adrik, they don't have any sleds they can sell."

Teddy looked up. "Sleds? Did you say you were looking for a sled?"

The big man nodded. "That's right. Do you know where we might buy one?"

"I have one," Teddy replied. "Oh, where are my manners, the name is Davenport. Thomas Davenport."

"Adrik Ivankov is my name," the big man said, extending his hand. "And this here is Jacob Barringer."

Teddy nodded. "I have a sled, and since I'll be staying throughout the winter, I'll have no need of it. You're welcome to purchase it."

"What kind of price are you asking?"

Teddy looked around the small confines of the hardware store. "Well, I'd not considered the price." He chuckled. "But then again, I hadn't considered selling the sled until just now."

"Well, we aren't wealthy by any means. Fact is, I'm taking part of my party out to a friend's claim and leaving part of it here. My wife's friend just had a baby, and there's no sense in risking their lives until things warm up a bit. Still, I need two sleds. I can work in a trade—chop wood or build just about anything you need."

Teddy shook his head. "I'm afraid I have little need of either of those things. I'm staying at the hotel across the street."

"We have a lot of extra meat," the young man offered. "We shot us an elk and a moose not too long ago."

"Fresh meat could be a real bonus. I would imagine the hotel might well be glad to get it," Teddy said rather absentmindedly. "All right, I'll trade you meat for the sled."

"How much do you reckon would be a fair amount for the sled?" The big man asked.

Again Teddy felt perplexed. He'd never dealt in such matters and the consideration of a fair trade was completely beyond his interest. "Why don't you give me what you believe to be fair. I'll trust the good Lord to watch over my end of the deal," Teddy finally said.

"Well, He watches over every deal I make." The big man smiled. "I'll tell you what. The boy and I will go load up the meat and bring it around within the hour. We're in a bit of a hurry, so why don't you show us where you'd like to meet."

Teddy motioned them to follow. "As I said, I'm just there across the street. Come along and I'll show you the sled. That way you can better judge for yourself a fair trade."

The men followed Teddy down the walk and across the frozen snow and mud of Second Avenue. Teddy heard them commenting on the blessing of running across this stranger, but thought little of himself as their rescuer. He was glad to unload the sled. It was of little use to him. Come spring he'd simply hire someone to pack him out to the cabin on horseback.

"We're heading out to Hunker Creek," the big man told him. "Have a friend with a claim there. This is certainly going to be an answer to prayer."

"Well, here we are, gentlemen," Teddy said, stopping behind a small storage shed. The alleyway behind the hotel was covered in undisturbed snow and the wind had blown drifts across the doors to the shed. Teddy used his booted foot to push aside a good portion of the drift before pulling a key from his pants pocket.

"This should do the trick," he said, unlocking the shed. Dim light filtered into the confines of the dark storage room. A variety of supplies and other articles were stacked atop each other. Teddy's sled was just inside, due to the fact they'd only just arrived.

The big man pulled the sled out into the alleyway and nodded. "It's a fine, sturdy piece," he commented, looking it over for any defect.

Teddy pulled out his pocket watch and popped open the cover. It was nearly lunchtime. How had he managed to waste half a day? He began to make a mental calculation of his morning activities, not clearly hearing what the big man told him.

"If that meets with your approval."

"What?" Teddy questioned. "I'm afraid I was a bit adrift."

The big man laughed. "No problem. I merely said the sled is worth a good portion of meat. I'll bring it by here right away. Can you meet us here in an hour and make the trade?"

"Certainly," Teddy replied.

He waited until the men had headed off at a trotting pace before wrestling the sled back into the shed. He fiddled around with the lock, finally mastering it. Securing the door before heading back around the side of the hotel, Teddy considered what he should do now. The day was clearly getting away from him and he still had to come back to deal with the man who wanted his sled. He might as well purchase the supplies and then head back to the hotel for a bite of lunch. It would no doubt be time to meet the man after that. After he squared things away with the sled, he could certainly set about organizing his work.

Once again he crossed the street, anxious to purchase his supplies and get back to his room. There was a great deal of work yet to be done, work that would no doubt keep him busy until spring.

"Teddy Davenport, is that you?" an older man called as Teddy once again approached the hardware store.

Teddy looked up and met the approaching man somewhat apprehensively. "Lawrence Montgomery?" The man's face was buried behind a thick fur cap.

"That's right. I say, what are you about this day?"

"I was going to purchase some supplies. I'm working rather diligently to catalog my newest findings."

"Still working on the book, eh?"

Teddy nodded. "Most assuredly."

"Well, that's fine. Just fine. Say, you wouldn't be interested in having a spot of lunch with me, would you?"

"I shouldn't. I truly have a great deal of work to do." Teddy had never really cared for Montgomery's company. They had little in common, save England. Montgomery had been a member of Her Majesty's Navy and he never failed to bore Teddy with tedious stories of life aboard ship. Teddy wouldn't have minded hearing about the foreign ports, but Montgomery was far more consumed with naval life than the scenery he'd experienced.

"Just a cup of tea, then?"

Teddy knew the man was lonely for company, but he really didn't want to lose anymore time. "Perhaps we could meet later today. I simply must get back to work at this time."

"Then it will have to be another day," Montgomery said, "for I'm off to meet with the Arctic Brotherhood after lunch. We're discussing the possibility of building a new hall. You really should join us."

"Perhaps at the next meeting," Teddy promised. He knew the organization to be one of good charity and good times, but the meetings were generally not to his liking.

Turning to head back to the hotel, Teddy had barely crossed the street when he realized he'd completely forgotten about making his purchases at the hardware store. With a sigh, he rubbed his gloved hands together and made his way back to the store. He doubted he had any chance of making this day a productive one. The best he could hope for was a time of peace and quiet in the afternoon. Of course, there was also the matter of selling his sled. Pulling his watch once again, Teddy noted the time. He didn't want to make an enemy of the big man by failing to show up at the appointed time.

"Mr. Davenport," the clerk called out from behind the counter. "Good to have you back in town. What can I do for you today?"

Teddy closed the case on the watch and thought for a moment. *Oh, bother.* Now what had he done with his list?

CHAPTER ELEVEN

MIRANDA LOOKED OUT the window of the hotel. Happily she found that the wind had abated, as well as the falling snow. The street below was covered with a thick layer of white powder, but already there were dozens of people forging a new path through the pristine blanket.

"This ought to be as good a time as any to go in search of the registration office," Miranda said, letting the curtain fall back into place.

Gathering her coat, Miranda slipped into the hall. She glanced briefly at Teddy's door, wondering if he was hard at work inside. She thought to let him know that she was leaving for a while, but remembering how irritated he became with interruptions, Miranda decided against it. She owed him no explanation.

After getting directions to the recorder's office, she rushed in the direction indicated. Miranda was eager to learn the whereabouts of her friends. She had prayed fervently for their safety and could only trust that God had kept them from the same fate she'd suffered.

"I'm looking for my friends and family," she told the official once she'd managed to work her way through the gathering of men.

An older man with a thick bushy mustache of red and gray, looked at her as if to consider the validity of her statement. "You ain't one of them gals from Paradise Alley, are ya?"

"I'm afraid I'm not familiar with that particular place. I'm from San Francisco."

The men around her laughed while the older man looked at her sternly.

"Paradise Alley is the entertainment center for men who are looking for female companionship. I'm just askin' if you're one them kind of gals."

Miranda felt her cheeks grow hot. "I should say not. I was coming north when we encountered a storm on one of the lakes. I was swept overboard and it's been many months since I've seen or heard anything of what became of my friends and family. I'm staying over at the Dawson Lucky Day Hotel."

The man nodded as if he'd known the truth all along. Apparently this was enough to satisfy his curiosity. "So what's the name?"

"I believe the claim would be under Ivankov. Adrik Ivankov."

"Hmmm, name don't ring a bell, but let me look through the records."

Miranda waited patiently while the man searched his ledgers. "Nope, don't see no Ivankovs listed here. I have an Ivanovich. Would that work?"

He suggested the name as though Miranda were picking out colors for new draperies. "No," she answered. "How about Colton? Do you have any listing for Colton?"

"That spelled with an E-N or O-N?"

"O-N."

The man flipped through the pages and ran his finger down a long, hand-printed list. "I got a Benjamin Colton marked down on the Little Skookum. Would that be them?"

Miranda shook her head. "No."

"Maybe this here Ben Colton would know about your Coltons."

"No, I don't think so. You see, that's my family name and I've never known us to have a Benjamin in the family."

The man rubbed his chin. "Well, guess I can't offer you much help."

"Do you have any other suggestions for locating folks in this area? If my friends haven't filed a claim, is there any other way I can learn if they made it this far?"

"You could check in with the Mounties. They're trying to keep tabs on the folks comin' and goin'. They might have something for you."

Miranda thanked the man and walked back outside. The air was crisp, almost painful to breathe. The frosty cold filled her lungs, causing her to bury her face against the lining of her collar. Looking up and then down the street in hopes of seeing someone familiar, Miranda tried not to succumb to the feeling of overwhelming hopelessness.

What if they were all killed on the lake? What if I'm the only one who survived? Oh, God, please don't let that be the truth of it. I can't imagine never seeing them again.

Of course, it was possible that upon arriving in Dawson and believing Miranda dead, they could have returned to San Francisco, or at least Grace might have returned. But Grace had said it wasn't her home and she couldn't go there without Peter.

Thoughts of her brother gave Miranda an idea. Perhaps she could telegraph Peter in Skagway. Of course, he might have gone back to San Francisco by now, but he also might have stayed. But where could she send the message to be delivered? She had no idea where Peter might have gone. The sensible thing to do seemed to be to send her parents a wire and make sure they knew she wasn't dead. From there, maybe they could get word to her about Peter. The only problem was it cost money to send a telegram—money she didn't have.

Perhaps I could ask for a loan from Teddy, she thought. He had certainly offered her plenty of other things—a room, clothes, food. Surely he wouldn't begrudge her a telegram to her family.

Spotting a Mountie, Miranda crossed the street. "Sir," she addressed, "can you tell me where I might send a telegram? I need to contact my parents in California."

"I'm sorry, miss. There aren't telegraph connections for that kind of contact. Your best bet would be to post them a letter. I can direct you to the postal office."

"How long will it take a letter to reach them?" Miranda asked, her heart sinking with every new discovery.

"It could be months. The mail is taken out on dog sled and sometimes it's very reliable and other times it's less than so." He smiled apologetically. "I wish I could be more encouraging."

Miranda nodded. So much for sending a telegram. In a spirit of complete dejection, she shuffled through the icy snow and made her way back down the street. Shivering from the cold, Miranda decided to take a shortcut through the alleyway. She could see the top of the hotel at the end of the narrow path and felt confident she could reach it more quickly by this route.

She'd not gone ten steps, however, when a bearded man popped around the corner from the opposite direction. She bristled, knowing that it had been foolish to get off the main street. What if the man meant her harm?

She sized him up. Although dressed in a heavy coat and hat, Miranda thought the man looked rather thin and gaunt. He looked at her for a moment, then raised a bottle and took a long drink. Lowering the bottle, he looked at her again and took several steps forward. The shock was clearly written in his expression.

Miranda studied him. Her momentary fear passed as she recognized something familiar about the man. The light was fading from the skies, however, and the shadows could have been playing games with her. Moving a step closer she called out, "Crispin, is that you?"

The man dropped the bottle at this and began backing away. "No!"

"Crispin, wait. Where are you going?" she called out. "Where are the others?"

The man fell backward over a barrel, but quickly regained his feet and shook his head. "Leave me be. Go away!" he shouted.

He turned and fled, disappearing almost as quickly as he'd appeared. Miranda hurried after him, but it was to no avail. She came out of the alley near the hotel and looked in both directions.

"Crispin!" she called. The word echoed back at her.

He had simply vanished, as if he'd never been there at all. She rushed to where the alley intersected a narrow passage between buildings and looked first one direction and then the other. He wasn't there. Perhaps the whole incident had been nothing but a figment of her imagination. Perhaps she longed so much to find her loved ones that her mind had begun conjuring them up.

"Oh, Father God," she whispered. "I cannot begin to understand what just happened. Surely if that man was Crispin Thibault, he would have come to me in greeting. Surely he would have taken me to my friends. What do I do now?"

She continued down the alley, feeling nothing but dumbfounded of the strange meeting. The sight of Teddy at the storage shed behind the hotel did little to lift her spirits.

"I say, what are you doing here?" he questioned as she drew near.

"I was just coming from the deed office. No one has heard of my friends. I thought to send a telegram to my parents, but a Mountie told me there are no such services here in Dawson." Miranda felt tears come to her eyes. "And just now, I thought I saw one of the gentlemen from my party, but he ran off in a fit of fear." Tears stung her eyes against the cold air.

Teddy put the key to the shed in his coat pocket, and then extended his arm. "Now, now. You mustn't cry. The air is much too cold and your eyes will positively freeze. Look, I've had a bit of luck in ridding myself of the sled. I made a rather nice trade for some elk and moose meat. What say we get the cook to fix us some of it for our supper? We can dine and discuss what you must do next."

Miranda was surprised at his generous offer of time. "What about your work?"

Teddy looked to the skies overhead. "I'll simply work into the night. Come along."

Miranda didn't know what else she could do. Reluctantly she reached out and took hold of Teddy's arm. "I'm completely confused," she told him, looking up into his warm brown eyes. She saw his expression soften. "I'm so alone."

"Nonsense," he replied, patting her arm with his gloved hand. "You have me. I shall help you in whatever manner presents itself to me."

Miranda turned to Teddy, captured by his gallant concern for her well-being, and felt that she was losing her heart to his quiet, gentle ways. Though she felt so vulnerable—so lost—he was like a refuge in the cleft of the rock. A shelter from a certain, otherwise unbearable, storm.

⊣{ C H A P T E R   T W E L V E }⊢

TEDDY FELT A STRANGE FLUTTERING and warmth in his chest. He typically didn't concern himself with the emotions of others—in fact, it wasn't something he'd really ever done before now. His mother had been a very loving woman whose strength and independence he had greatly admired. His father, a refined Englishman, was soft-spoken and gentle of spirit. Teddy had never had cause to deal with such depth of feeling—until now.

"I am sorry about your friend," Teddy said as he guided Miranda into the hotel. "But you truly shouldn't let his reaction upset you."

"Why do you say that? I've been gone for months," Miranda replied indignantly. She pulled away from him and shook her head. "They believe me to be dead. He acted as though I were a ghost."

"But they'll know the truth of it in the end." Teddy thought his argument to be perfectly reasonable. Miranda's expression suggested otherwise.

Taking hold of her well-worn skirt, Miranda crossed the lobby in obvious displeasure. Teddy could scarcely believe her reaction. What had he said that was wrong? He rethought his words as he followed her up the stairs.

"Miss Colton, I say, you surely misunderstand me."

"I understand that you believe my concern to be silly and unwarranted."

"I never said it was silly," Teddy replied, trying hard to remember any comment that might have given her this impression.

"You act as though it's nothing more than a simple misunderstanding," Miranda countered as she topped the stairs. She turned, pulling her wool bonnet from her head. "You suggest that the truth will come out in the end. Well, let me explain something to you, Mr. Davenport. My friends believe the end has already come and gone. They believe me to be dead in Lake Laberge."

Teddy nodded, trying hard to guard his words. "Yes . . ." he began hesitantly, "but you're not."

"Exactly!" She made the declaration and lifted her chin defiantly.

Teddy watched Miranda stalk down the hallway toward her room. He went over every piece of information, each comment he had shared. But her actions and attitude simply did not follow any rational response. Why was she so angry with him? Only moments ago she had been tearful.

"Miss Colton," Teddy called as he followed after her, "I must be allowed to say something—to explain . . ."

Miranda turned, her eyes narrowing. "To explain why you are so heartless?"

"Me? Heartless? I assure you that is hardly the case. I am trying my best to offer you comfort by presenting a reasonable explanation. Your friends cannot leave Dawson, short of heading out on dog sled. That is highly unlikely, as there isn't a sled to be bought in town. A man told me that just this morning, when I sold him my sled."

"What could that possibly have to do with any of this?"

"Just this," Teddy said, hoping she'd hear with her logic and not her emotions. "If that was your friend—the man you saw earlier—he won't be leaving Dawson until spring thaw. That won't come until May. That gives you months to track down your friends."

"I hardly have months, Mr. Davenport. I cannot expect to go on living here without a job. I have no clothes to speak of, no money for personal items, and I cannot pay for the room in which I'm sleeping."

"But the money is immaterial," Teddy assured her. Finally he felt confident of the subject matter. "I've given you the room without requirement of pay. I've offered to buy you new clothes, and I'd be happy to give you cash for your personal needs."

But instead of making her happy, Teddy could see that this announcement only intensified her irritation. "I'm not your responsibility," Miranda said firmly. "I'm not about to allow a strange man to keep me, almost as if I were his . . . his . . . mistress."

Teddy felt his cheeks grow hot. He was unaccustomed to women speaking in such a manner. He was befuddled. First Miranda had been upset because she found her friend and lost him. Then she was upset about being without money or clothes. And when Teddy offered to help, she was angry about that as well.

"I *never* suggested that I expect anything in return, Miss Colton," Teddy finally managed to say. "I don't know where you could possibly get such an idea."

Miranda put her hand on her hips. "I'm a woman and you're a man. You're keeping me in a hotel, in an adjoining room to your own sleeping quarters. You pay for my meals and now you offer to put clothes on my back. What will people think?"

"Well, I really don't care what people think. We know what the truth of it is. I don't think of you as a woman," Teddy said, suddenly halting, realizing his blunder the minute he'd spoken. Not only was it the wrong thing to say, it was a lie. He was only too aware of Miranda as a woman.

"You are without a doubt the most insensitive and simpleminded man in all creation," Miranda proclaimed. "You don't understand anything unless it grows out of the ground and can be pressed into your books for further study. In fact, I'm beginning to think you are incapable of understanding anything not associated with vegetation. I believe, Mr. Davenport, it very well may be possible that your brain is composed of nothing but mulch and compost. Good day!"

Abruptly she turned and opened her door without even looking back at him. When she slammed the door behind her, Teddy knew it had been done for his benefit.

"Mulch? Compost?" He shook his head and pulled the room key from his pants pocket. Women were queer creatures. So temperamental and emotional.

With a slow shake of his head, Teddy opened the door to his room and stared in stunned amazement. The room, which that morning had been in perfect order, now lay in complete disarray. Books, plants, jars, and clothes were scattered about the room like children's toys in a messy nursery. Months of work had been destroyed, completely obliterated in this attack on his personal belongings.

Teddy walked in, not even bothering to close the door. He picked up one of his journals and dusted the flaked pieces of dried *Calypso bulbosa*—fairy slipper—from the leather cover.

Who could have done such a thing? He wondered at the destruction, barely able to comprehend the situation. No corner of the room was untouched. The bed had been torn apart, the bedding left to lie on the floor, mattress hanging off on one side.

Teddy began picking things up without any real thought or order. He was standing there rather dumbly, his arms full of this and that, when Miranda Colton knocked on his open door.

He looked up to catch her expression of disbelief. "Who did this?" she questioned.

"I don't know."

"Why would they do this?" she asked, stepping into the room.

"Again, I cannot say."

He shook his head and looked back at the disarray. "I had nothing of value here—not in a monetary sense. However, in the sense of work and months of searching—these possessions are invaluable."

"I'm so sorry, Teddy." Miranda's soft-spoken tone soothed his frayed nerves. "Not only for this, but for the way I acted. I know you were only trying to help me, and I wasn't very kind. I'm sorry."

"No, I'm the one to apologize. You must understand—I've not had much experience with the fairer gender. I suppose myself to be rather remiss in dealing with the emotions and even the physical needs of women." Teddy moved to place the armload of materials on the table.

"Is there anything I can do?" Miranda asked, coming to stand beside him. "I could help you clean this up."

"The work will be extensive. I can't just tear into it. I'll have to take it a little at a time. It will be rather painstaking."

"I don't mind. I owe you much."

He turned and caught the compassion in her expression. How was it that she could be so sympathetic and concerned, when he had obviously hurt her deeply only moments ago?

"You owe me nothing. The law of the north is to do unto your neighbor as you would have done to you. The law of God's Word is to love your neighbor as yourself. I would have wanted someone to help me, had I washed ashore in the same condition."

"Yes, but I haven't acted very grateful. I really would like to help you here. But first, perhaps we should ask to speak with the management. I think the owner should know of this."

"He already does," Teddy replied. "I am he."

"You own this hotel? Why didn't you tell me?"

Teddy shrugged. "It never seemed important. When the rush first came on, I used funds from my parents' estate and built the nicest place I could."

"Well, at least that explains why you had no trouble putting me up," Miranda said smiling. "You are quite the man of many surprises, Mr. Davenport."

He looked away. "I could have done without this surprise." He thought of her offer and realized that, in the destruction of all that he held dear, he needed her. He needed her comfort, her gentle nature, and her companionship.

"I will allow you to help, but only if I may pay you a salary." He held up his hand to ward off any protests. "I will deduct the price of the room if that makes you feel better, but I would have to pay someone—so it might as well be you."

"But I would do the job without charge," Miranda replied, coming to stand in front of him. "Teddy, you've already done so much for me."

"Then allow me to continue. You have no other alternative, unless you would like to become a saloon dancer or scarlet woman. And while your appearance would definitely put the others to shame, such an occupation would never befit you. Let me pay you to be my assistant. But I will warn you—I'm an absolute bear to work for. The work will be tedious and the hours long. We've much to accomplish in order to right this wrong."

"Very well, Teddy. I will allow you to furnish my room and board and whatever else you feel fair. In return, however, I will work the same hours you work. So, if you plan to labor into the wee hours of the morning, I'll be right there at your side."

He smiled to himself and bent down to pick up a dried sample of fireweed in order to keep her from seeing his face. The idea of having Miranda at his side was most appealing. He'd grown very accustomed to her company, and though he didn't understand her emotional outbursts, he was drawn to her presence like no other.

He straightened and held up the plant. The fuchsia color had faded a bit since he'd picked it for his collection, but it was lovely nevertheless.

"Do you know what this is?" he asked, holding up the flower.

Miranda shook her head. "I haven't a clue."

"It's *Epilobium angustifolium*, commonly called fireweed or blooming Sally. It's generally considered to be a nuisance to those who garden. Some even call it a weed." He twirled the piece in his finger a moment, and then handed it to Miranda. "I've collected many of them in my explorations of the land, but I thought this one to be an exceptionally nice example."

"It is lovely—weed or no," Miranda said, taking the flower.

"I thought so as well."

"How shall I preserve it for your work?"

He nodded toward the table. "We shall gather the samples and lay them out atop the table. As we gather them, I'll try to categorize them again. It's not going to be easy."

"Well, as you said earlier, there's no place to go short of mushing out on a dog sled, and since you've sold your sled . . . well, that pretty much means we are here until spring."

"I suppose you're right," he replied.

———

After they had worked in companionable silence for several hours, Miranda felt a gnawing in her stomach and suggested they stop for a bite of supper. "I'm quite famished and I know I could work better on a full stomach."

"I suppose it would be best," Teddy said, pulling off his gold-rimmed glasses. He carefully folded the glasses and put them in his pocket. "I traded the sled for a large quantity of meat, so we're bound to have a pleasant supper."

Miranda stretched, glad for the rest. Her back ached from the constant bending to retrieve pieces of vegetation. How Teddy could identify each piece and correspond it to a place on the table was beyond Miranda. Most of the plants looked quite the same, especially the leaves.

"If you don't mind, I'd like to freshen up a bit," Miranda told him. "I won't be but a minute. I just want to wash up and fix my hair."

"Your hair looks lovely," Teddy said, then instantly appeared embarrassed by his outburst. As if to cover up his mistake, he continued. "I suppose I haven't told you this before, but the color reminds me of the bark of the mountain maple. The brown species—not the gray."

Miranda reached her hand to her hair. "I'm betting a few more years like this one and it will be all gray."

"I think not. You've many years before that will come about," Teddy replied.

"Well, just so long as the mountain maple is of sturdy stock," Miranda said, moving toward the door. "My people are all from sturdy stock. We are fighters, and I won't have it said that I resemble anything less than a strong specimen."

"Indeed, you are that," Teddy said, his voice dropping to a husky, barely audible tone.

Miranda smiled to herself. He wasn't such an unlikable sort. Just quaint and unique in his compliments. She'd had her hair praised and admired before, but never had anyone compared it to the bark of a tree. Coming from anyone else, it might have seemed insulting. Coming from Thomas Davenport, it almost seemed a term of endearment.

Part Two

MARCH 1899

And he hath put a new song in my mouth,
even praise unto our God:
many shall see it, and fear,
and shall trust in the Lord.

PSALM 40:3

CHAPTER THIRTEEN

PETER SAT ALONGSIDE his father in the law office of Mathias Hamilton. The news was all good, and Peter knew the blessing had come from God.

"The judge has agreed that the contract was not issued in a legal manner. The fraudulent manner in which Mr. Paxton conducted his business and the disregard for your son's legal partnership in the business has rendered the judgment in your favor."

Peter breathed a sigh of relief. He had fully planned to leave the month before, but the lawyer had deemed it necessary to keep Peter close at hand. Now, at last, he would be free to go north and find his sister. Already his mind raced with plans.

"I have also seen to that other matter," Hamilton continued, addressing Peter. "I have looked over the trust papers given to you by your mother-in-law. Everything is in order."

Peter could scarcely believe the news Myrtle Hawkins had brought him. Paxton had thought he could ruin Hawkins through his bank account, but her husband had been too wise for that. Knowing the ruthlessness of Martin Paxton, Frederick had secured most of his fortune in an irrevocable trust for Grace.

When Paxton discovered the truth—that Grace was the one who would hold the purse strings—he had forced Frederick into compliance, threatening to share the story of his adulterous affair. Poor Frederick Hawkins had had no choice but to give in. The last thing he wanted to do was alienate the affection of his wife and only child. What Frederick Hawkins had thought would offer his daughter protection from Paxton's evil schemes was instead the very thing that drove him to pursue her. The trust would be hers upon her twenty-first birthday, and was the real reason Paxton had pushed for marriage prior to her coming into her majority. He was determined to ruin Hawkins in any way he could, and all because Hawkins had broken Martin's mother's heart through their illicit affair.

Of course, Peter now felt, in the aftermath of knowing the truth of Paxton's actions, that he could understand—at least in part—what had driven the man. Had anyone tried to dally with his mother, he would have had similar desires to see that person ruined.

"In light of the information you've given me, in regard to your wife's death," Hamilton continued, "I shall send a post to the authorities in Canada and see what we can do to receive confirmation. After her death is confirmed, we can proceed on arranging the affairs of the trust."

Peter nodded, not wanting to talk about Grace's death. He didn't want to deal with any aspect of the situation that would remind him of his loss. Standing, he extended his hand and firmly shook the hand of Mathias Hamilton. "Thank you for your time."

Ephraim Colton did likewise and added, "You will see to transferring the company entirely to my son?"

"The matter is already being tended to," Hamilton assured them.

Peter and his father hailed a cab outside the law office and made the journey home. "I know Mother's spirits will be lifted by this news," Peter said.

"Indeed. Although she doesn't care as much for the business as she does for having the matter resolved and behind us."

"She worries about you—about your health."

Ephraim sighed and settled back against the leather seat. "I know she does, but in truth, none of us know how much time we have on this earth. We're here for a short time, the Bible says. We must make every effort to live our lives in a manner pleasing to God and to be a blessing to others for His glory."

Peter found his father's words to be inspiring. "I agree. That's why I'll head north at the end of the week. It's time I found Miranda and brought her home. By the time I arrive in Skagway, it should be close to spring thaw."

"I know it would comfort your mother to know what has become of her," Ephraim agreed. "She has worried incessantly about her all winter. She felt remiss in having encouraged her to go north with Grace, yet . . ."

"Give it no other thought," Peter interjected. "I believe God has had His hand in all of this from the beginning. I didn't always feel that way, but I most certainly do now. I know God has a plan for my life and a purpose that only I can fulfill. It's no less for Miranda or you—or Grace."

He felt the bittersweet sorrow of her memory come over him. He could almost see her dark brown eyes and smell her sweet fragrance. What was it—apple blossoms and roses?

His father's touch brought his senses back to the present. "Son, I know your heart is heavy. I loved her, too, you know."

Peter met his father's gaze. "I know."

"We are better for having had her in our lives. But let us not lessen that experience by focusing on the pain. Grace would never want us to live in a manner that would suggest that God is anything other than just and loving. She would want us to move forward in love for each other and for the God she so dearly loved."

"I know you're right, but sometimes it's just so hard." He paused. "I reach for her in the night and she's not there. I think I hear her come into the room and turn to find that it's only the wind."

Ephraim nodded. "It's not easy, but in time the pain will lessen."

"I'd like to believe that," Peter said, "but I doubt it could possibly be true. Still, I'm willing to leave it in God's hands. After all, there are few other choices."

"Especially choices that would honor Grace's memory and be in keeping with God's desire for your life."

The cab stopped in front of their townhouse, interrupting the moment. Peter paid the driver, and then helped his father from the steps. He looked up at the house, noting that it no longer felt like a home to him. Leaving San Francisco seemed the only hope of maintaining his sanity. He'd been happy here with Grace, despite the arguments and the painful words between them. Words he'd spoken in anger. Words that had driven her away.

"Come on, son. Let's tell your mother the good news."

Ephraim headed up the steps of the walkway, and reluctantly Peter followed.

Peter lightly fingered the pink silk gown that he'd given Grace shortly after their marriage. She had looked radiant in the dress, but then, she'd looked radiant in most anything she wore. Caressing the gown to his face, he breathed in her perfume—now faded and barely distinguishable.

"Oh, Grace. Why did I have to wait until it was too late to know what I had in you?"

"Peter?" Myrtle called from behind the closed bedroom door.

Putting the dress aside, Peter went to the door. Opening it, he found his mother-in-law looking rather expectant. "Yes, Myrtle?"

"I wondered if we might have a moment to speak together. I don't want to take you away from anything important."

"No, that's all right. I wasn't doing anything that can't wait until later. What did you want to talk to me about?" He stepped back to allow her to enter the room.

Myrtle walked past him, then turned and smiled. "Peter, your mother tells me that you're heading north by the end of the week."

"Yes, that's correct." He motioned to a chair. "Won't you sit down?"

Myrtle nodded and took a seat. Her black gown, a constant reminder of her widowhood and Grace's death, swished in gentle whispers as she straightened her skirts. Peter pulled up another chair from the opposite side of the room and sat down across from Myrtle.

"I figure to leave by Friday. I want to be north as soon as possible and find my sister."

"I pray God will grant you His favor in your search. I plan to leave by the end of the week, myself. I wondered if you would be so kind as to escort me to the train station on the day after tomorrow."

"I would be happy to do that," Peter replied. He had a hard time looking at Myrtle, especially at her eyes. She reminded him so much of Grace that it hurt. He had to look away.

"Do you suppose you will learn anything more of Grace?"

Her question pierced his heart. "I don't know. I don't expect to be shown a grave or anything like that. I don't imagine they would be able to ... to ..." He couldn't say the words.

Myrtle nodded. "No, I don't imagine they would have recovered her body." She folded her hands in her lap and looked down. "I just wondered if you thought there might be some further word on her. Maybe Miss Pierce would be able to share something more."

"It's possible. I'm sure if anyone would be able to give us further insight, Karen would be the one. Miranda, however, was also very close to Grace. She loved her like a sister, and they'd grown quite close." Peter hesitated before suggesting, "Why don't you stay here while I'm gone? I know my mother and father would love to have you here."

"No, I would rather go back to my aunt's place. She's old and needs the help. Besides, there is something renewing and invigorating in living in such a simple rural setting after having lived in Chicago."

"I'm sure that is true."

"I only ask that you keep in touch," Myrtle said rather sadly. "I don't wish to lose contact with you simply because Grace is gone."

"And you won't. I've already spoken to my lawyer. I am arranging to set up an account for you with the money Grace inherited. I want you to have whatever you need."

Myrtle's face reddened a bit and tears came to her eyes. "You are a good son-in-law, but really, you mustn't worry about me. I'm set well enough with my aunt."

"I insist. I'm not sure how long it will take to resolve, but should you need anything prior to that, please don't hesitate to contact us. I'll leave an account with my parents. Just let them know what you need, and we'll do our best to see to it."

"Oh, Peter, you are truly as remarkable and generous as Grace told me."

"I wish I'd been as generous of spirit with Grace. I'm ashamed to say that I wronged her terribly, Myrtle. I didn't tell you everything that transpired between us, but our marriage was not as pleasant or loving as it could have been. I'm afraid that before I knew God I was rather ruthless at times."

Myrtle wiped her eyes and smiled. "Marriage is hard work—for everyone. I remember times when I wanted nothing more than to throttle Frederick. He would speak to me as if I were a child without good sense."

"I know I did that to Grace on more than one occasion. I have a bad temper."

"Surely no worse than my Frederick." Myrtle reached out and took hold of Peter's hand. "She loved you—be certain of that. Her letters said that and so much more."

Peter's heart flooded with gratitude. "Thank you for saying so. It helps. I hate to think of Grace's last thoughts of me being how truly awful I was and how sorry she was for having married me."

"Then rest your mind and put your worries aside. She told me of difficult moments, but she always stressed that her love for you was stronger than anything that could possibly go wrong."

Peter gripped her hand gently. "We should have had this talk a long time ago."

"I didn't realize how much you were hurting until I came here. Watching you has shown me proof of your deep abiding love for my daughter. How I wish things could have been different." Myrtle's voice was tinged with regret. "I just wanted you to know that I understand. I miss her and Frederick more than I can say, but God alone will ease the pain—in His time."

"I only wish I had known what a priceless gem I had in her, before it was too late. When I come back from the Yukon, maybe I'll take some of her money and erect a monument to her in the cemetery."

"Why not put the money to some better use, something that would bring glory to God and make Grace proud?"

"Such as?" Peter questioned.

"I don't know. Pray about it, and perhaps God will give you a mission," Myrtle said, getting to her feet.

Peter immediately stood and embraced the older woman. "Myrtle, you were a godsend. You've given me comfort as no one else possibly could. When I return, I shall visit you in Wyoming."

"I would like that," she said, pulling away. "I would like that very much."

CHAPTER FOURTEEN

MONTHS OF WORKING with Teddy had given Miranda quite an education. She could now identify many flowers and dried leaves without having to ask Teddy for assistance. She had also come to realize that her frantic concern for locating her friends was lessening in the wake of her pleasure in Teddy's company. She'd become rather lackadaisical in her inquiries.

Truth be told, there were many days when she never even left the hotel room. She labored with Teddy, helping him catch up his research to at least the point where he'd left off when they'd come to Dawson in January. Now, with March winds alternating between freezing them to the bone and teasing them with a touch of spring, Miranda knew she needed to rededicate herself to the pursuit of locating her friends. However, Teddy was more adamant in their work than ever before. The summer would mean he could be back in the fields, and if his work from the previous year went uncompleted, he'd have to delay his trip.

As she poured over Teddy's journals and ledgers, Miranda wondered what course of action she should take. She had inquired around town about her friends when the opportunity presented itself. Many people knew of large, burly miners whose description fit that of Adrik Ivankov, but no one could tell her for sure that the men were one and the same.

At the same time, Miranda was torn by the thought of Teddy leaving for the wilderness. She tried to tell herself that it was only because they'd become such close companions in their work, but in her heart she knew it was more than that.

"I believe that," Teddy said, coming into the room unannounced, "if we persevere, we may well have this work completed by the end of next month. That will work in perfect accord with my return to the cabin."

It was almost as if he'd read her very thoughts. Miranda straightened from where she'd been bent over his books. She decided it would be best to broach the subject of what was to become of her once he was gone.

"Teddy, what am I to do if I cannot locate my friends?"

He looked at her rather blankly for a moment. It almost seemed to Miranda that he'd not given the possibility even a moment's thought.

"Why, I suppose you might stay here," he said, then turned to hang his coat on the peg by the door.

"I can't very well do that without a job," Miranda chided. "I could return home. After all, it's important to me that my family knows I'm safe."

Teddy looked at her for a moment. Miranda held his gaze, watching him search her face as if looking for something. "Passage would be expensive," he finally said. He walked to the window and pulled aside the sheer curtain. The skies were staying light for more hours of the day, and Miranda was grateful for this.

"I think it would be wiser to locate your friends rather than just leave. After all, they must be somewhere in the area."

"I've not seen Crispin again, and he was in the area as well," Miranda replied.

"Yes, but that could have been a man who just favored your friend. You said yourself that you couldn't be sure."

Miranda nodded and walked to the stack of drawings Teddy had asked her to file. Bringing them back to the table, she began to sort through them. Paintbrush, shooting stars, larkspur, and subalpine buttercups graced the pages of stiff paper. Teddy Davenport was quite an artist. The flowers, rendered only in charcoal and pencil, were detailed and labeled in such a way that they allowed for easy reference for anyone who wanted to study the species more closely.

Realizing Teddy had joined her at the table, Miranda looked up. "I know it could have been a complete stranger," she finally said. "It seems likely that it was, but I have to make a decision before you head out."

"You could come with me. I won't be staying at the cabin the entire time. I'll be traveling the area, in fact." His voice took on an excited tone. "Yes, that's it. You could accompany me. If your friends are not evident come the thaw, you could travel with me and look for them as I take collections of the vegetation."

"I suppose that's a possibility," Miranda replied thoughtfully. She looked up and caught the animation in his expression. "Are you certain it wouldn't be a hindrance? After all, you mentioned more than once that my arrival to your cabin had seriously altered your schedule and routine. And now you've had to endure my company here in Dawson as well."

"I'd hardly say that I've had to endure your company. You've been a tremendous help to me. I'd not have this work done by now if not for your help."

"It's been a great deal of fun," Miranda said, surprised by her declaration. "I've really enjoyed the education. I've always loved to learn, although my family never encouraged formal education past the normal schooling for girls. I often thought it would be fun to attend a university, but my brother was against the idea, feeling it wasn't proper. He prefers to see me at home." She smiled and rearranged the papers in her hands. "But that's unimportant. What I wanted to say to you was that I've also enjoyed feeling useful."

"Well, you've certainly been that and more."

Miranda looked into Teddy's eyes, lost in the warmth of his gaze, and the words she'd thought to say froze on her lips. Realizing he was now only inches away, she felt suddenly shy, almost nervous.

"I'm sorry that I ever said you had altered or interfered with my schedule," Teddy said, his voice dropping. "I never meant to hurt your feelings or give you the impression that you had caused me any grief. Your help has allowed me to reclaim the time lost to me because of the vandalism to my room."

Miranda licked her lips and struggled to form the words to reply. "I . . . I'm . . . glad to know . . . I mean, I'm glad I didn't cause you any real problem."

She felt her knees grow weak. Why hadn't she realized how handsome he was before now? She had known him to be attractive, even found his appearance to be quite nice, but he'd never affected her like this before. Now she could see every detail of his face—the furrows in his forehead from the long hours of concentration over his work, the fullness of his lips. He needed a shave, and she was sorely tempted to reach up and run her fingers over the stubble on his chin.

Like a child caught with her hand in the cookie jar, Miranda felt her face grow hot as they locked gazes once again.

"Miranda," he whispered in almost a reverent tone.

When she leaned forward, Miranda had no intention of initiating a kiss—yet that was what she did. Putting her hands on his shoulders, she stretched up on her tiptoes and kissed him lightly upon the lips.

He did nothing, and when Miranda pulled away, she put her hand to her mouth. "Oh, please forgive me." She hurried for the door, completely embarrassed at what she'd done. "I'm sorry. I didn't—I mean I shouldn't have—" She opened the door and turned to see him standing there still stunned by her actions. "That was a mistake—it won't happen again."

She hurried out of the room, not even bothering to close the door behind her. She ran for the comfort of her room, frightened by the emotions raging through her. Closing the door, she leaned against it, panting, struggling to draw a decent breath.

"Why did I do that?" she whispered.

Her stomach did flips, her emotions alternating between giddy and terrified. "I kissed him," she said aloud to the room, as if it might offer her some comment. "How could I have acted so wantonly?"

Shame flooded her soul. "Oh, forgive me, God. I never meant to be so forward. Mr. Davenport has done nothing but be the perfect gentleman. He's helped me every step of the way, providing for my needs, and I repay him by this. I'm so sorry."

She began to pace the room, the heavy navy wool of her skirt flaring out around her as she moved. He'd bought her the skirt, as well as the cotton blouse she wore. He'd bought her other things as well—shoes, boots, undergarments. At the thought of the latter Miranda felt her cheeks grow even hotter.

I've ruined everything, she thought. *I acted on impulse and now look where it's taken me. I deserve for Teddy to march over here and throw me out.*

As if on cue, a loud knocking sounded at her door. Miranda froze in place. "Who . . . is . . . it?" she stammered.

"Open the door, Miranda."

It was Teddy. He'd come to reprimand her and to ask her to leave. Gathering her courage, Miranda went to the door and opened it. Before she could offer another word of apology or even a plea to be given a second chance, Teddy swept her into his arms and kissed her ardently on the mouth. His lips lingered for more than a moment and Miranda lost herself in reckless abandonment. If this was good-bye, then she'd go out in style.

Releasing her rather abruptly, Teddy stepped back. His eyes were ablaze with passion. "I don't want it to be a mistake," he said, his voice husky and very different from the businesslike manner in which he usually communicated.

Grace Colton sat nursing her son after a long day of washing out linens and towels. Adrik had secured her a place with a local dentist, Dr. Brummel, and his wife, Georgia. As soon as she recovered from Andy's birth, Grace had gone to work for the couple doing housekeeping and laundry, along with some cooking. Her efforts were rewarded with room and board for herself and Andy and a small amount of pocket money.

She had very little time off, but that didn't matter to Grace. In fact, she preferred things that way. When working, she didn't have time to dwell on Peter. Not that she could ever put him totally from her mind. Looking down upon her brown-haired son, she knew she would be forever reminded of her husband—no matter his decision regarding their marriage.

Andy cooed as if knowing her thoughts. He pulled away from her breast and laughed, his tiny hand reaching up to take hold of her unpinned hair.

"Oh, my sweet boy," she whispered. "You are my very life. God was so good to give you to me."

She shifted him into an upright position and adjusted the neck of her night-gown. How she cherished these quiet moments in the late evening. This was her time with Andy. Hers alone. Had Peter been a part of their life, he would have shared in the time, and then he would have seen for himself how very special their relationship might be.

"Oh, Andy," Grace said sighing, "I wish your papa could know about you—see you. If he were here right now, I know he would adore you."

Andy made gurgling noises as Grace began patting his back in order to burp him. She rocked back and forth in her chair, humming to herself in rhythm. Andy's eyelids grew heavy, and after burping him, Grace lifted him to her shoulder and pulled his hand-knit blanket around him.

"Thank you, God," she prayed as Andy fell asleep—his face nuzzled against her neck. "Thank you for this child and for the protection afforded me by Dr. Brummel and his wife."

She rocked in the silence for several minutes, enjoying the simple pleasure that the moment afforded her. It was hard to imagine, given the peace she felt, that the entire world outside her window could be so caught up in the pursuit for gold.

There had been numerous claim jumping incidents and even deaths related to misunderstandings. Grace had found it far easier to remain in the safety of the Brummel house, rather than risk her life on the streets. She'd only gone out twice, and both times were to venture no farther than the corner dry goods store.

Each trip had been marked by an unusual event. The first one had brought her face to face with a group of "scarlet women," as Mrs. Brummel called the local prostitutes. The day had been warmer than most and Grace had decided the short outing would be good for both her and Andy. But babies were a fairly rare sight in the town, and Andy brought much unwelcome attention—especially by a group of prostitutes who had wandered over from Paradise Alley.

Grace had been rather uncertain as to how she should handle the moment. The girls, heavily painted and gaudily dressed, had each wanted to hold Andy. They cooed over him, reaching out to touch the pure and innocent child. Grace pitied them and allowed them their moment of pleasure.

One woman, not so much older than herself, held Andy longer than the others. She gently stroked his cheek and spoke in low, soft whispers. Grace couldn't hear what she said, but when the woman returned Andy to her arms, Grace saw tears in the prostitute's eyes.

The moment had moved Grace beyond words. She was certain she would always remember the woman's face and wonder what problems had brought her to such a sorry life. Was there a baby in her past—perhaps a child who had died or had been taken from her? The very thought left Grace deeply saddened.

The next time Grace ventured out, she had gone alone. This time the store was filled with raucous miners, and an argument ensued about which creek was bearing the best show of gold. Before Grace knew what was happening, the men had separated into two groups, and Grace found herself positioned between the two as she stood at the counter preparing to pay for her goods.

In the next moment, one of the men took a swing at another and Grace was pushed to the floor. As she looked up she was shocked to see the store owner bring down a large wooden mallet on the counter.

"You are a disgrace to mankind," the owner told the men as the sound of the mallet strike echoed in the small confines of the store. He came around the counter and helped Grace from the floor and then unfolded his handkerchief and laid it out flat on the counter.

"You all owe this lady an apology. A pinch a piece ought to say it well enough."

Grace watched as each of the hardened sourdoughs ambled up, muttered their regrets, and deposited a pinch of gold dust on the cloth. By the time they'd finished she had fifty dollars worth of gold to her name.

After that she had decided it would be best not to risk another trip. Andy needed her—she was all he had until Peter could be found. Of course, she knew Karen and Adrik would happily provide for the child, but they were two days away down on Hunker Creek. Only that morning she had penned Karen a letter, telling her how much she longed for their company and hoped the time would soon present itself for her and Andy to join the others.

With Andy asleep, Grace put him in her bed and rolled thick blankets in a circle around him. He needed her warmth for the cold nights, but she didn't want to risk rolling over on him. Mrs. Brummel had suggested the arrangement and had even rearranged the room to place the small bed up against the wall so that Grace needn't fear Andy rolling out once he became more mobile.

Yawning, Grace sat down to complete her final task for the night. She turned up the lamp just a bit in order to see better. Taking up a pencil and paper, she began writing a letter to Peter. In the letter she told of Andy's birth. She hadn't had the courage to do so until now. The baby was two months old, and she needed to let Peter know of Andy's existence.

What she dreaded most was that Peter would come to her only because of Andrew. She didn't want her husband to journey to the Yukon out of a sense of obligation or duty. She wanted him to come because he loved her and wanted her to be his wife. If he found out about Andy, how could she ever be sure of the reasons behind his return? She had prayed about the matter more than once, knowing it was only fair that Peter should know about his son's birth. She even wondered if God might use Andy to show Peter how important his marriage vows were—that his promise to God and Grace were the very foundation for the family he was called to lead. At the same time, however, she truly regretted having to break the news to him via a letter. She had thought to take a ship back to California, come summer, but now she wasn't so sure.

The letter she'd written to Peter's parents after Miranda's death gave him every indication of her whereabouts. It hurt her that they had made no contact. She had made it clear that their party had intended to winter in Dawson City. She had assured Peter and his family that she could receive mail at "general delivery" in town. But no letter had ever come, and in the months since Miranda's death, Grace had worried that maybe there would never be a letter from her husband.

"Lord, I don't want him to come only because of Andrew," she whispered, her tears falling upon the paper. "I want Peter to love me and to love you. I want Peter to come to me . . . but only if it's forever."

—{ C H A P T E R   F I F T E E N }—

"THAT LEG LOOKS INFECTED, Gump," Karen said as she assessed the week-old ax wound.

"Ja, I think you might be right."

"Adrik, I think you're going to have to take Gump to the doctor in Dawson before this gets much worse. It's already showing signs of proud flesh."

"You think it's that bad?" Adrik came over and upon seeing the swollen, red wound let out a whistle. "Gump, you should have told me it had festered."

"I figured it'd get better," the old man said, his voice betraying the pain he felt as Karen sopped at the wound with alcohol.

"Well, it hasn't. I guess we're going to have to make a trip to Dawson and get you squared away."

"You could also pick up Grace and the baby, couldn't you?" Karen questioned. While she enjoyed Leah's company in the small cabin, she longed for another woman to talk to. Especially one she knew as well as Grace. Grace was like her own daughter in so many ways.

"I suppose we could arrange for that as well," Adrik replied. "It's warming up a little at a time. Probably won't have any more of those forty-below temperatures."

"I hope you're right. Anyway, I miss her a great deal and hate to think of her being all alone with Andy in Dawson." Karen had only heard from Grace a few times. One letter had come just a few days ago, brought in by one of their neighbors who'd taken a two-week furlough in Dawson while his partner kept the claim.

"If you take me to Dawson," Gump said, "who vill be here to care for the place?"

"I'll be here," Karen replied. "As much as I'd like to see civilization again, I'm just as happy to stay here. Leah and Jacob and I can take care of things while you're gone."

"I don't like the idea of leaving you," Adrik said.

"We'll be fine, Adrik," Jacob Barringer promised. "I've cut enough wood to keep warm until May and you won't be gone that long." He laughed good-naturedly. "And if you are, well, I'll just cut more wood."

"Not that there's a lot left. Some of the areas are positively stripped of vegetation," Karen said as she wrapped Gump's leg with a makeshift bandage. "There, that will have to do until you can see the doctor." She gently helped him get his boot on. "Try not to walk around too much. I'm afraid you'll make it bleed again."

"A man's no good if he can't be helpin' out," Gump replied.

"You'll be no good at all if that poison gets into your bloodstream and kills you," Adrik told the man sternly. He looked at his watch and then to Karen. "It's too late to leave now. We'll head out first thing in the morning."

Karen knew Adrik was just as worried about the old man as she was. Gump had been good to them, and she'd grown to love the old man's stories. Of course, it would have been better had the cabin been bigger. Adrik had helped the matter by fashioning some collapsible beds. They folded up when not in use, which allowed them extra living space during the day and early evening. Still, the cabin was barely twenty-by-twelve feet, and at times Karen could swear the walls were closing in.

Turning from Gump, Karen focused her attention on helping Leah with supper. A large piece of elk roasted on a spit over the fire in Gump's hearth. The delicious aroma almost made Karen forget that she was sick and tired of elk. But she longed for fried chicken and creamy mashed potatoes. And she would have walked a mile for a piece of Aunt Doris's strawberry cream pie. She would have walked two miles in the snow for a glass of fresh, cold milk.

Leah sat near the fire faithfully turning the roast, and she smiled when Karen offered to take over. "At least it's warm here."

"Sometimes I doubt we shall ever be warm again, but Gump assures me the air heats right up in the middle of summer."

"And the sun stays up for hours and hours. I think that's so wonderful," Leah said, her voice edged with girlish wonder. "I think it's amazing how God gives the north so much light in the summer, to make up for not having much in the winter. It's like a little present."

Karen chuckled at the analogy. "I suppose you could say that."

"But I also like the northern lights," Leah continued. "They put on just about the prettiest show I've ever seen. God made that, too, didn't He?"

"You can be sure He did," Adrik answered for Karen. "There are a great many wonders in this world, and all of them come compliments of the Almighty. Why, you should have heard Karen's papa talk about God's glorious creation. When he was preaching the Gospel, he used nature and the beauty of the land to show the glory of God to the folks who were listening."

"Maybe that's why the natives liked him so much," Leah suggested.

"I know it was an important part," Adrik said, nodding. "Mr. Pierce always said in order to get people to take an interest in what you had to say, you had to meet them where they lived."

"What's that mean?" Leah questioned.

"It means," Karen interjected, "that most folks only take an interest in what's most important to them. If you want people to listen to what you have to say, you have to show them how it pertains to them—why it should matter to them."

"Exactly. You also give them examples they can relate to," Adrik added. "Mr. Pierce lived among the natives, especially the Tlingit. He lived as they lived and ate what they ate. He worked alongside them and never complained or judged them. He showed the love of Jesus in human form. He was one of the most godly men I've ever known."

Karen wiped a tear from her eye and turned back to the roast. "I think our supper is just about ready. Leah, did you get the bread sliced?"

"Yes, ma'am. I'll put it on the table." She got up and went to the cupboard.

Karen smiled at her husband. "Thank you for the nice things you said about my father. Sometimes I miss him and Mother so much. It still makes me sad to think of how I came north to find him, only to lose him."

"He's not lost to you," Adrik said, reaching out to take hold of her. The roast was forgotten as he embraced her. "He's waiting in heaven with your mother. You'll see them again."

"I know, but I made the trip and then . . ."

"And then you found me," Adrik said firmly, tilting her chin upward to meet his gaze. "And I found you, and now my life is so much better. I'm blessed and whole."

Karen looked into the longing expression of her husband. She knew how much he desired for them to have time alone. He'd promised her he'd build them a private room as soon as the weather warmed.

"I'm blessed as well," she whispered. "Blessed beyond all my expectations."

———

The next morning, Adrik kissed Karen soundly and waved good-bye as the dogs pulled the sled down the trail. She hated to see him go. What if something happened to them on the trail? What if wolves or a rogue bear that had awakened early from its hibernation attacked them?

Karen knew it was senseless to worry. "*Worry is a sin*," her mother had told her when she was young. It was like saying that God wasn't able to see to her needs.

Karen and the children busied themselves for the rest of the day with cleaning the cabin. They were all restless. The old timers called it cabin fever. But whatever it was, Karen longed for an end to it. She couldn't help but believe things would have been better if she had a home of her own—with real beds and walls. She wondered if she had what it would take to spend the rest of her life in Alaska or the Yukon. The uncertainty concerned her, at times to the point of making her fretful. Adrik would never be suited to life in the southern states. He had made that quite clear, and Karen worried that she might fail him in her longing for what once had been.

By dinnertime they were all exhausted and quite ready to settle down to warmed elk hash and canned peaches. Karen always tried to dole their food out in a responsible way. She wanted them to have variety, but too much variety would cause them to forfeit their supply. There was no way of telling how long it would be before they could buy additional food items. And then there was no way of telling how much the food might cost.

They were just finishing up the supper dishes when a knock sounded on the cabin door. Karen looked to Jacob, who immediately went for the rifle. He nodded his readiness and stood behind the door as Karen opened it.

Steadying her nerves, Karen opened the door. An unknown man loomed in the doorway. His gaze fixed on Karen, his eyes narrowing. She smelled whiskey on him almost immediately.

"Howdy, ma'am."

"Hello." Her tone was clearly cautious.

The man scratched his beard and pushed back his hat. "Well, ma'am, I was wonderin' if your menfolk are around."

"They are," Karen said, counting Jacob as man enough for the moment.

"Can I talk to them?" His gaze devoured her, making Karen feel extremely uncomfortable.

"No, I'm afraid not. They're busy right now."

The man stepped forward and looked into the cabin. "I don't see anybody but you and the girl."

Jacob stepped out from behind the door. "The lady said they're busy." The rifle did not go unnoticed by the man. He stepped back immediately and nodded.

"I was hopin' to talk to them about takin' some mail into town for me. I heard a rumor they was headin' into Dawson."

Karen stiffened. The man had probably been watching the cabin and knew Adrik and Gump had already taken off, but she felt inclined to pretend they hadn't. "You might catch them down at the creek," Karen said, feeling the moment merited the lie. Besides, she hadn't said *which* creek they might be by.

The man cleared his throat and spit on the ground outside the door. "Guess I could go lookin' for them."

Karen began to close the door. "That would be best."

"Or I could just wait here for them. Maybe beg a cup of coffee."

"No, I'm sorry. That wouldn't be possible. You might try the next camp if you're looking for coffee. I'm afraid we're completely out." At least that wasn't a lie. It was at the top of the list of items for Adrik to bring back from Dawson.

The man shrugged but refused to go. Karen continued to close the door. "I'm sorry, but the room is growing chilly." She closed the door in his face and quickly latched it.

She turned to Jacob and shook her head. In a hushed voice she said, "I don't like this one bit."

"Me neither. I'll make sure the shutters are closed tight and barred. You might want to put something in front of the door."

"Do you think he'll try to hurt us?" Leah asked fearfully.

"I hope not," Karen replied. "We must pray for God's protection." She glanced back at the closed door, grateful for the thickness of the roughhewn wood. Gump, being of good Swedish stock and familiar with cold weather, had made the entire cabin with thick walls and few windows. There had been a time Karen might have taken a great displeasure with this, but now she was quite grateful.

"I think we'd best load the other gun. Just in case." Jacob's voice wavered slightly as he spoke.

Karen looked at him and nodded. "Might as well be prepared." But she didn't feel at all prepared. She felt very vulnerable and frightened. *Oh, Lord, please shelter us from whatever harm that man intends. You know what he was up to, even if we don't. Please thwart any evil that might be planned against us. And please bring Adrik back quickly.*

A crash sounded as Jacob dropped the box of ammunition, causing Karen to jump a foot. She looked to the young man and tried her best to smile. She read the worry in his eyes, however, and knew she couldn't fool him. She might be able to convince Leah that things were all right, but Jacob was old enough to know better.

"Sorry," he said, picking up the bullets.

Leah walked over to Karen and wrapped her arms around her. "I'm scared," she whispered. "I didn't like that man at all. What if he comes back here tonight?"

"We'll be ready for him," Jacob stated firmly. "I'll keep watch. You two can sleep and toward morning you can take over for me. Then come daylight we can talk to the Jones brothers at the next claim and tell them what happened. Adrik figures them for good folk—Gump, too."

"Maybe we should go there now," Leah said, looking hopefully to her brother.

"No," he said and resumed loading the Winchester for Karen. "He might be out there hoping we'll do exactly that."

Karen trembled at the thought and Leah held her all the more tightly. "I wish Adrik were here," Leah barely breathed.

Karen nodded. "I wish he were, too."

───────────

Jacob Barringer sat alone in the silence of the night, his rifle across his lap as he sat poised—watching, waiting. Come what may, he was ready. At least he hoped he was. He didn't know what to make of the stranger who'd frightened them all.

He hadn't seen Karen so shaken since their store in Dyea had burned down. Jacob tried not to let the man's appearance bother him. He tried not to imagine that the stranger was out there in the darkness, plotting and planning against them.

What had he wanted? Had he known all along that the menfolk were gone, with the exception of Jacob? Jacob would never have admitted it to Karen or Leah, but at the moment, he didn't feel that much like a man. He wanted to prove himself to be brave and capable, but frankly the idea of having to shoot some-one—possibly kill him—was something Jacob didn't stomach well.

He supposed he wasn't intended to like the idea of shooting someone, but he'd seen so much destruction and death on his way to the Yukon that even the idea of dealing with one more confrontation was more than Jacob wanted to face.

What he did want was to leave the Yukon. He'd denied the discouraging truth long enough, but now he resolved to accept that his father had died in the Palm Sunday avalanche on the Chilkoot Trail. If his father were alive, he'd be here in the heart of it all—working his knuckles raw as he tried to find gold. If his father were alive, he would have at least sent word back to Karen at the store.

No, his father was dead. Jacob had to accept the truth, no matter how hard or painful. But with that acceptance, came another overwhelming truth. He was responsible for Leah. He needed a good job and he needed to provide her with a real home. The only trouble was, he didn't see how he could do both. He wanted to go to work for Peter Colton. He'd gotten to know Peter fairly well during their days in Skagway, when Jacob would meet up with him on the docks before transporting the goods to the store. Peter had promised Jacob he could have a job with Colton Shipping anytime he wanted one.

The real problem was Leah. He didn't want to leave her again. She'd been truly hurt when he'd left her to head north. They'd only talked about it once or twice, but he knew she had felt abandoned. How would it be if he took a job that kept him far away from her for long periods of time? And where would she stay? Karen had offered them both a home for as long as they needed it, but Jacob couldn't very well expect Karen and Adrik to give up their future to care for Leah forever.

Yet he'd seen how Leah and Karen interacted. Karen had become a mother to Leah, and Adrik had filled in the place of a father. It seemed right for her to be a part of their family. Leah would be all right with Karen and Adrik, especially if Jacob promised to come and see her from time to time. If he worked for Peter's shipping company he could no doubt do just that. Maybe he'd mention it to Karen tomorrow—see what her thoughts were on the matter.

The crux of all his problems was this: He didn't want to disappoint Leah. Not after all she had been through. He didn't want to hurt her, and he didn't want to make a mistake where she was concerned. God had given him a responsibility. And God would expect him to take the matter seriously and to make plans for their future—plans that would benefit them both.

A scratching noise at the door caused Jacob to jump to his feet. As silently as he could manage, Jacob moved to the door. He listened, waiting for something more.

The unmistakable sounds of movement on the other side of the door caused the hair on the back of Jacob's neck to stand up. His chest rose and fell in rapid, shallow breaths. Perspiration beaded on his forehead, even though the cabin was quite chilly.

Anxious to make sure the rifle was loaded, Jacob cocked the lever just enough to expose the breech. The sight of the cartridge reassured him. Next he checked the magazine. Finding it loaded with extra cartridges, Jacob let out the breath he'd been holding.

A loud thump sounded against the door. Jacob jumped back. He glanced over his shoulder to make sure the noise hadn't disturbed Karen or Leah. There was no sign of either one of them stirring.

Jacob didn't know how long he stood fixed and rigid at the door. After a good deal of time had passed, however, and no further noises sounded from outside, he decided to open the door and check outside.

The rush of cold air momentarily surprised Jacob. He glanced again over his shoulder to see if Karen or Leah had stirred, then focused his attention outside. Hearing a sound to his right, Jacob strained to see in the dark. As he leveled his rifle he saw the unmistakable outline of a bear. Cautiously, Jacob backed up and closed the door. There was no sense in shooting the poor animal and waking the entire valley. No doubt the bear had awakened early from its hibernating and was simply looking for food. Relief washed over him.

Yawning, Jacob realized how tired he was. A quick check of the clock on the mantel revealed that he still had a good two hours before dawn.

"Help me to stay alert, God," he whispered the prayer. "And give me the wisdom to know what to do." He paused and glanced again to the bunks where Karen and Leah slept before adding, "And the strength to do it."

─┤ CHAPTER SIXTEEN ├─

"THERE'S COME A MESSAGE for you, Mrs. Colton," Dr. Brummel stated, handing Grace a folded piece of paper. "Seems your friends are in town and are prepared to transport you and little Andy back to their cabin."

Grace looked up from the ironing she was doing. She'd worked all morning to wash and iron the sheets, and she was on her last one. A thread of joy wound about her heart at the thought that Karen and Adrik were in town.

Taking up the paper, she read the note. "It looks like Adrik had to bring that nice Mr. Lindquist in to the hospital. I do hope it isn't serious." She looked to Dr. Brummel as if for some insight to the man's condition.

"I couldn't say. I was only there to pick up some laudanum for a patient."

"I see. Well," Grace said, her tone quite animated, "I suppose I should pack my things."

"We're going to miss having you here, Mrs. Colton."

"Now, why will we be missing Grace?" the dentist's wife asked as she came into the room.

Grace turned to face the woman. "My friends have come to take me to their claim site."

"Why, it still gets down to forty-below some nights. You can't be traveling with a baby in that kind of weather," Georgia Brummel complained.

"I'm sure my friends have made provision," Grace answered. Already she was packing her things in a carpetbag. "I'm sure we'll be just fine."

Georgia looked at Grace as if ascertaining whether she could change her mind.

Finally she relented. "Very well. I'll pack you some things for the trip."

"Thank you, Mrs. Brummel. I do appreciate all you have done for me. I only hope I can one day repay you for your kindness."

"Nonsense," Dr. Brummel declared, "you've worked harder than any house girl we've ever had—and we've had plenty. Why, down in Sacramento, where we hail from, we had a new girl almost every week some months."

"He's right," Mrs. Brummel sniffed. "No one was ever as good to us as you are."

Grace looked at them both. "No one outside of my family and Karen Ivankov has ever been as good to me as you've been. Andy and I might have died were it not for you. We surely couldn't have made the trip before now. Thank you so much for all you've done for us." She reached out and hugged them in unison.

Dr. Brummel reddened in the face and stepped back. "I . . . uh . . . I'll take you and Andy over to the hospital when you're ready."

Grace nodded and hurried to gather her things. Andy slept peacefully, even when she bundled him into the warm beaver-skin bunting she'd made for him only days earlier. Pulling on her own coat and a fur cape given to her by Mrs. Brummel, Grace felt a bittersweet emotion in her departure. Though she missed Karen and longed for her company as much as she could anyone's, Grace knew she would miss Dr. Brummel and his wife. She would also miss being in a real house with wooden floors and rugs and curtains at the windows. She knew from Karen's letters that the accommodations at Gump's claim were desperately short of womanly touches.

"I guess I'm ready," Grace finally said, carrying the sleeping baby in her arms.

"I'll get your bag," Dr. Brummel offered and disappeared into Grace's room.

"I've packed a box of things for you," Georgia said. "Some things to eat along the way and a few items to remember us by."

"I won't forget you," Grace said. "And when I come back to Dawson, I will visit."

"Oh, do. And bring Andy as well."

Grace nodded. "You can be sure I will."

Grace allowed Dr. Brummel to carry everything but the baby and followed him out into the frigid morning. The walk to the hospital wasn't far, but even that short distance could freeze the lungs of a man—or woman. Grace had already secured Andy inside her cape, but now she buried her face down deep in order to keep from breathing the raw, painful air.

She hastened her steps to keep up with Dr. Brummel and felt great relief when the hospital came in sight. She felt a giddiness at the prospect of seeing her friends again. She was especially anxious for Karen to see the baby.

"Adrik!" she called as soon as she caught sight of the man.

Adrik turned and smiled as Grace came through the hospital doors. "Why, hello there, little mother. How does it go with you?"

"Wonderful!" Grace tried not to sound too exuberant. She didn't want to hurt Dr. Brummel's feelings, so she quickly added, "The Brummels have been so good to us. They have taken such good care of Andy and me."

"I knew they would," Adrik replied, nodding slightly to the older man. "They're good people. I wouldn't have left you with them if they hadn't come highly recommended."

"Well, it's me and the missus who are grateful," Brummel interjected. "Grace has been a great help. Georgia sometimes suffers great bouts of depression, but she wasn't upset even once while Grace was here."

"Oh," Grace lamented, "you don't think my leaving will cause her to become ill, do you?"

"My dear, you mustn't worry," Dr. Brummel reassured. "She'll be fine. I'll see to it. Now that I know she does better with the company of a good friend, I'll endeavor to find someone else to be a companion. No more of those bitter old women who clean house like prisoners forced to work against their will. No, I will find another sweet young woman such as yourself. Maybe even one with a child."

"I'll pray for her," Grace offered. "It's easy to fall into despair in such a cold and lonely place. Andy has helped me a great deal." She lifted the baby to her shoulder. "He's given me a will to live life anew."

Adrik put his arm around Grace's shoulder. "This little gal has a way of praying that goes right from her mouth to God's ear. If she's praying for your wife, then you can be sure things will come around right."

They bid Dr. Brummel good-bye and waited in the hospital corridor for Gump to reappear. When he did, he looked none too happy.

"Fool doctors are always trying to find vays to drain a man of every cent."

"What's wrong, Gump?"

"Oh, dat doctor vants to keep me here. Says my leg might be needin' surgery."

"Well, you ought to do what the doctor says," Grace said softly.

Gump eyed her suspiciously. "Who are you?"

"I'm Grace Colton," she replied.

"She's the one we've come to take back with us," Adrik added. "And I agree with her completely. You ought to do what the doctor says."

"Vell, I am," Gump muttered. "But I told him I von't be stayin' here, so I'm supposed to come back in two veeks if it's not any better."

Adrik nodded. "That sounds reasonable enough."

"Ja, I think it vill be better," Gump replied. "Either that or I take the leg off and get a new one." He smiled as if he'd made some great joke.

They headed toward the door, but Gump put his hand on Adrik's arm. "I vant to go to the recorder's office."

"Sure, Gump, but why?" Adrik questioned.

"I got me some business."

Adrik looked to Grace. "Will that be all right with you?"

"Certainly, Adrik. Andy and I are more than happy to comply with whatever plans you have."

Adrik smiled. "Well, you'd best bundle up, then. It's not warmed up enough out there so as a man can even breathe decent. I sure wouldn't want you comin' down sick. Karen would never let me hear the end of it."

————

The bottle slipped from Miranda's hand, crashing to the floor in a loud, disheartening sound, shattering into hundreds of tiny pieces.

"Oh, bother," she sighed, taking up Teddy's favorite saying. In a hurry to clean up the mess before Teddy returned, Miranda failed to give proper attention to the task. Without warning, her hand sliced across one of the larger pieces of glass, ripping a long cut on the side of her palm.

Stunned, Miranda stared at her wounded hand for a moment. Blood poured from the cut, spilling out onto the floor at an alarming rate. Her breathing quickened and a light-headed feeling washed over her.

"Oh my." It was all she could manage to say, and so she repeated it several times.

Humming a tune, Teddy walked in completely preoccupied. "I say, the cost of . . ." He fell silent at the sight of Miranda.

Seeing the way his expression changed to worry, Miranda hoped to reassure him that everything was all right. "I've made a mess," she tried to explain, her heart racing.

Teddy seemed to quickly assess the situation. He pulled a handkerchief from his pocket, taking long strides to cross the room as he did. Kneeling, he gently wrapped the cloth around her hand. His touch was so tender and gentle that Miranda very nearly forgot there was a problem.

"What happened?"

"I . . . I . . . dropped the bottle. Oh my." She gazed into his eyes. He looked almost frightened. Again, she felt the need to reassure him. "I'm so . . . so . . . sorry. You mustn't worry. I don't want to be a bother." Her voice sounded foreign, almost childlike to her own ears.

Teddy firmly held her wounded hand. "No bother at all," he said, helping her up by cupping her elbow. "Let's have a look at it in the light."

The cloth was already soaked a bright red when Teddy pulled it away from her hand. The wound was deep. Miranda could see that much.

"It will have to be stitched, I'm afraid," Teddy told her. "Let me find a better bandage and we'll go straightaway to the doctor." He looked around the room.

"Don't worry. I'll be fine." But in truth, Miranda wasn't sure about that at all. She felt dizzy and sick from the sight of so much blood. Her hand didn't really hurt all that much. Certainly it didn't hurt as much as the time she'd let the knife slip when peeling potatoes. That wound hadn't required stitches, but this one was clearly deeper.

"I'm not worried," Teddy said, coming back with the case that he'd pulled off a pillow. "This ought to do."

Miranda let him wrap her hand with the pillowcase, then waited as he retrieved her coat. She felt numb, almost senseless.

When Teddy returned he was already wearing his own coat and gloves. "Come along," he said, putting the coat around her shoulders.

As he half dragged, half carried her down the hall, Miranda's mind raced in a million different directions. *Who will clean up the mess?* she worried. *What if I get blood on this lovely hall runner? Will it hurt terribly to have stitches put in?*

Teddy led her down the stairs and to the front desk. "I'm going to take Miss Colton to Dr. Hauge's. She's broken a jar in the workroom and cut her hand. Would you get someone to clean up the mess?"

"Sure, Mr. Davenport," the clerk replied.

Miranda thought the man very kind as he offered her a smile.

"Hope you'll be feelin' better, miss."

"I'm fine, really. Thank you for your concern," Miranda replied. The man nodded at her with a look that suggested he didn't believe her.

Teddy helped her to secure her hooded coat. He carefully maneuvered her hand through the sleeve and then did up the buttons for her. Miranda felt rather flustered at his nearness. Her nerves were making her jittery, and she couldn't help but give a little giggle.

"I feel like I'm five years old. Silly glass and silly me for getting cut."

"Never mind that," Teddy said very softly. He put his arm around her. "Lean on me if you feel the need."

What a strange suggestion, Miranda thought. *Of course I don't need to lean on him. That would be entirely unseemly.* But in the next few steps, she wasn't at all convinced of the impropriety. Miranda felt as though she were floating. A weakness drained her legs of strength, and she found that all she desired was a chair and a warm fire. She felt so cold, and they hadn't even been outside for more than a minute.

"Oh, bother!" Teddy said as he came to a stop in front of the doctor's office. "He's gone to tend someone on a claim. Let's just go to the hospital and be done with it. We're bound to find a doctor there."

Miranda had no argument for him. She wasn't even sure at this point how much longer she could maintain consciousness. She felt strange and a peculiar heat seemed to penetrate her face and neck. Leaning against Teddy, she tried her best to keep up.

"Teddy," she whispered. "I don't feel at all well."

He stopped and, without giving her a chance to protest, lifted Miranda in his arms. "It's the loss of blood and the pain. You're going into shock. Stay awake, Miranda. Talk to me."

She looked into his eyes and lost herself for a moment. My, but he was handsome. If she died now, in his arms, she would at least know the contentment of being near him.

"Talk to me, Miranda," he ordered.

"I don't know what to say." She smiled weakly.

Teddy crossed the street and continued down the way to the hospital. "Tell me about San Francisco. Does it get this cold there?"

Miranda shook her head. "Oh no. Never."

"I wouldn't have thought so. Are the summers hot?"

"No, they're never hot. They're so very lovely. The flowers bloom all up and down our street." She tucked her head down against Teddy's neck. He smelled wonderful. She wondered what the scent might be. In fact, she hadn't noticed it when they'd been working.

"You smell good," she whispered. "Like spices and flowers."

"You're becoming delirious," he said with a laugh.

"I like spices and flowers," she countered, not at all sure why he would laugh. "I like you, too." Shadows in her mind beckoned her to rest. She could almost see their dark fingers motioning her to follow deeper into the black recesses of her mind.

"I'm honored and deeply touched," he replied, then added, "I like you, too, Miranda."

She smiled. He was such a pleasant man when he wanted to be.

They arrived at the hospital and once inside, Teddy set her down on the bench in the hall. "Stay here. I'll find the doctor." He studied her for a moment. "Maybe I shouldn't leave you alone."

"Nonsense," she managed to say, forcing herself to sound alert. "I'll be fine."

"If you're sure. I'll only be a moment."

Miranda nodded and leaned back against the wall and closed her eyes. She wanted so much to be a good patient for her worried friend. Opening her eyes, Miranda looked down the hall in the direction Teddy had taken. He had gone through one of the open doorways, but Miranda couldn't be sure which one.

Then her gaze caught something unexpected. A large, broad-shouldered man appeared at the other end of the corridor. She heard him laugh and recognized the sound. Struggling against her weakness, Miranda jumped to her feet and called out. "Adrik!"

The word barely made a sound in her throat, and then darkness consumed her and Miranda fell to the ground. *Not now*, she thought. *I can't faint now.* But it was too late. Certain that she'd finally seen another of her traveling companions, Miranda slipped into unconsciousness.

———

The recorder's office was surprisingly void of traffic. Adrik figured the cold had kept most folks hunkered down in their tents and cabins, or it might have been that a general malaise had settled on the community. At any rate, no one seemed to be too anxious to buy and sell claims if it meant going outside.

So much had changed. Adrik had heard the sad stories of those men who had figured to be able to get a claim for little or nothing. Stake your claim and rake up the gold—that was the battle cry. But it wasn't the reality. Claims had been quickly snatched up, and those who were willing to sell usually demanded a high price to transfer ownership. That, coupled with the Canadian rule against the selling of fractional claims, had left a lot of people without a chance to seek their dreams.

"Come with me." Gump motioned Adrik to follow him into the office. "It's too cold out here for you, much less that little lady and baby."

Adrik took the bundled baby from Grace, then helped her from the sled basket. As the trio followed the limping old man into the office, Adrik was anxious to see what business he had to tend to.

Adrik was more surprised than anyone when the old man requested that his claim deed be rewritten to add a partner.

"I vant Adrik Ivankov here to be my partner." The clerk looked to Adrik and then proceeded with the paperwork.

"Why are you doing this, Gump?"

"I vant to," the old man said. Then sobering a bit, he frowned. "I von't be much good to you for a time. Maybe not for a long, long time. You and Jacob will have to do most of the digging by yourselves."

"But we don't mind. I never expected you to give up half your claim," Adrik said. "You could be out a small fortune by doing this."

"Or you could be out a lot of hard vork for nothin', I'm thinkin'. I vant to do it this vay. Besides, somethin' could happen to me. Then the claim vould go back to the government. I'd rather give you the gold." Gump's singsong cadence was stronger when his emotions ran high. Adrik saw the determination in the set of the old man's jaw and decided not to challenge his decision.

Once the matter was settled to Gump's satisfaction, the foursome returned to the sled and were finally on their way back to the cabin. Adrik couldn't imagine why the old man had offered up half his claim. Sure, Gump was a bit incapacitated for the time, but there wasn't a whole lot they would be able to do until the weather warmed up, anyway. Maybe the situation with Gump's leg was more serious than he was letting on. Maybe the doctor had told Gump he could die. That idea bothered Adrik greatly. He wished fervently that he could make life easier for the old man.

I'd like to send him back to Kansas a rich, comfortable man, Adrik thought. *I'd like to see him retire from working so hard and just enjoy his old age.* But of course, that wasn't likely to happen. Gump's attitude and spirit was much the same as Adrik's. They'd probably die working.

Thinking of work, Adrik began to plan for the claim. There was gold to be had, but it would come only after a great deal of hard work was given in trade. Panning and sluicing, spending hours in the cold water washing the creek gravel— it was enough to drive a man quite insane and crush his dream of riches. Many folks believed the gold to be buried some fifteen feet below the surface. To dig down that far required hours and hours of backbreaking work—all in the hope that they could break through the frozen barriers of muck and rock and find the mother lode.

After a few feet of muck, there generally was a frozen layer of gravel, and sometimes, if a man had sunk the shaft in the right place, he hit pay dirt just under this. Gump had insisted that they'd strike it rich if only they kept digging, instead of panning. Most miners used a ground fire to thaw the surface, but that was time consuming and not always very effective—the digging went horribly slow. Steam boilers were making the job a lot easier for some miners who could afford the expense. Though Adrik wished they had a steam machine to thaw the ground, he knew they didn't have the money for anything extra.

He considered how he might rig up his own steam machine. He had a metal washtub they could use to heat water, but that wouldn't solve the problem of capturing the steam and focusing it into the ground. Adrik had studied the setup from a drawing at the mercantile. The display showed how a steam boiler could be fixed near the site, with pipes coming out one end for the steam and a chimney of sorts to vent the firebox. The pipes went into the ground where they would pump hot steam and thaw the frozen muck. Adrik wasn't sure that the time spent would produce a steamer that worked, but he decided to discuss it with Gump when they got back to the claim.

Adrik's attention turned to Grace and the baby, snuggled deep in a pile of blankets and furs, along with Gump. The body heat of the two adults would no doubt keep the baby plenty warm, but Adrik had other worries concerning their safety. He'd heard wolves howling along the trail on their way into Dawson, and he wanted no part of having to fight off a pack to keep his friends alive.

Then there were the two-legged wolves. Men who pretended to be sheep but were really vicious animals who would eat you alive. Trouble had been a natural companion to the gold rush. The Northwest Mounted Police, the pride of the Yukon, had done a wonderful job of controlling things in the area, but there would always be problems so long as there was a profit to be made from stirring up trouble. Adrik could only pray he was doing the right thing. He'd never considered becoming a part of the stampede. In fact, he thought those poor souls who pinned their hopes to gold instead of God to be misguided. The word gold was just one letter more than God, and Adrik had always figured the L to stand for *Lies*.

Much of the gold rush had been built on lies told by one man and passed on by another. People lied about what gold they found, and they lied about what they didn't find. They lied about their pasts and preyed upon others who'd believe their lies for the future. It was a kind of sickness born out of sin.

But as for me and my house, Adrik thought, remembering the Bible verse, *we will serve the Lord*. But here he was in the center of the rush, making his own scars upon the land, seeking his own methods to find the gold.

But I'm doing this for Gump and for the others, he told himself as he urged the dogs to pick up the pace. Self-examination questioned that declaration, however. Was he really doing this for the others? Or was there some small dream of gold in the back of his own mind?

⊣ C H A P T E R S E V E N T E E N ⊢

"BUT YOU DON'T UNDERSTAND," Miranda moaned. "I saw one of my friends."

"It's all right, Miranda," Teddy encouraged, "you probably just thought you saw him. I say, you lost a lot of blood. There's no telling how it played with your mind."

"I'm not crazy," Miranda said, growing angry. "I'm telling you, I saw him. He was standing down at the end of the corridor."

"The same corridor where I found you on the floor?"

Miranda turned away. "Never mind. I don't expect you to understand. You didn't understand the first time—the time I saw Crispin."

"Was this Crispin the same man you saw here at the hospital?" Teddy asked, gently.

"No, I . . ."

"Well, let's get this over with," the doctor said coming into the room. He didn't even bother to introduce himself, and Miranda thought him very rude.

Taking hold of her hand, he unwound the cloth and studied the wound for a moment. "Um, yes. I see," he murmured.

Miranda felt a wave of nausea as she caught sight of her bloody hand. Leaning back, she found Teddy there to support her. She looked to him, hoping he could somehow give her the courage she lacked.

"It will be fine. You'll see," he whispered.

"Will it hurt?" she asked.

"Most likely," the doctor said without emotion. He began to wash to wound, mindless of the pain.

"Talk to me, Miranda. Tell me about your friends," Teddy encouraged. "Don't think about what the doctor is doing."

"That's easier said than done," Miranda declared, wincing at the pain. "Must you be so rough?" she asked the doctor indignantly.

The man looked at her as though stunned by her words. "If I don't clean it out, miss, you'll most likely get an infection."

"I don't mind the cleaning, it's the way you attack the job as though you're gutting and cleaning a rabbit."

The doctor paused and actually smiled at her rebuke. "I do apologize. It's been a rather hectic day. I shall attempt to limit the pain I cause you."

"Thank you," Miranda replied, turning to Teddy as the doctor took up a needle and thread. "Adrik is the man who let me come on the trip. He and Karen got married in Whitehorse. Karen . . ." She closed her eyes as the doctor pierced her skin. Tears came unbidden to her eyes.

"Go on, Miranda, tell me about your friends," Teddy prodded.

She opened her eyes and licked her lips. "Karen was the nanny to my sister-in-law, Grace. You remember, Grace is married to my brother . . . my brother . . . Peter." She felt a strange warmth creeping up her neck, flushing her face and making it difficult to focus.

"I'm here," Teddy whispered. "Don't be afraid. I'll see to it that you're all right."

His words were comforting, and Miranda tried hard to keep them in her mind as she faded in and out of consciousness.

"There. All done. You are free to leave," the doctor said, wrapping a bandage around her hand.

"Thank you," Miranda murmured, leaning her head against Teddy. She felt so weak.

"Mrs. Colton, you will need to do as little as possible with your hand. I have made several stitches," the balding, heavy-set man continued. "You must keep your hand immobile." He turned to Teddy. "You must see to it that your wife keeps the hand dry, clean, and covered. We don't want to risk infection."

Teddy didn't bother to correct the doctor regarding their martial status, and Miranda thought it rather odd. Perhaps he was caught up in his concern over her wound. She had no more time to consider it, however, for Teddy was reaching out and helping her to stand.

"I'll see to it that the wound is well cared for. When should we return?" Teddy questioned.

"Two weeks."

The doctor turned to go, but Miranda called out, "Wait!"

The man turned, a brow raising. "What is it?"

"Did you see a big man at the end of the hallway?" she asked. "It would have been earlier, prior to my arrival. I saw him there and believe him to be a friend of mine."

The doctor looked to Teddy, who merely shrugged. "She's been separated from her friends and family and has been searching Dawson for them."

"I saw no one fitting the description. Perhaps the loss of blood gave you hallucinations," the doctor replied, then left without another word. The brief moment of kindness he'd offered her earlier seemed all but forgotten.

"I say, not much of a bedside manner."

"I know what I saw," Miranda said, feeling suddenly very weak. "I know it was Adrik."

"If it was, then he'll be around in town somewhere. We'll find him."

"The doctor thinks I'm crazy."

"Nonsense, he merely suggested that you might have . . . well, that is to say . . ." Teddy looked uncomfortably to her, as if expecting Miranda to rescue him from having to say anything more.

Miranda leaned heavily on Teddy, realizing she was completely spent by the entire affair. Perhaps Teddy was right. Maybe she had conjured up Adrik from the recesses of her subconscious mind. She longed to find her friends again and the long months of isolation and winter darkness had left her very discouraged. If not for her work with Teddy, she might have lost her mind to be sure.

"Oh, just take me home, Teddy."

Outside in the long corridor, Miranda caught sight of another doctor. Her hope surged anew. Surely it couldn't hurt to ask him if he knew Adrik, she thought. "Excuse me, Doctor," she said as Teddy started to walk toward the man.

The bearded man looked up from the chart he'd been reading. "Yes?"

"I saw a very large man—down there—earlier. Maybe an hour ago. He was very tall and broad shouldered. He had a beard."

"Oh yes." The man nodded. "I saw him, too. He came in with a friend of his who has an ulcerated leg."

Miranda let out an audible sigh. "I knew it. Did you get his name? I'm looking for my friend, and I thought it might be him."

"No, I'm sure I don't know the man's name. The patient was called Lindon or Lindberg—or maybe it was Lindquist. Yes, I believe it was Lindquist."

Miranda frowned. "I don't know any Lindquists. My friend's name is Adrik. Adrik Ivankov."

"That name sounds familiar," Teddy said, looking at her oddly.

"Well, it should, I have been talking about him—along with all my friends—

ever since I woke up in your cabin," Miranda countered. "You're certain you don't know the name of his friend?" she questioned the doctor again.

"No, I'm sorry. The man was only here a short while. He brought in his friend and then left to retrieve supplies. They were heading back to their claim, as I recall. I was called in to offer an opinion on the leg, but nothing more. The man wasn't even my patient."

Miranda nodded. "I understand. Thank you." She turned to Teddy, more drained and discouraged by the man's answers than by her wounded hand. "He's probably gone by now. That was some time ago, at least an hour. No doubt they've headed back to their claim." She felt as though her world were crumbling all over again.

"Please take me back to the hotel."

Teddy gave her a look of compassion. "Indeed. I shall take you back and see to it that you are put to bed. I'll bring one of the housekeepers to sit by your bed, as it would hardly be appropriate for me to care for you."

Miranda barely heard his words. She was certain she had seen Adrik, and the fact that no one else seemed to understand or know where she might find him was more than she could bear.

———

When they returned to the hotel, Teddy arranged Miranda's bed while the housekeeper he sent for stood by to assure propriety. Then he left the room while the girl helped Miranda change her clothes.

His staff had done a marvelous job of cleaning up his workroom. There was no telltale sign of the glass or the blood. He'd have to offer them a bonus for their good work.

Taking out his spectacles, Teddy bent over one of his journals and studied the drawing he'd made. *Epilobium augustifolium.* His gaze fell on the second part of the name. *Augustifolium.* The name made him think of Miranda's friend. What had she called him?

Adrik? Yes, Adrik Ivankov. The name sounded familiar to him, but for the life of him, Teddy couldn't remember where he'd heard it. Perhaps he was simply recalling the memory of Miranda speaking the name so often—but he didn't think so. The name seemed to attach itself to a vague memory of the same type of large man Miranda had described to the doctor.

"I have Miss Colton all tucked in," the house girl said, opening the adjoining door. "She asked me to keep the door open between the rooms."

Teddy was surprised but pleased with this news. He hated that propriety wouldn't allow him to tend to Miranda as he had back in his cabin. Of course, Nellie had been the one to actually care for her at that time, but he had been able to look in on her at his leisure. And for some reason, that was very important to him.

"I've arranged lunch," Teddy called in to the next room just as a knock sounded at the door. "That should be it now." He opened the door and a young man of about sixteen or seventeen stood holding a tray laden with food.

It was the boy, however, and not the food that caught Teddy's interest. The boy looked familiar, yet Teddy was quite sure they'd never met.

"Do come in. You may leave the tray on the table over there," he instructed the boy.

As the youth entered the room and passed by Teddy, the memory suddenly came to him. The boy reminded Teddy of the young man who'd accompanied the buyer of his sled. The big man with the beard.

The big man . . .

Teddy felt the wind go out of him. Adrik Ivankov. The man who'd bought his sled had introduced himself as Adrik Ivankov. Of course! Teddy looked to the open door adjoining his room to Miranda's. He should tell her, of course, but then what? He had no idea where the man had headed after purchasing the sled. He only recalled that the man and the boy had planned to depart immediately.

He supposed he could tell Miranda that much. But what if she hated him for failing to recognize Adrik? Granted, it had been a simple and innocent mistake, but she had been sharing information about her friends and family for months. Teddy simply hadn't bothered to listen carefully. He'd been too caught up in cataloging his plants and creating the book of his dreams—of his father's dreams.

"Do you need anything else, Mr. Davenport?" the boy asked.

Teddy shook his head, tossed the boy a coin, and glanced again toward Miranda's room. What could he say to her? He could tell her that he was a thoughtless oaf—a man given to his own selfish interests. But, of course, she already knew that.

And he could hardly say, "Sorry, old girl, I was just remembering that I had an encounter with your friends when we first arrived in Dawson City. Pity I hadn't paid attention to your stories or descriptions of them."

Teddy turned away from the open door and walked to the window. The hours of light had increased over the months and soon the thaw would be upon them. He would be ready to return to the fields to gather specimens. He had hoped Miranda would accompany him and prayed she would consider making their arrangement a more permanent one.

If I tell her the truth, she'll hate me, he thought. *She'll blame me for letting them get away all those months ago. She'll never speak to me again.*

He looked down on the streets below where a bustle of activity assured him that a change was in the air. The cold had kept people rather immobile for many months. Now whenever the sun was overhead and the weather higher than thirty-below, folks ventured out as if spring had come.

"I can't lose her," he whispered against the glass. "I can't." In that moment he made his decision. He would say nothing. He would keep his secret and pray that Miranda would never learn the truth.

⊣ CHAPTER EIGHTEEN ⊢

SKAGWAY HAD COME into its own during Peter's absence. The sights, sounds, even the smells, were different than the little mud-flat harbor town he'd known before. Hotels, stores, gambling halls, and drinking establishments lined the main thoroughfares and beckoned his company. Church spires, schools, and a train depot suggested a more civilized society.

The railroad, now running over White Pass, was rumored to make it all the way to Lake Bennett by summer. Peter thought it amazing, given the fact he'd worked on the railroad's inception only last year. The rugged terrain did nothing to welcome a railroad, that much Peter knew firsthand. They'd been forced to blast rock shelves out from the sides of the mountain in order to lay track. The work had been perilous and often deadly. Apparently the workers' temperaments matched that of the land. Stubbornness and pure grit would see the railroad built to Dawson City.

"Mister, want to buy some mining equipment?" a scruffy-looking man asked. "They've found gold in Nome, ya know. If you're headin' out to Nome, you'll need some gear."

Peter smelled the foul odor of the man before he turned to meet his gnarled expression. "I don't think so."

"I got me an outfit I bought off a man who was headed home. I need the money, mister. I can sell it to you for five hundred dollars."

Peter shook his head. "Sorry, I already have the goods I need."

The man spit and wiped brown tobacco juice from his beard with the back of his sleeve. "Ain't going to find a better deal. I'll make you a bargain. Let's say . . . four hundred-thirty."

"No," Peter said more firmly. "Now, if you'll excuse me."

He'd barely taken five steps down the street when yet another man, equally repulsive and odorous, offered to sell Peter a tent.

"I have no need for it, sir," Peter told the man.

The bum smiled, revealing multiple holes where teeth had once been. He scratched his belly, then shrugged. "I got snowshoes and sleds, as well."

"I'm sorry, but I have everything I need." Peter moved on, amazed at the number of people who walked the streets trying to sell him something. By the time he got to Jonas Campbell's house north of the city, he'd been offered everything from fruit to satin slippers.

Knocking on the door, Peter waited for Jonas to appear. It was late enough in the day that Peter was sure he'd find his friend at home, rather than down at the train shops where he worked repairing engines.

"So you found me," Jonas said with a smile as he pulled the door open wide and laughed at the sight of Peter. "I guess my directions were good enough, eh?"

"They were perfect," Peter replied. "I came straightaway without trouble. Unless, of course, you count trouble as being harassed by every other man on the street to buy their goods."

"Those cons are everywhere," Jonas said, ushering Peter into his small house. "They offer to sell you almost anything you can think to ask for. The law tries to keep them under control, but it's more than what this town can handle."

"Didn't seem so bad last year," Peter said, pulling his cap from his head.

Jonas motioned for Peter to take a seat at the roughhewn table. "I got some coffee for us." He poured the steaming liquid and brought the mugs to the table. "Things weren't this bad last year," Jonas admitted as he handed Peter a cup. "But then the height of the gold rush glory was just coming to a peak. Now things are dying down."

"Is the gold played out?"

Jonas shook his head. "No, I don't believe it is, but the people are. The winter wore most of them to the bone. Those that didn't collapse and die vowed never to endure another arctic winter."

Peter took a long drink from his mug. "I can well understand that. Here it is the twenty-fourth of April and it's still incredibly cold outside. Looks like it might even threaten snow."

"Most likely," Jonas replied. "So tell me about this trip of yours. You goin' to take the train north?"

"As far north as it will go."

"Well, it's over the pass, that much I can offer you. They're working on the tracks again, but not making much progress. The snows have kept them pretty buried. They've even broken into two teams—one working from the north and heading south, and the other is heading north from the front of the line. They hope to meet in the middle and have the thing at least as far as Lake Bennett."

"I had heard that destination mentioned. Jonas," Peter said, leaning forward, "what should I do after getting as far as Bennett? Can I hire a boat to take me to Dawson?"

"Oh, yeah, these days—or I should say when the water isn't three feet thick with ice—they run steamers through most areas. It ain't half the trouble it was last year. Why, you had people crashing on the rocks, losing their boats and lives. . . ." Jonas's voice trailed off. "Sorry, Peter. I just remembered about your wife. I do apologize."

"No offense taken. I'm glad they worked to make the route safer. I would pray that no other man be saddled with the pain of losing someone they love."

"Well, I'm sure your sister is glad to have you comin'. I wouldn't want no sister of mine alone and unprotected in Dawson City. That place is just plain wild from what I've heard."

"I've heard the same," Peter said, knowing only too well the horror stories. "That makes it all the more imperative for me to get there as soon as possible."

That night, Peter lay awake for a long time. He thought of the first time he'd come to Alaska. Grace had been aboard his ship, *Merry Maid*. She had been so gentle and soft-spoken—and so terrified. He had known there was trouble in her life, but something about her had drawn him so completely to her. She needed him for protection.

He thought of her first night aboard the ship. He'd unthinkingly assigned her a small, windowless cabin, which she shared with Karen Pierce and Karen's aunt. They didn't seem to have a problem with the lack of windows or fresh air, but Grace had grown ill. She left the cabin against his orders, and when he found her, he nearly scared her half out of her wits.

I spent the rest of our marriage causing her to fear my condemnation, he thought. *I left her with nothing but fear and hurt feelings.* The thought devastated him, and in spite of knowing God forgave him for his past failings, Peter would have given anything on earth to know that Grace had forgiven him as well.

"Oh, he's grown three times over," Karen declared as she lifted Andy Colton into her arms. "He looks just like you, Grace."

"He does favor me a bit," Grace replied. "I wish Mother could see him. I know she'd fall positively in love with him."

"Have you had any word from your mother?"

Grace shook her head. "I wrote shortly after the accident. I don't suppose the mail is very reliable up here."

"To be sure," Karen replied. She cuddled Andy on her lap and shared the quiet morning moments with Grace. Everyone else was about their chores, and Adrik had encouraged Grace and Karen to spend the morning together. Karen was grateful for the rest. She hadn't slept well with Adrik away, and waiting for his return had felt like forever.

"So what do you think of our claim?" Karen asked. "Did Adrik tell you that Gump signed half of it over to Adrik?"

"I was there when Gump did the deed. I'm so glad for all of you. Now I won't feel so bad when I go back to California."

"You're going back?" Karen said in disbelief. "I thought you planned to stay up here with us."

"I've given it a lot of thought," Grace told her, "and I've decided to return to California to introduce Andy to Mother and Father Colton and then head to Wyoming, where my mother is living."

"What about Peter?"

Grace shrugged. "I don't know. I wrote him a letter and had thought to mail it before leaving Dawson, but I couldn't bring myself to do it. I kept thinking, 'Why bother?' I mean, it's obvious that Peter could have come north to bring me home, if he cared enough to do so. But apparently he doesn't."

"You don't know that for sure. He might not even realize where you are."

"I left him a letter at the hotel and paid the owner good money to see to it that Peter got it. I told him everything in that letter. How his anger hurt me. How I couldn't bear his ugly words—the words he swore he didn't mean. I also told him how much I loved him." Her expression changed from passive to sorrowed. "If he received that letter . . ."

"*If* he received it," Karen interrupted. "You can't be sure he ever got it. He may not even know where you are. You know it's possible he never returned to the hotel to learn of your whereabouts. He may well have figured you to have returned with his parents to California. He may have gone there himself, not even knowing you were in the Yukon."

"Well, if that's the case, it's even more imperative that I get to California. Besides, this cold climate is no good for Andy. He's not all that strong."

Karen frowned. "Perhaps it wasn't wise to bring you here."

"Nonsense. It would have been just as cold in Dawson," Grace argued.

"Yes, but in Dawson you had doctors at your fingertips. Here, there's no one to help."

"I would have had doctors at my fingertips for two hundred dollars a visit.

Did you have any idea they were charging that much money?"

"No, I guess I didn't."

"Dr. Brummel even made that kind of money for his dental work and usually all he did was pull teeth. Look, you're here and I feel confident of your abilities. After all, you were my teacher. You gave me wise counsel and taught me a great deal. If anyone can keep us in health and good spirits, I say it will be you."

Karen felt uncomfortable with her friend and one-time student's adoration. She worried that perhaps by encouraging Grace to join them, out of her own selfish desire, she had somehow risked the lives of both her friend and Andy. Looking down at the happy baby, Karen knew she could never forgive herself if anything happened to him on her account.

Karen handed Andy back to Grace, then went to take her apron from the hook. "So what do you think of the place? It's crowded and dark, but it keeps out the chill."

"Anything would have to be better than the tent," Grace said, smiling. "I just hate feeling all closed in."

Karen laughed. "Well, after a few weeks here, you may change your mind. Adrik and Gump made the berth bunks. I feel like I'm living in a wooden box, but when you tack a cover up there to totally enclose the bed, it does retain the heat pretty well."

"I was warm enough last night," Grace admitted. "I hope Jacob and Gump didn't mind sharing a bed."

"No, I know they didn't. There were times through the coldest nights when they slept together and Leah slept wedged against the wall with Adrik and me. There wasn't any room to move even an inch, but we kept from freezing."

"Well, Leah and I could sleep together with Andy between us. He'll stay warmer that way, and then Gump and Jacob can each have their own bed."

"That was the plan, but we didn't know you'd be coming in last night and Leah fell asleep in the smallest bunk. It wouldn't have done any good to get her up and rearrange everyone then."

"Oh, I agree," Grace replied. "Although I am happy to learn my permanent place will be the lower bunk instead of the upper. I thought I'd break my neck climbing down this morning."

Karen turned to the stove and checked the cast-iron skillet. She tossed a few droplets of water into the pan to see if it was finally hot enough. The popping and sizzling was all the encouragement she needed.

"I'll fry up some bacon and then put the oatmeal on," she told Grace. "You sit there and relax, and we'll have breakfast on in a moment."

Leah appeared just then. She was bundled from head to toe and was still shivering from the icy morning air. Carrying a bundle to Karen, she held it up like an offering. "Adrik ... said to give this ... to ... to ... you." Her teeth chattered as she spoke.

Karen took the bundle and motioned Leah to the stove. "Come warm up, and next time don't stay outside for so long. A half hour in this cold could kill you." She directed Leah to stand near the firebox on the stove. "Gump hasn't stoked up the fireplace yet, so the stove will have to do."

"I could stoke up the fire," Grace offered.

"No, I want you and Andy to rest and warm up from your long trip. Leah will get warm enough right here." Karen unwrapped the bundle to find a half dozen good-sized potatoes. They were a little old, but never had anything looked so good. "Where in the world did he find these at this time of year?"

Leah shrugged. "He didn't say. Just told me to give them to you. Guess he thought they'd be good for breakfast."

"Indeed they will," Karen agreed. "I'll fry them up in the bacon grease."

"Hmmm, I can just taste them now," Leah said, looking rather wistful.

Karen thought it a shame that they all treated food with such enthusiastic, even wanton, behavior. She wasn't at all sure what she might or might not do for a piece of fresh fruit or a nice green salad.

Karen hurried to wash and cut up the potatoes, skins and all. She cooked the bacon and pulled it from the skillet. "I can't believe we're actually having potatoes for our breakfast. This will be wonderful." She dumped the plateful of cut up spuds into the grease and jumped back as fiery droplets spit back at her from the pan.

Just then Gump, Adrik, and Jacob entered. Each man carried an armful of firewood—just a portion of the supply they would need for the day.

"Smells near good enough to eat," Adrik teased.

"Ja, it smells like a good house should," Gump added.

Karen turned and smiled. "I don't know where you managed to lay your hand on potatoes, but I'm eternally grateful."

"I have my ways," Adrik said, depositing his wood beside the fireplace.

"Don't I know it," Karen said, smiling at her husband. "You probably sweet-talked some poor unsuspecting soul just when she was at her most vulnerable."

Adrik grinned roguishly. "My lips are sealed, Mrs. Ivankov. Just be grateful we didn't eat them on the trail, for we were sorely tempted."

A loud commotion from the dog pens caused Adrik to raise his hand for silence. Karen heard the awful racket and trembled. The team was awfully worked up about something, and that usually spelled trouble. Taking up his rifle, Adrik moved to the door. Jacob was right behind him, and Gump followed after the boy. Each man took up his firearm and moved outside with caution.

"What is it?" Grace asked.

"I don't know. What I do know is that I don't intend to wait here," Karen said. "Why don't you put Andy in the play box Adrik fixed for him and we'll investigate."

Karen heard Adrik yell something. "Hurry, Grace. Let's go see. Never mind leaving Andy—just grab that blanket and bring him. Here, we'll wrap it around both of you," she said, helping to maneuver the blanket around Grace's shoulders.

Leah followed close on their heels, still wrapped in her coat. *She's the only sensible one of the group*, Karen thought, as they rounded the edge of the cabin and looked to see what the men had uncovered.

The dogs were still barking up a storm. They'd congregated at the north end of the pen and were jumping at the fence and pouncing upon each other as they howled and carried on.

"What is it?" Karen asked.

Adrik shook his head. "Someone was messing around the shed. They've stolen the sled I bought in Dawson."

"Why would they take the sled and not the dogs?" Leah asked. "The dogs are worth three hundred a piece."

"Ja, she's right," Gump said, making certain the pen gate was secure.

"Why would anyone want that old sled?" Adrik questioned.

Karen was just as perplexed. "Who'd you get it from in Dawson?"

"I bought it off an Englishman—a botanist, to be exact. He was there putting together a book on plants of the Yukon. He didn't need the sled anymore and offered to trade it when he heard me talking in the store about needing one."

"Maybe he stole it from someone else," Leah suggested.

Jacob shook his head. "Nah, he didn't seem the type. He was one of those bookish fellows—the kind that studies all the time. I can't see him stealing a sled from anyone."

"Me neither," Adrik replied.

"Maybe the thief was a friend of the botanist," Karen suggested. "Maybe there was something of value that had been left on it."

"Can't imagine what it'd be. It was just an old sled."

Karen bit at her lip and rubbed her arms. She'd been foolish to come outside without a coat. "Did the man sell you anything besides the sled?"

"No. The only thing he sold me was this sled—oh, and the sled box. But we're using that for Andy. It's the box I fixed up for him to play in and sleep in during the day."

"Maybe there's something about the box," Karen suggested. "We should go check it out."

"Nah, it's just a wooden box, nothing special."

Grace had already started back to the cabin when Karen turned to follow. She heard Grace scream and feared the thieves had struck again. Adrik came running, whipping past Karen in a flash.

Karen then saw what had caused her friend's dismay. Smoke was pouring out the cabin door. "The potatoes!" she screamed and charged past her husband to enter the cabin.

She could barely see what she was doing, but somehow Karen managed to pull the skillet from the stove. She put the pan in a washtub and hurried outside, nearly knocking Adrik down at the door.

"Silly woman," he said, taking the smoldering tub from her. "You could have died from the smoke."

Karen coughed and sputtered for air. She looked at the charred potatoes and felt tears come to her smoke-filled eyes. "But our potatoes were burning."

"I'd say they're already gone," Adrik replied, this time in a less serious tone.

"No!" Karen declared. "I won't believe it. I was so looking forward to those potatoes. I won't let them go to waste."

Adrik laughed. "You go right ahead and eat 'em if you want, but as for me, I plan to find something a little less well-done."

Gump chuckled, as did Jacob and Grace. Leah was the only one who offered Karen any real sympathy. She came and put her arm around Karen's shoulder and patted her gently.

"Come on, boys," Adrik called, "let's get the cabin opened up and clear out the smoke. If we stand out here much longer, we'll all be frozen in our tracks."

"Not if we warm ourselves by the potatoes," Grace suggested.

They all broke into peals of laughter, and even Karen had to smile. Gone were her dreams of potatoes fried to a golden brown, a hint of bacon flavoring each morsel. Easy come, easy go. It was the story of gold, be it rock ore or potatoes.

—{ C H A P T E R N I N E T E E N }—

APRIL 26, 1899, dawned in Dawson City at forty-below. To say it was cold was to come nowhere near describing the painful bite of the northern wind. Very few people moved on the streets below, and those who did brave the cold were bundled like furry snowmen.

The cold seemed to permeate everything. It seeped into the very core and left a person with the desire to do nothing but bury himself under piles of covers. Teddy gave serious thought to making this his last winter in the Yukon. He felt trapped. As surely by his own conscience, as by the cold.

Teddy stood at the frosted window of his hotel room. His thoughts bothered him in a way he didn't want to acknowledge. He was keeping the truth from Miranda.

It wasn't hard to rationalize why he was remaining silent, but it was hard to see how much she longed for some kind of contact with her friends—and do nothing to help. Teddy turned from the window and paced the room. Miranda had gone downstairs to the kitchen to get some hot water for their tea. Teddy had suggested they simply have one of the staff bring it up, but Miranda had wanted the exercise. She was suffering a terrible bout of cabin fever and longed for sunny days and warmth. Teddy didn't blame her. He longed for the same, only he longed for such things with Miranda at his side.

"But surely she'll leave me when she finds her friends," he said aloud. "And how could I fault her for that? She has history with them that she does not share with me."

Teddy's thoughts went back to the day they'd kissed. He'd been so dumbfounded by her initiation of the act that he had initially said nothing—done nothing. Then when she'd fled from the room, looking as though she'd broken all ten commandments at once, he knew he was in love with her. He knew, too, that he wanted to kiss her again, and this time he wanted to be the one to initiate the kiss.

And he had kissed her. The thought of her lips upon his still haunted him. He would have kissed her many times over since that wonderful day, but Miranda had been skittish and shy around him ever since. The only time she'd really seemed her old self was when she'd cut her hand.

Teddy wouldn't have wished her pain for all the world, but he did enjoy her neediness when she was incapable of helping herself. He felt wonderfully necessary in her life when she was ill or injured—though he certainly had no desire for her to spend her days as an invalid. No, he really just wanted her to need him all the time. To need his company—his hospitality—his love.

His earlier fears of Miranda's interfering in his work had faded with the passing of each day. She was nothing like his mother. Eugenia Davenport had cared nothing for her husband's dream while Miranda Colton seemed quite enthusiastic about Teddy's desires. The only problem was that Teddy's enthusiasm for his work was fading in light of the revelation that he had fallen in love.

Already he could envision a future with Miranda working at his side. They'd complete the book and go on a lecture tour discussing the various aspects of Yukon vegetation and forestry. They'd spend quiet evenings in discovery—discovery of books, plants, and each other.

A cloud settled over him, making Teddy feel quite black in his mood. There would be no future with Miranda, however. She would hate him when she knew the truth. Maybe he could still figure out a way to keep her from finding out.

"I must tell her," he declared in defeat. Keeping the truth from her was making him feel quite heartsick. He argued with himself in his dreams from dusk to dawn, and when he would awaken from his restless sleep tormented with guilt, he'd start the whole process all over again with his conscious mind. No, it was best to get the truth out and tell her exactly what had happened and why he'd not told her the truth.

"But the setting should be special," he murmured. "Perhaps then she'd be more inclined to forgive me." *Please let her forgive me.*

An idea came to him to have the cook prepare a special dinner. They could eat privately in the little office downstairs. He'd have it all arranged. There would be candles and beautiful linens and, of course, crystal. He would see to it that the table was perfect.

Teddy began plotting the dinner, deciding on whatever fancy feast his money might buy. He'd heard that Muldoon's Saloon and Restaurant had some pork chops that they were selling for an outrageous sum. Perhaps he could get cook to secure a couple for their meal. They would be tasty with a bit of rosemary, which Teddy could provide from his supplies of herbs. He'd considered it his great fortune to have traded cash for a vast array of herbs from a woman he'd met in British Columbia. The herbs had served him well on many an occasion and would no doubt be just the thing to make their rather bland fare a bit livelier.

"Here we are," Miranda announced, opening the door. She balanced a tray of tea and Swedish cookies on her right hip, looking as if she'd been serving tables her whole life.

"Let me help," Teddy said, going to her. He took the tray and smiled. "What would you think about a surprise?"

"It depends on what the surprise is," Miranda replied. "Cutting my hand was a surprise. Falling overboard on Lake Laberge was a surprise. I'd just as soon know about the arrangement prior to deciding whether I'm for it or against it."

"It's a good surprise," he replied.

Miranda's expression turned to one of excitement. "Have you found my friends?"

Teddy felt bad for having given her false hope. "No, but I think you'll be pleased with my idea, nevertheless."

She lowered her face, and Teddy knew she was struggling to keep him from seeing her disappointment. She'd tried so hard to be stoic—for his sake. He knew he'd been less than comforting when she'd brought up the past and the long separation she'd endured. But in a town with some thirty thousand people, she was expecting the impossible. He had only wanted her to understand the situation and how difficult it was. He didn't want her to feel that she couldn't confide in him, yet sadly, he knew that was how she felt.

"So what did you have in mind?" she asked softly.

Teddy put the tray down and began to pour the tea. "If I told you, it wouldn't be a surprise."

Miranda moved to the table and studied him for a moment. Cocking her head, one brow raised ever so slightly, she questioned him again, "What are you planning?"

"I assure you it is all good. I would never do anything to hurt you." He swallowed hard, and this time it was his turn to look away. Of course, he hadn't meant to hurt her, but by being inattentive and not listening to the names of her friends, he had inadvertently kept Miranda from finding her loved ones months ago. There was no way he could keep that from hurting her.

"So when is this surprise to be unveiled?"

He handed her a cup and saucer. "Tonight. Tonight at seven."

She nodded. "Very well, Teddy Davenport. I shall trust you this once."

Her words went through his heart like a knife. *Oh, please, Lord,* he prayed. *Please let her understand.*

———

The candlelight dinner completely captivated Miranda. She had come to expect certain things from Teddy, and romantic displays didn't fit that list.

Upon his instruction, she had dressed in her finest gown, a pale cream wool trimmed in gold braiding. Teddy had purchased it for her from a local seamstress. The woman had fussed and fawned over Miranda until she thought she might very well faint from exhaustion. The experience, however, had merited her three new gowns, and of all of them, this was the most beautiful and elegant.

"Teddy, what is this all about?" she asked as she unfolded her napkin.

"I thought we deserved a special evening. I had an epiphany of sorts and needed to share it with you. But first, we shall dine on very fine food. I've had the cook scouring the city since this afternoon. He's procured for us two very thick pork chops, baked potatoes, applesauce spiced with cloves and nutmeg, and a brandied plum cake, which he assures me will be most rewarding."

Miranda thought the food sounded most delightful. She certainly hadn't gone hungry staying here at the hotel under Teddy's care, but neither did they eat all that well. This was Dawson, after all. They were isolated in the frozen Yukon without hope of major deliveries until spring breakup. Supplies were running low—and the variety was definitely lacking. Spring thaw couldn't come soon enough.

Miranda knew that date was to come upon them within a month or so, as people were already placing bets on when the river's ice would thaw enough to break free. It certainly wasn't going to happen if the days stayed at forty-below, as this one had. But it would come—soon enough.

One of the housekeeping girls acted as their server. She brought the plates, bearing the offering of the beautifully arranged meal, hot from the kitchen.

"Might I offer a prayer?" Teddy asked.

Miranda nodded. "I'd like that."

"Father, we thank you," Teddy prayed, "for this bounty and for the bounty you will provide on the morrow. We thank you for hearing our prayers and for tenderly caring for us. Amen."

"Amen," Miranda whispered.

They ate in silence for several minutes. Neither one seemed willing to let the food get even marginally cold. The serving girl brought in fresh hot rolls and Miranda nearly swooned when she saw they were accompanied by a small amount of butter.

"I've not tasted butter in ever so long," she said, taking a tiny bit to smear on her roll.

Teddy reached across and slathered the roll more sufficiently. "I'm not that fond of butter, but I know it is a treat for you."

Miranda felt overwhelmed by his kindness. Surely he longed for the comforts of civilization. He was of a fine English family, moneyed and educated. It must have been hard on him to be so isolated from the things he'd grown up with.

"What do you miss most about England?" she asked.

Teddy looked at her thoughtfully for a moment, then he turned his gaze to the ceiling above her head. He looked to be a million miles away.

"I miss the comfort of having everything neatly ordered. There is a settled feeling to the land—a knowledge of whom it has belonged to for centuries. Wherever you look, you have the feeling of a gentleness that cannot be had here." He looked back to smile at Miranda. "If England is a refined and elegant old lady, then the Yukon is her defiant and rebellious grandchild."

"I would love to see England some day," Miranda said softly. "The man I told you about, Crispin Thibault, the one I thought I saw in the alley, he was from abroad. He told such wonderful stories. He had skied in the Alps and sailed fjords in Scandinavia. He made it all sound so wonderful—so completely amazing. Before I came with my parents to Alaska," she said thoughtfully, "I'd never traveled outside of California. In fact, I'd hardly seen more than San Francisco."

"Perhaps one day you'll visit England. I'd love to have you stay at my estate. I would love to show you all the places I love so much."

Miranda sobered and looked into his dark eyes. She saw something in his expression that wasn't all together clear. There was a certain amount of passion and desire, but there was something else as well—something almost akin to regret.

The dinner passed much too quickly, and once the dishes had been cleared away and fat slices of plum cake had replaced the entrée, Teddy decided to speak more seriously.

"I have something to tell you. I'm not at all sure how you will take it, but I beg you to bear with me and hear me out before you comment."

Miranda felt a tightening in her chest. What was he about to tell her? Had he found out something horrible in regard to her friends? "What is it?" she asked, leaning forward.

"First promise to hear me out."

"I promise," she said without thought. "Now tell me."

"I came to realize the other day, the day you cut your hand, where it was I had heard the name of Adrik Ivankov."

"Is that all? I told you about him—and Karen and Grace and the Barringer children. How could you have not remembered?"

"Because I failed to really listen." He bowed his head momentarily, refusing to meet her gaze. "I was selfishly enveloped in my own affairs. I was focused only on completing my work. You see, this book was very important to my father, and I wanted very much to honor him."

"I don't understand." Miranda had the feeling she wasn't going to like what Teddy had to tell her, but she needed to know the truth.

"When we arrived in Dawson, do you remember that I sold our sled?"

"Yes."

"Well, the man I sold it to was Adrik Ivankov."

"What?" Her voice took on an alarmed tone. "You sold it to him and didn't tell me?"

Teddy pushed back from the table, his face betraying his anguish. "I didn't realize who he was. Please, just hear me out. I hadn't remembered you telling me the man's name."

"But . . ."

He held up his hand. "Please. I didn't know it, or I would have brought him back here and opened the door for the happy reunion. I ran into the man, quite literally, in the mercantile. He said he was looking for a sled, and I told him I had one. He was with a young boy of about sixteen or seventeen."

"Jacob Barringer," Miranda filled in.

"I suppose so. You see, I didn't pay either one of them much attention. Mr. Ivankov talked of his need for the sled and how he was moving his group to one of the creek claim sites. I didn't listen closely enough for the name to register."

"Oh, Teddy, how could you be so unthinking? You had to know I was looking for friends in those circumstances."

His expression contorted in misery. "I know. I've asked myself that at least a thousand times since you spoke his name at the hospital and I realized where I'd heard it."

"But that was over two weeks ago, Teddy. You've known all this time and still said nothing?" Miranda struggled to keep her temper. "Why? You knew how very much I wanted to find him—to find all of them. Why would you do something so selfish?"

"Because I didn't want to lose you," Teddy suddenly blurted out.

Miranda sat back stunned. "What?"

"You heard me. I didn't wish to lose your company. Don't you see, Miranda? I've fallen in love with you."

She felt her breathing quicken to the raging pace of her pulse. "You love me?"

He came to where she sat and got down on one knee. "I love you with all my heart. And the thought of losing you—of having to let you go—nearly breaks me."

Her heart softened toward him. It had never been her nature to hold grudges, and her anger fled in the light of his devotion. She loved him, as well. She'd known it for some time. His love of God made him perfect in her eyes. How could she not forgive him?

"Oh, Teddy, I'm so sorry. I shouldn't have lost my temper."

"I'm the one who is apologizing. Please forgive me. I promise to be more sensitive to your needs. I promise to listen more clearly and to give you all my attention. Please, just please say you'll marry me."

"Marry you?" Her voice left her as her breath caught in her throat. He was proposing marriage!

"I'll make you a good husband. I promise that with God's help, I'll be everything you need me to be."

"Oh, Teddy." She felt tears come to her eyes. "I . . ."

"FIRE!"

The shouts rang clear from the lobby. Teddy jumped to his feet just as the cook burst in on them. "Boss, the whole town's on fire!"

Adrik and Jacob had grown restless waiting for spring thaw. The gravel that Gump had dug up prior to their arrival beckoned them for sluicing and exploration. Adrik knew they couldn't wash the solution in water, as they had to fight the frozen creek just to get enough water to drink and wash with. But Adrik had another plan.

Taking a pick, he worked loose a chunk of gravel and frozen muck and brought it into the cabin. Diligently he and Jacob worked at thawing the mass by putting it in a wash pan near the fireplace. From time to time, one of them would turn the pan to offer heat to the various sides of the pan and, little by little, the mass thawed.

"You beat 'em all, Adrik. Yes, by golly. You beat 'em all."

Picking through the rock and mud, Adrik took Gump's good-natured teasing in stride. He knew Gump was just as interested in what he might find as everyone else. A few flakes of gold encouraged Adrik to keep at it. Gump had said there was enough gold on the claim to keep him comfortable, but they all needed a really strong show of color. And in the twinkling of an eye, that was exactly what they got.

"Gold!" Adrik declared and jumped to his feet. He held up a nugget the size of a peanut. "Look what I've found!"

Gump limped across the room. His leg had healed, but he still walked with a bit of difficulty. "Are you sure there? It could be fool's gold."

"No, this is the real thing!" Adrik dropped the rock in Gump's hand.

"Ja, it's the real thing all righty."

Karen and Grace moved in closer, while Leah played with Andy. "Is it true?" Karen asked. "Have we struck pay dirt?"

"I think it would be safe to say we're getting closer," Adrik replied, pulling Karen against him in a tight embrace. "I think once the warm weather comes, we're going to strike it rich."

"Ja ha!" Gump let out a yell, then quieted quickly. "No sense in lettin' the whole vorld know just yet."

Adrik shook his head and laughed. He'd never seen the old man so happy. "We're going to make it," he told Gump and the others. "We're going to find the gold!"

"OH, TEDDY, this is just awful," Miranda declared, looking at the charred remainders of Front Street. The town had suffered cruelly, the fire razing much of the business district, as well as Paradise Alley.

"What in the world could have happened to the fire-fighting equipment?" Teddy questioned, not really expecting an answer.

"I'll tell you what happened, mister," a complete stranger interrupted. "The fire department was on strike for more pay. They didn't keep the water heated so when the people tried to use the hoses, it froze in the lines before it could even come out the nozzle. Those hoses burst quicker than a spoiled melon. It's the firemen's fault so many folks are out of business."

"Do you have any room at the hotel, Teddy?" Miranda asked as her gaze followed hundreds of people who were wandering up and down the street in a daze.

"We have some room, but not nearly enough. We'll do what we can, however. Let's get the word out that we're open to take in those without homes. Let them come and share whatever we can offer."

Miranda smiled. "I'll start spreading the word."

———

From the looks of the crowd that had gathered outside the hotel doorway, Miranda figured the news had traveled rapidly among the citizens of Dawson. Tired and completely worn by the evening's events, Miranda worked until the wee hours of the morning to ensure that everyone at least had a place on the floor to throw down a blanket.

"Come on," Teddy said, pulling her away from the front desk. "We're going to have to get some rest."

"How can we?" Miranda questioned. "There are still so many people outside."

"The hotel staff can take care of them. You've done enough for one night."

"It seems like an entire week has passed instead of one night. If it wasn't for the heavy smell of smoke on the air, I would think it had."

Teddy smiled. "A good night's sleep will help a great deal. Once you are able to rest in your own bed . . ."

"But I can't," Miranda interrupted. "I gave my room to a group of women. I believe there are seven to be exact."

"Seven women are going to sleep in that small room?"

Miranda nodded. "I think they're used to a lot worse."

Teddy seemed to understand. "The soiled doves, eh?"

Miranda smiled. "I knew you'd understand."

"As long as they don't try to conduct business in my establishment. But the real concern, of course, is what you are to do now. I suppose you can sleep in my room, and I can try to find a place elsewhere."

"I had one of the girls move my things into your room, but I don't have to sleep there. I just didn't want to lose track of my belongings."

"If we were married, this wouldn't be a problem at all," Teddy said, a rye smile on his lips.

"Yes, well, we aren't married, and so it presents a problem," Miranda said, feeling the heat come to her cheeks.

"Do you trust me to remedy the situation?"

"What do you mean?"

Teddy shrugged. "Well, I could secure a license and see to our marriage—if you only give me a yes to my proposal."

"What about the sleeping arrangements now?" Miranda asked with a grin.

"I'll take a spot on the floor in the office, but only if you agree to my proposal."

"And if I don't?" She was amused with his teasing tone.

"Then you'll soon learn what it is to sleep eight women to a bed."

Miranda laughed. "Oh, Teddy, you are such a dear."

"Is that a yes?"

She leaned into his arms and wrapped him in her embrace. "Yes. Yes, I will marry you, Thomas Davenport."

"I knew I could wear you down with my genteel charm."

"Actually, I was pretty sure I would marry you that morning you overflowed the pan of oatmeal back at the cabin. I figured anyone that needy . . ."

"Oh, hush," he said, silencing her with a kiss.

Miranda cherished the moment, wanting nothing more than to go on holding him for a long, long time. She had found the love of her life, even with his absent-minded ways. He was hers, and that was all that mattered.

———————

Teddy and Miranda married in a simple ceremony on the fifth of May. By that time tents had sprung up all along Front Street, even while the blackened debris remained to be hauled away. The saloons and gambling halls were the first to be back in business, with the scarlet women following right behind.

Miranda marveled at the transformation, but no more than she did at the transformation in her own life and that of her husband's demeanor. The once shy, soft-spoken Teddy seemed to take on a manly pride about him. He strutted proudly with Miranda on his arm, never failing to introduce her as his new bride.

For Miranda, the joy of her new marriage was almost more than she could put into words. And she had tried. Writing to her mother and father, she had sought to explain her feelings and decision. She knew Peter would be livid that she'd not consulted him prior to speaking her vows, but she was a grown woman in her majority, and she'd been through enough adventure over the last year to know her heart and mind on the matter.

"Can you take this over to the charity hospital?" Teddy asked as he finished wrapping a bundle of labeled herbs.

Miranda looked up from her letter and nodded. "Of course."

"You might delay in case the doctor has another list. Tell him I will do what I can to secure whatever he needs to help the burn victims."

"It was good of you to help arrange the charity hospital," she said, coming to her husband's side. Kissing him lightly atop his head, she was unprepared for his sudden embrace. He pulled her onto his lap and kissed her passionately upon her mouth.

"I still can't believe you're my wife. The most beautiful woman in all the world and she belongs to me!" He kissed her again, this time a bit more ardently.

Miranda wrapped her arms around Teddy's neck and gave herself over to the emotions that welled up inside her every time he touched her. How she loved this man!

"Ah, you'd better take this and go," Teddy said, pulling away rather suddenly. He nearly pushed Miranda from his lap and then handed her the package. "If you don't go right now, it might very well be hours before I'm prepared to let you leave."

Miranda giggled. "Whatever you say, Teddy dear."

She was still grinning when she descended the stairs, package in hand. She had never known such happiness. *Oh, Father God, you are so good to me. You have blessed me beyond all my expectations and dreams. Thank you for helping me choose this godly man for a husband. Now I can truly thank you for allowing the storm upon Laberge and for my accident. If not for that, I might never have met Teddy.*

Walking the short distance to the hospital, Miranda lifted her face to the noon-day sun. The warmth was minimal, but it was wonderful nevertheless. The breakup of the ice on the river was impending, and daily there were reports to relay the situation on the Yukon River. She'd heard it rumored that the government had plans to load the winter garbage atop the ice floes just prior to the breakup and that way, what the river didn't claim as its own, the ice would carry away downstream. Miranda couldn't imagine those folks who lived downstream appreciating the gesture, but she had no say in the matter.

The hospital tent had been purchased by Teddy from a local man. In fact the structure was actually two tents fixed side by side. Miranda entered the structure and found an unoccupied desk and chair at the opening. Beyond this were rows of cots where writhing, pain-filled patients waited for some form of care.

Just then a young man of medium build passed by Miranda. "If you're looking for a patient, just take a walk down the aisle. My bookkeeper has gone off to purchase more bandages."

"Are you the doctor?" Miranda questioned.

The man stopped and turned on his heel. "I am. Is there a problem?"

"Not at all. My husband is Thomas Davenport. He sent this package of herbs for your use."

"Oh, that's a relief," the man said, stepping forward to take the offering. "I'm beyond myself in trying to treat these poor men."

"Teddy, my husband, wondered if you had another list of needs? Herbal or otherwise," she added quickly.

"I do indeed. Let me step over to the other tent and get it."

Miranda nodded and watched as the man hurried from the room. The moans of the men filled her ears, and without knowing why, Miranda turned her attention to the occupants of the tent. Slowly she walked down the aisle, looking first at this one and then that one. She prayed silently for each man, hoping God would be merciful. By the time she reached the patient at the end of the first row, Miranda could not suppress a gasp.

"Crispin?" she whispered his name, but it was enough to make the man open his eyes.

"Miranda," he breathed. "An angel come to take me to my death."

"No," Miranda tried to assure him, "you're not going to die. Not yet."

His eyelids flickered. "Are you really here? You're dead. You can't be here."

"I didn't die, Crispin. I fell overboard but was rescued." She knelt beside his cot and took hold of his bandaged hand. He was burned—badly. And for the first time, she wondered if she'd given him false hope in her statement regarding death.

"You didn't die? But we were certain." His raspy voice struggled to form the words.

"God watched over me and brought me safely to Dawson."

"I'm so glad," Crispin replied.

He closed his eyes, and for a moment Miranda thought perhaps he had passed away. Tears formed in her eyes. How awful to find him like this. "Oh, Crispin, I'm so sorry you've been hurt. Where are the others? Are they here with you?"

He rolled his head slowly from side to side. "No. We separated when we came to this place. I couldn't bear to stay on. I kept thinking of you—how I had failed you."

"Oh, but you didn't. Please don't think such a thing." She kissed his bandaged hand.

Crispin's breathing grew very ragged. Miranda feared he was nearing the end, and she knew that she had to talk to him about Jesus. "Crispin, where are you going?" She hoped he would understand exactly what she was asking him.

He looked at her and shook his head again. "I don't know. Can you show me the way?"

"But of course I can. Jesus said that He is the way, the truth, and the life. You have only to put your trust in Him and repent of your sins. He will do the rest. He will guide your way." She touched his forehead, noting the cold, clammy feel to his skin.

"I'm sorry that I doubted God. I was foolish. I thought I would never need such a thing in my life." He fell silent and once again closed his eyes.

Miranda wiped her tears with her free hand. For several moments she heard only his ragged breathing and the moans of those around her. The smell of death was thick on the air. Why hadn't she noticed it before? Unable to bear the thought, she finally offered, "I can pray with you, Crispin. If you want me to."

"No need," he whispered. " 'Tis done."

"I'm so glad. Now I shall see you again in heaven," Miranda said, trying to keep from sobbing. She couldn't believe the emaciated man, so burned and scarred, was the handsome Crispin Thibault who had wooed her with his charming intellect and stories of faraway places.

Crispin opened his eyes and looked up at her. "Thank you so much for coming. I told God I would be glad to do the right thing—only I didn't know what the right thing might be. I only wanted to go home, but I had no home to go to. I prayed for an angel and here you are."

He wheezed and struggled to breathe. Miranda turned to see if the doctor had returned. She felt frantic to find him. "I'll go for the doctor," she told Crispin.

"No," he whispered. "I shan't be here when he comes." He drew a ragged breath and added, "I have never stopped loving you."

With that he closed his eyes and surrendered his life. Miranda burst into tears and fell across him, knowing now she could do nothing to help him.

"Mrs. Davenport?" the doctor called her name, reaching out to help her to her feet. "Did you know him?"

She nodded, wiping her eyes and trying so very hard to regain control. "He was a friend."

"I'm sorry. Is there anything I can do?"

Miranda nodded. "Yes. Please don't send him away to be buried in some unmarked grave. My husband and I will pay for his burial. Please do what you must, but call the funeral parlor to care for him. I'll make the arrangements."

"All right," the man said sympathetically. "I'll send my man when he returns."

"Thank you. Now if you'll give me your list . . ."

"Oh, of course. Here you are."

Miranda squared her shoulders and pulled her wool cape close. With one last glance at Crispin, she hurried from the tent and nearly ran all the way back to the hotel.

Once inside the sanctuary of Teddy's hotel, Miranda darted up the stairs in an unladylike manner and rushed into their room. The sight of her husband caused her to break into tears anew. "Oh, Teddy. Something awful has happened!" She collapsed in his arms, her tears dampening the front of his shirt.

"What is it?" Teddy asked, his tone betraying his concern. "Are you hurt? Did someone bother you?"

Miranda lifted her face to meet his gaze. "No. No one bothered me. I found my friend Crispin Thibault at the hospital. Oh, Teddy, he'd been horribly burned."

"I'm so sorry." His expression of worry melted in the wake of her declaration. "Is he going to make it?"

"No. He died while I was with him." She sniffed back tears. "He was waiting for someone to come tell him what he needed to do in order to go to heaven. What if I'd not taken the herbs to the doctor? What if I'd come too late?"

"But you didn't, my dearest. Remember, God is never too late. He knew your friend's heart was ready to receive the truth. I'm so proud of you for sharing with him—for helping him in his final moments."

"But imagine all the others, Teddy. What if they're waiting, too? What if they're dying to know the way home, just as Crispin was?"

He nodded. "It's a possibility that we should seek to rectify. No one should die without knowing Jesus Christ and the gift He offers them."

Miranda put her head against his shoulder and let Teddy hold her close once again. No matter what happened, she promised God, she would see to it that each of the injured had a chance to know the truth about salvation. She didn't know how she might accomplish it, but she felt the inspiration of certain purpose course through her veins. She wouldn't let them die without knowing that God loved them and wanted to give them a home in heaven.

CHAPTER TWENTY-ONE

THE WARMTH OF MAY brought with it the thaw. The excitement built toward the last of the month when the ice finally began to crack and pop. Then loud moaning and muffled thunder rose from the frozen water, signaling the arrival of spring.

Daily, Miranda walked back and forth from the hotel to the charity hospital. And daily she sat for hours beside the various patients' beds. She listened to their stories, prayed with them, and offered them bits of hope laced with love.

Many of the patients died slow, painful deaths. There was little anyone could do. Some had originally come because of the fire, but after being evaluated it was clear they were dying for other reasons. Scurvy, cirrhosis, malnutrition, and a variety of other desperate conditions claimed more lives than the smoke and burns. They were the downtrodden and poor wretches of society. They were the forgotten of the gold rush—those souls whose lives could offer nothing of value— so no one cared to know where they had gone or what had happened to them along the way.

But Miranda cared. Her heart broke over the neediness of them all. She felt sorrow in their passing and attended their burials faithfully. If they had even the remotest family member still living, Miranda wrote their final letters and promised to mail them. She was an angel of mercy and love—an angel offering a light to guide them home.

"They tell me," Miranda said as she sat by the bed of an elderly man, "that the river is open and new arrivals are expected within the week."

"Tell 'em all to go back where they came from," the old man said. "Tell 'em the abundance of gold is a myth perpetuated by the devil hisself."

Miranda smoothed back the old man's white hair. "They wouldn't listen. You know that." She smiled and tenderly pulled his blanket to just under his chin. "You get some sleep now."

"Will you come again tomorrow?"

"Of course," Miranda whispered, not at all certain that the old man had any tomorrows left.

———

Peter Colton felt a sense of urgency as he stepped down the gangplank of the steamer. It was like a hunger driving him forward. He saw it in the faces of those around him, only they were in search of gold and he was in search of flesh and blood.

Sunlight poured down upon him like golden rain. It radiated around him, giving him hope. He had to find Miranda. It was all that he could think of. She would be alone and scared, no doubt, and he desired only to offer her comfort and to take her home.

"Lord, please help me to find my sister," he prayed in a hushed breath. All around him the crowds trudged through the muck and mud streets, eagerly chasing after invisible goals. The gold was all they sought. The gold was what they thought they needed.

From the moment he'd first stepped onto the steamer, Peter had heard nothing but tales of getting rich and fat on Yukon gold. He'd heard tales of the Klondike before, but these rivaled most he'd known. The frenzy of the early days, so questionable and uncertain, had been replaced by a passionate confidence that drove men to the gold fields. They were noisy, desperate witnesses to the age-old story of men who would sell their souls for the taste of wealth.

Peter's patience for the entire lot had worn thin. This greed and hunger for power, the desire for overnight fame and fortune, was all such a waste of time and effort. Peter could see that now. In light of his recent inheritance from Grace's estate, Peter knew that the money he'd worked so hard for all his life meant nothing. It was so very unimportant without the woman he loved.

Checking in first one store and then another, Peter asked each clerk or owner if he knew of or had seen Miranda. He produced a picture, several years old, but still bearing a strong resemblance to his beloved sister. When he stopped in at the government house to check with the mounted police, he got his first break.

"I believe I have seen that woman," the sergeant told Peter. "She looks like the lady who helps at the charity hospital."

"Where would I find that place?"

The sergeant gave Peter directions and wished him well. Peter, excited and grateful for the news, hurried off to his destination without even thinking to thank the man. His long-legged strides seemed slow compared to his usual gait. Peter knew this was only his imagination. He wanted so much to know that Miranda was safe and well. The months and miles that had separated them could no longer stand between them, and Peter thrilled to know he would soon be reunited with his sister.

Coming through the opening to the tent hospital, Peter met the youthful yet haggard man who sat as guard at the door.

"Yes, may I help you?"

"I certainly hope so," Peter replied. "I'm looking for Miranda Colton. She's my sister and I was told I might find her here."

"She was here earlier," the man admitted. "I think she's gone back to the hotel where she lives."

Peter frowned. "Can you direct me?"

The man pointed out the way. "It's just down the street," he said, walking Peter to the door. "The Dawson Lucky Day Hotel. You can see it from here."

Peter nodded and this time remembered to thank the man. He hurried down the street, feeling ever more sure of his reunion. She was really here. She was only a few hundred feet away.

Initially impressed with the elegance and grandeur of the Dawson hotel, Peter sought out the clerk, giving little regard for anything else. He was grateful to know Miranda wasn't staying in some run-down madhouse.

"I'm looking for Miranda Colton. I was told she had a room here."

"Yes, sir, she does."

Peter smiled. "Wonderful. I'd like the room number."

"I'm sorry, I can't give that information to you. Miss Miranda is a proper lady and doesn't receive gentlemen in her quarters unless . . ."

"I'm her brother. She'll receive me," Peter replied, his patience wearing thin.

"Mister, a lot of folks could say they were her brother, but that still doesn't prove it."

"Is there a problem?" a man called from the stairs.

Peter turned to spy the well-dressed, dark-haired man. "Are you the manager here?" he demanded.

"I'm the owner," came the reply. "Thomas Davenport."

Peter eyed Davenport suspiciously. "I'm trying to find Miranda Colton, and if one of you doesn't start talking, I'm going to lose my temper." He approached Davenport in what he hoped was a menacing stance. The man was only an inch or two shorter than Peter's own six foot height, but Peter felt confident he had a good twenty or thirty pounds on the man. Muscled pounds at that.

"I'm afraid I cannot allow you to know her room number. I do not know you and it wouldn't be prudent . . ."

Peter grabbed Davenport by the suit coat and slammed him up against the wall. "I'm Miranda's brother, Peter Colton. If I don't get some answers, I'm going to—"

"Peter!"

Peter looked over his shoulder and saw Miranda staring at him in disbelief. He slowly loosened his hold on Davenport, surprised by the changes he saw in his sister. Could a year have changed her so much? She looked so much older—wiser. Her brown hair was very simply pinned into a bun at the back of her head and her attire was just as plain and unassuming, but her countenance fairly glowed. She was radiant and lovely. Her cheeks were rosy and her eyes were bright with the joy of living.

Forgetting about Davenport, Peter rushed to Miranda and lifted her into the air. "Oh, but you're a sight for these eyes of mine," he declared. "It was a long and tiring journey, but here you are. I'm so blessed to find you at last."

"Peter, it's so wonderful to see you. How long have you been in Dawson?"

He put her back on the ground and laughed. "I just walked off the boat. I started searching for you from the moment my feet touched the shore. I've come to take you home. How soon can you be ready to leave?"

Miranda looked past Peter, her expression searching for something Peter couldn't quite comprehend. He turned to the Davenport man, then back to his sister. "Well? When can you be ready to leave? I told Mother I'd have you home as soon as possible."

"I'm not leaving, Peter." She walked by him and went to stand with the stranger. "Peter, I'd like you to meet my husband, Thomas Davenport. Teddy to his friends."

Peter felt as though he'd been gut punched. "Husband?"

She smiled and turned an endearing look on Teddy. "Yes, we were married on the fifth of this month. Teddy is a botanist and I've been helping him with his research. He's writing a book describing and detailing the vegetation of the area."

"I can't believe it." Peter felt the heat come to his face. Of all the nonsensical, crazy things for her to have done. No doubt a cold winter of isolation and loneliness had led her to make her choice.

"Oh, Peter, don't be angry with me. I love Teddy dearly, and he's a wonderful, godly man. You'll come to love him as well."

"This is madness. You can't possibly know this man well enough to have married him."

"Peter, if you'll recall, you once told me you fell in love with Grace upon first setting your gaze upon her—how was it you put it?—'angelic features'? You surely haven't been gone so long you don't remember how it feels to first fall in love?"

Peter winced. How could she so flippantly mention his dead wife? Didn't she know the pain he'd suffered because of his actions? "I suppose I didn't think of it like that," he said, at a loss for any other way to explain his thoughts.

Miranda's expression softened. "Please be happy for me, Peter. I'm so very content with my new life. Please don't be angry."

Peter saw her joy and knew he couldn't be upset with her. His chance for true love might be gone forever, but he shouldn't wish it away for Miranda. "I'm not angry, just surprised. I would never have imagined in a hundred years that you would meet and marry that quickly."

Miranda laughed. "Well, neither did I. But Teddy saved my life, and I lost my heart to him."

"Then it would seem I made this trip for naught," Peter said, feeling suddenly dejected. The excitement of the trip north and the anticipation of finding his sister faded in light of this new discovery.

"How can you say that? What about Grace?" Miranda asked, leaving Teddy's side. "What of your wife?"

If he hadn't known better, Peter would have thought she was angry with him. "What of her?" Peter asked softly. His heart felt raw at the very sound of her name.

"What of her? Don't you care about her? Why worry about me when you should be focused on finding her?"

"That's rather impossible, don't you think?" Peter said, feeling defensive.

"Why should it be? I've been searching for her, as well as the Ivankovs, since coming to Dawson. I did manage to run across one of our party, but he died in the hospital just a few days back."

Peter felt confused by her words. "Are you suggesting that it's possible to find Grace? What do you mean? Surely you won't find Grace here."

"Why not? This is where the party was headed. I expect her to be near to this vicinity, even if she's not here in the city. Of course, thirty thousand people venturing in and out of the city makes our work that much harder, but . . ."

Peter shook his head. "This is madness. What are you telling me?"

Miranda looked at him oddly. "I'm saying that Grace is somewhere nearby. She's probably no more than a day or two in any direction."

"But that's impossible. She was lost on Lake Laberge. We received a letter stating this from the Mounties."

Miranda blanched. "No, Peter. I was the one who went overboard on the lake. I was lost in a storm and washed ashore. They don't even know I'm alive, because I've not been able to find them to let them know. Some native people found me and took me to Teddy. He helped nurse me back to health with the aid of a wonderful old Indian woman. As far as I know, because my friend who died just a while back told me so, the rest of the party is fine."

Peter sat down hard on the staircase. He felt dizzy, sickeningly dizzy. "You're saying that Grace is alive?"

Miranda came and sat down beside him. "Teddy, get him some water, please."

Teddy went off to do as she asked while Miranda took Peter's hand in hers. "Peter, I'm so sorry. I didn't realize you'd believed her dead all this time."

He shook his head back and forth, hoping to clear his vision. Tears came unbidden to his eyes. Could it really be true? *Dear God, how many times have I pleaded for it to be true? Have you given me the miracle I asked for?*

Teddy returned and handed Peter the glass of water. Peter drank it down without pause and handed it back to Teddy. "This is so incredible. So wonderful and awful at the same time. If only I'd known she was alive—if only I could have come sooner."

"Peter, there's something else you should know," Miranda said, looking quite serious. "It's probably going to come as quite a shock, but you must hear it from me."

Peter felt his chest tighten. What could she possibly say that was so important in light of the news she'd already given him?

"What is it? Tell me everything."

Miranda took a deep breath. "Not very long before I fell overboard in the storm on Lake Laberge, Grace made an announcement to our group. Peter, Grace was expecting a child."

The news was impossible to comprehend. Peter leaned back against the stairs and stared in dumbfounded silence. A baby? Grace was to have his child? The misery he'd known—the anguish he'd endured—seemed to fall away in light of this latest declaration.

Grace was alive, and he was to be a father.

⊣ C H A P T E R   T W E N T Y - T W O ⊢

"THE WAY I SEE IT," Teddy began over breakfast, "we can put out word that Peter is here searching for Grace. As miners come in from their claims and new folks go out to find gold for themselves, we can pass the word."

"That can only help," Miranda agreed. "After all, it will be far easier to locate Grace if we enlist the help of the local folk."

"What about checking with the government?" Peter questioned. "Don't they have to keep records of who has a gold claim?"

Miranda took a sip of tea and nodded. "They do keep records, but I've already checked. I figured the claim would be under Ivankov. I even checked Colton, but there was only one name listed, and it was completely unrelated."

"Since she was already expecting when we parted company in Skagway," Peter said, "then she would have already delivered the baby. Are there no records for that? Surely she would have gone to the hospital."

"Not in Dawson," Miranda said. "There aren't many facilities that cater to women, but even when they do, they cost more than you could imagine. I heard a woman say the other day that she would have to pay fifteen hundred dollars to have a baby in the hospital. I know from our earlier days on the journey north that we never had enough money for Grace to deliver in a hospital. Now, if they struck it rich upon arriving in Dawson, then perhaps. We can always ask around."

"It was so simple to find you. Why can't it be just as simple to find her?" Peter pushed his food around absentmindedly. Never mind that he was privileged to have some of the first fresh eggs available in Dawson since the onset of winter.

"We'll commit it to prayer," Miranda said. "I've been praying all along, but now that you're here . . . well, maybe that was just what God was waiting for."

Peter suppressed a yawn. Apologizing, he shrugged. "I didn't sleep well last night."

"Of course you didn't," Teddy replied. "I can't say that I would sleep a wink if Miranda were lost to me—no matter how temporary."

"The thing is," Miranda continued, "I feel almost certain the party will return to Dawson for supplies. There's also Queen Victoria's birthday celebration tomorrow. Not many people will miss that, even if there are more Americans in Dawson than territorial folks."

"Do you suppose they'll come for the celebration?" Peter asked. His tone betrayed his eagerness.

"Up here, folks can't afford to miss out on a good party. The eating is always better, and the company breaks the tedium of the long winter. I think we should position ourselves throughout the town and spread the word," Miranda answered.

"I say!" Teddy exclaimed. "Let's offer a reward. I'll put up the money. Maybe folks will be inclined to dig deep into their memory if something profitable is at stake."

"That's awfully generous of you. I have funds of my own—back in San Francisco. I could easily reimburse you."

"Nonsense. I should have thought to do this earlier. Miranda has been so faithful in her search. I don't know why it didn't come to me before now."

Miranda patted Peter's forearm. "We will do what we can. One way or another, we'll find her. I feel certain of it now that you're here."

———

Miranda didn't expect Peter's appearance at her door. The hour was late and she figured it to be Teddy, so she opened the door wearing her nightgown and shawl.

"Peter! What are you doing here at this hour?"

"I couldn't sleep. I heard Teddy tell you he'd be late working with the bookkeeper, so I thought maybe we could talk for a minute."

"Sure, come on in."

Miranda closed the book she'd been reading and put it on a small table. She motioned to two chairs on either side of the table. "Have a seat and tell me what's on your mind."

Peter sat quickly and looked at the book Miranda had been reading. "Botany?" He looked up at her with a quizzical expression.

Miranda grinned and took her own chair. "I figure if I'm to be a help to my husband, I need to understand his line of work. I find it all quite fascinating."

Peter shook his head and smiled. A bit of the haggard look left him and Miranda felt encouraged. She worried about her brother. She knew he had been dealt a terrible shock and she actually feared it might wreak havoc with his mind. Men had gone crazy over things of less consequence. Peter had always prided himself on being the patriarch—even savior—of his family. She was certain this new revelation was a shock.

"So what did you want to talk about?" she asked softly.

"Grace."

Miranda nodded. It was the first time since Peter's arrival that they'd had a chance to be alone. *Peter must have a million questions.* Miranda only hoped she could offer him satisfactory answers.

"Did she hate me after I left?"

Shaking her head, Miranda tried hard to be reassuring. "No. Not once did she ever say anything that would suggest such a thing. Quite the contrary, in fact. She would often cry . . ." her words trailed off.

"Go on, I need to hear it all," Peter urged. "I know the truth isn't always pleasant."

"She cried a great deal after you left. She wouldn't let anyone near her know it firsthand, but we heard her crying and saw her reddened eyes." Miranda lowered her gaze and bit her lip. She knew Peter wanted the truth, but she wanted so much to spare him the pain.

"Grace never stopped loving you," she said finally. "She only wanted you to love her—to love God. She knew you two would be destined for misery if you didn't find the truth of God to be valid for your life."

"I know," Peter replied. "She was a very wise woman."

"She still is," Miranda said. "You have to stop talking about her in the past tense. She's alive. I know she is. I know we will find her, Peter. I feel very confident of this."

"I'd like to have that confidence for myself. It just seems that this is all a very bad dream. A dream sprinkled with teasing clues that refuse to allow me to solve the puzzle."

"I know it's difficult. Here I've been fretting that you and Mother and Father believed me to be dead, and all along you've been mourning the loss of your wife. I'm so sorry."

"I'm the one who's sorry. I've made a mess of things," Peter said, burying his face in his hands. "Tell me about your accident—when you were lost on the lake."

Miranda tried to remember back to those early days. "I really don't know what happened. I know there was a storm, but I don't remember falling overboard. I can't tell you much of what happened in the weeks that followed, either. I simply don't remember.

"I do remember waking up in Teddy's cabin. Nellie, the Indian woman who helped him, cared for me. She was so gentle. I remember she had these pudgy, calloused hands, but she was infinitely tender. It taught me a lot about not judging people by their looks."

"How so?"

Miranda smiled and gazed at the ceiling. "I think I always looked at things—the appearance of things—and judged for myself their value. Not in a malicious manner, mind you, but rather in a way so as to determine if I was safe—if the circumstance was prudent."

"Those are good things," Peter said. "I wish I'd been more cautious about a great many things."

"Sometimes we can be overly cautious. Sometimes we are afraid to live life."

"And sometimes we're not afraid enough."

Just then Teddy returned from his office work. He looked to Miranda and seemed to instantly understand the situation. He motioned to the bedroom door and then to himself as if to suggest he could slip away if she needed him to. Miranda shook her head and motioned him to join them.

"Come sit with us, Teddy."

At this Peter looked up, and there were tears in his eyes. Miranda was nearly undone by their appearance. She had always seen her brother as the strong one, the leader whose confidence was never shaken. Now, here he was, fallen from his pedestal, flesh and blood just like everyone else.

"I'm sorry. I was just leaving," Peter said, getting to his feet.

"Don't leave on my account," Teddy interjected. "We've a holiday tomorrow, remember? We can sleep late if the noise in the town doesn't get us up with the dawn." He smiled, then sobered. "Seriously, if you'd like to stay, I can send for tea."

"No," Peter said, moving toward the door. "What I really need is to spend some time in prayer."

Miranda got up and followed him to the door. "If you need me, I'm here. Please let me be there for you, as you've always been there for me. Being the strong one all the time must be an exhausting endeavor."

Peter smiled sadly. "I believe God has broken me of my craving for control. Now, all I long for is my wife and child."

Miranda closed the door after he'd gone and locked it. Shaking her head, she looked to Teddy for strength and support. "I just don't know if he can bear this."

"He'll have to. Pride is a harsh mistress," he said, coming to wrap her in his embrace. "So, too, is obsession."

Miranda looked up to meet his gaze. Puzzled by his words she asked, "What are you saying?"

"I'm saying, I've long been devoted to an obsessive desire. It almost cost me your love. I've been driven to work on this book—to fulfill my father's dreams. I thought that if I brought this book to life, it would in some small way give life back to my father."

"You loved him very much, didn't you?"

"As much as a boy can love his hero. I adored my mother, for she was fun-loving and sweet and gentle, but my father was the man I wanted to grow up to be. My mother never understood his passion, but I did. Not because it was plants and flowers—but because it was so much a part of him. It was his desire as much as she was."

"Didn't she try to understand?" Miranda questioned.

"I don't know. I think she must have. After all, she would tolerate the trips to Cornwall. But my father was always very much alone in his work. It was one of the reasons I took up the interest. I wanted to be close to him—to let him know that someone understood and cared."

"That's why I want to help you with your research. I know what this project means to you."

"I'm glad you know, because what I want to say—to offer—is given out of my deepest love for you."

"I don't understand, Teddy. What are you talking about?"

"I'm saying that instead of leaving next week for the cabin, we'll stay here and help Peter search for Grace. We'll purchase supplies and horses, and we'll hit the trail and look up and down every creek where they've had even so much as a dusting of gold."

Miranda knew the cost of Teddy's gift. Her heart swelled with joy and love for this man—her husband. That he would sacrifice for her in this manner was all the proof she needed that she had done the right thing in marrying him.

"Oh, Teddy, you are more wonderful than I can find words to say." She wrapped her arms around his neck and pressed his head down. Ardently, she kissed him, pouring out all her emotions in that one action.

He moaned and pulled her tight against him. Miranda felt him sink his hands into her hair. Pulling her head back gently with one hand, he used his free hand to gently touch her cheek. At this, Miranda opened her eyes.

"You may not have the words to say," Teddy said in a low, husky voice, "but I think I understand your meaning just the same."

———

The celebration started early, as expected, but it didn't awaken Peter. He had been awake for hours. In his mind he kept replaying the news that Miranda had given him. Grace was alive. She hadn't died as he had thought. She'd lived an entire winter in the Yukon. She'd carried his child—alone. Given birth—again alone.

He had no way of knowing if the baby was a boy or a girl, or even if it had lived. The uncertainty threatened his sanity. He had always considered himself a strong, sound-minded man, but now he questioned that.

He tried to pray, but he felt there was a wall between him and God. Why did God seem so far away? Peter had given his trust to Him—claimed Jesus for his Savior. So why did it seem he was standing here alone?

A carnival-like atmosphere was going on outside the hotel, but Peter could barely muster the interest to pull back the drapes and see what was happening. Outside, the entire world seemed to have put on its Sunday best. Women wore ribbons and feathers and gowns more beautiful than he'd seen in some time. The men were equally bedecked in their finest suits or at least their cleanest jeans.

An audience had gathered around one man who was juggling while balancing on a unicycle. Not far from this group, another collection of folks were intrigued by an acrobatic act.

There were barkers calling out their wares. Everything from food to colorful banners declaring best wishes to Queen Victoria could be had for a price. Peter despaired of stepping into the madness in hopes of finding Grace. The crowd was growing by the minute, and it was barely past nine.

"Peter?" Miranda called out as she knocked on his door.

Peter found his sister dressed smartly in a red-and-green plaid skirt and white blouse. Her hair had been perfectly coifed and her face was bright with the radiance of a woman in love. She looked the epitome of a reserved and proper lady. Their parents would be proud to know her manners and upbringing had not been forgotten in the Yukon.

"Are you ready to venture out? There are all sorts of planned events—pie-eating contests, ax throwing, and races, to name a few. People are so happy at the new shipments of food and supplies that, whether the queen had a birthday or not, we'd no doubt have a party."

Peter took up his jacket and pulled it on. "I'm nervous," he admitted. "I'm terrified and excited all at the same time. I've never felt so lost."

Miranda cocked her head to one side and looked at him rather quizzically. "Lost in what way?"

"I tried all night to pray—to seek guidance so that today I might do exactly the right thing. But I feel as if God isn't listening. I just feel . . . alone."

"Oh, Peter, I know how you feel. I went through that myself when I woke up at Teddy's cabin. There I was, with a man who hardly even knew I existed and an old Indian woman who barely spoke my language. I prayed and nothing seemed to make sense. But just when things seemed as lost and hopeless as they could be—God always sent me a sign."

"What kind of sign?"

"It all depended on the situation," Miranda admitted. "But when I felt my lowest—when I gave up and left it in God's hands—things were accomplished."

"So you're telling me to do nothing?"

"Not at all," Miranda said, reaching up to touch Peter lovingly. "I'm saying commit it to the Lord, and be assured that He hears you. Sometimes His ways are obscured and foreign to us—but it doesn't mean He isn't there. It doesn't mean He isn't listening."

"I know you're right. I feel like I have nothing left to give."

Miranda nodded. "When you get to the place where Jesus is all you have," she said with a smile, "you'll find that Jesus is all you need."

Peter pondered her words as they made their way out into the streets. Teddy waited for them at the entryway of the hotel. He beamed Miranda a smile, warming Peter's heart. At least Miranda was happy. He could see that. He couldn't have picked a better mate for her than she'd chosen for herself.

The crowd grew, and by noon Peter was convinced that no fewer than twenty thousand people had flooded the muddy streets. He had asked what seemed like ten thousand of that number if they knew of his wife, but no one seemed to have a clue about the dark-eyed beauty.

"Any news?" Miranda asked, coming with Teddy from across the street.

"No. No one knows her."

"We've not had any better time of it," Miranda said. She came to stand beside Peter while Teddy excused himself to go back to the hotel.

"I'll rejoin you both in about an hour," he told them. "I have an appointment that is of great importance."

Miranda waited until he'd gone before turning to Peter. "He's considering selling the hotel. He's been talking to some of his friends, and they believe the new finds of gold in Nome are going to send most of the people west. They worry that Dawson will dwindle back to nothing."

"Where will you go, then?"

Miranda shrugged. "I don't know. We still have work to do in this area. Teddy's entire focus for the past few years has been to compile this book on the plant life of Canada. He's rearranged his thinking, however, and now he seems more inclined to consider other possibilities."

"Such as?" Peter asked, as a man jostled him from behind. "Hey there, buddy," Peter said, turning to suggest the man go elsewhere with his rowdiness.

"I said you're a liar," the man called out, ignoring Peter. He turned away from Peter to throw a punch.

Peter quickly grabbed hold of his arm. "I'd appreciate it if you did your fighting elsewhere."

"That's it, mister, hold him for me," another man called out, rushing them.

Peter was appalled to see that Miranda stood directly in the line of fire, and rather than concern himself with the man he held, Peter threw himself in front of his sister and took a blow full on the mouth.

Blood spurted out of Peter's mouth, along with a tooth. He reached up in agony as Miranda screamed. The two men, seeing they'd caused a fuss that clearly couldn't benefit them, slipped into the crowd and were gone before Peter could gather his wits.

"Peter, are you all right?"

"I have a horrible pain in my jaw. I think that ninny loosened up every tooth in my mouth."

"Say there, son, I'm a dentist. Why don't you come with me? My office is just a couple of blocks away," a man urged, taking Peter's elbow.

"Yes," Miranda encouraged. "Let's go with him, Peter."

Peter reluctantly allowed himself to be led away. He could hardly think clearly, and his mouth hurt fiercely. A fire had started somewhere in his jaw and had traveled down his neck.

"Come on, right in here," the man said, pointing Peter to his office. The man opened the door and motioned Peter to the dental chair.

"Just sit back and I'll get some water and a bowl so we can rinse your mouth and see what's what."

The dentist moved quickly around the room, gathering what he needed. He offered Peter a glass of water and a bowl in which he could spit. Peter rinsed his bloody mouth several times, fearing each time that he would spit teeth out with the water.

Finally the dentist went to work. "Ah, it doesn't look too bad. Knocked out one of the back molars and it's bleeding a good bit. Loosened up the others, but they'll firm up again when the swelling goes down and the tissue has a chance to heal." He looked down at Peter. "I'm Dr. Brummel, by the way."

"Peter Colton," Peter managed to say when the dentist took his hands out of his mouth long enough to reach for a clean towel.

"Colton, eh? I know a couple of Coltons. Are you related to a Mrs. Grace Colton?"

Miranda dropped her handbag and stared at the man, while Peter came up out of the chair. "I'm her husband. I'm here looking for her." His hand went to his mouth as pain shot through his jaw. "Do you know where she is?"

"Sit back down, son. You're in no shape to go jumping around. I don't know where Grace is now. She lived with us for a time after her son was born."

"Son?" Dizziness overcame Peter as he sunk into the chair. "I have a son?"

"You sure do. Didn't you know? Well, I guess the mail being what it is, a fellow can't expect to hear anything in a timely manner. Yes, sir, you have a fine boy. She named him Andrew, but we all called him Andy."

Peter didn't even feel the procedure as the doctor continued to work him over. He had a son. "How long ago did Grace leave you?" Peter asked.

"Well, now, let me think. I believe it was March—might have been April. No, I'm thinking March. She met up with her friend—a right nice fellow name of Ivankov. He'd come to town to bring another friend of his to the hospital and then pick her and the baby up. It was still pretty cold, but they said something about only having a two-day trip by dog sled."

"Two days?" Peter looked to Miranda. "Can we get a map and have Teddy help us draw a perimeter that would mark the distance of two days surrounding Dawson?"

"I know we could. Teddy would be happy to help. He knows the land around here very well. He's already explored a good portion of it."

Peter eased up out of the chair as Dr. Brummel concluded his treatment. "Come back in a week and let me take another look just to make sure everything is doing what it's supposed to be doing."

"What do I owe you?" Peter questioned.

"Not a thing," Brummel replied. "Your wife was a joy to my household. My wife and I very much enjoyed her company and that of the baby."

Peter squared his shoulders. He felt his hope return. God had given him the sign he so desperately needed. Looking to Miranda, he smiled, and she smiled in return. *"Weeping may endure for a night,"* he thought, remembering the Scripture, *"but joy cometh in the morning."*

Part Three

AUGUST 1899

I have fought a good fight,
I have finished my course,
I have kept the faith.

II TIMOTHY 4:7

YUKON SUMMER WAS A SPLENDID thing to be certain, but Peter saw little in the way of the beauty around him. Desperation marred his vision as he traveled with Miranda and Teddy from one creek to another. There were gold mines staked out at hundreds, maybe thousands of locations along creeks and rivers too numerous for Peter to count.

They searched the banks of creeks called Bonanza, Eldorado, Skookum, Nugget, Too Much Gold, and All Gold. Back trails wound their way through defoliated lands where miners had made roughhewn cabins or pitched their tents.

They found men who were worn-out and ready to pack it in and men who were wealthy beyond their wildest dreams. What they didn't find was Grace or any sign of the Ivankov party.

"They have to be close," Miranda told her brother. She was trying desperately to keep up his spirits. "We've already checked so many different camps, I'm sure we'll find them soon. Teddy says there's a lot of activity on Hunker Creek. We can head there after returning to Dawson for more supplies."

"I'm beginning to think we've made a mistake in searching. Maybe it would have been better to just stay in town and wait for them to come to us. After all, everyone needs fresh supplies from time to time," Peter said, his tone dejected.

"Perhaps, but we've already talked to most of the storekeepers, and they allowed us to put up those flyers you suggested. If any of the party should venture into Dawson, they're certain to spy one of them."

"Maybe, but I just feel like I'm wasting my time out here," Peter said, kicking the dirt. "I'm not finding what I'm searching for any more than most of the rest of those men out there."

"They may never find what they're looking for, Peter, but I feel confident that you will find Grace."

Peter shook his head. "I can't claim your confidence. I wish I could, but it's been months. It's August now. The bugs have been fierce. The nights have grown cold, the sun is waning to the south, and even though there are plenty of hours of light left each day, it's clear that the weather will turn on us in the weeks to come."

"But that's weeks, Peter. You can't give up." She reached out to take hold of his arm. "God is still with you. He hasn't left you to fend alone."

Peter sat down on a rock. "I know that." He stared off in the direction Teddy had gone only moments ago. "How long do you suppose Teddy will be gathering plants?"

"Not long," Miranda said, coming to sit beside him. "Are you that anxious to get back on the trail?"

"I'm anxious to be at the end of the trail. I'm anxious to be done with the search."

———

Adrik had never seen Gump happier. The gold was proving itself with every new dig into the earth. The panning hadn't been nearly as productive, although it had yielded a little gold flake now and then. No, it had taken the rigged-up steam contraption and thawing of the land to really find the gold. At first, it had taken hours of backbreaking work—steaming, digging, hauling, and then sluicing and sorting—all to find a bit of gold now and then. But finally the gold was coming in more readily than it had before and Gump declared them all rich as kings.

The only problem was that strange things continued to happen around the camp. From time to time Leah or Grace would mention seeing someone darting in and out of the trees just to the back of their camp. Sometimes Adrik would go outside and find the cache door open and the dogs barking up a storm. Other times he would find something else amiss. But always there were footprints in the dirt to suggest the culprit wasn't a four-legged beast.

Because of this, Adrik had taken to keeping a guard on duty twenty-four hours a day. Gump took guard duty during the day while Adrik and Jacob worked. Adrik then went to sleep right after supper and allowed Jacob to take the first watch. Then around two in the morning, Jacob would wake Adrik for his turn. Since posting the men, there had been little disturbance, and that was just how Adrik wanted to keep it—especially now that they had accumulated several thousand dollars in nuggets and gold dust.

"I'm going out," Jacob said, checking the Winchester to make certain it was loaded.

"God be with you," Adrik said, same as every night. "You'd better wear your jacket. Felt like the wind was going to shift. Wouldn't be surprised if we were in for an early cold spell."

Jacob nodded and grabbed his coat on the way out the door.

"Do you think we'll have to continue standing watch until we leave?" Karen asked as she sat down at the table. She took up some mending and began working.

"I think it's probably going to keep us on the safe side of things," Adrik answered. He yawned and stretched. "Well, I think I'll head to bed." He got up, then crossed to where Karen sat.

She lifted her face and smiled. "I'll be glad when all of this is behind us. I miss sharing a bed."

Adrik nodded. The separation hadn't been his favorite development either. But it seemed only prudent to do things this way. Karen had taken to sleeping in the single upper berth, allowing the men to alternate using the lower bunk as they came and went in the night. Gump kept his own upper berth without the need to share it as he had done throughout the previous winter months.

"When are we going to leave?" Leah asked. She came from the kitchen area, where she'd finished cleaning up after supper.

"I don't know, sweetheart," Adrik said smiling. She was such a pretty little thing, and he worried incessantly about keeping her out in the wild among the miners and no-accounts. Karen schooled her every day as best she could, but they had no materials to make the situation very productive. At least the Bible afforded good reading.

"I hope we'll go south before the snows come," she said rather sadly.

Adrik studied her for a moment, not expecting her solemnity. "Why is that?"

"Well, Jacob said that with his share of the gold we'd buy Papa a gravestone. I want to make sure we do that before we lose the money or spend it somewhere else."

Touched by her request, Adrik nodded. "We'll do our best to get back to Skagway before the snow sets in."

"Jacob said we could always hire a dog sled to take us to the train. He said we'd be rich enough to buy tickets for the train and still be able to buy a real nice stone."

"That is an idea," Adrik replied. "I'll sleep on it and see what I come up with."

He slipped off his boots, then crawled into the berth, carefully arranging the blankets that draped out the light. Sometimes the heat made sleeping uncomfortable, but the light made it worse. The sky would be light until nearly midnight, wreaking havoc with their sleep patterns. Gump had made shutters for the few windows, but the light still seemed to permeate the room—peeking in through the door cracks and places where the chinking had fallen out.

Settling against the pillow, Adrik sighed. *Lord,* he began to pray, *I ask that you help me to make the right decisions. I see the needs of my loved ones, and I want to make it right for each one. I want to find Peter Colton for Grace and little Andy. I want to bring Bill Barringer back to life for his children. I want to be alone with my wife for weeks on end, with no one but each other for company.*

The future held many questions and few answers, as far as Adrik was concerned. Gump had already told him of his desire to sell his half of the claim and be out by the end of September. He had plans to head back to his parents' farm. He wanted to see his brothers and find out whether his folks still lived. Adrik couldn't blame him for that. It did pose a problem, however. Should they just sell the entire claim to strangers and take what they could get?

The gold was showing good color. Was it wise to leave now, just when the getting was good? Adrik turned restlessly and sighed again. Sleep would be hard in coming.

———

Jacob didn't mind standing watch in the evening. The summer sun kept things light for long into his watch, and by the time the skies darkened it was nearly time to wake Adrik for his shift.

The time alone gave him a chance to think things through—to make decisions about his future, and Leah's future, too. He wanted to get back to Colorado before the winter set in. He'd thought about that decision for a long time and knew that he had obligations to see to.

First, he would buy a stone for his father's grave. Then he would take Leah and return to Colorado to buy a stone for their mother's grave. After that, he hadn't figured out what was to be done. While Peter Colton had once offered him a job with his shipping firm, that didn't take care of what to do with Leah. Besides, no one had seen Peter Colton in some time. The offer of a job might not stand at this point.

Walking the perimeter of the claim was easy. It wasn't very big, and because other claims butted up against it, it was within easy walking distance of the neighbors. There were rumors among the creek folk that the Ivankov party had hit it big and thus the reason for the rotating guard duty. Adrik thought it best not to explain that their worries were related to the stolen sled and the unwelcome visits that followed.

Jacob had told Adrik about the stranger who'd come when Adrik had taken Gump to Dawson. The story hadn't set well with the older man. Apparently Karen hadn't told him about it, but then, she'd been caught up in the reunion with Miss

Grace. It was after that when Adrik started keeping a closer eye on the strangers who passed through the area. Gold brought out the thieving in men, he'd said, and Jacob could see that it was true. Why, just the day before there'd been a big fight among four brothers across the creek. There had been enough noise to raise the dead before it was all over. And all because the youngest brother felt the other three were cheating him out of his rightful share of gold.

Gold. How he hated the very word.

Jacob had seen his mother, sister, and father suffer because of gold and silver. He wanted to be done with it all—to be rid of such nonsense. He wanted to work at a regular job with regular pay and have a home.

A noise behind the cache caught his attention. Several of the dogs began to bark. Jacob immediately moved to the area, but found nothing amiss. *It might have been a bear,* he told himself.

Like many of their neighbors, Gump and Adrik had built the cache with two purposes in mind. One, the raised platform and enclosed storage area for their bulk food provided protection from wild animals. It also allowed them to store tools and other things that had become too plentiful in a house filled with seven people. Down below, Adrik and Gump had arranged a makeshift pen alongside the support posts for the cache. Here they quartered the dogs, while under the raised platform they found a perfect place to shelter the sled. Jacob felt certain that should anyone try to steal from them, the dogs would be the first to know, and from their apparent irritation, something had caused them to feel threatened.

The dogs quieted momentarily, then began letting up a wild howl, yipping toward the stand of trees behind them.

"Who's there?" Jacob called, leveling the Winchester. "Come out, or I'll start shooting."

"Whoa there, boy. I didn't save your life in Whitehorse just to get myself shot." A figure emerged from the shadows, and Jacob recognized the man as Cec Black-abee. Cec had indeed saved his life. It had been while Jacob was working in White-horse at Cec's saloon that Adrik had found him.

"What are you doing sneaking around our cache?" Jacob asked, lowering the rifle. "Don't you know it's foolish to threaten another man's supplies?"

The wiry old man stepped closer and Jacob could see he carried his own rifle and pack. Cec looked thinner to Jacob, maybe even sickly. He had a scruffy look to him that suggested it'd been months since he and a bath had exchanged pleas-antries.

"I wasn't so much threatenin' your supplies as trying to reclaim my own," Cec replied.

"What are you talking about?" Jacob asked warily. The old man was up to something underhanded. He could almost see it in his expression.

Licking his lips, Cec struck a casual stance as he leaned back against the trunk of a tree. "Well, it's like this, son, I came north after you left me. I figured to do me some gold pannin'."

"Thought you said there was more gold in whiskey than panning," Jacob interjected.

"I thought so, too. Maybe still think that, but I had a chance to make it big. Had me a partner who figured we could do well with a claim he'd discovered. He sold me half, and I sold off the bar to pay him his share. Then the double-crosser took off with our supplies. He stole our sled and dogs and left me for dead. If I hadn't been found by a Mountie on patrol, I probably would have froze to death."

"What's that have to do with us?"

The dogs continued to yip and howl at the intrusion, causing Jacob to motion Cec away from the pen. This quieted the dogs a bit. Jacob was surprised their barking hadn't roused Adrik by now. "I don't see what you need with us. Your ex-partner isn't here."

"No, I know that full well," Cec replied. "But he sold off our sled, and you folks ended up with it."

"The sled we bought was stolen . . ." Jacob stopped and looked Cec in the eye. "It was you, wasn't it? You're the one who took it."

"I did it, but it was mine to begin with. He had no right sellin' it off like that. He took all my gear and I figured he might have sold that to you as well."

Jacob shook his head. "No. The sled was all we bought."

"There weren't nothin' else? No sled box?"

Jacob wasn't about to tell Cec that they had a baby inside the house sleeping in the sled box, so he shrugged. "Could be, I don't remember too clearly. Adrik bought a lot of things in Dawson that day."

"Look, boy," Cec said, moving closer. The dogs didn't like the threat to Jacob and picked up barking again. Cec looked around him as if to make certain they were alone. "I'll give you a good amount of money if you'll help me get that sled box back."

"What's so important about it?"

"Call it sentimental value," Cec said, grinning.

"No," Jacob replied. "I don't want anything to do with you, and I certainly don't want anything to do with anything illegal."

"Now, hold off there, boy. Who said it were illegal?"

Jacob backed up a step in order to be able to better maneuver his rifle. "If it's not illegal, you won't mind coming inside to tell Adrik and Gump your story."

"We don't need to go bringin' them in on this. I thought you and me were friends. After all, I saved your life."

Jacob nodded. "Yeah, but Adrik paid you for your trouble."

"Look, I can make it worth your time if you just help me out."

"The truth, Cec. I want the truth."

The old man scratched his jaw and spit. "Well, guess it does no harm to tell you. That box held some important papers—a claim deed and a map. I need them."

"I never saw anything like that. The man who sold us the sled must have taken them out first," Jacob replied.

"Jacob! Jacob, what's going on out there?"

Jacob breathed a sigh of relief and turned toward the cabin. It was Adrik. "I'm out back, Adrik. Come quick."

Cec pushed Jacob forward, causing him to fall flat on his face. By the time he got to his feet, the older man was gone and Adrik was rounding the corner of the cabin.

"What's got those dogs all riled?"

"Cec Blackabee," Jacob answered. "Remember him? He's the guy who saved my life—the one you paid so you could take me out of Whitehorse?"

"Sure, I remember."

"Well, he was here. And get this, Adrik, he's the one who stole the sled. My guess is he's also the one who's been nosing around here these past months."

"Did he say what he wanted?"

"Yeah. He told me his partner had done him wrong. Said the sled and sled box were stolen along with his other supplies, and he wanted them back. That the box contained some papers—a claim. Adrik, he offered to make it worth my time if I helped him retrieve it."

"Did you let on that we had it?"

Jacob shook his head and picked up his rifle. "No."

"Well, that's good." Adrik looked toward the trees with a worried expression.

"I kind of doubt he'll come back tonight," Jacob said. "He seems more of a coward than I remember. I suggested he tell you about all this, but he wanted nothing to do with that."

Adrik turned back to face Jacob. "You did good, son. I'm proud of you."

Jacob warmed under his praise. Adrik had become a surrogate father to him, and he'd learned a great deal from the man. "So what do we do now?"

Adrik took one final glance back at the trees, then put his arm around Jacob and started for the house. "I think we'd better take another look at that sled box."

THE SLED BOX, however, proved to be nothing special at all. It was five simple, thin pieces of pine, nailed together with a hinged top to complete it. Adrik had taken the top off, in order to make a bed and play area for Andy.

"I can't figure why this would get anyone too excited," Adrik said, shaking his head.

"It's this place that gots 'em all messed up," Gump threw in. "The darkness made men mad, and long hours of light do no better. The vinter leaves 'em cold and hungry for the gold and a decent meal—it's more than enough to make a man foolish."

"I quite agree," Adrik said, forgetting about the box.

"That's vhy I'm gettin' out. Yes, sir," Gump said, scratching his chest. "This place vants to kill me. I von't let it. I think ve got to make our choices based on vhat's best for our own bodies and mind."

"I don't blame you, Gump. I'm just not sure what Karen and I will do. I'm not sure what direction God would take us now."

And he wasn't at all convinced that the answer would easily present itself. Adrik had prayed and prayed for a sign—something to show him whether he should sell out with Gump and return to Dawson or Skagway or whether he should stay put.

"I guess we can all sleep on it," Karen suggested. "You didn't sleep, Adrik. Why don't you go back to bed?"

Adrik looked at the clock. "It's already ten. I'll just relieve Jacob early and let him have some extra rest. I need the time to think and pray on what's to be done. Gump is right. We're going to make our choices soon."

Karen woke up earlier than usual and lay in the bunk, listening to the sounds of the morning. Reluctantly she pushed back her covers and crawled over the edge of the bunk. She wouldn't be sorry to leave the cabin and its lack of amenities. Every day was a challenge—whether it was for lack of a proper bathroom or need of a bigger kitchen with running water. She had never worked so hard to accomplish so little.

Moving around the room as quietly as she could, Karen smiled gratefully when she saw Gump had already stoked the fire in the stove. She'd have a quick time of it putting the breakfast on with the stove already hot and ready to go.

"Karen!" Grace called from her bed. Her note of alarm brought Karen quickly.

"What's wrong?" She looked at her bleary-eyed friend and then to the lethargic baby in her arms.

"It's Andy. He's burning with fever!"

Nothing struck fear in the heart of a mother more than to see her child ill. Karen didn't have to have children of her own to realize this. She remembered only too well, fussing and fretting over Grace's bouts of illness—and Karen had only been her governess.

"Well, we can wash him in a lukewarm bath and see if that brings the fever down," Karen suggested.

Grace nodded, but worry obviously consumed her. "He will be all right, won't he? I mean, I know he's never seemed like that strong of a baby, but surely this is just something simple."

Karen wanted to encourage her friend. "Maybe it's just teething. I remember my sister telling me her children all ran high fevers while teething."

Grace seemed to relax a bit. "Yes, maybe so."

Karen went around the room gathering the things they'd need for the tepid bath. "You go ahead and get him ready. It shouldn't take too long to heat up a bit of water."

Grace began unfastening the gown Andy slept in. Karen could see that her friend's hands were shaking from nervousness. *Lord, please give her strength to face this*, Karen prayed. They'd all heard of someone down the line who'd lost a child or a loved one. Grace had already endured the loss of her husband—it seemed unusually cruel for her to be forced to deal with the loss of a baby, as well.

Karen chided herself for such dark thoughts. There was no sense in imagining Andy dead and buried at this point, yet Karen couldn't help but worry over him. He was so precious. He offered them all the hope that one day—hopefully soon—

things would work out for good and that they'd all be safely back to the places they longed to be. Karen wasn't exactly sure where that place would be for her and Adrik, but she prayed daily for God to show her.

Grace brought Andy to the tub and waited until Karen nodded her approval of the temperature. He didn't so much as stir when they placed him in the water, and that was when Karen began to worry in earnest. She remembered Aunt Doris teaching her to make a tea from the white ashes of hickory or maple wood. It was an alkaline tea that, when taken several times daily in weak portions, seemed to reduce the fever. The only trouble was, she had no opportunity to go scouting for hickory or maple trees. She didn't even know if they had such trees in the Yukon.

"Oh, Karen, he's really sick. What are we going to do?" Grace looked up at Karen, fear eating away her usually cheerful countenance.

"I don't know. I'll talk to Adrik while you keep running the water over his body."

As Karen grabbed up her shawl, she heard Leah call from behind her, wanting to know what was wrong. She didn't wait to explain the matter but instead exited the cabin in search of her husband.

"Adrik?" she called out in the morning light. "Adrik?" She circled the cabin and found him in the back near the cache.

"What are you doing out here so early?" he asked. "Couldn't bear to be away from me?" He grinned and casually rested his rifle on his shoulder.

"Andy's sick, Adrik. Really sick. He's running a high fever, and when we put him in a tub of water, he didn't even open his eyes. I'm afraid he may die if we don't get help."

Adrik's expression quickly changed. "I'll come with you, and we'll see what's to be done."

Just then Grace's scream filled the air. Adrik and Karen ran for the front of the cabin, just as Leah came running from inside. "Hurry," she cried, "Andy is shaking all over the place."

Adrik stepped ahead of Karen, but Karen dogged his heels into the cabin. There in the tub, while Grace held him, Andy jerked in a strange, spasmodic rhythm.

"He just started doing this," Grace said, tears streaming down her face. "Oh, Karen, help me. Help him!"

By this time, Gump and Jacob were up and watching. Finally, Andy's body stilled just as suddenly as the spasms had begun. Grace looked to her son and lifted him in her arms. "He's still breathing," she sobbed.

Karen went forward and gently took the baby from her friend. "Adrik, we must get him to a doctor."

"I agree. I'll get the dogs hitched to the ore cart. We'll use it to pack Grace and the baby in. It won't be a fast journey, but they certainly can't walk all the way."

"I want to come with you," Karen said, wrapping the baby in a towel.

"Me too!" Leah declared.

Adrik nodded. "Jacob, you and Gump stay here and don't worry about mining. Just keep an eye on things. I'll take them down to Gold Bottom. That's less than two miles. There's a doc who shares a claim with his brother. He ought to be able to help us."

But the doctor had already returned to Dawson, the brother told them when they arrived some time later. They were encouraged to travel on toward Dawson with the possibility of another doctor who had come north for gold, taking up residency somewhere to the west of Last Chance Creek.

Karen knew the distance was considerable, but there was really no other choice. Adrik pushed out, urging the dogs to pick up the pace. By the time they reached Last Chance, more than ten miles away, Karen was completely spent. She knew they'd have to rest for a time and was relieved when Adrik suggested the same.

Andy's fever remained high and he refused all attempts by Grace to nurse him. His lethargic state terrified the group. There was no sense to it.

Once the dogs had rested a few hours, Adrik woke Karen and Leah and told them they'd have to push on. Grace felt bad for being the only one to ride in the cart with Andy.

"There isn't room for all of us," Karen said, trying to reassure her, "and you need to keep Andy quiet. You'll also need your strength to deal with his illness."

"Karen, will you please pray?"

Karen nodded and smiled. "I already am."

They seemed to travel forever, but without a doctor to be found along the claims on Hunker Creek, they had no choice but to head on to the Klondike River and Dawson. The minutes seemed to drag by, and Karen thought she might very well collapse from the pace they kept. Adrik and the dogs seemed hardly winded, but Leah wasn't doing well. Finally Karen suggested that there might be enough room for Leah to sit with Grace in the cart, if both ladies swung their legs out over the sides. It was a rather improper display, but it worked and the proprieties were forgotten.

Karen tried to focus on praying while she walked and jogged to keep up with the cart. The path was impossible in some places, with mud and debris left behind after the swollen creeks had receded back to their banks. In other places, the path was well-worn and fairly easy to navigate, but Karen was getting more tired by the minute.

As they drew nearer civilization—although she used that term quite loosely—

Karen was saddened by the state of the land. The once lush forests, full of pines and spruce and floored with thick vegetation, had been stripped of its glory. Denuded land was a stark reminder that gold came at a high price.

The natives of the area had been pushed out and away from the wealth of the rivers of gold. Karen felt bad for the way she'd seen the local natives treated. It was the same for the Tlingit and other tribes. The stampeders had come with a hunger for that which had never belonged to them. It didn't matter that a native had found the gold in the first place—it only mattered that others could come and take it away.

Karen knew her father would have hated the changes in the land. He would have mourned the passing of the beauty and would have been enraged at the treatment of the Indian people. He had loved his Tlingit brothers and sisters— had given his life in service to them. He wouldn't be pleased that Karen was a part of this maddening rush.

She wasn't pleased with herself. Seeing how people acted around her—how they fought each other for a slice of bread, how they murdered and stole from one another, all in order to have a little bit more than their neighbor. It was a sickness, a fever—every bit as deadly as Andy's.

God forgive us, Karen prayed. She knew her husband was considering what they should do for their future, but she was already coming to some of her own conclusions. She'd speak to Adrik as soon as the opportunity presented itself.

They arrived in Dawson in the late afternoon of the second day. Adrik quickly guided the team to the hospital. Karen was amazed at how dead the town seemed. There had once been people overflowing the streets and businesses, but things appeared oddly calm now. Only a few dozen souls ventured out as the group made their way through the town.

Adrik helped Grace from the cart, leaving Karen and Leah to see to each other. Karen didn't mind. She knew her husband was far more concerned for the deathly-ill baby. Karen and Leah joined hands as they followed Adrik and Grace into the hospital.

"Do you think he'll die?" Leah asked. Her tone suggested that she was near to tears.

"It's in God's hands," Karen said softly. "We've certainly done everything possible by bringing him here."

"What if the doctors can't help him?"

"I don't know," Karen said sadly. She knew Grace's entire life was caught up in that little boy. If he were to die, Grace would most likely follow him into the grave, a victim of a broken heart.

"He can't die, Karen. He just can't." Leah broke into sobs and buried her face against Karen.

Karen didn't know what to say to the child, for she felt the same way. Andrew had to live. He had to live so that Grace would have the strength to go on. He had to live so that Peter would come to them and take his family to the safety of their home far away. And that was really what Karen wanted for Grace, in spite of the pain it brought to think of being separated, perhaps forever.

The doctor refused to let anyone accompany Andy, save Grace. He directed the rest of the group to wait outside. Adrik appeared ready to argue with him, but Karen gently touched his arm and smiled.

"We can spend the time in prayer," she suggested.

And they did just that, waiting for hours on end to hear from the doctor as to what was wrong with the tiny boy. As time passed, Karen despaired of the news being good and finally excused herself from the group.

"I need to be alone for a few minutes. I shouldn't be long," she told Adrik. Walking out into the evening air, Karen marveled at the crisp, sweet scent—so different from the smells that permeated the hospital.

For several minutes she walked down the road, not at all certain where she was headed. She really had no place in particular to go, but she wanted to be away from the hospital so that she could clear her head.

"Father, we need a miracle," she prayed in a whisper. "Please heal Andy and give Grace the strength she needs to endure."

Mindless of her aching feet and sore muscles, Karen continued her walking prayer time. She had just about decided to head back to the hospital, when she spotted a woman who looked remarkably like Miranda Colton. From the distance Karen wasn't at all certain that it was Miranda, so she picked up her pace. A surge of hope coursed through her. Perhaps Miranda hadn't died.

Unable to keep up the rapid speed, Karen called out. "Miranda!"

The woman turned instantly, and then it was clear. It was Miranda! Karen hurried forward, calling her name again. "Miranda! Oh, it is you!"

Miranda put her hand to her mouth and looked as though she'd been robbed of her air.

Karen reached her and embraced her hard. "Oh, we thought you were dead."

"Is it really you?" Miranda asked softly. "I've looked so long and hard for you."

Karen pulled back and saw the tears in Miranda's eyes. "It's me. It's really me."

"We've been searching for you. We just now came back to town to gather supplies and were planning to head out again tomorrow," Miranda replied. "Did you see the flyer? Is that how you found me?"

"What flyer?" Karen questioned. "We, too, just arrived in town. Oh, Miranda, you don't know the situation at all. There's a problem. Grace needs you now, more than ever. She had her baby. It's a little boy and his name is Andrew."

"I know. I met up with Dr. Brummel. He apparently let her stay on with him for a time."

Karen nodded. "Yes. Yes, he did. Well, Andy is sick. He's at the hospital right now. You must come and help Grace stay strong. Oh, she'll be so happy to see you."

"But wait, we can't go without Peter," Miranda said, surprising Karen with her matter-of-fact statement.

"Peter is here?"

"Yes. He's been searching for Grace for months. He was beginning to think he'd never find them."

"So he knows about the baby?" Karen questioned.

"Yes. He knows. Come with me. I'll take you to him."

———

"Vell, I suggest five-hour shifts," Gump said as Jacob prepared to go out on watch.

"Five hours?"

"Ja, that would be enough time to sleep a bit and then be up to keep vatch."

Jacob nodded. "I think you're right. I'll wake you in five hours, then." He headed for the door, then realized he'd forgotten his rifle. "I guess it won't do me much good to go out on guard duty without a weapon."

"Ja, you might need it."

A knock sounded at the door. Gump and Jacob exchanged looks.

"Who could that be?" Jacob questioned. "You don't suppose they're back already."

"Nah, they vould just come in," Gump replied, moving to the door.

Jacob turned back to take up his gun as the urgent knock sounded again. Without picking up his rifle, he turned to see who it was as Gump opened the door.

In the blink of an eye, a gun fired straight into Gump's chest, sending the old man staggering backward. Jacob forgot what he was doing and rushed for the smoking barrel that was still stuck inside the door. The stranger cocked the rifle to fire again.

"What do you think you're doing?" Jacob cried out, grabbing the barrel.

Cec Blackabee was pulled into the cabin by the action. The shock of his appearance caused Jacob to hesitate for just a moment. It was a moment that gave Cec the edge. Pushing Jacob backward, Cec tried to free his rifle from Jacob's hold. It did no good, however. Jacob wasn't about to let Cec have the upper hand.

The wiry man threw his weight onto Jacob, wrestling him to the ground, the gun wedged neatly between them.

"I figured if money wouldn't bring you over to my way of thinkin'," Cec growled as they fought, "fear might. I'd just as soon blow off your head as to look at you."

"You'll have to kill me before I'll let you get away with this," Jacob spat, pushing Cec off of him. Still holding on to the rifle, Jacob struggled to his feet, careful to keep the barrel pointed away from him.

The gun exploded again, the bullet narrowly missing Jacob's face. "I don't mind killin' you, boy. You've been nothin' but trouble to me. I ain't had much luck since I found you half drowned." Cec pushed Jacob off balance and struggled to cock the rifle one more time. Lowering the gun directly at Jacob, Cec smiled maliciously. "You ain't got a prayer, boy."

Before Cec could squeeze the trigger, Jacob heard someone yell.

"It's the Lindquist cabin!"

Cec turned his head just a bit, as if to ascertain where the voices were coming from. Jacob let his rage direct him. He flew across the distance to Cec and fought with all his might to wrench the gun from his hand.

Another shot fired, and by this time they could hear voices growing louder. Cec dropped his hold on the gun and darted through the smoky room and out the door before Jacob could stop him. Standing there, the rifle in his hand, Jacob stared dumbly at the door, then turned to where Gump lay bleeding on the floor.

"Hold it right there!" a man's deep voice called out.

"Somebody grab him, he's killed the old man!" another man yelled.

Jacob turned just as two men grabbed hold of him, while a third firmly planted his fist in Jacob's face.

"Ride for the Mounties," one of the men commanded. "This boy just killed the old man."

"No doubt for his gold," someone muttered.

"No!" Jacob tried to yell, but the word came out very softly. "I didn't do it. There was someone else."

"I don't see no one else," the man replied. "Just you and the gun and the dead body. That's enough proof for me."

⊣ C H A P T E R   T W E N T Y - F I V E ⊢

GRACE COLTON SAT BESIDE the bed of her desperately ill son. She could find no reason in her mind or heart for why God would allow such a horrible thing to happen. Andy looked so small, so pale.

She touched him gently, stroking his cheek, so downy soft. She wondered how any mother ever found the strength to say good-bye to her child. Grace thought of her own mother and the boy she had lost. Grace had grown up without siblings—rather lonely and isolated. Her mother would rarely talk about her firstborn son, and Grace never really knew much about him, other than the devastating effect of his death.

He can't die, Lord, she prayed. *I can't bear the thought of losing him. He's my baby—my son. I've seen so much death and destruction—sorrow and pain. I just can't bear to see anymore.* She crumbled to her knees. *Please, God, hear my prayer. Please spare the life of my child.*

Grace sobbed into her hands. *Don't leave me here alone, God. Please don't leave me here alone.*

Someone touched her shoulder. At first Grace thought it was the doctor. Using the back of her sleeve, she dried her eyes and tried hard to square her shoulders. Getting to her feet with the man's help, Grace turned, only to realize the man was her husband.

"Peter." She spoke the name almost reverently. "Oh, Peter."

It had been well over a year since she'd seen him, but the time instantly fell away with the look of love in his expression. Grace thought perhaps it was a dream, or that she had gone mad, but either way, so long as he was there at her side, she didn't care.

She collapsed in his arms and buried her face against the once familiar chest. He smelled of fresh lye soap and hair tonic. As he tightened his hold on her, Grace thought she heard him draw a ragged breath. She pulled back just enough to see that he, too, was crying.

"I thought you were dead," he said.

Grace reached up her hand to touch his face. "Why would you think that?"

"Because the letter that came from the Mounted Police said it was you and not Miranda who fell overboard on Lake Laberge."

Grace shook her head. "How could that be?"

"I don't know, but I thank God you are safe and alive. You have no idea the hours I mourned your passing. The hours I pleaded with God for your return are too numerous to count. And now, here you are."

"It must have been a terrible shock to learn of Miranda," she said softly. She stroked his jaw, feeling the stubble of beard beneath her fingers. He looked so much older—he looked exhausted and spent. She feared he might even be sick. "I'm sorry about your sister."

"She's alive, Grace. There's no other way to tell you than to just come out with it. She's down the hall speaking with Karen at this very moment."

Grace let go of her husband, her voice catching in her throat. "She . . . she . . ."

Peter nodded, holding on to her shoulders. "She's alive. Apparently she washed up on the shore, and Indians found her. She was treated and cared for by an Englishman and his housekeeper. Her health was restored, and she came here to look for you and the others."

"I can't believe it. Oh, Peter, I think I need to sit down." Grace felt her vision blur and her head grow light. "I think I might very well faint."

Peter led her to a chair, but then instead of having her sit on it, he sat down himself and pulled her onto his lap. Cradling her there like a child, he held her tight. "You're as thin as a rail," he whispered, and then added, "I can't believe you're here and alive. I think of how things might have been—but I pushed it away, all because of my stubborn refusal to yield to God what was rightfully His."

Grace tried to clear her mind, but whenever she lifted her head the dizziness returned. She wanted to ask Peter a million questions but instead remained quiet. Perhaps this wasn't the time or place. For now, she could just be grateful he had come to her.

As if knowing what she needed to hear, however, Peter continued. "I cannot say the way was easy. Paxton continued to hound and plague me. I feared him more than I feared God or anyone else. He seemed to have a power to destroy my hope."

Grace nodded with a shudder, knowing only too well how Martin Paxton could be. She hoped she would never see the man again.

"In the course of my journey, God put me together with a great man named Jonas Campbell. Jonas helped me to see and understand what you'd been trying to tell me."

Grace raised up and looked at her husband. A flicker of hope warmed her heart as she met his loving gaze. "What are you saying?"

"I'm saying I'm sorry for the pain and misery I caused you—caused us. I'm saying I was wrong and that I hurt so many people because of that wrong attitude. I'm begging you to forgive me and take me back, because frankly, I don't know how to go on living without you." He paused and Grace thought he had never looked so handsome as he did in this vulnerable, apologetic state. "And I'm saying that I learned the truth of God for myself and gave my heart over to Christ."

"Oh, Peter," Grace whispered. She touched his face very gently and wiped away the tears that streamed down his cheeks. "God is so good. So faithful."

"Then you'll forgive me? Forgive me for all the ugly words, for the way I treated you?"

"I forgave you the moment they caused me pain. I love you, Peter. That didn't die in the wake of the battle, it was only bruised a bit."

She fought back her light-headedness to get to her feet. "Come here. I have someone you must meet."

Peter stood with her and went to the bed. "This is our son, Andrew. He's very sick and I don't know what the future holds in store for him. He was born last January here in Dawson."

"I know," Peter said, reaching out to touch their son. "Karen has told me all about him. He's beautiful, Grace. Thank you."

"The doctor isn't certain what's wrong. He fears it might be pneumonia or bronchitis. He says horrible things like, '*Such diseases are just stepping-stones to consumption.*' Imagine telling a mother that her child might well develop consumption. It seems most cruel."

"I'm sure he's not trying to be unreasonably macabre. Perhaps he's merely a realist. Maybe he just doesn't want you to have false hope. Maybe he doesn't know our hope is founded in God, and therefore is never false."

"I thought he might . . . might die . . . without you ever getting to see him," Grace said, stumbling on her words.

"He's a Colton. He's strong." Peter turned her in his arms. "But even if he isn't strong enough, God is. Oh, Grace, I see that now. I despaired during my search for you, feeling that maybe God was punishing me. For so long I believed you dead—your mother believes it, too."

"Oh, poor Mama!" Grace said, putting her hand to her mouth. The awfulness of the truth was settling in on her.

"We'll get a letter off to her as soon as we can," Peter promised. "There's so much more you don't know. Things that I must say, that you must know."

"What could possibly matter in light of all that you've already told me?"

Peter's expression grew very serious. "Paxton is dead. He's no longer a threat to us. He tried to make me believe you wanted a divorce. He knew things about our last fight that convinced me of his knowledge. But on the other hand, a part of me knew you would never give yourself over to him."

"He promised to return your company if I did," Grace said, shaking her head. The memory seemed as if it had taken place a million years ago.

"When I headed back to San Francisco after he told me you were dead, I found him on the same ship. There was an explosion and the ship went down. Paxton tried to leave me stranded on board, but instead, he was killed."

"Oh, the whole thing sounds just awful. Were you hurt?"

"Yes, but I healed eventually. Now Colton Shipping has been returned to the Coltons, and there is one more aspect of this story that you must know. You are a wealthy woman."

"What?" Grace could hardly believe she had understood him correctly. "For a moment I thought you said I was wealthy."

"I did," Peter said, reaching out to touch her face. "Your father protected most of his holdings by shifting everything into a trust for you. Paxton didn't find this out until your father was nearly bankrupt. When he realized he had been duped, he continued to threaten your father—promising to tell your mother and you about the affair. It's the reason Paxton suddenly showed up as your betrothed.

"When you ran away, your mother learned the truth, and Paxton was further frustrated to realize that she didn't care. She loved your father and stood by him, putting the past behind her. Realizing he'd been further thwarted, Paxton decided that the only way to get what he wanted was to go after you and force the marriage. He had documents forged to falsely proclaim his guardianship over you, then headed to Alaska once he knew where you were."

"It all makes sense now," Grace said. "But why didn't he follow me up here, if it was that important to him?"

"At first, he had no clue as to where you had gone. Then when he knew for sure you'd gone north, my guess is he was torn between whether to follow you himself or send someone after you. He was making a great deal of money in Skagway, plus he had Colton Shipping to think about. When the message came that you'd been killed, Paxton finally realized there was no hope of attaining what he'd worked so long and hard to have."

"That must have just about killed him," Grace said, glad that Paxton would have known the taste of defeat because of her. The man had been her family's undoing, and it made her feel better to know that he had been defeated.

"I'm glad he's dead," she said without thinking. "God forgive me if that is wrong, but the man was so horrible to me—to my loved ones. I feared that he'd find out about Andy and try to steal him away. I worried that he'd come here to Dawson and threaten our lives. I forgive him—I honestly do—but I'm glad it's over. I've had very little peace because of that man."

"You've had very little peace because of me as well, but I hope to remedy that. I'm not that same man, Grace. God has broken me, and I'm much better for it."

Grace wrapped her arms around Peter. "I love you so very much. I couldn't bear to lose you—again."

"You'll never lose me, darling," he whispered against her ear. "Never."

Just then Andy's faint cry could be heard. Grace nearly pushed Peter away at the sound. "Listen!"

She looked at her son and found his eyes open. His fussing was like music to her ears. Reaching out, Grace touched his forehead. The fever had broken—his skin was cool to her touch.

"Oh, Peter, he's better. This is the first time he's rallied since taking ill. Oh, thank you, God!"

Peter reached down to touch Andy's cheek. The baby began to cry a little harder at the appearance of this stranger. Grace quickly lifted her son, holding him tenderly to her breast. Andy immediately began rooting—seeming suddenly eager to nurse.

"I'd say he's hungry." Peter touched his head. "That must be a good sign."

"I'm sure it is. Oh, I'm sure it is!"

"I heard a baby's cry," Karen said, coming into the room. "Was it Andy? How is he doing?"

Miranda followed Karen and stood at the door, looking stunned. Grace felt as though she were in a dream. Karen moved beside Grace and reached out to touch Andy.

"The fever's gone," she announced.

Grace nodded. "I can scarcely believe what God has done." She felt the dizziness return to her head. "Would you please hold Andy for a moment? I'm feeling rather faint."

Karen quickly took the baby, while Peter took hold of Grace. Miranda came to her side and helped her to the chair.

"I thought you were dead," Grace whispered, tears falling anew. "I thought I'd lost my sister forever."

"I feared the same fate might well have happened to the rest of you," Miranda admitted. "I searched and searched but couldn't seem to make any headway. I couldn't find any of you. I found Crispin several months ago and he told me you were all well the last time he'd seen you. He died shortly after that, but he accepted Jesus as his Savior before he died."

"That's a great comfort," Grace said, remembering Crispin's gentle treatment of her while she labored to give birth to Andy. "I will always be fond of the man. He helped Leah deliver Andy, and for that I shall be eternally grateful. May he know peace now."

"I'm sure he does. His countenance was quite peaceful when he passed. I wish he could have been here to see us all reunited. I'm so happy, I can scarce take it in."

Grace embraced her sister-in-law with tears of joy, her heart overflowing with happiness. The lost was found and the prodigal had come home. The sick had been healed and the blessings of God's abundance flowed over them all like warm summer rain. All was right with the world once again.

―――――

"But I'm telling you, I didn't kill Gump," Jacob protested to the police officer. "He was a good friend. I wouldn't have done something like that. I had no reason."

The officer seemed unimpressed. "Did you kill Mr. Lindquist for his gold?"

"No!" Jacob declared, certain that if he spoke the truth they'd release him.

"So then did you kill him because of a disagreement?"

"I'm telling you, I didn't kill him."

The man looked at Jacob, his expression clearly betraying his disbelief in Jacob's statement. "You say a man came to the door and shot Mr. Lindquist through the heart. After this, you wrestled the gun away from him and the man fled before anyone else could come to the scene."

"That's right. The man's name is Cec Blackabee. He admitted to stealing our sled and wanted to know if we had some of his other possessions. He figured to strong-arm his way in and take them by force."

"I see," the Mountie replied. "Then how is it that no one else saw the man leave the cabin? Upon hearing the shots fired, your neighbors came to investigate. No one saw another man leave the scene."

Jacob felt sickened by the events of the past few days. He had no idea how to make the truth any more clear. This man believed him to have murdered Gump. The poor old man was barely gone and they wanted to blame Jacob for the death.

"I'm telling you the truth," Jacob said, sitting back down on a bench in his cell. "I didn't kill Gump Lindquist. I didn't kill anybody."

―――――

Peter and Grace lay entwined in each other's arms that night. Sharing his bed with Grace for the first time in over a year, Peter marveled at how very right it felt. With her brown-black hair spread out upon the pillow, her chocolate-colored eyes wide, looking at him with evident adoration, Peter had never been happier.

"I thought I'd lost you forever," he whispered.

"I felt the same when you didn't come for me," Grace murmured.

"I was such a fool." He reached out and touched her cheek, then trailed his fingers down her neck. "I can't believe I risked letting you get away."

"We were both wrong—immature and inconsiderate."

"No. You were perfect," he said, shaking his head. "You only stood up for what you believed."

"Yes, but I belittled you at the same time," she admitted. "Not only that, I went behind your back to accomplish my will."

"Well, it's behind us now. We have each other and we have a son." Peter smiled at Grace's contented expression. "I can scarcely believe it."

"I know. I felt the same way for so long. When I was carrying Andy, it was like something out of a fairy tale. I couldn't believe I would really bear a child—hold him and see him as flesh and blood."

"The doctor sounded very confident of his recovery," Peter whispered, pressing his lips against the hollow of her neck.

"Yes," she half whispered, half moaned.

Peter didn't know if she was replying to his comment or his kiss. He decided not to question it and instead turned out the light.

SEPTEMBER CAME UPON DAWSON with a threat of colder days to come. Miranda knew that her brother and sister-in-law were securing passage to return to California before the rivers froze and made travel a much greater risk. With Andy to think about, she knew they would take no chances.

Her heart ached at the thought of their leaving. She so enjoyed their company. Andy had regained his health, and they had taken up rooms on the floor above hers and Teddy's. It was wonderful having family so close after so many months of not knowing where they were or even if they were still alive.

Peter had seen to it that a letter was taken out in the first available mail packet. He'd included a note from Miranda to assure their parents that all was well. Miranda told her mother about Teddy and how very much in love she was with her Englishman. Still, she longed to see her mother and father—to know they were well and that her father had recovered from his heart attack.

Peter had told her about the recovery of the shipping firm. Miranda was certain that had to have been a boost to her father's health. He loved his ships and the sea, but most of all, he needed to know that his family was cared for.

Miranda looked at her reflection in the mirror. Brushing through her long brown hair, she couldn't help but think how the trip and all that had happened to her had changed her. She didn't even look like the same youthful girl she had once been. A married woman stood in her place now.

Turning to examine her figure, Miranda studied the flow of her quilted skirt. She had lost some weight, there was no denying that, but it was a pleasant sort of thing. Her waist appeared quite small, and her hips were pleasingly curved beneath the muted green-and-black print skirt. The pin-tucked white shirtwaist with its voluminous sleeves was another recent gift from Teddy. He loved to see her dressed up in pretty things and often spoke of the day when they would go to Europe together and he would buy her a wardrobe in Paris.

As if thinking of him had brought him to her, Teddy opened the door to their suite, wrestling a box marked FRAGILE.

"What's that?" Miranda questioned. She put down her brush, leaving her hair down, and turned to see what the contents might be.

"It's the shipment of herbs I ordered from England. I hope they were able to send everything." He acted giddy, like a child at Christmas.

Miranda crossed the room and pushed back the heavy green drapes in order to let in more light for better viewing. Teddy put the box on the table and pried off the top. He reached into the straw-packed box and began pulling jars and brown paper packages from within.

"Ah," he said, holding up a jar. "*Malva moschata*—musk mallow. This is a wonderful herb. It is used to reduce inflammation." He set the jar aside and unwrapped one of the packages. "This is *Pterocarpus santalinus* or red sandalwood—for treating fevers, inflammation, even scorpion stings. It comes to us all the way from India."

"How fascinating," Miranda said, catching Teddy's excitement. "What else is in there?"

Teddy pulled out another bottle. Miranda could read the label for herself. "*Mandragora officinarum.*"

Teddy nodded. "Mandrake. Very deadly if not used in the correct proportions. But very effective as an anesthetic for surgery if used properly. You can put a person to sleep quite effectively with this, but it must be handled correctly."

"How wonderful that God gave us so many needful things in the form of wild flowers and other vegetation. These herbs will be so very beneficial to the doctors up here."

"That is the idea. One doctor told me how hard it was to get shipments on a regular basis. I offered to see what I could do, and here we are. I say, not a bad catch."

Miranda laughed. "I should say not."

Teddy finished arranging the bottles and packages on the table, then set the crate aside. "I'll package up some of these and have you take them over to the hospital."

Miranda smiled. He was such a generous man. He had so much to offer and plenty of material wealth to share. Teddy Davenport was, in her estimation, a rare and wonderful find in a world of selfishness, greed, and ambition.

"What are you smiling at?" Teddy questioned as he looked up and caught her expression.

"I was just thinking nice thoughts about you, that's all."

He cocked his head to one side and raised a brow. "Oh, and what might those thoughts include?"

"I was thinking of how generous you are—what a wonderful giving man you are, and how so many people have benefited from your kindness."

"I'm doing no less than most would if they had the means."

"You and I both know that isn't true," Miranda replied. "This place is full of people who have gold dust a plenty, so much that it dusts their hair and sticks under their nails. They don't care about anyone but themselves. They think only of the gold."

Teddy pulled on his glasses and shrugged. "I suppose you are correct. There is a sickness among many of the souls here. Gambling and drinking thrive as the men seek to lose themselves and their past. Greed causes a man to do things he might never consider otherwise."

"I know that well enough." Miranda took a seat at the table and adjusted her quilted skirt. She was grateful for the warmth as September had turned cold and rainy. Today the sun had dawned bright and the skies were clear, but there was a taste of rain in the air, and Miranda knew that by evening they very well might be forced to endure yet another damp night.

"Oh, I nearly forgot. We're having dinner with your brother and sister-in-law this evening. Karen has agreed to keep the baby, so it will be just the four of us."

"I thought Adrik had said they had to return to the claim. He is upset they've already stayed so long in Dawson. If it weren't for those two sick sled dogs, I know they would have headed back to the claim the moment Andy recovered."

"Yes, Karen said he was quite upset at the delay of time. Apparently Mr. Lindquist desires to leave the Yukon and will need to pack out his things and reach Dawson in time to catch a steamer south." He continued looking over his herbs as he spoke. "I believe they plan to leave in the morning. They hope to reach the claim in a couple of days."

"Have they decided what they're going to do? I mean, are they staying through the winter?" Miranda asked hopefully.

"I don't believe so. When I spoke to Adrik he implied that they might be on the same steamer Mr. Lindquist would take south. Apparently there is some thought of their returning to Dyea. It seems Adrik has some distant relationship to the Tlingit Indians."

"Well, I shall be sorry to see them go," Miranda admitted. She tried to keep the worry from her voice, but in truth, she couldn't help but wonder how life would be once her friends returned to their various homes.

She lifted her face and found Teddy studying her. "Do you regret marrying me?" he asked.

The question completely stunned her. "Not at all. Why would you ever ask such a thing?"

He put down the bottle he'd been toying with and came to where she was sitting. Kneeling beside her, Teddy took hold of her hand. "I'm quite capable of dealing with the truth. If you are having regrets, I believe we should discuss it."

"My regrets have nothing to do with you," Miranda said, reaching out with her free hand. She gently touched Teddy's cheek. "I love you. I'm very happy to be your wife."

His worried expression seemed to relax just a bit. "But I hear a kind of longing in your voice."

Miranda smiled. "Oh, Teddy. You truly have learned to listen and to care. It blesses my heart in a way that I can never quite explain. No, the longing I have is simply one to see my mother and father. I know my brother will journey home and they will all be reunited. I suppose I miss them more than I realized. Seeing Peter and Grace, and knowing they will be a part of that life—well, I can't help but be reminded of my past."

"It's probably good we're having this discussion," Teddy said. "I had wondered what you would like to do with our future."

"Whatever you want is fine with me. My life is with you, and I'm not sorry for that. I want to help you with your book, if you desire to continue working with it. I want to see your homeland and to know the things that were precious to you as a child. As long as you are by my side, I don't care where we go or what we do. I only desire that we serve God as we do it."

"I am in complete agreement with that. The book, while important to me, is no longer my first priority. You are."

Miranda shook her head. "No, don't put me there. Put God there. If God is your priority, then I know I will be cared for."

"Of course, He is above all," Teddy agreed. "I just wanted you to know that I desire to make you happy."

"Oh, but you have, Teddy. You have." Miranda slid from the chair and knelt beside her husband. Embracing him tenderly, she kissed him gently upon the lips. "Since we're here," she murmured, "perhaps it would be most fitting if we were to pray together for guidance."

———————

"I suppose," Peter Colton began, "it shall be a long time before we see you again." He had shared a luxurious dinner of baked chicken and wild rice with his wife and sister and brother-in-law. Although a cold rain pelted the glass of the hotel dining room in a steady pulsating beat, he felt warmer and more content than he had in months. Maybe even years.

Teddy spoke up before Miranda could answer. "It might well be sooner than you think. Miranda and I have agreed that a trip to spend time with your mother and father would be good for both of us. I have work to complete here, but it's nothing that can't wait."

"Truly?" Grace questioned, leaning forward. "Will you travel with us?"

"No," Miranda said, looking with an endearing expression toward her husband. "We need a bit more time. Most likely we'd go to California in the spring."

"Oh, how exciting," Grace said, reaching over to squeeze Peter's hand. "Isn't that wonderful!"

"It is good news," Peter agreed. He watched his sister, seeing in her a confidence and strength that he had not recognized before.

"That's not all," Miranda said, her voice charged with energy. "After California, we're going to travel across America and then on to England. Teddy wants to show me all the wonderful things about his homeland."

"It's amazing what God has done in just a short while," Peter declared. "I look at the man I was just two short years ago—even a year ago—and I'm overwhelmed. God's hand was on me even then, but I couldn't see the need for His guidance. I was certain I knew where I was headed and how to get there. It took Grace to show me where I was in error."

"And grace to bring you beyond those errors into forgiveness and new life," Teddy said.

Peter chuckled at his brother-in-law's play on words. "Exactly," he agreed. He turned to his sister. "You've picked a good man for yourself, Miranda. I could never have done as well for you." Miranda beamed under his praise, and Peter knew just how important his words were to her.

An hour later, Peter and Grace left Teddy and Miranda on the second floor of their hotel and walked to the third floor where Adrik and Karen were caring for their son.

Knocking on the door, Peter and Grace were met by Leah Barringer's animated smile. "Andy's been trying to walk again!" she exclaimed.

"How marvelous. He's so early at this," Grace said, taking her son in hand. Andy clapped his hands together, then smacked his hands up against his mother's face. "You'd never guess he'd been sick so recently."

"Was the doctor ever able to tell you what was wrong?" Karen asked.

"No," Grace replied, hugging her son close. "I suppose it was just one of those things that we shall never understand."

"I think I understand it well enough," Peter said, looking at his son in amazement. He still had a hard time believing he was a father. "Andy's illness brought you all back to Dawson and to me."

"True enough," Adrik admitted.

"So when are you heading back to your claim?" Peter asked.

Adrik looked to Karen then back to Peter and Grace. "Well, that's what we needed to tell you. We're leaving in the morning. We know you're heading home soon, but we just can't stay. It's already been two weeks, and I'm sure Gump and Jacob are just about beside themselves."

"I understand. It looks to me like this town is emptying out rather quickly."

Adrik nodded. "That's for sure. I'd say the heyday of gold in the Klondike is pretty much over. There will be those who stay on and make a living for themselves, but I don't think you'll see Dawson sporting a population of thirty or forty thousand ever again."

"The steamers on the Yukon reminded me of when we first came to Alaska," Grace admitted. "They were so full of people a person could scarcely walk the deck."

"They're all heading to Nome—that's where the most recent gold strikes have been found. And once again they're spinning stories of how a man can just pick the gold nuggets up off the ground. Never mind that they didn't find that story to be true in Dawson. They're just hungry for the gold."

"It's so sad," Karen spoke up. "So many people are struggling to find something they think will make them happy, and they don't even realize that what's missing in their life is Jesus."

Peter nodded. "That's true. I know that for myself." He smiled at Grace and hugged her close. "I'm going to miss our talks. You and Adrik have been good friends to us."

Karen moved closer and Peter saw her dab tears from her eyes. He thought of how little he had cared for her when they'd first met. She was too independent, and he felt she poorly influenced Grace. Now he admired her very much and felt proud to call her his friend.

"You will always be welcome in our home," Peter said.

"And you in ours," Adrik replied.

Karen quickly agreed. "Oh yes. Do come back and see us. We plan to head to Dyea soon, but first we have to get Gump and Jacob and sell the claim."

"Jacob wants to get a job with your shipping company," Leah threw in.

"You tell him anytime he wants a job, it's his," Peter assured.

Andy began to fuss and Grace shifted him in her arms. "I think it's time we put this little fellow to bed."

"I suppose this is good-bye," Karen said, coming to embrace Grace. "I can hardly bear it, but I know it's for the best." They hugged each other tightly, causing Andy to howl in protest.

"Adrik, thank you. Thank you for caring for Grace when I was too blind and too selfish to do so myself." Peter looked to the big man and smiled. "God knew exactly who to send into my life and into the lives of my loved ones. I'm proud to call you friend."

"That goes the same for me," Adrik replied, clapping Peter on the back.

———————

The day of Peter, Grace, and Andy's departure was a brilliant sunny autumn day. The crisp air felt exhilarating rather than cold, and Miranda was grateful for that as she prepared to bid her brother good-bye.

"I'm so glad you and Grace are back together," Miranda whispered as she hugged Peter's neck.

Peter pulled away and winked. "And I'm glad Teddy took you off my hands."

Miranda nudged him playfully. "You will have your hands plenty full with that boy of yours. Just look at him. He's all excited about the trip."

Their gazes went to the baby who squealed with delight at the sights and sounds of the steamer *City of Topeka*.

"He will no doubt run me ragged, but what a pleasure," Peter insisted.

Miranda felt her longing for home rise with every minute that passed. When the final boarding call was given, Miranda went to Grace and embraced both her and the baby. She tried not to cry, but the tears came just the same. "I shall miss you so very much."

Grace nodded, tears forming in her eyes as well. "I could never have made it without you. When I thought I'd lost you on the lake, my heart nearly stopped. You have been closer and dearer than any sister."

"Oh, I will come for a visit as soon as I can," Miranda promised. She kissed Grace's cheek, then turned to do the same for Andy. "You be a good baby," she admonished, rubbing his rosy cheek.

Teddy came up behind her and put his arm around her. "We shall journey to see you soon," he told Peter.

"You do that. I know Mother will want to meet the man who has so clearly captured Miranda's heart."

Miranda looked up to Teddy with her tear-filled eyes. "He has done exactly that," she agreed. "He's taken my heart captive, as well as my mind." She looked to her brother. "I can speak more botanical Latin than a girl has a right to know."

They laughed and Teddy squeezed her close. "She makes a perfect assistant. But more than that, she makes a perfect wife."

"Then we are both truly blessed," Peter said, "for I feel the same about Grace."

Teddy and Miranda watched the trio board the steamer and waited until the ship had begun its journey up river. After they docked they would catch the railroad, now completed to Bennett, and be home within a matter of weeks instead of months.

"I know you will miss them, my dear," Teddy said, turning Miranda to face him, "but I promise you, I will take you home to your family. Do you trust me to do that?"

She nodded. "I trust you. I'm not unhappy, Teddy. Please understand that. I love you very dearly, and I am home wherever you are."

"Then I am doubly blessed, for I feel the same."

CHAPTER TWENTY-SEVEN

JACOB PACED THE CONFINES of his cell while, outside, an icy rain pelted the town. He was worn and exhausted from his daily work on the city woodpile—punishment for all who were incarcerated. For over two weeks now he'd been jailed for something he didn't do. No one would listen to him—not the officer who brought his meals, not the commissioner in charge, not even God. At least that's how it felt to Jacob.

He tried to pray, but he felt his words were bound up in anger and resentment. *Why did you let this happen to me, God?* he couldn't help but ask. It became his focal question. *Why? I liked that old man and enjoyed working with him. I would never do him harm. So why am I now being accused of his murder?*

He hated the Yukon. He hated everything the Yukon stood for. The greed. The lies. The gold. He wished fervently that his father had never brought him and Leah north. What good had it done any of them? His father was dead. He was in jail. And now Leah was alone.

Once again, he'd failed his sister, and once again, God had failed him.

Why?

Pounding his fist against the wall, Jacob wanted to scream out that they were all mad. He felt as though the entire world had gone insane and only he remained knowing the real truth.

He let exhaustion overcome him as he stretched out on his cot to stare up at the ceiling. Daily he heard the Mounties speak of the vast numbers leaving Dawson. *The rats are deserting the ship,* he thought. *Leaving it for a more lucrative ship called Nome.* Jacob shook his head, failing to understand any of it.

Here he was, sixteen. He wouldn't be seventeen until January of the new century. Would he even live to see it? Would they proclaim him guilty and end his life for the murder of Gumption Lindquist?

"It's not fair," he muttered. "I thought when a person trusted God, if they did what they were supposed to, that God would keep them from harm—that bad things wouldn't happen to them. But I've had nothing but trouble."

The first few days after they'd taken him into custody, Jacob figured everything would be resolved in a matter of hours. He figured that somehow Adrik would get wind of his incarceration and come to his aid. He'd even asked the Mounties to look Adrik up at the hospital, but he guessed no one had ever seen fit to do that.

To say he was discouraged didn't begin to reveal the scope of his emotions. The hopelessness that held Jacob captive seemed to breed other feelings that washed over him in waves. He was angry for the mistake—angry because no one believed him. He felt deeply grieved over Gump's death, sorry that Gump would never see his farm in Kansas and never know if his parents were still living.

Then there was the fear. Jacob hated being afraid most of all. What if no one ever came to his defense? What if the truth was never revealed and he remained in jail for the rest of his life?

He thought of Leah and worried about her incessantly. She was so young, just fourteen. What would become of her? He knew Karen loved her and would see to her upbringing, but Leah would have no family of her own. If they killed Jacob as punishment for Gump, Leah would be completely orphaned. The thoughts kept whirling through his mind.

Anger. Sorrow. Fear.

They were Jacob's cellmates—and they demanded their voice.

———

Adrik stared at the notice on the door to his cabin and shook his head. "This says that the property has been confiscated and quartered off by the Northwest Mounted Police."

"Why would they do that?" Karen questioned.

"I don't know."

"Where's Jacob and Mr. Gump?" Leah asked. She started to walk around to the backside of the cabin when one the Jones brothers hailed them.

"Ivankov, where have you been?"

"Jones," Adrik acknowledged and nodded. "We've been to Dawson. Baby took sick. Didn't Jacob or Gump tell you?"

"They couldn't very well do that, now, could they?"

Adrik had no idea what the younger man was talking about. "Do you want to explain?"

"You don't know, do you?" The dark-haired man shoved his gloveless hands in his pockets. "That boy killed the old man."

"What?" Karen exclaimed, coming around Adrik to face the man. "What are you saying?"

"I'm saying the Mounties took Jacob off to Dawson. He shot old Lindquist right through the heart. They figure he was after his gold."

"No! Not Jacob!" Leah cried. She rushed into Karen's arms, looking up mournfully at Adrik. "Jacob wouldn't kill Mr. Gump—they were good friends."

"Well, the old man is dead, nevertheless. Mounties took him away and posted the notice on the cabin. We've been keepin' an eye on things ever since."

"I thank you for that," Adrik replied. "How long ago did all this happen?"

"Right after you headed out. I figured you might even learn about it while you were there. I'm supposin' the *Nugget* carried the story."

"I'm afraid," Adrik said, looking from Jones to the women, "we weren't paying much attention to the events around us. Well, we'll just have to gather our things and head back to town."

"Ain't suppose to go through the door—it's posted to stay out."

"I see that," Adrik said. "We got some things we can gather from the cache, but our gold is hidden in the cabin and I'm not leaving here without it."

Jones nodded. "Seein's how you're the old man's partner and all, I don't see no harm in you takin' your fair share. I'm sure no one will be the wiser for it. Sure ain't my business."

"I'll check in with the Mounties when I get to Dawson. Jacob's going to need some help in clearing his name," Adrik replied.

"I don't think you can clear the boy of something he did," Jones said turning to go. "I saw him myself—standing there with the rifle in his hands—looking all crazed. He said it were someone else, but I never did see nobody." He then ambled off toward his own claim, as if not wanting to know or say anything more on the subject.

Leah's sobs tore into Adrik's heart. "Don't worry, sweetheart," he said, reaching out to stroke her hair. "I'll see that this gets figured out. We'll get Jacob out of jail—you'll see."

"Why did this happen?" Leah asked tearfully. "Poor Mr. Gump, he was afraid this land would kill him, and now it has. And poor Jacob. He must be so afraid."

Adrik looked into his wife's eyes. He wished fervently that he knew what to say to comfort Leah, but nothing made sense. "I don't know."

In a numbed state of shock, the trio worked to pack out what things they didn't wish to leave behind. Adrik knew it would most likely cause problems with the police when they learned of his entry into the cabin, so he refused to let Karen or Leah go inside.

"Better it fall on me than you two," he told them. "Just tell me what you need for me to retrieve and I'll do my best to find it."

Adrik stepped into the cabin and stared at the darkened shadows on the wall. He took enough time to light a lamp, dispelling the shadows, but to his horror, it revealed the bloody brown stain on the wooden floor. Gump had been so proud of that floor. He'd made it himself without much help from anyone else. He'd spent the winter months sanding it down to make it so smooth he could walk barefoot on it in the summer. Now his lifeblood stained the floor, forever marking it as a reminder of unfilled dreams.

Adrik felt his eyes mist. He'd loved Gump like a father, and now the old man was gone. Gone before he could take back his gold and surprise his family. Gone before he could see his mother and buy her the white leather, gold-trimmed Bible she'd always wanted. Gone.

"And that's what I plan to be as well," Adrik said, anger replacing his sorrow. "I'm taking my family and leaving this place. And if I never hear the word *gold* prior to stepping onto the golden streets of heaven, it'll be just fine by me."

Two hours later the cart was packed and the dogs were rested and ready to go again. Adrik knew if he never saw this land again, it would be perfectly fine with him. He longed for the simplicity of his life on the Alaskan coast.

They had what Adrik had been certain was several thousand dollars worth of dust and nuggets by now. As angry as the greed represented by the ore made Adrik, he knew he'd have to rely upon its bounty for a while longer. It was going to have to get them home and then some. They'd be able to buy the supplies they needed and the rest could be given away, as far as Adrik was concerned.

Adrik planned to send Gump's half to his family in Kansas, but first he'd have to convince the Mounties that he had a right to the gold. That might not be so easy to do in light of what had happened.

Karen wanted only her family Bible and a few sentimental trinkets she'd collected along the way. Leah asked Adrik to get Jacob's change of clothes and his winter boots, along with her things. He did this, wishing he'd been there for the boy when this tragedy had happened. There was no doubt in his mind of Jacob's innocence. What there was doubt about was who had been responsible.

"You two are going to ride," he said, lifting Leah into the cart. "I know it will be a tight fit, but we need to make good time. Jacob's already been all this time without us and he must be feeling pretty frantic by now. I've packed the gold under everything, but you should be comfortable enough. I put some blankets, along with our clothes, down as a cushion."

Karen and Leah nodded in understanding. "We'll be fine," Karen assured him.

She let Adrik help her into the cart and smiled. "We've forgotten only one thing."

Adrik looked back to the cabin, then to Karen. "What?"

"Prayer."

Adrik knew she was right. He felt the warmth of God's presence even in her words. They hadn't thought to pray. They had waited until their fleshly needs were met—their criteria and agenda tended to—and then they had thought of prayer.

Adrik pulled off his hat, in spite of the fact that it had started to snow. Bowing his head, he started the prayer with an apology. "Lord, we're sorry for thinking of you last. We know it isn't the way we're supposed to be. We let ourselves get caught up in the moment. We saw the problem, instead of the answer-giver. Forgive us.

"And Father, we ask that you would be with Jacob just now. Sustain his faith, Lord. This has to be a terrifying time for him. He's probably confused and scared, and Lord, I just ask that you would strengthen him. Make your presence real in his life, and help us to help him. I don't believe for one minute that he killed Gumption. I don't know who would kill such a kind old man—but Lord, you know exactly who did the deed. Help us to find that man.

"Give us safe passage back to Dawson, and give us the strength and courage we'll need to deal with the days to come. In Jesus' name, Amen."

"Amen," Karen murmured with Leah.

Adrik dusted the snow from his hair and put his cap back on. He stood on the ledge at the back of the cart and took up the harness reins. Pulling the brake, he whistled to the dogs. They sprang to attention, eager for the run. Adrik gave the reins a snap. "Hike!"

Jacob had never been so happy to see anyone in his life as he was to see Adrik and Karen.

"Where's Leah? Is she all right?" he asked.

Karen and Adrik nodded in unison. "She's just fine," Karen said. "They wouldn't let her come back here, however."

"They almost wouldn't allow Karen back here, but we wore them down," Adrik said, giving the guard a playful nudge.

"You can have ten minutes," the guard said as he pointed them to a small wooden table. He then turned to Jacob. "Don't even think of trying anything."

Jacob barely heard the man. He wanted only to hear Adrik tell him that he'd figured everything out and he would soon be set free. The trio sat down together while the guard watched on.

"You want to tell us what happened, son?" Adrik began.

"It was Cec Blackabee, Adrik. He showed up not long after you left. He didn't even give Gump a chance. Gump opened the door and Cec fired his rifle. He might have only meant to scare him, but Gump must have seen the gun, 'cause best I can figure, he tried to close the door and got the bullet in the chest."

"Then what happened, Jacob?" Karen asked softly. She reached out and touched his arm tenderly, motherly. He felt warmed by her presence.

"Gump fell over, and I charged for the man in the doorway. At first I didn't know it was Cec, 'cause he stood outside in the shadows. I grabbed hold of the rifle, but not before he had a chance to cock it again. The gun went off as we wrestled. Finally, he pushed me back and cocked it again, and aimed it right for me. It was then that we heard someone coming. The distraction gave me a chance to try again to take the rifle from Cec.

"When Cec heard the neighbors coming, he ran. When everyone else showed up, there I was holding the gun, and they all presumed the worst."

"What about Gump? Was he already dead?"

Jacob looked at the table remembering the horrible sight of Gump's bloody shirt, his pale, wrinkled face, his eyes glazed over, but open. "They told me he died pretty much instantly. The bullet went right through his heart."

"This is ridiculous," Karen proclaimed. "If you told them this, why aren't they listening? Why is he still sitting here in jail?" she asked Adrik.

"There were no witnesses who saw Cec leave," Jacob said.

"No one?"

Jacob shook his head. "Everyone focused on me. I was the only one they thought about. Cec was able to slip away without any trouble."

"I don't understand, son," Adrik said very softly. "Why would Cec Blackabee want to kill Gump?"

Jacob shrugged. It was a mystery to him as well. It was one thing to be a thief and cheat, but another to be a murderer. He'd known Cec to be underhanded at nearly every turn, but he didn't seem like a murderer.

"I know he said something about scaring me into helping him. I suppose he figured if I wouldn't help him for the money, I would do it if he threatened my life."

"Look, we're going to see this thing through until you're proven innocent and set free."

"I'd like to believe that." Adrik's words sounded good to Jacob, but promises weren't going to turn the key on his cell.

"You must believe, Jacob. God has a plan for you, and I am certain it isn't to leave you to rot away in a Yukon prison," Karen told him. Her gaze met his and refused to let him go.

Jacob appreciated her strength. He thought it might well be his imagination, but he already felt more hopeful. It seemed just seeing them here, sharing his plight and knowing the circumstances, helped him to bear his burden.

"We're going to leave now," Adrik told Jacob. "I'm going to have a talk with the commissioner to see what can be done. Keep praying."

"I'm trying, but God doesn't appear to be listening."

Adrik grinned. "That guard over there doesn't appear to be listening either, but I know he is. And I know God is listening as well. You have to trust that, Jacob. Faith in times of plenty and peace isn't really faith. It takes a trial like this to build faith that moves mountains. Just trust Him, Jacob."

Jacob heard Adrik's words and took them deep into his heart. A tiny flame sparked to life, spreading hope and courage throughout his weary limbs. "I'll try," Jacob said, knowing the alternative was unthinkable.

Jacob tried to sleep that night, but his mind came back to the words Adrik had given him. The counsel was wise, he knew that full well, but it was also hard to believe. Jacob felt done in. Trust and faith came hard in the shadow of a noose.

"I'm trying, Lord," he whispered. "I don't know if that's enough or not. I guess if it's not enough, then I need you to forgive me. And if it is enough, then I need you to help me. Either way," he said, closing his eyes, "I need you."

———

"I don't care how many witnesses saw Jacob standing there with the gun after the shooting had already been done. I'm asking, did anyone see Jacob pull the trigger?"

The Mountie sitting across the desk from Adrik and Karen did not appear interested in their questions. "Sir, that's really not a matter I can answer."

"I believe, based on my knowledge of the boy and the relationship he had with the old man, that it would be impossible for Jacob Barringer to have killed Gump Lindquist," Adrik declared.

"That's all well and fine, but you must remember, we have a situation here that doesn't always allow for the normal way of things. The gold rush has brought out the savage beast in many men."

Adrik stared at the man's balding head and then looked past him to the window. Outside snow was falling, reminding Adrik that the time was quickly passing and soon they'd be facing winter once again.

"I know who killed Gump," Adrik finally stated. He looked back to the Mountie. He sat so completely regal in his stately uniform. The look on his face was fixed, almost stoic. He was a soldier through and through. "A man named Cec Blackabee killed him. Jacob was there and witnessed the entire thing."

"Why would this man, whom no one saw, with the exception of Mr. Barringer, want to kill Mr. Lindquist?"

"For months we've been dealing with a thief and sneak," Adrik replied. "We had a sled stolen and evidence of other attempts to break in. Then one night a commotion arose while Jacob was on guard duty. Cec Blackabee had come to ask Jacob to help him. It seems his partner ran off with his property, including the deed to a claim and a map. He asked about these things and admitted to having stolen our sled. He said the sled was taken from him by his wayward partner."

"Not only that," Karen piped up, "but a strange man appeared at our door some time back when the men were gone. He made me feel most uncomfortable and appeared to be up to no good."

"Was this the same man who stole the sled and supposedly killed Mr. Lindquist?"

"No," Karen said shaking her head. "I'm sure it wasn't. Jacob was there that night. He would have recognized Cec Blackabee if he'd been the man. I'm suggesting that Mr. Blackabee may have a partner."

"This is all very interesting, but it doesn't prove Mr. Barringer's innocence. I have eye witnesses—"

"Who saw the boy holding the rifle," Adrik interjected. "But no one saw him commit the murder."

"I wish I could help you. I will be happy to check into this matter more thoroughly, but the truth is, you're going to have to have evidence to confirm the story—evidence that will stand up in a court of law. Otherwise, I'm afraid the judge will deal most harshly with this young man."

"Meaning exactly what?" Karen asked.

"Meaning if he's found guilty, he'll most likely be hanged."

⊣ CHAPTER TWENTY-EIGHT ⊢

"ARE THEY GOING TO kill my brother?" Leah asked, her voice quavering.

Karen looked up from the dining table. "We can't even think that way," she said. "Surely, God won't let him be punished for something he didn't do."

"Innocent people get blamed for things all the time. You said so yourself," Leah replied.

Adrik turned to her. "You can't let this kind of thinking rule your heart. It isn't fair that Jacob is having to endure this. Nor is it fair that you have to endure this heartache."

"It also wasn't fair that Mr. Gump had to die," Leah interrupted. "Nothing about this place seems fair. People hurt each other and cheat each other—and all because of the gold."

"No," Adrik said. "It isn't the gold, it's the sin of greed. The gold is just a metallic rock that lays there and does nothing. It has no thoughts or feelings, it simply exists."

"The wealth assigned it comes from human decisions," Karen added.

"Well, it's still not fair."

Adrik nodded. "You're sure right on that point. It's not fair."

"But then we should be able to do something about it!" Leah declared, pushing away her bread pudding.

"Sweetheart," Adrik began, "there is much in life that isn't fair—never has been, never will be. Innocence is lost, trust is betrayed, and love is misused. It's been happening that way since the beginning of time."

"It's sure been happening since the beginning of my time," Leah muttered.

"Leah, do you believe God is singling you out for trials? Look at Karen," Adrik replied. "She lost her mother and father. She left a good life in Chicago where she had plenty of everything she needed. She lost her aunt in a fire. And she got saddled with me." He grinned as he added the latter statement.

Leah couldn't help but smile as Karen interjected, "Yes, and he's been a troublesome burden ever since." She playfully nudged Adrik. "He's not at all easy to live with."

Leah enjoyed their playful spirit. It reminded her of her mother and father. Still, she also remembered times when her mother's heartbroken cries nearly broke her heart. "It's just so hard," Leah finally replied, sobering again.

Adrik gently touched her cheek. "I know it is. Jesus never said it wouldn't be. In fact, He told us life would be difficult. He told us we would have troubles, but that we could be of good cheer because He has already overcome the world and all the problems it could ever bring. That's in the gospel of John, sixteenth chapter. So you see, it isn't fair. And life is hard. But it's nothing new. Every person in the world has to deal with the same sort of thing at one time or another."

"They don't all end up in jail fearing for their lives," Leah protested.

"Maybe not the kind of jail your brother is in, but there are all kinds of ways to be imprisoned and all manner of dealings that threaten our very lives." Adrik squeezed her hand and smiled. "But Jesus is bigger than all of this. He's already seen it. Already dealt with it. It's as though when we have to go through it, we can rest in Him 'cause He already knows the direction to take to get us through in one piece."

"But Jesus could have kept the bad from happening," Leah said and tears came to her eyes. "He could have kept Jacob from being blamed for killing Mr. Gump. He could have kept Mr. Gump alive."

"Without a doubt," Adrik said, nodding. "And that really bothers you, doesn't it?"

Leah swallowed hard. "Yes. It hurts me to think of God just standing there letting Jacob get hauled away for something he didn't do. It makes me want to die inside when I think that things might keep going wrong—that God might keep standing back, doing nothing, while they decide to hang my brother."

It was Karen's turn to talk. "Do you trust God, Leah?"

The girl shrugged. "I thought I did. I sure want to trust Him."

"Sometimes the only thing we can do is accept that He knows best—that He has a plan and is just and loving."

"And sovereign," Adrik added.

"What does that mean?"

"Sovereign means that God is the absolute, highest authority. He's the final word on everything. He's the one in charge of how things will be. No matter what—no matter how it looks or feels. It means trusting that He's in control even when things seem very much out of control."

"That's really hard," Leah said. She lowered her head and wiped her tears. "My mama used to say that same thing. She told me when she was dying that God's ways were sometimes hard for us to understand, but that we have to keep on believing in Him—we have to have faith that He will take care of us."

She looked up to Karen and Adrik. "She said that was what being a Christian was all about."

"It sounds like your mother was a very wise woman," Adrik said softly, then added, "I'm figuring you're a lot like her. Maybe even more than you know."

———

Jacob sat at the same wooden table where he'd visited with Adrik and Karen only two days before. Now, however, instead of his friends, an American lawyer sat opposite him.

"Your friends have put me on retainer to see to your needs," the man said, adjusting his eyeglasses. "My name is Calvin Kinkade. I'm originally from Oregon, but I found it lucrative to journey north." He paused and, after fussing a bit more with his glasses, looked at the paper he'd brought with him.

"I'm afraid that there isn't much here to help me." He looked directly at Jacob, his eyes peering over the top rims of the silver-framed spectacles. "Unless we can produce a witness or this Mr. Blackabee, I'm not sure we'll be able to convince anyone of your innocence."

"I thought they were supposed to prove my guilt," Jacob said rather snidely. He wasn't feeling at all good about the fact that Adrik had brought a lawyer in on the situation. That had to mean that things didn't look good—that they were in desperate need of legal help.

"Yes, well, given the fact that so many people saw you standing over the dead man, gun in hand, I believe they feel they have sufficient proof of your guilt."

"That's what I figured. So why is Adrik wasting his hard-earned money by hiring you?"

The man was nonplussed. "I'm afraid I don't understand. Do you not see the need for legal representation?"

Jacob knew his anger would soon speak for him, so he took a deep breath and tried to calm his nerves. "I didn't kill Gump. He was a good friend, and the last thing I wanted to see was his death. I don't much care anymore what anyone believes. You aren't going to solve this case by sitting here picking at my brain. You need to be out there," Jacob pointed to the window. "Cec Blackabee is out there, and it doesn't much matter to him who ends up dead if it means that he gets what he wants."

"Yes, well, I suppose I can speak to your guardian on the details of this and see what is to be done."

When Jacob said nothing more, the man got to his feet. "I have arranged for you to have a visitor. Mr. Ivankov felt it was most important." The lawyer nodded to the guard, who in turn opened the door.

Leah Barringer ran across the room and threw herself into Jacob's arms. "Oh, I thought they'd never let me in here," she cried.

"I can't believe they did," Jacob replied, holding her away from him enough to get a good look. "Are you all right?"

"I'm fine, but you look terrible."

He laughed. It felt good to laugh. "I'm fine. I'm working hard, but it's not too bad."

"Working? What are you doing?"

"I'm cutting wood for the city. That's how they keep the prisoners busy around here, and sometimes it's how they sentence guilty folks. They end up cutting wood for so many weeks or months."

"How awful," Leah said, glancing down to see the irons on Jacob's ankles. "Are they afraid you'll run away?"

Jacob shrugged, trying to keep things light. He could see the fear in Leah's expression and wanted to put her mind at ease. "They do this to everyone when they bring them out of their cell."

"Oh," Leah said, seeming to calm with his response.

"I'll give you two a moment alone," Mr. Kinkade said, then went to speak with the guard.

"Leah, I want you to promise me that no matter what happens, you'll stay with Karen and Adrik and grow up sensible."

"I promise. But what about you?"

"It doesn't much matter at this point. I can't free myself. I can't leave the jail and go find Cec. If I could, I would."

"Adrik's looking for him," Leah replied. "He'll find him."

Jacob reached out and pushed one of his sister's braids back over her shoulder. She was growing up so fast, she hardly resembled the youngster she once had been. Soon she'd have beaus and then a husband and children. He wanted a better life for her. Better than their mother had known. Better than they had known.

"I'm sure if anyone can find Cec, Adrik's the man. Just don't go getting your hopes up. Cec may be far from here by now."

"You have to have faith, Jacob." Leah's expression grew quite serious. "We have to trust God, even though it seems like He doesn't care. He's always out there—

watching us and dealing with us. He hasn't left us, even if we don't understand why these things are going on."

"Sounds like you've thought this through," Jacob said.

"I have. I wasn't very happy when this all started, but while I'm still not happy with the way things are, I know God is in control of everything."

Leah's words were exactly what Jacob needed. He needed to know she believed in him—trusted him and loved him. But he also needed to hear her declare her faith. Somehow, for whatever reason, he felt as if he were sustained because of her faith.

"Karen and I have been praying. We know God has everything in His hand. He sees us and loves us, and He's not going to let you be falsely charged."

It warmed Jacob's heart to know that without even having to ask, Leah knew he wasn't capable of murdering Gump. He hugged her close. "Thank you. Thank you for coming here and thank you for believing in me."

Leah stepped back. "How could I not?" She smiled. "I have to go now, but just you wait. You'll see. We'll find that horrible Mr. Blackabee, and you'll be set free." She hugged him tight. "I love you, Jacob."

Her words broke through the wall Jacob had put around his heart. Holding her close, he countered her words with his own declaration. "I love you, too."

Long after she'd gone and Jacob was back to work on the woodpile, her words stayed with him. They gave him a rhythm to work with. "You'll be—set free. You'll be—set free." He lifted the axe and brought it down in an imagined beat. Then a verse from the Bible came to him. *Ye shall know the truth, and the truth shall make you free.*

"They'll know the truth," Jacob said bringing the ax down hard. "and I will be set free."

––––––––––

"I think trying to find Cec Blackabee will be rather like hunting for the proverbial needle in a haystack," Karen declared as she, Leah, and Adrik sat keeping company with Miranda and Teddy.

The night had grown late, but while Teddy would have just as soon gone to bed, he knew his new friends needed to discuss their strategies. He wanted to help as best he could, but nothing seemed reasonable.

"The man could well be back down toward Whitehorse by now," Teddy reasoned.

"I thought of that already," Adrik declared. "I gave his description to the Mounties and told them all about Cec's saloon in Whitehorse. Someone there is bound to know him and should be able to keep an eye open for him. But I really don't think he would have left this area. He desperately wants those missing papers. They mean a lot of money to him—at least that's how I figure it."

"And you say," Teddy began, "that the man figured them to be on the sled I sold to you?"

"That was his way of thinking. Why he figures that, I can't really say. He told Jacob that his partner had robbed him. He said the sled and sled box were a part of that thievery and that the sled box contained his documents."

"I say, why wouldn't the partner just keep the documents? Better yet, why not sell them to some poor unsuspecting fool."

"Well, as best as Jacob and I could figure out, the papers were hidden and the man wouldn't necessarily have known he had them."

"I see. Well, that does change things a bit."

"But if the man stole the sled, wouldn't he have found what he was looking for?" Miranda questioned.

"Well, apparently he thought the papers would be in the sled box," Adrik said. "But we'd taken the sled box inside and made a baby bed for Andy. It was a pretty nice box, simple, but nice. We put a well-worn crate in the sled for carrying supplies and tools. Cec probably didn't pay any attention when he took the sled. Once he got away and realized the box wasn't the same one, he had to figure on a way to get the box back."

"Well, now we have to figure a way to get Cec back," Karen said. "And we've got to do it soon."

⊣{ C H A P T E R T W E N T Y - N I N E }⊢

MIRANDA CURLED UP against Teddy's warm body and sighed. It was so very nice to have a husband to sleep alongside, especially when the weather turned cold. Her mind raced with thoughts. Even though she knew she'd be better off to fall asleep, she couldn't stop thinking about poor Jacob Barringer. She wished fervently there was something she could do for the boy, but she knew that, besides praying, she had no means with which to help him.

It seemed so little, and yet, she knew prayer was the ultimate weapon of a Christian warrior. She thought of all the times when she'd been truly afraid, and then remembered how God had soothed and calmed her. She prayed He would do that now for Jacob.

I'm sure he's not guilty, she thought. *He's too sweet a boy. He just couldn't have killed anyone.*

Miranda was just about to drift off to sleep when her attention was caught by a noise coming from the other room. Since marrying Teddy, they'd turned the other room into a large sitting room and work area. Teddy's tables and shelves consumed one end of the room, while the other end was used to receive guests.

The creaking sounded again, and this time Miranda sat straight up. She noticed a light threading through the space at the bottom of the door.

Slipping from the bed and pulling on her robe, she thought only to crack the door a bit to look out into the sitting room, but when she touched the knob, Miranda was no longer convinced she was doing the best thing.

She started to turn back when the sound of glass breaking caught her attention. Without thinking, Miranda threw open the door, hoping to scare the burglar into making a run for it.

"Teddy, wake up! We're being robbed!" she screamed. Stepping into the sitting room, she screamed again. "Teddy, there's a man in here!"

And indeed there was. The man quickly covered the distance that separated him from Miranda and clamped his hand over her mouth.

"Shut up. Do you want to wake up the whole hotel?"

She would have told him that she had exactly that in mind, but his foul-smelling hand made it impossible. Struggling against the man, Miranda tried to free herself. She pushed against him with all her strength, but it was to no avail. He held her fast in a steel-like grip.

That was how Teddy found them. Miranda saw his expression change from one of confusion, to anger.

"Let her go!" he declared, charging forth with uncharacteristic boldness.

"Stay back, mister. I've got a knife and I ain't afraid to use it."

Teddy halted at this news. "Please don't hurt her. You can take whatever you want. Just let her go."

"Look, mister, I don't know who you are, but you have my property and I want it back," the man said, pulling Miranda backward. The man turned her toward the worktables. "Where is it?"

"I don't know what you're talking about," Teddy said, moving very slowly to cross the room in front of them. "Please just let her go and tell me what this is about."

The man suddenly grabbed hold of Miranda's wrist and yanked her around, throwing her off-balance. She landed at his feet in a resounding thud.

She looked up at the wiry man. He was older than she'd expected. From his grip on her, Miranda had presumed him to be young. Instead, his face was weathered and wrinkled and his black hair was liberally sprinkled with gray, especially at the temples. He had a scar along his jaw, just under his chin. She might never have noticed it had she not been sitting at his feet.

"Please, tell me what you're looking for," Teddy said.

"You bought a sled from my partner. He stole it from me and also took some other things that didn't belong to him, including a sled box. I want it back."

"I don't have them," Teddy said. "I sold them."

Miranda realized that this had to be Cec Blackabee. She tried to scoot away from the man, but he stomped his muddy boot down on her robe. The foul odor told her mud wasn't the only thing he'd collected along the way.

"Stay put," he ordered. He turned back to Teddy. "I know you sold them. I followed the man you sold 'em to."

Miranda looked to her husband and realized by his expression that he, too, knew the truth of who this man was. He silenced her with the tiniest shake of his head.

"If you know this, then you know also that I do not have what you're looking for," Teddy declared.

"I think you're wrong, mister. I reclaimed that sled of mine—took it back from the man you sold it to. The sled box with my things was missin'."

"I'm sorry. What does this have to do with me? I sold the man both the sled and the sled box."

"I saw the sled box. It weren't the same one you were sold."

Miranda saw Teddy stiffen at this. "How would you know what the man sold me? You weren't there. He could have disposed of the item you're speaking of."

Cec nodded. "I suppose he could have, but I don't think he did. I think you've got it."

Teddy's expression changed at this. "Describe the box."

Cec shrugged. "It was about two foot deep and about a foot and a half wide. It was made out of good wood and painted white."

Teddy nodded. "Yes, I do remember it." He looked to Miranda as if to apologize.

She saw the misery in his expression and wished she could somehow comfort him. "Where is it, Teddy?" she asked softly.

"Back at the cabin."

"Where?" Cec questioned.

"A cabin I use that's out south of Dawson."

"Take me there."

Teddy shook his head. "It's a three-day trip and I have no transportation. The weather is bad, and we'd no doubt have a difficult time of it."

"I don't care. I can get us some horses," Cec said, scratching his chin. "The lady'll have to ride double with me."

"I say, why not just leave her here," Teddy suggested. "She can't help in this— she doesn't even know about the box."

Cec shook his head. "I don't think so. The minute you and me head out, she'd be over there telling it all to the Mounties."

"What if I gave you my word?" Miranda questioned. "I promise to stay right here in the hotel." She knew she could keep that promise and still go to Adrik for help.

"You must think me a fool," Cec answered. "Now you're both wearin' on my patience. Let's go."

"Look, we have to put on our street clothes. It's much too cold to travel in nightclothes," Miranda declared.

The man looked at her for a moment then turned his gaze to Teddy. He studied Teddy for several seconds. Miranda couldn't imagine what he must be thinking. The hard set of his jaw told her that he wasn't at all pleased with the delay, but he understood the logic of her statement. They couldn't very well go parading out into the night dressed as they were. If nothing else, the very sight of them would be sure to attract unwanted attention.

"All right. You go first," he finally told Miranda. "Get your clothes on—and no funny business or I'll cut him to ribbons. He can show us the way in pain, just as sure as he can without it."

Miranda nodded. "I promise I won't do anything but get dressed."

"We will need a few supplies," Teddy told Cec as Miranda got to her feet. "If you don't mind, I'll collect some of these herbs to take along. They're good for tea and medicines. You never know, the snow could come upon us, and we could find ourselves in grave danger."

"Take 'em if you like," Cec said without concern.

Miranda paused at the door, fixing her gaze on Teddy. She couldn't imagine why he wanted to take his herbs. Trembling, she reached for the door.

Once inside their bedroom, Miranda hurried to dress. She felt a foreboding creep over her. What if Cec killed them after he got what he wanted? She glanced at the hall door and thought about running to Adrik for help. They were just two doors down.

But if I don't hurry, Cec might hurt Teddy, and I could never forgive myself if that happened.

Miranda tried to figure out how best to dress. She knew it would be cold and possibly rainy. She layered her body in a variety of woolen stockings, petticoats, and even a pair of boy's trousers she'd used on the hike north. Finally, she topped the outfit with a heavy wool skirt and long-sleeved blouse. Her hands shook so badly that she had difficulty buttoning the blouse.

"'The Lord is my light and my salvation; whom shall I fear? The Lord is the strength of my life; of whom shall I be afraid?'" She murmured the verse from Psalms, praying it would give her comfort and calm her nervousness.

Haphazardly, she knotted her hair at the nape of her neck, then took up a jacket and pulled it on over her blouse. Glancing around the room, she quickly retrieved her coat and gloves. She hurried back into the workroom to find Teddy bundling up the last of the things he wanted to take.

"I'm ready," she said in shaky voice.

Teddy crossed the room and handed her the bundle. "I shall be only a moment."

True to his word, Teddy reappeared within minutes. Miranda could see that he, too, had dressed in his warmest clothes. "All right, let us be about this, then," he said, looking harshly at Cec. "I would like to appeal once more to your sense of decency. Please allow my wife to stay here."

"Get movin'," Cec said, pointing them to the door. "I got me a gun as well as a knife, and I'll use either one." He patted his pocket as if to emphasize the presence of his weapons.

Miranda opened the door and peered into the hall, hoping perhaps someone would be taking a middle-of-the-night stroll. The hall was empty, however, and the hotel was silent.

Cec grabbed hold of Miranda's elbow. "You go first, mister. That way if you try anything funny, I'll see it. I'll also have your woman."

Teddy's gaze met Miranda's once again. She saw the love he held for her in his expression. She knew he would die for her if necessary. He nodded slowly and headed out into the hall.

Miranda felt her courage giving way. She realized her only chance to alert someone would be to raise a ruckus in the hall. But what if no one heard her? She would only manage to irritate Cec and maybe even cause them to be killed. She saw Karen and Adrik's room door as they moved down the hall. If only Adrik could know what was happening. She made a quick decision.

"Ow!" she cried, and fell against the door to Adrik and Karen's room. Her impact made a terrible noise.

"What's wrong with you, fool woman?" Cec growled low. He yanked her back upright.

"I just twisted my ankle," Miranda offered apologetically.

Teddy turned, looking fearful. "What's wrong?" he asked quietly.

"Your woman took a wrong step," Cec replied, then grabbing Miranda, he thrust her forward again. "Don't let it happen again, missy."

"I'm sorry," Miranda said, not meaning it at all.

———

Adrik couldn't imagine who was coming to call in the middle of the night. He threw back the covers, disturbing Karen's sleep.

"What's wrong?" she asked groggily.

"I don't know—probably nothing more than a drunk wandering down the hall to his room," Adrik replied. "Go back to sleep." He went to the door. Throwing it open, he started to protest the interruption but found no one there.

It was just as he'd suspected. Probably nothing more than someone staggering down the hall in a state of inebriation. As he started to close the door, however, something came over him, and he paused. Stepping forward, he looked toward Teddy and Miranda's room. No one was there and the door was closed. He shrugged and glanced down the hall in the opposite direction.

He caught only the briefest glimpse of a woman and man, but he was almost certain it was Miranda, and he was even more certain that the man with her was Cec Blackabee.

—[C H A P T E R   T H I R T Y]—

ONCE THEY WERE OUTSIDE, Cec Blackabee led Miranda and Teddy around behind the hotel and down the alleyway. From out of the shadows, a thin, tall man appeared.

"You get it?" he asked.

Cec tightened his hold on Miranda and pulled her closer. "No. We've got to head out to his cabin to get it, Mitch."

"Where's that?"

"Three days out. You got the horses?"

"Yeah, but I don't got no three days worth of supplies," the thin man answered.

Cec growled, then turned to Teddy. "You got any supplies for the road?"

Teddy shook his head. Miranda hoped it would persuade Cec to forget about the journey.

"We'll just have to steal 'em," Cec told his partner.

The man shrugged. "Guess we can break into the dry goods store. Nobody is gonna be there at this hour."

"I wish you wouldn't," Teddy said. "It's bad enough what you're doing with us, but if you continue adding to your illegal activities—"

"I don't want to hear it," Cec told him, moving closer to Teddy. "I've killed when it was necessary. Stealing ain't that much of a bother for me."

Miranda couldn't see well in the dark, but she could sense the tension in Teddy. She longed to assure him that everything would be all right—that God would protect them—but she wasn't all that convinced herself. Her faith felt terribly immature at the moment. It was easy to quote the Bible verse that God was her light and salvation—that He was her strength. But putting it into practice was very difficult.

Cec and the man called Mitch conversed in low whispers for a minute or two before pushing Miranda and Teddy in a direction away from the hotel. Miranda struggled to keep from tripping over her skirts as Cec forced her to move faster and faster. When they reached the end of the alley, Mitch disappeared momentarily, then just as quickly reappeared with three horses.

Miranda knew horses were at a premium in this country. No doubt they'd been brought north on one of the summer steamers, but now that the weather was turning colder she wondered how convenient it would be to keep them. Poor beasts. They would no doubt suffer as most animals did in the frozen north.

"Get up there," Cec commanded Miranda.

She looked to the horse and back to Cec. In the darkness she knew he couldn't see her confusion, so she spoke. "How?"

"What do you mean, how?"

"I mean, I don't know how to mount the horse. I've not ridden a horse before."

"Well, if that don't beat all," Cec said. "Put your foot in my hand and take hold of the horn. Pull yourself up and over and I'll boost you up there at the same time."

Miranda had no idea whether she was doing it right or not, but she put her boot foot in Cec's folded hands and grabbed hold of the saddle as best she could. Pulling herself up, she nearly flew over the other side of the horse as Cec gave a mighty push.

He grabbed hold of her leg and steadied her, as Miranda fought to balance herself atop the horse. Once she was settled, Cec took up the reins from Mitch. Pulling something from his pocket, he motioned to Teddy. "Walk ahead of the horse. I'll be right behind you. We'll go to the end of the block and around the dry goods store."

Miranda gripped the horn of the saddle for all she was worth. Terrified beyond words, she could only pray in silence.

Once they'd arrived at their destination, Cec surprised Miranda by handing her not only the reins to her horse, but the other two as well. "I've got a gun on your husband. He's coming with me and Mitch. If you know what's good for you, you'll keep quiet and hold these horses right here."

"But I don't know anything about horses," Miranda protested.

"Keep your voice down," Cec demanded. "Ain't nothing for you to know. Just sit still and hold the reins. If the animal starts moving around, pull back on the reins. He'll stop quick enough."

Miranda trembled as she took up the reins in one hand and clung desperately to the saddle horn with the other. She feared for Teddy's life, anxious that he might try to do something foolish in order to keep her from having to make the journey.

It seemed to take forever for the men to break into the back of the store and return, arms laden with supplies. Miranda knew in truth it was only minutes, but her heart was pounding like a kettledrum and her rapid, shallow breathing made her light-headed. She tried to calm herself—to pray—to focus on anything other than what was happening.

Cec hoisted himself up behind her and pulled her back against him. Taking the other horses' reins from her, he tossed them to Mitch. "You go ahead and lead the way, mister," he said as Mitch handed reins over to Teddy. "Just remember, I've got your woman back here. Any stupid moves and I'll cut her."

"Don't hurt her. I'm not going to do anything other than what you direct me to do."

"Keep it that way," Cec demanded.

Teddy knew the way to the cabin, even in the dark, but what had him worried was where they might take refuge along the way. There were a few claim cabins here and there, but his own place was well away from most of the hubbub of the gold rush. Not that there hadn't been folks trying to find gold on the property around his place. But so far, he'd not heard of any great finds.

God was faithful to provide, in spite of Teddy's worries. By nightfall the next day, they'd managed to find an abandoned cabin on Baker Creek. The second night, they found a lean-to off the Indian River. Both nights Cec kept Teddy from Miranda, reminding him as they went to sleep for a few hours that he had the knife close at hand, should Teddy try anything at all.

The third day out it started to snow, and the snow quickly built into blizzard-like conditions. Teddy feared he'd never be able to make his way to the right path, but God was faithful, even in that. The snow lightened and the winds calmed, and as quickly as the blizzard had threatened, it departed. Teddy silently praised God for the blessing.

Glancing over his shoulder, however, he could see that Miranda was nearly done in. He felt bad for her, knowing how sore and stiff she must be from the ride. The first night she'd barely been able to walk when they'd dismounted, and by morning she was so stiff that Cec had to lift her to the saddle. Teddy resented the man touching Miranda, yet there wasn't anything to be done about it. He had a plan, but it would have to wait until they were in the cabin.

"There it is!" Teddy called back to the men. "That cabin tucked in the trees over there." He urged his horse forward, grateful the journey had come to an end. But even as he thanked God for a safe trip, Teddy began to fear what the men would do to him and Miranda once they had what they wanted.

Jumping from the horse, Teddy didn't concern himself with the others. He had a plan, and in order for it to work, he had to make certain that things came together. Rushing into the cabin, he went immediately to the stove, took up kindling and matches, and started a fire. He no sooner had that going when Cec came into the cabin, pushing Miranda ahead of him.

"What do you think you're doing?" Cec bellowed.

"I'm getting a fire going. She's half frozen," Teddy said, pointing to his wife. "I'm half frozen. I think some tea would do us all good." He added small sticks to the fire and watched as the flames greedily claimed the offering. Next he put in split strips of dried logs left over from the previous winter.

Miranda sunk onto the small bed and rubbed her arms vigorously. Teddy worried about her health, fearing the cold and continuous riding would be her undoing. Checking the fire again, Teddy was satisfied that it was going strong. He added a few more pieces of wood, then took up a bucket and, without waiting for Cec to comment, went out of the cabin.

Since it hadn't been cold for too long, he figured the creek would still be free flowing, but if not, there was the snow. Breaking through a thin crust of ice, Teddy filled the bucket and hurried back to the cabin. He hated to think of Miranda alone with Cec and Mitch. The two were the lowest kind of scum, and Teddy could only pray that God would deliver them before Cec could hurt them.

"Here's the water," Teddy said, entering the cabin as though they were all good friends.

"Look, I don't care about the water," Cec said angrily. "I want that box."

"I understand," Teddy declared, "but the tea is important." He poured the water into a pan and put it on top of the stove. Then, pulling a bundle from his coat, Teddy unwrapped the herbs he'd brought along with him.

"I ain't standing around while you play host," Cec declared.

Teddy measured out a portion of mandrake root and sprinkled it into the water. He could only pray that the amount was sufficient.

"I said, I want that box," Cec said, coming forward to take hold of Teddy's arm. "Let your woman fix tea, if that's what you want, but you get that box for me."

Teddy nodded. "Very well. Miranda, would you finish preparing the *Mandragora officinarum* tea?"

Miranda's brows raised in surprise, and Teddy knew instantly that she understood what he'd done. She nodded, getting to her feet slowly.

"Now, where is my box?"

"I believe," Teddy said, glancing around the room, "that I must have locked it in the cache outside. Let me check the other room, however. No sense in going back outside if the box is in the other room."

"Get to it, then."

Teddy saw Miranda take her place at the stove. She picked up the small bottle and studied the label as if to assure herself that she'd heard him right. "Darling, feel free to offer our guests tea after it has a chance to boil a minute."

Miranda nodded in understanding.

Teddy checked the bedroom knowing full well the box wouldn't be found there. He was buying time. Time to let the mandrake tea get hot. Time to see both men rendered unconscious.

Teddy made a pretense of digging through things, pushing blankets and boxes aside. Cec looked into the room about the time Teddy decided he'd done as much as he could. "It's not here," he declared. "Guess we'll have to take the ladder and climb to the cache."

"Hurry up! I've waited long enough."

"I'll only be a minute," Teddy said, seeing that Miranda was preparing to pour the tea. He took up a ladder that was stored by the front door. It was a simple homemade contraption that Little Charley had put together for him when he'd built the cache. "You go ahead and have some tea."

"I don't want tea," Cec fairly roared. "I want that box and I want it now. Mitch, you stay with the girl. I'm going with him."

Miranda was just handing Mitch a mug of tea when Cec made this announcement. Teddy saw her worried look. He knew she was thinking the same thing he was. If Cec went with him, then he'd return to find his partner unconscious and there would no doubt be a problem. Instead of worrying about it, however, Teddy ushered Cec quickly out the door. Mandrake worked fast, and if the man fell unconscious, Teddy wanted Cec completely removed from the scene.

MIRANDA WATCHED in wonder as Mitch slumped to the table. She felt a sense of relief as he appeared to sink into a deep sleep. She looked at the tea and smiled. Teddy had thought of everything. What a brilliant scheme.

Looking to the door, however, she frowned. Cec Blackabee would return with Teddy and see the man sleeping and know that something was up. She wondered what she could do. Perhaps she could drag the man to the back room and hide him. But though the man was thin, Miranda could clearly see that wouldn't work. She was tired and hungry from their journey. Cec hadn't figured it important to feed her much or see to it that she rested. Now, with complete exhaustion washing over her, Miranda knew she could easily fall asleep without the aid of the mandrake tea.

Still, sleep wasn't an option at this point. She had to think, and think fast. The cache wasn't that far away, and once Teddy retrieved the box, Cec would march him back into the cabin, and then he would see Mitch and demand answers.

Spying the cast-iron skillet, Miranda decided her course of action. She picked up the skillet and went to stand beside the door. When Teddy came back, he'd no doubt be in the lead. She would wait until he passed by her, and then she'd club Cec over the head.

The thought turned her stomach. Miranda tried not to think of the graphic scene of Cec's head wounded by her hand. She cringed. Could she really hit him? Her hand began to tremble. *God, please help me.*

The door opened and Miranda held her breath. She raised the skillet over her head and closed her eyes for a split second. Letting her breath out slowly, she waited.

"Move!"

She heard the demand but startled at the sound of her husband's voice. She waited and stared in wonder as Cec Blackabee entered the room first. He carried the white box in front of him and Teddy followed. Then to her surprise, Adrik Ivankov came in behind them both.

"Thank you, Father," she whispered.

All three men turned to see her standing, poised and ready to strike. Smiling, she lowered the skillet. "I thought maybe I could hit him over the head," she explained to her husband.

Teddy went to the table where Mitch had passed out. He felt his neck and nodded. "He's still alive. At the rate Mr. Blackabee was rushing me, I couldn't be sure that I'd put in the right amount of mandrake."

"Look here," Cec said in protest, "I got a lot at stake here."

"So does Jacob Barringer," Adrik said without feeling.

"That's right," Miranda threw in. "You're letting a boy take the blame for a murder you committed."

"Nobody can prove I did it," Cec said smiling. "Now maybe if you were to let me take my box and go . . ."

Teddy shook his head. "Put the box down." He went to the back room and returned with rope. "Adrik, would you mind doing the honors? I'm afraid my knot tying isn't all it should be."

Miranda watched the big, burly man smile. "I'd be pleased to help out." He took up the rope and fairly knocked the box from Cec's hands. "Thought he told you to put that down."

"You both can be rich if you help me," Cec said, even as Adrik bound his hands.

"What's in that box that makes you willing to kill?" Teddy questioned. He lifted the white box and looked it over. Miranda edged closer to see if there was anything special about the piece. Teddy looked up and caught her gaze. "Are you all right?" he asked softly.

"I will be," she assured him. Her heart swelled with love for her husband. He'd been so brave and bold. She would never have imagined the quiet, mild-mannered botanist she loved would dream up serving mandrake tea.

"We're taking you back to Dawson and letting the law sort this out," Adrik told Cec as he finished tying him to the chair.

"I'm tellin' you, if you'd just listen to me," Cec demanded, "you could be rich."

Adrik shook his head. "I don't want to be rich. I want Jacob Barringer out of jail."

"Well, he ain't never gonna get that way if you take me in," Cec said snidely. "I'll tell 'em all how I saw him kill that old man."

"You'll do nothing of the kind," Adrik said. "You'll tell them the truth or I'll beat you senseless."

"Go ahead. Beat me. That will only help my case."

"Why do you need this box to be rich?" Teddy questioned.

Miranda stayed close to his side, fearful that Cec might yet break loose or that Mitch might awaken. She didn't want to be anywhere near either man should they find it within their own strength to gain the upper hand.

"Look, you let me go," Cec tried to dicker, "and I'll give you half the claim. Mitch ain't much good to me anyway. I have a claim on Bonanza Creek."

"Those are some of the richest claims in the territory," Adrik said matter-of-factly. "Where in the world did you get a claim like that?"

"I had a partner," Cec replied. "He went north while I stayed in Whitehorse. We figured I could keep sellin' whiskey while he went up and scouted us out a claim. He found one, but we needed to sell the saloon in order to finish paying the owner of the claim his askin' price."

"So you paid him off, received the deed, and your partner decided he wanted the claim for himself? Is that it?" Adrik asked.

"That's about the sum of it," Cec declared. "Only thing is, I hid the papers and the map. He didn't know where, but he thought he did. He knew it had something to do with the sled and so he stole off in the middle of the night and took the sled with him. He tried to take the dogs, but he never had learned how to hitch 'em to the sled, so they got away from him."

"So the man who showed up here to sell me the sled," Teddy interjected, "was your partner?"

"That's right."

"So what does the sled box have to do with this?" Adrik asked.

"That's where I hid the papers. He didn't know it, though. He figured, like I said, that they were hidden somewhere on the sled, but he couldn't figure it out. I had a secret compartment on the box, a false bottom where I hid the papers. When he robbed me of the sled, he robbed me of everything."

Teddy examined the box and, to Miranda's surprise, quickly figured out the puzzle of the box and opened a panel in the side. Tipping the box sideways, Teddy spilled out several pieces of paper. Miranda quickly retrieved them and handed them to her husband.

"It's a deed, all right," Teddy replied. He handed the paper to Adrik. "I don't know too much about such things, but since you have a claim of your own, maybe you can tell if this is the real thing or not."

"Looks real enough," Adrik said, studying the paper.

"This looks like a bill of sale," Teddy said, handing Adrik yet another piece of paper. He unfolded the final piece of paper and held it up. "This is the map."

"See, I weren't lyin'."

"Well, perhaps that's the only one of the commandments you haven't broken yet," Adrik said, "but I doubt it."

Cec spit on the floor. "Look, if you want that boy of yours to go free, then you're gonna have to do business with me. Mitch was out in the woods waiting for me the night the old man died. I'll tell the law it were him and not Jacob who killed the Swede." He looked hopefully to Miranda and then to Teddy. "That way we'll all be happy."

"I don't imagine Mitch would be too happy," Teddy countered.

"And then you'd be breaking the commandment about lying," Adrik added, "and I know how that would just about break your heart."

"I ain't gonna rot in a jail. Not when this claim on the Bonanza is worth fifty thousand if it's worth a dime."

The front door, which had been left partially open after Adrik had passed through, now opened in full. Two Northwest Mounted Police officers entered looking for all the world as if they materialized out of thin air.

Adrik turned to the men. "Have you heard enough?"

"Indeed we have. We'll take the prisoner into custody for the murder of Gumption Lindquist, as well as the kidnapping of Thomas and Miranda Davenport."

Adrik chuckled. "Ah, I'm sure there are quite a few more charges you can figure out to pin on him. Just remember, lying isn't one of them."

"I have my serious doubts about that," the sergeant said.

"Well, to tell you the truth, I have my doubts as well," Adrik admitted.

Relieved at the Mounties' appearance, Miranda longed for the horrid man to be taken from their cabin. She wasn't at all pleased when her husband suggested the hour was too late to start back for Dawson.

"You're welcome to keep him in the back room. There are no windows and only one entry."

The Mountie nodded. "I believe it would be prudent." He motioned for his subordinate to take Cec in hand.

"You ain't gonna pin that murder on me," Cec declared. "They'll hang Jacob for sure now."

Adrik crossed his arms and stared hard at the older man. Miranda saw his eyes narrow. He opened his mouth to say something, then turned and walked out the door. Miranda looked to Teddy. "I'd like to go talk to him." Teddy nodded.

Miranda slipped away from her husband even as Cec continued with his protests—cursing them all for their stupidity. Following Adrik outside, she was relieved to see that the snow had stopped completely and the sun was out.

"Adrik," she called after him. He had walked away from the house, but paused and turned.

"Sorry, I just had to get some air," he said as she joined him.

"I can well understand. I've been in his company for three days now and feel like the only thing I want is a bath. The man is as bad as they come. He doesn't care about anything but himself."

"He'd have let Jacob die."

Miranda shuddered. "Yes, he no doubt would have."

"I can abide a lot of things, Miranda, but that isn't one of 'em."

"I know."

Adrik pushed his hat back. "I've seen enough corruption and evil to last me a lifetime. Here we are on the verge of new century, and it seems the entire world is so wrapped up in itself that most folks can't even see what's right or wrong."

"Teddy told me that many people believe the end of the world will come on the last day of the year."

"I've heard the same," Adrik replied. "They get all excited about dates on a calendar rather than focusing on what's real and true. And that includes folks in the church as well as those who aren't." He paused and shook his head. "I just don't get it. Makes me sorry I ever came north."

"I'm not sorry I came north," Miranda replied. "I might never have met Teddy. But I am sorry for the greed and the sins of the men who are driven by that greed. I rejoice in the Lord, however, that He made a way for Jacob to be found innocent without having to wait for a long trial. I'm sure he's miserable enough in jail."

"He is. His faith's been really shaken. Leah's, too. But I think they'll come out of the fire proven as gold. They're good folk and their hearts are right."

"Karen's done well with them, as have you. I know Jacob spoke to me of how much he admired you. You've become his only father figure. Do you mind taking on a ready-made family?"

Adrik grinned. "I hadn't figured to even marry, to tell you the truth. Didn't figure I'd find a woman up to the challenge. Karen proved me wrong on that. So I guess I can handle being father to a couple of orphaned kids. Especially when they're as great as Jacob and Leah."

"I'm glad. I wondered what would become of them since it's pretty certain their father never made it past the avalanche."

"I'll offer them both a home for as long as they want it."

Miranda smiled. "On the coast of Alaska?"

"Yes, ma'am. Back where I belong," Adrik replied enthusiastically. He looked to the cabin and then to Miranda. "You're good medicine. You've got me thinking back on what's important and right in my life, instead of what's wrong. Teddy's a lucky man. You're going to do him proud."

"Thank you," Miranda said, feeling suddenly embarrassed by his praise. "How about we go back now and figure what we can put together for dinner."

Adrik nodded. "The Mounties and I brought a few provisions. I couldn't rustle up much since we were struggling to keep pace with you, but what I have is yours."

Miranda looped her arm through his and pulled him forward. The big man kept an even gait with her steps, neither saying another word. *It is good to have friends like this,* Miranda thought. She knew no matter where the future took them, she'd always be able to count on Adrik Ivankov. He was just that kind of person.

Later that night, Miranda stepped out for a walk with her husband. The air was cold but not uncomfortably so. They walked hand in hand for a time without speaking a single word. Finally, Miranda looked up to catch Teddy watching her.

"What are you thinking about?" she asked.

"I was just remembering when you were brought to my cabin. You were so lifeless, I was sure you were already dead. Nellie was the only one who believed you'd make it. The men who brought you wouldn't even stick around for a meal, they were so certain you would die while they were there. And being very superstitious people, they didn't want to deal with your spirit being unleashed. Especially since it would be a most troubled spirit from having died so tragically."

"It was that bad, eh?"

Teddy nodded. "Gravely so. You were so very sick. With each passing day and no response from you, I felt confident that all I could do was pray for you to pass easily into God's awaiting arms." He stopped walking and pulled her into his embrace. "I'm so very glad He didn't take you then. I cannot imagine my life without you in it."

"I spent so many months angry that God would allow such a thing to happen to me. I imagined my grieving parents and friends and just thought what a horribly cruel joke it was to play on them," Miranda admitted. "Now, with that time behind me, I see how God took the bad and made it come together for good. He gave me you and he brought my brother back together with Grace. He was worried about leaving me here alone—about my being stranded and penniless. That's what brought him up here."

"Your brother is a good man," Teddy said, gently tracing Miranda's jaw with his thumb.

"He's changed a good deal—for the better, I'm happy to say. He never would have picked you to be my husband—not with the way he used to think and evaluate the potential suitors in my life."

Teddy dropped his hold and stepped away feigning hurt. "You mean I wouldn't have been good enough for you?"

Miranda laughed and the sound was lyrical and lighthearted. How good it was to be happy. To laugh again and have everything come together in proper order.

"To the way Peter Colton used to think, no one was good enough for me," she said, still smiling. "But he changed his thinking and suddenly realized I knew what was best for myself all along."

"And what was that?"

"You," she replied, stepping forward to wrap her arms around his neck. "Only you, Thomas Edward Davenport."

⊣ CHAPTER THIRTY-TWO ⊢

JACOB HEARD THE COMMISSIONER say he was free to go, but the words barely registered. His soul soared on wings—the wings of freedom. Leah jumped into his arms, laughing in her excitement.

"Did you hear that! You're free! I told you God would work it all out. I told you He wouldn't let us down."

"Yes, you told me," Jacob said, chuckling. Leah's laughter was contagious.

"We've been after this man for a long time," the commissioner said, leaning back in his chair. "Of course, we had no idea that the man who killed the true owner of the Bonanza claim and the man who killed Mr. Lindquist were one and the same."

Jacob loosened Leah's hold on him and sobered. "So he killed more than Gump?"

"Indeed he did. Mr. Blackabee killed the rightful owner of this deed." The man held up the paper as if for evidence to his statement. "We had witnesses to the crime, but no one knew the killer by name. We even had a drawing made up. See here?" He pulled a paper from his drawer. The likeness was very much like that of Cec Blackabee.

Adrik stepped forward. "We'd like to leave Dawson as soon as possible. How long before this can be cleared up? What with Jacob being a witness to Gump's killing, and all."

"It shouldn't be more than a matter of weeks at the most," the commissioner declared. "We'll do what we can to see the matter resolved in an expeditious manner. We have Mr. Barringer's written statement, as well as the statement of the Mounties who overheard Mr. Blackabee's confession. With the other charges against Blackabee, Jacob's testimony may well not be needed. Cecil Blackabee will most likely be hanged."

Jacob shuddered. It could just as easily have been him they were talking about. In spite of the way Cec had left him to take the blame for Gump's death, Jacob pitied the man. After all, he had saved Jacob's life. His mind protested too much concern, however, as Jacob knew Cec would have let him die in order to save his own neck.

Adrik and Karen led the way outside, with Jacob and Leah following close behind. Jacob drew in a deep breath as soon as his feet hit the muddy street. Freedom. How very precious it was. He had taken for granted the privilege and joy of just being able to come and go as he pleased.

Thank you, God, he prayed silently as they made their way to the Dawson Lucky Day Hotel. *I feel so blessed that you have delivered me from jail—from the possibility of death.*

"Peter Colton said to tell you that you could have a job with his shipping company whenever you were ready," Leah told Jacob.

Leah's news was just an added bonus to the day. "That's good to hear."

"What's this all about?" Karen questioned. "Are you making plans behind our backs, again?" She smiled and winked, making it clear she wasn't serious.

"I think I'm going to have to make some plans sooner or later," Jacob said, quite serious. "I'll be seventeen in January. I ought to find a decent job. I kind of figured if I got work with Peter, I could learn some kind of trade."

"That's good thinking, Jacob," Adrik said, slowing his pace to allow Jacob to pull up even with them. "Peter would make a good teacher. He'd be fair and honest, and those are traits you don't always see in your authorities on earth."

Jacob knew this to be true. He'd always admired the way Peter worked with Grace and Karen when the tent store had been a part of their lives. He didn't understand what had happened between Peter and Grace in their marriage, but he figured it wasn't his concern. He'd prayed for them both, however, as he had come to care about Grace as if she were family.

The foursome came to a stop on Second Avenue, as if the spot were some previously agreed upon destination. Adrik and Karen looked at Jacob as if searching for answers to unspoken questions. Jacob felt the need to continue.

"I want something better than what my pa had. He was a dreamer. Everything was always better one town over or at the next discovery of gold." He pointed down the deserted street. "You couldn't move along this street last year this time without running into someone or having to get out of somebody's way. Now it's almost worse off than when it started. That's always the way it seems to be. I've seen dozens of towns just like it. Leah has, too."

Leah nodded, as if to confirm his statement. Jacob reached over and gave one of her braids a playful tug. "I want something better. Something that offers more security to my family." He grew rather sheepish and added, "And someday I want a family—a wife and children. But I want to give them a home where they can live and know that every day there will be food on the table and a roof over their heads. I don't want them to worry about having to pack up their few belongings and head off to some new discovery of prosperity."

"Sounds like you've given this a lot of thought," Adrik said. "It also sounds like very wise planning."

"I figure it fits with what God wants for me, as well."

"Then God will point the way, Jacob," Adrik assured. "You can be guaranteed He'll show you the right direction."

———

October brought more snow and the promise of a cold and tiresome winter. Already there was less and less sunlight. Karen looked out the window of their hotel room and wondered how soon they would be able to leave. She was anxious to be settled in Dyea. Especially now.

She put her hand to her abdomen and marveled at the knowledge that she was to have a child. She hadn't told Adrik yet. She'd been waiting for a special moment. The baby, best as she could figure, would be born in May. It seemed a perfect month for a new life to come into the world. Even in the frozen north, new life could be found in May.

Karen thought of her mother and father and wished they could have lived to see her married to Adrik. They both had held him in such high regard, and Adrik had loved them even before Karen was a part of his life. Surely they looked down from heaven, happy for the union and proud of the choice she'd made.

She hoped they'd also be proud of her desire to pick up where they left off. After long hours of discussion with her husband, Karen felt confident that they were being called into ministry work with the Tlingit Indians. She particularly wanted to work with the children—teaching them everything she could so that they might be better equipped if and when they wanted to be a part of the White world.

"Well, it's settled," Adrik said, coming through the adjoining door to their sitting room. "Jacob is free to leave. The government released him."

Karen looked at Adrik and saw the joy in his face. He had been so worried about Jacob. He loved him as much as a man could love a son, and this warmed her heart. She knew he would be a good father.

"You look very pleased to hear the news," he said, sitting down to pull off his boots.

"I am. I'm also very pleased about the love you've shown Jacob and Leah. You have been so very good to both of them in the absence of their real father."

"They're easy to care about. Easy to love," he said, putting his boots aside. He pulled out his pocket watch and checked the time. "I didn't realize it was getting so late. The commissioner kept me even after announcing the news. He kept talking about the changes in the area."

Karen smiled. "It's no bother. I was too excited to sleep."

"I can well imagine. Waiting for this news has stretched our patience. But now that we have it, we can go back to Dyea and build us a cabin. Or, from the sounds of it, take one that's been deserted. I guess Dyea is hardly more than a few folks keepin' company these days. Skagway's suffering, too. I feel bad for the folks who poured so much time and effort, not to mention money, into building up those towns."

Karen nodded and unfastened the tie on her robe. "So do you think we can leave Dawson right away?" She slipped out of the robe and carefully draped it across the end of the bed. Turning down the covers, she waited for Adrik's answer, but none came.

She paused and looked back to see what had suddenly silenced him. "What's wrong?"

"Nothing," he said, getting to his feet. "I was just watching you. You are the most beautiful woman in the world. I still can't believe how blessed I am. I couldn't be any happier."

"Don't count on that," she murmured, getting into the bed. Her strawberry blond curls spilled out across the pillow as she leaned back. She watched her husband, memorizing each detail—his broad, strong shoulders, trim waist, and thick, muscular legs. He was a powerful man of great physical stamina. She wondered if they had sons if they would take after him. She smiled again at the thought of the child. How very blessed she was. God had given her the desires of her heart—so much more precious than rivers of gold or mountains that glittered with ore. A child!

Adrik quickly finished undressing and picked up the Bible on the stand beside the bed. It was their habit to read from the Word every night before retiring. He slid under the covers and eased back against the headboard of their bed.

"I have a request for tonight's reading," Karen said. She thought this the perfect way to break her news. "Read from the Psalms. Specifically Psalm 127."

"All right," he said, turning the lamp up a bit before flipping through the well-worn pages.

"Psalm 127," he began. " 'Except the Lord build the house, they labour in vain that build it: except the Lord keep the city, the watchman waketh but in vain.'"

He smiled over at her and Karen reached out to tenderly touch his bearded face. He continued reading. "'It is vain for you to rise up early, to sit up late, to eat the bread of sorrows: for so he giveth his beloved sleep.'"

Adrik grinned. "Now I see why you wanted me to read this. You're hoping I'll be quiet and let you go to sleep."

Karen giggled. "Not at all. I quite like being in your company Mr. Ivankov."

Adrik turned back to the Bible. "'Lo, children are an heritage of the Lord: and the fruit of the womb is his reward. As arrows are in the hand of a mighty man; so are children of the youth. Happy is the man that hath his quiver full of them: they shall not be ashamed, but they shall speak with the enemies in the gate.'"

He looked at her quizzically. "That's it. It's a mighty short psalm."

"Yes, but it says quite a bit." She reached over and took the Bible from him and put it on the stand on her side of the bed.

"'Except the Lord build the house, they labour in vain that build it,'" he murmured as Karen snuggled closer. "That's good counsel."

"Yes," she said. She reached over and took hold of his hand. Drawing it over to her stomach, she added, "'Lo, children are an heritage of the Lord: and the fruit of the womb is his reward.'"

Adrik said nothing. Karen heard his breathing quicken, but still he said nothing. She looked at him and saw the disbelief in his expression. Smiling, she pressed closer and kissed his lips very tenderly. "We're going to have a baby."

"I can't believe it," he finally managed to say. "A baby." The wonder of it all was written in his face as his expression changed from shock to acceptance.

"Yes, a baby," Karen said excitedly. "The doctor believes it will come sometime in May."

Adrik pulled her close, nearly knocking the wind from her as he squeezed her tight. As if realizing his strength, he quickly released her. "I didn't hurt you, did I?"

"No, silly. You just surprised me."

"I surprised you? You just about gave me heart failure with your little surprise."

Karen frowned. "You aren't pleased?" She hadn't even thought he might not want to have children right away.

"Of course I'm pleased," he said, sounding hurt that she would even suggest such a possibility.

Relief coursed through her body, and she settled down in his arms once more. "I'm glad you're pleased. I'm so excited I can hardly bear it. It's too wondrous."

He drew her to him more gently this time. Stroking her long hair, he studied her face for a moment. "I'm so very blessed."

She nodded, "We're so very blessed."

The next morning Adrik woke up before Karen. He watched her sleep for a long time, completely amazed at the news she'd given him the night before. He was going to be a father. The news was not what he had anticipated, and yet it was so completely perfect. He couldn't imagine her not being pregnant—it seemed so right, so completely of God.

He had thought for a long time into the night about their future. About the plans he should make. He would get them back down to Dyea before the hard winter set in. He had friends there. Family too. He would see to it that they had a good home in which to raise their new child.

For as long as he could remember, Adrik had longed for a family of his own. He hadn't figured any woman in her right mind would want to live the way he did, dealing with the people who were so very dear to him. He figured marriage would probably not be something he'd be blessed with. But God had proven him wrong. And now, God had given him a child.

Karen stirred and opened her eyes. She looked up sleepily and batted her eyelids several times as if trying to clear the haze.

"Good morning, love," he whispered, leaning down to kiss her.

"Morning." She yawned and shrugged her shoulders. "How did you sleep?"

"Like a man who'd just been told he's going to be a father."

She smiled. "That well, huh?"

"I just started thinking of all the things we'd have to do and sleep became an impossible task."

Karen stretched and sat up. Adrik pulled her back against him, relishing the way she felt in his arms. "So what is it that you figure we need to do?" she asked.

"Well, first off, we need to get back to Dyea," he began. "I want to secure a good place to live for the winter and make sure it's big enough for all of us. I don't know how much longer Jacob will be with us, but we'll plan for him as well."

"What else?"

"Well, we need to figure out what all you'll need for the baby. I can make the cradle myself, but we'll need to get some materials so you and Leah can start sewing up all those little doodads babies always need. We'll send a letter to Peter, and he can bring a load up the next time he comes to Skagway."

"That sounds wise. I'm glad you have this all figured out."

Adrik laughed. "I haven't had much of anything figured out since the day I first met you. But to tell you honestly, it doesn't matter. I'm enjoying myself immensely."

Laughing, Karen wriggled out of his arms and pulled on her robe. "You enjoy yourself far too much," she teased.

"Well, I figure—"

The knock at the door interrupted his thoughts. Karen tied her sash and went to the door while Adrik jumped from the bed and pulled on his jeans.

"Who is it?" she called.

"Miranda."

Karen glanced at Adrik. He nodded, then hurried to pull a shirt on over his long underwear.

Karen opened the door. "Good morning, Miranda. We slept a bit late. Hope you'll pardon our appearance."

"I'm sorry. I hadn't intended to bother you this early, but a man is downstairs waiting to talk to Adrik. I told Teddy I'd come and get him."

Adrik was surprised by the news. "I'll get my boots on and be right down. Any idea what the man wants?"

"He said he could offer you transportation to Whitehorse."

Adrik looked to Karen and laughed. "Well, God is certainly keeping us on the right path. That's a good start south. We'll be home before you know it."

"We're going to miss you terribly," Miranda said as Karen and Adrik told them the news of their departure later that night. They stood in the hotel lobby close to the fireplace in order to ward off the October chill.

"We certainly will," Teddy added. "You've been more than good friends. You've been a generous and loving family to both of us."

"We feel the same about you," Karen assured. "Don't forget your promise to look us up on your way to San Francisco."

"Since we probably won't be able to go until May or June, perhaps we'll get a chance to see the baby, as well," Miranda said excitedly. "I still can't believe the news. It's just so wonderful."

Karen looked to Adrik and laughed. "It is wonderful. I can't tell you how happy we are."

"May will take forever to get here," Miranda said mournfully. She looked to Teddy and forced a smile. She didn't want him to think her too sad so she quickly added, "At least, I'm sure you'll feel that way. Waiting for good things is always hard, especially when it involves a baby."

"And waiting with patience has never been easy for me," Karen replied. "I have very little in that area to draw from."

"Well, this child will come in God's timing and His alone," Teddy replied.

"Say, where are Leah and Jacob?" Miranda questioned. "Do they know about the baby?"

"They do indeed," Karen answered. "As for their whereabouts, they're upstairs packing. They're very anxious to leave Dawson. They're ready to begin anew and settle down to a different kind of life."

"Oh, we shall miss you so," Miranda said, hugging Karen and then Adrik. "You both mean the world to me. I'm so grateful you allowed me to come north with you."

"Despite the fact we lost you in the lake?" Adrik jokingly asked.

"Especially for losing me in the lake," Miranda replied, then went to Teddy's side. "I might never have found my true love, otherwise. You shouldn't feel guilty at all, but rather rejoice for having played a part in God's plan to put Teddy and me together."

"That's definitely one way of looking at it," Adrik replied.

"It's the best way of looking at it." Miranda's words gave her the strength to say good-bye to yet another group of loved ones. She wasn't left comfortless or without love. She reminded herself of her blessings and looked up to catch Teddy's loving gaze. Yes, she thought, it was the best way to look at the events of her life over the last couple of years. One event had been built upon another, and each had brought her to the place she was now.

Miranda would see all her loved ones again one day, and for now, she had her Teddy—her beloved Teddy.

CHAPTER THIRTY-THREE

CHRISTMAS 1899 PASSED with much joy in the Colton household. San Francisco was a far cry from the cold of the Yukon, and the spirit of celebration was upon the whole family.

Andy, now nearly a year old, was the apple of his grandparents' eyes. Walking with awkward baby steps, he delighted the family to no end. Still too small for the rocking horse his Grandfather Ephraim had given him for Christmas, Andy was content to merely slap his palms against the wooden seat and chatter, "Horsy. Horsy."

"There's news from Teddy and Miranda," Peter said, unfolding a letter. "Actually, the news is from Teddy. He intends to surprise Miranda with a visit much sooner than planned. He's discussed lecturing here in San Francisco on the botanical wonders of the Yukon. Apparently there's a great deal of interest, and he's decided to approach an American publisher in regard to his book."

"How marvelous," Grace declared.

Amelia Colton nodded enthusiastically. "Oh, I long to see Miranda."

"Mother Colton, it won't be long," Grace assured. "She'll be here before you know it."

"Indeed," Peter replied. "Teddy plans to leave the Yukon shortly after the first of January. Apparently his native friends have agreed to help them."

"Oh, that's just days away," Amelia said, looking to Ephraim with great joy. "How long will it take them to get here?"

"Well, it depends on the weather. Teddy wants to arrange passage out of

Skagway by the thirtieth of January. He worries that he might be delayed on the trail, but if that happens, they'll merely wait it out. I'll pick them up in Skagway. I'm planning to arrive there on *Merry Maid* the twenty-fifth of January. I'll be delivering supplies to the town anyway, as well as making a delivery to Karen and Adrik Ivankov in Dyea."

"Will Grace and Andy go, too?" his mother asked with concern in her tone.

"No, they'll stay here as the weather will probably be threatening. But I'm sure we'll make many more trips to the north."

"What of transporting gold miners to Nome?" Ephraim asked.

"We're already devoting *Summer Song* to that purpose," Peter explained. "I meant to discuss it with you last week. I've been using *Summer Song* for the past couple of months to take men and supplies into Nome. The biggest problem is that Norton Sound freezes solid. We end up having to harbor out deep and then transport folks and supplies across the ice. It isn't something I'm really comfortable with."

"I can well understand. What if the ice melts?"

Peter smiled at his mother. "They tell me it freezes many feet thick, but still, there's no sense in risking life and limb. The passage is long and risky, but the profits are good due to the tremendous need for supplies. I've received an order requesting I bring as many work dogs as possible, along with any fresh fruit I can find. I'll probably take *Merry Maid* up that way once the weather is better." He refolded the letter and put it into his pocket, adding, "Of course, we must get the Davenports here first."

"It will be so good to have Miranda home. Does Teddy say how long they can stay?" Grace questioned.

"No, but I'm sure if he's to lecture, it might well turn into a lengthy visit."

"Oh, I hope so," Grace said smiling. "I know it would do us all good to be a complete family again."

———

Miranda waited in the lobby of the Fairview Hotel. The elegance and grandeur of the once popular hotel had faded with the diminishing numbers of people still residing in Dawson. But it didn't matter. The citizens of the town had decided a New Year's Eve party was in order, and it had been a most entertaining and rewarding evening.

Miranda and Teddy had dressed in their finest clothes. Miranda wore a salmon-colored satin gown that was trimmed with black jets and lace. The full cut of the muttonchop sleeves were inset with ebony lace, which the dressmaker had assured Miranda had been handmade in Paris.

Teddy, ever the refined Englishman, sported the latest fashion—a black Prince

Albert–styled frock coat with satin lapels and gray striped trousers. Miranda thought him the most handsome man at the party. He moved with such grace that Miranda felt almost clumsy alongside him. But it wasn't long before he had her dancing comfortably in his arms. He was as gentle and tender a teacher on the dance floor as he had been in training her in botanical research.

"Here we are," Teddy said, coming from the cloakroom with Miranda's cape and his own coat. He put the fur-lined cape around her shoulders before donning his coat. "I'm certain the weather is quite frigid."

"Then I shall have to walk very close to you in order to stay warm," Miranda teased.

"You shall walk very close to me anyway," Teddy replied. "I wouldn't have it any other way." He pulled her near and held her close. "Did you enjoy yourself this evening?"

"Very much," she answered, looking up into his face. "I enjoy myself wherever you are."

Walking from the hotel, they left behind the gentle strains of a Strauss waltz. Miranda had enjoyed the music even more than the dancing. She had missed the concerts she and her mother had attended on occasion in San Francisco. The thought had never even entered her mind until coming here tonight.

Fact was, she tried hard not to think of San Francisco at all. Even though her family could not consider themselves as wealthy, Miranda had enjoyed many cultural programs that had given her great pleasure. Those things were few and far between in Dawson. It wasn't for a lack of trying, however. In its heyday, Dawson's Opera House and Palace Theatres were acceptable places of entertainment, but it wasn't the same. Miranda felt as though she were stuck at the end of the earth, with no hope of ever rejoining civilization.

She knew part of her depression was the lack of light. The winter months were very difficult to endure—especially for one who treasured the sunlight so very much. Then there was the cold and the snow. Miranda felt she'd endured enough of both to last her a lifetime.

"What are you thinking about?" Teddy whispered against her ear.

Miranda smiled. Teddy made it all bearable. She was so glad for his company—his love. "I'm just thinking how fortunate I am that God brought us together. You've given me so much."

"It helps that my holdings are vast," Teddy said laughing.

"No, not the material things," Miranda replied. "I know I shall most likely never want for those, but I'm speaking of your love and tenderness. I love being with you—learning from you. I feel as though a whole new world has been opened up to me."

"As do I. I know my focus for years was on one thing alone: the botanical book that would fulfill my father's dream. But it doesn't fulfill my dreams. You do that."

Miranda reached across Teddy's waist and took hold of his arm. Pulling it to her, she gently kissed his gloved hand. "And you do that for me. I adore you, you know."

"I hadn't guessed."

He paused outside their hotel and lowered his lips to hers. "Happy New Year, Mrs. Davenport."

Miranda forgot about the cold as her heart raced, warming her blood. "Perhaps," she whispered against his mouth, "we should go upstairs."

He pulled back grinning. "You are a bold one, Mrs. Davenport."

She giggled. "I wasn't implying anything improper. I'm merely confident that we will freeze to death if we wait out here much longer."

Teddy laughed and opened the door. "After you, my dearest wife."

They went directly to their room, ignoring the revelry of other hotel guests who were celebrating the new century. Miranda thought it all such a wonder that they should find themselves in the year 1900. What would the years to come bring? Would there be new wonders and innovations to bless them in their daily existence? Or would there be wars and tragedy? No doubt there would be both, and only a faith in God would help them endure the passage of time.

Once they'd reached their room, Teddy helped Miranda with her cloak, then saw to his own things. Shedding his frock coat to reveal a snug, white waistcoat and starched shirt, Teddy then pulled the gray silk ascot from around his throat.

Miranda watched as he put his things very carefully aside, then pulled his glasses from his pocket. She frowned. Usually this was the signal that he intended to work, but it was well past midnight, and she had not figured him to even be interested in such matters.

"Where are you going?" she asked as he walked from their bedroom into the sitting room and work area.

"I have something I need to tend to," he said.

Miranda dispensed with her handbag and gloves and followed her husband into the other room. "Teddy, it's very late. Couldn't it wait until morning?"

"No, I'm afraid that will be too late."

"Too late? What in the world could possibly be so important that it can't wait until morning?"

He opened his journal and motioned her to come to his side. "Come see for yourself."

She did and noted the calendar he had created for the month of January. The thirtieth was circled. "What's this all about? What is so important about the thirtieth of January?"

Teddy smiled secretively. "Well, that's what cannot wait."

"But that's thirty days away," she protested. "What happens on the thirtieth?"

"That's the day we catch a boat out of Skagway bound for California. In fact, if all goes well, it will be your brother's ship *Merry Maid.*"

Miranda stared at her husband in disbelief. "What are you saying?"

Teddy closed the journal and reached out to take her in his arms. "I'm saying that we're leaving Dawson tomorrow. Little Charley and his friends are coming to take us south by dog sled. Are you up for the trip?"

Miranda felt tears come to her eyes. Teddy's words were just too wonderful. "Do you mean it?"

"Absolutely. Can you be ready?"

"Of course I can," Miranda declared. She wrapped her arms around her husband's neck in girlish anticipation. "Oh, Teddy, this is the best news you could have ever given me. When did you decide to do this?"

"Your brother and I spoke before he departed Dawson. I told him I would write to him to confirm the date, but I was certain the plans we set into motion would work well for us."

"But what of your work?"

"I'll take it with me. There's no need to remain here. I've exhausted the area in my searching, and I've an opportunity to take what I've learned and present it in lecture form for various universities and lecture halls."

"That's marvelous. Why didn't you tell me sooner?"

"I wanted to surprise you. I figured I owed it to you. You've been so very good to endure the departure of your friends and family. You've not complained about being left behind in this dying town, and I knew it would do us both good."

"When I first met you," Miranda said, lovingly touching her husband's face, "I thought you were the most self-centered man in the universe. You were buried deep in your work, and you scarcely even noticed that I was alive."

"I'd never had reason to think of anything else. My work had become my life, and even my faith suffered for it. But no more. I've learned the importance of listening with my heart, as well as my ears. I've learned that God doesn't desire us to live in isolated little shells, thinking of nothing and no one but ourselves. He longs for us to reach out—to share His love and to make mankind our greater concern.

"I started that journey from isolation when I met you, and the rewards have been most amazing. There isn't a river of gold I would trade for the love I have with you or the friendships I've made through you. I had no idea what was missing in my life, until you came along."

"I knew what was missing," Miranda said softly. "I just didn't know where to find it. But God did." She melted against him, longing only for his touch.

"I suppose," Teddy said, his voice husky with desire, "that we should get a good night's sleep. Little Charley will be here for us around ten o'clock."

"I'm not sleepy," Miranda whispered against his ear.

"Me either," Teddy replied. He pulled away enough that Miranda could clearly see his face. "Do you want to help me pack my samples? Or you could log the information for each one in the journal."

She took hold of his hand and pulled him gently toward the bedroom. "I think I'm more tired than I realized."

He chuckled and followed her without hesitation. "Ah, Mrs. Davenport. How am I ever to get my work done with you to distract me?"

Miranda laughed and closed the door to their room. "I'm sure you'll figure it out in the years to come. After all, I intend for us to have several score of years together. That's a lot of time for figuring."

"Or loving," he whispered.

She nodded. "Especially loving."